HELEN MacINNES

HELEN MacINNES

Three Bestselling
Novels of
Terror & Espionage

Agent in Place
The Hidden Target
Cloak of Darkness

Published in 1993 by

Galahad Books
A Division of Budget Book Service, Inc.
386 Park Avenue South
New York, NY 10016

Galahad Books is a registered trademark of Budget Book Service, Inc.
Published by arrangement with Harcourt Brace Jovanovich, Inc.

Library of Congress Catalog Card Number: 93-70025
ISBN: 0-88365-814-3
Designed by Hannah Lerner

Printed in the United States of America.

Contents

Agent
in Place

If hopes were dupes, fears may be liars.
—Arthur Hugh Clough

To
Ian Douglas Highet
and
Eliot Chace Highet
—with all my love

One

THE MESSAGE HAD come at eight o'clock that morning as he was swallowing a first cup of black coffee to clear his head and open his eyes. But before he could cross over the short stretch of floor between him and the telephone, the ringing stopped. He started back to the kitchen, had barely reached its door before he halted abruptly. The telephone rang again. Twice. And stopped ringing. He glanced at the kitchen clock. He would have one minute exactly before the third call. Now fully alert, he pulled the pan of bacon and eggs away from the heat, did not even waste another moment to turn off the electric stove, moved at double time back into the living room, reached the telephone on his desk, sat down with a pencil in his hand and a scrap of paper before him, and was ready. The message would be in code and he had better make sure of each digit. It had been a long time since he had been summoned in this way. An emergency? He controlled his excitement, smothered all his wondering. Punctual to the second, the telephone rang again. Quickly he picked up the receiver. "Hello," he said—slow, casual, indifferent.

"Hello, hello, hello there." Two small coughs, a clearing of the throat.

He knew the voice at once. Nine years since he had last heard it, but its pattern was definite: deep, full-chested, slightly husky, the kind of voice that might break into an aria from *Prince Igor* or *Boris Godunov* with each of its notes almost a chord in itself. Mischa? Yes, Mischa. Even the initial greeting was his own sign-in phrase. Nine years since last heard, but still completely Mischa, down to the two coughs and the throat-clearing.

"Yorktown Cleaners?" Mischa was saying. "Please have my blue suit ready for delivery to 10 Old Park Place by six o'clock this evening. Receipt number is 69105A. And my name—" Slowing up of this last phrase gave the cue for a cut-in.

"Sorry—you've the wrong number."

"Wrong number?" High indignation. "The receipt is here in my hand. 69105A."

"Wrong telephone number." Heavy patience.

"What?" The tone was now aggressive, almost accusing. Very true to life was Mischa. "Are you sure?"

"Yes!" The one-word answer was enough to let Mischa know that his prize protégé Alexis had got the message.

"Let me check—" There was a brief pause while a dogged disbeliever riffled through a couple of pages against the muted background noise of

some lobby or restaurant. Then Mischa spoke again from his public telephone booth, this time with sharp annoyance, "Okay, okay." Angrily, he
banged down the receiver for an added touch of humor. He had always
prided himself on his keen perception of Americans' behavior patterns.

For a moment, there was complete silence in the little apartment. Mischa,
Mischa . . . Eleven years since he first started training me, Alexis was thinking,
and nine years since I last saw him. He was a major then—Major Vladimir
Konov. What now? A full-fledged colonel in the KGB? Even higher? With
another name too, no doubt: several other names, possibly, in that long and
hidden career. And here I am, still using the cover name Mischa gave me, still
stuck in the role he assigned me in Washington. But, as Mischa used to mis-
quote with a sardonic smile, "They also serve who only sit and wait."

Alexis recovered from his delayed shock as he noticed the sunlight shaft-
ing its way into his room from a break in the row of small Georgetown
houses across the narrow street. The morning had begun; a heavy day lay
ahead. He moved quickly now, preparing himself for it.

From the bookcase wall he picked out the second volume of Spengler's
Untergang des Abendlandes—the German text scared off Alexis's American
friends: they preferred it translated into *The Decline of the West,* even if the
change into English lost the full meaning of the title. It ought to have been
The Decline and Fall of the West, which might have made them think harder
into the meaning of the book. With Spengler in one hand and his precious
slip of paper in the other, Alexis left the sun-streaked living room for the
colder light of his dismal little kitchen. He was still wearing pajamas and
foulard dressing gown, but even if cold clear November skies were outside
the high window, he felt hot with mounting excitement. He pushed aside
orange juice and coffee cup, tossed the Washington *Post* onto a countertop,
turned off the electric stove, and sat down at the small table crushed into
one corner where no prying neighbors' eyes could see him, even if their
kitchens practically rubbed sinks with his.

Now, he thought, opening the Spengler and searching for a loose sheet
of paper inserted in its second chapter ("Origin and Landscape: Group of
Higher Cultures"), now for Mischa's message. He had understood most of
it, even at nine years' distance, but he had to be absolutely accurate. He
found the loose sheet, covered with his own compressed shorthand, giving
him the key to the quick scrawls he had made on the scrap of paper from
his desk. He began decoding. It was all very simple—Mischa's way of thumbing his nose at the elaborate cleverness of the Americans, with their reli-
ance on computers and technology. (Nothing, Mischa used to say and
obviously still did, nothing is going to replace the well-trained agent, well-
placed, well-directed. That the man had to be bright and dedicated was
something that Mischa made quite sure of, before any time was wasted in
training.)

Simple, Alexis thought again as he looked at the message, but effective
in all its sweet innocence. "Yorktown" was New York, of course. The "blue
suit" was Alexis in person. "10" meant nothing—a number that was used
for padding. "Old Park Place" obviously meant the old meeting place in
the park in New York—Central Park, as the receipt number "69105A"

indicated: cancel the 10, leaving 69 for Sixty-ninth Street, 5A for Fifth Avenue. The delivery time of the blue suit, "six o'clock" this evening, meant 6:00 P.M. minus one hour and twenty minutes.

So there I'll be, thought Alexis, strolling by the old rendezvous just inside Central Park at twenty minutes of five this evening.

He burned his scrap of jottings, replaced the sheet of paper in its nesting place, and put Spengler carefully back on the shelf. Only after that did he reheat the coffee, gulp down the orange juice, look at the still life of congealed bacon and eggs with a shudder, and empty the greasy half-cooked mess into the garbage can. He would tidy up on Monday—the worst thing on this job was the chores you had to do yourself: dangerous to hand out duplicate keys to anyone coming in to scrub and dust. When things got beyond him in this small apartment, he'd call for untalkative Beulah, flat feet and arthritis, too stupid to question why he asked her to clean on a day he worked at home. Now he had better shave, shower, and dress. And then do some telephoning of his own: to Sandra here in Washington, begging off her swinging party tonight; to Katie in New York, letting her know that he'd be spending the weekend again at her place. And he had better take the first Metroliner possible. Or the shuttle flight? In any case, he must make sure that he would reach New York with plenty of time to spare before the meeting with Mischa.

As he came out of the shower, he was smiling broadly at a sudden memory. Imagine, he thought, just imagine Mischa remembering that old fixation of mine on a blue suit, my idea of bourgeois respectability for my grand entry into the capitalist world. I was given it, too: an ill-fitting jacket of hard serge, turning purple with age, threads whitening at the seams, the seat of the pants glossed like a mirror, a rent here, some mud there; a very convincing picture of the refugee who had managed at last to outwit the Berlin Wall. (Mischa's sense of humor, a scarce commodity in his line of business, was as strong as his cold assessment of Western minds: the pathetic image always works, he had said.) And now I have $22,000 a year and a job in Washington, and a three-room apartment one flight up in a Georgetown house, and a closet packed with clothes. Eight suits hanging there, but not a blue one among them. He laughed, shook his head, began planning his day in New York.

He arrived at Penn Station with almost three hours to spare, a time to lose himself in city crowds once he had dropped his small bag at Katie's East Side apartment. That was easily done; Katie's place had a self-service elevator and no doorman, and he had the keys to let him into both the entrance hall and her three rooms on the fifth floor. It was a fairly old building as New York went, and modest in size—ten floors, with only space enough for two tenants on each of them. They paid no attention to anyone, strangers all, intent on their own troubles and pleasures. They never even noticed him on his frequent weekend visits, probably assumed he was a tenant himself. But best of all was the location of the apartment house between two busy avenues, one traveling north, the other south, buses and plenty of taxis.

Katie herself was a gem. Made to order, and no pun intended. She was out now, as he had expected: a restless type, devoted to causes and demonstrations. She had left a note for him in her pretty-girl scrawl. *Chuck tried to reach you in Washington. Call him any time after five. Don't forget party at Bo's tonight. You are reinvited. See you here at seven? Kate.* Bo Browning's party . . . Well, that was something better avoided. Danger for him there, in all that glib talk from eager Marxists who hadn't even read *Das Kapital* all the way through. It was hard to keep himself from proving how little they knew, or how much he could teach them.

But Chuck—now that was something else again. There was urgency in his message. Could Chuck really be delivering? Last weekend he had been arguing himself into and out of a final decision. Better not count on anything, Alexis warned himself, and tried to repress a surge of hope, a flush of triumph. But his sudden euphoria stayed with him as he set off for Fifth Avenue and an hour or so in the Metropolitan Museum.

By four o'clock he began to worry about his timing, and came hurrying away from the Greek gods' department, down the museum's giant flight of steps, his arm signaling to a loitering taxi. It would take him south, well past Sixty-ninth Street, all the way to the Central Park zoo. He would use that entrance, wander around the zoo itself to put in fifteen minutes (he was going to be too early for Mischa after all). Now he was thinking only of the meeting ahead of him. The initial excitement was gone, replaced by nervousness, even a touch of fear. It was a special encounter, no doubt about that: there was something vital at stake. Had he made some error, was his judgment being distrusted? Had his growing boredom with those quiet nine years shown in his steady reports? But they were good reports, succinct, exact, giving the foibles and weaknesses of the hundreds of acquaintances and friends he had made in government and newspaper circles. As a member of Representative Pickering's personal staff, with nine years of promotions all the way from secretarial adviser to office manager controlling an office swollen to forty-seven employees, and now to the top job of communications director, he had contacts in every major office in government. He was invited around, kept an ear open for all rumors and indiscreet talk. There was plenty of that in Washington, some of it so careless that it baffled him. Americans *were* smart—a considerable enemy and one that posed a constant danger—that was what had been dinned into him in his long months of training; but after nine years in Washington, he had his doubts. What made clever Americans so damned stupid once they got into places of power?

The fifteen minutes were up, leaving him seven to walk northward through the park to the Sixty-ninth Street area. Had he cut the time too short, after all? He increased his pace as he left the desolate zoo with its empty cages— animals were now kept mostly inside—and its trees bare-branched with first frosts. The Saturday crowd was leaving too, moving away from the gathering shadows. So he wasn't noticeable. And he hadn't been followed. He never was. But he was suddenly surprised out of his self-preoccupation by the dimming sky. The bright clear blue of the afternoon had faded. It would soon be dusk. The street lights were already on; so were the lamps posted along the paths, little bursts of brightness surrounded by darkening meadows, by bushes and trees that formed black blots over falling and rising ground. Fifth Avenue lay to his right beyond the wall that edged the park. Traffic was brisk, audible but not visible; only the high-rising apartment buildings, lining the other side of the avenue, could be seen. Their windows—expensive curtains undrawn, shades left unpulled—were ablaze with light. What was this about an energy crisis?

Strange, he thought as he came through a small underpass, how isolated this park can make you feel; almost as if you were on a lonely country road. The crowd had thinned, easing off in other directions. He was alone, and approaching a second underpass as the path sloped downward, edging away from the Fifth Avenue wall. Now it was almost dusk, the sky washed into the color of faded ink tinged with a band of apricot above the far-off black silhouettes of Central Park West.

The underpass looked as grim as a tunnel—a short one, fortunately. Near its entrance, on the small hillside of bushes and rocks that lay on his right, he saw a group of four men. No, just boys—two leaning against a crag, nonchalant, thin; two squatting on the slope of grass, knees up to their black chins: all of them watching. He noticed the sneakers on their feet. Keep walking and get ready to sprint, he told himself. And then his fear doubled as he heard lightly running footsteps behind him. He swung round to face the new threat. But it was only a couple of joggers, dressed in track suits, having their evening run. "Hi!" he said in relief as the joggers neared him rapidly.

"Hi!" one said, pink-faced and frowning. He glanced at the hill. Both he and his friend slowed their pace but didn't stop. "Like to join us?" the other one asked, thin-faced and smiling.

And he did, breaking into their rhythm as he unbuttoned his topcoat, jogging in unison. Through the underpass, then up the path as it rose in a long steady stretch. "Race you to the top," the thin-faced man said. But up there, where the outcrop of Manhattan rocks rose into a cluster of crags, he would be almost in sight of the Sixty-ninth Street entrance. Now was the time to break off, although he could have given them a good run for their money.

He smiled, pretended to have lost his wind, stopped halfway up the path, gave them a wave of thanks. With an answering wave they left him, and without a word increased their pace to a steady run. Amazing how quickly they could streak up that long stretch of hill; but they had earned this demonstration of their superiority, and he was too thankful to begrudge them their small triumph. He was willing to bet, though, that once they were out of sight, they'd slacken their pace back to a very easy jog. What were they, he wondered—a lawyer, an accountant? Illustrators or advertising men? They looked the type, lived nearby, and exercised in the evening before they went home to their double vodka Martinis.

He finished the climb at a brisk pace. Far behind him, the four thin loose-limbed figures had come through the underpass and halted, as if admitting that even their sneakers couldn't catch up on the distance between him and them. Ahead of him, there was a man walking two large dogs; another jogger; and the small flagpole that marked the convergence of four paths—the one he was following, the one that continued to the north, the one that led west across rolling meadows, the one that came in from the Sixty-ninth Street entrance. Thanks to his run, he was arriving in good time after all, with one minute to spare. He was a little too warm, a little disheveled, but outwardly calm, and ready to face Mischa. He straightened his tie, smoothed his hair, decided to button his topcoat even if it was stifling him.

He might not have appeared so calm if he could have heard his lawyer-accountant-illustrator-advertising types. Once they had passed the flagpole on its little island of grass, they had dropped behind some bushes to cool off. It had been a hard pull up that hill.

"Strange guy. What the hell does he think he's doing, walking alone at this time of day?" The red face faded back to its natural pink.

"Stranger in town."

"Well-dressed. In good training, I thought. Better than he pretended."

"Wouldn't have had much chance against four, though. What now, Jim? Continue patrol, or double back? See what that wolf pack is up to?"

"Looking for some other lone idiot," Jim said.

"Don't complain. Think of the nice open-air job they give us."

Jim stood up, flexed his legs. "On your feet, Burt. Better finish our rounds. Seems quiet enough here." There were three other joggers—bona fide ones, these—plodding in from the west toward Sixty-ninth Street and home; a man walking two great Danes; a tattered drunk slumped on the cold hard grass, clutching the usual brown-paper bag; two sauntering women, with peroxide curls, tight coats over short skirts (chilly work, thought Jim, on a cool November night), high heels, swinging handbags. "Nothing but honest citizens," Jim said with a grin. The wolf pack had vanished, prowling for better prospects.

"Here's another idiot," said Burt in disgust as he and Jim resumed their patrol northward. The lone figure walking toward them, down the path that led from the Seventy-second Street entrance, was heavily dressed and solidly built, but he moved nimbly, swinging his cane, his snap-brim tilted to one side. He paid no attention to them, apparently more interested in the Fifth Avenue skyline, so that the droop of his hat and the turned head gave only a limited view of his profile. He seemed confident enough. "At least he carries a hefty stick. He'll be out of the park in no time, anyway."

"If he doesn't go winging his way down to the zoo," Jim said. He frowned, suddenly veered away to his left, halting briefly by a tree, just far enough to give him a view of the flagpole where the four paths met. Almost at once he came streaking back, the grass silencing his running shoes, the gray of his track suit blending into the spreading shadows. "He won't be alone," he reported as he rejoined Burt. "So he'll be safe enough." Two idiots were safer than one.

"So that's their hang-up, is it? We'll leave them to the Vice boys. They'll be around soon." Dusk would end in another half hour, and darkness would be complete. The two men jogged on in silence, steps in unison, rhythm steady, eyes alert.

Two

THEY ARRIVED AT the flagpole almost simultaneously. "Well-timed," said Mischa and nodded his welcome. There was no handclasp, no outward sign of recognition. "You look well. Bourgeois life agrees with you. Shall we walk a little?" His eyes had already swept over the drunk lolling on the grass near the Sixty-ninth Street entrance. He glanced back for a second look at the two women with the over-made-up faces and ridiculous clothes, who were now sitting on a bench beside the lamppost. One saw him, rose expectantly, adjusted her hair. Mischa turned away, now sizing up a group of five people—young, thin, long-haired, two of them possibly girls, all wearing tight jeans and faded army jackets—who had come pouring in from Fifth Avenue. But they saw no one, heard nothing; they headed purposefully for the nearby cluster of rocks and crags and their own private spot. Mischa's eyes continued their assessment and chose the empty path that led westward across the park. His cane gestured. "Less interruption here, I think. And if no one is already occupying those trees just ahead, we should have a nice place to talk."

And a good view of anyone approaching, Alexis thought as they reached two trees, just off the road, and stepped close to them. The bushes around them had been cleared, so even a rear attack could be seen in time. Suddenly he realized that Mischa wasn't even thinking about an ambush by muggers at four forty-five in the evening—he probably assumed that ten o'clock to midnight were the criminal hours. All Mischa's caution was being directed against his old adversaries. "Central Park has changed a lot since you were last here," Alexis tried tactfully. This was a hell of a place to have a meeting, but how was he to suggest that? "In summer, of course, it's different. More normal people around. Concerts, plays—"

"A lot has changed," Mischa cut him off. "But not in our work." His face broke into a wide grin, showing a splendid set of teeth. His clever gray eyes crinkled as he studied the younger man, his hat thumbed back to show a wide brow and a bristle of graying hair. With rounded chin and snub nose, he had looked nine years ago—although it would be scarcely diplomatic now to mention the name of a nonperson—very much like a younger version of Nikita Khrushchev. But nine years ago Mischa had had slight gaps between his front teeth. The grin vanished. "There is no détente in Intelligence. And don't you ever forget that." A forefinger jabbed against Alexis's chest to emphasize the last five words. Then a strong hand slapped three affectionate blows on Alexis's shoulders, and the voice was back to normal. "You look like an American, you talk like an American, but you must never think like an American." The smile was in place again.

Mischa broke into Russian, perhaps to speak faster and make sure of his meaning. "You've done very well. I congratulate you. I take it, by the way you walked up so confidently to meet me, that no one was following you?"

The small reprimand had been administered deftly. In that, Mischa hadn't changed at all. But in other ways, yes. Mischa's old sense of humor, for instance. Tonight he was grimly serious even when he smiled. He's a worried man, thought Alexis. "No, no one tailed me." Alexis's lips were tight. "But what about you?" He nodded to a solitary figure, husky and fairly tall, who had walked along the path on the heels of two men with a Doberman, and now was retracing his steps. Again he didn't glance in their direction, just kept walking at a steady pace.

"You are nervous tonight, Alexis. Why? That is only my driver. Did you expect me to cope with New York traffic on a Saturday night? Relax, relax. He will patrol this area very efficiently."

"Then you are expecting some interest—" Alexis began.

"Hardly. I am not here yet."

Alexis stared.

"Officially I arrive next Tuesday, attached to a visiting delegation concerned with agricultural problems. We shall be in Washington for ten days. You are bound to hear of us, probably even meet us at one of those parties you attend so zealously. Of course I shall have more hair, and it will be darker."

"I won't flicker an eyelash." As I might have done, Alexis admitted to himself: you did not live in a Moscow apartment for six months, completely isolated from other trainees, with only Mischa as your visitor and tutor, and not recognize him when you met him face to face in some senator's house. But Mischa had not slipped into America ahead of his delegation, and planned a secret meeting in Central Park, merely to warn Alexis about a Washington encounter. What was so important that it could bring them together like this? "So you are an expert on food grains," Alexis probed.

"Now, now," Mischa chided. "You may have been one of my best pupils, but you don't have to try my own tricks on me." He was amused. Briefly. "I've been following your progress. I have seen your reports, those that are of special interest. You have not mentioned Thomas Kelso in the last three months. No progress there? What about his brother, Charles Kelso—you are still his friend?"

"Yes."

"Then why?"

"Because Chuck Kelso now lives in New York. Tom Kelso lives mostly in Washington."

"But Charles Kelso did introduce you to his brother?"

"Yes."

"Four years ago?"

"Yes."

"And you have not established yourself with Thomas Kelso by this time?"

"I tried several visits on my own after Chuck left Washington. Polite reception. No more. I was just another friend of his brother—Chuck is ten years younger than Tom, and that makes a big difference in America."

"Ridiculous. They are brothers. They were very close. That is why we instructed you to renew your friendship with Charles Kelso when you and he met again in Washington. Five years ago, wasn't that?"

"Almost five."

"And two years ago, when it was reported that Thomas Kelso needed a research assistant, you were instructed to suggest—in a friendly meeting—that you would be interested in that position. Your reaction to that order was negative. Why?"

"It was an impossible suggestion. Too dangerous. At present I am making twenty-two thousand dollars a year. Did you want me to drop fourteen thousand dollars and rouse suspicions?"

"Was eight thousand dollars a year all he could afford?" Mischa was disbelieving. "But he must make—"

"Not all Americans are millionaires," said Alexis. "Isn't that what you used to impress on me? Sure, Kelso is one of the best—and best-paid—reporters on international politics. He picks up some extra money from articles and lectures, plus travel expenses when he has an assignment abroad. But he lives on the income he earns. That is what keeps him a busy man, I suppose."

"An influential man," Mischa said softly. "What about that book he has been writing for the last two years?"

"Geopolitics. Deals with the conflict between the Soviet Union and China."

"That much, we also know," Mischa said in sharp annoyance. "Is that all you have learned about it?"

"It is all anyone has learned in Washington. Do you think he wants his ideas stolen?"

"You had better try again with Mr. Thomas Kelso, and keep on trying."

"But what has this to do with your work in Directorate S?" That was the section of the First Chief Directorate that dealt in Illegals—agents with assumed identities sent to live abroad.

There was a moment of silence. It was impossible to see Mischa's expression clearly now. Night had come, black and bleak. Alexis could feel the angry stare that was directed at him through the darkness, and regretted his temerity. He repressed a shiver, turned up his coat collar. Then Mischa said, "The brash American," and even laughed. He added, "It has to do with my present work, very much so." He relented still further, and a touch of humor entered his voice. "Let us say that I am interested in influencing people who influence people."

So Mischa had moved over to the First Chief Directorate's Department of Disinformation. Alexis was appropriately impressed, but he kept silent. He had already said too much. If Mischa wasn't his friend, he might have been yanked out of Washington and sent to the Canal Zone or Alaska.

"So," said Mischa, "you will persevere with Tom Kelso. He is important because of his job and the friends he makes through it—in Paris, Rome,

London—and, of course, in the North Atlantic Treaty Organization. They trust him there in Nato. He hears a great deal."

Alexis nodded.

"About Nato . . ." Mischa was too casual, almost forgetful about what he had intended to say. "Oh yes," he remembered; "you sent us a piece of information a few days ago about that top security memorandum they passed to the Pentagon. You said it was now being studied at Shandon House." He was being routinely curious, it seemed, his voice conversational.

"It is being analyzed and evaluated. A double-check on the Pentagon's own evaluation."

"What is the real function of this Shandon House? Oh, we know it is a collection of brains working with computers; but—supersecret? Capable of being trusted with such a memorandum?"

"It is trusted. Everyone has top clearance. Security is tight."

"Ah, patriots all. Yet you said that it might be possible to breach that security. How? When?" The tone was still conversational.

"Soon. Perhaps even—" Alexis restrained himself. Better not be too confident. Better not be too precise. Then if the project turned sour, he wouldn't be blamed for promising too much and achieving too little. "I have no guarantee. But there is a possibility," he said more guardedly.

"When will you know more than that?"

"Perhaps later tonight."

"Tonight!" Mischa exploded. "I *knew* you had something, I knew it by the way you worded your message!"

So it was his information on the NATO Memorandum that had brought Mischa chasing over to New York. He had read Alexis's message last Tuesday or Wednesday. By Saturday he was here. In person. Was the Memorandum so important as that?

"You are set to act?" Mischa demanded. "What is your plan?"

"I have three possible variants. It depends. But I'll deliver."

"You are using microfilm, of course? The Memorandum is in three parts— over forty pages, I hear. You will need time."

Another hazard, thought Alexis. "I'll make time."

"And when you deliver, do *not* employ your usual method."

"No?" Alexis was puzzled. It was a set procedure. Any photographs he had taken, like his own reports in code, were passed to his weekly contact in Washington. The contact delivered them to Control, who in turn handed them over to the Residency. From there they were speeded to the Center in Moscow. There had never been any slip-up. His contact had a gift for choosing casual encounters, all very natural.

"No!— You will make the delivery to Oleg. He will alert you by telephone, and contact you some place of his own choosing. On Monday."

"But I may not have the microfilm by Monday. It may be the following weekend before—"

"Then you deliver it to Oleg on the following weekend," Mischa said impatiently. "You won't have any chance to get the Nato Memorandum after that. It returns to the Pentagon, we hear, for finalized recommendations to the National Security Council. Before then, we want the particulars of that document. So press your advantage with Shandon House. You do your job, and Oleg will do his."

"Oleg—how will I be able to identify him?" Surely not by a lot of mumbo-jumbo, Alexis thought in dismay: recognition signals wasted time, added to the tension. He had always felt safer in knowing his contact by sight, although there his interest stopped and he neither knew nor cared who the man was. The contact followed the same rules. To him, Alexis was a telephone number and a face.

Mischa raised his cane, pointed to their watchdog, who had stationed himself at a discreet distance.

"He isn't near any lamppost," Alex objected.

"You will see his face quite clearly as we pass him. Shall we go?" Mischa tilted his hat back in place. "We separate before we approach the flagpole area. I shall leave by way of the zoo. You head for the Seventy-second Street exit. Oleg takes Sixty-ninth Street—his car is parked there. He will drive down Fifth Avenue, and pick me up at the zoo. Simple and safe. It will raise no eyebrows. You agree?" Mischa moved away from the trees.

Alexis, with a quick glance over his shoulder—he had thought he saw two lurking shadows in the rough background—stepped onto the path. Mischa noticed. "Scared of the dark?" he asked with a laugh. "At half past five in the evening? Alexis, Alexis . . ." He shook his head. They walked in silence toward the waiting man.

As they passed close to him, he was lighting a cigarette. The lighter didn't flare. It glowed, with enough power to let Oleg's face be clearly seen. The glow ended abruptly. The cigarette remained unlit.

"You'll remember him?" Mischa asked.

"Yes. But could he see me clearly enough?"

"He has examined close-up photographs of your face. No trouble in quick identification. That's what you like, isn't it? I agree. No doubt, no uncertainties." Behind them Oleg followed discreetly.

Some fifty yards away from the flagpole, Mischa said, "Now we leave each other. Take a warm handshake for granted." This time the smile was genuine. "I shall hear from you soon?" It was more of a command than a question.

"Soon." No other answer was possible. He had forgotten how inexorable and demanding Mischa could be.

Mischa nodded and left, drawing well ahead. Alexis slowed his pace slightly, letting the distance between them increase. Oleg passed him, intent on reaching the car he had parked nearby, possibly on Sixty-ninth Street itself. It was westbound, of course: just the added touch to Mischa's careful arrangements.

Alexis watched Mischa as he took the southward path at the flagpole. For a few moments a nearby lamppost welcomed him into its wide circle of white light, showed clearly his solid figure and brisk stride against the background of massive rocks that filled this corner of the park. Then he was gone, swinging down toward the zoo.

Oleg was now well beyond the flagpole and heading for Fifth Avenue. Alexis noted for future reference the way he moved, the set of his shoulders, his height and breadth; the way he turned his head to look at the drunk, now sitting with his head between his knees. A dog-walker, enmeshed in a tangle of leashes, merited only a brief glance. One of the prostitutes still loitering under a lamppost received no attention at all: virtuous fellow, this Oleg.

So now, thought Alexis with a smile when he reached the flagpole, it's my turn to branch off. Two steps, and he stopped abruptly as he heard a shout. One shout. He looked round at the path to the zoo.

Someone rushed past him—the prostitute, fumbling in her handbag, kicking off her high-heeled shoes with a curse, running swiftly, gun drawn. It's a man, Alexis realized: a policeman. Almost simultaneously, the drunk had moved, racing around the crags, pulling a revolver out from his brown-paper bag as he cut a quick corner to the zoo path. Alexis stood still. His brain seemed frozen, his legs paralyzed. He looked helplessly at the dog-walker, but that young man was already yanking his charges toward the safety of Fifth Avenue.

Keep clear of the police, Alexis warned himself, don't get involved. But that had been Mischa's voice. Of that he was almost certain.

He began to follow the direction the two undercover men had taken. Again he stopped. From here he could see a man left lying on the ground, and three or four thin shadows scattering away from him as the policemen closed in. The one dressed as a woman knelt beside the inert figure—was he dead, or dying, or able to get up with some help? The other was giving chase to the nearest boy—the rest were vanishing into the darkness in all directions. Then he noticed the hat and the cane—pathetic little personal objects dropped near the body.

The policeman beside Mischa looked toward Alexis. "Hey, you there— give us a hand!"

Alexis turned and ran.

He came out onto Fifth Avenue, collected his wits while he stood listening to the hiss of wheels as the cars and taxis sped past. The traffic signal changed, and he snapped back into life. He crossed quickly, and entered Sixty-ninth Street. Curbs were lined with cars, the sidewalks quiet, with only a few people hurrying along. Where was Oleg? He couldn't have gone far: there hadn't been time enough for that. Alexis's desperation grew, he was almost into a second attack of panic. Then, just ahead of him, not far along the block, he saw broad shoulders and a dark head moving out into the street to walk round the front of a car and unlock it. He broke into a run. Oleg looked up, alert and tense: a look of total amazement spread over his face. He entered his side of the car, and opened the other door for Alexis.

"And what is this?" Oleg began angrily.

"Mischa was attacked. In the park. Not far down the path. Police are with him—undercover police. They'll send for more police, an ambulance. Get over there! Quick! See what's happening, see where they will take him. Find out the hospital. Quick!"

"Why didn't *you*—"

"Because they've seen me with him. The undercover man who was in woman's clothes saw us both together when we met."

"But—"

"There's the first police car." The siren was sounding some distance to the north, but it was drawing nearer. "Quick!" Alexis said for the third time, still more urgently. And left the car. He walked over to Madison. He did not look round.

Now it was up to Oleg. And Oleg (thought Alexis) is aware of that. He must know a good deal more than either Mischa or he pretended: being shown photographs of me, for instance, and given other particulars too—which proves he had access to my files? If he did, he's aware that I am just an agent in place, a mole that stays underground and works out of sight. My God, I was nearly surfaced tonight. So let Oleg attend to the problem of Mischa. He would have contacts in New York. He would know how to handle this. And above all, Alexis told himself, I have my own job to do. With Mischa or without Mischa, I still have an assignment to complete. I'll send the microfilm by the usual route, if Oleg does not contact me in Washington. This is no time to delay. If I get the information I'm after, I'm damned if I'm going to sit on it. You win no promotions that way.

He hailed a taxi to take him a short distance up Madison. From there he walked the block to Park Avenue and took a second cab. This carried him down to Fifty-third Street. There, among the tall office buildings and the Saturday-evening strollers, he walked another block to find a taxi to take him over to Second Avenue and up to Sixty-sixth Street. A circular tour, but a safety measure. He had heard of agents who had traveled for two hours on various subways, just to make sure.

It was a quarter past six when he reached the entrance of Katie's building. He did not get off the elevator at her floor, but at the one above. For a moment he stood in the small hallway thinking—as he always did—what a stroke of genius it had been to find an apartment for Chuck Kelso right in this house.

Then he pressed the bell. He was no longer Alexis. Now he was Nealey, Heinrich Nealey—Rick to his friends—an odd mixture of a name, but genuine enough, a real live American with legitimate papers to back that up.

Three

THE JOURNEY FROM Shandon House in New Jersey to Charles Kelso's apartment in New York took about an hour and ten minutes. It was easy—first a country road to lead through rolling meadows and apple orchards onto the fast Jersey Turnpike lined with factories, and then under the Hudson, in a stream of speeding cars, straight into Manhattan. So Kelso had chosen to make the trip twice daily, preferring to live in the city rather than become a part of the Shandon enclave in the Jersey hill-and-tree country. Like the younger members on the institute's staff, he preferred a change in friends: he saw enough of his colleagues by day, he didn't need them as social companions at night or on weekends. As for the long-time inhabitants of the various estates that spread around Shandon's own two thousand acres, they kept to themselves as they had been doing for the last forty years. If they ever did mention the collection of experts who had invaded their retreat, it was simply to call them "The Brains."

So too the village of Appleton, five miles away from Shandon—it had been there for almost three hundred years and considered everyone arriving later than 1900 as foreigners, acceptable if they provided jobs and much-needed cash (cider and hand-turned table legs had been floundering long before the present inflation started growing). On that point, the Brains were found wanting. They had their own staff of maintenance men and guards to look after Shandon House. Even the kitchen had special help. Four acres around the place had been walled off—oh, it didn't look too bad, there were small shrubs to soften it up—but the main entrance now had high iron gates kept locked, and big dogs, and all the rest of that nonsense. And those Brains who lived outside the walls in renovated barns, or farmhouses turned into cottages, might be pleasant and polite when they visited Appleton's general store; but they didn't need much household help and they never gave large parties, not even for the government big shots who came visiting from Washington.

The village agreed with the landed gentry that old Simon Shandon had really lost his mind (and it must have been good at one time: a $300,000,000 fortune testified to that) when he willed his New Jersey estate, complete with enormous endowment, to house this collection of mystery men and women. Institute for Analysis and Evaluation of Strategic Studies: that's what Simon Shandon had got for all that money. And even if the outside of the house had been preserved—a rambling mansion with over forty rooms, some of them vast—the interior had been chopped up. Rumor also said there was a computer installed in the ballroom. The villagers tried some computing themselves on the costs, shook their heads in defeat, and found it all as meaningless as the institute's title. Strategic studies—what did that mean? Well, who cared? After twelve years of speculation, their curiosity gave way to acceptance. So when Charles Kelso, taking the quickest route back to the city, drove through the village on a bright Saturday afternoon, when sensible folks were out hunting in the woods or riding across their meadows, no one gave his red Mustang more than a cursory glance. Those fellows up there at Shandon House came and went at all times: elastic hours and no trade unions. And here was this one, as usual forsaking good country air for smog and sirens.

But it was not the usual Saturday afternoon for Kelso. True, he had some work to catch up with; true, he sometimes did spend part of the weekend finishing an urgent job, so that the guard at the gatehouse hadn't seen anything strange when he had checked in that morning. And he was not alone. The computer boys were onto some new assignment, and there were five other research fellows scattered around, including Farkus and Thibault from his own department. But they didn't spend much time on one another, not even bothering to meet in the dining hall for lunch, too busy in their own offices for anything except a sandwich at their desks. They hadn't even coincided in the filing room at the end of the day's stint. It was empty when Kelso arrived to leave a folder in the cabinet where work-in-progress was filed if it was considered important enough.

Maclehose, on duty as security officer of the day, let him into the room through its heavy steel door—he always felt he was walking into a giant safe, a bank vault with cabinets instead of safe-deposit boxes around its walls. Maclehose gave him the right key for Cabinet D and stood chatting about his family—he hoped he'd get away from here by four o'clock, his son's seventh birthday, pity he hadn't been able to take today off the chain instead of Sunday.

"Then who's on duty tomorrow?"

"Barney, if he gets over the grippe." Maclehose wasn't optimistic. "He's running a temperature of a hundred and two, so I may have to sub for him. Thank God no one—so far—is talking about working here this Sunday."

"I may have to come in and finish this job."

"Pity you didn't keep it in your drawer upstairs." Maclehose could see his Sunday being ruined, all on account of one overdutiful guy. That was the trouble with the young ones; they thought every doodle on their think pads was worthy of being guarded in Fort Knox. "Then we could have locked up tight. Is that stuff so important?" He gestured to the folder in Kelso's hand.

Kelso laughed and began to unlock Cabinet D. He was slow, hesitating. Once its door was open, he would find two vertical tiers of drawers, three to each side. Five had the names of each member of his department, all working on particular problems connected with defense. The sixth drawer, on the bottom row of the right-hand tier, was simply marked Pending. And there the NATO Memorandum had come to rest. For the past three weeks it had been dissected, computerized, studied, analyzed. Now, in an ordinary folder, once more a recognizable document, it waited for the analyses to be evaluated, the total assessment made, and the last judgment rendered in the shape of a Shandon Report which would accompany it back to Washington.

"Having trouble with that lock?" Maclehose asked, about to come forward and help.

"No. Just turned the key the wrong way."

And at that moment the telephone rang on Maclehose's desk in the outer office.

It was almost as though the moment had been presented to him. As Maclehose vanished, Kelso swung the cabinet door wide open. He pulled out the Pending drawer, exchanged the NATO folder for his own, closed the drawer, shut the door. He was about to slip the Memorandum inside his jacket when Maclehose ended the brief call and came hurrying back.

He stared at the folder in Kelso's hand. "Taking your time? Come on, let's hurry this up. Everyone is packing it in—just got the signal—no more visitors today."

"How about Farkus and Thibault? They were working on some pretty important stuff."

"They were down here half an hour ago. Come on, get this damned cabinet open and—"

Kelso locked it, handed the keys over with a grin. "You changed my mind for me."

"Look—I wasn't trying to—"

Sure you were, thought Kelso, but he only tucked the folder under his arm. "It isn't really so important as all that. I'll lock it up in my desk. Baxter will see no one gets into my office." Baxter was the guard who would be on corridor patrol tomorrow. "Have a good birthday party—how many kids are coming?"

"Fifteen of them," said Maclehose gloomily. The door to the filing room clanged, was locked securely. Its key, along with the one for filing cabinet Defense, was dropped into the desk drawer beside those for the other departments—Oceanic Development, Political Economy, Space Exploration, Population, International Law, Food, Energy (Fusion), Energy (Solar), Ecology, Social Studies.

"Quite an invasion." Kelso watched Maclehose close the drawer, set its combination lock, and turned away before Maclehose noted his interest. "All seven-year-olds?"

"Good God," Maclehose said suddenly, "I almost forgot!" He frowned down at a memo sheet lying among the clutter on his desk. "There would have been hell to pay."

What's wrong now? Kelso wondered in dismay, halting at the door. His hand tightened on the folder, his throat went dry. Some new security regulation?

Maclehose read from the memo. "Don't forget to pick up four quarts of chocolate ice cream on your way home."

"See you Monday if you survive," said Kelso cheerfully, and left.

Kelso drove through Appleton, hands tight on the wheel, face tense. His briefcase, picked up in his office, lay beside him with the NATO folder disguised inside it by this morning's *Times*. He had opened the briefcase for the obligatory halt at Shandon's gates, but the guard had contented himself with his usual cursory glance through the car's opened window. After four years of being checked in and out, inspection of Kelso had become routine. Routine made everything simple.

All too damned simple, Kelso thought now, turning the anger he felt for himself against Shandon's security. I should never have got away with it. But I did.

He had no sense of triumph. He was still incredulous. The moment had been presented to him, and he had taken it. From then on there had been no turning back. How could he have done it? he wondered again, anger turning to disgust. All those lies in word and action, the kind of behavior he had always condemned. And yet it had all come so naturally to him. That was what really scared him.

No turning back? He slowed up, drew the car to the side of the narrow road, sat there staring at his briefcase. Now was the time, if ever. He could say he had forgotten something in his office: he could slip downstairs to the filing room—Maclehose would have left by now. He had the combination of the key drawer—127 forward, back 35—and the rest would be simple. Simple: that damned word again.

And yet, he thought, I had to do it. There was an obligation, a need. I've felt it for the last three weeks, ever since I worked over the first section of the Memorandum along with Farkus and Thibault. Yes, we all agreed that the first section should have been published for everyone to read. Now. Not in ten, twenty, even fifty years, lost in the highly classified files until some bureaucrat got round to releasing it.

The other two sections—or parts—of the NATO Memorandum were in a different category. From what he had heard, they *were* top secret. Definitely unpublishable. Unhappily, he glanced again at the briefcase. He wished to God they were back again in the Pending drawer. But he had had only a few moments, less than a full minute, not time enough to separate them from Part I of the Memorandum and leave them in safety. All or nothing: that had been the choice. So he had taken the complete Memorandum. The public had the need to know—wasn't that the current phrase, highly acceptable after the secrecies of Watergate? Yes, he agreed. There was a need to know, there was a moral obligation to publish and jolt the American people into the realities of today.

He drove on, still fretting about means and ends. His conduct had been wrong, his purpose right. If he weren't so sure about that . . . But he was. After three miserable weeks of debating and arguing with himself, he was sure about that. He was sure.

He was late. First, there was a delay on the New Jersey Turnpike, dusk turning to night as he waited in a line of cars. A truck had jackknifed earlier that afternoon, spilling its oranges across the road, and it was slow going, bumper to bumper, over the mess of marmalade. Next, there was a bottleneck in Saturday traffic on the Upper East Side of Manhattan—huge Caterpillars, two cranes, bulldozers, debris trucks, even a powerhouse, were all left edging a new giant excavation until Monday morning. If there was a depression just around the turn, these hard-hats didn't know it. And then, last nuisance of all, with night already here, he found all the parking spaces on his own street tightly occupied. He had to leave his car three blocks away and walk to Sixty-sixth Street, gripping his briefcase as though it contained the treasure of Sierra Madre. Yes, he was late. Rick had probably called him at five exactly; Rick seemed to have a clock planted like a pacemaker in his chest. It was now ten minutes of six.

"One hell of a day," he said aloud to his empty apartment. Switching on some lights, he placed the briefcase on his desk near the window and looked for any messages that Mattie, his part-time help, might have taken for him this morning. There was one. From his brother's wife, Dorothea. He stared at it aghast. Mattie had written out the message carefully, although the hotel's name had baffled her. "Staying this weekend at the Algonekin. Can you make dinner tonight at seven thirty?" God, he thought angrily, of all the nights for Tom and Thea to be in town! And then he began to remember: Tom was on his way to Paris on one of his assignments, and Thea was here for a day or two in New York. But surely they hadn't told him it was *this* weekend? Or had he forgotten all about it? His sense of guilt deepened.

He left the desk, with the typewriter table angled to one side of it, navigated around a sectional couch and two armless chairs in the central area of the room, skirted a dining section, reached the small pantry where he stored his liquor, and poured himself a generous Scotch. Of all the nights for Tom to be here, he kept thinking. He dropped into a chair, propped feet on an ottoman, began trying several excuses for size. None seemed to fit. Best call Tom and say that he just couldn't make it. Not this time, old buddy. Sorry, really sorry. See you on your way back to Washington. No, no . . . that was too damned cold.

He sighed and finished his drink, but he didn't move over to the telephone. He went into the bathroom and washed up. He went into the bedroom and got rid of his jacket and tie. He put some disks on his record-player. And when he did at last go to the desk, it was to open the briefcase. Plenty of time to get in touch with Tom—it was barely six fifteen. Yes, plenty of time to find some explanation that would skirt the truth ("Sorry, Tom. I forgot all about it") and yet not raise one of Dorothea's beautiful eyebrows.

The doorbell rang. Rick?

Four

I⊤ WAS RICK. "Sorry I couldn't phone. Spent the last hour getting here from La Guardia. Traffic was all fouled up." He was at ease as he always was, a handsome man of thirty-three, blond and gray-eyed (he had that coloring from his German mother); but at this moment his face looked drawn.

It's the harsh light in this hall: I'll have to change the bulb, thought Kelso. He caught sight of himself in the mirror, and he looked worse than Rick— everything intensified. His dark hair and brown eyes were too black, his skin too pale, the cheekbones and nose and chin had become prominent, his face haggard. "What we both need is a drink," he said, dropped Rick's coat on a chair and led the way into the room.

"Nothing, thanks." Rick's glance roved around, settling briefly on the desk and the open briefcase. He restrained himself in time, didn't make one move toward it. Instead, he watched Chuck pour himself a drink. "You look wrung-out. A bad day?"

"Hard on the nerves."

"What happened?"

"I took the damned thing." Chuck lowered the volume of *Daphnis and Chloe*.

"You've got it?"

"Yes. It's in the briefcase."

"All of it?"

Chuck nodded. "There was no other way."

"You aren't thinking of typing out the whole thing?"

"Not bloody likely. Part One is all we need. What about a reporter? You said several would jump at the chance to use it. Have you contacted any?"

"Yes. There's one on the *Times* who is interested."

"How much did you tell him?"

"Only that there might be something important for him to report in a week or two. Top-secret material, but no breach of national security if it were published. He sensed something big. Investigative reporting—that's got the appeal, all right."

"But why the *Times?*" Chuck objected. "That's Tom's paper."

"What does it matter? He's stationed in Washington—has never been near Shandon House. Besides, you aren't using your name, are you?"

"I don't want it used." Chuck insisted on that.

"Too bad, in a way. Think of all the lectures you'd be invited to give." Rick's smile widened. "The college circuit would really—"

"I want no publicity whatsoever. None. This is not an ego trip."

"I know, I know. Just joking."

"Does your reporter know that he can't use my name?"

"I didn't even mention it to him. I just spoke of Shandon House."

Chuck frowned. "Did you have to bring that in?"

"Yes. He knows who I am and what I do; in fact, he knows me quite well. But that wouldn't be enough to take to his editor and get the go-ahead to use the material. Shandon House carries real clout. Not to worry, Chuck. He isn't talking to anyone until I hand him a copy of the Nato Memorandum, Part One. Do you think he wants this story filched away from him?"

"Name?"

"Holzheimer. Martin Holzheimer. You've seen his by-line, haven't you?"

Chuck tried to remember, then shrugged his shoulders. If Holzheimer had a by-line, he was good. And Rick was an experienced judge: he met a lot of young journalists in his job as communications director for publicity-hound Pickering. Communications director. What titles these congressmen could dream up for their swollen staffs! "How old is he?"

"Old enough. Twenty-nine. On his way up. Besides, the useful thing is that he lives in Manhattan, so I can get hold of him easily."

"When?"

"Why not tonight?" Rick crossed over to the windows and pulled down the shades. "By the way, once you finish the typing, would you pick up Katie at Bo Browning's party? She's expecting me, but I have to meet Holzheimer." He adjusted one shade to his liking. All I need is some time to myself, he was thinking as he moved over to the desk. "Now, let's see how much work we have to do. How many pages?"

"Just a moment—I'd better call Tom first."

Rick stared. "Are you crazy, Chuck?"

"He's in New York, wants to see me for dinner."

"Oh." There was a brief pause. "Why not go? I can start the typing, and you finish it when you get back."

"No."

Rick tried a smile. "Then may I at least read the Memorandum? Just to get an idea of what we are into?"

"Sure. I didn't want you typing anything—you've been dragged into this business far enough."

"No worry about that. Holzheimer won't use my name or mention it to anyone. You and I are confidential sources. Privileged information."

"So is Shandon House," said Chuck firmly. "That name is strictly for his eyes alone. And for his editor's."

"Oh, come on, Chuck—"

"No. Its name does not get into print."

"I wonder if he'll agree to—"

"He'd better. Or else, no Memorandum. Besides, he will be reporting that it came from Nato. That's enough."

Rick nodded. "I suppose he will do some digging, check around, and find any possible leak in Washington—from State or the Pentagon—that would link Shandon House with the Nato Memorandum. That should convince him he is dealing with authentic material."

"I hope to God no one starts leaking too much."

"Beyond admitting that the Memorandum is now at Shandon? That's about all anyone does know. Except the top brass." If none of Mischa's agents in Washington—he must have one or two planted in both the Pentagon and State—had been able to get close to the NATO material, then no Washington informant was able to leak anything of value. "It's a well-kept secret. That will whet Holzheimer's appetite."

"Didn't he want to know *why* I was passing on this information to him?" I'd be curious about that myself, thought Chuck.

"Yes. And I told him the bare truth. You're a man who believes in détente and wants to see it work. The Nato Memorandum shows very clearly that détente is under attack. You thought the American public ought to know. And be warned." Rick studied Chuck's face. "Right?"

Chuck nodded. He was over at the desk now, taking out the Memorandum from the covering newspaper. Then he began removing Parts II and III, loosening them carefully from the close staples that bound the pages together. It would be a slow job.

"Have you read all the material?" Rick asked.

"Just glanced at the second and third sections. I wasn't working on them."

"What's so important about them? Part One—you told me last week—is a statement about the threats against détente. But what follows?"

"Part Two gives facts and figures about Nato's defense capability and dispositions, along with facts and figures about the Warsaw Treaty Organization's accretion in strength. Part Three gives the sources of all information presented in the preceding sections, to back up their credibility."

"Sources?" That could mean intelligence agents as well as reports from military attachés. Intelligence agents—wasn't that what Mischa was interested in? "Don't tell me they were *named?*" Rick looked shocked.

"Of course not. Kept anonymous. Just identified by location."

By location. But possibly identifiable by the quality of their reports. Any good KGB analyst could place them by their area of interest and their selected targets. Mischa's department would know just where to look for them, might be able to confirm a suspicion and make identification. No wonder Mischa had been so eager to get his hands on the NATO Memorandum. "I suppose," Rick said, "that that much had to be disclosed, to make their reports acceptable on this side of the Atlantic. I've often wondered how any intelligence agent ever gets believed if he stays completely unidentified. A weird kind of life. Did you ever regret refusing it when you had that chance with Military Intelligence in Germany?"

"Not my line. Codes and ciphers weren't either. I soon backed out of them: remember?" Chuck had removed all the staples without breaking one. He put them carefully into an ash tray for later use in reassembly. He gathered Parts II and III together, slipped them into the desk drawer, and locked it.

Rick lifted Part I. "Yes, you backed out of codes all right—into a job at the Pentagon." He laughed and began to flip over the loose pages.

"Go on, say it. I backed out of the Pentagon, too."

"No, you didn't. You jumped up the ladder and caught the Shandon rung." Rick was taking the pages more slowly, frowning in concentration.

"And there I am. Stuck." The chief of his department was only three years older than Chuck's thirty-two.

"Not you." Rick waved him into silence, seemed intent on reading. But he did not have to go beyond the first four pages to realize this was dynamite, and not the kind he had expected. He had assumed—and he cursed his stupidity—that this NATO statement on détente would aim some sharp criticism against the West. And it did. Danger lay in blind acceptance of détente as the magic word. Danger also lay in its complete rejection by prejudiced cold warriors. NATO's advice lay between these extremes: détente was good—as far as it went; it merited support—but only with a clear understanding of its limitations. Without that, public opinion in the West could be exploited and splintered, weakening NATO's defense capabilities at a time when the Warsaw Pact countries' armed strength had increased to a point of superiority in many areas. (This sharp reminder was a natural lead-in to a plea for continuing American military strength in Europe. Depleted numbers of tanks and planes, as a result of Middle East requirements, must be replaced. Any decrease in Western defense would only lessen the West's bargaining power.)

But that was not all of NATO's unpleasant warning. To bolster its thesis, it included a careful study of the Soviet interpretation of détente: military and economic agreements could be signed, but that in no way precluded Soviet interest in exploring the weaknesses of the West and pouring acid into open wounds. The old methods of cold war—open or threatened confrontation, brutal tactics such as the Berlin blockade—were now out of date. The new strategy of détente was "the conquest of the system," a phrase much used by German Communists. By this was meant the destruction of political democracy in the West, by *covert* attacks on its constitutional foundations and by the discrediting of fundamental political and social ideals. For this purpose, Disinformation (Department A of the First Chief Directorate, Committee for State Security) had become increasingly important in Soviet planning.

Disinformation. Mischa's department. What would he have to say about these details on the recent successful take-over of the Free University in West Berlin, for instance? His agents and their methods clearly described? Rick drew a deep breath to steady himself, then went on with what he had been discussing. "You'll be at the top of the ladder in ten years—director of the institute by Tom's age. How does that grab you? Better than being a foreign correspondent." He placed some of the pages on the desk, squared them off neatly. He pursed his lips.

"What's the verdict so far?" Chuck was eager to know.

"Packs a hefty punch. But—don't you think—it might be considered a low blow against Kissinger and Ford?"

Chuck stared at him. "I told you what it was about, didn't I? What made you change around?"

"I haven't. I still think it ought to be published. Perhaps a little later. Not at this moment. Ford is in Vladivostok right now."

"All the more reason—"

"Why don't we wait until after Kissinger attends the Nato meeting on December twelfth in Brussels? That's not too far off." And, Rick thought, that would give me time to squelch Holzheimer's interest.

"And that is exactly why we are going ahead as planned. We'll make sure that the Brussels meeting is going to listen to Nato's assessment of détente, and talk about it openly. It isn't just the American public that needs a jolt. There's far too much secrecy about things that should be out in the open. How can people decide, if they get no choice? They've got to know the alternatives. . . ."

"Okay, okay. It was just a suggestion. You've convinced me that it wasn't a good one."

"You know your trouble, Rick? You're too damned conservative."

"You know both our troubles? We need some food. I've had nothing to speak of since breakfast. And you? I bet you didn't eat much lunch. What's in the refrigerator?"

"You can fix us a sandwich while I'm typing."

"Right. But first let me finish reading. I could use that drink now. A dry Martini?"

"Coming up." Chuck left for the pantry.

Rick moved quickly. He dropped the sheets of paper on the desk, turned toward the typewriter, and lifted off its cover. Then he selected the *A* key, raised its type bar, and bent it. He did the same with the *S* key next to it. That should be enough, he decided as he pushed the type bars back in place as far as they would go. He slipped the cover over the machine and wiped his fingers clean of ink before picking up the Memorandum again. By the time Chuck returned, he was sitting at the desk, a study in complete concentration. He finished the last page and placed it with the others.

"Well?" Chuck asked.

"It's good. Someone worked hard over all that. Nato Intelligence, I suppose?"

"It's something like our own work at Shandon. A matter of analyzing facts, and evaluating, and wrapping it all up with judicial opinion. Prognosis is always the hardest part, and yet it's the most necessary. Here's your Martini—dry enough? I'm out of onions and olives. Like some lemon peel?"

"No, this is fine. Just fine."

Chuck looked at the clock on the desk, checked his watch. "I'd better give Tom a call before I set to work." He was suddenly worried. "Hope I have enough carbon paper. I'll need a copy for myself—just to make sure that the *Times* prints all I give them." He went to the typing table and pulled out its drawer. "Enough," he said as he checked the box of carbons. "But there's no extra ribbon."

"Now you're starting to fuss over details." Any old excuse, thought Rick, to postpone the call to Tom. Has there been some brotherly quarrel?

But Chuck was pulling off the typewriter cover and inserting a sheet of paper into the roller. "Just testing the ribbon. If it's weak, you'll have to borrow a spare from Katie. No typewriter-supply shop is open at this hour on a Saturday night."

"Tom will be waiting—"

"Time enough yet." Chuck began typing, and stopped. He tried again. "Damnation."

"Something wrong?"

"Two keys stuck. They're out of kilter." He tried to straighten their type bars, and then looked up at Rick in complete dismay. "No go," he said. "What the hell do I do now? And who—"

"Mattie? She has a strong dusting arm."

"She wouldn't touch the type bars."

"She could have dropped something on them by accident."

"A load of bricks?" Chuck asked bitterly.

"Or she backed her two hundred pounds into the table and sent the machine flying."

"What the hell do I do?" Chuck said again. "Try Katie, will you? She'll lend us her typewriter." Katie had an old and hefty machine, a period piece that amused her, along with her stand-up telephones and big-horn phonograph.

"It's on the blink. It would chew up every ribbon you had."

Chuck stood very still. Then his face cleared, and he reached for the telephone book. "Algonquin, Algonquin . . ." His finger ran down the *A* section. "Here we are." He put through the call. "Tom? I just got in and found Dorothea's message. Look—I'm sorry: I have a load of work to do here. Can't manage dinner. But could I drop down to the Algonquin right now? Have a quick drink with you? . . . And say, could I borrow your portable? . . . I'll return it tomorrow without fail. . . . Yes, I know you need it. I'll have it back long before you take off for Paris. Okay? See you in twenty minutes or so."

Chuck dropped the receiver, and was off to the bedroom for jacket and tie. He made a whirlwind exit, calling over his shoulder, "Back in an hour."

So I lost that round, Rick thought: he will have his typewriter, and a completed script by ten or eleven tonight. But I've been given the time and opportunity I need. Better than I planned. So take it. He began clearing the desk, moving the section of the Memorandum he had been reading out of his way. One hour, probably more. He would aim at forty minutes, and be on the safe side.

He produced a small bunch of keys and selected the skeleton one—that was all he needed for this simple lock. Deftly he manipulated it, pulled the desk drawer open, and lifted out the two top-security parts of the NATO Memorandum. He only glanced at the number of pages, wasted no time in reading them, although he had a strong temptation to examine Part III. He adjusted the strong desk lamp to the correct angle. Then he took out a small matchbox-size camera from his inside pocket, and placed the first page in position under the circle of light. He began photographing.

The whole job was completed—the sheets all back in order and replaced in the drawer exactly as he had found them—within thirty-five minutes. The precious film was left in the camera: he would extract it when there was less chance of any mishap—his hands felt tired, his eyes strained. The inside pocket of his jacket, fastened with a small zipper, would be safe enough.

Now he could put the desk back in shape again. The pages of Part I were neatly placed, ready for Chuck's use. He would make some sandwiches, get coffee percolating, and show some signs of a well-spent hour.

Lose one round, win another, he told himself, as he searched for his glass— he had laid it quietly aside on one of the small tables, unwilling to risk Chuck's potent mix while he still had problems to work out. The Martini wasn't worth drinking now. He carried it into the kitchen, emptied it down the sink, and poured himself a double vodka. He had earned it.

Five

Tom Kelso got back to the hotel at ten past six, after a day divided between meetings—one with an editorial staff member at the *Times,* to discuss the shape of his visit to France; another with a television reporter who had just ended a three-year assignment there; a third with an attaché on leave from the embassy in Paris—and found Dorothea, clad in a black chiffon negligee and a white felt hat. She was seated before her dressing-table mirror, studying a profile view of the upturn-and-dip of the hat's wide brim. She turned to welcome him, as he came through the sitting room and halted at the bedroom door, and gave him a smile that would lift any tired man's heart. "What do you think?" she asked him.

"A lot of things." He lifted the hat from her head, tossed it onto a chair. And I've only got fifteen minutes to shower and change, and order drinks from the bar, he thought in sudden frustration.

"Don't you like it?"

"It gets in the way." He bent down and planted a kiss on top of her soft smooth hair. She raised her face, still flushed and pink from her perfumed hot bath, to offer him a proper kiss on his lips. She smelled delicious, damn it. "I'll take a two-minute shower. Would you get out my blue shirt and red tie, honey?" He was on his way to the bathroom, pulling off his clothes as he went. "And you'd better start dressing, Thea."

"But Chuck won't be here till seven thirty. There's plenty of time."

"Not as much as you think. Tony Lawton is coming up for a drink. Brad Gillon, too."

"When?" she called in alarm, rising from the dressing table and going into quick motion. First the shirt and tie. Tom was already in the shower, her question drowned out in a flood of water. She began pulling on panty-hose and bra. Gillon she knew well, an old friend of Tom's, once attached to the State Department but now out of Washington and into New York publishing. Tony Lawton? She started creaming and powdering. Yes, she remembered, she had met him once before—on a quick Washington visit; English; lived in London when he wasn't traveling around—another of Tom's friends from abroad. Some eyebrow pencil, lipstick, hair combed into place. She was almost ready for her little black dress, in fashion again like the hat she had bought on impulse at the end of a hard day's shopping. Saturday wasn't her choice, exactly, to find Christmas presents, but that was the way Tom's schedule had been arranged, and so—she shrugged her shoulders. Tom was out of the bathroom, rubbing his hair dry. "When are they due?" she asked, dress in hand.

"At six thirty, damn it."

"Oh, heavens!" She began stepping into her dress.

"It's always the way—" He stopped combing his hair. "I'm getting an awful lot of gray at the sides," he said worriedly, looking into the mirror.

"It suits you, darling." She took a minute off dressing, and studied him. At forty-two, he was a healthy specimen: muscles firm, waistline still trim (he brooded about it, kept swearing off second helpings and desserts, but that was a vanity he shared with a million other men), dark hair plentiful even if graying at the temples, dark eyes watching her with a smile as he studied her in turn.

"Come on, blondie," he said, "get that dress on, however much it spoils the view. Old Brad would lose the sight of his good eye if he were to see you like that."

"Oh, Tom!" Her even eyebrows were raised, black eyelashes flickered, pink lips parted into a gentle protest.

"Yes, it's always the way," Tom said again, pulling on his own clothes. He had been delighted today when Tony Lawton had called him at the office, suggesting a drink this evening—and would Tom invite Brad Gillon, too? "Why didn't I say seven o'clock?"

"Because Chuck is coming at seven thirty. You'd never have time for any of that old-boys-together talk."

"Better order the drinks," Tom reminded himself, moving quickly to the telephone.

"How did your day go?"

"Not too bad." Tom waited for bar service to answer, speculating again why Lawton had been so eager to arrange a meeting here this evening with Gillon, rather than going straight to Gillon himself. Tony's wiles always amused Tom: they gave him good copy too, although they weren't always immediately publishable. "Not too bad at all. I was well briefed. I'll know where to start digging for information in Paris, get the French points of view about the Brussels meeting next month. They've got a kind of—" He broke off to tell bar service that he needed Scotch, bourbon, spring water, soda, and plenty of ice. Pronto.

"A kind of what?" Dorothea asked as he left the phone.

"We-are-with-you-but-not-of-you complex. Tricky to evaluate. It could mean more than we think, or less than we hope." The French, dissociated since de Gaulle from NATO's military problems, would attend only the diplomatic and economic sessions of the Brussels meeting, but they still held definite opinions about European defense.

"So," she said slowly, "you'll be covering the Nato meeting on December twelfth." She was still hoping that he wouldn't have to return so soon to Europe. With this Paris visit, he would miss Thanksgiving at home. He might miss Christmas with his trip to Brussels. "It's all definite?"

"Definite," he said, and hoped there would be no more argument about that. "I'll be back before Christmas. All the Nato meetings will be over well before then."

But, she wondered, will your business be over, my sweet? Emergencies could stretch an assignment, as she well knew. She ought to be grateful, she reflected, that Tom wasn't staying on for extra weeks in Paris while he waited for the Brussels meetings to begin—a lot of men would have done just that.

"You look like a girl who needs help with a zipper," said Tom, and fixed her dress. "Perfect," he decided, swinging her round to look at the total effect, and it was no diplomatic lie. He kissed her gently.

"So are you. I like that dark red tie."

"Matches my eyes," he told her, and let her go, to hurry into the sitting room as a waiter arrived with the tray of drinks. He heard her laugh. But his eyes were tired, he had to admit. As well as listening today, there had been a lot of reading and note-taking; and a head now filled with a collection of odd facts that kept swimming around. All he wanted was a relaxed evening, a pleasant dinner, and early to bed with his beautiful blonde. "Any message from Chuck?" he called to her.

"Not so far." Dorothea was selecting the right earrings. Tom's voice had sharpened. She could imagine the frown on his face. "Chuck will be here. Even if he didn't get my message, he'll turn up."

And there came the old twinge of guilt, whenever she mentioned Chuck: her fault, probably, that he had drifted away from Tom in these last five years. Before her day, they had enjoyed a fairly comfortable setup from Chuck's point of view. Until she had entered the scene. Then, he had left Washington behind him for a job at Shandon House and a life of his own in New York.

About time, too, she had believed: Chuck, except for college and army service, had been on Tom's back since he was eight and Tom eighteen. At that ripe age, Tom had become father and mother combined, and found a cub-reporter's job to pay the bills (their parents' life insurance could scarcely meet the rent of the New York apartment). As soon as Chuck was safely into college, Tom seized the chance to travel: Vienna, for the Kennedy-Khrushchev meeting; Athens, for the last two years of the Caramanlis democracy. With that over, he was back at the dutiful-brother bit, seeing Chuck through a youthful and disastrous marriage, remaining a bachelor himself—partly because he was into international politics and the new excitement of travel, partly because there was his move to Washington, but mostly because being a bachelor had become a habit hard to break. (After all, if the boy of eighteen was loaded down with family responsibilities, the man he became had already had enough of them for a while.)

And then Tom and she had met.

In a television studio. (She was arranging interviews on the Bud Wells Talk Talk Talk Show, and Tom was one of the victims that day.) Ten minutes, no more than that, ten minutes together, and there it was, bingo. The hard-case bachelor of thirty-seven, the career girl of twenty-six—good-by to all set plans and determined ideas; hello to a future of whatever it took to make it work.

She smiled at the memory, and carefully fastened her earrings into place. They dangled brightly. The rope of mock pearls was discarded. Enough was enough. Looking critically at her image in the mirror, she wondered what kind of woman Chuck had imagined for a suitable sister-in-law: plump and speechless, or gray-haired and motherly? He resented her; she could feel it, although he hid it well. Just as she resented the way Tom still worried about him. But one rule she had made right from the beginning: never criticize Chuck, that delightful, brilliant, and forgetful young man. Why didn't he call? Tom hadn't seen him in almost two months. And it hurt Tom: of course it must.

Dorothea went into the sitting room. "You know, darling, he may never have got my message."

"Chuck? You worry too much, my pet." Tom's voice was carefully casual.

Do I? she wondered. Then she smiled in relief as the telephone rang. But it wasn't Chuck. It was the desk clerk announcing Mr. Bradford Gillon.

Brad connected in her mind with another thought. "He *is* going to publish your book, isn't he?"

"Hasn't backed out so far."

"If only you could get some time to yourself and finish it. Just six months—"

"Would you settle for three?" He was laughing at the surprise he had given her. "Meant to keep the news for dinner, but you really coax things out of a man. You'd be a good reporter."

"Oh, Tom—did the *Times* tell you today, actually promise—?"

"They'll consider a three months' leave." He caught her, held her close. "But that will depend on how the world news breaks," he added to keep their excitement in check.

"Oh, Tom—" she said again, her arms flung around his shoulders. "I've got plans too. I'm taking a year off. Oh, I know, I may never get that job back again, but—"

"A year?" He looked at her quickly.

"Two, if necessary. There's more to life than having my name painted on my office door. Besides, I saw Dr. Travis first thing this morning. She says I'm in great shape now. No further risks. She sounded definite about that. Everything's fine. All systems go."

"Thea—"

A quiet knock sounded on the door. Tom released her and went to answer it. "Hello, Brad. Isn't Tony coming?"

"Sure. I saw him circling around the lobby." Brad's usually serious face was showing definite amusement. "He'll be arriving by himself any minute."

"By the stairs?" Tom asked with a grin. He left the door ajar.

Brad was now wholly absorbed with Dorothea. "You look wonderful." He gave her a brotherly hug and a warm kiss on the cheek.

"So do you." A little heavy, perhaps, but he was a tall, big-boned man, so he carried his weight well. Strong features, hawk nose, heavy eyebrows, almost somber in repose. White hair waving back from a large brow—plenty of brains inside that massive head. Gentle eyes, blue and quietly observant. "How is Mona?" Dorothea asked, minding her manners.

"Just recovering from her third attack of flu this fall."

"It's a hint to make you take her to Florida sunshine for ten days."

"Wish I could. Haven't had a week off the chain since last Christmas."

Recently he had been in France and Germany, Dorothea remembered, to discover some new authors and round up a belated manuscript or two. (Brad had reverted to his early interest in French and German literature— he had a degree from Harvard, way back in the early 1940's—which provided a pleasant niche for him in the publishing field.) "Why not take Mona with you on your next trip abroad?"

"Children," said Brad briefly. As a man of fifty-two who had married young, he now had all the problems of two divorced daughters and four grandchildren. "Why people can't stay married!" He shook his head. It seemed to him that after bringing up two strong-minded females, it was a bit much to have their offspring dumped on Mona. "Never own a house with five bedrooms," he said. "Should have got rid of it years ago."

"Well," said Tom, pouring bourbon for Brad and Scotch for Thea and himself, "when home becomes unbearable, there's always the office."

"Is Brad long-suffering, again?" Tony Lawton asked, as he stepped into the room and closed the door firmly. His voice and smile were amiable, and they all responded with a laugh, even a small one from Brad, who knew his own weaknesses better than most men. "Don't you believe him. He's addicted to work. Take that away, and he'd really be miserable."

"Overwork was never your complaint, Tony," Brad reminded him. But the indirect compliment pleased him.

"Wouldn't dream of allowing it to interfere with my pleasures. Yes, I'll have bourbon, Tom. And how are you, old boy? Mrs. Kelso—" Tony turned all his easy charm on her, and it was considerable—"how very nice it is to see you again. Or don't you remember me?"

He wasn't a particularly memorable man: nondescript features: brownish hair; gray eyes level with hers; no more than five foot seven. Age? Late thirties, early forties? His voice was attractive. He was dressed in gray, the suit well-cut; his tie was subdued, his shoes gleaming. Clothes definitely made the man in this case, Dorothea decided: without that cut of suit and those polished shoes, she never would have identified him so quickly. Unless, of course, he retained that warm smile and gentle humor in his talk. "I remember," she said. "The wine merchant who likes to drink bourbon and branch water."

"Split personality," Tony agreed, and didn't even flinch at "wine merchant." He rather liked that description of his wine-shipping firm, headquarters in London, branches all around the world.

"It's safer drinking bourbon than Bordeaux nowadays," Brad suggested, and that launched Tony into a hilarious version of the "Winegate" scandal in France. He had just come from there, seemingly. He does get around, thought Dorothea, and sat quietly watching the three men absorbed in one another. The talk was veering from French wine to French politics, then over to Algiers (wine as the lead-in to politics again), and next to Italy (Chianti troubles and—yes, there it was once more—political problems). It wasn't that the men had forgotten about her: there were smiles in her direction to keep her in touch, as it were. And she was fascinated. Free-flowing conversation like this seemed to bring out each man's character. Tom was the journalist, pouncing on a statement, questioning. Brad still retained much of his reserved and thoughtful State Department manner—everything weighed, and often found wanting. And Tony, eyes now alert and interested, tongue quick and explicit, must be a most capable businessman. In some ways, a strange trio; but friends, most definitely. She had a sudden vision of getting all three of them onto the Bud Wells talk show—they'd take it over. That would really freeze Bud's platitudes into astonished silence. She laughed. They stopped discussing Yugoslavia after Tito's death, and looked at her in surprise.

The telephone rang. Saved by the bell, she thought, as Tom went to answer the call and attention switched away from her. Gentlemen don't listen to other gentlemen's phone calls, she reminded herself, amused now by the low-voiced conversation that Brad and Tony had begun. But I'm no gentleman. It was Chuck on the phone. She could tell from Tom's face as he listened. Her heart sank.

Tom stopped beside her chair. "He forgot all about this evening," he said quietly, and managed a smile.

"Did he actually say—" she began, indignation showing in spite of all her resolutions.

"No, no. Pressure of work. He's dropping in here for a quick drink. Needs to borrow my typewriter."

"I'll get it ready for him." The portable's traveling case was in the bedroom closet with Tom's bags. She left Tom explaining his brother's visit, and when she came back they were on the topic of Shandon House—old Simon's brain child, Tony called it. Simon Shandon would have been astonished to see how big it had become.

"Not in numbers," said Brad. "They've held that down. But in impact—yes. Your brother must be a whiz kid, Tom, to get in there."

"He's got most of the family brains."

Not true, not true, Dorothea thought in quick defense; but she let Tom have his moment of modesty. Damn it all, why did he always downgrade himself with Chuck? A long-standing habit, meant to encourage the young and bolster their confidence?

"What is Shandon going to do with its new property?" Tony asked. "Expand into Europe?"

I'm at sea again, thought Dorothea: what new property?

Brad noted her expression, began to explain. Simon Shandon's widow had never liked New Jersey, never even liked living in America. She preferred their villa on the Riviera. So, under the terms of old Simon's will, that was what she had been left—the villa, and a yearly allowance for the extent of her lifetime. When she died—no children, no near relatives to complicate Simon's wishes—the Riviera estate would become the property of Shandon House. She had obliged them by dying three weeks ago at the age of ninety-two, still fuming against her husband's will and all the wealth he had invested in New Jersey.

"Probably that's why she stayed alive so long—out of sheer pique," Tony said. "So now Shandon has a place near Menton. How very snazzy! Will it be a rest and recreation center for tired intellects?"

"They could treat it in the way Harvard dealt with the Berenson villa near Florence," said Brad.

"A sort of Shandon-by-the-Sea?"

"Without computers. Just a gathering of brains, American and European, setting themselves problems to solve. A series of evening seminars after a day of solitary meditation." Brad's smile widened.

Tony said, "Each man with a private office and his feet up on his desk, thinking great thoughts as he stares out at the blue Mediterranean? It's a marvelous racket, this institute business. Cozy little setup, and tax-free."

"They do justify their existence," Tom reminded him.

"Every now and again. But—" Tony sighed. "It can be a dangerous situation, too. Get it under political control, and where will we all be? Listening to advice that will leave us more bewildered than ever." He smiled for Dorothea. "I bewilder very easily," he told her. She wondered about that.

The telephone rang—the desk in the lobby announcing Chuck's arrival. Dorothea packed the portable typewriter into its case. Tom had already opened the door and was waiting in the corridor, no doubt to tip Chuck off about the guests inside.

Chuck entered, his arm round Tom's shoulder. "Really sorry," he was explaining, "but I've got a rush job to finish. You know what deadlines are like, Tom." He relaxed as he saw that everyone—even Thea, or rather Dorothea: Thea was Tom's privilege, she insisted on that—accepted his explanation. He looked tired enough, God knew. And it was a relief to find others here: he could beg off staying for a twenty-minute chat. With this group there would be no chance for a tête-à-tête with Tom. He gave Dorothea a brief kiss on her cheek and one of his best smiles. A polite nod to the Englishman, a small word or two to Brad Gillon, whom he remembered from Washington days, and he had the typewriter in his hand and an apology on his lips. "No, I won't sit down—I might not get up again for another hour. Besides, I have a feeling I'm interrupting a good party. When do you get back from Paris, Tom?" He was already moving to the door.

"Sunday. A week from tomorrow."

"I'll see you then. Come and stay at my place—I've a couch that makes into a fairly good bed."

"I may do that."

"Wonderful!"

Dorothea said, "By the way, Chuck, you'd better clean the type. Some letters are a little blurred with ink and gunk. I meant to do that yesterday, but—"

"It works, doesn't it? Which is more than can be said for my machine. Thanks, Tom. Thanks a million. And I'll have it back tomorrow morning. Okay? I'll drop it off on my way to Shandon."

"Sunday on the job?" Tom asked. "You really are in a bind."

"It happens, every now and again."

"Doesn't it, though?" Brad agreed. "Bye, Chuck." Good-bys from Tom and Dorothea, too. Tony Lawton smiled and nodded. The door closed and Chuck was on his way.

Throughout the brief visit, Tony had said nothing at all. His interest in Chuck had been politely disguised. Now he said, as he stopped examining his drink, "So that is one of Shandon's bright young men."

"Never met anyone from there before?" Brad asked. "If you like, I'll introduce you to Paul Krantz, the director. He's an old friend of—"

"A waste of his time. And of mine: Shandon isn't laying down a cellar of French wines, is it?"

"Hardly," said Tom. "At lunch, I hear, they are more apt to grab a ham on rye with a gallon of coffee."

"Then I'll stick to our customers in Washington. That," he said to Dorothea, "is where I am bound now. You'd be surprised how many embassy cellars need replenishing."

"I'll take the hint and replenish *you*." Tom reached for their glasses. And there's a gentle hint for Tony, he thought. "And then Thea and I are leaving for dinner. That mention of ham and rye made me remember my own lunch today."

"Go right ahead," Tony said easily. "I'd like to stay for a few moments with Brad, and dig into that memory of his. Nice to have a friend who goes back a long way."

Tom stared at him, said briskly, "Come on, Thea, we'll leave them to it. Get your wrap. We'll eat downstairs, make it an early evening." He looked pointedly at Tony, as Dorothea left for the bedroom to collect scarf and bag.

"We'll be away from here long before that," Tony promised. "Where are you staying in Brussels? The old hangout? I'll look you up if I'm around."

As he would be. "Do that," Tom said. "And don't make all your nice little news items off the record. Give me something I can write up. Here's the key to this room. Lock up tightly, will you?"

"That's Brad's department."

"Oh, I forgot, he's the one who will be dropping it at the desk. Exits must match entrances."

"Always kidding." Tony smiled blandly.

Brad laid the key well in view beside his drink. "We'll talk about the book when next we meet," he said apologetically. "How is it coming?" His rule with authors was never to press them, never harry or hurry.

"Needs some spare time, but I think I may get that."

"Oh?" Brad probed gently.

"I'll stop in to see you at the office, on my way to Brussels. I'll explain then. Okay?"

"Very much so."

Dorothea returned, her bewilderment growing as she was led in Tom's firm grip out of the room, her little good-by speeches cut down to a bright smile. At a safe distance along the empty corridor, she let her feelings explode. "And what on earth is going on?"

"Nothing."

"Nothing?"

He calmed her with a kiss on her cheek. "They needed a place to meet. Why not in our room?"

She dropped her voice to a whisper. "What are they plotting?"

"It's no conspiracy against the United States, if that's what is worrying you," he said with a grin. "It's just some information that Tony wants from Brad."

There was no one in the elevator. Dorothea said, "But Brad isn't with Intelligence, is he?"

"Definitely not." No more. Brad had resigned from that kind of work almost twelve years ago.

"But Tony is, isn't he?"

"Now, what gave you that idea?"

"Just a feeling, somehow. You know, I only remembered him tonight by his clothes. And I thought, What if Tony was dressed as a stevedore and I bumped into him on the docks—"

"*That's* a wild notion!" It amused Tom.

"Or, if he was dressed as a pilot and I saw him on board a flight to Detroit—"

"If my aunt had whiskers, she'd be my uncle."

"Some women do have whiskers," Dorothea reminded him coldly. "All I'm trying to say is that Tony's the kind of man I'd hardly remember unless I could place him by his clothes."

"Not very flattering to Tony, are you? I don't think he'd be too amused to hear all that. In fact"—Tom was suddenly serious—"I think we should drop the whole subject right now and enjoy our dinner."

He steered her through the lobby into the dining room. He wasn't too worried. In five years of living together Thea had never repeated a confidence he had given her. Discreet. No gossiper. That was Thea. But he didn't like the little frown shading her bright blue eyes. "We'll talk later," he promised.

"It's just that I'm so sick of the word Intelligence," she began.

"Later," he said firmly. "Now, smile for the maître d', and get us a good table."

"And you'll really answer all my questions?"

"Do my best. I'm no oracle, darling, just a newspaperman who is very very hungry."

She smiled then, for him entirely. They got a good table in any case.

In the sitting room Brad Gillon had been listening intently to Tony. No more jokes, no more flights of fancy.

"Come on, Brad, dig into that memory bank. You must have heard of Konov in your OSS days. That time you raced into the ruins of Hitler's Chancellery neck and neck with Soviet Intelligence. Konov was with their team."

"The one that went through a mess of Hitler's private papers, trying to find some evidence that Churchill had been conspiring with him to attack Russia?"

"They wanted to believe it, too," Tony said, shaking his head.

"A Soviet intelligence officer's dream of glory? *Alone I found it.*"

"But there was nothing to find. If only Konov had been in Disinformation at that time, he would have invented a document then and there. Thank God he wasn't. He is now." Tony paused. "During the fifties and sixties, Konov worked in their Department for Illegals. Does that catch your memory? A lot of intelligence reports must have passed over your desk in that period."

"I left State by 1962," Brad reminded him. "But just around then—yes, I begin to remember Konov." His voice quickened. "There was that episode in Ottawa—left in a hurry just before the Canadians could arrest him. He was in the U.S. too, I recall. A busy little beaver."

"North America was his field. Still is."

"Then why is Nato worrying about him—or don't you think our intelligence agencies can cope?" Brad asked with a wry smile.

"*If* they'd start co-operating with each other again—" Tony suggested, but refrained from a sharp criticism of Hoover in the late sixties—"or with us. But that happy state got cut off abruptly. It's the root reason for all their present troubles isn't it?"

"Could be." Thank God, I'm out of all that, thought Brad; but he couldn't bury his memories, or the latest headlines either. "I'm afraid for my country, Tony. These are bad days."

"Head-rolling time," Tony agreed. "I must say—when you Americans start swinging, you use a hatchet. Couldn't a neat scalpel and some precision surgery do the job?"

"You get no big headlines with a scalpel."

There was a brief silence.

"Look—I didn't bring you here to depress you," Tony said briskly. He rose and freshened their drinks. "All I want is a little help from you on the problem of Vladimir Konov."

"How?" Brad was wary.

"Konov is arriving here on Tuesday. He's with a grain-buying team meeting your agricultural experts in Washington."

That was a shock. "Cool customer, isn't he? After his exit from Canada—what is he doing here, d'you think? Gathering background for future Disinformation use?"

"He'll sound out those who are soft and those who are tough, and no doubt he'll go to work on the easy marks, and arrange some future approaches through his Illegals. They were his specialty during the sixties. He provided them with American passports and life histories—sometimes belonging to real Americans, remember?"

Brad nodded.

"But Konov has another reason for coming here, just at this time. A reason he has been trying to keep to himself. So we've heard, from one of our agents in Moscow."

"Nato Intelligence has an agent in place? Close enough to Konov to know his plans? Pretty good. In fact, damned good."

"So far, yes. He and Konov are in the same Department of Disinformation. He's actually senior to Konov, but they are rivals for the next big promotion. Tricky."

"That's one of your better understatements."

"So here's the setup. Konov has suspicions—they are his meat and drink. Konov has ambitions. Konov is out gunning for our agent. And he will succeed if he can get his hands on a Nato Memorandum that was sent to Washington. He knows it exists, but hasn't the particulars so far. And that's what he needs, to be right on target—a piece of evidence that would disclose our agent. Several others, too, but our man in Moscow would be the first casualty."

"What evidence? Surely Nato didn't mention names?"

"No, no. The evidence would be in the kind of specialized information that was sent to Nato. Konov could track the source down. At least, that's what our agent feels. He's jittery. No doubt about that. We had word from him yesterday."

"So you took the night flight out of Brussels," Brad said thoughtfully. "Washington next?"

Tony nodded. "I'm on convoy duty—making sure the Nato Memorandum gets safely back to Brussels, once the Pentagon releases it to me."

"But what help do you need from me?" Brad's somber face was perplexed.

"Just sound the tocsin. Warn any of your old friends at State that Konov is in town. They'll get in touch with the Justice Department and see that the message gets through to the right investigative agencies."

"What about your own CIA contacts in Washington?"

"Paralyzed at the moment. You've been reading the papers, haven't you? How do you expect them to act—boldly, effectively?" Tony's face was grim. "This is important, Brad. One good man's life is at stake; and eight others too. And Nato *is* America's business. Without it, you'd really go bust in Western Europe."

"The FBI has a lot on Konov—they must have."

"We hope," Tony said, a trifle bitterly.

"You have no friends there?"

"Once upon a time. They resigned in Hoover's latter-day period of saint-hood. All communications with European Intelligence cut off. No more quiet interchange of information. Let's wait until the dam breaks, and then we can all rush together. Hands across the sea, tra-la!"

Brad finished his drink. "I'll see what I can do."

Six

CHUCK RATTLED OFF a short line of connected dashes to mark the end of the text. The typewriter sounded triumphant, but he had no sense of exultation. No excitement: not even relief that the job was over. He pulled the last page out of the machine, separated it from its carbon copy.

"Twenty minutes past ten," Rick said. "Not bad at all." He placed the carbon copy with the others, studied the page for any errors. "Clean. Except for those damn letters." The *m* and *n* were ink-blocked, the *t* thickened. "Pity you didn't have any type cleaner around. Still, it's legible. Quite professional. I'd hire you as a secretary any day."

Chuck said nothing at all. He gathered up the NATO Memorandum, Part I, and opened his desk drawer. Carefully, he placed all three parts together, and began fastening them into one complete document.

Rick spoke again. "Can't I have a look at the two last sections?"

Chuck went on with his job, finished it, and replaced the NATO folder in the drawer. "I'd rather we didn't handle it any more than necessary."

And Rick, who had been congratulating himself on his display of complete innocence in that last question, looked suddenly surprised. I didn't wear gloves, he remembered, and his face went rigid.

"You'd better phone Holzheimer."

Rick tried to recall whether he had really grasped the sheets of the Memorandum between thumb and forefinger: he had lifted them gingerly by the tips of his fingers, but there had been speed and pressure. No, he decided, he hadn't left any identifiable traces of his work. But he ought to have gone downstairs to Katie's and got the gloves he kept there: then he would have made sure that there were no fingerprints. He was almost certain now: what he was really nervous about was the expression on Mischa's face if he ever heard of this carelessness. Mischa . . .

"Holzheimer," Chuck repeated sharply. "You said he would be waiting until ten thirty. It's almost that now."

Rick nodded and reached for the telephone. And there went a perfectly natural excuse, he thought as he concealed his annoyance. Ten thirty had been a time that he had pulled out of the air: he hadn't expected Chuck to finish the typing job until eleven o'clock at the earliest. Too late, he would have explained, to get in touch tonight; better leave it till tomorrow. And tomorrow could have another tomorrow . . . any pretense to let him delay and postpone and delay. But now he could feel Chuck's eye on his fingers as he dialed the number, so he kept it accurate. When he got through, there was enough background noise in the newsroom to give him a second chance at an excuse. "No go. I don't think he's at his desk. Gone home, perhaps. Or out on the town. There's so much damned racket—"

"But someone answered you—"

"Sure. And left the phone off the hook."

"Keep trying."

"It's the wrong time to call him. Obviously."

Chuck reached out and seized the receiver as Rick was about to replace it. "What the hell—" Rick began.

"We'll wait this out." And simultaneously, a voice was saying angrily into Chuck's ear, "Who's this? Do you want to talk with me—or not?"

"Martin Holzheimer?"

"Speaking."

"Here's Nealey. Hold the line." Chuck handed the receiver back to Rick. "Tell him you'll meet him in Katie's apartment, as soon after eleven o'clock as possible."

"What?"

"Downstairs. Apartment 5A."

"But—"

"Tell him."

Rick did all that. He ended his call, and smothered his anger as he turned to face Chuck. "Just what do you think you are doing? This was my end of the business—to meet him some place where it would be safe and quiet—"

"Katie's apartment will be very quiet. She's out until dawn, isn't she?"

"But why *her* place?"

"Because it's handy. I'll be there, too."

Rick was nettled. "I thought you were going to keep clear of—"

"I want to see this man, get a kind of feeling about him," Chuck said.

"Totally irrational behavior."

"Possibly. Just following my instincts, I guess. I'm going to make quite sure that he won't publish the name of Shandon House."

"And what about you?" Rick asked.

"You can introduce me as the man who has access to Shandon House. That's all. We'll keep the Kelso name out of it."

Rick shook his head. "So that's why you chose to bring him to Katie's apartment? He will see her name on the doorplate. Not yours. And you can slip down—"

"Okay, okay. Let's get ready. Lock up tight. Check the windows, will you, Rick?"

As he spoke, Chuck pulled the couch well to one side, and turned back the rug that lay underneath. Next, he was over at the desk again, lifting the folder with the precious Memorandum. He laid it under the rug, which he then smoothed into place. Satisfied with the look of it, he began heaving the couch into its original position.

"That should do. I won't be gone for any length of time, but I don't trust that desk lock: any nitwit could force it open. Windows okay? Put four records on the player. Leave a couple of lights on." Chuck picked up Holzheimer's copy of Part I to carry inside his jacket. His duplicate copy was shoved inside a magazine, a folded newspaper flung carelessly on top.

"See this?" he asked as he opened the front door. "It's said to be burglar-proof."

Rick stared at the new lock on the door. "When did you have that put in?"

"A couple of days ago. The old one was too easy."

And so, thought Rick, if I had slipped downstairs for a pair of gloves, I'd have been locked out. My key for this door would have been useless. He began to laugh.

"It's no joke," Chuck said. "That damned lock set me back thirty-six dollars."

So it's this way, Rick was arguing with Mischa (or with Oleg, if it came to that): we got the second and third parts. Wasn't that worth the disclosures in the first part? And Mischa (or Oleg) would have to agree. Neither of them would pin a medal on him, but they couldn't say he had botched the assignment either. He looked at Chuck as they reached Katie's door. "You really are full of surprises," he said, and shook his head.

"As soon as you identify me to Holzheimer as his source—"

"I still can't imagine why you are taking the risk of letting him see you."

"Insurance."

"Against what?"

"Against a delay in publication. He'll carry more weight with his editor if he can say he has actually met me. And also—" Chuck paused.

Rick braced himself. He had underestimated Chuck tonight. "Also what?"

"I'll be able to identify him again, if necessary."

"Suspicious, aren't you?" Rick unlocked Katie's door and they stepped into the disordered hall.

"Yes," Chuck said frankly. "That's the hell of this kind of business," he added with distaste. "You have to think twice about every move you make, judge it from all angles." There was another pause. "I wish to God I had never—" He broke off.

"Backing out?" Rick concealed a rising hope.

"No." Chuck looked straight ahead, and was depressed by the view. The living room was dark except for one light somewhere round the corner, but he could feel, if not see, the combined clutter of objects inside. It was one unholy mess, he thought: no expense spared on the furnishings and pictures, and yet everything—like Katie's own styles of dressing (they varied each month according to whim)—looked as though it came from some attic or flea market. "How can you stand this?"

"Stand what?" asked Katie's voice. Rick and Chuck looked at each other, stepped into the living room and got a full view of the dining alcove at its lighted end. Rising from its marble-topped table were four startled people: Katie, dressed in her current style of satin blouse, turquoise jewelry, and Indian headband; a squat blond man, with shaggy hair and full beard, his eyes glaring at the two intruders; a tall thin black man with a rounded Afro and large dark glasses; a woman with Alice-in-Wonderland hair, sweeping its long locks round a middle-aged face, and a good pair of breasts (but beginning to sag) showing braless under a tight cotton shirt pulled over patched blue jeans.

"Pigs," the woman said, gathering up a map and some scraps of paper from the table, her head knocking lightly against the shade of the overhead Tiffany lamp to send it swinging. The men's faces went blank and watchful. Katie was trying to laugh. "They're all right," she kept saying. "Just friends."

"Get them out!" said the woman. The two men, impassive, sullen, kept staring.

Rick recovered. "Katie, why the hell aren't you at Bo Browning's?"

"What the frigging hell are you doing here?" Katie replied in her Philadelphia Main Line accent.

"We're raiding your refrigerator for a late supper," Rick told her, moving toward the kitchen. "And then I was going to pick you up at Bo's party. That was our arrangement, wasn't it?"

"It was not," Katie flashed back. Normally she was an extremely pretty girl, dark-haired and slender, with a face that smiled gently. At this moment she looked almost ugly with fear, her large blue eyes watching her companions' faces, her mouth taut with anxiety.

The tall thin man moved first, straight for the hall, measuring Chuck as he passed him with bitter contempt. The middle-aged woman followed, silent now and angry as she stuffed the map and the scraps of paper into her large shoulder bag. So did the short bearded man, his face averted, his hands tucked into the pockets of an old army jacket. Katie paused only to snatch up the woman's cardigan and her own coat. "I'll get them to leave—" she was pleading as she ran after them. "Don't go."

"Come on!" the woman told her. "Or stay behind with your pet pigs." Permanently, the angry eyes seemed to say. Katie didn't even hesitate. She closed the front door behind her, leaving Chuck to stare at its elaborately painted panels.

In the living room, his amazement grew. Rick was selecting two books and some small personal objects, throwing them into his bag on top of clothing and shaving kit. He moved briskly, checking the overpiled bookcase again, then the bathroom shelves. "That's it," he said, closing the bag.

"You're leaving?"

"As soon as you meet Holzheimer."

"Why? If ever there was a time to stay and argue Katie out of all this—" Chuck looked over at the table where four heads had huddled in a tight little conspiracy. "I mean, she's way into something that's too deep for her."

"That's obvious. Too deep for any of us." Rick was hearing an early warning signal from Mischa: in America, you'll make friends with all kinds of people—conservatives, liberals, even Marxists. But stick to the ideologues; avoid the anarchist groups, the activists. Even if they are far to the left, they can't be trusted. They need a tight control, and you haven't got the capacity to do that: you can't supply them with money or weapons or training. You have no hold over them. Therefore, for you and your work, they are dangerous. They will involve you in trouble you can't handle. Keep clear of them and attract no suspicion.

Rick locked his bag.

"She needs someone," Chuck insisted.

Rick carried his bag into the hall, placed his coat and scarf on top of it.

Getting ready for a quick exit, Chuck thought. "Why don't you call her father, at least?"

Rick looked at his watch. "Almost eleven o'clock." He sat down to wait for Holzheimer. Mischa, he was thinking again, where was Mischa now? And how was he? Any use telephoning the nearest police station, keeping everything anonymous, just an inquiry about a missing friend?

"Why not call her father? Or someone? She has a sister—"

"Married to a State Department man. And one brother who is a Wall Street banker, and an uncle who owns a newspaper chain. What do you think they could do? Argue? How far has that ever got them with Katie?"

"Well, they were just letting her have her little games. No one took her seriously. You didn't, did you? You never knew she was in so deep. It must be recent, though. Wouldn't you say?" Chuck looked over at the marble-topped table, and remembered the hard sullen glares from three pairs of cold eyes. "Rick, you can't just leave her to those people. She'll—"

"She's a spoiled brat."

"She always was. That didn't keep you from shacking up with her for two years. Look—if you don't stay around to persuade her out of this mess, I will."

"Will you? Then you are a goddamned fool." More of a fool than I had even guessed, Rick thought. "Those who want to dig their own graves supply the measurements."

"An old East German saying?" Chuck gibed angrily. It was the first time he had ever referred to Rick's childhood. And then he felt a twinge of remorse: it had been no fault of a six-year-old, Brooklyn-born, that he had been taken by his German mother to visit her parents in Leipzig once the war was over. No fault of his, either, that the two of them had been kept there until eleven years ago, when Anna Nealey had died and Rick had at last been able to escape to the West.

"No." Rick was smiling, unperturbed. Just one of Mischa's little bits of peasant wisdom, he recalled. He kept on smiling, said nothing more. The doorbell rang and ended the slight impasse. "I'll introduce you as Jerry, and then I'll slip away. No need to stay," he told Chuck as he rose to let in their visitor. "Shall I switch on some more lights?"

"No." Chuck pushed Katie and her friends out of his mind. "Ready," he said.

The meeting in the semidark room was brief. Martin Holzheimer was a tall lank man who curled up in his armchair like a question mark. Let's change that attitude to an exclamation point, Chuck decided, once his own curiosity was satisfied—Holzheimer's never would be unless he had a three-day session of probing—and reached inside his jacket for the document.

"Okay," he said, "here it is." He laid Part I of the NATO Memorandum on the free corner of a coffee table laden with bric-a-brac.

"Just like that?" Holzheimer asked. "No further stipulations?" His legs had stretched straight.

"You've agreed to everything I've asked."

Holzheimer was on his feet, reaching for the document. "As of this moment, you are privileged information. Turn on a light, will you, and let me have a look at this."

"Read it at your desk." Chuck was already in the hall, opening the front door. He came back into the room. "Just close the door behind you," he said. "Good night, Mr. Holzheimer."

Holzheimer looked at him with a suspicion of a smile. "Where can I reach you, Jerry? Here?"

"No."

"I thought not," Holzheimer said. Jerry's clothes didn't match this weird world around him. "Then where?"

"I'll call you. Every second day, until your story is published. How's that?"

"Not good, but not bad either." There was nothing to be gained by staying. It could be counterproductive, in fact. Holzheimer could sense when a man was obdurate. This one was granite. "Good luck," he said, and then wondered why that phrase had slipped out instead of "Good night."

"And to you." Chuck turned away. He heard Holzheimer pull the door shut. He checked the lock. And waited. Five minutes later he was back in his own small apartment. After Katie's, it seemed spacious. And safe. The folder under the couch and rug was safe too.

He sank into a chair and relaxed completely for the first time that day. He was too exhausted to go to bed. No sense of excitement, no feeling of a major victory. He couldn't even tell if the whole damn thing had been worth it. Then a strange thought came to him as he glanced round the room—would he ever see Rick here again? Possibly not. Rick was running scared tonight, no doubt worried about what Representative Pickering would have to say if he ever found out about his bright-eyed aide's liaison with a pretty little activist in New York. That was why Rick had cut off Katie with a karate chop. Would he do the same to me, Chuck wondered, if and when necessary? It was a disturbing idea, so he turned away from it. Tomorrow, he preferred to think, Rick would be laughing at his attack of panic, and probably telephoning Katie, too. God, what a mess some people make of their lives. Chuck thought of Katie: all the advantages in the world, yet searching for more and more. Strange restless ambition that drove some people. What was it that brother Tom used to say? People's lives are shaped by the choices they make. That was Tom, all right, trusting in each person's capacity to think and decide for himself. But what about people like Katie, all emotion and no forethought? If there was a wrong choice, pretty prattling Katie would take it.

Suddenly he went tense. What about my choice today? The right one, he told himself again, and dropped that subject. He had plenty of other things to keep his mind occupied: a typewriter to be returned; a Sunday visit to Shandon House; the Memorandum to be safely filed in the security room.

Yes, an early start. He rose briskly and went to bed, plunging almost at once into a sleep untroubled by doubts.

As for Rick, he had no easy night. There was no late train, no late flight to Washington. He found a room at the Statler Hilton, just across the avenue from Penn Station, for an early departure tomorrow. The sooner he was out of Fun City the better. And what could he do about Mischa? Nothing, he told himself for the hundredth time. That was Oleg's problem. Or was it, entirely? As Alexis, Rick would have to make his weekly report on Monday. His Washington contact would call him without fail. And he would have to give an account of his meeting with Mischa. If he kept quiet about that, there could be harsh questions from the Center in Moscow. It would be a different matter if Mischa were well and functioning: then the meeting need never be mentioned. But now? How would Oleg handle it? What would be his story? Rick had no way of knowing until Oleg met him in Washington. And would he?

No, the best thing was to make his usual report, stating he had been called to New York by Mischa. They had met in Central Park. The NATO Memorandum had been discussed, and subsequently secured. Mischa had been attacked after they left each other. Alexis had warned Oleg. He knew nothing more.

And then, he thought in alarm, in an emergency like this I must report immediately—not wait until Monday. I'll have to call my contact tomorrow in Washington. I'll have to give him a message to pass on to Control, then to the Resident. And let's hope that the microfilm I have secured will stop all questions. But what would Oleg have to say to that? He was to get the film from me—so Mischa ordered. Well, let the Center settle it: Oleg may be the one to be disciplined—and Mischa, too. After all, my first loyalty is to Moscow, not to Mischa.

But there was enough of the old loyalty to Mischa to drive him downstairs into the lobby. (He needed cigarettes anyway, he told himself.) At one of the public telephones he put in a call to the Nineteenth Precinct of the New York Police Department. It was on Sixty-seventh Street—he had passed it often enough—and surely it would deal with any mugging around the Sixty-ninth Street area. A woman answered and passed him over to an officer at the desk.

Rick's voice was polite and anxious. "My cousin went out for a walk on Fifth Avenue this evening and hasn't returned. I'm worried. Perhaps he was assaulted—have you any reports about a mugging? Somewhere near Sixty-ninth Street? That's where he lives."

"No, sir. No report of any assault in that area, as yet."

"Not as yet? But this was at half past five!"

"Where was your cousin taking his walk, sir?"

"He probably went into the park."

"In that case, try the Central Park Precinct."

"But don't you know—"

"They deal with anything that happens *inside* the park," the officer said patiently. "We deal with *outside* the park. You could also try Missing—"

He stared at the receiver that had suddenly gone dead in his hand. He said to the sergeant, "It's always the same. Someone goes out for a walk and doesn't get back when he's expected, and his relatives start thinking he's been assaulted. What a town!" Then he added, "But how did he know the time when his cousin could have been mugged?"

It was a question, half-amusing, half-puzzling, that made him call the Central Park Precinct some ten minutes later. "Did you hear from the joker who knew what time his cousin got mugged in the park? . . . Yeah, five thirty. That's what he said. . . . Sixty-ninth Street entrance? Hey, he knew the place too! Somewhere near Sixty-ninth Street, he said. . . . Yeah, sounded like a fairly young fellow. American? Sure. He was American, all right. Okay, okay. Just thought I'd let you know."

"What's going on?" the desk sergeant asked.

"Central Park Precinct has a John Doe problem. Unidentified victim of assault in Lenox Hill Hospital. But as soon as this cousin got the info, he hung up. Didn't say he'd come around to identify, dodged giving his own name."

"Could be he was in a hurry."

"Too much of a hurry, if you ask me."

The desk at the Nineteenth Precinct went back to its other problems. But its phone call hadn't been pointless. The sergeant at the Central Park Precinct was making a note of it: any small piece of information about the unidentified victim now in Lenox Hill was worth adding to the bits and pieces of strange little items that—so far—constituted the file on this John Doe.

Rick returned to his room. Yes, the telephone calls had been well worth his while. Now he knew where Mischa was—Lenox Hill, the nearest hospital to the scene of the mugging—and that Mischa had carried no identification on him. These were two facts which would look good in his report tomorrow: he had done all he could. Oleg could have done no better.

He went to bed, only to lie staring at the ceiling. In all, he managed three hours of sleep before he rose to leave for Washington.

Seven

OLEG, ALONG WITH a drift of other curious spectators, had seen the ambulance arrive and noted the name of Lenox Hill Hospital. The next thing was to find out its address. He did that from a directory in a phone booth. And then what? His English was good; he could pass for the John Browning of Montreal that his passport and driver's license said he was. Which papers, if any, had Mischa been carrying? Canadian, or American? Or none at all? (That would be best under the present circumstances.) A complete mess, Oleg decided, anger growing out of his fears. That son of a bitch Alexis, running scared, leaving everything to be cleaned up behind him.

Oleg chewed over his ideas along with a hamburger at a Madison Avenue quick-service counter. He had several options, but calling the Soviet Mission to the United Nations was not one of them. Mischa had outstepped his authority this time. Unless his own assignment that had brought him secretly to New York was fulfilled—and its results worth the risks taken—Mischa was in trouble. And so was Oleg. All for the purpose of nailing down a high-placed traitor. Exemplary, if their plan had worked: praise and promotion. But now? It would still have to work, even with this unforeseen accident. Or else . . .

So, first, he would have to get Mischa out of the hospital before any identification became possible. Maintenance of security (and that was Oleg's own particular field in the Executive Action branch of Disinformation) was now the primary consideration.

From the Madison Avenue coffee shop he made his way on foot toward the Lenox Hill district. What with the surfeit of automobiles parked along the streets that crossed the various avenues, he had decided to leave his Chevrolet exactly where it was, on Sixty-ninth. Once he had scouted the hospital area, he would know whether it was easier to use a taxi rather than his rented car for Mischa's removal. And how was that to be effected? By open legitimate means—such as a friend of the family come to take an injured man home? Or (if that was impossible) by a careful survey of the position of Mischa's hospital room, and later, with outside help, a well-planned abduction? That would take time, and there was danger in any delay, even if there was no fear of Mischa talking. Mischa would plead amnesia if he couldn't get away with feigning unconsciousness.

Oleg walked six blocks up Park Avenue, noting its spaciousness and its high-rising apartment houses. Against the cool blackness of night, lights seemed intensified. And there were too many of them: windows glowed with life, high overhead street lamps cast no shadows, traffic signals—stationed along the three-mile stretch of broad pavement—sparkled bright red or green at every corner. Above all, it was too quiet for his taste; there were some pedestrians, some taxis and cars, but not enough movement to make sure of an absolutely unnoticed departure from the hospital. (There were doormen, for instance, inside every well-lighted lobby he passed.) No, Park Avenue wasn't suitable. Madison, to the west, had been a busier place—although its small expensive shops, which reminded him of the Faubourg St. Honoré, were all closed and tightly shuttered with heavy iron grilles. He cut over to Lexington Avenue, a block away to the east, and decided it was his best bet. It had a life of its own—nothing blatant, a district of neighborhood stores, overhead apartments, cafés and bars and small restaurants. Taxis and buses, too. Enough animation for his purpose.

He was a stranger in this Upper East Side district. His last assignment in New York had taught him a lot about the west of Manhattan, from Ninetieth Street right down to Chelsea. He knew his way around Greenwich Village. Off Manhattan, he could even find his way around parts of

Brooklyn, which was no mean feat. And in Queens there was the safe house where he and Mischa had intended to spend tonight. With this experience behind him he had been considered an expert on New York City by Mischa: one of the reasons why he had been approached for this current assignment. Again he cursed Alexis, who (from the files on his activities) spent many a weekend in this section of the city. Alexis could, at the very least, have given him a number to call; could have waited by its telephone for further instructions; could have helped in several small ways without endangering his own security.

Oleg left the bright bustle of Lexington, walked back to Park Avenue to approach the hospital, logically, from the front. The layout was simple. The building, high-storied, occupied a whole block on the avenue, and stretched along the two side streets—Seventy-sixth and Seventy-seventh—as far as Lexington Avenue. But the first difficulty in his plan of escape quickly became apparent: a huge project of construction work was going on, a new corner wing was being added, the building's height increased, and the entrance from Park was blocked by high wooden hoardings and heavy equipment stretching round to Seventy-sixth Street—and there, the door was closed for the night. This narrowed his search to Seventy-seventh Street itself, a quiet thoroughfare, occupied on its north side by some apartment buildings, two houses, and a Christian Science church to challenge the doctors across the road in direct confrontation.

He walked past the hospital's main entrance, with glass walls and wide windows giving him a clear view of the brightly lit hall and a large desk. A busy place, complete (and this aroused a sardonic smile) with a gift shop just inside its door. One policeman outside—no, a hospital guard in dark blue uniform, who was having a sneak smoke on an eight-inch cigar. America, he thought contemptuously, his confidence growing. Beyond this there was another entrance, smaller and more businesslike. EMERGENCY was the sign overhead; and, adjoining it, a shuttered garage marked AMBULANCE.

So that is the target, he thought. But he walked on, and soon reached Lexington again. Too early to make his move. Besides, he wanted to find out more about this whole area.

It was a clear night, a dark sky reflecting the city's glow: fine November weather meant no rush on taxis. He would hail one without much delay when it was necessary. There were plenty of them here, all cruising south, Lexington's one-way direction. And enough people on foot, dressed very much in the style he and Mischa had chosen for themselves. Prosperous bourgeois, with only a few long-haired types in jeans and leather jackets, and some weirdos dolled up with heavy platform shoes and other whimsies. A variety of facial characteristics, he noted: many Central Europeans, judging from the small Hungarian, Czech, and German restaurants; Chinese too, and Cuban, Greek, Italian eating places. And Irish saloons, of course. The usual New York hodgepodge, he decided. Easy to pass unnoticed in this racial mix.

He dropped into a café and had a cup of coffee with a sandwich, sat smoking his way through several cigarettes as he arranged a flexible plan in his mind. He would have to play it all very loose, perhaps improvise as he went along.

By half past ten, he had explored enough, and turned back to Seventy-seventh Street. The hospital ambulance was coming out of the garage. Some new casualty, he thought, and perhaps an opportune moment to begin his inquiries in Emergency. He drew a deep breath, and entered a brightly lit hall: small, square, unfurnished. The short stretch of wall to his left was occupied by a glass-enclosed counter, revealing an office behind it where several people milled around. Opposite this, to his right, was the wide entrance to a room edged with plastic chairs, where waiting relatives sat in solemn silence. Facing him was a blank wall with a closed door and a clearly printed warning that it was for patients' use only. That was all: a bare no-nonsense place where he felt dangerously noticeable. Mischa's departure, unless it were authorized, would be impossible to arrange through this boxed-in trap. How much easier it would have been in the large hall inside the main entrance, with its moving currents of people, its busy desk, its lack of curious eyes.

He was being watched right now. A young black woman was already at the counter, sliding one of its windows open. In the office behind her there were three other women and two men, busy people, but interested in him, even momentarily. He decided on his best line of approach. He was a worried and bewildered stranger from Canada, searching for an old friend who had failed to keep an appointment tonight. But what name would he use for Mischa—the one on his Canadian or his American passport? Or had Mischa not been carrying passport or papers? So Oleg sounded harassed and vague.

"The police sent me here," he began. "They say there was an attack on a man in the Sixty-ninth Street area of Central Park, this evening. He may be my friend—I am searching for him."

The girl looked at him, no expression on her face, no reaction visible.

"The police said the man was brought here. About six o'clock," Oleg rushed on. "Would you please verify?"

The girl turned toward another clerk, called out, "About six o'clock, Central Park victim."

There was a quick check with some records. "Admitted at five fifty-eight," came the abrupt answer. Then someone else looked up to say, "Hey, wasn't that the guy with no identification on him?"

Oleg felt a jump of hope. Better than he had expected. He looked crestfallen. "There is nothing to identify him? Then how do I know whether he is my friend? And I'm the only one who knows he's missing. We were to meet this evening at six o'clock. I waited for over an hour. Then I kept phoning and—"

"You telephoned his family?"

Smart girl, he thought, in spite of her expressionless manner. "No. He lives alone. His wife lives on Long Island. In Patchogue. They are separated. I'll call her when I find out what has happened." Oleg raised his hands helplessly, let his voice trail off. "If I could see this man—" He paused, waiting for the right response. And he got it.

"Just a moment," the girl said, and went over to another section of desk, one that faced a broad interior corridor. She spoke to a nurse on duty there,

who telephoned to some other part of the hospital. There was a brief explanation: we have a man down here who is inquiring . . . The rest was lost in
the sudden flurry of activity as the ambulance returned. But the nurse had
received an answer and the girl came hurrying back to Oleg.

"Yes," the girl said, "they want you to identify him. But you'll have to
wait. Take a seat in there." She nodded toward the room opposite. Behind
her the office had turned into a whirlpool of action.

"But why wait?"

"He isn't available right now."

"Why?"

"He is not available." That was all she had been told, seemingly.

"But I can't wait." He backed a couple of steps. "I must know. If this
man is not my friend, I shall have to do a lot of searching tonight. I can't
waste any time—they might keep me waiting for an hour. Even more." He
half turned and said angrily, "I'll come back tomorrow."

"Just one moment," she said again—a much-used phrase, obviously. This
time, after a glance at the hustle and bustle around her, she did the telephoning. "You can go up," she told Oleg. "You can't see him as yet. But
you can give the police some particulars."

Police? He looked at her.

She didn't explain. She pointed to the closed door that led into the hospital. "Through there straight ahead. One flight up. The elevator is on
the right. Near the end of the corridor."

"Police—is anything wrong?"

This amused her. "They always stay until identification has been made."
Then her telephone rang and she was busy with some other inquiry.

Straight ahead, she had told him. Beyond the door he ignored the busy
nurses' desk, the harshly lit operating room facing it, the large room on his
right with several emergency beds separated by yellow curtains. It was all
clean and bright and modern, with expertly controlled pandemonium near
the ambulance area far to his left. His pace quickened as he reached the
end of the broad corridor, further progress barred by a door that must lead
on to other stretches of this bewildering place. That might be useful, he
thought, but he did not risk exploring it. Not at this moment. One flight
up: that was where he was expected now. Police? he wondered again as
he entered the elevator. And why was Mischa not kept downstairs in that
room with the yellow curtains? In one way Oleg was pleased by this:
privacy was better for his purposes. But in another way he found it somehow disquieting.

Yet, as he stepped off at the second floor and came down a corridor to
reach the desk (it was all similar in setup, he noted, to the first-floor area.
except that here there seemed to be private rooms), his alarm about police
vanished. There was only one officer in sight, and he was young. Inexperi-
enced, Oleg thought with relief. So there were no suspicions brooding
around Mischa. This was just standard procedure, as the girl downstairs had
said.

As for the two nurses at the desk, one was middle-aged and pleasant-faced;
the other young and pretty—at least the police officer seemed to think so.

It was a relaxed picture, even if the light walls, bright lights, antiseptic smell all spelled hospital. Oleg felt his worry subside. "Is this where I have to identify a man?" he began, lowering his voice halfway through his question as he noticed the sign behind the desk: QUIET, PLEASE. "Or am I on the wrong floor? This is Emergency, isn't it?"

"Intensive Care," the older nurse told him. "But we take the overflow from Emergency when necessary. You've come to the right place."

Oleg's eyes followed her glance, to a closed door. "My friend is in there?"

"He is recovering from the anesthetic."

"What happened to him?"

"A severe injury to the arm. But he is resting comfortably." She busied herself at the desk. The younger nurse, her smooth dark hair crowned by a saucy white cap that perched miraculously on top of her head, began to help her stack a pile of clothes into neat order. Mischa's clothes, Oleg saw.

He said, "Do these belong to the man in that room? If he turns out to be my friend, he'll need them. I am taking him home."

The senior nurse exchanged a glance with the policeman. "The wound required many stitches. The doctor will tell you when he can be—"

"But my friend would prefer to leave now. I know him well. He has a fear of hospitals."

"He has lost a great deal of blood. It would be dangerous to move him."

"I could hire an ambulance."

"He requires hospitalization. His wound has to be dressed professionally. If he dislikes hospitals, there would be no point in moving him to another. Now, would there?" The tone was decided even if subdued, the argument over. She picked up a clipboard, consulted the instructions on it, and hurried off.

And I, thought Oleg, defeated myself in that interchange. Still, it is easier to extract a man from a sickbed in New York than it would be in Moscow. There, they really know how to be on guard. Here—one policeman, soft-spoken and hesitant, who is only now coming forward with a notebook and pencil in hand. He is about as urgent as if he were going to give me a traffic ticket.

The officer had completed his own quiet study of the stranger: just under six feet in height, husky, strong shoulders, dark brown hair worn short, eyes blue and deep-set, features strong, manner argumentative. He spoke now, keeping his voice low-pitched. Pity he had to ask the questions right here. But where else? He must keep an eye on the door of that room. "Could you give me some particulars about your friend—height, weight, general description?"

"It's two years since I saw him last, in Montreal. You see, I am here on a short visit, just arrived this morning—"

"Height and weight, sir. Then we'll know if there is any reason for you to stay around."

Better keep the details fairly accurate, thought Oleg, or else I'll be dismissed. "He is about five feet six inches tall. Weight—I'd say one hundred eighty pounds. At least, that's what it was when I—"

"Yes, sir. Hair? Eyes?"

"Gray eyes. Hair turning gray, worn long. Age—fifty-one."

"If he has had a haircut since you last saw him, he may be the right man," the officer observed. "You better wait and have a look at him. How did you learn he was in Lenox Hill Hospital?"

The surprise question fazed Oleg only for a few moments. He plunged into an amplification of the story he had told the girl downstairs. His friend, the tale now ran, had telephoned him at five o'clock, just before he set out for his usual evening stroll down through Central Park. They had arranged to meet on Fifth Avenue at Fifty-ninth Street and then have drinks and dinner together. His friend never arrived. "So I waited. For almost an hour. Then I telephoned his hotel. The clerk said he had left for the evening. I had dinner. Then I telephoned again. And again. He hadn't returned. I went out for a walk trying to think what I should do." Oleg paused. Better not mention any police station—that could be too easily checked. "I saw a police car and asked them for help." The young nurse, he noticed, was enthralled by his story. She had finished her listing of Mischa's clothes, and was now listening wide-eyed. Encouraged, he went on. "They called in their precinct—"

"Which one was that?"

Oleg shook his head. "It's all very confusing to a stranger. Their precinct called some other police station—one that had a record of—well," he demanded suddenly, "what record would it have? You know the procedure better than I do. Anyway, the patrol car directed me to this hospital—as a possibility." By now, he had memorized all the doors and exits that lay within sight. He might not need them. He would have another try at persuading the nurse. She couldn't stop him if he insisted on hiring an ambulance and taking his friend to a hospital in Patchogue. Ex-wife or not, she was the only family he had in this country. And so on and so forth.

The officer had listened patiently. "Yes, sir. Now I'd like to have some names."

"I am John Browning," Oleg volunteered, giving himself a moment to think up a name for Mischa. "I'm at the Hotel Toronto."

The senior nurse returned, frowned a little when she found them still talking at the desk.

The officer persisted, dropping his voice even more. "Your friend's name?"

"Robert Johnstone."

"Johnson?"

"No." Oleg spelled out the name, watched the slow pencil record it in the officer's book, and was ready for the next question when it came.

"His address?"

"Somewhere on East Seventy-second Street. He's been living there since he separated from his wife. That's all I know."

"You had his telephone number," the officer reminded him.

"Oh, yes, he gave me it when he called, and I jotted it right down. I've got it right here—" He began searching his pockets, became frustrated. "Must have left it on the telephone table in my room."

"We can get that later." The officer seemed amused by something else. "Johnstone," he said with a grin, looking at the young nurse. "A good old Russian name."

She reacted at once, large brown eyes widening with indignation. "But that man *is* Russian." Her tone was definite, her accent tinged with Spanish. "I know Russian when I hear it. I was in Havana in 1963." She flashed a glance at Oleg's startled face. The senior nurse shook her head over this display of Cuban temperament. The officer enjoyed it quite obviously.

Oleg had to be sure. "The man spoke Russian? My friend can speak French, of course. But Russian?" He looked at her in disbelief.

"Ask Dr. Bronsky," she told him sharply, quick to defend herself. "Dr. Bronsky knows Russian well. He was there when the man was fighting the anesthesia. We *both* heard him."

"That's right, we've got it all down in Dr. Bronsky's statement," the officer said, trying now to calm the little storm he had helped to raise.

"Some patients do curse and swear when they are under an anesthetic," the older nurse said. "I have heard some surprising things myself." Nothing to worry about, her crisp manner implied.

But Oleg had to know. "Perhaps my friend did learn some Russian in New York—enough for a cuss word or two. That isn't so bad, is it?" he asked the girl.

"There was more than that. He cried out, began struggling and calling for his friends to help—"

"If we *must* talk here," the older nurse broke in, "then let us keep our voices as low as possible. Haven't you finished yet?" she demanded of the officer. I'm willing to co-operate, she thought, but really! This is a hospital, not a police station.

"Almost," the officer told her. He had been watching Oleg. "Alexis," he said very quietly.

Oleg stared at him.

"Alexis," he repeated. "Does that mean anything to you, Mr. Browning?"

Oleg shook his head.

"His wife's name, perhaps?"

The Cuban nurse said quickly, "Alexis could be a man's name. Alexis and Oleg—he called on them both for help. And he cried out—"

"Yes." The officer cut her short, added placatingly, "It's all noted down, every word of it." He looked at Oleg again, sensing something he couldn't explain. And yet the man's face was expressionless, almost blank. "His wife?"

Oleg forced a smile. "His wife is called Wilma."

"Wilma Johnstone." It was written down. "Her address?"

"Patchogue, on Long Island. She may now be using her maiden name. Konig, I think." Oleg could feel the cold sweat breaking over his brow.

"Do you have her full address so that we can notify her if necessary?"

But at that moment, Oleg was saved. The door to Mischa's room had opened, and all heads turned toward it.

Two men came out, both in ordinary civilian clothes. One carried a camera, the other a small hand-case. Behind them was a tall man dressed in white trousers and white tunic. A doctor?—No, an attendant, Oleg decided. After the two violent shocks that had almost paralyzed him into this stiff and foolish smile, his brain was coming to life again. And the other two men? Detectives? The police officer seemed to know them, anyway. One of them was saying to him, "You can tell the lieutenant that we've finished here. Got a good set of prints. They'll be on his desk tomorrow first thing."

Prints?

"Is he conscious yet?" the older nurse wanted to know.

"Sure, he's conscious," said the attendant. "And hating every minute of it. When they took his fingerprints, he—"

"Did he tell you his name was Johnstone?" Oleg burst out; and drew a censuring look from the nurse. "I'm sorry," he said, dropping his voice back to the proper level for a hospital corridor.

"He's telling nothing to nobody," the attendant said as he left. "Doesn't remember a thing about anything."

Oleg measured the distance to the room with its open door: twenty steps, perhaps less. Then his ear caught the Cuban's words to one of the detectives. "What do we do with these things?" He looked back at the desk where she had placed a cane, a pair of cuff links, and a cigarette lighter. "We were told to keep them aside for you."

"Not for us. The lieutenant probably wants to have a look at them. He'll be here shortly."

The police officer couldn't resist saying, "Try the lighter, Ed."

The man with the camera picked it up gingerly. It was just the usual throwaway-when-finished lighter that had become popular in the last few years. This one was white in color, like the one he had bought for his wife last week. He flicked it on. There was no flare from the flint. Instead, a strong light glowed through the white plastic, turning it transparent. "Well, what d'you know?" He laughed, shook his head, released his finger pressure, and let the glow disappear. "A flashlight."

"Useful for a keyhole in the dark," the older nurse said as she left for Mischa's room.

"Pretty strong for that," the policeman suggested. "It's got no brand name on it. No patent mark, either. That's what caught my eye. And then I couldn't see any butane inside. Empty. So I flicked it on."

"Real cute."

Not half as cute as the cuff links, Oleg thought, as he watched the group gathered at the desk. It would take more than that young pig's curiosity to open them. But let someone with more experience get his hands on them, and the cuff links would be quickly identified as a tool of espionage. He hesitated only for one moment. All his plans were abandoned. The situation had become impossible. He walked over to the door of Mischa's room, his hand searching deep in his pocket.

The nurse had checked the tubes attached to the vein in Mischa's left arm. Now she was adjusting the bottle of glucose overhead. "Come in, come in," she said briskly.

The room was deeply shaded. Oleg said, "I can't quite see," and came nearer, drawing his hand out of his pocket. Mischa was lying very still, his eyes closed against the world.

The nurse went to the door to switch on the ceiling light. But before it blazed over the room, Oleg's hand had grasped Mischa's wrist and pressed.

That was all. For a second, Mischa opened his eyes, almost smiled. He knows, thought Oleg, and took a step backward.

"That's better," said the nurse. "Now you can see him."

"Yes." Oleg's hand slipped deep into his coat pocket, and edged the small empty vial with its broken needle into its hiding place. Then he couldn't speak. He stood there, looking down at Mischa as if he were a stranger.

"You don't know him?"

Oleg shook his head. He turned away abruptly, made for the door.

The policeman was there. "Any identification?"

"None," said the nurse.

The officer closed his book and tucked it into his breast pocket. He said nothing at all.

She glanced back at the bed. "Sleeping peacefully. And about time, too." She switched off the light, leaving only the small night lamp gently glowing over the side table. The door she left ajar. She looked at the watch pinned to her stiff apron front. "The rush begins any time now. Saturday night, you know." It was a hint to the officer to go sit on a chair and stop upsetting her routine. Thank goodness, the two others had left. Really, as if she hadn't enough to do without all this interruption. What had been gained by it, anyway? A lot of notes in a police officer's little book, which were now useless.

Oleg had hesitated at the desk, as if he had lost his sense of direction. "What do I do now?" he asked her. He eyed the cuff links.

"Try Missing Persons. The police will help you," she said not unkindly. Her voice sharpened. "Maria—put all that stuff on the desk out of sight until the lieutenant gets here. Safely, now!" She moved the cuff links well aside from Oleg's hand. "You know," she told him to give him a little encouragement—he seemed so depressed—"you should be glad that the man is not your friend. He is in trouble." She tapped the cane. "Because of this. Carrying a concealed weapon."

"It didn't protect him much," the officer said. "That happens: your own weapon turned against you."

"That happens." Oleg nodded a good-night to the nurses, and started toward the elevator.

The officer came with him. "As we figure it," the young confident voice went on, "four perpetrators attacked and the victim drew the sword to scare them off. But there were three too many for him. One seized the sword and slashed him as he put up an arm to defend himself. Two officers were in the vicinity and intervened before he was killed. Yes, you can say he's a lucky man."

"You got the sword back, I noticed." Oleg's pace slowed almost to a halt.

"Thrown away as the perpetrator tried to evade arrest."

"But no wallet?"

"We have it. It wasn't lifted. Not enough time."

"And there wasn't even a credit card inside?"

"Just money. Plenty of that," the officer said briefly.

Yes, thought Oleg, almost a thousand dollars. Mischa had always put his trust in money. It was more reliable, he used to say, than any false documents.

What's his interest in these details? the officer speculated: first he was too impatient to wait, and now he's dawdling around.

"And not one label on his clothing?" Oleg asked.

"None. But we have the clothes. The lab can start work on them, if necessary. There's always a way. Good night, sir."

"Good night." Oleg stepped into the elevator.

"We'll let you know if we hear anything about Mr. Johnstone. The Hotel Toronto?"

The elevator door closed, leaving Oleg to his own thoughts.

Slowly, he walked back to his car on Sixty-ninth Street. There could have been no other solution. There was too much information packed inside Mischa's brain. Too many chances that he would be interrogated by experts. Too many question marks around him, too much risk for all of us. "There's always a way," the young officer had said, a trite phrase, but one that Oleg had found to be true. Given the right men, properly trained, complete identification of Mischa could be made within a few days. There it was: no other solution possible. His pace quickened.

Reaching the car, he thought of Alexis as he stepped into the front seat. Alexis was now on record. So was the name of Oleg. And Alexis must have been seen tonight when he met Mischa. *Two officers were in the vicinity. . . .* How many more? Had he himself been observed? Almost certainly. Yet no cause for alarm, he concluded as he eased the car toward Fifth Avenue—he had kept his distance from both Mischa and Alexis. But the sooner he left New York, the better. He gave up the idea of spending any time in Queens. Instead, he would drive to Trenton, where he knew the location of another safe house. From there, too, he could send out the news of the assault on Colonel Vladimir Konov—place, time, and hospitalization.

And his report would state, quite simply, that he had tried to save Colonel Konov and failed. Konov had died before he could be reached. Unidentified. The body would remain in the hospital morgue for three days: after that, it would be moved to the police morgue for one week. (This he knew from a previous incident, on his last visit to New York.) Therefore any plan to claim the body should be made as soon as possible, although he himself would advise against it. End of report.

Eight

Tom Kelso, with a successful visit to Paris behind him, arrived back in New York only one day late. Which was pretty good going, considering what he had packed into the preceding week: lunch with an editor of *Le Temps;* two interviews with foreign affairs experts (on the record); two sessions with other

Quai d'Orsay men (off the record); a brief but important meeting with a cabinet minister; four encounters extending past midnight with journalists ranging from far left to right wing in their opinions; and a relaxed dinner with an old friend (Maurice Michel, once assigned to NATO, and now back at his desk job in Paris at the Quai d'Orsay), a purely personal evening which was passed amusingly, a welcome interlude in a week of hard business.

The twenty-four-hour postponement of Tom Kelso's return did mean that he couldn't take up Chuck's suggestion to spend Sunday night at East Sixty-sixth Street. But the invitation had been casual enough: Chuck had probably sensed that Tom would be heading home to Washington and Dorothea.

He delayed in New York just long enough to drop in at the *Times* and deliver his final article on Paris and its current attitudes to NATO. "Sorry about the typing," he told the copy editor. "Finished the piece at three o'clock this morning."

"Seems okay."

"It gets messier toward the end. Three of the letters have started acting up. I cleaned them, but they keep gathering ink. The type face is worn. Needs replacing, I guess."

"What have you got against a new typewriter?" the copy editor hinted. Reporters' loyalty to their old machines always amused him: brought them luck, they thought, although they'd never admit it openly.

"I'm attached to this one. Easy action. Rattles off a fair copy in no time flat."

"This looks clear. I've seen worse. At least you can spell."

Tom glanced at his watch. He had twenty-five minutes to board the Metroliner for Washington, and none to spare. He gave a casual wave and was on his way.

The editor began reading Kelso's copy with more concentration. Then, as he reached the third page, he stopped and frowned. I've seen worse, he repeated to himself; and I've also seen another just like it: these letters, *m* and *n*; that blocked *t*. . . . Identical. He looked up, startled, but Kelso was already out of sight. "Who the hell does he think he's kidding?" he asked aloud. He signaled to the girl at the next desk. "Hey, Melissa, get me that copy we were working on yesterday. The Holzheimer story."

"Just his piece, or the attached Memorandum?"

"The Memorandum, damn it."

When it arrived at his desk, he needed only one glance. "Well, what d'you know?" he said softly. He had never thought Kelso was one of the smart alecks, but this put him right at the top of the list. "That guy is full of surprises."

"What guy?" Melissa asked.

He didn't explain, just sat there grinning as the meaning behind Kelso's trick became quite clear to him. Then he rose and went to see if some of his friends had ten minutes to spare: this joke was too rich not to be shared around. It would cause some small earth tremors, but Holzheimer would feel most of them. And serve him right, too cocky by far: all that contemptuous dismissal of the "oldies," all those paeans for the "new" investigative reporting, hallelujah amen. As if that concept of journalism had just been invented, and never practiced for a hundred years or more before this latest crop of *Wunderkinder* made the newspaper scene. What had a good reporter ever been, except investigative?

Tom had a standard rule about his arrivals in Washington. He never wanted to be met at the station or airport. What he liked was to reach home and find a wife with arms outstretched, ready to meet his, as he dropped his bag and closed the door and shut the world away. Dorothea had her own rules: everything prepared to welcome the traveler—steak ready to broil when needed, flowers arranged, candles waiting to be lit on a supper table for two, ice bucket filled, Ravel or Debussy gently playing, bathroom tidied up from her own hasty dressing, a large towel folded near the shower; and her own appearance, from brushed hair and careful make-up right down to house gown and pretty slippers, never betraying the mad rush around the apartment since she had got back from the office barely one hour ago.

Tonight had been more of a wild scramble than usual. She was fixing the second earring in place, congratulating herself that she had possibly ten minutes to spare for a last check on things—when she heard the key in the lock, and Tom's voice. She came running, cheeks pink with haste, eyes dancing with amusement at her undignified scamper that suddenly changed into a more decorous approach. But it didn't last. Tom's arms swept her up as he kissed her, swinging her off her feet. One sandal was lost, an earring dropped, hair sent flying free. And "Oh, darling," was all she could say once his grip was loosened and some breath came back into her body.

He looked round the room, looked back at Dorothea. Nothing had changed: everything was just as he had been remembering it. Strange, he thought as he relaxed, that this is the one fear I take traveling with me: that someday I'll come back and find it all different, all lost. This is the only truly permanent thing in an impermanent world. He kissed her again, long and gently.

On the flight across the Atlantic, he had worked over his report, editing, clarifying. He had managed to catch some light sleep on the Metroliner to Washington, which kept him going until he reached home. But the preceding week had been a tight stretch of work, and Tom was tired, admitting it frankly. It was difficult to shake off the tyranny of hours: Paris time had been seven thirty when he rose Monday morning; and now, after he had showered and changed and had supper (but not steak tonight—a chicken sandwich and a drink were all he wanted), Paris time would be 3:15 A.M. Tuesday. The glamorous life of a traveling journalist, he told himself wryly. There was Thea, radiant, desirable, glowing with life and love; and here he was—adoring her, yet longing, as he thought of the big beautiful bed in the next room, for deep instant sleep between smooth cool sheets. But his will power was adrift too: he seemed incapable of moving, of breaking away from this quiet happiness. He sat at the table, relaxed and content, finishing his last drink slowly, listening to Dorothea's soft low voice filled with interest as she questioned, watching the subtle changes in her expression and mood as he answered.

Now she was talking about her own week in Washington. Yes, she had burned all bridges, faced Bud Wells in his TV den. "Oh, of course there were all kinds of objections and counterarguments. But I was firm; I really was, darling. That's the side of me you don't know."

"Don't I?"

"Anyway anyway anyway, I'm free as a bird from the first of January," she said lightly. "Have you heard any more about your own leave of absence?"

"Didn't have time to check."

"It will come through?" she asked anxiously.

"I suppose." Then he grinned and added, "Yes, it will come through, darling."

"Oh, Tom—stop teasing! Where shall we spend it? Not here. That telephone will never stop ringing, and you'll be yanked back to the office."

"That happens," he agreed.

"I've been making a list of places where we could find a small cottage. It keeps getting shorter as I cross them off, one by one. I'd like some spot where we don't have to dig ourselves out of the snow before we can collect the morning mail. No sleet or cold rain, either."

He said nothing, only watched her with growing amusement.

"You don't really want to go into the wilds of Vermont for the winter months, do you?"

He shook his head, smiling now. Thea's concern touched him. He knew what her own choice would be. "You'd like some sun and sand," he suggested.

"But the trouble with Florida or the Caribbean is that I can't see you beachcombing. All very well for a week, but for *three* months?"

"You don't finish writing a book by staring up at blue skies," he agreed.

"And then," she said, "you need a place where you can keep in touch with everything that's going on—newspapers sold at every street corner, isn't that your idea of bliss? Bookstores, too. A museum, galleries, interesting little streets to wander around in—after all, you can't be glued to your desk forever."

Again he shook his head, his smile broadening, letting her run on, keeping his own suggestions to the end.

"And what with the way you check and double-check, you'll need a reference library nearby, won't you?"

"Or else ship three crates of books."

"Then I give up. There's no place that feels like a holiday and yet offers all that. We'll have to settle on some college town—oh Lord, I had *enough* of college towns when I was a faculty brat. Where else, then?" She was disconsolate. Perhaps they'd stay right here in Washington, after all. An end to all her dreaming of something different, something new. Vacations in the last five years had been few and interrupted: either her job or his was always tugging holidays apart. "All I wanted was some place where you could finish the last two chapters of your book as well as—" she paused—"oh, just being together. Or does one cancel the other?"

"Only if I get sidetracked."

"I won't—"

"You sidetrack me very easily."

"This time, I promise. Truly."

"Truly and seriously, I'll need six clear hours at the desk each day. And a couple more to rewrite what I put on paper the night before."

"I promise, darling," she repeated most solemnly. "I'll start a book of my own. *The Talkative Great*—all about the tongues swinging loose on TV interviews. Or I could call it *Strip Tease in Words*. Or *The Day of the Exhibitionist*. Or *Leaking Secrets—Drip Drip Drip*."

"At least, you've got plenty of titles," he teased her. "No problem there."

"The only problem we have at this moment is—not how we'll spend these three months, but where."

"What about the South of France?"

She stared at him. "Don't joke!"

"I'm dead serious," he assured her.

"But it's impossible—out of our reach, darling."

"Not as I see it."

"I had a look at our savings account last week," she told him. "We've got to put aside a large dollop for income tax in April. Remember, April is the cruelest month."

"And that leaves us about six thousand dollars flat."

"Which isn't so much, once you pay fares across the Atlantic and—"

"We make use of this apartment. I've found someone who wants it."

"A stranger—here? Can you trust him with your books and records and—"

"Not a stranger. Maurice Michel."

"Your Paris friend? The diplomat?"

"He and his wife are coming to Washington in February for a couple of months. So we've agreed to trade. We get three months in his place for his two months here. Fair enough."

"We're exchanging?" She was still astounded, scarcely believing.

"Why not? I had dinner with him last night. It's all settled. He has a cottage on the Riviera—nothing elaborate—his father once lived there, owned a small flower nursery. It's simple and rustic."

"Running water?" she asked.

"I don't see Michel fetching a bucket from a well."

She began to laugh, remembering the immaculate Frenchman who had visited them here last year. And to think of all the lists she had made of possible places and expenses—and Tom had arranged everything. No fuss, no trouble. In one night. Over dinner in Paris. "Darling, you are *wonderful*." She rose, came round the table to meet him with a tight hug and a wild kiss.

"And that's a pleasant idea to take to bed. Come on, Thea." He put out the candles, began switching off the lights, and checked the front-door lock. "No, no," he said as he came back to the table and found her beginning to gather the supper dishes together. "Let's just relax tonight."

"I'm too excited to sleep." It was barely ten o'clock. Even if she had an office to remember each morning, her idea of bedtime was usually midnight or later. Days were always too short, somehow.

"I'll persuade you into it." Then he looked *at* her quickly. "What's wrong, Thea?" Her eyes were wide as she stood so very still, watching him. She was close to tears.

"Nothing's wrong. Everything's wonderful." Her voice trembled, and she tried to cover the surge of emotions with a little laugh. She failed quite happily, as he smoothed away the threat of tears with a kiss. "I love you love you love you."

He kissed her again. And again, straining her close to him, saying in a voice that was almost inaudible, "Never leave me, darling. Never leave me."

The morning came, bright and beautiful as far as he was concerned. Thea had let him sleep on for an extra hour—he had a dim memory of her, fully dressed, dropping a good-by kiss on his cheek as she was about to take off for a nine o'clock appointment at her office. Complete metamorphosis, he thought now: the girl of last night, all floating chiffon and soft shoulders, teasing lips and hands, sweet seduction complete, had become the success-ful woman, neat in sweater and well-cut pants suit, attractive and compe-tent, equaling the male competition in brains, surpassing it in looks and natural warmth. What poor man had a chance against all that? Fifty-fifty, Women's Lib insisted, and with every right on their side of the argument; but weren't they forgetting some natural advantages that tipped the scale? And long live those natural advantages, he thought, leaving the disordered bed as he recalled that he too was due at an office this morning. Nine thirty now, he noted: time to get a move on.

The supper table's remains had been cleared, his breakfast tray ready along with a note warning him that Martha came in to clean around eleven. He'd be well out of here before the vacuum cleaner—one of his minor dislikes—started breaking up the peace of this apartment.

He scrambled some eggs, and had a leisurely breakfast with four news-papers for company. Recession was deepening, inflation swelling, the Middle East seething as expected. Vietnam making its unhappy way back into the headlines, the CIA a cripple and perhaps to become a basket case, terrorism in London, floods in Bangladesh, drought in Africa; and oil spill over every-thing, from prices and veiled threats to bitter denunciations. By comparison with all this gloom, his own piece on current French reactions to NATO seemed almost reassuring, although, when he turned it in yesterday, he had thought, Here goes another report to ruin a lot of breakfasts tomorrow. There was only one misprint in it—*fare* instead of *fire*—to wrinkle a few eyebrows. His lucky day, he thought: no transposed lines, no broken paragraphs.

On the page opposite his own by-line was another column, with Holz-heimer's name heading it. So young Holzheimer was starting to dig into NATO too, was he? And with considerable help from someone: the full text of a NATO Memorandum "now under serious consideration in Washing-ton" was printed along with Holzheimer's analysis and comments. There was no hint of the source for this piece of information, beyond the usual "official who preferred to remain anonymous, but who verified the authenticity of the document." Also, of course "The Pentagon has not denied the existence of the Memorandum" and "The State Department offered no comment in response to this reporter's repeated questions."

So here was another abominable leak. Tom Kelso thought: We are becoming a nation of blabbermouths. It wasn't only on harmless TV programs that there were (in Thea's words) "Leaking Secrets—Drip Drip Drip."

He had heard of this Memorandum—some evasive, upper-echelon gossip had been seeping around for the past few weeks, but no one knew the details. (Maurice Michel, last night in Paris, had quizzed him about it. If the French hadn't been able to learn its particulars, then it was pretty secret stuff.) What was it all about, anyway? With professional interest as well as private misgivings, he began reading it carefully.

It was a warning bell, he decided when he finished its final paragraph: an attempt to shock the Americans into taking a closer look at détente and its actualities, at pitfalls ahead for unwary feet. It wouldn't make NATO more popular with several segments of the public, he decided, but when did Cassandra ever have an easy role? He'd question some of NATO's statements himself—there was no proof offered, for instance, of certain ominous trends, unless one allusion to certain facts and figures meant that there was some appendix, some other part of the Memorandum perhaps, that had not been included in today's publication. But as it stood now, the document was simply an unpleasant shocker: not an actual breach in security, as far as he could see—except that some son of a bitch had taken it upon himself to make it public. He wasn't blaming Holzheimer: few journalists could resist a chance of a scoop. But the point was simply this: NATO's opponents would use it to help weaken the Western alliance still more. He could hear them even now. "Scare tactics," the right-wingers would say, "to get more men and money out of old Uncle Sap." Or, from the left, "shocking belligerence . . . cold warriors . . . imperialist aggression." As for Holzheimer himself, he carefully avoided giving his own private judgment. (Perhaps he hadn't made up his mind. The by-line was everything, was it?) He had contented himself with heaving a brick through a plate-glass window: often tempting enough, Tom admitted, but definitely resistible. Holzheimer shared one belief with his unknown source—he mentioned it twice so that no one would fail to understand his high motives. The public has a right to know, he stated. And who could quibble with that, when (apparently) no real breach of security was involved?

Well, Tom decided as he got ready to leave the apartment, I'll find out more about all this at the office. The first day back at work was always a heavy one, with a pile of mail and a list of possible news items all waiting for his attention. He'd be willing to bet that the first joking comment he got would be "Hey, Tom—do you see Holzheimer's out after your job?"

Is that what's really worrying me? he asked himself. No, not altogether . . . Yet why the hell can't I shake myself free of this small depression? Last night, even early this morning, I was on top of the world. Now—

No, he couldn't explain it. But his misgivings didn't vanish either. It was a serious-faced man who strode into the office, and once the greetings were over, the first joking comment was made and he had won his private bet. There was an additional remark, too, a question that he hadn't been prepared for. "What was your idea in giving Holzheimer this break? Or didn't you want your own sources to dry up on you?"

Tom stared blankly. "I don't follow—"

"Come off it. They would freeze stiff if you'd given it your own by-line."

"That's a pretty sick joke."

A small stare back at him, a laugh and a shrug of the shoulders. "Okay, okay—if that's the way you want to play it."

Let's get to the bottom of this, Kelso told himself, and he telephoned his oldest friend at the *Times* in New York. The replies to his questions were meant to be soothing. Not to worry, just a rumor flying around, based on very little actually and the *Times* saw no cause for any alarm.

"What rumor?" Tom demanded. Everyone seemed to know what they were talking about, except himself.

"The typescript of the Memorandum."

"What about it?"

"Your machine, Tom."

"*What?*"

"Yes. But even if you did copy the Memorandum, what harm really? You didn't break any—"

"I didn't copy it. Never saw it—"

"And of course we wouldn't have published it if we felt there was the remotest chance of breaching the security of the United States."

"But I didn't—"

"Tom, listen to me! The less said about this, the better for you. We're trying to contain it within the paper, don't want it spread abroad. You could get hurt by it, Tom, if your Nato friends thought you had pulled this off. Actually, I think you were right to want to see the Memorandum in print. Otherwise, we wouldn't have published it. So relax. We aren't criticizing you, even if your method was slightly—well, odd. We'll stand by you, in any case. You know that, Tom."

Tom said slowly, "I repeat, I did not—"

"See you before you leave for Brussels on the tenth. We'll have all this under control by that time."

The telephone went dead, leaving Tom staring at the receiver with grim set eyes. And what would be the use of going to Brussels if this gossip was not only controlled but completely disproved? He had seen journalists' careers smashed by less than this. He was in deep trouble. And the hell of it was that he didn't know why. Not yet, he told himself in sudden cold anger; but he'd find out, that was one thing for damned sure.

Nine

ALONG WITH THE New York *Times,* there had been a series of shocks delivered that morning.

First, there was Tony Lawton, who—within two minutes of reading the Holzheimer page—was calling the Pentagon.

The Pentagon, in turn, was telephoning Shandon House.

There the director had left a ruined breakfast for an all-hell-breaking-loose session in the filing room. The entire NATO Memorandum was there, he could report. Completely safe. Security had not been breached. Of course, he'd make further checks, find out more details about access to the Memorandum at Shandon; of course, he understood the future implications for the institute if the fault lay with it. And, testily, he added the suggestion that the Pentagon might start investigating its own security: it had had the Memorandum in its possession before sending it to Shandon.

Washington then stepped in, quietly, to contact the *Times*'s New York office. There, questions were coldly received and answered. No source could be divulged. Surely it was understood, in this day and age, that there was freedom of speech guaranteed in the Constitution? The *Times* stood by its reporter, Martin Holzheimer. What was more, this morning's news had contained nothing to injure U.S. security.

The office of the Secretary of Defense chose its own tactics. Again there was a long telephone call to the New York office of the *Times,* but now an attempt at conciliation: yes, yes, yes, total agreement that there was no breach of security in the publication of this part of the Memorandum. And then, with everything flowing more smoothly, came a sudden stretch of white water: had Holzheimer known that there were two additional parts to the Memorandum? Had he seen them? If so, security had not only been broken, but a highly dangerous situation created that could involve all members of NATO (and that, don't forget, meant the United States too).

The *Times* went back to square one. The second and third parts of the Memorandum, if they existed, were not its concern. Mr. Holzheimer had neither seen nor heard of them. He refused to divulge his source of information on the first part of the Memorandum, which was his constitutional right. Prior to publication there had been intensive study of the text of this section of the NATO Memorandum, as well as considerable investigation of the place from which it had originated. It was found (*a*) to be authentic and (*b*) to contain no actual military information. In fact, its publication was a service rendered to the American people, who ought to know some of the vital opinions that were held in certain influential circles of Western Europe, opinions that possibly might influence the future of the United States.

The impasse seemed complete.

It was then that Tony Lawton decided to make his own move. Frankly, today's little bombshell might be a fascinating debate for some people in New York or a red-faced embarrassment to others in Washington; but for a NATO intelligence agent in Moscow (and for eight others scattered through Eastern Europe in sensitive assignments) there could be imminent arrest, interrogation, death.

You can't bloody well waste any more time, Lawton warned himself. Ninety minutes already wasted in well-meaning talk. Get hold of Brad Gillon.

He telephoned Brad at once, using his private number and avoiding the office switchboard. "Brad—I'm flying in to New York. I'll be there by two o'clock. Cancel the three-Martini lunch, and see me in your office."

"See you here?" Brad sounded startled.

"That's right. And if you haven't read your *Times* this morning—" A delicate pause.

Gillon reflected for a moment, and came up with the proper assumption. "I have. But what's the excitement? No infringement on security as far as I saw."

That's what *you* think, old boy. "No?" Tony asked blandly.

Gillon said, "Okay. Come to the twenty-second floor. I'll tell the receptionist that Mr. Cook is delivering his manuscript. She'll announce you at once."

"Two o'clock," Tony reaffirmed. That would give him time to drop in at Shandon for a quick check on his way to New York. Bless the Cessna that he could call upon in an emergency, making this hop-skip-and-jump journey plannable.

From its marble-coated walls to its array of high-speed elevators, the large and busy lobby of the building, in which the publishing house of Frankel, Merritt and Gillon occupied three floors, was definitely impressive. Tony Lawton was both subdued and amused as he faced the young woman who sat on the other side of a vast gun-metal desk in the twenty-second floor's reception office. It was an interior room, small and antiseptic, with one giant abstract mural representing—? Tony had several interpretations, but repressed them as he looked at the virginal face of this latter-day Cerberus. "Mr. Cook," she repeated, voice frank Midwestern, dress chic Madison Avenue. Languidly, she picked up the telephone and announced him; but her eyes, outlined with heavy black fringes, took a visitor's measure as efficiently as any guard back at Shandon's main gate. "You can go in, Mr. Cook. That door—" She nodded to one of three. "I'm sorry that Mr. Gillon's secretary is still out to lunch, but if you go straight through, you can't miss his office. It's the corner one—on your right."

Tony entered an enormous stretch of windowless space, divided by shoulder-high partitions to form a beehive of cubicles. Bright lights, the air conditioned to Alaskan temperatures, people beginning to gear up after lunch (mostly young women; only two men in sight), machines machines everywhere, a forest of them, ready to add and subtract, and type, and transpose, and copy, and possibly do your thinking for you. But "straight through" did bring him to a row of closed doors. The corner one, on his right, had Gillon's name in very small letters—typical of Brad, Tony thought with pleasure.

"How to deflate a male author," Tony said as he closed the door behind him. "By the time he reaches here, he's walking on his knees."

"Or demanding a flat twenty-per-cent royalty," Brad Gillon said with a shake of his head.

Tony gave him a warm handshake and the room a quick glance: a wooden desk piled with galley proofs and manuscripts, jacket designs in the raw stage propped for consideration on a battered leather armchair, books climbing the walls wherever there wasn't a window. "Now I know I'm really in a publishing house," he said, as he cleared a small space on the desk, zipped open his brief-case, and brought out a crushed felt hat and a newspaper. "Ballast," he explained. "Tried to look like a pregnant writer. How am I doing?"

"Not bad at all," said Brad, eying Tony's tweed jacket, turtle neck, disarranged hair, and unpolished loafers. He himself was in shirt sleeves, with a slight loosening at the broad knot of his restrained blue tie. "You do throw yourself into your role, Tony."

"I was a writer, once: mostly aspiring," Tony reminded him. He was already taking a chair to face Brad across the desk. And then, just as abruptly, voice and manner changed. "You still know some people over at the *Times,* don't you?"

Brad recovered from the direct approach, and made a guess at Tony's train of thought. "Don't ask me to try and persuade them—"

"To reveal the source of Holzheimer's little piece? Of course not. The idea never crossed my mind."

"Didn't it?" Brad's serious face was lightened by a wide smile.

"I simply want you to take a wise, reliable friend aside, and tell him what he should know."

"And that is?"

"The real reason behind all this fuss from Washington about the surfacing of the Nato Memorandum."

"I'd like to hear that myself."

"You shall, you shall. But first let me give you the background."

"Off the record?"

"For you and your wise, reliable friend—no. For others, yes."

"Good. If you want me to approach anyone about the Nato Memorandum, I've got to be able to tell him—"

"All the facts," Tony agreed. "Here they are. The Memorandum consisted of three parts, all interrelated. The second and third parts were considered so important for future American policies that the entire document was given top-secret rating and a transatlantic journey to Washington by courier. After being studied there, it was delivered—again by courier—to Shandon House. And, as at the Pentagon, only people with the highest security clearance were put to work on it."

"The Pentagon wanted a double-check on its own long-range projections?"

"Perhaps to strengthen its own final report, which would be submitted to your policy-makers for their serious consideration." Tony shrugged. "But the point is this: no copies of the Memorandum were ever made; all working notes were shredded and burned at the end of each day; there was constant supervision, even surveillance. Once the job of analysis and evaluation was over, the various parts of the Memorandum were linked together again by heavy staples, placed in one folder, and filed securely away. That was ten days ago."

"Why the delay in returning it to Washington?"

"It was waiting for Shandon's own top-secret report to be completed. Tomorrow is the deadline on that."

"And they go back together to Washington?"

Tony nodded. "Standard operating procedure." He added, trying to control his annoyance and not succeeding, "But why the Pentagon ever sent it to Shandon in the first place—" He buttoned his lip.

"Supercaution. Understandable, if some of the contents of the Memorandum might influence American policy. There has to be double and triple checking of the facts, Tony."

"I can see that," Tony said, but he was still depressed.

"You think the leak came from Shandon?"

"It's possible. That is what we are trying to nail down. I've been in Shandon's filing room—a couple of hours ago, in fact. It's a bank vault. No outsider could get in there without dynamite. And no insider without supervision. So they say." Tony frowned, not so much at that problem as at the way he had sidetracked himself. Brad's questions had been good enough to let him stray. "The point I want to make is this: the Memorandum, intact, is now filed in its correct folder at Shandon. So, if someone at Shandon did take it out, he must have separated the three parts, copied one of them to hand over to a reporter, and then put everything all back in place again. But here's the main question: what happened to the second and third parts while he was typing out the first?"

"Perhaps Part One was all that he took."

Tony shook his head. "He wouldn't have the time needed to separate the three parts. Remember, he was in that filing room *under supervision.* He might get a chance to snatch the Nato folder and put it under his jacket, but that would be all the time available to him—a minute or less. No, he took the whole bloody thing."

"You think he actually photographed the entire Memorandum and sent it to Moscow?"

"The KGB wanted it. We know that."

"Ah—" said Brad, remembering his last meeting with Tony—"Vladimir Konov? Now I see what is really bugging you. Konov arrived last Tuesday in Washington, didn't he?"

"No, he did not," Tony said shortly. There had been some disturbing developments that he couldn't explain at this moment. Konov had not arrived with the agrarian experts in Washington last week. Instead, there had been a coded message for Tony, relayed via Brussels from NATO's man in the KGB. *Warning: Konov has left the Soviet Union four days early, departure secret, destination New York. Possibly accompanied by Boris Gorsky, colonel, KGB, Executive Operations (Department V, Disinformation).* "He was already in New York nine days ago."

"And when did the *Times* reporter hand in his material for publication?" Brad asked.

"A week ago, we were told."

Brad was now both worried and angry. "And you think the man who filched the Nato material might have handed it over to Konov?"

"Indirectly—yes. But directly? No, I don't think so. He's responsible for taking it out of deep security and making it accessible to others. That's all. Bloody fool. He's a thief, but he isn't a traitor."

"Why not?"

"If he had been one of Konov's agents, the first part of the Memorandum would never have been supplied to any reporter. It contains some hard facts about Konov's Department of Disinformation and its use of détente. *The conquest of the system,* remember?"

"That was only a small part of the published document. Most readers will concentrate on Nato's unwanted advice. I'm willing to bet that Konov's propaganda boys are going to play up that aspect: see how Nato is trying to influence the United States—another Vietnam being prepared—Nato still pushing the cold war."

"Et cetera, et cetera," Tony agreed. He lapsed into silence, kept staring out at the shapes of disguised water towers on the roofs of the high-risers opposite. Blue sky, unclouded. Everything in sharp focus. He wished his thoughts were as clear as the picture through the window. He went back to the essential problem, arguing it aloud. "There *must* be one other man involved—one man, at least, who played traitor without any compunction. And the only way we can uncover him is to find the idiot who took the Memorandum in the first place. Then we might learn a few leading facts— how did he protect it, did he let anyone else know about it? If so, who? And that's the fellow I'd really like to know about."

"But how do we discover your idiot? We can't get a definite name, that's for sure. Holzheimer will go to jail rather than tell. There was a case, last year—"

"I know. I read about it. We don't *ask* for a name, Brad. We find it out for ourselves." Tony was recovering from his depression. There was a sudden sparkle in his eyes at some amusing prospect.

"How?"

"You could have a short conversation with Holzheimer. He might be just enough shaken by all the fuss he has created to tell you the place where he met his informant."

"No, that wouldn't work—"

"Not even if his bosses wanted to know? They might, once they have a close look at the typescript of the Memorandum—at your suggestion, of course. I'd like you to examine it. Carefully."

Brad frowned, puzzling out the reason for that. Yes, several details about that typed copy of the Memorandum could be useful. "You want me to examine the brand of paper, the spacing, the margins—"

"Exactly."

"—and the type itself."

"That's hardly necessary."

"But to trace all those things will take time. It's the long way round to uncovering— Hey, what was that you said about the type?"

"It has already been identified. There's a whisper starting up—one of my Washington friends heard it this morning—that Tom Kelso must be the man responsible. He got the Memorandum from one of his high-placed informants, possibly in Paris."

"Tom? I don't believe it." Brad was shocked.

"His typewriter did the copying."

"Impossible!"

"If it did, then someone borrowed it. That's the simple explanation. The gossips prefer a more cynical interpretation."

"Ridiculous," Brad exploded. "If Tom wanted that Memorandum published, he'd have done it under his own by-line."

"And lose future confidences from his Paris informant? Tom was safeguarding himself. So the rumor goes."

Brad rose abruptly, began pacing the room. For a few moments, there was only the sound of three sharp curses.

"I agree entirely." Tony waited for the storm to subside. "Why else did I ask you to look at the typescript?" He paused for emphasis. Then he said, "We all have our own way of arranging a typed page, don't we?"

Brad nodded. There could be small but definite differences, a matter of personal preference, of habit or training. "And so we get closer to finding Holzheimer's source," he said slowly. It was a start; small, but perhaps a lead.

"You clear Tom—and that would please the *Times*, wouldn't it? They might be more amenable to letting you talk with Holzheimer."

Brad almost smiled. Tony's old practice of the honest *quid pro quo* always amused him. Tony never expected to get something for nothing.

"So," Tony summed it up, "no name is requested or divulged. Holzheimer is kept happy and virtuous. Tom is exonerated. And I get a chance to start tracing the second man."

"You are really hipped on that second-man bit."

"I can smell him. There has to be someone on the side lines—the direct connection with dear Comrade Konov."

"If," Brad said with heavy emphasis, "Konov did receive the Memorandum."

"If," Tony echoed, offering no argument. Then he added, "But I'd prefer to start action on the problem now, and not wait until I heard some disastrous news from Moscow."

Your agent there? Brad wondered. He moved back to his desk and reached for the phone. "I'll get onto this, right away."

Tony picked up his briefcase and the newspaper. For a moment, he seemed about to leave. Then he changed his mind and walked over to the window. So far below him that he couldn't even see it was Fifth Avenue. And in that direction to the north lay Central Park. That's where it had happened, according to his newspaper, which he had folded back to the page with the police report, brief and simple but headlined in bold print.

Brad ended his call. "Okay. The first hurdle is taken. I'm now heading for the *Times* itself. I'll be leaving in ten minutes."

Tony made up his mind and decided to risk his hunch. "Can you spare me two of them?"

"Something more for me to tell my—"

"No, no. Just your opinion on this." He handed his copy of the *News* over to Brad, and tapped the small paragraph with his finger. "What do you make of it?"

Brad began reading. "The *News* has a corner on crime stories in New York. This is just another case of mugging in Central Park, the body still awaiting identification in the morgue." And then he looked up in surprise. "Carrying a swordstick, and a lighter that could be used as a flashlight?"

"I wonder," Tony said thoughtfully. "I saw a couple of jokers keep a secret rendezvous in West Berlin last month. They used that kind of lighter for identification. They met casually at a dark street corner. One needed a light for his cigarette. All he got was a brief flash. So he said he would use his own lighter, and flashed right back. It's a new gadget. Simple-minded, but quick and sure."

Brad glanced back at the newspaper. "This fellow was mugged over a week ago."

"On the Saturday when we met at the Algonquin. Interesting date, don't you think?"

"There is only a bare description of him—about fifty years old, five foot six." Brad looked up sharply. "No mention of eye color. Or hair. Or build."

"Naturally. Do you expect the police to make it easy for anyone who'll try to make an identification?"

"No, it can't be," said Brad, staring at the newspaper.

"Probably not."

"A coincidence, that's all."

"I suppose so. I'd still like to see the police file on this case though."

"Now look here, Tony—I don't know anyone in the Police Department," Brad said in alarm.

"All right, all right." Tony put the *News* back into his briefcase. He would just have to find a less easy solution to that problem. But he'd find it.

"It's a long shot."

"They are the interesting ones."

Brad said slowly, half-persuaded in spite of good common sense, "I wouldn't mind seeing that police file myself."

"At this moment, you've got another job to do."

"That I have. But the hell of it is—even if you and I and my friends over at the *Times* know that piece of gossip is ridiculous—is Tom really cleared? Rumors in Washington have a way of seeping through all the cracks."

"It would take some publicity to kill this one dead. Perhaps an open admission from the man who started all this damage?"

"Publicity . . . No, I don't think that would be too popular with my friends." Brad paused, then added, "Have you any notion who that man might be?"

"Perhaps. And you?"

Brad said nothing at all, but his lips tightened.

Tony said, "I hope we are both wrong." They shook hands. "I'll call you. When and where?" He zipped up the briefcase and tucked the hat under his arm.

"I should be back here by half past four. I'll be working late this evening. Until eight, possibly." Brad glanced at his watch. "Good God!" Quickly he reached for his jacket and adjusted the knot of his tie.

Tony left. The huge office was now a humming hive of machines and voices. Outside, at the reception desk, the girl interrupted a call at the switchboard to give him a bright smile and a parting wish. "Have a good day," she told him, and sped him happily on his way to the police morgue.

Entry to the morgue was not too complicated. Identification of the mystery corpse had obviously been given top priority. It was Konov. Definitely.

Tony stood looking down at Konov's face.

"You know this man?"

"Perhaps."

"Perhaps?" Another kook, the attendant thought, as he stared at the visitor: he appeared normal enough, English voice, quiet manner, but definitely a kook.

"I'd like to see the detective in charge of this case."

That's a new line, the attendant thought, and ignored it.

"Do I have to go to the FBI?" Tony asked. That got a quick reaction from a couple of men in plain clothes, who had drifted in to keep an ear open for any possible identification. "The detective in charge," Tony insisted as they accompanied him out. "And possibly an interesting exchange of vital information." He jammed on his hat, pulled a scarf from his pocket.

"You don't say!"

"I do indeed." The scarf was in place, covering his sweater.

The two men eyed each other, then studied the Englishman. Their well-developed instincts gave them a final prod. "Follow us, sir," the senior man told him. "What did you say your name was?"

"Let's make this more private, shall we? Take me to your leader." His grin was infectious, and his accent slew them. They were glad to have an excuse to enjoy the small laugh that each had been repressing for the last full minute. Suddenly their smiles vanished, as Tony flipped open his Pentagon identification and held it briefly in clear view. "And if we must argue about this, first get me to your top brass. Let him check me out with Washington," he added very softly.

They were watching closely, still hesitant but no longer so doubtful. Exchanging a glance, they made a silent decision. "This way, sir," the senior detective said. Any bit of information about that stiff on the slab back there was worth a risk.

At five minutes to eight, Tony called Brad's office on its direct line. "Like to buy me some lunch?"

"Haven't you eaten—"

"Thought I'd visit the morgue on an empty stomach."

"You actually—"

"Yes, actually. Where do we meet?"

"Can't you talk now?"

"Too much to tell. What about your news?"

"Good, I think. Yes, on the whole, good. Are you near this office?"

"Around the corner."

"Then meet me at Nino's on West Forty-ninth Street. Italian food. Two stars. It's crowded, of course."

"How are the tables? Close-packed?" Tony asked doubtfully.

"That won't matter. The noise level is intense."

"Well—as long as we can get our heads close together—see you at the bar in ten minutes?"

It may have been the recession that was affecting people's willingness to spend, but Nino's had four tables empty. Brad chose a back-corner one, insulated from the service door by a thin row of plastic plants. "Fine," said Tony with approval.

He had a plate of minestrone, a little Bel Paese with Italian brown bread, a glass of white wine, and that was all. Brad, deep into his *calamari,* didn't question the choice. Tony wasn't living on food today.

Yes, it was Konov all right, laid out like a mackerel on ice. "And you know what? I felt sorry for him," Tony admitted. "Can you imagine that? I felt sorry." He studied the wall panel, across the room, of Vesuvius about to spew its ashes over Pompeii. "And then I kept wondering—why was the body left unclaimed? You've seen how the KGB takes care of its own. It always does."

Brad skewered a piece of white bread on his fork and mopped up the excellent sauce. "Yes. Like inventing a wife and daughter and touching family letters for Colonel Abel. They even had the woman—he had never seen her in his life—meet him, all tears and embraces, at the exchange point in Berlin."

"Yes, I remember those letters. They seemed to be in every newspaper I picked up."

Brad nodded. "Wide coverage. Everyone loves a hard-boiled spy with a much-loved wife. It must have turned Abel's stomach, though. He was a cool professional." Abel had slipped into this country just after the war, via Canada, and set himself up in the New York area at two separate addresses, with two different names and identities, as Control for a communist spy ring.

"Abel was GRU, wasn't he? Still, the KGB usually looks after its men too. Why not in Konov's case?"

"Interesting question."

"I'm thinking about it." Tony poured himself a second glass of Valpolicella. "This is better," he said with slight surprise, "than the Montrachet I had in Washington last night." He studied the bottle with a touch of indignation.

"Something else to investigate?" Brad asked with a smile. He hadn't felt as good as this for a long long while. He thought of the novel, the newest output from France, waiting for him back on his desk. All very well, but— He sighed, watching Tony and remembering the days when.

"How did *your* investigation go?"

"At the *Times?* Couldn't have asked for a more attentive audience. Unpleasantly shocked, just as I had been. I saw the typescript. And also a couple of pages of Tom Kelso's last copy. Tom always uses plain inexpensive paper. The anonymous typescript had the best Basildon Bond. The left-hand margins were about the same width. But I noticed that Tom likes to get as much on a line as he possibly can, while the typescript finished each line neatly—no runovers onto the right-hand margin. And its end was marked by a series of dashes. Tom finishes off with three asterisks in a row. You were right, Tony. There were differences, small certainly, and not eye-catching unless you were on the lookout for them."

"Reassuring to everyone, I hope."

"They never really doubted Tom."

"Of course not. But a little proof is always comforting, even to non-doubters. Did you get to meet Holzheimer?"

"No need. He had already told his editor where he met his unidentifiable source."

"I hope to God it wasn't in a subway station or on a street corner. No lead, there. Except that we'd know that we were dealing with a professional."

"We are dealing with an amateur. He arranged a meeting with Holzheimer in an apartment."

"Where?"

"In New York. Holzheimer hadn't given the full address."

"And is that all we get? A New York apartment?"

"I couldn't push too hard. Contraproductive. Everything is being treated very low key. No publicity, of course. The rumors will be scotched wherever they are met. And they'll die away—no real substance in them. Tom can handle the situation."

Tony said nothing. How did a reporter deal with a sudden lack of confidence in his discretion? There were no cagier informants than those in high government circles. Anything they leaked was off the record unless they wanted it to go public.

"Well," Brad said as he concentrated on lighting a cigar, "is that all our news?" His gentle blue eyes, in such marked contrast with his hawk nose and strong mouth, were studying the younger man. He could sense something more, well hidden as it was behind Tony's quiet control. A pleasant face, conventionally good-looking with its even features and bland expression, quickly accepted by most people when Tony produced his charm, too often underestimated when he adopted his blank-innocence routine.

Tony smiled. "You haven't lost your touch, have you? No, that is not all our news. I saw the police file."

Brad's lips nearly lost their grip on the cigar. "And how did you manage that?"

"By a neat *quid pro quo*. I'll tell you who the dead man was, if—in return—you let me see the file."

"No, no, it took more than that."

"Well, I got one of my pals at the Pentagon to vouch for me. After that, there was no real difficulty."

"He must have packed a real punch."

"Heavyweight class, definitely. Besides, the police are now in a contest with the FBI to see who hits the bull's-eye first. I was delighted to give whatever help I could. After all, the police had done all the real work. The FBI were called in when no record of Konov's fingerprints was found in New York. But there was no record of them in Washington either."

"What about Konov's clothing—material, cut, place of origin?"

"The experts are working on that."

But it took time. And the results might be inconclusive, too. Konov had been a careful operator. "What did happen to Konov? Was he shot or stabbed?"

"Sliced deep." Tony paused. "Gruesome conversation for this kind of place," he added, glancing at the brightly lit room: people eating and drinking and talking; waiters flashing around like so many hummingbirds; no one loitering nearby, no one interested in anyone but themselves, everyone having one hell of a good time. "Yes, I have to hand it to the New York cops. They really had gathered a lot of material, but none of it made any sensible pattern. That's why they allowed me to see the police reports, of course. They needed an identification to give them a steer in the right direction: not organized crime, not narcotics, just plain old-fashioned espionage. All they had was bits and pieces of information. Tantalizing, when you don't know what is the *type* of jigsaw puzzle you have to fit together."

"Bits and pieces." These had always fascinated Brad. Puzzles had at one time been his specialty. "What, for instance?"

"For instance, two police joggers were trotting in their rounds in Central Park, and reported meeting a young man whom they escorted, for his safety, as far as the flagpole at Sixty-ninth Street. Where, as one of the undercover policemen further reported, he saw the young man meet the victim. An hour later the two were back at the flagpole, this time walking separately. There was a third man near them, at first seemingly unconnected with the other two, but observed again later, when he watched the ambulance leave. And one more thing—the young man who had been rescued by the joggers actually witnessed the mugging, but kept his distance. He ran off when a police officer called to him to lend a hand. Yes, your cops really do take notice."

"As a city taxpayer," Brad said, "I find that very comforting."

"The clincher is this," Tony went on. "The man who appeared at the hospital to identify Konov—and he was the only one who did turn up there—seems to bear a decided resemblance to the man who watched the ambulance leave Central Park. A composite picture was made, you see."

"But why?"

"None of his story checked out."

"He saw Konov and disowned him? Then why did he go to the hospital—risk being seen?"

"A scouting expedition, perhaps." Tony's voice hardened. "After he left the hospital, about twenty minutes later, Konov was found dead. Heart failure."

They were both silent. Tony was thinking now of a call for help, cried out in Russian. Alexis and Oleg. The two men in the park? Two names to remember, at least. And that composite picture might be useful too. Alexis and Oleg . . .

Brad was saying, "Did you identify Konov by his real name?"

"By one of them." Tony smiled. "No lies, Brad. I kept my story most checkable."

"Thank God for that."

"Relax, old boy. I don't plan to get the law on my back."

"You actually blew your cover?"

"As little as possible. After all, the Pentagon vouched for me. Probably stamped me top secret. I wasn't asked to identify myself further."

"Dangerous. Going down to the morgue—"

"What isn't dangerous?" Tony asked lightly.

"It was probably being watched."

"Everyone was watching. Big strong detectives—"

"Damn it all, Tony, you know what I mean."

Yes, thought Tony, was Alexis or Oleg around, waiting to see who was interested in Konov? "I know," he said abruptly.

"It was a risk." Brad was really worried. The brief mention of Konov's sudden death had sounded an alarm.

"Calculated, I assure you."

"When are you leaving for Europe?"

"Want to get rid of me?"

"You're too much on your own here." Too vulnerable, Brad thought: not enough backup.

"Leaving on Friday."

"Don't try to solve all your problems before then. You may work them out more easily in Europe, anyway."

Yes, thought Tony, that was where the biggest problem was now rearing a very ugly head. Why had there been no more messages relayed from Moscow? By this time the NATO Memorandum must have arrived. By this time, too, the death of Konov must have been reported. So why the hell was there no message from Moscow? No call for an arranged escape? "Let's pay the bill and get out of here," he said, suddenly stifled by the laughter in the room.

Ten

THIRTEEN DAYS HAD passed since Rick Nealey kept his appointment with Mischa. Almost two weeks of silence. Each morning, he would rise and go through the motions of making breakfast, an ear cocked—even when he was taking a quick shower—for the expected phone call before he left the apartment. In the evenings, with all engagements canceled, he waited once more. But the signal never came. Oleg made no attempt to get in touch with him.

There were no Monday messages, either, from his usual contact, and when he tried to reach him (five times in all) there was no answer. All communications were cut off. He was isolated. Temporarily, of course. But why? Either there was an alert, a time for caution; or he was being disciplined. And again, why?

Not disciplined, surely. There was no cause for that. He had taken grave risks and acted promptly to procure the NATO Memorandum for Mischa. Any divergence from his instructions had been made necessary by the mugging incident in Central Park: he had delivered the microfilm on Sunday as soon as he returned to Washington, instead of waiting to hand it over to Oleg on Tuesday. Just as well that he had acted as he did. Otherwise he would still be sitting here, with the microfilm of the Memorandum to worry him every waking hour. It was too big a responsibility, too dangerous, and far too urgent.

But how long would this isolation go on? he wondered as he cleared away breakfast and prepared to leave for the office. This was Friday, the sixth of December. He couldn't go on playing the hermit without arousing some suspicions in his friends. There was a limit to excuses about overwork or flu. Which reminded him that he would have to call Sandra and cancel their weekend in Maryland. As for Katie, in New York—no, he wouldn't be back there for a long long time. She'd get that message without being told. And Chuck—well, the less he saw of Chuck the better. In any case, Chuck's usefulness was over.

He was about to pick up the receiver and dial Sandra's number, when the telephone rang right under his hand. Startled, he almost answered at once. And then checked himself in time. Two rings; then silence. He waited. Again, there were two rings and a breakoff. Now only one more minute . . . When the ring came again, he was ready with pencil and paper for the coded message that would come over the wire.

The voice was not his usual contact's. Oleg? He was almost sure of that, but he had to concentrate on the words. To his surprise, they weren't in code. They were disguised, of course, and sounded innocent enough to any curious ear. "I am sorry I could not keep our engagement last week. There was illness in the family, and a great deal of work to be done."

"Sorry about that." Yes, Alexis thought, that is Oleg's voice.

"What about lunch?"

"Today's impossible. I have an important engagement—" The luncheon at the Statler, to be exact.

"I know."

So Oleg was probably in Washington. The luncheon had been well advertised locally. Four speakers (including Representative Walter Pickering, on the lookout for a cause to tide him over the next election) and eight hundred guests. Theme: Responsibility in the Media. But was Oleg actually going to be there too? *Lunch,* he had suggested. What was he pin-pointing—time, or place? Or both? Alexis cleared his throat, gave a small cough to indicate that he was about to use code, and calculated quickly. He could slip away from the luncheon by ten past three. "Half past four," he said. "I'll be free by that time."

"Why don't you telephone me as soon as you leave?"

"I'll do that."

"How is your cousin Kay?"

"She's fine."

"Just had her sixteenth birthday, I hear."

"Right."

"You can give me all the family news when I see you. Don't forget to telephone." Oleg rang off.

He's a bold type, thought Alexis; he didn't even follow my lead and go into code, except for some disguised words: "telephone" meant "contact"; Kay and her sixteenth birthday emphasized the Statler at K and Sixteenth Street; and "family news"—if that meant a certain microfilm, then Oleg was going to be disappointed. His own fault, damn his eyes.

Now, let's see: I slip away from the luncheon toward its end, and contact Oleg at ten past three. Where? In the lobby? He's brash enough for that. It will be crowded, of course. In any case, the contact will be visual. He leads, and I follow at a discreet distance. Or it may be the other way around: I may have difficulty in picking him quickly out of a mob of people—he may have changed the color of his hair or added a mustache—but he will have no difficulty in identifying me. Yes, that is how I will play it. I'll leave the lobby, taking my time, giving him the chance to see me and follow. But a meeting in daylight? And a message sent with so little attention paid to code? Oleg's style is certainly different from Mischa's. He scares me, Alexis admitted.

He selected a subdued blue tie as suitable for a public appearance as Representative Pickering's aide. (The congressman was the first speaker of the day, with his eye on the clock and his own private plans for that afternoon.) He surveyed the full effect—gray suit, pale blue shirt for possible television—and added a navy silk handkerchief to his breast pocket. Yes, Rick Nealey was a personable character, quiet, dependable; and a damned good speech-writer, too. What would huff-and-puff Pickering have done without him in these last nine years?

The hotel was large, its lobby a constant stirring of people: arrivals and departures, guests waiting around either for friends or for reservations, visitors drifting in and out of the restaurant and coffee shop. A town within a town, thought Tony Lawton as he left the notice board with its verification of various luncheons—a formal one big enough to need the ballroom, offering four speeches on Responsibility in the Media as special enticement; something smaller on the mezzanine for environmental science; a third room booked for the Fife and Drum Historical Society; a special meeting of agrarian economists. It made him feel inundated: facts and figures, statements, pleas, warnings, perorations were pouring out all over this building. Its thick-carpeted floors must be ankle-deep in eloquence and good will.

He went over to the newspaper stand, a small shop in itself, and walked slowly along its rows of magazines, trying to decide which he would buy to keep him company on his way across the Atlantic. It was almost three o'clock, and he had a full hour to spend before he left. There was nothing to delay him here, now that the NATO Memorandum was being sent back—with some embarrassment—to Brussels. If Shandon House had been dilatory, Washington had been prompt. And serious attention had been given to the Memorandum. When the NATO meetings started next week, there might be more consensus and less disagreement on future planning. So this week, bad as it had been, could have ended worse.

He was far from cheerful, though. From Brussels yesterday had come a brief but disturbing message: Palladin, the NATO agent, had left Moscow for a short vacation in Odessa. That was all. Was he playing it cool? Nothing he couldn't control? Or was it the beginning of flight, and the proof that the worst fears about the NATO Memorandum were realized—it had reached Moscow?

Grim thoughts for a bright talk-filled lobby . . . Tony forced them out of his mind, concentrated on buying his magazines—one on travel (the kind of travel he never had the time to do), another on food and wine, a third on foreign affairs (must keep up with what the great minds are prognosticating, he told himself). Two paperback novels completed his armory against possible delays and certain boredom. And a couple of newspapers, of course. One of the headlines caught his eye—some young bombers blown up by their own concoctions—and he began reading as he walked slowly through the lobby, apparently purposeless.

There was a sudden thickening in the crowd around him. A stream of serious-faced men had drifted out of the elevators. The agrarians, Tony noted with satisfaction, including some of the Soviet delegation. He could place them all: ever since Konov had been scheduled to attend the Washington meetings along with his equally mysterious friend called Boris Gorsky, Tony had made a point of identifying each face with its announced name. Most of the Russian delegates were for real, the usual hard-headed farmer and businessman types now turned bureaucrats. Konov's absence had not been explained, either by a fabricated excuse of unexpected illness or by the announcement of his actual death. In fact, whatever name he might have used was no longer on the official list. He had become a nonperson. As for Boris Gorsky, he could be any of three secretarial aides and translators, or even one of the two Russian journalists who had been touring the Midwest with the delegation. Tomorrow was their departure date. The luncheon today was a cordial and sympathetic farewell.

Still absorbed by his newspaper, Tony took up his position behind a family group—mother and two children waiting for Dad to pay the bill—and let his eyes study the scene. Some of the agricultural experts were now debating a point: they had gathered in a tight knot in the center of the lobby, voices firm but expressions friendly. The translator was busy. And who was he? He hadn't been around last week. Covertly, Tony studied the stranger. Powerful shoulders, about five foot eleven in height, dark hair liberally streaked with gray. Well, thought Tony, the hair color doesn't correspond to the New York police report, complete with composite sketch, on the man who had visited Lenox Hill Hospital; but the height and build, the heavy dark overcoat, seem just about right. (Bless that young police officer who had noted so many details about the man who came to view Konov.) Now, if I could only see his face and his bone structure—blue eyes, too—then I might have found Boris Gorsky. . . . A long shot, of course. Still, who else but Gorsky would have gone to the hospital and talked his way into Konov's room? Who else? The two of them had arrived secretly in New York: that we do know. Both were coming to Washington, and then touring Chicago and the Middle West along with the agricultural experts. Cancel Konov. But that left Gorsky to fulfill their mission here. So he was probably still around. And what easier way to return to Moscow than accompanying the delegation home? No suspicions aroused, no need for any covert and complicated escape route via Canada or Mexico.

And still the broad-shouldered man kept his back turned to Tony. A lot of talk going on, over there. Impatiently, Tony glanced at his watch. Seven minutes past three. Come on, he urged silently, turn around, let me see your face. From the direction of the ballroom, others were now emerging, no doubt slipping away before the last speech had ended—they had the slightly harried look of people who had to get back to their offices. A woman, young and smartly dressed and—even from this distance—decidedly pretty, caught Tony's eye. Dorothea Kelso? Yes, it was Dorothea. She was now pausing at the cloakroom, speaking to a man who waited to retrieve his coat. A youngish man, Tony noted automatically: fair hair, pleasant face, excellent gray suit and blue shirt. A smart dresser. And with curt manners. He had made a quick good-by to Dorothea and was already walking away from her. And that, Tony found, was astonishing. Particularly as the young man was now crossing the lobby at a most leisurely pace, even pausing halfway to pull on his topcoat and fold a blue scarf around his neck. He was looking around him, and yet giving the impression that nothing interested him. Which was less astonishing than leaving a very pretty woman so abruptly, but still—to Tony's expert eye—a little peculiar. He's looking for someone, Tony decided; I've seen that kind of frozen expression before.

Then Tony's senses sharpened even more. The fair-haired man was about to pass the group of agricultural experts. At last, they were showing signs of leave-taking. Tony's attention switched to the man with the gray-streaked hair. He was saying good-by, speaking clearly and in English, thanking everyone, a neat little speech. Dorothea's friend, still adjusting the blue scarf at his neck, paused for a second as he glanced at the speaker. Had he recognized the voice? Tony wondered. Or perhaps it was a natural hesitation, a curiosity about all those foreigners blocking his path. At that moment the Russian ended his farewell, and, without waiting for the rest of his friends, walked with smart decisive steps toward the front entrance. He passed barely six feet away from Tony, who caught a glimpse of piercing blue eyes before he dodged behind the shelter of Mom's bouffant hairdo. And there was no doubt about the man's features. Strong: determined chin, high-bridged nose, broad brow. It was the composite sketch come to life.

Drawing a deep breath, Tony stepped away from his camouflage group (the two children were becoming impatient; poor Mom was losing her temper) and prepared to follow. It was an instinctive movement, and it brought him almost into collision with the young fair-haired man, no longer fussing with his scarf but leaving in a definite hurry. "Sorry," said Tony. The man barely nodded, turned his head away, continued on his set path to the main door.

Tony checked his step, and stood irresolute. Yes, it could be interesting to follow the possible Gorsky. But what was the use? This wasn't his territory, he was about to leave anyway, his job was over. A telephone call to Brad Gillon should be enough. Brad would know where and how to drop this piece of information. For what it was worth, Tony added. Perhaps his own curiosity had led him into exaggerating the importance of this small discovery. Now, if he were only playing on his home ground, with plenty of backup—yes, that would be another kind of game altogether. And yet, and yet . . . On impulse he began walking to the front door. Just ahead of him the fair-haired man with the blue scarf quickened his pace. Gorsky had already left.

Coming out into the broad busy street, Tony mixed with a small cluster of people waiting for taxis in front of the hotel entrance. He looked left along K Street and saw neither of the two men who had interested him. To his right was K's intersection with Sixteenth Street. And there, at least, was the younger man, waiting to cross—no, it seemed as if he hadn't quite made up his mind. Perhaps, thought Tony in quick dismay, he isn't following Gorsky at all, yet I'm damned sure I heard a voice contact being made in the Statler lobby: Gorsky spoke, the younger man noticed him, and everything went according to schedule after that. Until now. Then suddenly, with a last glance around him, the man in the blue scarf crossed Sixteenth Street at a smart clip. Tony followed, trying not to hurry, and reached the other side as his quarry was halfway along to Seventeenth Street.

Careful, Tony warned himself. There weren't too many people around in this stretch of handsome buildings, and no shops to give him the excuse of window-gawking. But he didn't have far to travel. There, some distance ahead, was Gorsky, stepping smartly into a parked car. His young friend had marked the spot, and headed for it. As he reached it, he glanced back, but Tony had already stopped two passing girls to ask them the way to Lafayette Park. They were a pleasant and diverting screen, delighted to set him straight with wide smiles and repressed giggles—you go *down* Sixteenth Street, can't miss it. What he didn't miss was the open door of Gorsky's car, ready and waiting for the fair-haired man to slip out of sight. All very neat, thought Tony.

He said thank you to the two girls, and retraced his steps to Sixteenth Street, letting them draw well ahead so that they wouldn't notice he was losing his way again as he crossed over to the hotel.

Dorothea's attendance at the media luncheon was one of Bud Wells's bright ideas: she had been seated between two prospects for his Sunday Special—interviews in depth, as Wells liked to subtitle it—so that she might gauge, between shrimp cocktail and tournedos and raspberry sherbet, the way they talked about what and where. The journalist on her right was easy in manner, with a wry humor about his recent assignment in Indonesia: he'd make an interesting guest on television. But the writer, expatriate by choice and now on a buy-my-new-book tour of his native land (it galled him, obviously, that the country he continually criticized should make him the most money, although he concealed that with his usual deft barbs about the American scene), was in one of his spiritually constipated moods. Apart from initial remarks calculated to annoy the journalist, and a mild pass at Dorothea herself, he relapsed into heavy concentration on food and drink. A difficult guest, Dorothea decided, to be handled with metal gauntlets. Or a hatpin, she added to that, dodging a leg that slid over hers just as the fourth speech of the day began. She left with a smile and a whispered excuse for the journalist.

There were other early departures, so she wasn't alone in her long walk through the ballroom. Ahead of her was Rick Nealey, making his way carefully through the array of tables. Immediately she thought of Chuck, and wondered if Rick had any news of him. She increased her pace and reached the cloakroom outside, only a few steps behind Rick. She hesitated but briefly. Her anger with Chuck was mixed with worry: his silence was incomprehensible. Tom hadn't heard one word from him all this hideous week. "Hello, Rick."

Startled, he swung round. His smile of recognition was slow in coming, almost nervous. "Hello there. Just dashing back to the office," he explained unnecessarily.

"How have you been?"

"Fine."

"And Chuck—how is he?"

"Chuck? I haven't seen him in ages."

"Oh, I thought you went to New York for weekends."

"Haven't been able to get away for several weeks." Rick reached for his coat and scarf. "Nice seeing you." He gave a parting nod.

Dorothea didn't even have time to say her good-by. He was off, heading for the lobby. How odd, she thought: scarcely the same man who used to visit us and stay and stay. Oh damn, why did I even bother to talk to him? The feeling of rebuff grew sharper. Angry with herself, with Rick, with Chuck, she turned toward the powder room, there to comb her hair, and wash, and apply lipstick. In the mirror she was glad to see she looked normal and not someone infected with hideous leprosy. Lighting a cigarette, she allowed herself five minutes to let her emotions subside. Also, to let Rick Nealey be well out of sight before she braved the lobby again. She tried not to think of what Tom would say when he heard about her attempt to get news of Chuck. (She wouldn't mean to tell him, but it would slip out: it always did.) Tom was refusing to discuss Chuck at all. He was waiting—of that she was certain—for Chuck to call him. An explanation was more than due about that borrowed typewriter. But Tom wasn't making the first move. He was right, of course. How did you go to your brother and say, "You were responsible for breaking security, and you did it with my typewriter, you bastard"? No, you waited for your brother to come to you and admit what he had done. That was all Tom wanted: an honest admission. After that, there could be frank argument. And for my part, thought Dorothea, I'd tell Chuck to resign from Shandon House and find a job designing chairs and tables, something where his ideals wouldn't do any damage to other people's careers.

She had a second cigarette.

Then she went back to collect her coat, just ahead of the grand rush out of the ballroom. Still thinking about Chuck, still worrying about Tom, she paid scant attention to anyone in the lobby.

"Dorothea!" a voice said delightedly, and she turned to look. At first she scarcely recognized him, with his hair wind-blown and his tie carelessly knotted. He was wearing a tweed jacket and flannels today, and carrying a bundle of magazines and papers under one arm; he looked like a college professor rather than a wine merchant. "Mrs. Kelso," Tony Lawton said, more restrained, "how very nice to see you." There was no doubt he meant it. "What about a cup of coffee with me?"

"I really have to get back to the office—"

"Ten minutes, twenty minutes?" He had a most disarming smile. "I'm just about to leave Washington. There's nothing more depressing than waiting around in a giant hotel by oneself."

"The café may be closed."

"Then we'll try the drugstore." He took her arm in a gentle but firm hold and steered her toward the café. "How is Tom?"

"He's in New York today."

He noticed the evasion. "It has been pretty rough on him." And will be rougher, he thought. "I visited Shandon a couple of days ago." She looked at him inquiringly. Her step no longer lagged. But he said nothing more until he had managed to persuade a waitress in the empty café that they only wanted two cups of Irish coffee and a quiet place to sit. He selected an unobtrusive corner, helped Dorothea slide her coat back from her shoulders, took a chair directly facing her, and studied the picture she made, blond hair, blond wool dress. "The color of champagne," he said with approval. "You should always wear it."

Dorothea laughed, and surprised herself.

"Much better," he told her. "You had a bad day, I take it."

"And a very bad week. Does it show?"

"It did. I saw this beautiful creature walking across the lobby and said to myself, 'Tony, if ever a girl needed a cup of coffee with a slug of Irish whisky topped with cream—' And here it is. To order." He gave the elderly waitress a warm smile of thanks. "Now, have a few sips, and I'll tell you about Shandon House."

"You saw Chuck?"

"Briefly. He was buried in work." A slight smile played around Tony's lips.

"He's the best excuse-manufacturer I know."

Tony nodded, his smile deepening, his eyes studying her with some surprise.

"I shouldn't have said that," she retracted quickly.

"Why not? It's the truth."

"Tom—" She paused and sighed, shrugged her shoulders.

And that tells the whole story, Tony thought. "Tom hasn't got in touch with Chuck? No, I don't suppose he could. Perhaps it's just as well. I tried. And got nowhere."

"Nowhere at all?"

"I talked about the Nato Memorandum—it's the main topic at Shandon these days. But Chuck is admitting nothing. He answered in generalities. The fellow responsible must have had very good reasons for doing what he did. It couldn't have been for money; and it certainly wasn't because of lack of patriotism. There were no traitors at Shandon. In fact, if this hypothetical fellow was keeping silent now, it was probably to protect Shandon and keep its good name untarnished by publicity."

"What?" She stared at him.

"Yes. There was no proof that the leak had come from Shandon. So why should this hypothetical fellow supply that proof?"

"And what about the typewriter—or didn't you mention it?"

"A mild suggestion: wasn't it a little odd, most peculiar indeed? But his reply was rather lofty. I shouldn't believe all the gossip I heard. The whole thing had been blown out of all proportion. Anyone could borrow a portable typewriter—slip into a hotel room and use it when the owner wasn't around. A couple of hours were all that was needed." And that, thought Tony, had been an interesting admission.

"Oh, come now—" Dorothea began.

"Besides, as Chuck pointed out, no one who knew Tom was going to believe any of that gossip. The whole idea was best treated with complete contempt. And silence."

"And Tom, meanwhile?"

"Tom could handle anything."

Dorothea stared out, through the wall of windows, at the open stretch of Sixteenth Street with its quiet houses and placid traffic. "And that is that," she said, trying to mask her anger and failing.

"The truth is," Tony said slowly, "Chuck is a very scared young man. He is suddenly faced with the unpleasant realization that his whole career might be ruined. So he rationalizes; and persuades himself he is right."

"And that will really break Tom. Far more than any gossip could do. Oh, Tony—"

"I know."

Here I am, thought Dorothea, discussing family with a man I once disliked. No, not exactly disliked; not exactly distrusted, either. A man I couldn't understand, perhaps a man whose job scared me. Too mysterious, too much out of my world. And yet now—"How do I tell Tom about this? He ought to know." She waited anxiously for his advice.

"Let Brad Gillon do it," Tony suggested. "He's coming to Washington this weekend, isn't he?"

Dorothea half smiled. Tony was really a most perceptive character, she thought. "I just can't discuss it with Tom," she admitted. "I'm too impatient with Chuck. Prejudiced, perhaps. So I back away from any criticism. Family loyalty—" She shook her head. "I wish it weren't so one-sided, though. Doesn't Chuck realize what his actions have done to Tom? It *was* Chuck who copied the Nato Memorandum, wasn't it? You and Brad were there when he came to borrow Tom's typewriter. You both know and Tom knows and I know. And Chuck knows we know. Oh, how can he *not* come to Tom and admit it?"

"Because the natural reaction in most people who have made a big mistake is to cover up. It takes a very honest man, and there are damned few of them around, to admit an unpleasant truth. Not right off, at least."

"I hate to believe that."

"Why?"

"Because—because I want people to be honest."

"And all things bright and beautiful?"

"What makes you so cynical, Tony?" she asked softly. "Your job?"

His smile vanished. "Cynical? Realistic is a kinder word." Then, very quietly, he added, "What job?" His anger was sharp, even if concealed. "Has Tom been fantasizing?"

"He doesn't do that!"

"Not usually."

"I'm the one who thought you might be—well, attached to some kind of—" She hesitated and dodged. "Tom argued me out of it, told me to stop speculating about people. It's one of my bad habits. But, Tony, you really are a mystery man."

"Me?"

"Yes, poor little innocent you."

"What on earth gave you such a mad idea? Flattering, of course. I'd hate to be considered just a routine type."

"You'd never be that." This pleased him in spite of himself. Encouraged, Dorothea said, "And anything I've noticed about you is strictly for my eyes only. I don't chatter, Tony. Not about serious matters."

"And just what have you noticed?" He had decided to play this for laughs.

"Well . . . The way you met Brad in our room at the Algonquin."

"Old Brad rather likes that kind of mystery. Reminds him of the best years of his life."

"Yes," she agreed, and her eyes sparkled bright blue with amusement, "there's some truth in that."

"What else?" he asked lightly. How could he explain that he had been followed all the way from Brussels, kept under tight surveillance until he had managed to dodge it in New York? Even then, he had been forced to move with the greatest care. There had been no purpose in dragging either Brad or the Kelsos into any possible danger. Contact with them had, for their sakes, best been kept disguised. Now, of course, in this last week—since the Memorandum had actually been filched—interest in him had dropped. It would be revived again, once he was identified as the man who had been so interested in viewing Konov's corpse. So far that had not happened. Either he had actually avoided being photographed as he came out of the morgue, or the KGB had been slow for once—it was possible that Konov's death had meant a lot of rearrangement in their priorities. At any rate, these recent days had been blissfully free of any surveillance.

Dorothea was saying nothing at all. The smile in her eyes spread to her lips.

He changed the subject by glancing at his watch. "I'm being picked up here by a friend at four o'clock. Before that I'd like to phone good-by to Brad. Too bad I can't be here for this weekend, but I'll see Tom trailing Kissinger in Brussels next Thursday. He's still going there, isn't he?"

"Yes. Not very enthusiastically, though."

"A delicate situation," Tony agreed. He helped her with her coat. "By the way, wasn't it Basil Meade I saw you chatting with? I didn't know he was in town."

"Basil Meade?" She was puzzled.

"You met at the cloakroom—"

"Oh—that was Rick Nealey. He's one of Chuck's friends."

Tony left a good-sized tip and led her to the cashier's desk at the door. "From Shandon House?"

"No. He's communications aide or something to Representative Pickering."

Tony paid the check, and guided her into the lobby. "Does he still see Chuck?"

"On weekends."

"You mean he goes to New York each week?"

"Yes. At least, I always thought he did. But he hasn't seen Chuck in ages—so he said."

"Does he stay with Chuck in New York?" Tony asked, his voice casual.

"He's at the same address, but in the apartment underneath. It belongs to his girl friend." Dorothea frowned. "Perhaps he and Chuck have quarreled." That might be the reason for Rick's embarrassment at meeting her. "But they always got along so well. It's really very odd. Oh, I'm sorry, Tony. This can't possibly interest you. I'm only trying to find some reason why Rick practically cut me dead. You saw it?"

"I saw it. And I thought he was a bloody idiot." That brought the smile back to her face. "How long have they been friends?"

"From away back. Ever since Germany."

"Old army buddies?"

"Rick was a refugee, actually. From East Germany."

"With a name like Nealey? The Irish do get around."

"Rick was born in New York. His mother was German. The Nealeys were Brooklyn. His father was killed in the Pacific, and so Rick ended up in Dresden or Leipzig—some place like that."

"A beautiful sequitur. Clear as mud."

Dorothea laughed. "But perfectly normal. His mother wanted to see her own people as soon as the war ended."

"And once in, they couldn't get out?"

"Yes." She was studying him thoughtfully. "You seem to know his story."

"Just the pattern. It happened often enough. When did Rick escape from East Germany?" Tony's voice was conversational.

"As soon as his mother died. She became an invalid, you see, and Rick couldn't leave her there alone."

"Rick—short for Richard?" The question was casual.

"Heinrich." Then Dorothea challenged him, her eyes widening. "This really *does* interest you."

"I always like a sad romantic tale." He took her hand. He held it gently, his face suddenly serious. "Good-by, Dorothea." And always my luck, he thought: the beautiful woman out of reach.

"Good-by." Then, as their hands dropped, she said with undisguised amusement, "And who *is* Basil Meade?" She left before he could even think of an answer. He watched her as she walked toward the door and passed out of sight. He was smiling too.

He had six minutes for his call to Brad Gillon. He wasted no time on explanations. "Listen, Brad," he said as soon as he got through. "Remember the

chap in the composite sketch I saw last Tuesday? He's here. In Washington—with the same delegation that our late unlamented friend should have
been accompanying. Possibly leaving tomorrow. Today he has been meeting Rick Nealey, a friend of Chuck's and some kind of factotum to a congressman—Pickering by name. Nealey visits New York on weekends—apartment in same building as Chuck's. Got all that? Okay. I leave it in your
hands. You have such interesting friends. Good-by, old scout. Take care."

Tony left the public phone, gathered up his magazines and papers (now
slightly crumpled), and was out at the front door as the small army car drove
up. His luggage was already waiting for him at the airport, along with the
NATO Memorandum under heavy guard. The stable door was securely
locked, he thought.

"Had a pleasant lunch, sir?" the sergeant-driver asked civilly.

"Very pleasant."

"Nice hotel. You'd enjoy staying there some time. There's a lot going
on in the evenings."

There's a lot going on any old time, thought Tony. Not a bad day after all.

Eleven

NOTHING HAD GONE as he had planned. Rick Nealey's irritation increased.
First, there had been the unexpected encounter with Dorothea Kelso, detaining him, wasting precious seconds when each one of his minutes had
been carefully estimated. Next, Oleg had chosen to make contact by voice
and lead the way out of the hotel. His own preconceived ideas of how to
deal with a difficult meeting, far too dangerous for his taste, had been swept
aside. And now here he was, as Alexis, following this madman along a public thoroughfare on a bright afternoon, neither the place nor the time appropriate, and far from his choosing. Insanity, he thought.

Grudgingly, he had to admit it was paying off. So far. The lobby was safely
behind him, and no one was on his heels. To make sure of that, as he walked
along K Street—keep nonchalant, no haste, let the space between Oleg and
him widen—he took the usual precaution of dropping a book of matches,
which gave him a quick glimpse of the Statler entrance as he bent to pick it
up. He saw only a cluster of people outside its door waiting for taxis, no
solitary figure, no head turned his way. At the corner of Sixteenth Street he
hesitated, as if in doubt of his direction—a harmless excuse to look around
him. At the Statler, there was still the cluster, and no one following him.
Quickly he crossed Sixteenth Street and continued along K. Well ahead of
him was Oleg, halting beside a parked car.

Irritation flared into alarmed anger. In broad daylight, for God's sake:
Oleg stepping into a car as if he were an old-time Washington bureaucrat,

not even glancing back. He's leaving that job for me, thought Alexis. Perversely, he didn't look over his shoulder until he had almost reached the car: only two women standing in front of the Fiji Legation, talking with a man—legs were all that was visible. Beyond that, a mother and small child; two priests on the other side of the street; some automobiles driving at a quick steady pace.

The car door was open. All he had to do was step in. Somehow the simplicity of it only angered him more, proving Oleg was right and himself overworried and fearful.

"You weren't followed?" Oleg asked, as he eased the car out into the traffic.

"I could say no, and I could say yes."

"And what does that mean?" Oleg's mouth was tight.

"Anyone could be following us. Secretaries, priests—"

"And your own shadow."

There was a long silence. "Where are we going?" Alexis asked at last.

"Driving around, like good Americans."

"You take a lot of risks. That telephone call this morning—"

"Stop talking and let me pay attention. There are bigger risks in getting a traffic ticket than in walking out of a hotel." As Oleg spoke, his eyes kept watching the rear and side mirrors. "No one did follow you," he said at last. He was concentrating carefully now on the one-way streets, avoiding the busy circles or the underpasses and the giant avenues. It was as if he had memorized a certain number of blocks in this part of town and wasn't going to venture into strange territory. As it was, Alexis had to admit, Oleg was doing not at all badly for someone who didn't know Washington too well; and how typical of the man, to keep the wheel himself instead of asking him to drive. Within six minutes Oleg had found the parking spot he wanted, back once more on K Street, but this time farther east, near the bus terminal for Dulles Airport. It was a busy section with plenty of movement. Their car, a rented Buick in unobtrusive brown, was not conspicuous; nor were they. Just two people waiting for friends to arrive from a flight to Washington.

But Alexis could not resist raising an eyebrow. It wasn't unnoticed. Oleg, switching off the ignition, said, "Less risk, too, in not driving far afield. And to what purpose?"

True enough. The shorter the time they spent together, the safer. They had not been followed. No other car drew up within view. That was all that mattered. But Alexis was still nervous and unsettled. He searched for a cigarette.

"Ah, the microfilm. You had enough sense to bring it with—"

"I've already sent it to Moscow." Alexis lit the cigarette, only remembered then to offer his pack to Oleg. It was impatiently brushed aside.

"There has been no report of its arrival," Oleg said, eyes angry, face tense. "When did you send it?"

"As soon as I got back to Washington."

"You were instructed—"

"I know. Mischa told me to give it to you on the Tuesday. But that was before he was injured. Which changed everything."

"Who told you it changed anything?"

"You did not contact me. You could have been back in Moscow for all I knew." And if Oleg wasn't notified about the arrival there of the microfilm, Alexis thought, then he isn't as important as he thinks he is. Encouraged, Alexis said in a cool crisp voice, "The Nato Memorandum went by the usual channels. It is in Moscow now—has been for the last seven or eight days."

"Usual channels," Oleg repeated, his eyes narrowing. "Which means it reached the desk of the wrong man."

"Wrong? It would reach the usual office—"

"Where one man has sidetracked it, misfiled it, kept it hidden for as long as he dared." Oleg's cold anger mounted with his voice.

"But why?" Alexis was instantly alarmed.

"To let him make his escape. He is a traitor. And you gave him a week to perfect his plans. By this time he is well away from Moscow. And he's laughing at you, Alexis. You were too clever by far. You played right into his hands."

"I don't believe it," Alexis said, fighting back. "A traitor? In such an important job? He wouldn't have lasted one hour."

"He lasted twelve years."

Alexis stared, aghast. "If you knew he was an enemy agent, why didn't you—"

"Mischa had suspicions, that was all. The proof could be in the Nato Memorandum, Part Three." Oleg's bitter face was accusing. "Which you sent, so obligingly, so kindly, straight to him."

"His office always has received my reports. Mischa did not warn me, nor did you. I only followed—" Alexis broke off, his worry doubling as he saw a new and immediate danger. "All these years, he has known who I am."

"No. We are not as stupid as that. He only knows that there is an Alexis, established in Washington, who sends weekly reports."

"If he is as good an enemy agent as you say he is, he could analyze the material I sent him, and know what kind of job I have here, even trace—"

"At this moment, he is too busy saving his own skin. If he gets clear—*if* (and we'll see about that)—then he may start tracking you down." Oleg looked as though he might enjoy that idea. "In the long run you may have damaged yourself. And others too. Unless we find him."

"He is CIA?"

"No. He's an agent of Nato."

"The same thing."

"Only in our propaganda." And that, thought Oleg, is at least one recent success. The slogans and chants against a NATO-CIA combination were growing stronger each week in Europe. "It even impressed you," he said contemptuously. "You have become an American."

The sneer reminded Alexis of Mischa. He had said something like that too, but jokingly. And then Alexis wondered why Oleg had given no news of Mischa. "How is—" he began, and was cut off by Oleg's next question. It dealt with the problem of Chuck Kelso.

"I see no problem," said Alexis. "He is reliable."

"He may endanger you."

"I don't think so." But Alexis frowned.

"How did you procure the Memorandum?"

Alexis told him, keeping it brief, and waited for a word of praise. Instead, "Kelso may tell his brother that you were with him on that evening."

"Even so, would that matter?"

"The brother has several friends in Nato. That would matter."

"Intelligence officers?"

"They could be. And they would certainly be interested in anyone who handled the full text of the Nato Memorandum."

"Chuck doesn't know I touched it. He has no way of guessing."

"You had better find out. Exactly. What is he feeling? What is he thinking? Will he talk? Make your report next week."

"Too soon. I can't get away to New York until—"

"Next week. And direct it to me personally in Moscow. Make sure of that. It will be your last report for some time. Do nothing. Keep quiet. I shall let you know when you can be active again."

So he is giving the orders now, thought Alexis. "Where is Mischa?" he asked. Had Mischa been demoted, blamed perhaps for the escape of a traitor?

"Mischa is dead."

"Dead?" A moment of disbelief. "But how? Where?"

"In New York."

Mischa is dead. Oleg is in command. The shock died away. "But how?" Alexis repeated. Oleg kept silent. "The result of the mugging, I suppose."

"The result." Oleg drew out something from his pocket. Three small photographs. "Have you ever seen this man with Chuck Kelso? The one in the tweed jacket?"

Alexis studied the snapshots of three men. There was no clear view of the face above the tweed jacket. The man had his hand up, coughing, in one picture. In the second, he held a large handkerchief at his nose. In the third, his head was bent as he looked at the ground. Hair and brow were hidden by the drooping brim of his hat. A scarf muffled his throat. "No," Alexis said slowly. "But these photographs don't help much. Who is he?"

"An expert," Oleg said.

"And the other two?" Their faces were clear enough.

"New York City detectives."

"Arresting the expert?" It was the kind of small joke that would have amused Mischa. Oleg said nothing. Reproved, Alexis became serious again. "Where were the pictures taken? That could be a clue."

Oleg came slowly back from his own far-ranging thoughts. Suspicions, always suspicions that couldn't be pinned down . . . Anthony Lawton, wine merchant . . . Or NATO intelligence officer? On a tip from an informant, he had been followed from Brussels to New York. (Possible close connection with Memorandum, the informant had said.) In New York he vanished. Reappeared in Washington. Reported to have entered Shandon House this Tuesday, the morning of the newspaper publication of the first part of the Memorandum. What reason for this visit—Chuck Kelso and NATO security? Or had it been merely wine business? The only detail the report had given was that Lawton was casually dressed in tweed jacket and sweater.

Tweed jacket . . . yet many people in New York dressed casually, even wildly. Oleg stared down at the elusive figure in the photographs. Yes, Lawton—if he were a NATO agent—would certainly have an interest in Mischa. But how had he found out Mischa was dead? Oleg slipped the snapshots back into his pocket. "They were taken at the morgue," he said.

Alexis looked uncomprehending. But there was no further explanation.

"I'll be waiting for your report on Kelso," Oleg said, and gestured to the door. "Give me five minutes before you take a cab." He started the engine. Alexis got out. The Buick edged into the traffic and was soon part of a steady stream of cars.

Alexis walked into the bus terminal. Five minutes, Oleg had said. Alexis wondered where he could find a drink, a stiff Scotch. And then, remembering that cold look on Oleg's face, he found a telephone booth instead. He would call Chuck now. At Shandon. Catch him before he left for the day, keep the conversation generalized and innocuous, try to arrange a meeting, something. Something that would look adequate in his report to Oleg. Adequate? He would have to do better than that.

"Rick here," Alexis began.

Chuck sounded surprised, then diffident. No, he wasn't going to be in New York tomorrow. He had a pile of work to finish at Shandon. And Sunday too was impossible. Anything wrong?

"Of course not. Just thought I'd like to see you, chat about everything. What did you think of that item the *Times* published last Tuesday? About Nato. Caused quite a sensation."

"Yes," said Chuck. He didn't sound enthusiastic.

"I thought you'd have liked it. It sent me. It's good that we know what's really going on, isn't it?"

"Yes," Chuck said again.

"You seem—disappointed."

"Oh, it's just that—" Chuck hesitated. "I don't know whether it was worth printing that kind of thing. Who listened?"

"Plenty. Here are you and I discussing it, for instance. It really was an attention-getter."

"In the wrong direction."

"What do you mean?"

"People are more interested in how it came to be printed than in what it said. The message itself got lost."

"Far from it. It came over loud and clear. Say—aren't you feeling well? You sound as though you were coming down with grippe."

"That's all I need," Chuck said. "By the way, Katie is in real trouble."

"Katie?" Alexis braced himself.

"She was arrested last night."

Alexis was silent.

"Rick—are you still there?"

"Yes. Arrested for what? Hiding a marijuana joint in her pocket?"

"Arrested in a bomb factory down in Greenwich Village. There was an explosion. Two of her friends were injured. Katie was found wandering in a daze."

"That's Katie, all right."

"It's no joke, Rick."

"No joke," Alexis conceded.

"And, Rick, I don't think we should talk, either of us, about—about that Saturday night."

"I agree. Button our lips."

"About Katie, I meant."

"We'll say nothing. About anything. *Anything*," Alexis repeated with emphasis. "Got that?"

"I suppose you're right."

"I am. Katie has complicated everything in her own sweet way. You see that, don't you?"

"Yes," Chuck said reluctantly. "Yes, she certainly has," he added, and now he sounded definite.

"Signing off, Chuck. This call is ending and I've no more loose change. See you sometime."

"Yes. Sometime."

He wants to see me as little as I want to see him, Alexis thought as he went to find a cab. And now he is really worried about admitting he handed over a copy of the Memorandum to that reporter—what's his name, Holzheimer?— in Katie's apartment. If he was on the point of breaking down and confessing to big brother Tom, Katie and her friends have taken care of that noble impulse. My report next week about Chuck Kelso will be simple: Chuck is depressed and worrying, but holding fast. (He has to, now. Unless he wants Holzheimer breathing down his neck with questions about his connection with a mad bomber.)

He found a cab, but he didn't take it to the garage where he had parked his car that day. Instead, he directed it over to the Mayflower, where he slipped into the bar for a much-needed drink. He didn't think he was being followed, but it was just as well not to have his movements traceable.

And what about you? he asked himself after a second drink. Your report next week will deal with Chuck. It will also have to pass on this newest information about Katie. How does it affect you? (Oleg knows you've been shacking up with her. It's on your file.) Lucky that you already stated you were going to keep clear of her: dangerous situation developing. So they can't blame you for being blind. But there's danger still around. Once the police start searching her apartment, inquiring about her associates—yes, that's something to be really concerned about. Katie won't talk. Not to the pigs. To her lawyer? Yes. He won't talk either. And yet, something can slip out, some damned investigative reporter can start digging. . . .

He finished his drink. In his report he would ask to be transferred from Washington, from the United States, for that matter. Oleg wouldn't like that—all of Alexis's expensive training had been geared to let him mix freely with Americans. Okay. He had done that. Now it was time to move: he was bored with all-things-to-all-men Pickering, anyway. How the hell could he have put up with that shoulder-thumper for nine long years? Time to move on—where? There were places, plenty of places outside the good old U. S. of A., where he could work with Americans. Be one of them. No training lost. That was it: a brilliant idea. He'd suggest it to Oleg, and let Oleg take it over as his own bright solution. Yes, that was it. Alexis paid and left. A brilliant idea.

And now he was out on Connecticut Avenue, dark with sudden night. He felt safer in its shroud. This was the way he and Oleg should have met. It would have given him more confidence, caught him less off balance. Or perhaps Oleg had been trying to dent his self-assurance. Had Oleg been testing him? An unpleasant meeting, certainly: everything tight and strained. Why? Wasn't Oleg sure of him?

He put that spiky question out of his mind by hailing a taxi and driving to the station. There he spent a couple of minutes buying a paper at the newsstand to see if anything had yet been printed about Katie; and if so, how much. There was only a bare description of the explosion, no details about the girl. They would come later. Unless her family succeeded in clamping down on any information about her. They would certainly try. My unwitting allies, he thought, as he took another cab, this time to a street corner a block away from his garage. He'd be home by six, a normal enough routine. And now he'd no longer have to wait for any contact to telephone him. Lie low, stay inactive, Oleg had instructed him. So he could call some of his friends, arrange some dates, enjoy himself. He might even go on that weekend with Sandra to Maryland. Why not?

His spirits lifted. White buildings, spacious and majestic, raised their lighted columns into the darkness. Trees and grass and stately monuments, broad avenues and streams of cars. Another working day was over. Speeches made, committees attended, letters dictated and signed; offices closing; and now the scurry through the giant mausoleum to neat houses in neat gardens where humans could come into their proper proportion again. Yes, he thought as he persuaded himself he would be glad to leave Washington, I have been too long here. It bathes you in dreams of glory, entices you with power and rewards, blinds you to the reality outside its magical radiance. These people, and he looked at the cars' lights sweeping steadily in front of him, are doomed.

For a moment he felt sorry for them, kindly and blundering as they were. And then he repressed his touch of emotion. Sympathy was treacherous, self-defeating. He had been Americanized, Oleg would say. Next time he heard that, he would have a reply ready for Oleg: "Just part of my job." Or would he ever meet Oleg again? I hope not, he admitted to himself.

Twelve

AND THERE SHE was, in view, exactly on time, sitting at a small table near the window of the café, smooth dark head bent over the *International Herald Tribune,* one hand holding a cigarette, the other about to raise her cup of midmorning coffee to her lips. She was frowning either in complete concentration on the paper's English, or in bewilderment over some of the news.

Tony Lawton stepped out of the cool breeze that blew along Menton's waterfront, entered the café, looked for a vacant table, and chose one a short distance from the girl. She didn't look up. They had worked together often enough in the past, so that old routines came back quite naturally. He slipped off his leather jacket as he ordered his coffee, and prepared to settle down for a pleasant half hour like the other Riviera visitors scattered around the room. Naturally, he glanced around him. Naturally, he became aware of the girl. He gave an obvious second glance, a double take, and looked both astounded and delighted. "Nicole!" he said, rising and coming over to where she sat.

Nicole's dark brown eyes stared up at him, at first blankly, and then with astonishment. Pink lips parted in a real smile. "But how extraordinary! What are you doing here?" She spoke in slightly accented English, with emphasis on the *r*'s as any Frenchwoman would.

Now don't overdo it, darling, Tony admonished her silently. "I'm on holiday—supposed to be sailing along the blue Mediterranean with a couple of friends." He signaled to his waitress to bring the coffee to this table. "May I?" he asked Nicole as he took the chair opposite her.

"Sailing? What happened to that idea?"

"The engine. It began hiccuping just as we rounded Cap Martin yesterday, so we made for the nearest port, and here we are."

"Your friends?"

"They are still over at the harbor, trying to fix what has gone wrong. They know boats. Frankly, I don't. We had hoped to leave today, but the experts aren't sure about that. I think if we make it out of Menton by tomorrow, we'll be lucky."

"Tomorrow is Saturday," she reminded him. "The weekend is taken seriously here. If your experts aren't already at work, you'll be ashore until Monday at least. Why don't you use the sails? You have sails, I suppose."

"We've already had a taste of a southeaster off Cannes. Thank you, but I'm no enthusiast about sails when the blowing gets rough. And what about you, Nicole? On holiday, too?"

"I live here."

"You do? So you have deserted Paris?"

"I prefer the weather in Menton. Besides, I have a job. I'm secretary— really a research assistant—to a writer: an American. W. B. Marriot. You must have heard of him."

"You know me. I never open a book unless it's to sign a check." Tony drank the last of his coffee and lifted the two tabs which had been tactfully tucked under a saucer. Prepare to move out, was his unspoken suggestion. "And what is your Mr. Marriot working on now? Or perhaps he is just enjoying a happy life like a thousand other writers and artists on the French Riviera."

"Côte d'Azur," Nicole corrected in liquid French. "Actually, Mr. Marriot is writing a script for a movie about the Americans who landed in Menton and joined up with the French Resistance."

"Way back then?"

"Well, if Dunkirk and Normandy are worth a war movie, so is the Côte d'Azur. In fact, it was a marvelous operation." She had to laugh at her own enthusiasm.

"So you are now an expert on World War Two," he teased her. He studied the tabs as an added prod: establishing your cover was all very well—and necessary—but it was time for more serious talk.

Nicole got his message, and began folding up the *Tribune* to slip it into her large leather bag.

"And this is your day off?" he went on. "My luck has turned. Let's have lunch together."

"It isn't my day off. I came in to collect the mail and buy some typewriter ribbon."

"So I see."

"But I always come here for a cup of coffee when I'm shopping in town," she protested. "I've stayed too long today. Your fault, Tony. I must go."

"What about dinner tonight?"

She had risen, picking up her cardigan—a bulky thing of giant stitches, the newest chic this spring—and smiled her good-by to the couple, man and wife, who stood behind the counter. They wished her a warm good day. The waitress echoed it, politely ignoring the five francs that Tony had dropped beside the tabs on the saucer. Even allowing for the fifteen-per-cent tip already added to the bill, the prices came high these days. "I'm sorry," Nicole was saying. "If only I had known you were in Menton, I could have rearranged this evening."

She began walking to the door, followed by several appraising glances from various tables. She was a fragile-looking girl, small-boned, who could carry the latest fad in fashion: a casual shirt topped by a heavy sweater, covered by an outsize cardigan above a wide skirt, its mid-calf hemline flaring over her long dark red leather boots. Yes, thought Tony, as he jammed one arm into his jacket and hurried after her, she was very good in every way: a natural part of the prevalent scene. And all her words, chosen carefully, had told any listening ears (possibly innocent in their curiosity, but always interested: a part of the nothing-much-to-do holiday feeling when the weather, if sunny and bright, was still too cool for the beaches) only what the local people already knew and could verify if questioned.

"Well," he said as he reached the heavy glass door in time to push it open for her, "perhaps you could rearrange something tomorrow?"

"If you are still here," Nicole said over her shoulder.

Standing on the scrimped sidewalk, jammed tight with rows of empty tables and chairs hopefully set out with bright-patterned tablecloths fluttering in the breeze and hanging on by a miracle, Tony Lawton only paused to zip up his jacket and say, "I'll walk you wherever you are going."

"To the market. I parked my car not far from there. It's a small red Opel, secondhand, just the right price for a secretary's salary."

"Which direction? East?"

"Yes. Toward the port."

Couldn't be better, he thought. The street, fronting the Mediterranean, was a one-sided affair, with a continuous row of small cafés and bars crowding the sidewalk. On its opposite side there was a promenade edging the shore, only a few strollers now taking the salt air along the wide curve of Menton's west bay. The port and the market were some distance ahead.

Nicole and he would have ample time to talk without any danger of being overheard. And on the promenade they'd be protected, by the constant rush of cars along the narrow street, from any observant eyes across the way in one of the interminable cafés. "Let's walk by the sea," he said, catching her arm, choosing a moment when the cars and taxis slackened their pace. They ran, hand in hand. She was laughing as if he had just made one of his better jokes, and he was smiling: two carefree and happy people, not a thing in the world for them to worry about.

"Well arranged," he told her when they reached the promenade. He squeezed her hand affectionately as he released his grip. A few couples, women with children, retired people having their morning constitutional, resident English still clinging to their favorite Riviera town in spite of inflation, several visiting foreigners. Not too many at this time of year—today was the last day of February—but enough. In summer this promenade would be pure jammed-up hell. What vacation place wasn't, nowadays? "Couldn't be better."

Nicole's face, always pale-skinned even in deep-tanning weather, flushed slightly with his compliment. He gave them rarely. "I was worried," she admitted, "that my description of the café hadn't been clear enough to let you find it easily." Now her English was both fluent and perfect, although a Londoner might have quibbled at a touch of American in an occasional phrase. But she had spent four years in New York as well as ten in England. Her French was authentic: she had been born in Paris and lived there for the first fifteen years of her life. Her Russian was better than adequate: her grandparents had come from Moscow, settled in France as czarist exiles in 1912 and rejected Lenin in 1917 as no solution for any true liberal. Her father was Swiss, and international-minded. She believed fervently in the necessary survival of the West. And with equal sincerity she saw NATO as its main defense.

"No problem," Tony assured her. "That yellow-striped awning over the pink and green tablecloths would have been hard to miss."

"When you called me this morning, I just couldn't think of any other place where you could find me quite naturally. Was it all right?"

"It was your usual morning routine, wasn't it?"

"Yes."

"Then it was best to stay with it and raise no questions." She relaxed then. So now he could get down to business. "And how is our friend?"

The sudden change in Tony's voice caught her by surprise. "He is well."

"No new developments?"

"None. He really has recovered. He feels safe here."

"Has he remembered any further details to pass on to you?"

"No. And I don't imagine there is anything to add. He was thoroughly debriefed in Genoa."

Tony nodded. Genoa was where Palladin had stopped running. He had insisted that the NATO team of debriefing experts come to him. He wasn't going anywhere near Paris or Brussels, or even into Switzerland—all too obvious, all dangerous. He was ill, exhausted, and had come far enough by difficult routes. He had had enough of travel and tension: from Moscow to

Odessa, to Istanbul, where he made contact with a NATO agent. From Istanbul, his journey had been arranged for him, step by step—to the island of Lesbos by fishing boat and then on a mail boat to the Piraeus, with a quick change to a decrepit freighter bound for Brindisi near the heel of Italy. Italians had smuggled him by truck westwards to Reggio, and then north to Naples: another freighter—this time bound for Genoa; and there, in a safe house, he decided to call a halt for three weeks. He had won that battle of wills. The specialists slipped into Genoa one by one, in order to gather all the information that was still so fresh in his mind. And he had won the second battle too: Menton, just across the French-Italian border, was where he had decided to start his new life.

"And he really is safe," Nicole went on, "as safe as a man like him can expect to be." Palladin had been one of the most important NATO agents in Moscow, a top-ranking KGB official. "He has changed his appearance, of course. He will really astound you when you see him." Then, as Tony still kept silent, she said, "You do want to see him, don't you?"

"I wish I could. But I think not. Your report will be enough."

"But—"

"It isn't necessary. Let's keep his visitors to a minimum." Especially the ones who might be traced, at some time, in some way, to NATO Intelligence. Nicole, of course, had been chosen for this assignment because her cover was secure and her connection with NATO unsuspected. W. B. Marriot ("Bill" to his friends) was also unknown to Soviet agents; and his household help, Bernard and Brigitte—a reliable couple from Switzerland, where Bill had supposedly spent the winter—were an efficient part of the team. Palladin completed the W. B. Marriot ménage as chauffeur—his own choice of occupation for his new identity as a French-Italian from Nice, name of Jean Parracini. (Bill carried his arm until recently in a sling, and leaned on a crutch when he walked—a skiing accident last winter, the story went. It was obvious to everyone that he needed a driver.)

"But we've made arrangements to take care of any special visitors. They'll bow in as Bill's associates from the movie world—dropping in to see him for consultations on his new film script. So, if you want to come up to the villa, it would be safe enough. Look—" She searched in her bag and found a small tourist folder with a map of Menton. "I've marked our house, very lightly. It's a difficult place for strangers to find."

He knew where it was—high on the eastern side of the town, where houses and gardens were scattered around on a steep hill slope. But he took the folder without comment and slipped it into his pocket. "And you've noticed no unusual interest in you or Bill?"

"Just ordinary French curiosity—no more. It dropped away within two weeks."

"And no interest in Brigitte or Bernard—or the chauffeur?"

She shook her head. "We've been accepted as part of the local scene."

"And Brigitte and Bernard don't know Jean Parracini's real identity? Or any of his past history?"

"Nothing. He insisted on that right from the beginning. And the setup *is* working. He is very pleased about that."

"I bet he is. He wrote most of the scenario, didn't he?" Palladin had insisted on that too, including exchanging his original role as W. B. Marriot the writer for Bill's part as Jean Parracini the chauffeur. Tony could see the reason behind Palladin's change—any interest in the household would be focused on the writer. A chauffeur wouldn't rouse local speculation or gossip.

"And you still don't like it." She shook her head, half-amused by Tony's excessive concern.

"There isn't enough protection for him. It's too open, too simple. And why did he choose Menton?"

"He says simplicity is his greatest protection. No one will expect him to be living in a busy little resort town with so many approaches."

"Far too many. It's impossible to watch them all." Tony glanced at the small port ahead of them, with its moles and jetties and anchorage for fishing vessels and pleasure boats. And beyond that crowded harbor, lying at the far eastern end of Menton under the shadow of a giant wall of red cliffs that marked the French-Italian frontier, was a new large marina, filled with yachts and cruisers. The land view was equally disturbing. There was this shore road, linking all the towns along the whole stretch of the French Riviera. And there was the old Corniche, and the new Corniche topping it, each twisting its tricky way along steep hillsides above the coast. And then there was the Marseilles-Genoa expressway, which had been completed three years ago straight across the mountain slopes, way high up there, supported on tall cement legs as it crossed ravines and deep glens, as direct and fantastic as any Roman aqueduct. They all had their own tunnels, too, to let them stream through the red cliffs, Les Rochers Rouges, and pour right into Italy. Even the damned railway line, thought Tony, had its tunnel. "Just too many quick ins and outs," he said of Menton. "And too many bloody foreigners wandering around." He glowered briefly at two innocuous visitors from West Germany.

"But that also works for Palla—" She caught herself in time. "For him," she ended weakly.

"If he wants to make a quick break for it—yes."

"That isn't what he's planning."

"He's a great planner, isn't he?"

"Wouldn't you be, if you had spent the last twelve years—"

"Yes," Tony said quickly, and silenced her. For twelve years, Palladin had worked right under the sharp eyes of men like Vladimir Konov. With each passing day, he must have wondered at his success in skirting detection, prepared himself for sudden disaster. When it came, he was ready. He had been lucky, luckier than Konov stretched out on a slab in a New York morgue, but he had made his luck. With some help from us, thought Tony, he had made it. But no amount of help could take away full credit to Palladin for brains and guts.

"You don't trust his judgment?"

"It's Menton that is worrying me," Tony admitted frankly. "I just wish he hadn't been so determined about it. That's all."

"But no one, no one, would expect him to come to a small resort town, so open and innocent. The opposition will expect us to send him to a country of our choice—and one where he can speak English. It's his best foreign language. He knows it well. Also some German, some Italian."

"What about French?" Tony asked quickly.

"He has been learning French. And fast. He spends every free hour on it. Talking records, books, papers, TV, and conversations with me."

Tony stared at her. "So he comes to live in France because he doesn't know French? Does he think the opposition will look in every other direction because of *that*?" And the opposition was not the KGB alone, enormous as that intelligence force was. It had control over the intelligence services of the Soviets' allies. They'd all swing into action.

"Yes," said Nicole quite simply. "He believes that the opposition will search in the English-speaking countries. They'll expect him to be hidden in a large city like London or Liverpool or Toronto or Glasgow—some place where crowds would make him feel safe. And if that fails, they'll try the opposite extreme—look for a remote Canadian farm, a lonely ranch in the United States."

Tony's pace slowed. They would soon reach the end of the promenade. Near the harbor area a lot of construction work was in progress: men and machines, digging and filling, and bottling up traffic. This was already complicated by the density of people attracted to the market; they cluttered its sidewalks, moved in and out of its giant entrances, and gave—from this short distance away—a good imitation of bees swarming around their honeycombs. They were even spreading across the final stretch of promenade itself. Soon no more serious talk would be possible. He halted, looked out at the Mediterranean admiringly. "Okay," he said, as if his doubts about Menton had been cleared away. He came in on them from another angle. "Does our friend have much to say about Shandon House?"

Nicole had been startled, but she kept her eyes fixed on a view of blue sky, blue sea. "At first, yes. Now, very little." She drew the cardigan's collar more closely across her throat. "His anger doesn't show any more. And he had every right to be bitter about Shandon's criminal stupidity. They let someone steal their Nato Memorandum right out of their top-secret files, and it ended up in Moscow. Jean lost two of his Moscow contacts through that piece of idiocy. Arrested in December, executed four weeks ago. Did you know?"

"I heard."

For a long moment they were silent.

Then she said, "We have been reading in the local newspapers about a villa owned by Shandon, right here in Menton. The same Shandon—as in New Jersey?"

"The same. They inherited the villa last year."

"Another think-tank?"

"Mostly a talk-pool—on a very deep level, of course." His smile had returned. Somehow the idea of Shandon owning a villa on the Riviera appealed to his sense of comedy. Although there were now other villas strung along the Côte d'Azur, quiet retreats in vast gardens, taken over by Institutes of This and That for the Betterment of Thee and Me. Shandon, situated in the wealthy enclave on Cap Martin, was only following a very pleasant pattern. "And what else do the papers report about it?"

"Not much. It's all played down. Does that mean Shandon Villa is a hush-hush operation?"

"Officially, no. The aim is 'free discussion by delegates from various countries on topics of general concern.' So they say. But—" Tony paused—"I shouldn't be surprised if there are some private exchanges between delegates which deal with very sensitive material indeed. Have you noticed that people just can't keep their lips buttoned when they want to assert themselves? Or win an argument? Or when they are feeling relaxed—sun and sea and flowers and palm trees and no journalists around to print off-the-record talk?"

"Surely Shandon wouldn't bug its own guests?"

"Not Shandon itself."

She didn't quite follow. "They've been discreet enough about their guest list for the first seminar. Even the local newspapers weren't given the names. Security precaution, I suppose."

"No names at all?"

"Only those of the permanent staff in a kind of Welcome-to-Menton paragraph. The director is an American, of course. Now, what's he called?" Her brow wrinkled.

"Maclehose. Security officer of the day when the Nato Memorandum was taken out of Shandon House."

"Oh no!"

"Oh yes."

"Do they never learn?"

"No blame could be pinned on Maclehose. Unthinkable. He's a stalwart fellow. His wife and children will *love* living in Menton." Tony's sarcasm ended. "But, secretly, he did embarrass them: so the easiest solution was to kick him sideways across the Atlantic. It's a cushy job. With some prestige, too. His guests will be cabinet level." Then Tony asked the question that worried him most. "What is Jean Parracini's reaction to Shandon-by-the-Sea?"

"None."

"He reads the local papers—part of his French lessons, aren't they? Didn't the mention of Maclehose raise any comment?"

"Maclehose was just a name. Jean didn't recognize it."

"He must have. He saw my report on Shandon."

"You gave it to him?" She couldn't believe it.

"Not my idea. Someone in Genoa thought he deserved to know how his cover had been blown—he kept asking about that. Naturally enough. And we owe him a great deal." Tony shrugged. "But not to the point of letting him carry a grudge. In our business, there's no room for a personal vendetta."

"Surely he wouldn't—"

"You know him better than I do."

"He isn't a maniac. He has a cool detached mind. He wouldn't do anything wild and endanger us all."

"I hope not." Tony was remembering the description of Palladin's sudden rage in Genoa when he had read the report on Shandon. By all accounts, it had been a painful and terrifying scene. "Let's head for the market," he said abruptly, and turned away from the laughing sea, little white teeth gleaming in the curving lips of each small wave.

Nicole shivered. "I feel frozen," she said. But it wasn't altogether the cool breeze that had caused this momentary chill. She stepped out smartly, her wide skirt swinging around her red leather boots, her dark hair blowing loose in the wind.

"By the way," he said in his most casual manner as they waited to cross the street, "does the name Rick Nealey ring a bell?"

"Nealey," she repeated, frowning. "I've seen it." The frown deepened; and then disappeared. "Yes. He's on the new Shandon staff, isn't he?"

"Executive assistant to Maclehose."

She stared at Tony's too expressionless face. "Another name in your report?" she asked, her voice almost inaudible.

"You may be frozen, but your brain is still cooking," he said and won a small but delighted smile.

And then it vanished just as quickly. Jean, she was thinking, must have recognized Nealey's name in the newspapers. And yet there had been no comment at all. None. And none about Maclehose. None at all . . . As though he had no interest in them whatsoever. Not natural behavior, she told herself. A danger signal? But Tony's hand was on her arm, guiding her, giving her some comfort. "When do you leave?" she asked in midstreet.

"The boat is going to take some time to fix." He had seen to that, with a neatly applied hammer. "Georges and Emil will come on shore, take rooms in the Old Town. I'll wander around."

"Will you come up to the villa? Bill would like to see you."

"Georges will be in touch with him," he had time to say before they reached the sidewalk.

"We could use some extra help," she admitted. "We now have two problems." The first was to keep Jean Parracini safe from the KGB. The second—to keep Jean Parracini safe from himself.

"At least two," said Tony, thinking of Rick Nealey, and stopped at a mass of flowers for sale. Tables, set up roughly outside the market, were covered with them. "Buy some carnations." They were the only flowers, apart from roses, that he recognized.

He waited for Nicole to choose, heard her discussing prices with one of the ruddy-faced women behind the flower display. But his thoughts were still with Nealey: sudden resignation in late December from his job as Representative W. C. Pickering's aide (nicely explained, of course, no hard feelings), and a quick exit from Washington in early January; nothing against him in FBI files; unknown to CIA's informants in East Germany (but they'd keep digging); papers in order, according to U.S. Army, who had employed him as civilian interpreter, 1963-1965, after his escape to West Germany; 1941 birth certificate (Brooklyn); total acceptance by Grandmother Nealey, sole surviving relative but since deceased, on his return to U.S.A. (A newspaper account of that happy reunion seemed to think it perfectly normal that an eighty-four-year-old woman should recognize a grandson she hadn't seen for twenty-seven years.) Blank-Wall Nealey: all Tony had got was one large headache from butting his head against it. You didn't have the evidence, not a shred of hard proof, he told himself. So how did you expect the Americans to act, especially when they are all walking on eggs these days? Nealey's apartment *and* his office, too, would have needed to be bugged. Just try that on for size in a newspaper headline.

"Aren't they divine?" Nicole asked, thrusting a bunch of red and pink carnations under his nose. "They grow all over the hillsides around here, in plastic-covered greenhouses. Imagine the work!" She dropped her voice. "Do we drift apart now?"

"Too open. Let's get under cover."

The market was a huge cavern of a building, filled with stalls, rows and rows of them, piled with all varieties of produce. And the crowd was large enough to please him: his leave-taking of Nicole could pass ignored in this mass of people, buying, selling, or simply strolling among the good things to eat. "No one in this part of France will ever starve," Tony said. "Almost tempts me to take up cooking." Half the shoppers, he noted, were men. "Admirable place." And he wasn't only referring to its gastronomical delights. He relaxed, felt secure.

Nicole touched his arm. He looked at her sharply as she drew him behind a poultry stall, with ducks and geese and chickens swinging from overhead hooks. It was the first time, he thought, that he had used a screen of plucked hens to dodge behind. "Jean," she said quietly. "He's over there, next to the sacks of onions."

"What the bloody hell does he think he's doing?"

"I don't know." Her eyes were troubled. "He does go out on errands, of course. A chauffeur doesn't sit in a house all day."

There were several people, a mixed group, crowded near that stall. "I don't see him," Tony said.

She laughed, then. "I told you he had done wonders with his appearance. He's the man in the dark suit. Why don't you come and meet him—hear his French accent, too?"

Tony studied the man. No resemblance. Palladin's hair had been blond, thin on top and straight, above a cheerful round face and pale complexion. He had been a permanent wearer of glasses, and definitely corpulent. Jean Parracini had dark brown hair, thick and wavy. His tanned face was haggard and furrowed, the cheeks fallen, the eyes (with no glasses) deepset and shadowed. He had grown a mustache, dyed it black. And he must have lost about forty pounds in weight. Even his height, the usual giveaway, seemed to have increased slightly with the way he now held his shoulders. New posture and thick-soled shoes, judicious use of subtle make-up, an expensive hair-piece fitted securely over a head shaved bald, and—above all—a crash diet: these were the complete transformers. "Contact lenses, too," Tony murmured. He was fascinated. But Jean wasn't walking around picking up any purchases. Jean was waiting. Even when he moved on a few steps, seemingly engrossed with onions and the neighboring potatoes, he was waiting. "He may be looking for you. Did you tell him you were going to buy some artichokes?"

"No. I left as soon as you called me this morning on Bill's private line."

"Would Bill tell him you had gone into town?"

"Possibly. But not to meet you." Of that she was sure. "Perhaps he came here to buy something Brigitte had forgotten to order."

"He's pressing his luck too hard."

"I'll go over and join him," Nicole decided. "Ease him out of here." But Jean was already leaving.

Tony's eyes still stayed on the dark suit, watched it move slowly toward another entrance.

"That leads into the town itself. He has probably parked Bill's car—"

"What make?"

"A Mercedes, black, four-door, Nice registration."

Jean had almost disappeared behind the fruit stalls. "Think I'd like to get a closer look. See if that disguise is as good face-on as it is at a distance."

"Meet him? I thought you were avoiding—"

"He won't know me." A one-way mirror in a small Genoese room, old dodge, had made sure of that. "I hope," Tony added along with a good-by smile. "Go buy your artichokes, my pet. And tell Bill what I told you. All of it." He drifted away, seemingly in an aimless wandering between the rows of stalls. He too was heading definitely for the market's townside entrance.

Once he was far enough away from Nicole, who was now absorbed in the price of poultry, his pace could quicken. But he had delayed too long, and Jean Parracini was no longer visible. Lost between the fruit and the cheeses, Tony thought, and swore silently.

He came out into the sunshine, wondering which direction to take. He noticed a parked black car, nearby. But it was a Citroën, newest model, with a swoop of its hood to give it a sporting air. The man who was dumping his packages onto the back seat before he stepped in to take the wheel was obviously alone. He wore a suit and tie, too; but he was not Jean Parracini. He was Rick Nealey.

Slowly, Tony lit a cigarette. The Citroën drew out into the traffic. And from some distance behind it, a black Mercedes left its parking place. It increased speed as much as it dared in the busy street, and then—as it came nicely up behind the Citroën—slackened its pace to keep a decent following distance.

We have a maniac on our hands, thought Tony, and crushed his barely smoked cigarette under his heel. Better warn Nicole at once; explain Rick Nealey just enough to let her know how deeply Parracini was endangering himself. This was no ordinary American he was following. Nealey could outfox even a Palladin, when he was blinded by bitter rage. And Nealey wouldn't be here alone. He must have some backup, a contact. . . . "Hell, bloody hell," Tony said softly, and turned to reenter the market.

He stopped abruptly, almost bumping into a woman carrying a wicker basket filled with a morning's shopping.

"Tony!" Dorothea Kelso said.

Thirteen

Typed, retyped, torn up. The discarded pages filled the wastebasket. A typical morning's work, thought Tom Kelso, and pushed his chair away from his desk. Maurice Michel's desk, to be exact, in Maurice Michel's library, no longer looking the neatly ordered place where a diplomat had worked. Tom's notes and maps were scattered everywhere; even the small room's name (a little too grand for ten feet square, walls lined with bookshelves that encased door and window too) had been changed to "study"—his own quiet corner, far removed from living room and kitchen. Much good its peace had done him. Thea and he had been here since the beginning of January, and the last two chapters of his book refused to shape up. Tomorrow was the first of March, the last month here before their return to Washington. Return to what?

Every aspect of his work now seemed to have become uncertain. Who the hell will want to read this book anyway? he asked himself angrily. Who in the United States worried about long-term policy and what they would have to cope with ten years from now? Short-term, that's us—jumping from one crisis to another. "We'll cross that bridge when we come to it"—and that we will, even if the bridge blows under our feet and we have to swim for it.

Thoroughly despondent, restless, he rose and made his way through the silent house to the pantry where the Michels had installed a little bar. He'd better bootleg a drink or two before Thea got back from the market in Menton.

She wasn't saying anything about his change in habits, but she must have noticed. She was too smart a girl not to be aware of them, and too sensitive not to feel the perpetual state of worry and dejection that had seized him, away back in December, after his return from the NATO meeting in Brussels.

It hadn't been a complete failure for him—real friends at Casteau rallied round and talked with him as they had always talked, but few of them could hand out vital information. And the others, important sources for sensitive material in the past, had become tight-lipped, even evasive. He had never thought he was a particularly prideful man, but the snubs struck deep. And the results, in his reports back to the *Times*, were clearly seen—by himself, at least. The journalist was the first to know he was slipping; next his editors; and then the public. End of a career. Any newsman was only as good as his sources. ("Like a policeman?" Thea had asked when he discussed this problem with her. "They need informants too. Don't they?" He had laughed and agreed, but wondered how journalists' high-placed sources would react if they were called informants. "Let's say," he had answered, "that Watergate would never have been explained if there hadn't been leaks of information.")

He poured the second drink, another double, and wandered back through the living room, a place he usually found cheerful and pleasant. Solange Michel had taken great care with the colors and chintzes. (*"Toile!"* Thea had corrected him. "Chintz, my eye.") And Maurice had made sure that his wife hadn't sacrificed the old fireplace and the beamed ceiling in her splurge on remodeling an old house. The Michels had spent money, time, and energy on fixing up their place in Roquebrune; but Tom wondered how long it would take them to sell it, once they came back to see the huge condominiums that were being built farther up the hillside behind them. Nothing, he thought, nothing ever remains perfect. In deepening gloom, he went out onto the terrace.

The trouble—or rather today's trouble—was the telephone call that morning. From Chuck. At the airport in Nice.

The first time I've heard from him . . . Tom tried to stop brooding about Chuck, and stared down at the olive trees in front of the house. Condominium builders hadn't yet got their hands on that long stretch of descending terraces, but no doubt they would. And they'd be eying that nice piece of real estate lying below the olive trees, a cape that pointed its long finger into the Mediterranean, a promontory of very private land occupied by expensive villas and perfect gardens. Cap Martin wouldn't listen to the jingle of big promoters' coins. It could buy and sell them with cash still left in the till. It probably wasn't even aware of the glass and concrete spreading over the Roquebrune hills above it: a density of trees, a richness of foliage, covered and protected and hid it completely.

That was where Chuck was spending the next few days. At Shandon Villa. Transportation from Nice? That was taken care of—Nealey had met him at the plane. No, he couldn't make it for lunch. Catching up on his sleep, he had said: he never could handle overnight flights. After that, he had some business to attend to. He would drop in to see Dorothea and Tom this evening. Sixish. Okay?

The first time since November—and all I got was a drop-in promise. Not, "Tom, I wanted to see you." Not, "Tom, I have a lot to talk over with you." Not, "Tom, let's have a quiet evening together, and get a lot of things straight." Just—"sixish."

Tom finished his drink at a gulp, wondered about another, decided not. His career might be slithering downhill, his book might be choking itself to death, but he still had Thea. And this, he knew, as he looked at his glass, was no way to keep her. He knew it, and yet he kept slipping away from his resolution. How else did you blot out the feeling of failure?

He had made a real effort to stop thinking about Chuck; and Shandon; and the Memorandum; and that goddamned Olivetti. (He wasn't using it any more.) He wouldn't even discuss these subjects with Thea. But the subconscious was a real devil, eating away at him. No matter how determinedly he dropped the hurts and disappointments out of his conscious mind, they only sank below the surface; and lay there.

So now Chuck was here, and perhaps ready to talk. . . . There had been a slightly too jocular manner in that phone call. Is that what we are going to have—an hour of chitchat and sweet evasions? Goddamn it—Tom nearly walked back into the house to pour himself a third drink. At least he had started counting: a step in the right direction. But this meeting with Chuck— He dropped all speculation, tried to let his emotions subside and his mind stop questioning, and concentrated on the far stretch of coast line. It was a continuous sweep of cliffs and bays, with a back screen of mountains whose rocky spurs ran out into the sea and sheltered the indentations of beaches. To the west, he could see the bold plunge of Monaco's headland. Then came the bay, where Monte Carlo had tucked itself into one corner, curving eastward to the green-covered promontory of Cap Martin lying below him. In jutted the shore line again, to form the wide bay where Menton lay with its Old Town built high above the port. And beyond that, the bay curved farther inland before it came sweeping out again to the red cliffs, a mountain wall of sheer rock that formed a most definite frontier. Next stop—

Italy, and the Riviera dei Fiori, and a distant view of Bordighera. And then nothing but a horizon where blue sky met blue sea. Florida, he thought, had started with several strikes against it when it went up to bat against the Côte d'Azur.

Nerves calmed, mind more at rest, he turned away. That view was better medicine, he admitted frankly, than the empty glass in his hand. Keep remembering that, he told himself. He set the glass down on the table at the side of the terrace, a private corner shielded by lemon trees, and began walking down the rough driveway that led, from the east side of the house, to the Roquebrune road.

Thea was late. Menton, adjoining Roquebrune (or was it the other way round? One moment you were driving in Menton; next block you were in Roquebrune), was only a couple of miles from here. It was just like her to go dashing off to the market, to buy extra food—and no doubt some special items that their tight budget didn't usually allow. (Money was another of his hidden worries: it melted, like first snowflakes on a city sidewalk, in this spreading inflation.) "Chuck may stay for dinner," she had said when the phone call from Nice was over. Tactfully, and again true to Thea, she hadn't said what was really on her mind—and on my mind too, thought Tom: why the hell doesn't Chuck stay here with us? We've got two unused bedrooms, damn them.

Back to Chuck again, are we?

He quickened his pace, putting distance between himself and the silent house and a desk littered with discarded manuscript. I've become too critical, too hesitant about my own work, he thought now. I'm not fit company for Thea these days. The only time we are really happy, and not often enough either, is in that big beautiful bedroom upstairs. Solange—so she had told them proudly—had furnished it after the style of the Byblos Hotel over at Saint-Tropez: white carpet everywhere; white plaster walls cleverly finished to look as if they were carpeted too; outsize bed, practically floor-level, covered with a white rug. "A love nest at first sight," said Thea, setting them both laughing. Well, if we can both laugh together and love together, there is hope for us. Without that, we'd have started drifting apart in these last months. It could yet happen, his common sense warned him. If he didn't get a better grip on himself—I'll get over this, he told himself. I must. I don't need a sense of guilt to add to my problems.

The last stretch of driveway ran through the old Michel flower nursery, still functioning, now owned and worked by honest Auguste and his stalwart Albertine, who came up the hill to "oblige" once a week with a thorough house-cleaning, or, for a special evening, to cook. There had been too few of those. Not fair to Thea—I'll have to take some days off, drive her around, visit the hill towns, explore. We'll do that next week. The hell with my work, it's getting nowhere as it is. I've got to do some rethinking of the last chapter, organize its material better, reshape and—or should I just throw the whole thing out and start over again? Remake it, fresh and alive?

He passed the rows of flower beds, some bright with bloom, the rest promising flowers next month, and halted at the clump of mimosa by the gate. He could see no sign of their car—a small Fiat they had rented—in the rush of traffic to and from lower Roquebrune. The road was narrow, twisting up the hill, built in the days when people walked or used real horse-power. His worries sharpened as he watched the stream of cars and trucks and buses. Where was Thea anyway? he wondered irritably. What had delayed her so long in Menton? She was usually back by noon. And it was certainly noon—the nursery was deserted, all hands now engaged in their midday meal.

And there she was at last, safely returning. The accident he had begun to fear hadn't taken place. But it nearly did, at this very moment, as Dorothea took a wild chance to make a left turn across the path of the descending traffic.

"For God's sake, Thea!" he yelled as she stopped inside the gate and waited for him.

"I didn't even chip a taillight," she told him cheerfully. "Jump in. I'll give you a lift to the house if you'll trust my driving. And there's nothing wrong with it either," she reminded him. Hadn't he noticed? If she had pulled up and waited to make the turn, the car behind her could have rear-ended the Fiat? He is too much on edge these days, she thought unhappily. And all her excitement about her meeting with Tony Lawton drained away. Silently, she made room for him on the seat beside her.

"You're late." He picked up the sheaf of papers and magazines she had bought in Menton: the *Herald Tribune* and *Le Monde* from Paris, the *Observer* and *Economist* and *Guardian* from London, the current *Time* and *Newsweek*. "What about the New York *Times*?"

"It's later than I am." Besides, it always arrived two or three days old. Another day wouldn't hurt. "Headlines are hideous, aren't they?"

His eyes scanned them. "Yes," he said briefly. That's where I should be, he thought: right back where the wires are bringing in all the latest alarms and excursions, the stuff that journalists' dreams are made of.

"I picked up the mail on my way into Menton. You'll find it in my hand-bag."

"More bills?"

"A letter from Brad Gillon." She brought the car to a very smooth halt beside the row of orange trees near the back door.

Tom searched in her purse and found the envelope. It had been opened. He looked at her.

"It's addressed to me as well as you." Dorothea's lips tightened. "Oh, really, Tom—do I *ever* open your mail?"

"What's he saying? Telling you to keep after me about the book?"

"He isn't badgering you about anything. He had a meeting with Chuck. Brad took him to lunch at the Century. There was a lot of serious talk."

Tom said nothing. The serious talk should have been between Chuck and me, he thought bitterly. He was about to slip the letter unread into his pocket—he'd have a drink first and feel more able to deal with it—when the stamp on the envelope caught his eye. "Just look at that postmark, will you? February fourteenth! Two weeks on the way!" he said in disgust. "And by air mail, too."

"Normal delivery nowadays." Dorothea thought of her own postcards to Washington that had taken four weeks. "Better read the letter, Tom." It was important. Doubly so because its arrival was so late.

Tom stuck the letter into a pocket. "It's all old news by this time." And he had a feeling he didn't want to hear it.

"It's still urgent enough." She glanced at his face, saw worry increasing. So she made an effort to lighten her voice, and her manner, and the news. "He had planned to come and see us last week, after some publishers' meeting in Paris. But Mona was in Acapulco and guess what she did? She developed pneumonia. In Acapulco—I ask you! So Brad had to cancel Europe and fly down to bring her home."

"Stop circling, Thea. You're getting into a pretty constant habit of doing just that recently. You can give me the bad news."

Can I? she wondered. If I circle around it, you are the one who evades it. She drew a deep breath. "He must see us, Brad says. And so he is arriving in Nice on March eighth, straight from New York."

"But that's next weekend."

"Yes. Before he goes on to Paris. He wants to talk with you."

"So we are getting top priority." He didn't like that idea either. "What's his problem? Is it the book? Or—" he forced himself to say it—"about Chuck?"

"About Chuck." She reached over, kissed him on the cheek. "I'm sorry I was late, darling. But I met—"

He silenced her with a kiss on her lips. "I'm sorry I was so damned sharp-set. It's just that—" He hesitated, fell silent.

"You are worrying far too much these days," she told him gently. "I was barely thirty minutes late. And you can blame twenty of those on Tony. We bumped into each other just outside the market."

"Tony? Tony Lawton's in town?"

"Come on, darling. Let's get this basket of food into the kitchen, or the Brie will be melting over the lamb chops."

"What's he doing here?"

"On holiday. Sailing. The boat needed emergency repairs, so it's stuck in Menton for today. I invited him to come back here with me for lunch, but he had some phone calls to make. So I asked him to come up this evening and have a drink." She was already heading for the back door, carrying the smaller packages. Tom gathered papers and basket, and followed her into the kitchen.

"When?" His voice was sharp.

"Oh, around five."

"But Chuck will be—"

"Chuck will be late." He had a habit of lateness whenever something unpleasant was on the horizon, and this meeting with Tom wasn't going to be easy for either of them. "And before you meet him, Tony wants to have a word with you. Sort of background information, I think. Necessary, Tony said. Otherwise, you'd—"

"I don't need advice on how to handle my own brother."

"Oh, Tom! Tony's only trying to—"

"What the hell does he think he's doing, sticking his nose into—"

"Read Brad's letter." Abruptly, she turned away and began unpacking the basket: cheeses and meat into the refrigerator; fruit and vegetables to be washed and dried. Tom turned on his heel, walked into the pantry, but the letter was now in his hand. She found she was waiting, tense and nervous, for his footsteps to stop at the bar, and chided herself for even listening. But there was no sound of a bottle set down on the tiled counter, or of ice dropped into a glass. He must be reading, not pouring another drink. Not yet, at least. She faced the window, tears in her eyes as she stared out blindly at five little orange trees trying to screen the torn-up land farther up the hillside.

Then Tom was beside her, one hand slipping around her waist, the other holding Brad's letter. "He's so damned diplomatic. As far as I can make out, he had something important to tell Chuck at that lunch. And Chuck didn't like it." He frowned at a closely written page, trying to read between its lines. "I wish he had been more explicit. I suppose he couldn't be—not old Brad, at least."

"He was giving Chuck some off-the-record information. So he said."

Tom liked the look of the whole matter less and less. "Brad wouldn't entrust it to a letter," he agreed, "or to a phone call." His frown deepened and he looked once more at the paragraph dealing with Chuck. Brad's script was as discreet as Brad himself.

> . . . *And so I tried some frank talk with your brother. He didn't believe me, not then. But I think I've jolted him enough to start him thinking about the net result of his actions last November. Some of it can be told now, off the record. (I had to take this chance with Chuck; and he will be the last person to want it publicized. It goes far beyond personal matters.) We parted coldly, yet I still have hopes that my news will have some effect on him. He has some extra worries, too—new developments which must trouble him: Katie Collier has jumped bail, leaving her family to forfeit a hundred thousand dollars; and Martin Holzheimer has stumbled on a story that seemingly convinced him to get in touch with the police. So my guess would be that Chuck is a deeply troubled young man, and more than a little scared by the way things are turning out, although—so far—he is persuading himself that he can cope. I gave him your address and telephone number, by the way; and I shouldn't be surprised if you have a letter from him, as the first sign that my words had some effect. I hope I didn't overstep our friendship, Tom, in trying to handle this tricky situation. But I knew the facts, and I was on the scene. That's my excuse, anyway.*

Tom slipped the letter back into his pocket, and loosened his hold on her waist. "I'd better cable Brad at once—let him know we did get the letter. He's probably been worrying for the past week why he had no answer from us." Tom thought over that, and impatience returned. "Why the devil didn't he call and ask if his letter had reached us? That wouldn't have broken security."

"And risk having his ears pinned back for interfering?" More nervous than she let herself appear, she glanced at Tom. "I'm just following your advice, my love. I've stopped circling."

"Does Brad think I'm so damned touchy as all that? And you know me better than to even think I'd—" He checked his rising temper. "I'm sorry, Thea. Sorry." He took her in his arms, felt her stiff spine begin to relax. "I know, I know. I've had my moods recently. They're over. All over. Believe me. I can't afford them now. I've got more to worry about than myself." He kissed her, hugged her close, kissed her again. Now her body felt soft and warm, supple against his.

She said, "I've been difficult too. I—"

He silenced her with another kiss before he let her go. "I'd better start sending that cable. Or perhaps I'll risk a telephone call."

"It's seven in the morning in New York."

"All the better. I'll get him before he leaves for the office." Tom halted halfway across the kitchen. "Who is this Katie Collier?"

"Oh, that's the girl who nearly got blown up with her friends when their bomb factory exploded."

December headlines, he remembered then. "But what has that got to do with Chuck?"

Dorothea could only shake her head.

"And what's this flap about Holzheimer? There's no reason why he shouldn't be in touch with the police—he's a reporter. And a good one."

Dorothea was less generous. The man who started all our troubles, she thought. She said, "Couldn't he at least have told you where he got that copy of the Memorandum? After all, you're fourth estate, too."

"I didn't ask him. Because I knew. Because I didn't want to hear." He began walking to the pantry door, stopped there, said, "He got the Memorandum from Chuck."

At last, she thought, at last he has actually said it out loud. She heard his footsteps go briskly past the bar toward the telephone. Relief surged over her. His mood had indeed changed. Permanently? Certainly for this afternoon, making Tony welcome—like old times. And thank God for that.

She began pulling leaves of lettuce into small pieces for a *salade Niçoise*. Radishes to be sliced. Chop up some of that red thing that looked like a blood-soaked cabbage. (She never ate it, was that why she could never remember its name?) Anchovies. Small black olives. Pieces of tuna. Croutons, garlic-flavored. Hard-boiled eggs—"Damn and blast," she said aloud. She had totally forgotten them this morning. Okay, okay. Almost *salade Niçoise* but not quite. Blame it on a telephone call from Chuck.

But at least he had telephoned. Give him credit for that first gesture. He had sounded normal enough. Perhaps Brad had exaggerated the trouble around him. And yet, if the situation wasn't as bad as Brad had seen it, why had Tony changed his own plans so suddenly when she mentioned Chuck's call from Nice? Yes, that was when Tony had dropped all interest in the busy street outside the market, even in the pretty girl (well worth admiring, conceded Dorothea) who was passing by with her long wide skirt swinging over dark red boots, and had shifted his entire attention to Dorothea.

"Chuck?" Tony had asked. "In Nice?"

"He must be in Menton right now. Rick Nealey met him at the airport."
Tony whistled softly; an eyebrow went up.

"I agree. A little unexpected, isn't it?"

"Frankly, I'd have bet on a letter. That's always easier than direct confrontation. Is he staying long?"

"I shouldn't think so. He's at Shandon Villa, and there won't be much room for him when it starts filling up next week."

"Why stay at Shandon at all?"

"Oh—some business, he said. But he does want to see Tom. At least he invited himself for a drink this evening."

"Shandon . . . I'd have thought Tom would have advised him against that."
"But why?"

He stared at her for a moment, openly puzzled. "Let's walk a little—to your car? You lead the way and I'll carry this." He took the basket over one arm and began steering her through the midday crowd. "Now tell me what Brad had to say last weekend—didn't Tom believe him?"

"Brad never got here. Mona fell ill. He hopes to see us next weekend."

Tony's lips tightened. He walked in silence for several paces. "When do you expect Chuck for that drink?"

"At six."

"I'd like to have a word with Tom before then."

"Come up and have lunch."

"Wish I could, but I've some heavy telephoning to do." He plunged into a quick explanation about the boat, engine failure, two of his sailing chums now working on it down at the harbor and waiting for his return with some supplies.

"You have a busy day ahead of you. Come and have lunch tomorrow. Bring your friends too."

"How about five this evening?" Tony asked. "All right with you?"

"Can you manage it without too much trouble?"

"I'll make sure I manage it."

"And stay to dinner?"

"Better not. I'll disappear before Chuck arrives. Strangers, keep out. Isn't that what Tom would say? How is he, how's the book, how are *you?*"

"Worried," she said frankly. "Your news for Tom—unpleasant, isn't it?"

"But necessary. Believe me. Someone has got to give him the details, provide some argument-power when he is dealing with Chuck." He had noted the disbelief in her eyes. "Tom," he said gently, "is accustomed to dealing with facts. He would want to know the situation. Wouldn't he?"

"Once—yes." Her voice was unsteady. "But now—"

"Once and always," Tony insisted. "He can take it."

And then Tony had made one of his conversational leaps into the charm of southern French towns, red-tiled roofs rippling, light walls and brightly painted shutters, flowers and palm trees popping up all over, nineteenth century hodge-podging with the twentieth, and wouldn't it be wonderful if you could have tourist money without the tourists? But why this good bourgeois street, along which they had walked, was named in honor of the naughty president Félix Faure, he would never understand.

By the time they reached the car Dorothea had even begun to smile again. He stowed away the basket, glanced over at the heap of newspapers and magazines lying beside the driver's seat as he opened the car door for her. He misses nothing, she had thought, not even the way I looked when I spoke about Tom.

Then, as she was about to enter the car, she turned to give him a quick tight hug and a kiss on his cheek. "Thank you, Tony."

"Not at all. Delighted to carry baskets for pretty girls, any day."

"I wish I had dark red boots too."

That had startled him. Briefly. "You are a proper caution, you are. See you at five, love."

Fourteen

"Some heavy telephoning," Tony had said—a truthful excuse—as he backed away from Dorothea's lunch invitation. But now, first of all, he had some heavy thinking to do. And quickly.

He watched her gray Fiat safely on its way, and then began walking back to the market district. Slow steps, racing thoughts. Two problems now: Jean Parracini's safety—the damned fool must be restrained somehow; Chuck Kelso at Shandon Villa. Why couldn't that self-assured idiot have stayed with his brother? Here on business, was he? What kind of business? Chuck was a young man who surrounded himself with question marks, Tony thought as he found a small café where he could have a ham-and-crusted-roll sandwich— a difficult feat in a country devoted to table d'hôte menus.

Twenty minutes later he was out in the street again, plans made, searching for a safe telephone. (The café's phone had been the free-to-all-ears type.) Streets were almost empty, shops closed, restaurants crowded, in deference to the midday ritual of eating. The main post office, large and capacious, usually packed but possibly half-empty at this time of day, was his best bet. Its telephone booths, nicely tucked into one corner of its ground floor, had doors to insure reasonable privacy. And he had a sufficient supply of the mandatory *jetons* in his pocket—in France, where coins for public telephones were distrusted, he always made sure of that.

He put in his first call—to Bill and Nicole, up in their hill house in the Garavan district. (Thank God, he thought, that Jean Parracini's hiding place, on the other side of town from Cap Martin, was so far from Shandon Villa.)

"Keep a better eye on Jean," he began, wasting no time.

"But he's safely back. He's eating dinner now," Bill said.

"Where?"

"In the kitchen with Bernard—as usual. Everything normal. Don't sweat."

"When did he return?"

Bill consulted with Nicole, who took over the receiver. "He arrived only eight minutes after I did," Nicole said. "I was here by quarter past twelve."

"That's odd." Impossible, in fact.

"Why?"

"When I last saw him, he was tailing Rick Nealey from the market. And that was at five minutes to twelve."

"Then he couldn't have followed for very long. Perhaps it was a coincidence—he just seemed to be—"

"It was a tail." That silenced Nicole. "Who does Parracini think he is? The Invisible Man? He is taking too many chances." Curious, thought Tony: he hadn't had time to tail Nealey all the way to Cap Martin—so why had he followed at all? Or hadn't Nealey returned to Shandon Villa? Stopped a few blocks from the market area? And Jean, curiosity or ego satisfied, had headed home? A puzzle . . . "Let it go meanwhile. Keep him under wraps this afternoon. Don't lose sight of him."

"Even when he's resting in his own quarters?"

"Where are they?"

"Above the garage, of course."

"Separated from the house?"

"Yes."

"Put Bill back on the phone. . . . Bill, move Jean over to the main house—into one of your spare rooms. For his own security."

"He will refuse. He likes his privacy. And the only room available is right next door to Brigitte and Bernard."

"Who's in charge, anyway? You and Nicole better start sweating along with me. Now—here's some other business. I want you to phone Shandon Villa, see if Charles Kelso is around. Have a good story ready if he is there to take your call: you've just heard that his brother, an old friend, is staying in Menton—can Chuck give you his address? Then I want Nicole to call Shandon—yes, she's to phone too. She will ask for Rick Nealey, try to find out if he's there. She can be a reporter from Nice, wanting an interview. I'll call you back in twenty minutes, get your answers."

"Planning a visit to Shandon?"

He's too damned smart, Tony thought irritably. He didn't answer the question, said, "And now hear this. I'm sending out for reinforcements. And I want you to accept their invitation to take you and Jean sailing tomorrow."

Bill said, "What if he refuses to go with them?"

"They'll be senior men, they'll pull rank. Besides, it is a matter of security. He'll listen. Explain to him that they want to clarify some of his earlier information. What better place than a boat?"

"We're using the *Sea Breeze*? I thought you had engine trouble."

"Not so much as all that. We'll be ready by the time the reinforcements fly into Nice tomorrow morning."

"Serious problems?" Bill was really listening now.

"When weren't they?"

"Sounds like an alert," Bill said reflectively.

Tony hung up, checked his watch with the post office clock. He had used up several *jetons,* and his next call was to Paris. But all he'd have to do, when he did make sure of the right connection, would be to identify himself by his code name (Uncle Arthur) and leave a message with significant phrases for further relay. "Weather deteriorating, heavy winds possible. Advise dual repairs, best available, at dockside by 11:00 A.M. tomorrow." They'd know where the *Sea Breeze* was moored, its exact location in the harbor— all that had been reported on arrival yesterday evening.

And let's hope, he thought, once the brief talk with Paris was over, that the best they have available for this repair job will be a couple of men senior enough to keep Jean Parracini in place. Bloody nuisance: protecting an ally could be more difficult, and definitely less rewarding, than tracking down a hidden enemy.

His third call was to Georges, in the room he had rented at the seaside edge of the Old Town. (Excellent position, right across from the harbor, with a view of the *Sea Breeze* neat in a row of small boats, large boats, old boats, spanking-new boats; short masts, long masts, or none at all.) "Cancel your visit to Bill," he told Georges. "And Emil is still working on repairs? . . . Fine. Get in touch with him. Everything has to be ready by eleven tomorrow morning. And he is to lay in supplies for five people— better make it enough for three days—perhaps more. Did you rent that Citroën?. . . Oh, a Renault, cream-colored, two-door. Okay. Pick me up near my hotel at two thirty. And wear a collar and tie—and a jacket. We're turning respectable."

Back now to Bill on his hill. Four minutes later than arranged, damn it. Would Bill notice? Of course he did.

"Four minutes late," he said in mock surprise. "Run into trouble?"

"Napped too long. Forgot to set the alarm clock."

Bill laughed. "I believe you. Okay, listen to this: Charles Kelso lunched at the villa with the director and his family, but he seems to have gone out. The girl at the phone didn't know where. Couldn't care less, if you ask me. There was a lot of banging in the background. I joked about it. Apparently there are a lot of workmen still around, trying to get everything finished for next week's grand opening. And here is Nicole to add her little piece."

Nicole said, "Rick Nealey hasn't been on the scene since he delivered Chuck at the villa this morning. He had to dash off to Eze and La Turbie— making arrangements for next week's guests. He should be back late this afternoon."

"Good. Now, how's Jean, our intractable friend? Sulking in his tent like Achilles?"

"He balked at first, but now he's packing his things to move over to the main house. Regrets his good TV in the chauffeur's quarters, though. His new room isn't set up for television."

"Has he a telephone there?"

"No."

"But there was a telephone in the old room?" There would have to be one, linking the main house and its garage.

"Of course." Nicole sounded puzzled. "Two, actually."

"An outside line as well?" Somehow, a disturbing thought.

"It came with the place."

"And no one thought of having it disconnected."

"Why should we? He'd avoid using it, wouldn't he? He's more security-minded than—" She paused, realizing her tactlessness.

"Than I am?" Tony suggested. "Okay, okay. Glad all is under control at your end. One thing you can do for me, Nicole—scout around the harbor near the Petit Port this afternoon. *Not* the new marina in Garavan—the old one. And mark where the *Sea Breeze* is berthed. She's lying just under the big mole—you can stroll right along it, many people do. Got that? About the middle of that row of boats. She's a one-master: a cabin sloop, porpoise bow, inboard engine." But although she might look slow, she could make ten knots, and there was space enough for six people, even if slightly cramped.

"*D'accord.*"

"Put Bill back on."

Bill spoke at once. "Here."

"Get Parracini down to the *Sea Breeze* tomorrow at eleven A.M. On the dot. Can you manage that?"

"Yes. I've already told him that he will have two Nato visitors."

"His reaction?"

"Just what you'd expect. Thinks their visit here could be dangerous for all."

"Tell him that's why you've decided, as a security precaution, to make arrangements for him to meet the visitors elsewhere."

"Will do. But aren't we going to a lot of extra trouble—"

"Yes." Indeed we are, thought Tony. "But it's a safety measure. And keep him happily occupied at the house for the rest of the day."

"He has already arranged with Bernard and Brigitte to take in a movie tonight. It's one they all want to see."

"Where?"

"At the casino."

"*Where?*"

"The movie house is part of the building."

There was a deep silence.

"I'll tell him that idea is out," Bill said. "It won't make anything easier for tomorrow morning, though."

"What showing of the movie? Early or late?"

"There's only one show. This is off season. Eight thirty, I think."

Tony calculated quickly. "Let him keep his engagement tonight, and have him in a good mood for tomorrow. How did he get away with arranging a visit to the movies, anyway?"

"Said it looked unnatural if he stayed cooped up here all the time, like a prisoner. Some people might start wondering."

"I see. He has got his confidence back, has he?"

"Well, it's true enough: if a fish doesn't want to be noticeable, it had better learn to swim with the school."

Seems to me, thought Tony, that I've heard that dictum before. "His phrase or yours?"

"His. And a good one. Don't you think?"

"Yes." Now, where did I hear it? Tony wondered. He glanced at his watch. It was one thirty-five. "See you tomorrow, dockside. You can throw away your crutch. Use a cane and limp slightly."

"I'm going for a sail, too?"

"You know how to handle a boat. It looks better—chauffeur goes along to help you board. Right?"

"And you?"

"Vaguely in the background. If you need to contact me before then, leave a message with Georges. He has rigged up an answering device on his phone. You have his number? And you won't see him this afternoon. He's needed elsewhere." Tony rang off.

He took a taxi to his hotel, one of the new ones on the Quai Laurenti that stretched east along the waterfront from the Old Town and its port. He had registered there that morning, left his bag. He'd change into something more in keeping with a visit to Shandon Villa—his new tweed jacket and flannels. He could risk bumping into Chuck Kelso; the important thing was to keep out of Rick Nealey's way. Meanwhile.

And his ostensible reason for the visit?

He had found a good one before he had left the hotel and was strolling toward Georges and the waiting Renault. Certainly, over the phone, it had impressed Maclehose enough to let him extend a welcome for a brief tour of Shandon Villa. He couldn't very well snub a visitor who brought direct greetings from the director of the Shandon Institute in New Jersey: Paul Krantz's name packed a punch even at this distance. Hadn't Krantz given his own guided tour to Tony, on that unpleasant morning back in November when the Memorandum crisis was in full flap? "Of course," Maclehose had said "I remember you. Drop out here any time. This afternoon? If you could make it early—I'll be here to show you around. And how is Paul?"

"Couldn't be better. I'll be with you before three."

"Good enough."

"Oh, just one thing—what's the quickest road to take through Cap Martin to reach Shandon?"

Maclehose gave him the directions—much needed, he told Tony with a laugh—and the call ended amicably.

Now, as Tony stepped into the Renault, he could say, "All set. We'll head for Cap Martin. And stop at the casino on the way. I've a brief visit to make there."

And Georges, tall, thin, dark-haired, a thirty-year-old Frenchman, fluent in English and Italian, carefully selected for this assignment in Menton—he knew this area well from family vacations as a boy—said in his usual offhand way, "Don't expect much action there until the evening. At this time of year, you'll probably find the casino closed for the afternoon."

"All the better to let me see the layout clearly."

"Planning a night on the town?" Georges's sharp brown eyes looked both interested and amused. "You won't find it pulsing like Monte Carlo's casino."

"Where the busloads start arriving in the morning?" Tony's smile was wide, his spirits rising. All arrangements made, nothing forgotten.

Georges smiled too. "And I thought this trip was going to be all dull work." He approved of the change. His manner was deceptively mild, cloaking his natural exuberance. Like Tony and Emil and Bill and Nicole, he wasn't in this profession for money. He had brains, a contempt for danger, and deep convictions. He had lively curiosity, too. It surfaced now. "Any excitement this morning?" he couldn't resist asking.

And Tony, sketching in the details, put him neatly into the recent picture. Enough of it, anyway, to let him know what was on the agenda, and why. (Later, Georges would fill in Emil, who was now superintending the repairs to the boat's engine.) There were moments, Tony believed, when a need-to-know was the best safeguard for concerted action. He enjoyed teamwork (strange as that would seem to some people who thought of him as a loner) and based it on his old *quid pro quo* maxim. You got good co-operation if you gave it. To those you could trust, of course. And Georges, with whom he had worked for the last seven years, was a man who was dependable. Even to the way he now drew up the car a short distance from the casino's entrance—not too far to walk, not too near to be noticeable.

The entrance steps faced a square, complete with flowers, palm trees, and small taxi rank. (Tony noted it for future use. There weren't many taxi stands around this town.) Inside, a small vestibule and more steps and no one to stop him. He found himself in a totally deserted hall, spacious, light—the wall directly opposite the vestibule's steps was of glass—giving a view of terrace and large pool, and beyond that, a glimpse of the front street where Nicole and he had walked along the promenade. There were two wings to the hall, the left one consisted of the *Salle Privée*—well-marked, well-screened from curious eyes—but a thin young man, dark-suited, pale-faced, appeared out of nowhere at the sound of Tony's footsteps, and politely barred him from pushing open its curtained door. Nearby was a large and empty dining room, handily adjoining that side of the pool's terrace; and across from it, close to the vestibule steps, was a pleasant (and equally empty) bar. The main hall itself had two large green-covered tables, where play would be less private and certainly easier on the budget. Beyond them, occupying the right wing of the building, there actually was a movie theater.

That was all he needed to see. He headed back for the vestibule, nodding his thanks to the dark-suited young man still guarding the other end of the hall, and emerged onto the busy street. He was thinking automatically that there must be other ways in and out of the building. The movie theater must have at least one emergency exit: even two? The pool, with its garden and colonnades along the waterfront view, had possibly an entrance of its own. The dining room? After all, it was a public place, this municipal casino—except for those who enjoyed high stakes in a *salle* kept *très privée*.

"Quiet as the tomb," he told Georges. And about as cold. Some summer sun was needed to heat that high-ceilinged hall. "Only one character bobbed up, near the *Salle Privée* door. What did he think I was going to do, anyway? Jiggle the wheel? Place marked cards in the shoe?"

"You don't gamble, do you?"

"What do you think we are doing right now?" And the stakes couldn't be higher.

As Georges drove past the wooded gardens, past glimpses of large houses surrounded by flowering trees beyond impressive gates, he said, "I think this address you've given me lies on one of the private roads. In that case, we'll be stopped. Only residents' cars and their friends' cars and taxis can get through. Everyone else—well, drive around some other road if you must, but keep out of this one."

"Taxis allowed?"

"It's a local rule. There's logic to it, I suppose. People in taxis are usually going to a definite address."

"We are, too."

"I hope your Mr. Maclehose told the guards you were expected."

"Guards? We aren't visiting the Élysée Palace."

"Not really guards. More like—well, guardians."

They turned out to be a fresh-faced woman in a cotton dress and cardigan, and her elderly husband with a cloth cap almost as old as he was. They looked like small stall-holders, down in the marketplace, ready to sell Tony a dozen oranges. But they took their job seriously, checked the name Lawton on their list (Maclehose had remembered) and—with a nod from the man and a smile from the woman—let the car proceed.

Georges took it easy, for the road was narrow and twisting. "I know what you're thinking," he told Tony. "They couldn't fight off more than their shadows. They might not stop a jewel thief, but they could certainly identify him to the police."

"The strangest Keep Out notice I've ever seen." But Georges was right: no stranger could come wandering round here unescorted. Jean Parracini, if he were tempted to seek payment for the damage done to him and his friends by Shandon (justice, he would call it), would find a direct approach impossible. "Wonder if Shandon Villa has a beach, a landing place for small craft?"

Georges stared at him, and then went back to keeping count of the houses. "That's the second on the left. And Shandon's the fifth?"

Tony nodded. The villas were generously spaced, securely separated from one another by walls and hedges, scarcely visible behind the screens of shrubs and trees that decorated smooth lawns. "And here we are, gates wide open. Shandon Villa doesn't subscribe to the closed-door theory, I see."

"But they have two muscular gardeners working close to the driveway," Georges pointed out with amusement.

They studied the villa before them. It was a massive assertion of an architect's dream of Italy with Spanish memories creeping in. The gardens, even from a view mostly blocked by pink stucco, were lush and extensive. "A touch of Eden. All right, Georges. Let's find the snake."

The door to the villa was impressive: two tall bronze panels, one of them ajar, both of them encrusted with decorative scenes depicting myths and men. "A slight echo of Florence?" murmured the irreverent Tony, not quite sure whether to let the massive door knocker clatter down on Aphrodite's backside as she received the apple from Paris, or to heave the door fully open and enter. "If the Duchess of Shandon couldn't have Ghiberti, she hired his great-great-great-great-grandson." He compromised by both knocking and pushing. "A fake," he added sadly as the panel swung back easily: wood covered with copper. "Now what?"

A broad hall stretched before them, running through the villa until it ended in a wall of glass. Sunlight and a terrace lay out there, making an inviting vista from this dark threshold. "Aren't we expected? Where the devil is everyone?"

Beside them a door opened, and Maclehose came bouncing out from his office, his hands outstretched in a slightly effusive, if belated, welcome. "Come in, come in—just finishing off some dictation." His face was tanned and healthy, his large and cumbersome body several pounds heavier, his smile beaming, his eyes wary but clearing, as Tony conveyed warm greetings from Paul Krantz. Delighted to see Tony again, delighted to meet his friend.

"Georges Despinard," Tony explained, "a journalist from Paris. He is writing a series of articles for *La Vie Nouvelle* about social changes in the Côte d'Azur. Naturally he is very much interested in Shandon Villa. We were lunching together, and when he heard I was coming here—"

"Of course, of course. Delighted," Maclehose said for the third time. "Yes, we are changing things. But for the better—I hope."

He's nervous, Tony thought: under all that exuberance is uncertainty. He's wondering if I'll mention that unpleasant morning back at Shandon House, when heavy flak was flying around and unhappy Maclehose was dodging the fallout. I'll do him a real favor: I won't even breathe a reference to the NATO Memorandum.

"Let me show you around," Maclehose was saying, leading the way past the open door of his office—really an anteroom tucked near the front entrance—where his secretary was pretending to be unaware of the two visitors. A handsome redhead, Tony noted: tight sweater, slender legs, face pretty but expressionless. Maclehose waved a hand to her. "Find that guest list for the first seminar, Anne-Marie. Bring it to me." He went on his way, hurrying along the hall, gesturing to right and left as he identified the rooms. "That's the library—I'm afraid I must leave in twenty minutes—the dining room is over there—but as I explained to you on the phone, I have engagements for this afternoon—and here's the main sitting room, must have some place where our guests can relax between serious business—this place is a madhouse today, last-minute checks on electrical work—" He nodded to two men who were carrying their toolboxes down a broad staircase. "Bedrooms up there, of course—ten of them, not counting the quarters for my executive assistant, he has his office and bedroom in the corner suite, he's constantly on the job, I tell him he even sleeps with his problems—and next door to him, two very sizable rooms which we've turned into group-discussion areas. Now, down here, we have the main seminar room—it was a large drawing room at one time—and across the way, the terrace room just beside this door, of course." He swept them through the large glass panels that slid apart at their approach, and brought them out onto a terrace overlooking a series of descending gardens that stretched to the sea.

"Remarkable," said Tony, thinking of the executive assistant's suite. "And your quarters, where are they?"

"Oh, we thought it better to keep the family at some distance from our distinguished visitors. So Mattie and I have set up house in that cottage over there, you can't see it because of the acacias. Very comfortable—seven rooms—Simon Shandon used to live in it when his wife had her friends to stay here." Maclehose looked around. "Beautiful, isn't it?"

"Remarkable," Tony said again. So the director has only a small office in the main building, and placed right at the front door as if he were the concierge. Doesn't he realize he is giving up his power base? Distinguished visitors were going to see much more of his executive assistant than of the director. Cozy chats and late-night conversations would not be shared with Maclehose. And at dinner, who would be the host? Seldom Maclehose, I'm willing to bet: he can't leave Mattie and the children night after night, can he? Not his style. A nice good-hearted family man, as virtuous and well-meaning as they come. "An ideal place. Don't you think so, Georges?"

Georges came out of shock: what wealth could build, when it set its mind upon it, always stunned him for a few initial moments. "Extraordinary!" Georges lapsed into French and let off a run of sentences.

Maclehose looked embarrassed, covered his perplexity with a wide grin.

"My friend is saying that you have done an outstanding job of transforming this place," Tony obliged. "He is deeply impressed. And so am I." Tony's eyes were now on the gardens, green terraces with bright beds, edged by shrubs and groupings of trees. "Georges would also like to stroll among your flowers—he is interested in gardens too. In fact, he was a landscape architect before becoming a writer."

"By all means. Tell Monsieur—" Maclehose was uncertain of the name— "tell your friend to go down to the pool—it's just above the beach—we've had some workmen fixing the lights there—underwater illumination." He glanced markedly at his watch. "I'd like to spend the next five minutes showing you the guest list for our first seminar." He looked around for Anne-Marie, but she wasn't in sight.

"See you back here in five minutes," Tony called after Georges. And don't forget a visit to the beach.

"I envy you your French," Maclehose admitted. "They speak so quickly—that's my trouble. A pity my executive assistant can't be here to meet you. He's an expert linguist. But he had some final arrangements to make for our guests next week—up at Eze—they'd enjoy lunch up there—a very fine restaurant."

"That's a pleasant idea: relaxation for tired minds."

Maclehose laughed. "All part of public relations. That's my executive assistant's main job, but he really can turn his hand to anything, don't know what I would have done without him. He took charge of the alterations, found a reliable contractor with a team of first-rate men—carpenters, painters, electricians—and the work was completed yesterday—except for a few corrections. And all in less than eight weeks, imagine!"

"And who's that? The contractor himself?" Tony asked as a quietly dressed man came climbing up from one of the lower terraces along with an obvious workman.

"No. I think that's the inspector, who is checking our wiring system. We had a certain amount of trouble with it."

"He looks satisfied now," said Tony. "All must be well. Your executive assistant will be relieved."

"Nealey? Yes, indeed. He had to call in two other electricians to get the final adjustments made."

"And the contractor himself didn't blow a fuse?" And what about his team of first-rate workmen?

"Oh, Nealey added a bonus—the work was finished in time, except for a few modifications we wanted to make. The contractor has nothing to complain about."

We wanted to make? Tony let that go, although it was tempting to hint that a bonus might be construed as bribery. But he resisted putting at least one warning fly into Maclehose's too trustful ear, his full attention now on the man who called himself an inspector.

The man drew near, the workman a step behind him. And suddenly Tony was on the alert, memory stirring, another scene floating up to the surface of his mind. Washington. The Statler Hotel. A group of Soviet agricultural specialists. An interpreter, who left, and was followed . . . and Rick Nealey slipping into the car where the man waited. A man in his early forties; five feet ten or eleven; broad-shouldered, strong build. The dark hair was no longer streaked with gray; the placid face was now tanned. The eyes were the same, blue, cold, and confident. Boris Gorsky.

He passed close enough to make Tony (now admiring the profusion of the nearby flower beds) feel a touch of cold sweat at the nape of his neck. Boris Gorsky, good God . . . Yes, Gorsky himself, as cool as when he had walked into Lenox Hill Hospital, and couldn't identify his old comrade Vladimir Konov. "These huge pink and purple patches, what are they?" Tony asked.

"Cyclamen," Maclehose told him. "Certainly," he was replying to the inspector's query, "go right upstairs. I'm sure you'll find it's all in order now."

The two men reached the house as the redhead at last stepped onto the terrace.

"Cyclamen? Massed close like that?" Tony shook his head in wonder, and managed a glimpse of the redhead's brief hesitation, a momentary question on her pretty face and a small smile on her lips, as she glanced at Gorsky. Then she came forward to Maclehose, a sheet of paper in her hand, her face once more expressionless. She isn't as dumb as she looks, thought Tony; she knows Gorsky. He looked at Maclehose, standing proudly on his beautiful terrace, in front of his beautiful house, above his beautiful gardens, and he fell silent.

Maclehose took the list with a warm smile of dismissal for Anne-Marie, and began explaining the prominent names it contained. The subject they would discuss was of paramount importance to the allies of the United States: *The Weakness of Super-Strength.* "A good title, don't you think?"

"Applicable only to the United States?"

"For this seminar, yes. Later we'll examine Russia's response to challenge."

"Responses," Tony corrected gently. "And when will that be?"

"Oh—sometime, I hope, this summer. It's a matter of getting the right specialists together."

"And there are more of them on America's weaknesses than on Russia's?" Tony asked blandly. Then glancing at his watch, he exclaimed, "Our time is almost up. Disappointing. I did want to hear about the rest of your staff, too. Surely you can't run a place as important as this only with Nealey."

"Oh, he will have an assistant. Besides that, there are two seminar aides, three translators, four secretaries."

"A neat progression."

Maclehose laughed. His anxiety about this visit from Krantz's friend had left him. The report back to New Jersey would be positive.

"Will they live on the premises, too?" Tony asked. "A bit crowded."

"I agree. There's no room—domestic staff and storage take our top floor. They'll stay in town."

"And go home early?" Tony was smiling. "Very nice work, if you can get it."

"No, no. They'll work a full day. They start on Monday—no need to have them around with all the hammering and sawing going on." Maclehose looked at his watch and tried not to frown.

"We are detaining you, I'm afraid. Why don't we say good-by now, and I can find Georges—"

"Would you?" Maclehose's hand was out.

"There he is at last," said Tony, looking down over the garden. Georges had been running, and now—as he saw them standing on the high terrace—halted abruptly, signaled urgently. He called out something unintelligible, ending with a shout of *"Vite! Vite!"*

At the first signal, Tony had already begun moving and was ten paces ahead of the startled Maclehose. Georges, turning on his heel, raced back the way he had come. A gardener lifted his head from setting out masses of begonias in a lower-terrace bed, rose from his knees as he saw the running men, and, trowel still in his hand, followed Georges. Someone else—a workman in dungarees—emerged from some trees to stand bewildered at this madness. He let Tony and Maclehose pass him before he too started downhill. There was a shout from the gardener, now hidden on the last terrace by a hedge of trimmed shrubs. Another yell from him—a warning? An answering shout from Georges.

Behind Tony, Maclehose called out, "They're at the swimming pool. My God—the children—" And he put on a desperate burst of speed that brought him slithering over the steep slope of grass to end up crashing against the hedge. He tried to see over the top of the clipped yews, but they were chin height, and dense. "Oh, my God!" he said again, as he followed Tony down the short flight of steps to the last terrace. Then his fears calmed as he caught sight of the pool.

It was only half full of water, probably had been emptied that morning for work on the undersurface lights—some heavy wires still snaked over the terrace as evidence that the electricians had been busy there, perhaps still were. At the shallow end, floating face down with arms stiffly spread, was a man. He was fully clothed, tweed jacket and all, except for his shoes. They lay haphazardly, scattered below the body, on the pale blue floor of the pool.

The gardener, in a mixture of Provençal and French, was shouting at everyone. Georges translated as best he could. "He says the water's dangerous—he was warned to stay away from this terrace—work was going on here."

Tony stared down at the pool. The back of the dead man's head, dark hair, was all he could see. Sharply, he glanced at Maclehose, who stood there, absolutely speechless, his eyes bulging in a face whose tan had faded to a pale yellow. Then, as a woman appeared on the far side of the terrace, Maclehose came to life. "Get back, Mattie, get back there! For God's sake don't step on those wires. Keep off the wet paving! Get back!"

Mattie stood still, incredulous. "Chuck Kelso," she said slowly. "It's Chuck!"

"I know, I know," Maclehose shouted angrily. "Get back to the house, Mattie! Keep the children away from here."

"The children—but they're safe at the garage. We were all waiting for you, and I came down to see what was delaying—"

"Get someone else to drive you into town."

Unbelievable, thought Tony. Here we all are standing in the exact same spot where we stopped short on this terrace as if we were in a bloody mine field, a man is telling his wife he can't drive her into town, and there's a corpse floating in the water beside us. And as background to all this, a three-way argument was going on between the gardener and Georges and the workman. The gardener said there were live wires all around; the electrician said the current was shut off—no one, but no one, would work at the pool with the current still on; and Georges was trying to get an answer to a sensible question. "Where is the main switch?" he kept asking. "Where?"

Tony walked over to the gardener, took the trowel from his hand, threw it into the pool. It broke the surface without a flare or a sizzle, and sank. "Let's get the body out of there," Tony said, and looked round for a rake.

Fifteen

"WE'LL STOP HERE for a few moments," Tony said, breaking their long silence, as they reached the Roquebrune road. Georges nodded, found a parking space near a group of small shops, and turned off the Renault's engine.

Neither had spoken since they left Shandon Villa. The police were still there, questioning the electrician, interest now focused on what power near the pool area had been turned off, what turned on, when and why. The pool itself was safe enough, all work there completed. Only one section, containing the lights that would illuminate the trees at one end of the pool, was still under repair. The power switch controlling that small area was still active. A regrettable oversight, a case of human failure; judgment against which the unfortunate electrician kept protesting. (The power had been off today on all areas of the pool and its surroundings. No, he hadn't seen this done: he had just assumed it to be so. As for the other electricians, they'd be back tomorrow to clear up the mess they had left: his job was to check the lights on the upper terraces, and that's where he had been working, hadn't heard or seen anything.)

Yes, everyone had been thoroughly baffled. And Maclehose gave the verdict that possibly would stand. "An accident, a terrible accident," he kept repeating. It seemed a plausible explanation: the trees at the dangerous corner of the terrace screened the small pavilion where Maclehose had installed his visitor. "Official guests at the villa, our own friends in the pavilion beside the pool— Mattie fixed up the upper floor nicely for them, just no room over at our place. Poor Kelso, he was the first to use our guesthouse. Arrived this morning, was only going to stay here overnight. Tomorrow he'd be on his way to Gstaad— always takes a winter vacation—two weeks, he said. Suicide? Ridiculous. He wasn't depressed. Preoccupied, perhaps. Certainly, he was in a serious mood at lunchtime, seemed ten years older than I remembered him. Just wouldn't let us plan his afternoon. He said he was going to wait for Rick Nealey's return. And after that he was going to see his brother. His brother—good God, Lawton, what do we do about his brother?"

And Tony said, "You let him know."

"Yes. Yes. I'd better call him right away. You are leaving?"

"The police have our names and addresses. They'll know where they can reach us." Which was true enough. And if the police wanted to check further than Tony's hotel or the *Sea Breeze*, they'd end up at a wine shipper's office in London and a journalist's desk in Paris.

"I don't think they'll trouble you," said Maclehose. And I hope, his anxious eyes were praying, they won't trouble Shandon Villa either. "No publicity about this," he added, glancing at Georges. "The less the better, don't you agree?"

"I agree."

"Accidents will happen," Maclehose said miserably. He sighed a deep sigh as he shook their hands, and went back to staring at the figure, covered now by a blanket, as if he could by sheer willpower bid the stretcher-bearers move it out of sight, out of his life.

Tony turned abruptly away, said nothing more. He began climbing up through the gardens, with Georges hurrying to catch up.

"Accident?" Georges wondered aloud. "Perhaps it was. When I passed across that terrace on my way to the beach, there was nothing to see. No one, nothing. Just a pool that was half full of water. And five minutes later, there he was—Kelso."

"And a few minutes before that two men had come up from the terrace."

"Two men? But I saw nobody—or were they inside the pavilion—?"

"Where else?"

Then Georges remembered Tony's brief visit to the upper floor of the pavilion in search of a blanket to cover Kelso's body. "What did you find there?"

"A bed where a man had been lying. Tie and sweater on one of those valet stands. Keys and wallet on a dresser. Jacket certainly off—who sleeps in a jacket? Shoes probably off, too. They managed to get the jacket back on him, hadn't time for the shoes—you had given them a scare, walking down toward the beach—so they heaved him into the pool and the shoes after him; turned on the power to look as if he had stumbled over a live wire and been jerked into the water by the shock."

"How was he killed? There was no sign of a wound."

"An injection, possibly: enough to knock him out and let the pool do the rest."

"Expert."

"They should be. I recognized one of them. Boris Gorsky."

"Gorsky is here?" Georges was dumbfounded. My God, he thought, Nealey has some real support: he must be of major importance. He glanced back over the placid gardens. None of the stress and strain down at the pool was either audible or visible from this upper terrace. Sheltered by hedge and trees, it was all peace and tranquillity.

In silence, they had entered the house and passed through the hall. A policeman was taking statements from two electricians. But there was no sign of Gorsky. "Expert," Georges had murmured again. Tony's only comment had been a tightening of his lips.

And then, on the Roquebrune road, as Georges switched off the ignition and sat back to wait for further instructions, his eyes on the traffic, his thoughts on Boris Gorsky, Tony startled him by saying vehemently, "Jean Parracini—that's our best bet. Our only one, now."

Georges, his mind still circulating around the pool, the body, the guest pavilion, looked blankly at Tony.

"He must have something tucked away in a corner of his memory that could help us. Just one small lead, that's all we want to find Rick Nealey's true identity. Goddamn it, Parracini must have tried to uncover that. His chief Washington source—surely it was something he would try to ferret out."

"He did name Alexis as his chief source in Washington," Georges volunteered.

Tony brushed that aside. "No big deal. We had guessed that. But who *is* Alexis?—Rick Nealey?" Tony paused for emphasis. "And who is the man who calls himself Nealey?"

"And what happened in East Germany to the real Heinrich Nealey?" Georges asked softly. Silenced, as Chuck Kelso had been silenced?

But Tony was following his own train of thought. "You worked with Gerard, when he was in charge of Parracini's debriefing in Genoa. Did you talk with Parracini himself?"

"No. Never met him. My job was background research on all the reports Parracini—as Palladin—had sent us from Moscow. The idea was that I might find certain pieces of information in them that needed more clarification or expansion. Gerard questioned him about them. Results were satisfactory."

"With occasional blackouts?"

"What did you expect? Palladin's reports from Moscow covered twelve years."

"How many altogether?"

"Just over a hundred—only about nine or ten each year. He was a very careful operator. Didn't send them regularly, and never from the same location twice running. A broken pattern like that makes it more difficult to recall every small detail stretching over twelve years."

"I know, I know." Tony was irritated. Not with Georges. With Gerard. "He didn't press Parracini hard enough."

"Gerard? He did shoot off the names you had suggested. Alexis. Oleg. Heinrich Nealey."

"And no impact on Parracini?"

"None. Except for an educated guess about Alexis: someone with important contacts and friends in Washington; someone who could supply all varieties of information, from facts and figures to scurrilous gossip. So he could be a political journalist on an important newspaper, or a television reporter, or a columnist. Not a young man—too judicious, too experienced— possibly in his forties or even fifties, judging by the age groups with which he mixed."

"An educated guess," Tony echoed in disgust. "Was that the most that Gerard could get out of Parracini?"

"It doesn't sound much like Rick Nealey," Georges admitted. "Could it be that there's another agent—"

"There were only two of them in Central Park with Vladimir Konov on the night he was mugged."

He's really stuck with his theory that Alexis must be Nealey's code name, Georges thought, and Parracini's analysis doesn't back it up. "Take it easy, Tony."

"Two of them. Alexis and Oleg," insisted Tony, exasperated with everyone, himself included. "One was security; the other was Konov's Washington agent. Which name fits Nealey?"

"Are you certain he was in Central Park that night?"

"The New York police have a description that matches Nealey exactly. Also a composite picture of the other man. He is a ringer for Gorsky."

"Ah," said Georges, "I didn't know that."

You might, thought Tony, have assumed that I did know. Or were you actually thinking I was just frothing at the mouth? He glanced at his watch. Surely Maclehose had called Tom Kelso by this time. "All right, Georges— let's get cracking. Up the hill until you see, on the left-hand side, a nursery marked Michel. There used to be yellow mimosa trees to mark the spot. Drop me just inside the gate."

Georges switched on the ignition, released the brake, kept his eye on the traffic and waited for the first safe chance to join the procession of cars. "We really may trigger some new detail in Parracini's memory tomorrow. He's had time to rest and think. And remember."

"He'd better."

"That was a devilish journey he had. He almost lost his life in an Aegean northeaster—the fishing boat that was taking him from Istanbul to Lesbos nearly foundered. Most of their gear went overboard, and two of their men."

"I know, I know." Tony restrained himself, tried to smile. "I'm short on patience today. But we haven't much time. Shandon Villa is a perfect setup for Nealey's kind of work." Nealey could gather all kinds of information, some hard intelligence, some dealing with the personal quirks and indiscreet remarks of prominent men. The Disinformation boys in Moscow would have a propaganda bonanza. They'd take the facts and twist and magnify and drop them into a willing journalist's ear for his next exposé of Western chicanery. It was all too simple nowadays to drive a wedge between democratic friends and allies: they were in a self-destructive syndrome, always willing to believe the worst about themselves and the best about their enemies. "Yes," he said as Georges at last joined the stream of traffic, "it's a perfect setup."

"And Nealey won't be working alone. We'll have a nest of agents—"

"That we will."

"Who's directing them? Gorsky?"

"Could be. He's senior enough." Or perhaps he was only acting as protector-in-chief.

"He doesn't hesitate, does he, when he thinks security is threatened? Could Chuck Kelso really have been such a hazard to them?"

"You saw the action they took." Which only proved, in its desperate haste, that Rick Nealey was an agent of prime importance. "One more thing: memorize this telephone number in New York." Slowly Tony repeated Brad Gillon's private number. "Call it immediately. Speak only with Bradford Gillon, tell him the message is from me. Give him the news about Chuck Kelso. Advise him to warn Martin Holzheimer to keep his mouth shut and get an assignment in Alaska."

"Alaska?"

"Don't be so damned literal, Georges. *Any* place that's out of sight, out of mind. We've got to keep at least one witness alive. I don't want any more convenient accidents on my conscience."

The yellow mimosa shimmered in the sunlight, air-spun gold, as heart-lifting as a host of daffodils. Georges was signaling for a left turn into the gate, and Tony's hand was already gripping the release knob on the door beside him. He wasn't a man of protracted good-bys, thought Georges with amusement.

But Tony had some afterthought. As the car drew up under the powdery blossom of the mimosa trees, he sat very still. "What are Parracini's plans?"

"Plans?"

"His future? There must have been some discussion about that."

"Oh, he will keep a low profile in Menton for the next few months. And once it's safe enough he can move into a new job. With us."

"With Nato Intelligence? What branch?"

"Gerard could use him in his department."

"Gerard's idea, or Parracini's?"

"Does that matter? It was a natural, whoever thought of it. Of course Parracini will keep his cover as chauffeur." Georges studied Tony's frown and tried a small joke. "Bill and Nicole will give him excellent references." But Tony wasn't in a mood to smile and make one of his usual quips. He's exhausted, thought Georges. He doesn't need this visit to Tom Kelso. He needs a couple of hours' rest; an evening to relax, enjoy himself. Tomorrow will be a heavy day.

Tony said, "Like to join me this evening for a drink in the bar at the casino?"

"Shall I be literal about that?" The word still stung. "Or do we just keep an eye on each other?"

"A very close eye. And ear. Eight o'clock. Okay?" Tony stepped out of the car and began walking uphill toward the house high above the olive trees.

Georges noted the slow footsteps, the slightly bowed head. He could have ditched going up there, Georges thought, as he reversed and turned to point the Renault in the right direction for the drive down to Menton. Damned if I wouldn't have telephoned my sympathy and condolence, and let it go at that.

From the olive trees came a persistent sound, a light and steady tapping of wood on wood. Tony halted to look. The house was only fifty yards away, and perhaps he wanted any excuse to delay the first meeting with Tom and Dorothea. If I hadn't promised her, he thought, I'd never have faced the next half hour. What good would it do, anyway? I can't tell them what I know or fear, can't drag them into this bloody bloody mess. It's safer for them, for everyone, if they just stay out and accept what will be reported as a tragic accident. Tom is too intelligent not to ask questions: that will be my worst problem. And Dorothea—God, I wish she hadn't so much quick intuition. Not now, at least.

The constant sound of small firm blows didn't miss a beat. He could see, far below this driveway, a white cloth spread under a tree, and, perched on its gnarled branches, two men with long canes. What the devil were they doing?

"Tony!" Thea called, and she came hurrying down to meet him in spite of high-heeled sandals. She had dressed up for this afternoon—a white frock whose pleats floated around her as she moved, some thin soft material that was as fluid as the swirl of a chiton on a Greek vase. "Tony, are we glad to see you!" she cried, happy and breathless, her smile radiant. "You're early, and that's sheer luck. Come on, come on." She caught his hand, urging him forward.

They don't know. Tony halted, looked away from her. They don't know. He stared down at the olive trees. What now? Blurt everything out, or wait till I get them both together? That was the thing about news: if it were good, you'd tell it and repeat it and go over it a third time willingly; when it was bad, you only wanted to say it once, briefly, and then wish you hadn't been forced to do even that. "What's going on down there?"

"They are tapping the olives. They sit up in a tree and beat it gently, and the ripe olives fall to the ground." She looked at him curiously. "Does the sound annoy you? Tom said it was getting on his nerves. So we'll probably avoid the terrace and sit indoors—too bad on such a heavenly day. Come on, slow coach!" She pulled his arm gently, and started him toward the house.

"Where's Tom?"

"Oh, the telephone rang just as we were coming down to meet you. He went back to take the call."

He checked the time on his watch. Ten minutes to five.

"You're early and Chuck is late. But that's all to the good—Tom has some questions he needs answered before he sees Chuck."

"Dorothea—"

"Just like Chuck," she was saying; "he decided he couldn't wait till six o'clock, so he phoned—"

"When?"

"After lunch. Around two, I think."

"What did he say?" The fool, Tony raged secretly, he actually called them from Shandon Villa; and told them—how much?

Dorothea's smile had vanished. "He was going to give Rick Nealey exactly until four o'clock. If Nealey was still avoiding him by that time, he was coming up here. By half past four. He said he had a tremendous problem and would Tom help him solve it? Tom had friends who worked in Intelligence—or even Brad Gillon—people who could act, take the right measures. What measures, Tony?"

They had reached the terrace, and Tony stood there silent, his face averted, his whole interest seemingly on the view of coast line that spread before them.

"Tony—what is wrong? Oh, I know Chuck must have had a bad quarrel with Rick. But why?"

"Didn't he tell you?" And I hope to God the answer is no, thought Tony. Let the pros deal with Nealey, not the amateurs.

"Hints, mostly—but they were strong enough."

"What kind of hints?"

"About Rick Nealey. Chuck's anger was all directed against him. What could have happened between those two? They were so close." She drew a deep breath. "But out of bad news there comes some good. Chuck's call ended abruptly—he was using the telephone in Maclehose's office—his own was out of order. But as he signed off, he sounded less worried, even relieved. When Tom promised to help in any way he could, Chuck said, 'I've been a goddamned idiot. I know that now. And I'm sorry, Tom. I'm sorry.' Which, you know, was a considerable admission: I've never heard Chuck say 'sorry' like that, meaning it, truly meaning it. For once, he wasn't going through his usual routine—all charm and little substance. He was really contrite." She studied Tony's impassive face. "But that *is* good news," she insisted. "Tom needed it. Oh, he's worried about Chuck—yes. But contact between them is re-established. And that counts, you know. Tom—" She broke off, unwilling to admit just how difficult those last months had been. And then, still watching Tony's face, she asked quietly, "Is Chuck's news as bad as that?" Her eyes widened, pleading with him for the truth.

There was no evading the directness of her gaze. "It was bad enough. And now it's worse—the worst possible kind of news for you and Tom. I didn't want to break it to you, not alone. Better that you and Tom should hear it together. But possibly he already knows—if the telephone call was from Shandon Villa. Chuck has met with an accident. A fatal accident."

For a moment, Dorothea stood rigid. Then she turned and ran into the house. Its silence paralyzed Tony. The Shandon call must be long over. And

Tom? Tony slumped into a chair, lit a cigarette, listened to the insistent tapping on the olive trees below.

I handled that badly, he thought. But how could news about death ever be handled well? And now Tom would come out here, start asking questions once the first shock had worn off. (And, as a seasoned reporter, he was adept at questioning.) I'll tell him everything that's possible to be told. No mention of Palladin's escape, or that he's still alive as Jean Parracini. Enough to let Tom know that the NATO Memorandum had been lifted from his brother's New York apartment and ended up in the hands of the KGB in Moscow; that Nealey seems to have been the only man who had access to Chuck's apartment on that Saturday night. Yes, we'll have to talk about Nealey—Chuck made sure of that. But I'll keep silent about Mischa and Alexis and Oleg, and not only for security reasons. A matter of safety, Tom's and Dorothea's.

Chuck was true to the last: lost in his self-centered world, righteous anger at being duped, hints blurted out about the source of his problem, sharing trouble when it overwhelmed him. Involving others, endangering them?—No, Chuck hadn't thought of that. Or he would never have unburdened himself in a telephone call. From Maclehose's office. Where a red-headed secretary had monitored every word. Why, oh why, couldn't Chuck have stayed in New York, made contact with Brad again once the truth began to get through to him? Perhaps he still couldn't believe he had been duped until he had a chance to confront Nealey and demand an explanation. Whatever Nealey had told him, on that ride from the airport this morning, hadn't worked. And Nealey knew it.

Tony lit a second cigarette, and then threw it away. If Brad hadn't pushed Chuck into facing unpleasant realities—and that was my doing: I suggested Brad see Chuck, lay the facts on the table (two men executed, several still under rigorous questioning, others scattered and hunted)—yes, if I hadn't urged Brad to talk frankly, pierce through Chuck's rationalizations with some truth, Chuck would probably be alive today. Skiing merrily in Gstaad, no thought of Nealey or Shandon Villa in his head, all things right with his own world; and who worried about what happened to other men in other places? Especially when they were espionage freaks, spooks wandering in a maze of threat and danger—their own choice, wasn't it? Probably their own creation, too. They did it for kicks or the money, everyone knew that. (Read your friendly local newspapers.) Saving the West? Me included? That's a big laugh. All part of their own hothouse fantasies. Who's threatening me—little men in black pajamas? Look, get rid of the ego-trippers, the paranoiacs. Then we can all make nice profits and get promotions and enjoy our skiing (or bowling or golf or fishing) and our sun-tanning (or dining or wining or women) and live in a better, still better and better, world without end amen.

Tony lit a third cigarette. It tasted worse than the others.

Yes, Chuck would have been alive if I hadn't wakened him to the truth. (He awoke. That's something. Millions wouldn't have.) He'd be safely far away, in happy Switzerland. And when I visited Shandon Villa today, Nealey would have been on hand to give me a guided tour, all wreathed in smiles and innocence. But Boris Gorsky would not have been there. Not visible, certainly.

And so I'd have learned nothing, and known less.

Not that I know too much. But now I make that knowledge count. This I owe to Chuck Kelso.

Behind him he heard Tom's footsteps on the terrace. He rose and faced him.

Sixteen

SUNSET HAD COME, a blaze of vermilion and gold dissolving into an amethyst sky. The olive trees, twisted ghosts rising out of deepening shadows, rested in peace. Down on Cap Martin, the heavy foliage became a massive block of blackness against a sea of faded ink. The air had turned shrewd and cool, but the two men still talked and walked on the terrace. Dorothea, chilled perhaps as much by Tony's information as by the evening breeze, had long since retreated into the warmth of the Michels' living room.

Tom's manner was quiet, dangerously quiet. From the first moment he had come out onto the terrace, he had been in taut control of himself. His first words to Tony were cold, totally unemotional. "How did you learn about Chuck's death?"

"I was visiting Shandon Villa."

"You saw what happened?"

"No one did."

"Tell me what you can. Exactly."

And Tony had done just that.

Then came the questions. And answers. And long pauses. And more questions. And now, with the sun already set, color and warmth drained from the land, Tom halted his steady pace and stared out at the bleak scene.

"And who," he asked at last, "is to deal with Nealey?"

"We will."

"How? You haven't had much success in these last months."

"There wasn't enough hard evidence to support official action. No witnesses to back up some of the statements in my report on Nealey."

Grimly Tom said, "And you've lost your best witness now. Holzheimer, if you could get him to tell what he knows, could only testify that Nealey approached him, put him in touch with my brother, was present when the first part of the Memorandum was handed over. . . . Where did that happen?"

"Holzheimer supplied his editor with the address—the apartment below Chuck's. Nealey spent the weekends there. But that's still not enough evidence." Then, as Tom's face twisted with sudden emotion, Tony said, "We have one possible lead." And Parracini had better come through, he thought. "I can't tell you any more than that. Not now, Tom. There's no need to know. And it's much better not to."

"I'm going down to Shandon Villa tomorrow, look around, question Maclehose."

"You'll get no information—"

"I'll pick up some details. That's my job, Tony. And I don't expect much from Maclehose. He didn't even telephone me this evening. Bugged out."

"Then who—"

"Nealey. All-purpose Nealey. Yes, that little bastard called me himself to tell me that my brother was dead."

"Good God."

"I let him talk. You know what I think? He was trying to find out how much I had learned from Chuck. He even brought up the subject of the quarrel they had this morning. About a girl—Katie, he called her—all a misunderstanding. So Nealey blamed himself for not having canceled his engagements today and stayed with Chuck, explained more, made him understand the truth of the matter." Tom struck a clenched fist against the palm of his hand as his anger broke loose. *"His* phrase. The truth of the matter."

"And what did you say?"

"Is that important?" Tom asked bitterly.

"It could be."

"I said, 'You son of a bitch.' And I hung up."

Tony was silent. Nealey had caught Tom at an agonizing moment when all defenses were down.

"You think that wasn't too smart of me," Tom said, suddenly truculent. "But that is what Nealey is. He's one—"

"I know, I know. I agree completely. I'd probably have called him worse."

"Not you. You wouldn't have given him a hook onto which he could latch his suspicions. Sure, he now probably thinks I know too much. So let's see what he will try with that."

"Stop goading him, Tom."

"How else do you trap him into a false move?"

"Don't you try it."

"That's right," Tom said, "leave it to the professionals. And what use have they been so far?"

Tony's fatigue suddenly caught up with him. His voice sharpened. "Ask that question of your own people. Who has been building up public opinion against your professionals? Nothing but denunciations, imputations, revelations, recriminations—how the hell do they manage to work at all?" He turned away. "I have to get back into town. I'd better call a taxi." He headed for the living room. At the French windows, he paused. "I'm sorry, Tom. Forget what I said."

Tom didn't answer, didn't even look round. He stood staring out at the lights circling the bay, hearing nothing, seeing nothing.

Tony found the telephone easily enough. It stood on the same old, rickety, eighteenth-century table he remembered from his week spent as a guest here. Solange had put him to work—she believed in keeping her visitors busy. These wall panels, on the other side of the room, testified to that. He had painted them and Maurice had added the finishing touch by smearing them with a dirty rag. Antiquing, Solange had called the process.

"You know," said Dorothea as she appeared quietly beside him and noticed his interest in the paneled wall, "Solange did that. She's really very clever about such things."

"Indeed, she is." He opened the telephone directory, and actually smiled. There was relief, too, to see that Dorothea was avoiding an emotional scene. "That's sensible," he observed of her change of clothes: the thin dress had been replaced by a heavy sweater and tweed pants.

"I was frozen." She studied his face. "I've made some coffee. Boiling hot. Sandwiches, too. I think you need both."

It was twenty to seven, he noted in dismay. The half hour planned for this visit had stretched considerably. "I'd like that. I'll have some coffee while I wait for a taxi."

"No need to call a cab. We'll drive you down to Menton."

"Wouldn't hear of it." He glanced back at the terrace.

"Tom often stays out there by himself. Don't worry. Please don't. And, Tony, don't let his words disturb you. He didn't mean them. He—he often has these moods."

Tony concentrated on dialing. "Tom's had too rough a day to drive anywhere tonight."

"He's going down to Menton anyway."

"Why?"

"To see the police. They phoned him just after Rick Nealey's call."

"Time enough to talk with them tomorrow. They'll know more by—" He broke off as he made the connection with the taxi stand near the casino. (A cab for seven thirty without fail, at the gate of the Michel nursery, Roquebrune. Night rates, of course, and a hefty tip, if punctual.)

"That's what the police suggested. But Tom wouldn't wait. He's a man who needs action." She hesitated. "These last months have been difficult for him."

And for you? Tony wondered. He remembered his first glimpse of her today, down at the market. An unhappy girl, he had thought. "Let's have that cup of coffee." Possibly a sandwich too, just to please her. Besides, she was right: he needed it.

"Rick Nealey—" she began, as they sat down at the kitchen table, and then fell silent.

Tony braced himself. More questions, more answers. The only way to handle them was to plunge right in, keep everything brief and restrained, and—above all—generalized. "He's been working in Washington for the last nine years."

"As an enemy agent?"

So she had either heard talk from the terrace, or added up her own suspicions to score a solid guess. He shrugged a reply.

"And never discovered?" That horrified her.

"He's good at his job."

"Good? How can you say that? He's a monster."

"To us, yes—he's one of the bad guys. To the opposition he's the hero, and we are the villains. It just depends on what side you stand."

"But you can't approve of what he has done."

"No. If I did, I wouldn't be interested in him."

"Were you following him on the day we met in the Statler lobby?"

"Frankly, until I saw him there, I didn't even know the fellow. It was you who told me who he was, remember?"

"But you *were* interested. Immediately." She looked at him angrily. "Why didn't you tell the CIA?"

"And have them up before another investigatory committee for more interference in domestic affairs?"

"Then the FBI—"

"From that day at the Statler until he left Washington, Nealey kept his head down. No peculiar phone calls, no contacts with anyone doubtful: just an innocent citizen going about his own business."

Her anger faded, leaving only bewilderment. "How can these things happen? The cold war is over."

"A matter of terminology. You can call boiled cabbage a *pourri* of roses, but it still smells and tastes like cabbage. There's too much rhetoric, too little thought nowadays—mostly our own fault: we keep accepting words and ignoring acts."

"You don't."

"Which makes me a very bad guy indeed. And, it hurts me to say, not just to the other side," he reminded her.

"Yes," she admitted. "Once, I thought you were—were—"

"An anachronism? A bit of a fake? Like that antiqued paneling, cheap pine pretending to be weathered oak?"

"Not a fake," she said quickly. "Never that. I just thought you were wrong, all wrong—a waste of a good brain."

"I'm a pretty good wine-taster. Doesn't that justify my existence?"

"Oh, Tony!" She almost smiled, checked herself and frowned. Tears were not far away.

In alarm, Tony said, "I didn't mean to—"

"You didn't. It's just me. . . . I feel—I feel terrible. About Chuck. I always found something to criticize in him—oh, not openly. But I had a lot of hard thoughts, especially when Tom kept excusing—" She shook her head. "Chuck didn't like me very much either. I wish now it hadn't been that way. And I'll always keep thinking that I—"

"No, you won't keep thinking about that," he told her. "Everyone feels guilt when sudden death comes to someone close to them. There's always remorse as well as regret. The last tribute. But no brooding, Dorothea: you aren't the morbid type. And how much would that help Tom? What guilt is he feeling right now, do you think?" He rose from the table. "Restrain Tom, will you? Don't let him do anything on impulse. That's usually disastrous." He raised her hand and kissed it. Just as abruptly, he left.

He took the exit through the living room's French windows. The terrace was in darkness. Tom called to him, "Hey—wait there, Tony! I'll run you down to Menton." Voice normal, friendly. Tony halted in relief. Tom's arm went round his shoulders. "Why don't you stay and have some supper?"

"Wish I could. But I have promises to keep. Besides, I'm bulging with sandwiches and coffee. You could use some yourself."

"Let me give you a lift."

"Thanks, Tom. But the taxi will arrive any minute now. I'm meeting it at the gate." Tony began walking toward the driveway with Tom at his side, relaxed and friendly.

"No direct connection with this house?" Tom asked, making the right assumption.

He has recovered, Tony thought: he's using his brains instead of his emotions. "Better not, don't you think?"

"Anyone been following you?"

"Hope not."

"How many of them are there, I wonder?"

He has recovered too damn well, thought Tony.

Tom went on, "Who arranged the accident? Not Rick Nealey. He must have had help."

"They're around. And all the more reason for you to watch your step, old boy. Keep Dorothea safe, will you?" He grasped Tom's hand. "Take care. Both of you."

"I'll walk you to the gate."

"Not even that," said Tony. A final handshake, a grip that reassured both of them, and Tony was off.

Where is he bound for? Tom wondered as he turned back to the house. *Promises to keep.* Business or pleasure? No, not pleasure: not tonight. Business that dealt with Nealey? That was Tony's main preoccupation now. *We have one possible lead.* His words. Was that what he was searching out? A possible lead . . .

Tom burst into the kitchen. "Look, Thea," he said, "I think I'll go down to Menton right away. Get it over with."

"But—"

"I don't feel like eating. I may as well learn what the police have to say." He put his arms around her, kissed her anxious face. "Lock up after me. Thoroughly. And go upstairs. You'll be all right, won't you? I'll be as quick as I can."

"Must you, at all? Tonight?"

"Yes." He left as abruptly as he had entered.

Obediently she locked the kitchen door, the front entrance, and the French windows. In the study she searched for a book to take to bed. Nothing in English, all in French. The television was black-and-white, a discussion from Paris with solemn novelists disagreeing at great length. French intellectuals talked in paragraphs, not in sentences. She picked up *Time* and *Newsweek,* switched off most of the lights, leaving just enough to welcome Tom back.

Then, with a last look at the lonely rooms, at the empty terrace, she broke into tears. I wish I were home, I wish I were home.

Down by the gate, headlights swooped into the driveway and stopped, their beam casting a wide arc around the flower beds as the taxi turned to face the road again. One moment more, and it began moving out.

Tom was already in the Fiat, its engine running. Smoothly he started downhill.

He knew what Tony would say. Or perhaps he would be so tight-lipped with anger that the words would choke in his throat. But this, thought Tom, is when I must take some action of my own. I will not be stuck on that terrace, knowing little, doing less.

Once past the gate, he abandoned caution until he picked up the rear lights of the taxi. Then he kept an even speed at a safe distance.

From the front road along Menton's west bay, the taxi made a left and cut into town. Not far. It dropped Tony just short of the English Church, at the corner of the square—if that's what you could call it: really an open stretch of central flower beds bordered by two avenues, a pleasant prospect for the casino's entrance.

Tom found a spot to park, and took it. What now? His first impulses were draining low: he felt both foolish and uncertain. But he got out of the car— he wouldn't have far to walk from here to the Commissariat de Police in any event—and began strolling toward the church.

Menton, in the off season, was an empty place by night. There were few people around at ten minutes of eight, as if everything had closed up tight for dinner. Tony could be easily seen in the well-lit streets. Which means that I can be easily seen too, Tom reminded himself. As a small protection he hunched up his coat collar—he needed that too, in the cool wind blowing up from the sea—and stared into a shop window. As he risked another look, he saw Tony cross the street, start up some steps, and disappear.

The casino? It couldn't be. Tom followed, his mind incredulous. But yes, it was the casino. First, there was the shock of disbelief; next, a sense of frustration. Damned if I'm going in there, he told himself, his face grim as he turned the corner at the church, and strode past the taxi rank, the stretches of flower beds and palm trees. So he had come chasing into Menton after Tony, and got nowhere. At the last moment, he had balked. Totally irrational behavior. But he had been in no mood to step into a world of fun and games. His emotions were too raw, unpredictable. Better get them under control and his mind working again—this was no way to enter a police station.

Halfway up the avenue, he halted and looked back at the casino. Even if he had put his own feelings aside, entered there, what good would he have done? What purpose served? He would have been too noticeable—the casino trade hadn't begun as yet. This wasn't Monte Carlo, with all its slot machines, Las Vegas style, packing in the busloads of people from early afternoon until dawn. No, he realized now, I'd have accomplished nothing at all, only caused unnecessary complications. Tony wasn't here for amusement: Tony was strictly business tonight. And he had no part in it.

For a moment even now, something of the old urge to know, to help, to do, reawakened in Tom. He hesitated. Cursed this feeling of uselessness. Turned away. Walked on.

The Commissariat lay a short stretch to his right, somewhere off these avenues. Few people around here: everyone enjoying their *bonne petite soupe*. The idea of eating still nauseated him—it was something else than hunger that gnawed at his guts. He had judged his direction and distance accurately, at least: the police station was just where it should be. It was func-

tioning, too: a visitor was leaving. The figure, clearly seen under the brilliance of the street lights, was familiar. Automatically Tom ducked behind
a row of parked automobiles, the new-style barricades of every Western city.
He hoped he looked part of a logical explanation: a man, with head and
shoulders bent, about to unlock his car door. For the figure, young, well-
dressed, fair-haired, now hurrying across the broad street, was Rick Nealey.

Tom kept motionless, attracted no nervous eye. Nealey had reached a black
Citroën, new model—and waited for a man to leave an automobile parked
just a few yards ahead. The meeting was brief. Sentences were exchanged.
That was all. Within three or four minutes the stranger returned to his car
and Nealey got into the Citroën.

Thinking of his Fiat parked snugly several blocks away, Tom damned
himself for an idiot: he couldn't even follow, only watch. He felt vulnerable,
though, and testing the door he stood beside, he found it was unlocked.
He slid into the front seat, kept his head well down.

Nealey's Citroën passed him, traveling westward. Back to Cap Martin?
The other car—an Opel, green in color—passed close to where Tom sat,
and then made a left turn down the avenue that led to the casino area. At
least, thought Tom, I could partly describe that stranger in the green Opel,
Nice registration: from a distance, he was about my height but heavier, and
broad-shouldered; near at hand, his features were strong, his hair dark. And
who the hell was he?

Thoughtfully Tom crossed the street and entered the Commissariat.

He was politely received, with just the right touch of official sympathy. They would know more about his brother's unfortunate death by
tomorrow. Yes, it did seem as though it possibly might have been a most
regrettable accident, a tragic error on someone's part, responsibility still
to be allocated. Meanwhile, Monsieur Kelso might consider what arrangements he would desire: cremation or burial here, or perhaps he would
prefer transport to the United States and interment there? There were local
agences that were fully capable of handling such matters. De rien, monsieur.
But one thing more: he could now take possession of the suitcase that held
his brother's belongings, including his wallet, cuff links, engagement diary
with addresses, wristwatch, traveler's checks, keys and key chain, air-flight
reservation for tomorrow to Switzerland, Hotel Post booking in Gstaad—
all intact, all carefully listed in triplicate on this official police form of
inventory. Be so good as to examine them, and then sign here. Merci, monsieur. À demain.

"Until tomorrow," Tom echoed. His voice was flat, unnatural, his movements slow and uncertain. He stood at the doorway, Chuck's case in his
hand, hesitating. Something else, he kept telling himself, something else . . .
"Mr. Nealey was here, wasn't he? From Shandon Villa."

"But yes—the assistant director. Naturally, he wanted to hear about the
results of our investigation. He had the fear that your brother's death might
have been suicide. But with your brother's plans for travel tomorrow—" A
Gallic shrug indicated suicide was not a likely theory. Then the hint of a
tolerant smile covered the next remark: "Perhaps Monsieur Nealey was also
afraid of the adverse publicity that Shandon Villa might receive. But he can

rely on our discretion. There were two visitors at the villa today, and he was worried about how they might talk. However, he was happy we could provide their names and addresses. He intends to visit them and make a friendly explanation about the necessity for restraint. Shandon Villa, after all, is beginning its meetings next week."

Tom asked bitterly, "Did he not want to view the body?"

A small shocked silence. And then a mild reproof. "Monsieur Nealey wants only to help, in any way he can. He offered to take your brother's suitcase to your house, spare you the trouble."

"But naturally," said Tom, mustering his French, "that was impossible. My signature was required."

"And you yourself were coming here. So Monsieur Nealey left."

I bet he did, thought Tom. He knew better than to meet me here tonight. But at least this proved that the police were efficient: they had removed Chuck's belongings from Shandon before Nealey could examine them, make sure there was nothing to endanger him. What the hell had he expected? Or was it just part of his training that he always must make sure? "Thank you very much," he told the police sergeant, a round-faced middle-aged man with a drooping mustache and kindly brown eyes. "You have been most helpful. Thank you."

"*De rien, monsieur*. And we regret—"

"Yes," said Tom, and left.

He locked Chuck's suitcase safely inside the trunk of the Fiat before slipping into the driver's seat. He switched on the ignition, and then turned it off. For fully ten minutes he sat there, his head bowed, thoughts giving way to grief within the darkness of the car. At last he raised his eyes, looking along the bright street. There were people entering the casino now. Not many. But enough. He wouldn't be too noticeable.

Pocketing the car keys, he got out, and began walking. Remembering the meeting between Nealey and his contact which he had witnessed tonight, Tom sensed urgency. Nealey's moves had been too quick, too immediate, not to convey a warning. Okay, thought Tom, I'm taking it. He entered the casino.

Seventeen

It was almost eight o'clock. The main hall of the casino was brightly lit and practically empty. Seven people, all told, and employees at that: a woman, behind a glass-enclosed booth at the far end of the hall beside the cinema; a young usherette, arriving for duty; four croupiers—young, tall, lean, darksuited—paired off at the two adjacent gaming tables; a fifth man, similar in dress and manner, on duty at the *Salle Privée*. The dining room, facing Tony as he took brief inventory—a natural pause after mounting the stairs that led up from the foyer just inside the front entrance to the casino—was equally lethargic: three tables occupied. And the bar beside him? He turned and entered, dismay rising. Empty too, except for an attendant polishing glasses and a couple of men—one at the bar, the other at a corner table. Two: count them. Tony almost exploded in a laugh.

He halted just inside the doorway, letting his eyes adjust from the hall's brilliance to this small room's imitation moonlight glow. *Très chic, très moderne,* but mostly disconcerting: it had taken him half a minute at least to see that Georges was the man seated at the bar. And shall we remain aloof, keeping that promised eye on each other, for the benefit of one stranger and a bartender?

The subdued lighting was evenly spread, giving twenty-twenty vision a chance to reassert itself. Tony could soon recognize the man who sat at the corner table and faced the room. He might now be wearing a gray lounge suit instead of this afternoon's work clothes, but he still had the same fair hair, sharp features, and slightly popeyed look of the electrician, climbing up through the gardens of Shandon Villa at Boris Gorsky's heels. And, thought Tony, he has recognized me. Probably Georges as well.

"Hello there!" he said as he joined the young Frenchman at the bar. "Sorry if I kept you waiting. Had a hard time parking the car."

Georges turned his head to stare in amazement, perhaps in disbelief.

Unperturbed, Tony ordered a Tio Pepe. "Do you want to perch, or shall we lounge? More comfortable over here." He led the way to one of the low tables flanked by four squat armchairs. It provided, as he had hoped, an excellent view of both the bar's doorway and, beyond that, part of the main hall—the most important part as far as Tony was concerned. It lay at the head of the stairs leading from the foyer: arrivals and departures easily noted. "Much better," Tony pronounced, flopping into the chair that faced the bar's entrance—and indicated, with an almost imperceptible nod, the chair close to his left elbow. From there Georges could watch the man in the far corner as well as observe the doorway by a turn of his head. Just as necessary, they could talk at close quarters and yet look natural, no table between them. "Now let's relax and have a couple of drinks before we move in for dinner. There's nothing like sight-seeing to exhaust a man. Any ideas for tomorrow? But someplace, I beg of you, where we don't have to walk and climb." He rattled on until his sherry arrived, but his voice was dropping gradually until it would reach a level that neither the barman nor Popeye could hear.

Georges caught on to Tony's stratagem quickly enough. But he still hadn't recovered from his first shock. "You're crazy, Tony," was his low-voiced comment. "Here we are, like two sore thumbs, as noticeable as hell."

"We'd be more noticeable if we were sitting apart. Have a look at that man in the corner. He probably saw you passing through the Shandon pool area."

"He and Gorsky—they were together?" Georges asked softly.

"Very much together."

Georges's eyes were grave, his lips tight. Gorsky was a name he knew only too well. The man himself he had seen only once. But there was enough in the Gorsky file to make that face memorable.

"Let's laugh it up a little, shall we? Heard any good stories recently?" That's better, thought Tony as Georges produced a convincing smile. "What did you find down at the beach? Can a boat dock safely there?"

"A rowboat. Not much more. There's only a small jetty. The water is shallow at the shore edge." As he talked, Georges's eyes had followed a couple coming into the bar—a nice chance to look at the man in the corner. It was a quick but thorough study. "Rocks on either side of the beach. Property boundary, as it were. The beach itself is stony, a romantic but uncomfortable place to swim. The jetty is in shallow water—no good for diving."

So, thought Tony, anything larger than a rowboat would have to lie offshore; and anyone—if Shandon was his target—would use a dinghy to get to the beach. But would Parracini really take all that trouble to get at Shandon? And he couldn't be too much of a sailor; he had been landlocked all his life. Nor did he have enough cash to let him hire a boat and a crew to manage it. And, Tony concluded, I just don't see Parracini rowing all the way around Cap Martin to reach his objective. So he'll have to reach Shandon by car, and that isn't such a simple operation either: too many restrictions on free access. Perhaps he'll give up his whole idea; or perhaps I was wrong—he never had it. Just an unnecessary fear on my part. And yet, his hatred for Shandon must be real enough: he has a large score to even out with Nealey. "Did you reach Brad Gillon in New York?"

"All taken care of. I also got in touch with Brussels via Lyons."

"You did?" Tony was impressed. "So you're all set up? Quick work."

Georges nodded. That morning he had transferred all his special equipment from the *Sea Breeze* to his new room in the Old Town: good and safe communication with Brussels was a first necessity. He eyed two more couples entering the bar. "That's a smasher," he observed of one of the girls.

"Things are looking up all over. Two sore thumbs begin to seem normal. Swelling much reduced."

"I hope that guy in the corner is beginning to believe that too. An odd place to choose. Not much visibility from there."

"My guess is that Popeye isn't here to watch the hall." And thank heaven for that: Parracini could arrive at any moment. A few people had already been drifting toward the cinema.

"Waiting for someone to make contact?"

"And keeping a low profile until he gets the signal. You know, he ought to attend to that thyroid condition before his eyes really bug out."

Georges's laugh was spontaneous. Interesting, he thought, how Tony's attention never drifts far from that hall outside. "Expecting someone?"

"Any minute now. Our friend Jean is going to the movies tonight."

Jean Parracini? Georges's head turned casually toward the hall, as he lit a cigarette. "I don't like it," he said softly. Far too much risk, he thought, and stopped watching the hall. He'd have to keep the same balance as Tony, between looking and not looking. No staring allowed.

"Oh, he won't be alone. He's bringing Bernard and Brigitte with him—Bill's devoted cook and butler." And devoted they were. Loyal and trustworthy. But the weakness was that they knew little. Only that Bill's household, and Bill's guests whenever they appeared, had to be safeguarded. Parracini was someone who spoke Russian and was learning French: that much was obvious. Parracini was important: that much they had been told. Palladin was a name they had never heard. Few had. "Keep smiling, old boy. We're on camera." More people had drifted into the bar. So far none of the tables near the entrance was occupied, but soon Tony and Georges might be surrounded, and that would make any further exchange of information a very tricky business.

"I still don't like it," Georges insisted. "Why couldn't the idiot stay at home? He's safe there."

"And getting bored. Wouldn't you be? Besides, he's quite confident he can fool anyone. His appearance has changed. Completely."

"I see—he's trying out the transformation on the movie-goers. But I wish—" Georges checked himself.

"So do I. Perhaps he'll get more sense talked into him tomorrow. Is the boat ready?"

"Everything's repaired. Emil is sleeping on board."

"You've radio contact with him?"

"Of course. Weather reports aren't too good for tomorrow, but improving on—"

"Here they come." Tony's eyes looked away from the three new arrivals in the hall and studied his sherry with disapproval.

Georges registered all three of them: a light-haired man, balding, of medium height; a woman with short red hair, a patterned dress and a cardigan; a man, also of medium height, tanned face, thick dark brown hair, a black mustache. Both men wore blue suits, white shirts, black ties. Georges shook his head, finished his drink. "I give up."

"The dark-haired one."

Nothing like his photograph, thought Georges, remembering its details. Nothing. In Genoa, Parracini had been blond, thin on top, with a round fleshy face and a heavy body—corpulent, in fact. "He doesn't even wear glasses." Georges's voice had dropped to a whisper. "Contact lenses?"

"The miracles of modern science," Tony said. "Why don't you slip out, have a closer look at him? See they all get into the movie safely."

"All the way?" Georges suggested.

"Might be an idea to mark their position. We may join them later." And as Georges shot a quick glance at him, Tony said, "Why not? We have to put in an hour and a half until the movie ends. Better there than here, perhaps." Then, very quickly, "Make sure no one is tailing them."

So that's it, thought Georges, already on his feet, excusing himself, moving into the hall. We're here as added protection for Parracini. And for once Georges didn't think old Tony (nine years older than Georges's thirty) was overworrying. Georges was still slightly shaken by Parracini's self-confidence, even if an outing of the domestic staff from Garavan House would seem to be normal downstairs procedure: cook, butler, chauffeur out on the town for their night off. He caught up with them as they were about to pass the roulette and baccarat tables. (So far, no customers there.) Brigitte was already complaining about the coolness of the air, while the two men, in comfortably warm jackets, discussed the lighting overhead. Parracini seemed totally natural and quite oblivious to those who passed him. He put on a good show, Georges had to admit. Searching for the price of admission, he angled himself near enough to Parracini to have a front view of the new face. Totally unrecognizable. Reassured, Georges made his way just ahead of them into the cinema, felt its cold air strike the back of his neck, and wondered how long Brigitte in her thin dress and skimpy cardigan would last.

The bar was now almost half full, and a couple of men had taken the table next to Tony. It had to come sometime, he thought: when Georges returns (four minutes gone, allow him ten at least to get Parracini & Co. nicely settled), we'll be reduced to discussing Uncle Joe's gall-bladder operation, or the weather, that good old stand-by. Which reminds me that tomorrow's forecast, according to Georges, is not promising. Let's hope that a rising sea won't distract Parracini too much from our questions—or us from asking the right ones to start unlocking his memory. He must know more about Alexis than he has been able to recall so far. It's all a matter of deep recesses in the mind which have to be explored: we all need that now and again. Yes, I'm convinced that he knows more than he realizes. Or am I being too insistent that he can lead us to Rick Nealey through Alexis? No. I don't think so. Why?

What, for instance, would I myself have done if I had been Palladin? On that day in Moscow when I was faced with disaster? When I knew there was no option but escape? My plans would have been long made, ready for such an emergency. What would I have done with the time left me before I could set these plans safely into action? We *know* from the delay in Palladin's alarm signal to us that several days had elapsed before it was safe for him to set out for Odessa. He hadn't just received the NATO Memorandum, with Alexis's covering report, and walked out of his KGB office, there and then. He had played it cool, probably sidetracked the report for at least a few days of respite; no sign of panic to arouse suspicion, no precipitous flight. So how would I have used those last three or four days in Moscow?

Of course, it's easy to *say* how I'd have reacted: I am sitting here in a quiet bar; not in my KGB cubbyhole with wary eyes all around me. Still, as Palladin, I'd have done some things automatically—I was a top-flight operator, with a built-in sense of what was vital information, and powerful enough to make a try for it. I'd have damned well found out every possible detail about this Alexis in Washington, the man who had ended my career and smashed everything I had built up over the last twelve years. And I'd have brought those details out with me. Not just an educated guess—but hard information, even if it was in small bits and pieces. Every little bit helps. That's the first rule of the good investigator. And you were that, Palladin.

An educated guess . . . The phrase rankled in Tony's mind. Alexis was middle-aged, was he? A Washington reporter or columnist? Oh, come on,

Palladin, you were one of the best we've ever had as an agent in place. But as Parracini, you're a real pain in my—Tony's thoughts were chopped off. The man entering the bar, looking directly at the corner table without even having to let his vision become accustomed to the understated lights, was Boris Gorsky.

As Popeye rose obediently, payment for his drink already calculated down to the obligatory fifteen-per-cent tip, Gorsky turned to leave with a sweep of his eyes around the other tables. Tony sat unmoving, totally uninterested, a picture of boredom. He had resisted his first impulse to drop his cigarettes under the table and go looking for them. Too obvious a maneuver, enough to solidify Gorksy's suspicions of him. What has he chalked up against me so far? Tony wondered. Someone who always seems to turn up where he isn't wanted? I hope that's all, I hope to God that's all. . . .

Gorsky had left, trailed by Popeye at a short distance. Keeping that formation, they strolled toward the other end of the hall, and soon were out of sight from Tony's vantage point. A new worry lunged at him, gripped his mind. Somehow, some way, they had managed the impossible. Gorsky knew who Parracini really was: he had found Palladin.

How?

A traitor among us?

No. Couldn't be . . . Bill, Nicole—both were unthinkable. Bill's faithful retainers? Unlikely. Someone closer to home, like Georges or Emil? Totally impossible. Gerard, receiving reports of Operation Parracini in far-off Brussels? Or someone on his staff, a trusted aide? Hell and damnation, Gorsky is turning me into a paranoiac, throwing suspicions around like streamers at a New Year party. Tony signaled to the bar attendant, made a sign for his bill. Pointless now to keep on sitting here. He had to see for himself. His fears might be unfounded: Gorsky could be here on other business than Parracini.

"You didn't drink your sherry," said the attendant. "Perhaps it was too dry for you, sir?" Only appreciated by true connoisseurs, his manner implied.

"I had a sip." And that had been quite enough. "Of both of them," Tony added with a smile.

The man was uncomprehending, counted out Tony's change in silence.

Resist complaining, Tony decided. He wouldn't believe me anyway, that someone had accidentally mixed two sherries together, an amontillado with a Tio Pepe, and hadn't thought it mattered—both were dry, both light in color. Who'd notice?

What was more important, thought Tony as he left for the hall, was to find Georges and alert him, and then keep Gorsky under judicious observation. Now I can be thankful that this is a quiet night in the casino—no mob scene to increase our difficulties. Gorksy must have bought some chips: he was one of a small group forming at the opened roulette table. Some distance away Popeye was circulating aimlessly. And Georges, equally nonchalant, was walking back toward the bar.

Tony halted to light a cigarette, let Georges do the approaching. "Gorsky is here."

Georges stood still. "That's big trouble."

"More so if he and Popeye had headed for the movie house. Where's Parracini?"

"On the aisle, third row from the back. Right-hand side of the theater as you enter."

"Watch Gorsky. At the roulette table. Can you identify him? He's wearing—"

"I know him. Not all my identifications are made on the strength of photographs," said Georges. Or perhaps it was the sudden increase in worry that had spurred his sharp response.

"Then he knows you." Tony's voice was extra-mild.

"Not necessarily. There were at least a hundred journalists milling around Kissinger at that Paris press conference on the Vietnam peace talks. Gorsky was there, calling himself Zunin, a representative from Tass. He had no reason to be interested in me."

"But you had a reason to be interested in him."

"He was masterminding that West Berlin kidnapping—" Georges forgot Berlin. He was looking past Tony's shoulder. "Someone's just arrived. Very uncertain. But he keeps watching you. Almost six feet, dark hair graying at the temples, rugged features, light tweed jacket."

Kelso? Tony risked a glance behind him and met Tom Kelso's eyes. "Hold the fort," he told Georges. "Don't let Gorsky out of your sight. I'll be back as soon as I can—a matter of minutes."

"Something wrong?"

"I hope not. Something important, though." If it wasn't, Tom wouldn't be here. Not tonight. And he had stayed only long enough to catch Tony's attention. He was already out of the front door into the street, as Tony walked (don't run, show no sign of haste) down the short flight of stairs into the small foyer.

The convergence of avenues and streets around the casino was placid enough; there was little automobile traffic and less people; bright lights over empty sidewalks, a town dozing off into early sleep. Tom was maintaining his head start: he had crossed over to the English Church, was striding on without one turn of his head to make certain that Tony was still with him. And for his part, Tony was keeping to his side of the avenue—he had no wish to catch up with Tom until he was reasonably sure that no one was interested in their movements. Apparently no one was. Not one loiterer or follower in sight. A short distance beyond the church, Tom stopped at his car and got in. Within seconds, Tony was slipping into the front seat beside him.

"Neat," Tony said. "But I can't drive around and talk. Have to get back—"

"This won't take long. It may not be as important as I think it is. But you ought to hear about it." Tom, without wasting a word, plunged into a brief résumé of what he had seen and heard tonight on his visit to the Commissariat de Police. "So," he concluded, "they know where you are both staying in Menton. The way Nealey went after your addresses was just too purposeful."

"We'll disappoint them. Thanks for the warning, Tom. And for the other details too." Boris Gorsky was driving a green Opel with a Nice plate, was he? "Most useful."

"What did they want with Chuck's suitcase? There's nothing of interest to them inside it, as far as I saw. No letters, no documents. Not even a diary—just an address book with a section for engagements."

"Have a careful look through that," Tony advised him.

"For what?"

"Anything that catches your eye. And you've got a good one, Tom. I'll call you later, around midnight. If possible."

"Call me as late as you like. I'll be awake."

"And one thing more. When Brad Gillon puts in a call from New York, any hour now—yes, we let him know about Chuck—ask him to start working hard on Katie Collier. The FBI must have made a thorough check of her phone bills. Get Brad to find out the calls that were made from her apartment *during the weekends.*"

"Made by Nealey?" Tom asked quickly.

"Always a possibility. Sorry to lay this on you tonight, Tom. Really sorry."

"Don't be. I need something to do. Take care, Tony."

Tony half smiled. "You know me, old boy," he said as he stepped out of the car and began walking back to the casino. The deserted streets were still innocent, so he made no detours but concentrated on speed. Sixteen minutes since he had left Georges, whose usual *sang-froid* must now be simmering with anxiety.

Georges met him as he reached the hall. "Thank God," he said. "It's all breaking loose. Haven't enough eyes to keep watching everyone. They've left the cinema."

"Parracini and party?"

"Brigitte insisted on leaving. Her complaints about incipient pneumonia were loud and clear. She's walking around the hall, trying to warm up, while Bernard has gone to pick up his car and bring it here to take them all home."

"And Parracini?"

"Walking around too. Damn his eyes."

"Gorsky?"

"Deep in a game of roulette. His friend is playing at the other table."

"Let's move in their direction. By the way, Gorsky has discovered my hotel. And the *Sea Breeze* too. Don't go near her tonight. You've left nothing of your special bag of tricks on board?"

"Nothing but Emil's transceiver—enough to keep contact with my room. I'll alert him when I get back there."

"Do that. Where's Parracini?" Tony couldn't see him. The red-haired Brigitte was now alone, standing still, hugging her cardigan close to her body, looking around her in rising alarm like an abandoned waif.

"He was near the big window—only a minute ago. With Brigitte." Georges's face was as tense as his voice.

"We'd have seen him leaving," Tony said reassuringly, but his own stomach tightened. Then he relaxed a little. "I spot him." Almost in despair, he added, "I could wring his bloody neck."

Georges had followed the direction of Tony's eyes, looked aghast at the carefree Parracini sauntering around the tables. Roulette seemed to fascinate him. He halted, found a place in the small grouping of onlookers, listened to the croupiers' calls, watched the turn of the wheel with obvious interest.

"Let's join the spectators," Tony suggested. But not too close to Gorsky, and keep behind him: nothing noticeable. And as Tony was about to congratulate himself on finding a place where they could see without being observed, Parracini made his move.

He reached Gorsky. Halted. Stood beside him. Seemed absorbed by Gorksy's play. He bent down to drop a few friendly words of advice in Gorsky's ear. There was a brief but amiable exchange between them. All most casual, it seemed, all perfectly natural, the polite smiles included. Gorsky went on playing, concentrating on his winnings. And with a final remark, Parracini turned away, his gaze now sweeping around the spectators. Both Georges and Tony, apparently absorbed in the game like the others who crowded near the table, passed muster. Parracini gave them neither a hard look nor a second glance. He strolled off in search of Brigitte.

There was a long, long silence between Tony and Georges.

At last it ended. Georges said, "I think the roof just fell in."

Tony had no reply. For once he was quite speechless. They began their leisurely walk back toward the other end of the hall.

"A drink?" suggested Georges as they neared the bar.

Tony shook his head. "We'll leave."

"Right now?"

"Right now." Tony led the way downstairs.

Eighteen

THEY CAME OUT of the casino into the cool night air. The streets seemed more deserted than ever, although it was barely half past nine. Tony halted for a moment, took a deep breath to steady himself. "God," he said, "what a fool I've been."

"We've all been," Georges reminded him. "And you," he added with painful frankness, "least of all." There was I, he thought, reporting back to Gerard earlier this evening, relaying Tony's apparent doubts; and there was Gerard, convinced that Tony might really be going off half-cocked about the Parracini debriefing in Genoa. Gerard's final comment had been acerbic. *Lawton not completely satisfied? Indeed. Or is he too intent on finding a quick solution for his Nealey problem?*

But Tony was in no mood for post-mortems. After that brief pause on the steps of the casino, he had set a smart pace, cutting along the avenue toward their left, then taking the first road down to the sea. It was as dark and restless as his surge of emotions.

They crossed the front street to the promenade. Is this, wondered Georges, where we cool off? Yet after a brief stretch of salt air and lonely beaches, Tony plunged back into the town once more. Making sure that no one followed, Georges decided: that was obvious. But as well as that? They were still not far from the casino; had been circling around it, in fact. If no one was interested in them—and Georges, in his own mind, was sure that no one was—then this was the time to take up position within safe view of the casino's entrance. "We could keep an eye on Gorsky," Georges suggested, breaking the long silence. "We can sit in the car. I parked it not too far—"

Tony brushed that aside. "Not tonight." His emotions had subsided; jumbled thoughts were coming back into order. At least, he thought, we know the worst. We can start from there.

"Let him think he has won?" Even if that gave Gorsky a false sense of security, Georges still didn't like it.

"Why not?" Reappraisal, decided Tony: see how we stand; then act.

"We're missing a first-rate opportunity. We may never have a second chance to find out where he is holed up."

"And risk raising his suspicions still more?"

But Georges persisted, found good reasons to bolster his own impulse. "We didn't add to them tonight. We showed absolutely no interest in him at the casino. Why shouldn't we have been there? We're tourists. And our visit to Shandon Villa was equally understandable. We haven't given Gorsky any reason to suspect—"

"Then we'll keep him unsuspecting for as long as possible." And that won't be too long, Tony thought. How much did he actually learn about my movements in New York, last December? Or at New Jersey's Shandon, or in Washington itself? His voice sharpened. "Damn it, Georges, you are a hard man to persuade."

"That makes two of us."

"I'm telling you to forget Gorsky. Meanwhile."

"How can we? He's in charge of this operation."

"Not he. Think back to that scene at the table."

"I see," Georges said with a touch of sarcasm. It strengthened. "That's why Parracini was the one to make contact? Here I am, sir. Reporting for duty. Any new instructions?"

A matter of protocol? Tony repressed a smile. "He had no other choice. Where's your car?"

"Next street," said Georges stiffly, and led the way. But he was thinking back, as Tony had advised. True enough: Parracini had had no other choice than to make the first move: he had come out of the cinema earlier than expected; he hadn't had much time at his disposal—five or six minutes at most—before Brigitte would find him. "He's good," Georges admitted. "He's flexible. Decisive. Isn't fazed by any variant in a set plan. But that doesn't prove he's important enough to outrank Gorsky."

"Which of them had the last word?" Tony didn't wait for a reply, stepped into the car as if to close the argument.

Parracini—yes, Parracini. Administering a final piece of advice? Or instruction? "If this is true—" Georges began, and paused. The idea of Parracini's importance was still too shocking to be easily believable. What have we been protecting—Bill, Nicole, all of us? Keeping him contented, comfortable, worrying our brains out about his safety? Yes, the joke is on us, a very sour joke indeed. Georges got into the driver's seat, sat there, staring at the wheel. We haven't only been fooled: we'll become a laughingstock when this news gets out. And Gerard, for one, may find his career—a good one, too—suddenly amputated. "If this is true," Georges repeated, but he was less doubtful now, "Nealey is here to run the Shandon Villa operation. Parracini is here—among other things—to supervise Nealey. And Gorsky, Executive Action Department, is here to supply protection." Which meant that Shandon Villa must be of far greater importance in future KGB plans than either he or Tony had first guessed. "You know," he admitted frankly, "if you hadn't been so intent on Nealey, we would never have stumbled on all this. It's one hell of a situation."

Tony had been keeping a careful eye on the street, fore and aft. It seemed as safe as those they had walked through in the last ten minutes—no more than twenty people encountered: couples, homeward bound; an occasional singleton, self-absorbed; but no one dodging into a doorway, no one dogging their footsteps. He relaxed now, lit a cigarette, offered one to Georges. "It could be worse."

"That is what appalls me." Georges was remembering his discussion with Tony only that afternoon, about Parracini's future in a cozy career with NATO. "My good God," he said, "what have we escaped?"

A KGB agent in perfect place, thought Tony. "Let's get moving. Take the tunnel, head for the other side of town." I've had enough of this one. "Can you put me up for the night?"

"Of course." Georges turned on the ignition and maneuvered the car out of its parking place. "We can always toss a coin to see who sleeps on the floor." His high spirits were returning with the thought of some action. There would be plenty to do before either of them stretched out to sleep. There would be a sense of decision, of accomplishing something important: the good feeling of being in the center of things. His luck had been in today, and Emil's had been out, stuck as he was on board the *Sea Breeze*. That was the way it went: stretches of boredom, of patient duty. And then—suddenly, like tonight—the big chance. "We'll have to move fast, Tony. And Gerard could be a problem, so paralyzed with shock that we could lose two good hours. Parracini has been his pet project, remember. How do you deal with that, I ask you?"

"That," said Tony, "is what I am trying to think about."

It was a gentle reminder to stop talking and leave Tony in peace. Georges grinned, said "Yes, sir," and concentrated on the rearview mirror. No car was following.

The casino, the shopping area, the public buildings and private houses all vanished behind them as they entered the tunnel and sped through the hill on which the Old Town stood. This was a short cut, the underpass that linked the two other sections of Menton, west and east. A strange way for a town to grow, thought Georges. First, the mass of medieval houses and churches packed together on a steep spine of rock. Then centuries later, a spread of people to lower ground, with their houses and markets and churches clustering around the base of the hill on either side. Three towns, actually, with the most ancient of them still functioning—not a historical relic, but a place with a life of its own. Today he had settled in nicely *sous les toits de Menton,* and had imagined that he'd be part of the Old Town for a pleasant week. But now, it was possible he'd be out of there by tomorrow. Parracini had changed all plans.

They swept out of the tunnel, entering on the broad avenue that followed the shore of Garavan Bay. The Old Town, dominating the harbor, rose up behind them. "The quick way up to my place," Georges said, pointing backwards.

Tony jerked round, but saw only a solid cliff of highrising tenements above a stretch of small stores and eating places.

"It's the street—a flight of steps, really—that lies about halfway along that row of shops and Italian restaurants."

"I'll find it."

"Are you sure? Perhaps we'd better make the climb together."

"Negative. We'll stick to our usual routine. Except that I'll follow you more closely than usual."

"We won't have far to go. My room is on the bottom layer of the Old Town. Lucky it isn't up on the pinnacle. And it faces the Mediterranean. I have a front-row seat to all this." He gestured with his right hand toward the dark in-curve of water edged by the continuous lights of promenade and avenue.

Another night, thought Tony, and I can admire the view. But now—his eyes followed the shore line ahead of them and reached the new anchorage for yachts and cabin cruisers. "That marina at the east end of the bay— wonder if it has boats for hire. Nice big boats with powerful engines."

"We've already got a boat. With a good engine."

Not good enough, not for what I'm thinking. "Let's go to your room." There was sudden urgency in Tony's voice. "Make the turn back at the next traffic light. I have to call Bill before we start sending any message."

"All right, all right." Georges took the next turn and headed back to the Old Town, traveling now along the waterfront apartments and hotels that had recently mushroomed on this side of the avenue. "Sorry about all this delay," he said too politely. It wasn't too much, he thought, only six or seven minutes altogether.

"I've been admiring your caution."

"I always take care when I'm approaching my place. It's the only base of operations we've got."

"I am still admiring your caution."

George's defensiveness ended in a laugh. He brought the car to a smooth halt, stopping short of the Old Town to leave them still about two hundred yards to cover on foot. The spot he had selected for parking was well calculated, too: the Renault had merged with a dozen cars that were drawn off the avenue, herded near a garden wall of one of the large apartment hotels. "Now for that damned walk," Georges said, eying it with distaste.

"I'll give you three minutes, and then follow."

"Remember—it's the first street you reach. Lies between the pizza palace and the beauty salon with yellow curtains. Forty-seven steps up, and you take the street on your right. I'll be waiting."

"Fine."

Georges had one last look around him before he stepped out of the Renault. "I wish this place wasn't so deserted at night. What we need is a good thick crowd for comfort."

"Next time we'll arrange our assignment for July."

Georges eased into a smile, started along the empty sidewalk.

I don't feel too happy about this either, thought Tony. Yet we've taken every precaution. There was some traffic—a few cars, an occasional taxi—but it was all fast-moving. No car had drawn aside and parked. And no one was suddenly stepping out of a doorway to follow Georges. Tony's glance flickered to his watch. The three minutes were almost up. Now it was his turn to step onto that lonely sidewalk, singing the off-season blues.

As he approached the Old Town, he had a closer view of the harbor. The mole, its clawlike arm thrown around the anchorage, was well lighted. One or two people walking out there, he noted; and one or two people, land side, on the promenade. The boats were hidden, but he could see rows and rows of masts, the long and the short, the slender and the thick, and those of the *Sea Breeze* riding peacefully among them. Yes, he thought, the *Sea Breeze* is another thing I don't feel too happy about. Gorsky will not only have her under surveillance, but he will find out that three of us arrived; and now only one is left aboard. He knows I'm at the Hotel Alexandre. But Georges—where? He won't rest until he traces Georges's real address. He can sense its importance: why else did Georges keep it out of the police records? And he can easily discover that the *Sea Breeze* has been taking on supplies—more than necessary for three people who say they are sailing along the coast. And he may do exactly what I was tempted to do, at that marina on the other end of the bay. He may hire a cabin cruiser. Not a pleasing prospect for the *Sea Breeze* when she sails out of harbor tomorrow.

So we cancel our plan? Tony heaved a sigh of regret. It would have been so simple, a neat clean operation: get Parracini aboard the *Sea Breeze,* but instead of cruising—the original idea—sail direct to Nice, coax him onto a plane for Brussels. Using what as the incentive? An interview for that job in NATO Intelligence? Yes, he wouldn't have refused that invitation. So simple. Like all might-have-beens.

What else was there, to take its place? Convey Parracini to Nice by car? He'd balk, most definitely. A secret meeting with two senior NATO officers on board the cruising *Sea Breeze*—that would seem logical enough: privacy and security combined. But a sudden switch to a car? He'd sense a trap. He'd never go of his own free will. Messy. A drugged man needed a stretcher and bearers to get him into a plane. I'm no kidnapper, Tony thought, and shook his head.

Even a helicopter—there was a stretch of open ground near the marina at the other end of the bay—wouldn't serve our purpose. We'd need local permission, and how do we get that before eleven tomorrow morning? And again there is the unpleasant problem of carrying an unconscious man—no,

Tony told himself sharply, that isn't the way you work. Just think harder, Lawton, will you?

Pizza advertisements, boldly printed and plastered all over a restaurant's window, shouted at him for attention. Beyond it, a small shop with its hair dryers showing, and curtains that might look yellow by day, but now, under the electric lights, were the color of porridge. And between the pizza and the porridge was tucked the street—a flight of stairs—that would lead him up into the Old Town. He began climbing.

It was a steep pull, the stone steps made sway-backed by centuries of clattering feet. On either side, no more than two arm-lengths apart, were the gable ends of houses, reaching high, cutting the night sky into a sliver. But the lights on the walls were evenly spaced, and adequate enough to keep a man from breaking a leg. Tony didn't have to fumble for his footing, grope his way. He could concentrate on moving as quickly and silently as possible. There were scattered windows above and around; sounds of muffled voices, of a radio muted behind shutters. And always, at his back, the night breeze that came funneling up this narrow street from the sea.

Forty-seven steps, and he could turn, breathing heavily, muscles taut, into a slightly broader street. And flatter too, thank heaven. Three boys, chasing one another, jostled a young man and his girl out of a tight embrace. An older man, fisherman type, walked slowly. Tony kept on his way as if he too were en route home. He passed Georges leaning against a wall, heard him whisper, "Second entrance on your right, and all the way up."

Tony reached the top landing, sat down on the last step to wait for Georges. If there hadn't been so many neighbors behind the closed doors he had passed, he might have laughed out loud.

Nineteen

GEORGES HAD ALREADY drawn the curtains across his window and pulled the shade over the glass panels of the door that led onto the midget terrace, before he turned on the lights and let Tony enter his room.

It was of medium size and sparsely furnished: a heavy wooden table and two hard chairs, a narrow bed, a chest beside it with a radio on top, a small wardrobe, a scrap of rug. The paintwork was orange, the plaster walls covered with the self-expression of a previous tenant—abstract murals in scarlet and purple. "Cheerful," Tony said, investigating a narrow door to find a tight squeeze of toilet and hand basin. "And running water, too." There was a definite drip from the small overhead cistern.

"It may not be the Ritz, but it has a better view." Georges took off his jacket, hooked it on a peg at the door.

"And things to tempt the gourmet," said Tony, examining the contents of the wardrobe, which Georges had selected as his pantry.

"I think you could use some of that right now," Georges said. It was his only reference to Tony's inexplicable attack of laughter that had met his cautious arrival on the landing. Thank God, Tony had suppressed it. And there was nothing funny about all this—nothing.

"Business first. Where are your miracle workers?"

Georges pointed to the radio beside his bed. "That's one. Didn't you have dinner before we met?" And he certainly hasn't had much lunch today, thought Georges worriedly. Hunger makes a man lightheaded.

"Not quite."

"It's five past ten—"

"And time to call Emil."

There was nothing lightheaded about that voice. Georges opened a drawer, picked out his transceiver, and made the call.

Tony took over. "Emil—this is serious. You may have some curious strangers wandering near the *Sea Breeze* tonight. How's the situation at present?"

"Normal," Emil's placid voice said. "A few people on the mole, one or two on the quay. And three fishermen practically next door, fixing something on their boat—been working hard on it.'

"Since when?" Tony asked quickly.

"Since this afternoon."

"Then they're okay. Anyone you've noticed before eight o'clock tonight is probably all right too."

"So that's when the whistle was blown?"

"Around then. And look—if someone tries to board, don't be proud. Yell for those fishermen."

"If they are still here."

"They like a bottle of beer, don't they, after a stretch of work?"

"Invite them on board?"

"Why not? Give them a friendly hail, anyway. Let them know you're around. See you tomorrow."

"Sleepless," Emil said with a laugh.

"Who won't be?" Tony flipped off the connection, looked thoughtfully at the transceiver, balancing it in his hand before he laid it on the table. It was little bigger than a pack of cigarettes.

Georges said, "All right, Tony. I read you. I'll carry it next to my heart from now on. The truth is, I didn't expect any excitement on this assignment." Just a simple little tour of inspection, hadn't that been our idea when we came sailing into Menton this morning? Make certain that all was going well with Parracini? *"Quel con,"* was Georges's final comment on that subject, as he fished out a neat object, disguised as a portable phonograph, from under the bed, along with an equally portable machine pretending to be a typewriter. He placed them on the table where he had already set out his versatile radio, some tapes, a pad, and pencils. "Any time," he told Tony, readying typewriter and phonograph for their proper functions. His entire equipment covered less than one half of the table.

"Compact," said Tony. "The wonders of modern technology." Georges worked on. He was taut and angry and much too solemn. "No more aerials draped out of windows?"

"It runs on batteries." Georges was intent on the final adjustments. "Ready when you are."

"And no sending keys? I don't even see you looped up in earphones?"

"That's all past tense. Nowadays, we—" Georges checked his reply and saved himself in time. He joined in Tony's smile. His voice eased. "What's the first message? To Gerard, I suppose." He looked at his watch, nodded his approval of the remarkably brief time it had taken to set up the preparations. "First, you run over the various points you want to make, then I can either tape or scramble—"

"First," said Tony, "I think we ought to get in touch with Bill. But by less exotic means." He picked up the telephone and dialed Bill's private number. He had to wait, impatience growing with each unanswered ring. "This call *is* necessary," he reassured Georges, who was watching him in dismay. "We must know where we stand, before we—" Bill's voice interrupted him.

"Already in bed?" Tony asked.

"No, no. I was in the next room watching television with Nicole. Sorry for the delay. Something new to report?"

"Nothing. Just wondering if they all got safely home from the movie."

"Early," Bill told him. "Brigitte couldn't take the air-conditioning."

"What about Bernard? Is he around?"

"Playing chess with Parracini downstairs."

"I don't suppose—no, you couldn't."

"Couldn't what?"

"Tell Bernard to slip quietly down to the harbor. But that's impossible now."

"Oh, I don't know about that—"

"I said *quietly*, Bill. We don't want to alarm Parracini—or the others, either. It's nothing much, anyway. Just a feeling I have about the *Sea Breeze*. I don't like having only one man aboard tonight."

"Why?"

"This afternoon—" and keep the casino and Gorsky out of this—"I saw evidence of the opposition."

Bill went into high alarm. "They're on the track? They've actually uncovered Parracini?"

"No, repeat no!" Just the opposite, Tony would have liked to say. Instead, he led into the question that had impelled him to call Bill. "And don't set Parracini into a panic about them. Shandon Villa is where the action is. Better say nothing to him. Keep his mind at ease—he has a big day ahead of him. When will you tell him that we've decided to have the meeting on board the *Sea Breeze*, and not at your place?"

"Oh, that's already done. Thought it better to break the news tonight, didn't want to spring it on him at the last moment."

"Tonight?"

"Just before dinner. We were having drinks, and—"

"I hope he wasn't unhappy about it."

"Far from it. It took him but a couple of minutes to see our point of view. I emphasized additional security."

So, thought Tony, Parracini needed only a few minutes to decide. No consultation necessary with anyone. He's the man in charge. No doubt left about that.

"Did I act out of turn?" Bill asked, puzzled by Tony's silence.

"Relax, relax. All that's bothering me is the *Sea Breeze*. She could use some of that additional security. If anything goes wrong with her tonight—" Tony left that idea hanging in the air.

Bill said slowly, "If you feel you need some extra support, I can get in touch with a couple of good men."

I knew it, I knew it: Bill wouldn't be here without some backup, some kind of insurance, Tony thought. "How soon?"

"They're on stand-by notice today. I don't want to call them, though, unless it's absolutely necessary. Is it?"

"With the opposition in town?"

"But not in connection with us, you said," Bill reminded him sharply. "What's their business here, do you know?"

"It was Chuck Kelso."

"That has nothing to do with us."

"I know, I know. But I'd still feel more comfortable with a couple of good men around."

"I'll call them." Bill wasn't too enthusiastic. He liked keeping his insurance well covered. "Where do you want them?"

"No need to go aboard—unless, of course, something breaks. Tell them to keep a close eye on the *Sea Breeze*. That's all."

"Okay." Bill was reassured. "We play it cool."

"All of us," Tony emphasized. And, for God's sake, don't disturb Parracini's sweet dreams, he thought as he rang off with a cheerful "See you— early tomorrow."

And that was that.

Georges, sitting with his feet up on the table, looked with undisguised impatience at his watch.

"I agree. It took far too long," Tony conceded. "It was like pulling teeth. But we did learn something important. Parracini was told about our *Sea Breeze* project before he went to the casino."

"Then Gorsky knows!"

"He knows." Either this room is getting hotter or my blood pressure is rising, thought Tony. He pulled off his jacket, dropped it on the bed.

Georges swore softly. "That alters everything." He shook his head in commiseration. "Too bad, Tony. It was a good plan."

"It still is. Sail straight to Nice; and then by air to Brussels. Couldn't be simpler. Why, even the Nice airport is in the perfect spot for us—right at the water's edge." Tony added softly, "We really can't refuse an opportunity like that, now can we?"

"Drop the whole idea, Tony. We can't pull it off. Not now."

Tony said nothing at all.

"Gorsky will hire a cabin cruiser, and keep the *Sea Breeze* well within sight.

The moment he sees we aren't having a leisurely cruise, he will send out a general alarm. We'll never get Parracini anywhere near Brussels. We won't even reach Nice—if Gorsky has a boat that can outrun the *Sea Breeze*—the best we can do in our motor sailer is ten knots. And his men will be heavily armed: he does nothing by half-measures. We'll have a couple of handguns, if that." Georges stared at Tony, his thoughts now back with the Gorsky file. "You know, if he couldn't board us, Gorsky would blow us all out of the water, Parracini included. He'd do that rather than let Parracini remain our prisoner. It's not the first time he has killed one of his own—for the sake of security."

Hands in pockets, Tony had been studying the equipment on the table. "Let's begin," he said, pulling the other chair into position opposite Georges. "But I want to know what to expect here. First, you tape my message, and then—"

"A waste of breath," Georges said. "You didn't listen. The plan is out, Tony. We need—"

"I listened. And you gave me a new idea. Always a pleasure working with you, Georges, my boy. Now, where were we?—Oh, yes. First, you tape the message; then you speed it up in transmission—turn it into a screeching background to harmless chitchat. And at the receiving end, there's a tape recorder to pick up the screech. Right?"

Georges nodded. Tony always knows more than he pretends, he reminded himself in surprise.

"And when the taped screech is played back and slowed down to the original recording speed, it becomes intelligible. Is that how we'll do it?"

"That's one way. But there's a new and quicker variation."

"Equally safe?"

"Safer. The latest in scrambling devices. Produces screeches that can be directly untangled as they arrive at the receiving end from any ordinary conversation."

"Simple and secure. I like that."

"Highly sophisticated and secure."

Tony's smile broadened as he pulled the writing pad in front of him. "Contact Brussels." He began jotting down what needed to be said.

"Geneva, you mean. Gerard is there this weekend. He's working late in his office in case we have anything further to report. You really worried him this—"

"Brussels," repeated Tony. "Straight to the top, Georges. Where do you think our message will get some real response? Special Service Division? Attention Commander Hartwell?"

"If he can be reached."

"He can be. Did you think I picked his name out of a hat? He's in charge of night duty this week. Sleeps in his office, stalwart fellow. He's American, so we'll jolly him up with a starting signal he'll recognize: *Officer requires assistance.* Next comes *Urgent call for immediate help, highest priority.* And then we follow with this—" Tony pushed the pad over to Georges. "You'll compress it for coded transmission, but don't drop out any words or phrases such as *vital—necessary—threat of attack—officers' lives in extreme jeopardy.*" And that last phrase, thought Tony, might be no exaggeration.

Pencil in hand, Georges was already abbreviating Tony's notes as he read them back. They were concise enough, but slightly more dramatic than Georges himself would have risked. "High-ranking enemy agent under arrest, escorted by four NATO officers, will sail tomorrow, Saturday, on *Sea Breeze*—maximum speed ten knots, departing Menton harbor eleven hours, arriving Nice around thirteen hours, weather permitting. Request immediate air transport to Brussels. Warning added: operation now seriously endangered by Soviet agents (Department V—Executive Action) known to be in possession of sailing information. *Sea Breeze* will be followed, intercepted. Real threat of attack. Officers' lives in extreme jeopardy. Require vital support. Necessity for immediate action. Most urgent request for—"

Georges looked up, his pencil poised in mid-air. "For a naval vessel?"

"A very small one."

"But—"

"How many navies does Nato have?"

Georges laughed, finished the job of abbreviation, began coding. "But why navy at all?" he asked as he completed the message for transmission. "Nato could find us a medium-sized cabin cruiser. There must be hundreds of them all along this coast."

"If Hartwell can arrange for it, I'd settle for that. In fact—" Tony had an additional idea, and smiled—"I'd like both. A cabin cruiser, not too big to dock in Menton harbor beside the *Sea Breeze;* a navy cutter out in the bay, waiting, ready to escort. Tell Hartwell that too. From me."

"You know him?"

"My old and good friend."

"Even so, you're asking too much."

"And making sure we get at least half of what we need." Tony pushed his chair away from the table, stretched his back muscles, and rose. "Sign off with one last nudge: we are here all through the night, awaiting instructions and final arrangements."

"You're as confident as that?" Georges asked. But there was a renewed assurance in his own voice, an added zest when he made contact and could begin transmitting.

Confident? Tony had wondered, walking aimlessly around the room. If hopes were dupes, fears may be liars. Certainly, doubts never win any argument, and we'll get plenty of that. But I'm damned if Gorsky is going to blow any of us out of the water, and then report that the *Sea Breeze's* engine must have exploded. Explosion? Another possibility to take into account . . . But later, Tony decided, deal with that later. Now, there was a message for Gerard to be whipped into shape.

Difficult, this one. Gerard would have no supersophisticated gadgets in a small room in Geneva: nothing as costly as the newest equipment available in Brussels. It wasn't only security that was the problem. Gerard was a problem in himself. First, there would be shock, disbelief. But once he was convinced, he'd start sending messages to prepare the two officers who were arriving in Nice tomorrow morning. The name of Parracini would be loose in the air, ready to be picked up by monitors. Or even by KGB ears—it only needed a dutiful little secretary or a bugged telephone in Gerard's office to blow everything wide open. Gorsky would warn Parracini to clear out, and Parracini would be into Italy tomorrow morning before Bill had poured his first cup of coffee.

So, Tony thought as he sat down on the bed, we talk with Gerard, make him realize we're faced with a major problem, and say nothing about Parracini. Not even a circumlocution like *high-ranking enemy agent*. Nothing. Yet we can't keep Gerard out of this. Tempting, but not possible. How do we warn him?

Tie loosened, belt unbuckled, Tony stretched out on the thin mattress. How? he asked the ceiling.

He felt a tug at his arm and was instantly awake.

Georges was saying, "Time we called Geneva. Sorry to do this, you were sleeping so deeply that I—"

"Just drifting in and out." Tony swung legs onto the floor. Exhaustion had left him: he felt as clear-eyed and brisk as if he had been asleep for several hours, but his watch told him it was barely twenty minutes since he had stretched out on the bed. "What about Brussels?"

"Completed. Don't worry, they received the message. Now, we wait."

"And what will we get—pie all over our face?"

We'll get worse than that, thought Georges, if we have miscalculated Gorsky's possible reactions. What if it could be all plain sailing to Nice, and no interference? Hastily he put that thought out of his mind. "By the way, I expanded that reference to Department V—Executive Action. Just a little. A neat insert, I thought. Hope you don't object."

"Too late, anyway. What did you add?"

"Gorsky's file number. Okay?"

"Wish I had thought of it," Tony admitted, walking over to the table, looking at the equipment, wondering if a telephone call using voice code might not be the quickest way to contact Gerard. He noted that Georges hadn't only been busy expanding references, but had found a spare minute to dump a small hunk of boiled ham, some Brie and *chèvre* cheeses, along with a loaf of bread and a bottle of wine, on the free end of the table. "Is Gerard as fascinated by Gorsky as you are?"

"More so. And with good reason."

"What, for instance?"

Georges hesitated.

"Come on, come on. This info could help us now."

"Gerard had a Soviet defector from Disinformation three years ago—sequestered him in a safe house, twenty-four-hour guard. But Gorsky got at him, through one of the kitchen staff. The defector died, and two of our men with him. Food poisoning."

"What was his code name in Gerard's casebook?"

"That's Gerard's private property. It wasn't even listed—"

"All the better. Less chance of its being recognized by outside ears. Our talk with Gerard could be monitored if we use the telephone. You know that."

Georges nodded. For at least a year, Soviet Intelligence had been able to intercept and record telephone calls in all foreign countries, not only between government officials but between private citizens. Computerized scanners could monitor and separate the microwave frequencies. Fixed antennae on the roofs of Soviet embassies were picking up signals between foreign relay stations—even signals beamed to American communication satellites. "They've been using our technology," Georges burst out, suddenly as much American as he was French. "That's how our telephone call to Geneva could be monitored—by Telstar! Ironic, isn't it?"

Tony said thoughtfully, "Now wouldn't it be nice to cause a hiccup or two in those busy little Soviet computers?" He paused. "What was the code name Gerard gave to his dead defector?"

"Hector."

The Trojan hero, dragged around by his heels at the tail end of Achilles' chariot . . . "Well," said Tony, "do we use the telephone? Or have you a better idea of how to contact Gerard?"

"Yes. But he will want to talk with you. And that could tie up our transmitter for the next hour." Further explanations requested, counter-suggestions—"No," said Georges, "we've got to keep our lines of communication open with Brussels."

"Then we haven't any choice, have we?"

"We could always use the old-time scrambler for telephone conversations. That might help."

"What would, nowadays? Twinkle, twinkle satellite, shining in the sky so bright, what d'you hear up there tonight?" That at least brought a small smile to Georges's worried face. "All right," Tony went on, "get Gerard on the line. You speak first, soften him up with a few friendly phrases. He likes you." And the sober truth is that Gerard and I have never liked each other. We are two Englishmen with clashing personalities, which can make for disagreeable sounds. Remember, Tony warned himself as Georges at last handed him the telephone, don't let Gerard's bloody bullheadedness get one rise out of you. Sweetness and light and firm persuasion. And keep it brief.

And brief it was, four minutes of talk, with Tony in control most of the way. For once, Gerard gave little argument: perhaps the initial shock was so great that its tremors lasted through the remainder of the conversation. Tony plunged right in with "Bad news about the condominium you are planning to build here. Serious difficulties have developed with the construction plans; a real crisis, in fact, that needs your personal attention. I know you were sending your two architects to consult the builders, but you ought to be here yourself. Why not fly down with them? We'll meet all three of you, and we can go over the blueprints without delay. I'd suggest an hour earlier than previously arranged—we have a lot to discuss about building specifications. They must be met—and that means you should oversee the necessary changes in the blueprints. A brief visit should be enough, but your presence is imperative. We need your guiding hand—just to ensure that your special project goes smoothly and agreeably."

"The blueprints were excellent. They met all building specifications. Who's objecting to them?"

"One of your rivals in real estate. He has an eye on your property. An aggressive type. The Achilles complex, you might call it. Remember Achilles? He was the fellow who killed poor old Hector and dragged his corpse around the walls of Troy."

"I've read my Homer," was Gerard's icy reply.

"And so you have. Stupid of me to forget. Three years ago—was it? Yes, three years ago you used to have a passionate interest in the Trojan heroes."

There was a short but painful silence. "Achilles is actually in—"

"Intolerable, at times," Tony broke in, blotting out any mention of Menton. "I agree. A memorable character, though: not easily dismissed. Stays in mind, doesn't he?"

"Yes," said Gerard. He began to recover. "I'll make arrangements to join you."

"Good. And you'll inform the others about the time of arrival?"

"They won't like it. It means a very early start."

"A proper nuisance," Tony commiserated, and gave Georges, listening in with an earphone, a slow and solemn wink. He rang off abruptly before any other question about Achilles might come blundering forth.

"Okay?" he asked Georges.

"Not for me." Georges smiled. "Gerard won't like me giving away the name of Hector—or 'three years ago' either."

"How else could we have warned him that Gorsky is here?"

"But not one word about Parracini's true identity? You could have disguised it, meshed it in with your reference to Gerard's special project."

"Sure, I could have said his pet project had changed shape, got twisted, had an ugly face, turned into a monster to haunt his dreams."

"Don't you trust Gerard?" Georges asked bluntly.

"That isn't the point. If I had told him the truth about Parracini, how do you think he would have behaved? Kept quiet? No. He'd now be sending messages, sounding the alarm, putting his department on red alert—other departments, too. He'd have started some action. And coopered ours. Look, I'm hungry." Tony settled himself at the table, checked the St. Emilion label. "Not a bad year," he said, and began breaking bread.

They made a good supper. "It will help keep us awake," Tony suggested, serving a second portion of Brie along with a large slice of *chèvre*—the ham already sliced to the bone, the St. Emilion at its last glass. There hadn't been much talk during the meal. But even as it ended and Georges lit a cigarette, his silence continued. "My voluble French friend," said Tony, relaxed and expansive, "what's worrying you now?"

"Gerard. Do I meet him at Nice airport tomorrow?"

"You meet all three, and give them the full report as you drive them to the Menton dock. You've got all the facts. I don't need to be there. I'd like to stay near the harbor."

"I wish you had trusted Gerard more. He's no fool."

"Not always."

Georges said sharply, "It *was* a good debriefing in Genoa. Gerard handled Parracini well. Nothing slipshod, I assure you."

"I believe you."

Georges tried some diplomacy. "If it hadn't been for you, Tony, we'd still be accepting Parracini at face value. I know that. He'd even be on his way to a post in Gerard's department. But—"

"But nothing! How could he have been accepted in Genoa? *That's* the first question to ask."

"He came guaranteed all the way. Made his first contact with us in Istanbul. He knew the address of our agent there, gave all the right identification signals. That *was* Palladin who reached Turkey."

Was it? Tony wondered. He said, "How long was he in Istanbul?"

"Several days. Had to get passport and documents, clothes, money—all that."

And in Istanbul, too, he was given the right recognition signals for his next contact in Lesbos, passed on from agent to agent, each giving him the next name to contact, the next signal to use. *Guaranteed all the way*— beginning with our agent in Istanbul who had accepted him as authentic. Tony said slowly, "Didn't any of you in Genoa know him personally? Was there no one who had been in Moscow and could identify him?"

"Palladin was a careful character. Didn't meet foreigners, avoided all contacts with the West. How do you think he stayed safe for twelve years?"

"There must be someone in Nato Intelligence who saw him in Moscow, knew him as Palladin."

"Palladin wasn't his real name. A cautious type, I told you."

"Even so—there must be someone who could have identified him. What about our agents who recruited him twelve years ago?"

"He recruited himself—as his private protest about the renewed campaign against Russian intellectuals. He volunteered, using a Polish journalist to contact a Nato agent who was briefly in Moscow. He wasn't really taken seriously at first, but the information he started sending—using his own methods to get it out to us—was of excellent quality."

"Where's the Polish journalist now?"

"Dead."

"Where's that Nato agent?"

"Retired. In London. He was hospitalized over Christmas—badly smashed up in a traffic accident. So he couldn't attend the debriefing in Genoa."

"Such a convenient and well-timed accident," Tony murmured. "What did they use to run him down—a truck?"

Georges let that pass. "It seemed merely a piece of bad luck at the time," was his only comment. "And now, of course, even if the old boy came out here on his crutches—well, we've seen how Parracini has changed his appearance. Right under our eyes, too. Ironic touch, isn't it?"

Tony had risen and was moving over to the balcony door. "I could wish the irony wasn't always turned against us these days. Time to start dealing out some of it, ourselves. Switch off that light, will you, Georges?" As the room darkened, Tony prepared to step onto the balcony. "Coming?" he asked.

"No, I'll stay here and watch for a radio signal. What's troubling you now? The *Sea Breeze* again?"

Tony closed the door gently behind him. Yes, the *Sea Breeze*. And Palladin's arrival in Istanbul, too. Or had Palladin actually arrived there? He could have been trailed to Odessa—taken into custody, and questioned under torture. A substitution wouldn't be too difficult: find a KGB officer who worked in Palladin's department and knew the same files. He only needed to be Palladin's approximate age—and possibly close to his height too, in case someone out in the West recalled that Palladin was of medium size. (Coloring could be faked or changed. Heights were always the giveaway.) Facial differences wouldn't matter: it was the impersonator's photograph and general description that would appear on the new Palladin travel documents. Odessa . . . Yes, that could be the place. There had been a delay there, before the next step had been made to Istanbul. And the man who was to replace Palladin could have increased that delay. He didn't need to make a tortuous journey from Odessa to Istanbul; he could have been flown to Turkey direct, at the last moment, giving him that extra time he needed to question Palladin. And Palladin himself? If not dead then, certainly by this time.

Tony stared down at the harbor and its protecting walls. All was silent, all was at peace. Within the giant horseshoe of black water, white hulls floated side by side, gently, easily. Neatly spaced lights, like hard bright nailheads, studded the edge of land, secured it from the dark bay. The sea was gentle; small ripples, glinting even and constant under the gibbous moon, stretched to the dark rim of the horizon. The stars were brilliant, barely veiled by the thin clouds teased over the night sky. Silent and peaceful, Tony thought again. He gave a long last glance at the *Sea Breeze* before he stepped back into the warm room.

"All quiet out there?" Georges asked, as he switched on all the lights again. "No signal, so far, on my receiver."

"If we have to use the *Sea Breeze* tomorrow—"

"Better wait for Brussels' answer before you start thinking about that."

"Tomorrow," repeated Tony, "we'll have Emil check under the water line."

"What?"

Tony saw once more the quiet line of boats, all neatly moored, dark waters lapping at their sides. We aren't the only team around with an experienced underwater swimmer, he thought. He said, his smile self-deprecating, "I keep thinking of an explosion set off by remote control. Don't look at me like that, Georges; it was you who gave me the idea to start with. When do you think we might hear from Brussels?"

"It's barely midnight. And the longer we have to wait for an answer, the better. A flat refusal comes back in no time at all."

"Midnight?" Tony asked, suddenly remembering Tom Kelso. "Damnation." He reached for the telephone, dialed from memory. No answer. "Georges, look up the local directory—under Maurice Michel. I must have got the number wrong." But the telephone book listed the same number he had dialed. He tried again, more slowly. And still there was no answer. He waited for the space of twenty rings before putting down the receiver. "I don't like this," he said.

"They're asleep. Or perhaps they turned the phone off."

"Tom said he'd be awake to take my call—whenever it came."

"They may have gone for a late-night stroll."

"I don't like it," Tony said. He held out his hand. "The car keys, Georges." He was pulling on his jacket as he moved toward the door. "Not alone," Georges warned him.

"How else?" Tony pointed to the electronic gear on the table. "You keep your ear on that."

"And if questions come in?"

"We don't budge from our requests. I'll stay in touch with you. Have you a spare transceiver?"

Georges produced it from a drawer, along with a small automatic. "For reassurance," he said with a grin, knowing Tony's objections to firearms.

Tony didn't argue. He slipped the pistol into his belt. With a parting nod, he closed the door carefully behind him.

Twenty

THE HOUSE LAY in darkness. Tom Kelso drew up beside the deep shadow of the orange trees, stepped out of the Fiat, and opened its trunk for Chuck's suitcase. His earlier emotions, a paralyzing mixture of grief and rage, had left him. The visit to the casino and the brief talk with Tony Lawton had actually been good for him: pain had been cauterized, mind braced. He could look at the facts, as far as he knew them, and see the shape of things that had to be done.

Thea had carried out his final instructions almost too well. Not only had she drawn curtains and closed shutters and locked doors both front and back; she had also bolted them, so that his keys were useless. He returned to the kitchen entrance—the one they generally used, near their parking space—and knocked hard. Perhaps she was asleep upstairs, and he'd have to go round to the side of the house and throw pebbles up at the bedroom window. He knocked again, called her name, had a moment of real fear—his emotions weren't so deadened after all, he admitted—before he heard her voice answering. Fear subsided as quickly as it had risen. As he waited for her to open the door, he looked around him at the sleeping hillside. Down by the nursery, lights glinted cheerfully from the close group of three small cottages where Auguste and his two married sons lived. Lights, too, from the houses scattered up and down the Roquebrune road. And brighter by far was the rising moon, almost full, silvering the open ground, blackening the shadows of trees and bushes. Nothing stirred. Even traffic sounds were thinned and muted. Peaceful and quiet and reassuring. The door opened, and he could take Thea in his arms and hold her.

"Gardenia," he said, kissing her neck. "So you were having a bath. I was beginning to think I'd need a battering-ram to get in here." He lifted Chuck's suitcase across the threshold, closed and locked the door behind him.

Relief spread over Dorothea's face as she heard him sound so normal. She matched her mood to his. "I heard the car, but I had to dry myself and get some clothes on—"

"And that isn't warm enough, either," he told her. She had only a thin wool dressing gown, belted and neat, over silk pajamas.

"I'll be all right." And her outfit was practical, chosen, in spite of haste to get downstairs, to let her cook something for Tom's supper. Besides, with all those windows and doors closed—

"Not warm enough," he repeated, "once you've cooled off from your bath." Her face was flushed to a bright rose, her hair was pinned up with damp tendrils curling over her brow and at the nape of her neck, her smile delighted with his concern but totally disbelieving. She was fastening a checkered apron around her waist, getting eggs and parsley out of the refrigerator. "I'm really not hungry, Thea," he said gently. "And I've some work to do."

"No trouble—and no time at all." She glanced at the suitcase in his hand. Was that the work he had mentioned? "I'll have an omelet ready in five minutes. Why don't you wash and have a drink?"

He nodded, dropping the suitcase on a kitchen chair before he went into the pantry and poured himself a single Scotch. That was something, he thought, a gesture of trust—the first time Thea had suggested a drink in the last five or six weeks. He went to wash in the study's small bathroom, took off jacket and tie, replaced them with a sweater, listening to the clank of a pan on the stove and the sound of eggs being beaten. The smell of the omelet cooking in butter, and coffee beginning to percolate, spread through the house. Appetizing, he had to admit as he returned to the kitchen. And a normal scene, with Thea at the stove gently shaking the heavy pan, her face intent as she judged the omelet's consistency. Now she was snipping the parsley into its center, working deftly. Tom put out the mats on the kitchen table, napkins and forks, resisted a quick visit to the pantry for another drink. "I'm hungrier than I thought," he told her as she folded the omelet, prepared to slip it onto a plate. We've stepped back into our own lives, he thought—except for the closed doors and windows, except for the suitcase lying on the chair.

Thea had guessed something of his thoughts. "Must we keep everything locked up tight?" she asked as she joined him at the table, with a triumphant omelet, oval and golden, green-flecked with parsley, firm on the outside, slightly *bavant* within.

"It's cozier," he said, evading the true explanation. "Come on, darling, share it with me. You must be hungry too."

"Tony's idea, I suppose," she said, discarding the apron, still thinking of closed windows and locked doors. "But isn't he being overanxious? Poor Tony . . . I suppose that's his way of life—an obsession with danger." She shook her head in amused disagreement, a lock of hair escaping farther over her brow. "We had a telephone call from New York—Brad Gillon—he had just heard." And as Tom dropped his fork and was about to rise, she added quickly, "Brad will call again as soon as he gets home from the office. That should be around eleven o'clock our time. I told him you'd surely be back from Menton by then. It's only half past nine now. So we can eat in peace. What about a mild Camembert to follow—and some

Châteauneuf du Pape? Then fruit and coffee, and you can tell me what happened down in Menton."

"Feed the brute?" Tom asked, but he was actually smiling. He felt better, much better. Nerve ends were being smoothed down. "I'll start telling you right now." So he began a full account of his visit to the town.

Dorothea listened in silence. As she rose to clear the table, she said, "You must look through Chuck's suitcase tonight? Oh, really—" she frowned angrily as she stacked dishes into the washer—"Tony *is* impossible." Hadn't he any imagination? Any sensitivity? "Why all this rush? Couldn't he have left us alone—"

"I'd like to know, myself, just why Rick Nealey wanted to get hold of that suitcase," Tom reminded her. "I must search through it. No way to avoid it, Thea."

"Then let me help," she suggested, glancing worriedly at Tom. He sounded fully in control, but—even with food and wine relaxing him—his face was haggard and drawn as he lifted the suitcase and heaved it onto the table. He opened it, looked down at the neatly packed contents, and hesitated. Slowly, he picked out a small book and two manila envelopes.

"I'll look through the clothes, if you like. The diary—"

"It isn't a diary. Just addresses and engagements." But there were some pages at the back that were headed Memoranda, partly filled by very small writing, close-packed, words abbreviated. "Expenses," was Tom's first judgment. "Chuck always kept a close account of what he spent in restaurants and theaters and—" He stopped short. There were other items, too, and a few notes. "I'll need some time to decipher all this. Let's move into the living room."

"Decipher? Is it in code?" Dorothea asked as she turned off the kitchen lights, checked the door's lock and bolt. Tom was already carrying the suitcase through the pantry. He had it open again, placed on one of the couches to let her more easily examine the clothes, before she reached him.

"No," he answered, as he took the address book and envelopes over to the writing table in the corner of the room. "Not code. Just abbreviations— an old habit of Chuck's. He used to put as much news on a postcard as most people could get into a couple of pages." He sat down, turned on the small light at his elbow, and began reading.

Dorothea looked down at the opened suitcase. She shivered, and then forced herself to start unpacking the dead man's clothes. Unfold, shake, search every pocket, she told herself. It would be a heart-wrenching job. Chuck had crowded a lot into his suitcase, ready for his winter vacation: ski pants and jacket, turtleneck wool sweaters. The only touch of formality was a navy blue blazer, gray flannels, dress loafers, and a white shirt and three ties—for special evenings, presumably. Or perhaps as a concession to Menton, if his stay had lasted a full weekend.

The police, she thought as she unfolded the blazer, had been as expert in packing as Chuck. Everything looked as though it hadn't been touched since he had filled his suitcase to the brim, back in New York. Perhaps the police had only made a cursory examination of the clothes, like a customs officer when nothing roused his suspicions. Why should they bother with clothes, anyway? They were what they seemed: the usual belongings of a young man who had been planning a holiday and not a suicide.

There's nothing here, she decided, finding only a folded handkerchief in one of the blazer's outside pockets. Inside, there was a slit pocket without one bulge showing in the silk lining. Nothing, she thought again, but dutifully searched inside the slit. Her fingers touched something light and thin, and drew out a folded sheet of airmail paper.

She opened it, and found a half page of typing: a letter, dated 26 February, to Paul Krantz, Shandon House, Appleton, N.J. Across its top left-hand corner were the words *Copy to Tom.* And at the bottom of the page, a hurried postscript, in pencil, with today's date—28 February: *Tom—I'll hand this to you as I leave this evening. Didn't want to discuss it directly until you had time to read, digest, and think it over. The original letter is signed, sealed, ready to mail—if Nealey doesn't accept my first alternative. He began by denying everything this morning, then ended—after we had a bitter argument which I won—by a tentative admission of guilt, saying he needed time to consider, etc., etc. I have given him twenty-four hours to resign from Shandon Villa. If he does, then I needn't send the letter to Krantz, and you can destroy your copy. If he doesn't, I'll see you before I leave for Gstaad. Any improvements to suggest on what I've written? As ever, Chuck.*

"Tom!" Dorothea called across the room. "I've found something. In the blazer pocket. A letter to Shandon House, telling them about the Nato—"

"Mentioning Rick Nealey?" Tom had risen, the address book and a newspaper clipping in his hand. Quickly he reached her, seized the typed sheet, and scanned it. Yes, there it was, brief and neat in two decisive sentences: Heinrich Nealey was the only person who knew about Chuck's possession of the entire NATO Memorandum; Heinrich Nealey was the only person who had access to the second and third sections of the Memorandum, on the night of November 23, 1974.

As for the rest of the letter, equally concise, it began with Chuck's admission of responsibility for the removal of the Memorandum from Shandon House. It ended with Chuck's resignation from the institute, together with the statement that he had acted out of conscience and with the belief—which he still held—that the American public had the right to know the full contents of the first part of the NATO Memorandum.

Tom read the postscript again. And again. At last he said, "Chuck never had a chance, had he? He didn't even realize that Nealey was a trained foreign agent—probably thought of him as an American who had been sidetracked into treason. Why else—" Tom looked challengingly at Thea—"did Chuck give him twenty-four hours, why delay in sending the letter when he wrote it on Wednesday?"

Because, she thought unhappily, Chuck was hoping he could avoid mailing the letter. "Perhaps," she said, "he still couldn't believe Rick Nealey had—" quickly she canceled the word *duped* and found a kinder substitute—"betrayed him. Not until he met Nealey face to face."

"But Chuck *knew*, before he met Nealey, that he had been tricked." Tom gave her the small newspaper clipping. "I found this tucked between two of the memo pages. It's from the Washington *Post,* published last Tuesday. One of those 'now it can be revealed' items."

It was a brief report by one of the more sensational, but accurate, columnists that the NATO Memorandum, part of which had been published by a prominent newspaper as a public service on December 3, 1974, had been delivered in its entirety to Soviet authorities. A reliable source at the Pentagon admitted that damage to allied intelligence agencies had been severe, and "in several cases, disastrous to agents in the field."

"Yes," Tom repeated, "he knew he had been tricked. Brad Gillon had told him, and he didn't want to believe it. And then this appeared on Tuesday." Tom put the newspaper clipping back inside Chuck's address book. "By Wednesday Chuck was ready to admit he had been duped. Duped. No other word for it. So he wrote the letter to Paul Krantz, changed his travel plans, came to Menton to confront Nealey—" Tom shook his head. "Good God, what a mess poor old Chuck made of everything! And always so sure he was right. Always so confident he could handle—" He broke off, turned away, said, "Chuck was out of his league."

Dorothea began packing the last clothes back into place. "First alternative," she said reflectively. "What did he mean by that? It was in the postscript, remember?"

As if I'll ever forget that postscript, Tom thought. Chuck, still vacillating, trying to show he could be tough. And would he have handed me that letter to Krantz if Nealey had come to him this afternoon, accepted his terms? No, possibly not. Chuck would have taken the letter out of the blazer pocket, destroyed it, persuaded himself there was no longer any need to disturb me about it. And our talk together would have been nothing but evasions and reassurances.

"Tom—" Dorothea was saying, her eyes wide with anxiety as they studied his face.

"'If Nealey doesn't accept my first alternative,'" Tom quoted back exactly. "It's a reference to some jottings he made as a memo in his engagement diary. Talking points with Nealey, I suppose. He was nervous—" The telephone rang. "Here, take it," Tom said, giving her the little diary, pointing to the page, and hurrying to answer the call in his study.

Dorothea looked at the few lines of small writing. *Alternatives: Either N. resigns, removes self from Shandon Villa or any govt. or official posts, or I send letter to Krantz at Shandon House, including statements for necessary authorities.*

Chuck was always hoping, Dorothea thought, that his ex-friend Nealey would accept the facts, disappear gracefully, cause no more trouble for anyone. And spare Chuck himself the necessity of resigning, of publicly admitting— Oh, Chuck, she thought in despair, why didn't you go to Paul Krantz as soon as Brad Gillon had talked with you? Why did you believe a newspaper columnist more quickly than a friend of your brother's? Everything would have been over by this time: Nealey dealt with, and you—yes, I know you'd have lost your job, but you'd still be alive.

Tom came back into the room. "That was Brad. Wanted to fly over here and help in any way. But I told him to stay in New York. There's a job for him to do—Tony's idea, actually—concentrating on Nealey's New York girl friend and the phone calls made from her apartment. Nealey may just have slipped up there. I don't think there's much of a chance, though. He's a wary devil. Still, sometimes they make mistakes. And every little—"

"But haven't we got enough on Rick Nealey now?"

Tom took Chuck's engagement diary from her, folded the letter to Krantz around it, placed them together behind the clock on the mantelpiece. "Your hands feel like ice," he was saying worriedly. "Better get upstairs and put some warm clothes on. Or why not go to bed? I'll join you as soon as Tony calls."

"I couldn't sleep."

"Then find a sweater and I'll light the fire." He began striking matches.

Dorothea moved toward the hall. It would take more than a fire and a warm sweater to get this chill out of her heart, she thought. "But we *do* have proof now, don't we?"

"About Nealey?" Tom watched the first flames curl round the twists of paper, catch the kindling. "We have nothing that Tony and Brad didn't already know. There's no proof that Nealey *is* a KGB agent. Not a shred of hard evidence." He remembered Tony's frustration this afternoon. Now he was swallowing the same bitter brew.

"You mean," said Dorothea, scandalized, angry, "he could get away with all this?"

"Darling, go upstairs and put some sensible clothing on your frozen back."

"It isn't right, it isn't just—"

"It seldom is," said Tom. "Upstairs, Thea!"

When she came down again, dressed in wool pants and heavy sweater, the logs were flaring, two glasses of brandy had been poured, and the room was darkened except for one small table lamp.

"Where's the suitcase?" she asked.

"In the hall closet." And let's not talk about it, Tom's voice seemed to say. He drew her down beside him on the couch and handed her a brandy. "We'll soon get you warm, my girl. I was beginning to think you had gone to bed after all." He tightened his arm around her shoulders, drawing her close, tried to relax and forget problems and worries in the gentle peace of this green and gold room. But he kept thinking about the information from Brad Gillon which he'd pass on to Tony when his call came through. A small item—and not worth mentioning to Thea, building up her expectations only to have them choked by more disappointment. But the small item was interesting enough to keep his mind harking back to Brad's voice: "And tell Tony that the long job of examining the pages of the Memorandum is almost complete. There was a jumble of fingerprints, but the experts have managed to isolate a few examples. They've got a couple—thumb and forefinger, at the top corner of two pages in Section Three of the Memorandum—which they haven't identified as yet." As yet . . . But the fingerprints could belong to Chuck, and that would land us right back at the beginning. "What delayed you upstairs, anyway?" Eleven forty on the mantelpiece clock. Tony's call should be coming through soon.

"I just had to tidy the bathroom—I left it in such a mess when I heard the car returning."

"You didn't open that damned window to air the place, did you?"

She almost had, and then remembered Tom's warnings and left it closed. The window was one of Solange Michel's brilliant notions. It was placed along the back of the tub, giving a daytime view of the hillside framed by the wisteria outside that climbed up and around to reach the overhang of roof. For modesty's sake, when darkness came and the bathroom lights were on, the heavy silk shower curtains could be drawn all around the tub, encasing it like a four-poster bed. "Too much trouble," she admitted. To reach the window, she would have had to step into the bath and get all those heavy folds of curtain drawn back. "I thought this wasn't the night to risk a displaced vertebra. When do you expect Tony's call? Do you think he'll have any further news?"

"I don't know." He cut off any speculations and rising hope on that subject by predicting, "Someone's going to break their neck in that tub."

"But it has the most beautiful view. You can sit in it and look out at—"

"Bulldozers and condominiums?"

Solange had never envisioned that. Dorothea laughed, and said, "Poor Solange."

"Poor Maurice. How the hell does he stand all her high-falutin ideas?" It was good to hear that soft laugh, Tom thought: she's relaxed and warm and she'll even sleep tonight, once Tony calls and we get upstairs. (No place for a telephone in any bedroom had been another of Solange's ardent beliefs.)

"But the effect *is* attractive," Dorothea said, coming to Solange's defense.

"Give me comfort, any old—" Tom stopped short, his body stiffening. "What was that?"

Dorothea felt a current of cold air circle around her bare ankles. "That," she said, dropping her voice, "could have been my omelet pan. I left it in the sink and someone has just put his foot in it."

"Coming through the window?"

"It's open. I can feel a draught—"

Tom put a finger across her lips, set down his brandy glass, drew her quietly to her feet. He picked up a poker. "Leave by the terrace, get down to the nursery and waken Auguste. Tell him to call the police."

"Not Tony?"

"Don't know his number. Quick!" He was listening intently as he talked. Yes, a second sound, muffled but stumbling, came from the direction of the kitchen. He pushed her toward the French windows.

"And you?"

"Get the police," he urged.

She pulled aside the long curtains just enough to let her open a window and step outside. A hand came out of the darkness, gripped her shoulder, and threw her back across the threshold. She half fell, regained her balance, and then—as the man followed her into the room—retreated in panic toward Tom.

The man was saying, "No violence, *monsieur*. One movement from you, and my men will shoot both of you."

And Tom, halfway to the window, the poker raised, froze in his tracks as he glanced back over his shoulder and saw, at the doorway, two other men with pistols drawn. Dorothea reached him, stood close beside him. He heard her quick intake of breath as she looked in horror at the two men now advancing into the room. Black ski-masks over hair and face, gashes of white skin at eyes and mouth; black coverall suits, tight over lean bodies; black gloves and rubber-soled shoes: completely anonymous, and because of that, more menacing. He caught her hand, gave it a reassuring grip, thought a hundred wild thoughts, and felt the despair of total helplessness.

Twenty-one

For a long minute, nothing moved. The two black figures in their grotesque masks had halted. paying no attention to Dorothea or Tom. Their white slits of eyes were on the man who had stepped inside the French window. He preferred the shadows. Certainly he wasn't risking one step nearer the light of the table lamp beside the couch, although his identity was disguised by a nondescript dark coat, a black silk scarf loosely covering his chin and mouth, and a hat that was pulled well down over his brow. About my height, almost six feet, Tom noted; but of heavier build—powerful shoulders. Even the voice, distorted by the scarf, will be hard to recognize again. But he's the boss, there's no doubt about that. Those two others are waiting for their orders. He will make the decisions.

And he did. "Begin!" he was saying in French. "You upstairs." He nodded to the taller of his two subordinates. To the other, "You—this floor!" He drew a revolver from his coat pocket, folded his arms, kept his aim directed at Tom and Dorothea.

"Chuck's case?" Dorothea asked Tom softly as she turned her head away from the watching man.

"Yes. And don't let him think you understand French."

She murmured, "That will be easy."

"No talking!" the man commanded in French. "Drop that poker. Drop it. At once! Do you hear?"

Tom kept his grip on it, said to Dorothea, "They'll speak more freely if they think we don't understand what they're—"

"Silence!" Again in French. "Or do you want me to let a bullet give you orders?"

Tom paid no attention. "You're doing fine, darling," he told her. And it was true. The initial tremble in her hand was gone. Panic and fear might still be there, but her face showed little sign of them. She stared at the man uncomprehendingly.

He broke into English. "No talking! Drop that poker. At once!"

Tom obeyed, and took Dorothea into his arms. "You've no objection to this?" he asked as a mild distraction from the poker—he had let it fall as near him as he could risk. "My wife hasn't been feeling too—"

"Quiet!"

"May she sit down?" That could get Thea out of range.

"Stay as you are. Both of you!"

So they stayed. Overhead, light footsteps searched through the bedrooms.

On the ground floor, light footsteps padded through study and dining room. Drawers and doors were being opened and shut. But once they had found what they wanted, what then? They will know we've learned too much, Tom realized. Why the hell didn't I leave everything in the suitcase? Then we could have seemed ignorant; then we could have stayed alive. How will they fake an explanation for our deaths? Something that could be accepted as purely accidental, a tragic occurrence. But what?

The masked figure who had been searching upstairs was the first to return. Nothing and no one, he reported. Only one bedroom in use, along with its adjacent bathroom—an interior one. The rest of the upper floor, unoccupied: drawers and wardrobes empty, no closets. No luggage. No guests. No servant. These two were living here quite alone.

"And so, no interruptions." The man by the window unfolded his arms, slipped his revolver back into his pocket. "Start searching this room. There may be closets behind the wood paneling."

The telephone rang.

"Let it ring!" he yelled, so that even his man still at work in the study could hear his command. "Don't cut the wire. People are living here. You understand?" Then he fell silent, seemed to be listening intently. "No telephone upstairs?" he asked as the ringing ended.

"None."

"All right. Get on with your search." He lifted back the cuff of his coat, studied his watch, compared the time with the clock on the mantelpiece. "Hurry, hurry! And what's this?" he demanded of his second assistant, who had just entered from the study holding a sheaf of papers.

"Tom—your manuscript—" Dorothea said, her voice rising in indignation. "What do they want with—"

Tom silenced her with a kiss on her cheek and a murmur in her ear. "Show them the suitcase. Get into the hall. And up the stairs—"

Her eyes questioned him.

"Lock yourself in the bathroom and—"

The telephone rang again. And kept on ringing, making his whisper inaudible. Had she understood?

Dorothea tightened her hand on Tom's arm. She raised her voice to be heard clearly above the ringing phone. "That manuscript is of no interest to you. But if you are looking for something special, then tell me what it is. I'll show you where you can find it." She took several steps away from Tom.

"We shall find it," the man by the window told her, riffling through the pages of Tom's manuscript. "Get back, there!"

Dorothea didn't retreat. "Have you the time to search all through the hidden corners of this old house? It could take you hours."

That's my Thea, Tom thought, smarter than I am. I'd have blurted out "suitcase," and let them realize we knew more about them than was good for us. And there's Thea, wide-eyed and innocent, nudging them into the first move. But hurry, Thea, for God's sake, hurry. That guy in the ski-mask who is thumping on the paneling is just about to reach the mantelpiece. And behind that damned clock he'll find everything they are searching for.

The telephone ended its twentieth ring.

"Hours," repeated Dorothea.

The man actually hesitated. He said carefully, "We want the valuables you have stored in a suitcase."

"A suitcase?"

Thea, my darling, we haven't time to waste. Tom eyed the masked man, who was now only six feet away from the mantelpiece.

"Oh," said Thea, seemingly enlightened, "you mean this suitcase?" And now she was walking rapidly toward the hall.

"Stop!" The manuscript was thrown onto the floor, scattering widely. "You tell us where it is."

"I'll have to show you." Thea walked on. "A difficult closet to find. The owner of this house simply hates doors that look like doors." She was in the hall now. The two masked figures ran after her, caught her arms. "How can I show you—" she began angrily, struggling to free herself.

"Let her go," the master's voice called out, and his two obedient servants released their grip. "Get that suitcase."

Dorothea pointed to the *trompe-l'oeil* panel. Idiots, she thought, they must have passed this closet, never even recognized the baroque symbolism of plumed hats and draped capes and silver-headed canes. "Just press your hand against that section—oh, stupids, where the grease marks are—and why the hell don't you speak English?" She pressed for them, just enough to let the panel open slightly, and drew back to let them finish the job. The staircase was behind her. She turned and ran.

There was a shout from the living room. One of the men left the closet, started after her. But she reached the bedroom door, slamming it in his face as she raced for the bathroom. She had its door—heavy, thick, a solid antique of hard oak—locked and bolted before he reached it.

She threw a towel into the bath for sure footing, remembered to turn on the faucets in the hand basin to cover any screech the curtains might make as she pulled them partly open—just enough to let her unfasten the sliding windows. The cool night air rushed in, and she stood looking down at the top of an acacia tree, yellow blossoms silvered by the moonlight. Behind her, the angry hammering on the door urged her on.

I can't do it, she thought, I can't. But she sat down on the sill, slid one leg over it, and clutched the side of the window frame. A pause. Then, gingerly, she reached out for the wisteria, slowly slowly until her fingers touched one of its strong ropes. Her hand closed around it, and tugged. It gave a little, then held firm. If a wisteria could tear a roof apart, then surely it can support you, she told herself. And if not—jump for the acacia.

She edged herself along the last few inches of sill, her hand tight on the wisteria. Now her second hand, and her body swinging loose for a wild moment, her legs dangling, shoulders wrenching, and fear screaming silently in her throat. In desperation, she searched for a toehold on the gnarled trunk, found it, and released some of her weight from her arms. Hand over hand, feet blindly testing each twist on the spreading vine, she lowered herself through the fronds of tender leaves and their drooping lanterns of mauve flowers.

She didn't fall until the last three feet, when her arms gave out and she dropped with a jolt. I'm sorry, she told the wisteria and its shredded flowers, as she picked herself up from the ground. She tried to steady herself with a few deep breaths, and began running. But her legs were weak, her feet uncertain. Her pace settled into a stumbling walk.

Did she make it? Tom kept wondering. Did Thea make it? He paid no attention to the suitcase, brought triumphantly into the room. He kept watching the hall, the first few stairs that were visible. He kept listening. There was only the distant sound of heavy beating against solid wood. Then it ceased. But there was no scream, only light footsteps running downstairs. The man tried to be nonchalant. "She shut herself into the bathroom. We might as well leave her there."

"No window?"

"None. I told you. So I locked the bedroom door in case she decided to come out." He held up its key.

"Bedroom windows?"

"Too high—a sheer drop down two stories onto a stone terrace." He pocketed the key and laughed. "A real vixen, who would have thought it?"

"Get on with your job! Search the rest of this room." For nothing except the two envelopes had been found in the suitcase, so far. These were being examined with excessive care, even Chuck's passport, his air-flight tickets, his hotel reservations, a timetable, a letter from a girl in Gstaad. Anything of paper, anything with writing, anything that could conceal between its pages. Two paperbacks were shaken and searched; so were two magazines. The minutes passed; time was awasting.

And now, thought Tom as he felt the rising anger of the leader, things are going to turn ugly. Once that suitcase is emptied, they'll start on me. His one way of escape, through the French windows onto the terrace, was still blocked: two men there, one kneeling as he pulled clothes onto the floor, went through pockets, even linings. And the third man, continuing his slow, methodical search of the room, was at the small table near the mantelpiece: it would be next on his list. The kitchen door was locked. So was the front door, seldom used, double-bolted. In any case, a bullet in his back would catch him before he could even reach the hall. The poker—no chance with that against three pistols.

And then, he thought, why not use some direct shock? Anything to throw that son of a bitch off balance?

Tom said, "If you're looking for an engagement book, you'll find it on the mantelpiece. There's a letter there too, which might interest you."

The man looked away from the suitcase at his feet, stared at Tom.

"It's a copy," Tom went on, "and there are four other copies in various hands. Did Rick Nealey actually think he could wipe the slate clean by this little attempt at robbery? He's a fool. And so are you. He's a marked man. He has been under surveillance for the last three months."

The man at the window hadn't moved, hadn't spoken. And then, from the thin black figure now searching the mantelpiece, there came "Here's something." His gloved hands were holding up a small book and a folded sheet of paper for all to see.

The man at the window came to life, moved forward, arm outstretched, eyes on the letter.

Tom made a sudden dive for the poker, swung it sharply against the man's shins, threw it at Ski-mask still on his knees by the suitcase, wrenched the window open, and side-stepped onto the terrace. A bullet passed close. He raced for the lemon trees. As he leaped into their shadows, two men rushed out of the house, revolvers aimed blindly. And then, suddenly, a loud report that echoed over the hillside. That, thought Tom, was no pistol shot.

He didn't wait to see the effect of it on the terrace, where three men now stood together. He seized that moment of their surprise, and ran for the nearest olive tree, dodged behind it, waited for another bullet to sing past his shoulders.

But there were no more bullets.

He heard quickening feet, heels slipping in haste over gravel and earth. They were on the driveway, heading down to the road. And the nursery. And Thea?

Tom left the shelter of the olive tree, began running.

Twenty-two

TONY LAWTON MADE a high-speed journey through the sleeping town. As he left Menton and passed through the lower spread of Roquebrune, he assessed the time it had taken him to come this far from Georges's hideaway. No, it couldn't have been done faster than this: three breakneck minutes down the stone steps, another three to the car, including the brief drive along the *quai;* less than a minute to zoom through the empty tunnel; three more for the next four kilometers through deserted back streets and abandoned avenues. Making ten, to this point. Plus another two, at full tilt up this little hill, and he'd be arriving at the Michel driveway by eleven or twelve minutes past midnight. Not bad, even if distances were short in this part of the world. And impossible, if there had been any traffic on the road. Bless all these sweet obliging people who tucked themselves into bed by midnight.

There were always afterthoughts, of course. It could be that the Kelsos had given up the idea that he would call this late, were already deep in sleep—no telephone upstairs, he remembered, and an old house with thick walls and heavy doors. Yes, it could just be that he had come chasing out here on a wild surmise. And yet, whenever he hadn't listened to the alarm bell that sounded off in his subconscious mind, he had always regretted it. Tonight the alarm had been sharp and clear. Foolish or not, here I come, he thought, and eased his speed, with the nursery just ahead, preparing for a sharp left turn into the driveway.

He began the turn, saw a car, a dark solid mass drawn close to the mimosa trees. He swerved back, traveled a hundred yards farther up the road until he could make a left into Auguste's compound—three small houses grouped near the nursery's own entrance. He brought the Renault to a halt right under Auguste's bedroom window.

He hadn't risked a short blast on the horn—no point in giving any warning to that car down at the Michel entrance—but surely the slight screech of brakes, as he pulled up to avoid the truck and the light delivery van at one side of the yard, must have roused someone around here. It had: a dog barked, and was silenced. To make sure Auguste hadn't turned over and gone back to sleep, Tony got out of the car and scooped up a handful of coarse gravel to toss at the windowpane, knocked on the door, rattled its handle, and started the dog barking again. And again it was silenced. Above him the bedroom curtains parted. A face looked out. Tony stood back to let Auguste have a clear view of him in the moonlight.

The face gazed down. Tony waved his arms. The face disappeared. A brief wait, the door opened, and he found himself looking into the double barrels of a shotgun.

"Old friend, don't you know me?"

Auguste stared. Then his arm relaxed. Three years it had been since Tony used to visit this yard, sit on that bench under the trees, and listen to Auguste's stories about the Resistance. He laid the shotgun against the door, called a few words back over his shoulder, as he stepped outside, his flannel shirt half tucked into trousers, suspenders dangling, boots unlaced. A broad smile creased his weather-tanned cheeks. There was a firm handshake, a warm greeting thumped on Tony's back. But the shrewd face was speculating hard.

Tony wasted no time on explanations. "There's a car stationed inside the Michel driveway. My headlights picked out one man at the wheel. So it isn't two lovebirds having—"

"Hand me that gun, Lucien," Auguste told the boy who stood just within the doorway. "Tell your mother to call the police." He turned back to Tony. "There has been thieving going on. Yes, even here it has started. They come by night, and load up. Plants taken and—"

"No, no—I think the trouble is up at the Michel house."

"Trouble?" Auguste demanded, alert as a hawk, his beak of a nose jutting out, his dark eyes narrowing as if they were ready to swoop on their prey. "Burglars?"

"That's what I'm going to find out."

"Not alone!" Auguste's son had been quick. He returned now with a sweater added to his shirt and a heavy jacket for his father. Auguste drew it on, zipped it to the neck, said, "Now we go together, eh?"

"Could use some help," Tony admitted. "But first—block off the entrance to the Michel driveway."

"With what?"

"The truck."

Auguste considered the idea, didn't like it much. His truck was valuable property.

"I'll drive it," the boy volunteered eagerly.

Lucien must be sixteen now, but he was thin, all his growth going into his height. One of Auguste's older sons, huskier, would be a safer choice. "Better wake one of your brothers—"

"Them!" said Lucien scornfully. "They'd sleep through an earthquake."

Recently married, both of them, Tony remembered. Lucien was making the decision for him, anyway. He was already halfway to the truck.

Tony, starting along the nearest path, called back, "Once you park it, get the hell out. And wait here for the police." Lucien looked disappointed, but he waved and climbed into the driver's seat.

"He can handle it," said Auguste, still frowning, as he caught up with Tony and settled into a quick jog.

"There will be no damage to the truck," Tony assured him. "And if there is, I'll pay for it," he added with a grin. He pointed obliquely across the nursery, to its far corner where the flowers ended and the rough ground of the hillside began. "We'll head up there." Near enough to the driveway without actually being in it; and, to be hoped, not noticeable. A quiet approach to the Michel house could be half the battle.

"This way," said Auguste, catching Tony by the arm, guiding him onto another path between the rows of flower beds and plastic-covered greenhouses. It was a zigzag course, and Tony might have found himself being forced to retrace his steps if Auguste hadn't been there to lead. The moonlight had become less dependable: cloud cover was beginning to move in from the sea. In another half hour there would be nothing but deep shadow spreading over the hillside.

And what about Lucien? Tony worried. The truck had moved out of the yard, and must be running downhill, but so quietly that he couldn't hear it. Had Lucien, the young idiot, put it into neutral? The next thing they'd hear would be a crash against the stone wall at the entrance to the driveway, and they'd have to veer off course to pick up the pieces: one truck, with gears stripped and fenders smashed, and Lucien jammed up against the wheel. But as they reached the end of their lope through the nursery, he heard the loud—but normal—sound of brakes as the truck pulled up; and then dead silence. "He managed it," Tony said, "Lucien actually managed it!"

Auguste only nodded, didn't seem the least astonished. He had halted, his eyes on the hillside. "Someone's out there." He studied the sparse cloud-shadows that blotched the stretch of open ground above them. Scattered boulders and bushes made it difficult to see. Only the Michel house, a dark silhouette, quiet, peaceful, was clearly visible. Auguste crouched low, pulled Tony down beside him, listened intently. "One man. Running."

"Stumbling," Tony whispered back. "He's having a hard time." Then they both saw him slide down onto the surer surface of the driveway, come running—slowly, blindly, too worried about his footing to notice either them or the car down by the gate. Quickly, Tony glanced in its direction. The driver was out, staring at the truck that had blocked his exit; now he swung around to face the running man.

"A woman," Tony said, rising to intercept her. Dorothea . . . He ran, but she was making one last desperate effort to reach the acacias. And then her head came up as she halted, suddenly aware of the car, of its driver. They stared at each other. She turned and came stumbling back onto the hillside, into Tony's arms.

She cried out in fear, struck him, struggled to free herself, beat weakly at his face with her fists. He caught her wrists, pulled them down, saying, "It's

Tony. Just me—Tony. Dorothea—it's Tony!" Suddenly her rigid body relaxed, sagging against his. He held her tightly, felt her flinch with pain as
his hand grasped her shoulder.

Auguste was beside them. "What about him?" He pointed his shotgun
toward the car.

Dorothea was saying, her breath coming in painful gasps, "The police—
call the police."

"It's done," Tony told her. "How many at the house?"

"Three. All armed. Tom only has a—"

The silence of the night was cut through by a pistol shot. It came from
the house.

"Tom—" Dorothea cried out, "Tom—"

"No, no," Tony tried to calm her. "It need not be." But his own heart sank.

"I'll deal with this one," said Auguste, grim-faced, and moved toward
the car. Its driver had only hesitated for the fraction of a second after the
revolver had been fired. He was already on the run, dodging downhill
through the olive trees, leaping from terrace to terrace. Auguste cursed, could
only aim the shotgun blindly into the darkness, and fired. "I scared the rascal
off, anyway. Do we go after him?"

"No—up to the house." Tony pushed Dorothea toward the acacias. From
there, she'd find a straight path through the nursery. "You get to Albertine.
The police will soon be there. Tell them about the burglars."

"Burglars?"

"What else?"

She nodded, partly understanding. "But I want to come with—"

"No. Get off this hillside!" Tony called back to her, already on his way.
He was running hard now, keeping to the driveway for the sake of speed.
Behind him Auguste's heavy footsteps tried to catch up.

Dorothea hesitated, attempted to follow, gave up after the first slow steps.
She turned away, began walking toward the acacias and the abandoned car.
Rick Nealey . . . It had been Nealey whom she had clearly seen in that one
terrifying moment when she thought she was trapped after all. But now he
had vanished. There was only the dark green car, its door still open, and
behind it—strangely—a truck drawn across the entrance to the driveway.
From the Roquebrune road she could hear a singsong siren drawing nearer
and nearer. They are all too late, she thought, and burst into tears. They
scalded her cheeks, searching out the scratches, stinging them, reminding
her of the wisteria. The pain in her shoulder screamed. And for the first
time, she became aware of a bruise on her hip, a dull steady ache that sent
her limping into the nursery.

All too late, she thought again, all of us.

Another forty yards, Tony was calculating as he drew out Georges's neat
little Beretta from his belt, and we'll be at the lemon trees; I can take the
French windows, Auguste the rear of the house. And at that moment he
heard Auguste's warning shout. In front of him, suddenly appearing around
the curve of the driveway, came a tight cluster of three dark figures. They
halted as abruptly as he did.

Surprise only lasted for one intense moment. Tony dived for the bank of grass beside him, chanced a shot, and missed. The three had already separated, two scattering onto the hillside above the driveway, with Auguste after them. The third man had darted into the row of olive trees on his right.

Tony picked himself up, ready to follow, and dropped once more as a shot came from behind one of the trees. Only one shot. Perhaps the man was in full flight, didn't want to give away his direction by any more firing. But he was bound to circle around, head for the car. Tony got up, quickly scanning the darkening terraces that descended, row upon row, toward Cap Martin. The moon was failing him: she had retreated into a swarm of clouds, dimming all chances of seeing the fugitive for at least several minutes. The car, Tony warned himself: that was to be the quick getaway. He began running toward it.

From above him, on the hillside, came the blast of a shotgun. Tony smiled, kept on his way. There were lights now, near the Roguebrune road. And voices. The truck was still there. So was the car, its door wide open. The minute he saw it, he stopped running, his angry eyes searching the terraced slopes of olive trees that fell toward that heavy dense band of blackness, the thick woods encircling the bottom of this hill. "Damn it to bloody everlasting hell," Tony said aloud. That car, abandoned—the man had seen it, veered off.

Behind him, on the driveway, there was a slip and a stumble. He whirled round.

"Hey, don't shoot at me!" a voice yelled.

"Tom?"

"Tom."

Thank God. Tony's head jerked back to the olive trees.

"Thea?" asked Tom as he slid to a halt beside Tony.

"Okay."

"Okay?"

"Safe." Tony's eyes never left scanning the terraces below him. "One of them is down there. The others took to the hill with Auguste at their heels."

"The two in ski-masks?"

So that's why they looked like a couple of black skeletons. "Yes."

"Then that's the guy we really need," Tom said, pointing toward the terraces. "He was in charge. Gave the instructions, knew what he wanted."

Tony said quickly, "Get down to the gate. Tell the police to put out an alarm, search the woods, check the Cap Martin roads. Two men headed there."

"Two?"

"The driver of the car—ran off—deserted—wouldn't like to be in his—" Tony felt sudden hope; and then major disappointment. No, that had only been a shift of cloud over the moon, a swaying of branches touched by the early morning breeze. "Get moving, Tom!"

But it's useless, he realized as Tom raced away. Only shadows out there, shadows and twisted trunks that looked like crouching men. You could call it luck, he thought of the armed man's escape, but he's the kind that makes his luck: instant decision, no hesitations. I must have been an inviting target, standing up here on the driveway; but he resisted the impulse to fire, drew no attention to his escape route, and slipped safely away. As for the other one—the driver—I'd like less and less to be in his shoes. Instead of running, he could have got into his car, gunned it uphill to the house, given them warning. They'd all have scattered, and neither Auguste nor I would have glimpsed them. And we'd have found Tom dead—he had seen them at work, had known what they were after—yes, Tom would have been silenced like Chuck. How the devil did he escape, anyway? Or Thea? These amateurs, Tony reflected, shaking his head in wonder.

He stayed where he was, still watching the wide stretch of terraces. The driver must have reached the woods some time ago; but it was always possible that the armed man—the leader of this expedition—was still hiding behind a tree trunk, waiting for all interest to ebb before he risked another step. From the direction of the gate, Tony could hear the truck being moved, and voices raised in urgency. One quick glance reassured him: two policemen had arrived, one of them still listening to Auguste, the other leaving Tom to run back to his Citroën, possibly calling for reinforcements, certainly putting out an alert. At least, Tony decided, some action has been taken, and he went back to watching those damned olive trees.

Tom, and Dorothea limping along with her husband's arm tightly round her waist, came up to join him. In time, he remembered to tuck the Beretta out of sight. "The alarm has gone out," said Tom. "And two more policemen arrived. They've been sent down to the woods—young Lucien is with them to show them the short cuts. And Auguste caught one of the ski-masks—wounded him in the leg. The other is being chased right now by Auguste's two older sons. So relax, Tony, relax." Then Tom's voice began to race with excitement. "That car down there—it's a green Opel, same registration as the one I saw earlier this evening. I now think the guy who ordered everybody around was the one who was driving it then. Same height, same build. Yes, could be."

Tony stared at him. Colonel Boris Gorsky?

Dorothea said, "But he wasn't the driver tonight. That was Rick Nealey. I saw him clearly—just before he ran."

Tony began to smile. The best piece of news I've heard today, he thought. He said gently, "How did you manage to escape?"

"By way of the wisteria." She tried to laugh, and failed.

"And you?" he asked Tom.

"Oh—I sort of threw him off balance."

Gorsky? "How?"

"First, by telling him where he could find Chuck's letter—he didn't even know one existed."

Nor did I, thought Tony. But there's no time now for explanations. "It mentioned Nealey?"

"It nailed him. Then I said there were four copies of it, now in other hands, and that Nealey—" Tom paused. "I blew it, Tony. Sorry. But I had to. No other way out."

"Blew what?"

"Told him that Nealey had been under surveillance for the last three months. Slight exaggeration, of course, like these four copies. Still, it worked. And then I caught him with a poker across the shins, and bolted."

Tony's smile broadened. "Threw him off balance? You yanked the rug right out from under his feet. And you settled Nealey's future, too. Both of you." He kissed Dorothea, clapped Tom's shoulder. They looked puzzled, but he'd explain later, another day, another place. He nodded toward the police car that was starting up the driveway. "They'll want a guided tour and a lot of answers from you. But there's really no need for me to hang around, is there? See you later—when we've all had some sleep."

Dorothea had noticed his second quick look at the approaching car. "Auguste has told them all about you."

"All?"

"You just happened to be passing by. You saw a mysterious Opel in the driveway, you wakened Auguste, and the two of you went after the burglars."

"Burglars," Tom said with amusement.

"And why not? Everybody knows that all Americans are loaded with cash. Think of all the jewels I have hidden away, darling."

She has recovered, thought Tony. He kissed her again, and began moving toward the police car.

"Hey, there—two in a row?" Tom asked with a laugh. Old Tony was going quite emotional tonight. Tom tightened his grip around his wife. "You think Nealey and his friends will be caught?"

The man in the ski-mask, possibly. Gorsky? Improbable. "Nealey will be dealt with," Tony called back over his shoulder. Of that, he was sure. He was still smiling when he reached the police car. "Good morning, officers," he began briskly, and then stared as Auguste, ending a long description of tonight's skirmish, got out to join him.

"That's all," Auguste told them. "Monsieur Lawton could add nothing."

One of the policemen wasn't so sure. "I believe two bullets were fired. Two pistol shots, *monsieur*?"

"Yes," Tony said, and could only hope the Beretta's small bulk wouldn't show through his jacket. "And two misses."

"You were the target?"

"I thought so."

Auguste broke in with "Instead of hugging the ground to dodge a couple of bullets, you'd have done better following me. I caught one of them, lost the other. Together we would have captured them both. Now let's go. I'll guide you back through the nursery. Don't want any more feet trampling over my freesias." He looked at the policeman and tilted his head.

Both of the officers smiled. They seemed to know Auguste well. Tony seized the relaxed moment to say, "If you need me, gentlemen, I am staying at the Alexandre."

"Your passport?" the younger policeman asked.

"The concierge still has it. I arrived only this morning."

"How long do you expect to stay?"

"Two or three days. I'm on a sailing holiday along the Côte d'Azur."

"Be so good as to notify us when you leave. We may need you to identify anyone we apprehend. Could you recognize the man who shot at you?"

"By height and build, only. And that isn't too certain. The moon was clouded—only patches of light."

Auguste said impatiently, "I've told you all that, Louis."

Louis had one last question. "Do you own a revolver, Monsieur Lawton?"

"Yes."

"Let me see it."

"It's in London, actually—in a bedroom table drawer."

Auguste said, "Much good it did you tonight." He grinned for Louis. "And you know where to find me if you need any more information." That raised a small laugh. The two officers saluted informally, and the car drove on.

I hope, Tony thought, that Tom will keep his mouth shut about finding me with a gun in my hand. Yes, he's got enough sense not to complicate life unnecessarily. "That's a smart young man," he told Auguste.

"Both good lads. They know me well. But why did he ask about your pistol?"

"He may have heard the two shots from a distance. One might have seemed louder, heavier, than the other."

"Were they?"

"Yes." Tony unbuttoned his jacket, showed the Beretta briefly. "Belongs to my friend who owns the Renault I am driving."

"And you happened to find the gun in the glove compartment? You'd have been a fool to leave it there, when you were going out to hunt down trouble. But you could have told Louis—"

"And used up everyone's valuable time? That doesn't catch any of your burglars, Auguste."

"Do you have a gun in London?"

"Of course. I kept strictly to the truth. Always do, with policemen. And with my friends."

They had entered the nursery, walking slowly along the paths, now dark, between the soft fragrances and muted colors of the flower beds. "Two shots of different caliber," Auguste ruminated, and smiled. "Yes, that Louis is smart. His father was a policeman too, and in the Resistance, fought alongside me against the Nazis. It was on a night like this, just about the same time of year, we helped guide a small group of Americans and Canadians—Special Forces, landing ahead of Tassigny's five divisions—right up through the mountains behind Menton. Didn't use the road, of course, kept to the hillsides all the way to Castellar, rough country, not like this but rough as the devil's backside. Now, that was a real battle. The Germans were deep inside the mountain, quadrilateral fortifications. But we took it. Yes, a real battle. There were twenty American and Canadian graves up at Castellar, and many of ours." Auguste shot a quick glance at Tony. "And now, when I tell my sons about it, they only count the lives that were wasted. Why not wait for the troops to come in, with tanks and artillery? That's what they ask." Auguste shook his head, a mixture of anger and sadness. "But there was no waste. Many of us died, all the rest were wounded, we silenced the German guns. They didn't blow the troops to pieces down on the beach, or coming up the pass. Yes, we won that battle."

"You won that war."

Auguste said nothing more. Then, as they entered the yard, his step became as brisk as his good-by handshake. "Next time you choose to visit, make it in daylight." A parting nod, and he was on his way to bed.

"I will," Tony promised. "And tell Lucien he did a fine job."

And that reminded Auguste. "If you see him down by the road," he called back from the doorway, "send him packing up here. He has a full day's work ahead of him tomorrow."

The door closed, and Tony stepped into the Renault. For a moment, his eyes rested on the glove compartment. It was just possible that the alert was in force, and there could be police checks on all drivers and their cars in this area tonight. He opened the compartment and placed Georges's Beretta inside, everything nicely legal, for the ride to Menton.

Quietly, he started the car, drove out of the yard and down the Roquebrune road, back to the Old Town.

Twenty-three

THE ALL-NIGHT VIGIL ended at five o'clock, when the final message was received from Brussels.

"All set," Georges said, coming over to the bed where Tony had been having one of his periodic cat naps.

At once Tony was awake and on his feet. "They've agreed?"

"More or less. Some advice, of course. And one alteration."

"What?" Tony shot out.

"Their cabin cruiser is in the fourteen-meter—"

"Forty-six feet, almost? That's something. How many knots?"

"Over thirty."

"That's about thirty-five miles an hour, more than three times the speed of the *Sea Breeze*," said Tony. "So what's the reason for any change in plans?"

"The length and bulk of the *Aurora*."

"I like her name." But Tony was beginning to see the problem.

"She has ample room for our party and her three-man crew, but that size would be difficult to maneuver inside the anchorage. It might be a very delayed departure."

Tony nodded. The harbor was small, and jammed with boats. "So what do they suggest?"

"That we board the *Aurora* where she is now docked—in the *port privé* at the other end of Garavan Bay. It's big, three times as big as the harbor. Can hold eight hundred boats in its private anchorage, another two hundred in the public section. Actually, it's more convenient for us—quicker to reach from Bill's house."

Tony's voice was clipped. "And just how do we persuade Parracini to accept this changer?" Our whole plan will end before it begins, he thought, if Parracini's suspicions start being ruffled.

Georges laughed. "That, they said, was for you to work out."

"Very funny." For once, Tony's sense of humor failed him. "And what about that escort?" he asked, bracing himself for more complications.

"Provided."

"We got it?" Tony's surprise changed to delight. Old friend Jimmy Hartwell had really pushed and pulled. "We actually—"

"Yes, you got what you wanted."

The two men looked at each other. "Then let's see what we can do with it," said Tony. Together, smiling broadly, they moved over to the table.

The next half hour was an organized jumble of big and little things to be done, all of them necessary. While Georges dismantled his equipment and turned it back into innocuous objects, Tony burned the clutter of notes and scraps of paper in a metal basin after he had memorized some last details—the *Aurora's* exact position in the *port privé*; the name of Vincent, their chief contact in the crew; radio signals for communication. Coffee was brewed and drunk while they drew up their timetable for this morning. They washed and smartened up, finished the coffee, and went over their schedule once more.

Outside, it was still dark, with only a hint of diffused light spreading from the east. "Time to call Emil," Tony said. "We'll give him a predawn swim."

"You mean you are actually serious about—"

"Better to look foolish than be stupid." Tony pulled out the transceiver and called in the *Sea Breeze*. Emil was awake. A peaceful night—no actual approach made to the boat. Two men had patrolled the mole. They had been quite obvious, making no effort to hide themselves from the *Sea Breeze*. Two of ours?

"Yes, could be. Possibly Bill's men trying to reassure you. And you heard nothing at all? Not even the lapping of the mere?"

Emil, not a literary type, was puzzled but definite. "Nothing."

"All right. Let's take out some insurance. Get into your wet-suit and slip over the side. Examine the hull—keel—rudder—every damn thing under the water line. How quickly can you do all that? Twenty minutes? Less? Good: get started before the light strengthens. Call us back."

Tony switched off, saw Georges's amused eye studying him. "Need something to do? Then listen to the weather reports." He himself walked restlessly around the room and then went out onto the small balcony for a few breaths of cold dank air. The sky was slowly turning a bleached black, banded with gray at the horizon. The last of night lingered over the lighted harbor. There the *Sea Breeze* nestled cozily with the other boats, all at rest, everything tranquil. Looking down at her, watching for any sign of Emil—nothing to see, Emil was good at his job, as slippery as a seal—Tony was already working out his own immediate problem: Parracini's tender suspicions.

As the gray of the horizon softly, surely seeped into the sky like water over a riverbank, Tony returned to the room. "It looks calm enough out there. Some clouds, but nothing threatening. What's the forecast?"

"Bright sun. Cool. And possibly heavy winds from the southeast this afternoon. But we'll be in Nice before then."

"With luck." Tony picked up the telephone and dialed Bill's number—not his private line, just the ordinary one that would ring at his bedside and rouse him from sleep. He kept his call brief, once he had Bill fully awake. "I'll drop in to see you this morning. In half an hour? No, nothing is wrong:

everything's fine. I just want to go over your timetable, make sure that it matches ours. Meet me down at the gates, will you? A walk in the garden will be just what I need to work up an appetite for breakfast. Yes, at the gates. See you."

"Cryptic," said Georges. "Giving nothing away. Just like your call to him last night."

"Had to be."

"Why? Do you think his telephones are bugged? But Bill's no fool. He makes a regular check on them—a matter of routine."

"And on nothing else?"

"The whole place was thoroughly gone over before Bill and Nicole arrived there. Oh, come on, Tony. Parracini must know about Bill's regular checks—he wouldn't risk a bug in a phone."

"What about a small listening device in the calendar on Bill's desk—or the blotter? Or how about a lamp bulb with sensitive filaments, near every telephone?"

"Very specialized stuff. Where would Parracini get—oh, I see." Georges was conscious of Tony's raised eyebrow. "From his kind friends in Menton? But still . . . Does Parracini know enough about installing sophisticated devices? That wasn't his line of business."

"It doesn't take much know-how to screw a light bulb into a socket."

"No, but it takes someone constantly monitoring. Parracini couldn't sit around in his room all day, listening—"

"There could be a monitor installed in a nearby house on the Garavan hillside."

It was a disturbing thought. Georges had no comment.

Tony said, "Look—they must be guarding Parracini as closely as possible. He's too important. And they've had time to arrange all necessary precautions."

Georges nodded. "One thing has been puzzling me. Surely he must have radio contact with Gorsky; so why did he have to meet him? Why even meet Nealey at the market yesterday morning?"

"I've been thinking about that too. There could be two very different reasons why he had to meet either of them. Nealey—because Nealey was handing him something more solid than a verbal message: one of your sophisticated gadgets, perhaps? Gorsky—because Parracini had been moved out of his cozy corner over the garage into a room next to Bernard's and Brigitte's. Perhaps he could only risk a very quick message on his transceiver, giving time and place for a meeting and important instructions. Possible?"

"Very possible." Georges smiled as he added, "How he must have cursed Bill for moving him into the main house. No privacy for anyone these days."

And then all their speculations ended with Emil's signal. Tony answered it.

Emil's usually placid voice was uneven and hurried. Tony listened quietly. "Put it together again, can you? Just as it was. Stow it on deck— some place unnoticeable but reachable. Don't worry, the *Sea Breeze* will be safe as long as she is in harbor. So there's no danger to anyone. I'll join you well before eleven. Get ready to move out by then, Emil. Yes, you and I—we can handle her, can't we?" A laugh that was genuine, a cheerful good-by, and the exchange was over.

Georges said slowly, "He found something?"

Tony nodded. "It was taped to the starboard side of the hull, near the engines. He detached it, examined it. There was no time mechanism, just a remote-control device."

"And you told him to put the damned thing together—"

"We can always heave it overboard once we are far enough offshore."

"Now, Tony," Georges began warningly.

"Mustn't keep Bill waiting." Tony looked at his watch, moved toward the door. "All clear here?" Together they gave the room one last quick check.

"All clear." Georges locked the door behind them, and they made their way down the staircase into the narrow street.

The Renault began climbing the twists and turns up the hill above Garavan Bay. It was a heavily wooded area, with a spread of houses and gardens hidden by walls and trees, dark, silent, mysterious in the somber light between night and day. Bill's place was as secluded as the others on this narrow road, but he was standing outside the gates to make sure Tony could identify it easily. So Georges's arguments were cut short. Why, he had insisted, couldn't he join Emil and Tony on the *Sea Breeze* once he had brought Gerard and the others from Nice, seen them safely aboard the *Aurora*? By that time he would have briefed them thoroughly.

"No," Tony said as they came round one of the sharp turns and saw Bill ahead. "One of us has to stay with Gerard and his traveling companions. We know what's been happening here; we know the arrangements. They don't. That's it, Georges. You've got to stick close—all the way. To Brussels. You're in charge, actually, but don't let Gerard notice it." The Renault drew up. Tony had the door open. "Good luck, old boy. See you next week." He was out, shaking hands with Bill, entering the gates with a last wave toward the car.

Georges drove on uphill to reach the highroad along the crest of Garavan. Tony was right, of course: Gerard would need a lot of extra details to persuade him to follow Tony's plan without adding some variations of his own. Better not say it is Tony's plan, Georges decided, not until we reach Brussels. Better let him think we have been following Commander James Hartwell's instructions right from the beginning. And so to Nice airport. And to a most exacting cross-examination from three razor-blade minds, once they came out of shock. In Tony's words, dicey, very dicey.

He put Tony out of his thoughts, concentrated on what he would say and how best he could tell it.

"Did my phone call awaken the household?" Tony asked as Bill closed the gates behind them.

"Left them all sleeping. Who was that in the car with you—Georges? Why didn't he stop off, say hello?"

"He's on his way to the Nice airport."

"Early, isn't he?"

"Wants to make sure he arrives in time."

"He's a bright boy. Easy to work with."

"That's Georges," said Tony. Looking at Bill's handsome and honest face— oh yes, he could be as devious as the best of them, but basically Bill was a straightforward, no-nonsense-about-me type—Tony began thinking back to

Georges's remarks. About Parracini and sophisticated bugging devices that he could manage to install without much specialized knowledge. But what had he used to overhear Bill's conversations? Because, Tony reminded himself, not all talk was made over a telephone. Apart from devices in set places, like a desk or a night table, what the bloody hell did Parracini use to listen to Bill having a private word with Nicole on the terrace, or with Bernard in the garden? Or even to conversations like this one, with Bill's now suggesting they'd head for the kitchen and rustle up some breakfast?

"Sounds good," Tony said. The house was about a hundred yards away. Not far enough, he thought unhappily. "Let's walk a little. I need the fresh air. Cooped up most of the night. You've a lot of garden here. How far does it stretch?"

"About five acres. We've kept a flower bed or two near the terrace and pool, but all this—" Bill pointed to hedges and trees that sheltered elaborately shaped plots—"we just let go. Too much work for Bernard." Then, as Tony took the nearest brick path, leading away from the villa itself, Bill said, "You didn't haul me out of bed to talk about horticulture. What's your problem?"

At this moment, thought Tony, you are. I've got a rising suspicion that Parracini knew your telephone rang, is now up and around, and listening to every word we say. "Two things," he replied. "The engine trouble we had on the *Sea Breeze,* and the weather."

"Thought you had got the engine fixed."

"We are still working on it. Oh, it's safe enough, unless we run into any strong weather. The latest reports are predicting a possible southeaster by this afternoon. And that's not a pleasing prospect, Bill, with an engine you can't depend on."

"Then the cruise idea is off."

"No. It's too good a security measure to pass up. But the cruise may have to be cut short if the weather prophets are right. As soon as the wind freshens too much, we can easily slip into the nearest harbor before anyone starts feeling queasy. Wouldn't want Gerard to be seasick, would we?"

"Gerard? Is he coming, too?"

"That's the word this morning. He's got some news for Parracini. A job with Nato—did you hear about it?"

"No."

"Nor I, until Georges cued me in."

"Does Parracini know? If so, why the hell didn't he tell me?"

"Well, it wasn't definite until Gerard pulled some strings and used his powers of persuasion. But it's all set. One caution, Bill: let Gerard break the good news to Parracini. That's Gerard's pet project, you know. He really will be hopping mad if we jump in ahead of him."

"This job for Parracini in Nato—"

"Very hush-hush, very important. That's all I know."

"A bit soon, isn't it?"

"Gerard thinks not. It will depend, of course, on the debriefing during our little cruise. But I'm sure Parracini will be able to help clear up the outstanding questions."

"About what?"

"About whom. Heinrich Nealey. He's been under surveillance for the last three months. We know he worked for nine years in America as Alexis; and one of his last contacts there was a man called Oleg." *Are you listening, Parracini, are you listening?* "It's just possible that Parracini can add to our file on Alexis. And on Oleg, whose real name is Gorsky, Boris Gorsky."

"I don't think Parracini has much to add to his previous debriefing."

"Memory can play tricks—blot out small facts that don't seem important, recall them later by some new association of ideas."

"Where is Gorsky now?"

"Haven't a clue." And that was true, in its way. Gorsky might be on Cap Martin, or in a cottage up on Garavan, or six miles away in Monte Carlo.

"Could he be in contact with Nealey again?"

"If he is, we'll get him."

"Through Nealey?"

"Yes. And we'll pull in several of the smaller fry too—a pretty redhead who's secretary to Maclehose, out at Shandon Villa, and at least three others working around the place. And they are bound to have set up a system of outside contacts. It could be quite a haul."

"Contacts," Bill said slowly. His gray eyes looked somber, his pleasant features grim, his usual smile—white against a permanently tanned face—vanishing. He smoothed back his longish sun-bleached hair, now ruffled by the breeze, pulled the collar of his suede jacket up around his neck as if he suddenly felt chilled. "You think Nealey is on to us?"

Tony didn't answer. He had been studying Bill closely. Casual dress—no cuff links, this morning; and no tie for any clip to hold in place. The suede jacket would only be worn at odd moments, so forget the possibility of buttons being wired for sound. No rings. A belt buckle, yes. And Bill's watch, that old favorite he had worn for years. Or was it? As Bill's wrist came up to smooth down his hair, then adjust his collar, the watch was in clear view.

Bill's worry was growing. "You think this house could be under surveillance?" With his setup Nealey must have gathered a lot of information—mostly for his own security—about recent rentals, strangers signing long-term leases.

"I'm sure they've been taking a close look at all new arrivals who've set up house in the last two months. That's the reason why you and Parracini are going to meet these Nato intelligence officers, instead of them coming to visit you here. We'll have them waiting for you, keeping out of sight. All you and Parracini have to do is get on the boat as quickly and discreetly as possible. And don't be late."

"Sailing when?"

"Didn't I tell you eleven o'clock? So get to the dock half an hour before that, and you step on board by ten thirty-five at latest. Can do?"

"Why not sail as soon as we reach the *Sea Breeze*?"

"Better let us make sure that no one at the harbor is too interested in her—or you. Can you lend me your two men to help me keep watch?"

"Sure. You're taking a hell of a lot of trouble for Parracini. Or is it for the Nato guys?"

"See right through me every time, don't you? It's the Nato guys who are my responsibility. And they are some of our top men. Nealey would give an arm and a leg to know their faces and put names to them."

"A high-level meeting, then." That at least pleased Bill.

"Yes. So let's get down to the last details, synchronize watches, and—hey, Bill, yours is running ten minutes slow."

"Can't be. Only got it yesterday." Bill peered at the elaborate watch face. "Does everything but talk," he said, "or show the time clearly. These damned numerals—" He froze as Tony held out his wrist, let him see his own watch. The two timepieces showed only one second of difference. "What's the matter with—"

Quickly Tony put a finger up to his lips for silence, pointed at Bill's watch; then jerked a thumb back in the direction of the house, and tapped an ear. Bill stared back at him. "Needs winding," said Tony. "Or has it stopped altogether?" Tony unbuckled its strap, drew it off Bill's wrist.

"What the hell—"

"Damned annoying," Tony said. "You'd better use your old one." He was feeling the weight of the new piece—it wasn't excessive, seemed perfectly normal.

"Can't," Bill said. "It got smashed up last Sunday."

"How on earth did you manage that?"

"Not me. It was Parracini and Nicole horsing around the pool. I laid my watch beside my chair while I went for a swim. They knocked the chair over, and the watch ended up under Parracini's heel."

"How much did you pay for this one?"

"It was a present—Nicole went half-shares on the purchase price and Parracini bought it yesterday morning."

"Now that's what I mean by his taking too many chances, wandering around town like that." Tony had his all-purpose knife out, resisted trying to open the back of the watch—it would be tightly sealed anyway—and worked on its winder instead. Anything, he thought, to give Bill an excuse for not wearing it. "Careful, Bill," he said. "You'll break off that key if you—damn it, you have broken it!" Tony snapped it off as he spoke, hurled the watch into a nearby bush with bright purple flowers. "Let's get one of your acres between it and us," he said softly as he drew Bill far up the path. At last he was satisfied, and came to a halt in a one-time rose garden. "Now we can get down to business."

"You think there was a bug in that watch?" Bill demanded, half-angry, half-bewildered. "Who the hell could have—"

"Parracini. I'll begin with him, and then go on to details about plans. Be prepared for a shock, Bill. But just listen, don't ask questions—we haven't time for that." Tony plunged into the story of Parracini.

"I'll say this for you, Bill," he ended. "You got a grip on yourself more quickly than I did last night. It took me half an hour to calm down."

"I'll let go once he's trapped in Brussels," Bill said through his teeth. "Now, what about your plans?"

"Here's our schedule." Tony gave their timetable, the *Aurora*'s name and exact location in the marina below this hillside. "Got all that?"

Bill nodded. "We get there by ten twenty-five. No later."

"And sail by ten thirty. Wait until you've got Parracini in the car, on your way to the *port privé*, before you mention the *Aurora*. That will take all your tact, Bill."

"I'll manage. I can tell him I just had a signal from you delaying the *Sea Breeze*, engine acting up again. As for the weather—you took care of that angle. If Parracini was listening, he caught an earful this morning."

"And he is now locked in your bathroom, far enough away from Bernard and Brigitte or Nicole, trying to get a message to Gorsky on his transceiver. About Heinrich Nealey, *requiescat in pace*. And about Parracini's triumph—accepted into Nato. I don't think he will balk at the change from *Sea Breeze* to *Aurora*."

"You baited the hook too well," Bill said as they left the rose garden, started walking down the series of paths and steps. He frowned at some new problem. "Nicole—when do I tell her?"

"You don't. She's too attached to Parracini."

"To Palladin, you mean. She admired him. He never took a nickel, worked for the West because he believed in us—such as we are," Bill ended abruptly.

"To paraphrase old Winston, democracy may not be perfect, but it's a damn sight better than anything else around."

"Nicole—" Bill was still troubled about her.

"Just leave her in happy ignorance. I'll tell her tonight, once I hear from you in Brussels."

"She wants to come on the cruise too."

"Impossible!" Tony was really startled. "Keep her out of it, Bill. She stays here. With Brigitte. And what about Bernard?"

"He was going down to the harbor with us, so that he could drive the Mercedes back here."

"May I borrow him—and your car? Just briefly. I'll tell him what I want done, myself. And where do I reach your two men by phone?"

"I'll call them and pass on your instructions." And then, as Tony raised an eyebrow, Bill reconsidered. "No, I won't. Those damned bugs—I suppose I'll have to leave them in place and not rouse Parracini's suspicions." So he gave Tony the phone number and the two names, with the identification password.

"Bless your sweet understanding heart. Won't forget this," Tony said, and he meant it.

"Okay, okay. Any other pointers you need to give me? Then what about some breakfast?"

"I'd better not meet Parracini. He may have noticed me last night among the onlookers at the casino. If he sees me here with you—" Tony shook his head.

"How are you getting back to town?"

"I'll start walking down the road. You send Bernard after me in that old rattletrap of his, and he can leave me near my hotel."

The bush with the bright purple flowers was coming into sight. "I'll pick that damned watch up and drop it into my desk," said Bill. "Have you another one?"

"I'll borrow Brigitte's. I don't imagine she has been wired for sound." As they reached the bush, Bill took out his handkerchief and went searching for the watch. Like a lost golf ball, he thought, and just as elusive. At last he found it and placed it in the center of his handkerchief, wrapping it up into a thick wad. Then, clutching it tightly inside his fist, he jammed his hand into his jacket pocket and kept it there. There was a smile on his face as they walked on in silence, avoiding the sound of footsteps on the brick path by moving onto a slope of dew-wet grass. But the joke would have to remain untold till he met Tony again: that damned watch actually had stopped.

Tony chose an oblique approach to the gates, using a row of tall thin cypresses to hide him from curious eyes at the house. Have we forgotten something, left anything undone? he wondered as he walked down the road to its next curve. There he sat on a low wall, waited for Bernard's car, and looked at the view. Far below him Garavan Bay stretched from its eastern boundary of russet cliffs, towering over the *port privé*, to the western harbor sheltering under the Old Town. The red sky, sailors' warning, now fading into a reassuring blue puffed with small white clouds, briefly touched the high cliffs and turned them into a wall of flame. The Mediterranean sparkled in the clear pure light, promising the mere landlubbers a perfect day.

"Good morning to you," Bernard called out, and opened the car door.

I hope it is a good morning, Tony thought. He climbed in, and they began the serpentine descent.

Twenty-four

RICK NEALEY'S QUARTERS at Shandon Villa consisted of an outer office, handsomely furnished with couch and chairs, where business could be conducted or important guests entertained, and an adjoining bed-sitting-room for private use only. There, one of the closets had been fitted with the necessary equipment to keep him in touch with his own secret world. Its installation had excited and pleased him, given him a feeling of increased status, a sense of widening power. Until yesterday. Until then, everything had been progressing smoothly and well. And now—

He pulled himself free from the twisted blanket, and rose. Dawn was breaking. He hadn't slept, partly because he had spent the night on the couch in his office, partly because of Gorsky's presence in his bed-sitting-room. It had been the only solution to the emergency that had arisen so unexpectedly on that disastrous visit to the Kelsos' house. Shandon Villa had been the nearest refuge. Impossible, said Gorsky, to continue along the shore road to his rented cottage, even if it was only two kilometers farther west. Impossible, Gorsky had repeated, to risk traveling on foot: the police had been called in, the alert was out, the search was on. So Gorsky had taken shelter in Shandon, with Nealey guiding him safely out of view of the two yokels on their guard duty against jewel thieves.

He must give me credit for waiting for him on the road below the olive trees. I watched him scrambling down those terraces, gauged his direction, was there to meet him. Without me, where would he have been? (I didn't have to wait for him—in an emergency, it was each man for himself.) Will Gorsky admit it? No, thought Nealey, he'll blame me for the whole of last night's fiasco. But it was he who was up at that house, not I. Will he blame me for that too?

Nealey, in dressing gown and slippers, padded silently downstairs. It was too early as yet for the cook and her helper to be working in the kitchen. Some food and hot coffee, and perhaps Gorsky's mood would be mellowed before he had to leave—soon, within another hour, while kitchen staff and Maclehose family were still asleep.

As he started back upstairs with a loaded tray, he remembered those other mornings when, in dressing gown just like this, he'd get his own breakfast in his snug apartment in Georgetown. A simple life compared to his present one. Suddenly he felt an unexpected nostalgia for the years when he was Alexis, and worked alone. Not actually alone, of course, but he had felt a certain independence: delivery of reports to agents who stayed anonymous; telephone calls that came from voices without faces; meetings arranged and kept in reassuring secrecy. Yes, it had been a useful life, and comfortable. But here, he had been drawn deeper in. He had learned more, been told more. Yesterday, it had excited him, pleased him. Today, it roused a strange disquiet.

He re-entered the office, set the tray down on the nearest table. He could hear Gorsky's harsh but muffled tones droning on, as they had done at several intervals through the night, making contact with someone locally. But this time, the someone had as much to say as Gorsky. I'll never know what this is all about, Nealey thought; from now on, Gorsky will tell me little. I am demoted. And why? It was the Kelso incident that made the abrupt change in Gorsky's attitude to me. It had never been a friendly association, but—on Parracini's orders—not inimical either. Until last night. Apart from two single words (one of them, "impossible," used twice, the other, "idiocy," uttered in blistering rage), Gorsky had only opened his mouth to say, "Where do you transmit?" Not one particle of praise for either the neatly arranged closet or the clever combination lock that would defeat more than a curious housemaid. Not one word, either, about the Kelso house. What had actually happened up there? Nealey wondered once more. Probably he would never learn. Gorsky was not the type to admit his mistakes. Gorsky . . . Oleg. The man he had hoped, in Washington, never to meet again. And now, thought Nealey, he is on my back: I can feel his teeth in my neck.

There was complete silence in the bedroom. Nealey hesitated, then knocked on its door and waited for a response. At last it opened and Gorsky, fully dressed, ready to leave, came out. His face was calm, his eyes cold. He looked at the breakfast tray and poured himself a cup of coffee. Nealey, helping himself to bread, butter, and honey, was suddenly aware of sharp scrutiny, and lost his appetite. The continuing silence unnerved him. He didn't even drink his coffee. He blurted out, "There was no other way. The old man shot at me. I had to run."

"Before he shot at you," Gorsky said, not even concealing his contempt. "After."

"And he missed? Yet he could aim well. He wounded Gómez and handed him over to the police."

"And Feliks?"

"He got away—with much difficulty. He is at the cottage. I have instructed him to leave, remove what he can, destroy the rest."

"But Gómez will give no information—"

"The cottage is no longer possible. You have ended its usefulness."

"I? I'm not to blame for Gómez—"

"If you had dealt with Charles Kelso effectively, there would have been no need for our visit to his brother's house. We could have concentrated on our real mission here, not on a distraction that should never have been allowed to develop."

"How else could I have dealt with Chuck? He threatened me and I persuaded him to postpone action. That gave you time to—"

"Not time enough to examine the suitcase before his body was discovered! You should have stayed here, yesterday afternoon. You should have gone through his belongings while we dealt with him. But no—you had to run off to Eze, provide yourself with an excuse for not taking part in his death. You could even have stood watch, like Gómez. Yes, Gómez. Who is now in the hands of the police. If he can be recognized as one of the electricians who were working at Shandon yesterday—" Gorsky's lips tightened as he stared down at Nealey, who sat with head bent, coffee cup pushed aside and forgotten, on the edge of his chair.

Gorsky's recital of mistakes continued. "You told me that Kelso had threatened you, that he showed you notes for a letter he was about to write—if you didn't resign. You did not tell me that the letter was already written."

Nealey roused himself. "It was only drafted, not actually written."

"No? Here is one copy." Gorsky placed it in front of Nealey. "There are four others. You do not have copies without an original. And it is ready to be mailed. Did he tell you to whom he sent it for safekeeping?"

"He only warned me he was drafting a letter," Nealey insisted.

"And you believed that?" Gorsky's scorn ended in a brief laugh.

"The letter is probably hidden in his apartment," Nealey suggested quickly.

Gorsky's contempt increased. "I had a thorough search made there yesterday, as soon as you told me about Kelso's notes. And no search would have been possible if there wasn't a time lag between here and New York. But your luck stopped there, Nealey. We found nothing. Nothing!"

"Then perhaps he was bluffing—there was no draft—"

"And therefore no letter ready to be mailed? What a comforting thought. Idiot! Read that postscript to his brother. There *is* a letter, now in the hands of someone he trusts—someone who is waiting for Kelso's instructions whether to send or destroy it. As soon as he hears of Kelso's death, he will either mail or open the letter. In either case, disastrous for you. Impossible to stay here. You resign today, and leave by tomorrow morning. I will send two men with you, to make sure your journey to Moscow is without incident."

Moscow? Recall. For what? Nealey said, "How can I resign? I am in charge here. The first seminar begins next week. Do you actually mean to sacrifice all my work, all this project? Parracini would never agree with that."

"Parracini has a bigger project in view than even Shandon Villa. If there is a choice between them, he will concentrate on the success of his own mission."

"And what is it that's so important?" Nealey countered. "To throw away our control over Shandon Villa—that's madness! And Parracini couldn't substitute one of his agents to take over my position here. There isn't time. The job will go to my chief assistant, perhaps permanently if he shapes up. And you know I selected him because he is excellent cover—politically a middle-of-the-road liberal who is against extremes, right or left. How far would you get with him?"

Nealey had made a good point, Gorsky conceded. "When does he begin work here?"

"Tomorrow or Monday. He arrives in Menton today."

Gorsky was silent for almost two minutes. "Then we shall arrange it this way. You don't resign: you will ask for a leave of absence, with your assistant taking charge for the next week or so. This will give us time enough to have another candidate ready for your job—someone who has more distinguished qualifications than your assistant. We will push him hard, just as we pushed you—use every bit of influence, pull every string we can find in Washington. And when we are ready to insert him into your slot at Shandon Villa, you can then turn your leave of absence into resignation."

"But how could I ask for any leave at this moment? The first seminar—"

"You have been working too hard, you've done too much. The death of your friend Charles Kelso has caused you great distress—you need two weeks to rest and regain your health."

"Two weeks?" Nealey was scornful. "You'll never be able to install anyone in—"

"Two weeks." Gorsky was adamant. "And if there is a delay in our plans, all you have to do is to request an extension of your sick leave." Gorsky's anger, held at a low simmer, was beginning to boil. "Any excuse, you fool, to prevent your job from being filled. You keep Maclehose expecting your return. Can't you do even that?"

Nealey moistened his dry lips. "What about Anne-Marie, or the others?"

"They will be sent elsewhere."

"But why?"

"Because of Nato Intelligence."

"*What?*"

Gorsky didn't explain. He continued with the problem of Anne-Marie. "You will reprimand her this morning, for incompetence. You will create a scene. She will leave in anger. And after that you will ask Maclehose for sick leave. A most appropriate request after the performance you have just given."

"You are clearing us all out of Shandon?" Nealey couldn't believe it. "All our work—all our organization—"

"We take the loss, and wait, and begin all over again. But carefully. Nato's agents will keep Shandon Villa under close observation for several months."

"It could be a false alarm about Nato Intelligence."

"Their agents are here in Menton. Three men came in yesterday, aboard the *Sea Breeze*. One, Emil Baehren, has been identified—he is guarding their boat. Of the two others, only Georges Despinard can be definitely connected with the *Sea Breeze*."

"Yes," Nealey was quick to remind Gorsky, "it was I who found out his name, and the *Sea Breeze* address, at the police station. And the third agent is Lawton, who is staying at the Alexandre? It must be. They were together at Shandon yesterday afternoon."

"It doesn't follow. An agent like Despinard could have used Lawton to arrange a visit to Shandon." It had been Despinard who had prowled around the gardens, not Lawton. "All we know definitely about Lawton is that he is a friend of Thomas Kelso. He is a friend of many journalists—including Despinard."

"But you have your suspicions?"

"I've had them for many months." Gorsky was enigmatic.

"Haven't you acted on them—had him followed, his rooms searched?"

"If we had discovered anything at all," said Gorsky, as if he were talking to a child, "do you think I would only have suspicions?"

Nealey said bitingly, "I've never known a lack of proof to keep you from taking action." And that, he saw by Gorsky's face, had been a mistake. He hurried on. "So we have three low-grade operatives in Menton, sent by Nato on a fool's errand—to protect Parracini."

"And at least two very senior officers arriving today. But the most senior of them all was already here, yesterday. According to one of our best informants, he sent a brief message to Paris requesting dual repairs for the *Sea Breeze*—two more agents, of course—and identified himself by one of his code names, Uncle Arthur." And that, he thought as he watched Nealey lose his cockiness and revert to being suitably impressed, restores the correct balance between us. No need to spoil the effect by admitting that Uncle Arthur's real name had never been identified—it was only known to four NATO officials in Brussels, and none of them were talking. As for his colleagues, they were ignorant of his rank and importance, accepted him as one of themselves. It had proved, so far, to be the best possible cover. So far . . . But he was here in Menton. And Lawton was here in Menton, as elusive as ever. And these two had coincided before. Accidentally? There never had been any proof that Lawton and Uncle Arthur were the same man. And yet—"When two suspicions become one," Gorsky said, watching Nealey's baffled face with a smile, "then I act."

"But if Lawton is a Nato agent—how could he have any interest in Shandon? We've covered our tracks, we've—"

"Nato *is* interested. Because of you. They have been watching you for the last three months, according to Kelso."

"Tom Kelso? What does *he* know? He was bluffing."

"I received further confirmation only half an hour ago—from Parracini. He was trying to reach you here, give you orders to clear out. I took the message. I am now passing his instructions to you."

"Something is wrong," Nealey protested. "No one has been watching me. Not for three months, or three weeks, or three days."

"Are you contradicting Parracini's judgment? Or mine?"

"No, no. But why didn't Nato move in on me as soon as I reached Europe?"

"Have you forgotten that a suspected agent is watched for his contacts, that the net is drawn around him until a large haul can be made?"

"I know," said Nealey, and didn't conceal his irritation. He was certain he hadn't been followed, either in Washington or in Menton. "But the point is—"

"The point is that you leave here by Monday at latest. For Aix-en-Provence. A natural choice for a man who needs rest and medical treatment. It has thermal baths, many doctors. More important for you—crowds and a confusion of streets. Feliks will meet you without any trouble. It can easily be reached from Menton—a two-hour drive. And it is near the Mediterranean."

Ten miles from Marseilles. "You are shipping me out on a freighter?" Nealey tried to conceal his anger.

"If we have to, yes." Gorsky noted Nealey's rigid smile. "But," he added, "we can offer you more comfortable quarters than that. We have a cabin cruiser available." His voice had lost all harshness, had become almost friendly.

Nealey thought over that idea. Yes, once it was time for him to slip out of Aix-en-Provence, it would be easy to travel to the coast, be picked up at one of its numerous small harbors. NATO agents would concentrate on the Marseilles docks, the obvious place for a man in flight. A cabin cruiser available? "All right. Shall I type out my request for sick leave now? Make sure it suits your—your scenario?"

"Write it by hand."

Nealey sat down at his desk, found paper and pen. Is this a trap of some kind? Or is Aix-en-Provence the trap? If I am under suspicion, the French police could easily detain me there at the request of NATO. "How long will it take you to find my replacement?" he asked as he dated his note to Maclehose. "Any delay could be dangerous. Extradition is possible, once the Americans receive Chuck Kelso's information. Or have you forgotten that I am supposed to be an American citizen?"

"You will not have long to wait before your replacement is here. A week, perhaps. Not more."

"A week?" He's lying, thought Nealey. He is ensuring my complete obedience by promises. Does he think I will defect? But this time Nealey hid his anger well. He began writing, pleading this and that, exactly as it had been dictated. He signed the letter, handed it over to be read.

Gorsky nodded his approval, and watched Nealey as he sealed the envelope and addressed it. "A week," he emphasized, as if he felt reassurance was necessary.

"I begin to think you have my replacement already chosen."

Gorsky concealed his chagrin. "Every important actor must have his understudy."

"You mean there was always a substitute, waiting to—"

"But of course. You could have met with an accident, or needed a serious operation. Such things happen."

Yes, thought Nealey as he stared back at Gorsky, accidents do happen. Thank God that Parracini is in charge. If he weren't here to restrain this man . . . And once again Nealey felt the same cold fear that had seized him in Washington.

"Get some clothes on," Gorsky told him. "You'll drive me into Menton, leave me at the market. And don't take long to dress. Two minutes." He had switched off the lights and opened the shutters, and was now making a quick check of the terrace and gardens. He was at the office door, his hat in his hand, his coat over his arm, waiting impatiently, by the time Nealey had pulled on trousers, shirt, and sweater, and slipped bare feet into loafers. Less than two minutes, thought Nealey, but Gorsky had no comment. His eyes and ears were intent on the silent house as he hurried downstairs, led the way through the hall, ghostly in the first light of morning.

He did not speak, even when they reached the garage safely—no one in the garden, no one at any window—and entered the car. Only as they left Shandon's gates did Gorsky say, "Hurry! Drive as fast as you can." He threw his coat and hat into the back seat. "Get rid of them," was his final command. Then, slumping low, head kept well down, eyes on his watch, a frown on his face, Gorsky seemed to forget Nealey completely.

Nealey made one last show of independent judgment. He halted the Citroën a couple of blocks from the market. "Too many trucks pulling in, too many farmers opening their stalls," he said briskly. "I'm not going to be caught in a traffic jam. You get out here."

Gorsky had no other choice: to keep the car standing while he argued would only draw attention to them. He got out.

Nealey had a parting word. "You shouldn't be seen with me, anyway. Or have you forgotten I'm under surveillance?" He smiled and drove on, cutting away from the shore, heading back into town. Surveillance, he thought with contempt, just one of Gorsky's lies to keep me in line. No one has been following me. I'd have sensed it. And, to prove he was right, Nealey spent a few extra minutes weaving in and out of streets and avenues, keeping his eye on the rearview mirror. As he expected, no one was tailing him.

There's only one real danger as far as I'm concerned, and that is Chuck Kelso's letter. How long will extradition take? If I'm faced with that, before Feliks arrives in Aix-en-Provence to—what would be Gorsky's word? Oh yes—to escort me safely to that cabin cruiser (another convenient lie to keep me trusting Gorsky?), then what do I do? What do I do? On sudden impulse, he swung away from the center of the town, entered the tunnel that led to Garavan Bay. The Hotel Alexandre was along there somewhere.

How easy, he thought, it would be to walk into the Alexandre, ask for Lawton, and make a pretty little speech: I am not the American citizen, Heinrich Nealey by name, born in Brooklyn, 1941. I am Simas Poska, born in Vilnius, 1940. As a trained agent of the KGB, I adopted the identity of Heinrich Nealey when I "escaped" from the German Democratic Republic in 1963. Since August 1965 I have fulfilled my duties as a Soviet intelligence officer in Washington. In January of this year I came to Menton to continue these duties. I have no connection with the death of Charles Kelso. Murder is not my bag, my dear Mr. Lawton. And so I defect, if you'll guarantee me this and that, etc., etc.

Yes, how easy. But defection is not my bag either. In spite of Comrade Colonel Boris Yevgenovich Gorsky, affectionately called Oleg by his friends—all two of them if that isn't an exaggeration—I am still a capable, intelligent, and loyal officer of the KGB.

Nealey reached the Alexandre, making a quick U-turn onto the westbound avenue, so that he could pass its door. He slowed down. So easy, he thought again, and laughed. Why not throw Gorsky's hat and coat, unwanted relics of last night, right into the hotel garden? Smiling broadly, he put on speed and headed back toward the tunnel underneath the Old Town.

As arranged, Gorsky had met Feliks, waiting in a dilapidated van, near the flower stalls outside the market. "The harbor," he told Feliks. "I want to see if the *Monique* has arrived."

"She's here." Feliks wasn't speaking French this morning. That had been part of his disguise for the Kelso assignment last night, like the black coveralls and ski-mask. His thin face was gaunt, and his voice depressed. The capture of Gómez was a real setback. Together they had made a good team. For almost eight years. Who would be his partner on today's job? Some new arrival from the *Monique,* no doubt, who would want his own way or need everything explained twice. Better to work alone, Feliks thought. Yes, a real setback.

"Then I want to verify her exact position." It had taken a generous payment and some rapid arrangements to get a fishing boat to leave well before dawn, and let the *Monique* slip into its mooring place.

"I'll take the tunnel," said Feliks. "It's the quickest route."

As they emerged onto the waterfront, Gorsky scanned each pedestrian, each car. "That black Citroën—just ahead of us," he said quickly. "Nealey. What's he doing over here?" The wide avenue that edged Garavan Bay would never lead to Cap Martin.

"Follow him?"

"Yes."

Well ahead of them Nealey made his U-turn, slowed down as he approached the Alexandre.

Feliks was roused from his state of gloom. "What *is* he doing?" He too made the turn, drew to the side of the westbound avenue as if he were going to make a delivery. His face was now as sharp and eager as a ferret's.

In bitter disgust, Gorsky said, "The man who knows when he is under surveillance. Just look at him, Feliks. He hasn't even noticed us."

That would be difficult, thought Feliks, hidden as we are by the high sides of this closed van marked Alimentations: eggs and butter, that's us. Still, Nealey's mind wasn't on his proper business. "He's stopping!" But as he spoke, the black Citroën picked up speed, began traveling at last in the right direction for Cap Martin.

"Let him go," said Gorsky. Yes, he was thinking, Nealey always runs. In Central Park with Mischa, or last night at the Kelso place—he runs. He saves himself. Always. And now he is about to defect. I know the signs. I can smell them. "Did you manage to salvage our communications equipment from the cottage?" he asked suddenly, and gestured toward the interior of the van. "Guns, ammunition?"

"Everything. All packed in cartons, ready to be set up or stored on the boat. Also, I brought some changes of clothes for us both."

Gorsky nodded his approval. "The *Monique,*" he directed Feliks. Then, back to thinking about Nealey, he lapsed into silence.

Twenty-five

THE ALEXANDRE, ONE of the new hotels facing Garavan Bay, was constructed in Siamese-twin style: an apartment house for long-lease tenants had been built directly onto its side, seemingly independent but conveniently linked by their jointly shared restaurant. For anyone who wanted to approach the hotel discreetly, it was fairly simple to stay unobserved, provided, of course, that he had previously scouted the area and discovered its possibilities.

Tony Lawton had done just that, as soon as he had checked in yesterday morning. Future insurance. It paid off now. Once Bernard had deposited him a good hundred yards away from the Alexandre and the KGB agent on guard duty (a minor character, this must be, Tony reflected, but still an annoyance), he walked briskly to the apartment house and nipped into its hall. There were other early strollers, too, out for a prebreakfast constitutional or the morning newspaper. Gorsky's man, glued to the hotel entrance, paid little attention.

From the apartment-house hall—one elderly lady, with hair curlers wrapped up like a pound of sausages, being pulled by her small white poodle toward the sidewalk—Tony entered the restaurant. (No patrons: croissants and coffee, standard breakfast, only needed a tray and room service.) Avoiding the kitchen door, he made his way between the rows of tables and entered the small lobby of the Alexandre. Empty, at seven in the morning, except for the night clerk still on duty and half asleep. Tony didn't approach the desk or the self-service elevator. He took the stairs, nicely carpeted, silent, and only three flights to his floor. His room key, behind a mezzotint on the wall near his door, was still in place, jammed between the picture frame and its cord.

Tony's room was modern—small, everything built in as on shipboard, with a stretch of sliding windows opening onto a balcony and a view of the bay. He resisted both, flopped down on one of the narrow beds. "Bliss," he said, feeling his spine stretch, his back muscles ease. But not yet, he reminded himself, not yet.

First, a call to Bill's two bright boys. They must be, to have chosen their identification routine. No humdrum weather talk from them. He was to ask, "Is Jeff around?" And the answer would come back, "No, he's out looking for Mutt." Yes, thought Tony, I rather like their style. Their names were Saul and Walt—Canadian, British, American? Bill hadn't said: only that there would be no language hang-ups, and thank heaven for that. Tony's instructions would be quickly understood. And then, to make his message authentic, he was to end with Bill's customary sign-off: "No more muffins for tea— make mine jelly doughnuts." Happy idiots, all three of them; but their touch of light relief was just what he needed to break up this morning's strain and tension. Tony's mind relaxed along with his body. He stopped worrying about the difficulties and dangers of making an open call to two unknown agents. He rose from the bed and dialed their number.

"A return visit to last night's scene," he began, once the formalities of Mutt and Jeff were over. "But this time, come as VIP's and pay us a visit. Be our guests. For arrival, manner should be dignified, dress restrained. Perhaps a dark raincoat to cover more normal clothes? The kind of thing that is worn around that area? Can do? A briefcase would look good, too. Ten o'clock prompt. Sea is calm. Breeze is slight. Understood?"

"Understood," said Saul—or Walt. "Anything to add?"

Tony gave them Bill's jelly doughnut routine. It was received with a brief and businesslike "Okay."

So that was settled. Next, a check with the *Aurora* itself. Vincent, the man to contact there, was very much on duty. Identification went briskly by a series of numbers. Tony's message was equally crisp: Georges arriving at ten, with party of three, all four with identity cards; two men, both known to Georges, entering marina ten twenty-five, boarding ten twenty-eight, sailing ten thirty.

"*D'accord*," said Vincent. "Will transmit sailing time to escort. *Bonne chance!*"

And that too was settled, thought Tony as he laid aside his transceiver. Any gaps left? There always were, of course, and then you had to improvise quickly and hope for the best. Too bad that he couldn't be down at the marina to make sure Georges and his party had reached it, or to see Bill and Parracini actually board the *Aurora,* watch them all sail safely out to sea. It would have been a satisfying moment. But impossible, with the time schedule necessary to keep Parracini from thinking up some demanding questions. Such as: "*Why* are we leaving the house so early? We don't arrive at the harbor until ten thirty; we board the *Sea Breeze* at ten thirty-five. Isn't *that* the arrangement?" Bill had difficulties enough without those queries being raised, intent as he was on getting Parracini into the car before the *Aurora* was even mentioned. Otherwise Parracini would head indoors for the bathroom, nice excuse, to make contact with Gorsky and pass the word that *Sea Breeze* was off and *Aurora* was on, *Aurora, Aurora,* find the *Aurora.* And Gorsky would. . . . Yes, the original time of departure from the house on Garavan Hill had to be kept. And that, Tony told himself, is the reason why you won't wave good-by to the *Aurora.* Uncle can't be in two places at once.

He ordered the usual *café complet,* began laying out the necessary change of clothes, shaved and showered. Breakfast still hadn't arrived. The hell with it, he thought, and got into bed. He set the alarm for nine o'clock. That would give him an hour and a half for sleep: enough to set him up for the rest of this day. He needed it.

But fifteen minutes later the waiter unlocked the door, brought the breakfast tray shoulder-high, triumphant delivery, into the room. Tony came awake as the lock turned. "*Scusi!*" said the young Italian, his good-morning smile transfixed as a naked man leapt out of bed with hands raised karate-style. "*Scusi, signore!*" The tray, almost dropped, was laid hastily on the nearest table.

"Just a nightmare, *un incubo*," said Tony, draping a sheet around him.

Two francs for a tip, and the boy's nerves were partly restored. At least he managed to get to the door and close it carefully.

The coffee had spilled over the paper tray-cloth. Half a cup was still pourable, croissant and brioche only fit to be eaten with a spoon. He turned away from the unappetizing mess, drank the coffee in two gulps, and dropped once more into bed. Just as he stretched back, preparing to drift off, his transceiver on the table beside his pillow gave its insistent buzz. He reached for it, switched on the connection. It was Emil reporting from the *Sea Breeze*. "Something new was added during the early hours. Must have been between four and five, when I was having some shut-eye. There's a cabin cruiser, the *Monique*, not far from us. She has taken the place of a fishing boat—"

"Your friends—they cleared out to let her—" Tony began in alarm. Good God, he was thinking, what kind of beer-guzzling pals did Emil welcome aboard last night?

"No, no, that was one of the other fishing boats. My friends are still here, working away. Two of them dropped in for breakfast. I couldn't call you until they left. All is quiet now. But—" Emil hesitated. "But the *Monique* seemed too interested in us. You'd better have a look at her. When do I expect you?"

"Now. Give me twenty minutes."

"No need to rush. As I said, all is quiet."

"Twenty minutes." Tony signed off, grim-faced. The *Monique*—Gorsky's? Could be. A cabin cruiser . . . And right in the harbor, not waiting out in the bay until the *Sea Breeze* sailed. Which meant the *Monique* could watch all the moves that Tony had planned, instead of relying on observers stationed at the dock, sending out radio reports on the exact number of men arriving at what precise time. Gorsky, if he was on board the *Monique*, would certainly have his binoculars trained on the *Sea Breeze*, and, unlike his observers, even if he had never seen Bill, he knew the difference between Parracini and Bernard. But how, Tony kept wondering as he called for a taxi to arrive in ten minutes at the apartment house next door, how the bloody hell did Gorsky manage to get his damned cabin cruiser into an anchorage that was already jammed full? Money, influence, or sheer luck?

He dressed rapidly: blue jeans, rough navy sweater, an old denim Windbreaker that could reverse into a tweed Eisenhower jacket, rubber-soled shoes, a knitted cap pulled down to cover his hair except for the wild fringe he had combed over his brow, eyeglasses with plain glass lenses, a temporary mustache. In the mirror the effect was good—a workaday sailor, with hands in pockets, hunched shoulders, and a slight roll to his walk.

From the false bottom of his bag he selected two hairpieces, one dark brown, one blond, found a dark mustache, and shoved them into the tweed lining's pockets. Transceiver, Gauloise cigarettes, a small box of coarse matches, and he was ready to leave. Again, his room key was hidden behind the mezzotint; again, he used the staircase, avoided the hotel lobby, and made his way through the dining room. He reached the front entrance of the apartment house as the cab drew up. He was inside before the startled driver could even get out of his seat to open the door.

"The *petit port*, and double the fare if we reach it in five minutes," Tony said, bending down to tie his shoelace as they passed the Alexandre's entrance. Gorsky still had a man there, leaning against his car's fender. Either Gorsky had agents to spare, and Tony doubted that, or he had become much too interested in Lawton.

He stopped the taxi not far from the harbor's steps. The double fare was ready, and a good tip added. "Meet me here at ten fifteen," he said. "Can you be sure of that? It will be a short journey, but I'll pay well." The driver, an old sailor type himself, looked at the money in his hand. Ten fifteen, he agreed. Without fail.

Now, thought Tony as he altered his walk to suit his appearance, we'll have a look at the opposition.

"Did you see her?" asked Emil. He had recovered from his attack of astonishment: he hadn't expected Tony to arrive so quickly; he hadn't even recognized him, mixing with the small groups of sailing enthusiasts and fishermen that gathered for the usual talk or early-morning stroll around the harbor area. It wasn't until a seaman detached himself from three other nautical types as they passed the *Sea Breeze* that Emil actually identified the man as Tony.

"Couldn't miss her." The *Monique* was a sleek and classy lady, with good lines and a capable look. She was smaller than Tony had expected, which accounted for the ease with which she had entered this harbor. She lay just four doors away, as a landsman might put it, cheek by jowl with the fishing vessel under repair. (Emil's friends were now having trouble with one of the sails.) Tony had had to pass her to reach the *Sea Breeze:* a bad moment when—like the three sailors to whom he had loosely attached himself on their walk along the wharf—he paused to admire the smooth and shining cabin cruiser. "She is being loaded," Tony said, as he took a mug of coffee from Emil.

"That only started about twenty minutes ago—just after I called you—with the tall fellow carrying down cartons onto the dock. He got one of the crew to stand guard over them while he went back for more. Didn't want anyone else to touch them, can you beat that?" Emil's good-natured face, round and blunt-featured, was tired and drawn this morning, but his usual cheerful humor had reasserted itself with Tony's arrival. He grinned and shook his head. "Don't know which is funnier—that man carrying those cartons, one at a time, all by himself; or the way you look." He noticed the mug of coffee was already emptied. "Like some breakfast?"

"A lot of breakfast," said Tony, and went on brooding about the loading of the *Monique.* At least eight cartons (extra valuable; contents delicate?), four suitcases, three baskets of hastily packed food supplies. Two men at work on the project: one of them, slow-moving and deliberate, using a makeshift gangplank, was now doing the heavy work, lifting and carrying; the other, still guarding his precious cartons on the dock, stood close beside them and gave out instructions. He had paused to rake Tony's little group with a very sharp look. Just the usual nuisance, he seemed to decide—curious locals without work of their own to do. His glare was enough to sour all their interest, and they moved on. Impatiently he had turned back to the job of loading, without even a second glance at Tony. But Tony had recognized him. The gaunt face, fair hair, prominent eyes now popping with annoyance, belonged to the electrician who had come hurrying up through

Shandon Villa's gardens along with Gorsky. "Where's that explosive you found?" Tony asked suddenly.

Emil lowered the heat under the bacon. "I did as you said. Stowed it in a coil of rope. Want to see it?" He left the cabin, returned in a few seconds with a small waterproof bag. "Plastic and detonator inside. What do we do with it? Give it the deep six once we're out of harbor? The sooner we get rid of this surprise package, the happier I'll be. Who made us a present of it, anyway?"

Tony took the lethal little bag, no bigger than the palm of his hand, studying it thoughtfully as he twisted the wire that tied its neck into a tighter knot. Time was passing: he might be too late. He rose, saying, "Won't be long."

Emil stared after him. He was already outside, stepping onto the dock.

He passed the three intervening boats—a sailing craft, a motor launch, a fishing vessel with Emil's friends communicating in hoarse yells—but kept his eyes on the *Monique*'s loading area. The tall thin man was now boarding her along with the last suitcase. Only the three baskets were left, large and bulging with food, obviously of less importance. They could wait until the two men had got the cartons, still on deck, safely stowed below.

Tony halted, lit a Gauloise, let it droop from one corner of his mouth. The two men, each carrying one of those fascinating cartons (electronic equipment?), made their way aft, heading for the rear door of the cabin. They entered. And Tony moved.

He ignored the two baskets that contained perishable items—bread, vegetables, fruit, cheeses. He went for the one that held a clutter of cans and jars, food that wouldn't need immediate unpacking. He tripped heavily against it, giving it a hard shove with his knee. The basket toppled on its side, and at least half of its contents spilled out. He made a grab for it, dropping the small waterproof bag among the lower layers as he set it upright once more.

"*Mon Dieu!*" exclaimed a woman behind him. "Did you hurt yourself?"

A man told him, "They shouldn't leave their stuff lying all over the place. Could have broken your neck."

Three small boys laughed, began picking up cans and jars, tossing them back into the basket. Fine fun. Several other people had gathered near Tony, attracted by the bang and clatter of his little accident. And on the *Monique* the thin fair-haired man, his eyes popping out of his head, had raced forward. He checked his cartons; relaxed a little; shouted at the boys.

It seemed a propitious time to retreat. Tony walked back to the *Sea Breeze*, leaving the makings of an argument behind him. The could-have-broken-your-neck fellow was taking no snash from any luxury cabin cruiser. Popeye retreated to his cartons—a scene was the last thing he wanted—and it was left to his slow-moving comrade to disembark his considerable bulk and pick up the remaining cans and jars.

"Hurt yourself?" Emil asked as Tony entered the cabin, noticing the slight limp. He turned back to the frying pan, concentrated on breaking a couple of eggs beside the curling bacon.

"Only temporary." Tony rubbed his knee, restored the blood flow, and was thankful that—so far—he wasn't a candidate for gout.

"What was all the racket about?" Emil glanced around. Tony was pulling off his knitted cap, smoothing his fringe of hair back in proper place,

removing jacket and eyeglasses. Then he sat down, looked blandly innocent. There was no sign of the small waterproof bag. "Where's that surprise
package?"

"I thought we'd better return it to its rightful owner."

"Sure you got the right man?"

"Yes. He'll be on the *Monique* before she sails." As Emil gave him a hard
but worried look, he added, "He has to be. Who else could decide whether
or not to press the button and blow the poor old *Sea Breeze* sky-high? He'll
be aboard, that's certain. His chief assistant is there now—that lean popeyed
blond fellow. The two of them left a dead man floating in Shandon's pool
yesterday."

"One of ours?"

"No, he wasn't one of anything. Just a danger to their security. So they
silenced him."

"Drastic."

"That's what they are, drastic, the special-action boys of Department V."

"The hell they are," Emil said. That changed the picture considerably.
He served up the eggs and bacon, filled two mugs with coffee, produced
half a loaf of crusty bread.

"Fresh," Tony remarked, cutting off a thick slice. "Been doing some
baking?"

"I didn't leave the boat," Emil assured him with an answering grin. "My
fishing friends brought it along—their contribution to breakfast. They brought
some bits of news, too. Harbor gossip, of course. But they don't like their new
neighbor. That fat crew member who helped with the loading—he's the only
one visible—told them to cut out the hammering: people were trying to sleep."

"People?"

"Three in the crew. And a man who came down to have a look at the
Monique. Then he walked past here, had a good look at the *Sea Breeze* too.
Didn't stop, just walked past, then turned and went back to the *Monique*.
He boarded her. He's probably still there. Haven't see him since. Or two
of the crew."

"The underwater experts?" Tony suggested. "Well, they had a busy night.
Now they are resting from their labors and preparing for the day to come."
He noted Emil's expression. "No more qualms about returning unwanted gifts?"

"No," Emil said most definitely.

"After all," said Tony, "it is really up to the button-pusher, isn't it?" A
case of holding your fate in your own hands, he thought. "What was this
joker like—the one who pretended he wasn't interested in the *Sea Breeze?*"

"About my height, dark hair, handsome. Husky, too. Good shoulders.
Carried them straight."

"Wearing what?"

"A dark suit, a black turtleneck."

"So he didn't have time to change his clothes, just ditched his coat and
hat. Yes, I guess we all had a busy night."

Emil's blue eyes questioned him.

"I know," Tony agreed. "I have a lot to fill in for you. And I will. But
let's finish with the *Monique* first. Any more particulars on her?"

"Nine-meter class, but deceptive. Her power is high for her size: thirty knots. She sailed from Monte Carlo early this morning. Not her usual crew, but owner's permission granted. All in order. The owner is an oil heiress who jets around."

"One of the liberal chic? Excessively liberal this time."

"Not too much. The *Monique* is only her second-best boat."

"And where did you pick up all that information? Is it pure gossip, or part-way reliable?"

"Well, I took a bet with Paul—one of my fishing friends—that the *Monique* couldn't do more than twenty knots. He said at least twenty-five. So he went along to the harbor master's office, where his cousin works. And checked. And I paid up."

Tony's eyes gleamed. "Do you think you can interest him in another bet? How long does it take him to hoist the sails? That would block the *Monique*'s view of us nicely. Around ten thirty, I'd say. Or if you can think of something better—anything to distract attention."

"Distract attention from what?"

My God, Tony thought, he knows practically nothing; he's been hugging this boat for the last twenty-four hours, while Georges and I have been chasing around. All he got from us was a cryptic warning, and a very unpleasant swim. "Let's get the facts out," he said. "Turn on the radio, Emil, and we can talk."

Emil smiled. "There are no bugs here, Tony. I've checked. I was only once off the boat last night—to ask my friends over here for a glass of beer."

"Twice," Tony said gently. "You had that underwater trip around the old *Sea Breeze*. But you did a fine job," he added quickly. Emil was twenty-six, and his feelings bruised easily. "Just fine."

"At least there was some action." Emil set down his coffee mug, and rose. He began a quick but methodical search of the cabin. It was small: could sleep four, seat six, or stand eight. Yes, Tony thought, Gerard wouldn't have enjoyed his conference with Parracini here: much more comfortable for all of them on the *Aurora*. He glanced at his watch. Five past nine. He had about fifty minutes to brief Emil, tell him the important details: Parracini; the original plans for the *Sea Breeze*; the switch to the *Aurora*; the *Sea Breeze* deception beginning at ten o'clock; their own time schedule. Fifty minutes would be more than ample. Tony relaxed, poured himself another slug of coffee.

"Nothing," Emil said with relief, finishing his self-appointed task. "Completely clean."

"Sorry to have troubled you, but I've been seeing some dicey examples of electronic magic. Bill's house is a complete trap. As Shandon Villa will be. You know, the opposition even wired Bill for sound—with a watch, no less, that he only takes off to go swimming. Cute?" And then Tony's amusement ended. "Christ—" He stared at Emil. "Does Parracini own a watch like that one?"

For a long moment, Tony sat completely still, completely silent. "I think I've messed things up," he said softly. His voice sharpened. "There *was* a gap, goddamn it, and I didn't see it." His face was white and tense. He could hear Bill's patient voice explaining to Parracini, in the car, about the necessary change from *Sea Breeze* to *Aurora*, perhaps even giving the advanced time of sailing. And every single word would be sent out by Parracini's watch, to be picked up near at hand, and relayed to Gorsky down in the harbor. "God," he said, and closed his eyes.

Whatever this is, it's bad, thought Emil. "What do we do?"

Can't reach Bill to warn him. Can't risk those blasted bugs near every telephone. Can't leave here either, got to brief Emil at once, let him know what to expect. "Do?" Tony asked heavily. "We don't give up. That's certain." And, he told himself, if I see the *Monique* suddenly preparing to leave at ten thirty, I'll ram her right in the harbor, damned if I don't. "All right. Let's talk."

Emil nodded. He decided to turn on the radio anyway, and sat down to listen.

Twenty-six

A T TEN O'CLOCK, prompt to the minute, two men came walking down the dock. They kept a steady unhurried pace, making their way politely but firmly through clusters of people, paying little attention to anything except their own grave conversation. They wore navy-blue raincoats. Their shoes were polished, their heads neat and well brushed, their collars and ties restrained and impeccable. And one of them carried an attaché case.

Lounging at the bow of the *Sea Breeze*, Emil was the first to catch sight of them. He took out his cigarette case and turned his back on the *Monique* as he spoke two words into it. "Looks good," he told Tony, who was still keeping out of sight in the cabin. He lit a cigarette, took a couple of drags, and only then did he seem to become aware of the two visitors. His nonchalance left him. He flicked the cigarette over the side and went to meet them, jumping onto the dock with—apparently—a smile of welcome. Actually, it was the Mutt and Jeff identification, delivered in a quick murmur, that was amusing Emil. He gave them a small salute, brought his voice back to normal. "Hope you had a pleasant trip. This way, gentlemen." He even steadied them by the elbow as they stepped on deck.

"You're overplaying it, buddy," the taller of the two said. "We aren't as decrepit as all that." He looked about sixty or a little less, gray-haired, slightly stooped, with a white indoor complexion.

"Just the VIP treatment," Emil assured him. "We're being watched."

The other one said nothing, merely pursed his pale lips. He was of medium height, putting on weight like his friend, his reddish hair fading with age. He too looked as though he spent most of his time at a desk.

What a pair of elderly ducks, thought Emil; where did Bill find them? And these are the men who patrolled up and down the mole last night, making sure no one boarded the *Sea Breeze*! If that had happened, they might have needed more help than I did. Emil was smiling broadly as he ushered them into the cabin.

"Hi there," said the gray-haired man. "I'm Saul."

"Walt," said the other. "Tony? Emil?"

They shook hands, looked round the small cabin, noted its tightly drawn curtains. "Who's doing the watching?" Saul asked.

"That cabin cruiser you passed. The *Monique*."

"We saw her arriving just as we were knocking off duty last night. Neat-looking piece. So that's our target."

"Rather," said Tony, "we are their target." His study of the two men ended. "Excellent," he told them, "an excellent job. But you can start stepping out of character."

"What?" asked Walt. "No more VIP treatment? And just as I was beginning to like it." But without wasting a second they shed the raincoats, pulled off the ties, stripped themselves of shirts and neatly creased trousers. They were now in tight-fitting jeans, coarsely knitted sweaters (Saul's was navy; Walt's, a dirty white). The wigs were next to go, revealing Saul's hair to be light brown, longish, sun-bleached at the edges, with a loose wave falling over his brow. Walt had black hair, thick and heavy, curling close to his head. From the attaché case, out came one pair of faded espadrilles, one pair of old sneakers, a small jar of cold cream, tissues, a mirror. With lightning speed they went to work on greasing and wiping their faces. The white indoor look vanished, was replaced by their permanent tans. And once the polished shoes were changed for espadrilles and sneakers, the transformation was complete: two young men, not much older than Emil and equally lithe and lean.

Emil's admiring stare was cut short by Tony. "Time to jolly your fishing friends into making a bet," he was told. He left immediately.

Tony studied the two quick-change artists. "Congratulations," he said. Three minutes it had taken them, no more.

"What now?" Saul asked.

"As soon as some diversion starts on board the fishing boat, you can slip out and stroll back down the dock."

"That all?" Saul didn't hide his disappointment.

"It's plenty. Did you know you were photographed?" Just wish, Tony thought, there had been three of them; still, Gorsky might possibly deduce, when he saw two men, that Gerard had substituted for one of the officers who were originally coming to meet Parracini. Did I mention "three" to Bill when he was wearing that bloody watch? Or did I have enough sense to keep my big mouth shut, only talk of Gerard? No time now to start recalling that garden scene—and stop worrying, there's nothing you can do about it, anyway. "You'll drive some guys crazy, back in Moscow, trying to fit names to your faces."

"Who's running their show here?"

"Gorsky."

"Who's Gorsky?" asked Walt.

"A tough customer. He had his underwater experts attach an explosive to the *Sea Breeze* last night. Emil found it." They seemed to know what that must have entailed, for they looked impressed and were no doubt reassessing Emil. Tony continued, "There is something else you could do. Risky, of course; you'll possibly be on camera again. What I've got in mind—"

But Emil had returned. "No need to place a wager," he told Tony.

"They've been working on the mainsail, got it hoisted halfway, and it's stuck. Quick," he urged Saul and Walt, "now's your moment."

Walt didn't budge. "What did you have in mind?" he asked Tony.

"At ten thirty, wait at the head of the dock. You'll see me, wearing this checked tweed"—Tony picked up his denim jacket, showed its lining—"accompanying a man, dark hair and mustache, dark suit. Run some interference for us when we pass the *Monique*. Will do?"

They were on their way. "Ten thirty," Saul said as he and Walt stepped on deck. Quickly, they passed Emil, leaning against a rail, watching the fishing boat with amusement. So far, its sail hadn't come slithering down, exposing the bow of the *Sea Breeze* to curious eyes on board the *Monique*. Emil drew a breath of genuine relief: the two men were now on the dock, with no connection observed between them and the *Sea Breeze*.

Behind him Tony's voice said, "I've got three minutes to catch a cab. See you." And Tony left, too, almost on the heels of Saul and Walt. He was once more wearing his denim jacket, knitted cap, eyeglasses; his walk—when Emil risked another glance at the dock—was a brisk seagoing roll. He caught up with Saul and Walt, passed them, and was lost in the crowd.

Definitely thickening, Emil noted. The harbor had come to life. Now there was constant movement on the dock and on the long mole above it. In the anchorage itself, some boats had already left for a cruise, weather permitting; some were being sluiced down and polished; others, with less optimistic owners, were being secured against any afternoon storm. It was the usual Saturday crowd of weekend sailors, wandering around when they weren't on board, interested in anything new and different. There were tourists, too, taking the air, feeding the sea gulls while they had their photographs snapped. And the old salts, gathered in twos and threes, watching this waste of good bread on birds who knew how to scavenge for themselves, were more convinced than ever that foreigners were crazy.

Emil left his post at the rail. It was ten fifteen. Better get the cabin straightened up, he warned himself. And what do we do with the clothes that Saul and Walt have left strewn around? Sure, stow them away in a spare locker meanwhile; but how and where do we return them? He went inside, shook his head over the wild disorder that met him, and set to work.

The taxi was waiting, just as arranged. Thankfully Tony got in: at least this was something that hadn't gone wrong. He gave the driver exact instructions that would take him halfway along the bay front, a brief run that would only last four or five minutes. There, at the same red light where he and Georges had stopped last night—good God, was it only last night?—the taxi made its left turn into the westbound avenue. "Just here," Tony said, money ready in his hand as the cab drew up.

He waited until it was bowling back to the Old Town before he moved over to a row of shops, so new that some were still vacant like the apartments above them. This was where he would meet Bernard, just outside the tearoom.

He had let Bernard choose the rendezvous as they had driven down to the Alexandre that morning, to give the quiet unassuming man a touch of needed confidence. Bernard might be Bill's faithful retainer, but he was the

last man Tony would have recruited for the job on hand—except that there
had been no other choice available. The tearoom with cakes for sale, Bernard had suggested at once. He and Brigitte often went there; Brigitte liked
their napoleons, cream inside instead of custard. It had lime-green curtains
and pots of cyclamen. Couldn't be missed.

"All right," Tony had said. "Once you drop Bill and Parracini at the boat,
at ten twenty-five, start driving like the hammers of hell. I mean that! And
pick me up near your tearoom."

"Not at your hotel?"

"No. At the tearoom. And waste no time, Bernard. This is pretty urgent.
And also our own top-secret plan." That had impressed Bernard, even if he
was mystified. "Say nothing to Brigitte or Parracini or Nicole. Bill knows I'm
making arrangements with you, so there's no need to discuss them with him."

And Bernard, still perplexed but always obliging, had told Tony to rely
on him. He'd be at the tearoom as soon as he could. He wouldn't forget
Bill's walking stick. He'd wear a dark suit, as Tony had suggested. And he
wouldn't say a thing to anyone.

So, thought Tony, here I am now, looking at green curtains and splashes
of cyclamen, waiting for Bernard. I am far enough from the harbor, where
Gorsky must have someone stationed as lookout for the arrival of Bill's
Mercedes; I am far enough from the Alexandre and its weary watchdog.
The taxi wasn't followed. I may actually be in the clear, unobserved except
by that girl behind the counter arranging her cream puffs.

He moved away, farther along the row of shops, chose a safer place to
loiter unnoticed—a window display of real-estate photographs, desirable
properties for sale—but kept a constant eye on the avenue that led from
the marina. Bernard wasn't late. It was Tony, overanxious about traffic jams
and distances to be covered—he kept forgetting how short they were in
Menton—who was five minutes early.

But so was Bernard.

In astonishment Tony caught sight of the Mercedes speeding toward him.
He had scarcely time to get his mustache peeled off without taking three
inches of skin before Bernard was about to reach him. And pass him without recognition. Tony whipped off his glasses and cap, waved, brought the
Mercedes to a startled halt. "Well done," he told Bernard. But, he was thinking, I'm glad that none of my friends were around to see that messy
encounter: amateur night at the Palladium. I'd never have heard the end of
it. And he wondered briefly, as Bernard followed his instructions and drove
on past the tearoom with its roving-eyed girl, if Bernard was able to do what
was expected of him without blowing the whole show. "How did it go?"

Bernard burst into a quick and excited story. Bill had made them leave
the house early, insisted on driving, said they could be followed, kept watching the rearview mirror, taking the winding curves of the narrow road like
a crazy man. Then, once round a sharp turn, Bill had pulled up short. And
there *was* a car following. It came round the curve, saw the Mercedes standing there, avoided it, sideswiped a wall at the edge of the—

Tony caught Bernard's arm, interrupting the flow of words. "We'll stop
here." He was drawing off his denim jacket, pulling out a dark brown wig
and mustache from a pocket. "We'll change before we reach the harbor,

arrive as expected. So—" he told Bernard, applying the mustache for him—"press hard on it. Hold your fingers there. Yes, that's right. And now this wig. Get it well down. Cover your own hair completely."

Bernard, after his first astonished moment, was quick enough. His own thin reddish-fair hair vanished. He studied the transformation in the car mirror, took out a comb to arrange his heavy dark waves in place, fingered the mustache once more, and nodded his approval. "It alters a man," he admitted, and smiled.

Tony had pulled on his own wig, changing his medium-cut hair, indeterminate brown, into longish blond locks. "Serious business," he warned. "No more smiles, Bernard. We could be watched every step of the way, from the Mercedes to the *Sea Breeze*. Let's get moving."

They started on the last lap of the journey toward the harbor. "What did Bill do?" Tony asked, prompting Bernard back into his story. "Did he drive on?"

Yes, that was what he had done. He had driven like a madman, and turned on the radio, and talked through it—about a change in the arrangements.

"And Parracini? How did he take it?"

"At first, angry. Told Bill to turn around, he was going back to the house. And Bill said, 'You don't want to meet Gerard? Because he's not coming near the house. It's no longer safe. You saw that car—it knew where to pick up our trail. What's your choice? Go back? Or go on, as arranged?' So we didn't go back."

"And Parracini?"

"As relieved as I was to arrive at the marina. Six minutes early." Bernard shuddered, remembering the speed with which they had made that wild descent. "We were lucky, I think. But Bill's a good driver—I'll say that for him." He pointed ahead. "I can park there. All right?"

Tony nodded. Yes, he was thinking, Bill is good. If he hadn't remembered Parracini's watch—well, he did; and I didn't.

The Mercedes came to a halt. Bernard's hands were still on the wheel, his grip tightening until white knuckles showed.

A case of stage fright, Tony thought, and at this moment I'm not too certain of my own lines. "Now, all we have to do is walk along a dock," he said reassuringly. "Look at no one, Bernard. No one. Just keep talking to me."

"Am I supposed to be Parracini?" Bernard's doubts were growing. "We'll never manage to—"

"You're his height, and that's the important thing."

"But if you are Bill, then—"

"I know. I'm three inches shorter, but he never was seen around town, was he? I've got his color of hair and his limp and his cane. So we'll manage. Shoulders back, Bernard, remember the way Parracini walks. And keep to my left side, your face turned toward me and away from the boats. Ready? Here goes." He reached over to the back seat for the walking stick, gripping it in his right hand, and got out of the car. Bernard had no choice. He got out too. "Left side, Bernard, left side! And you look fine."

As they crossed the avenue to reach the harbor, Bernard asked, "Are we doing this because of Parracini?"

"Yes."

"To distract the KGB?" Bernard's face was grim.

"Yes," said Tony again, and repressed a smile. "Just a little distraction." And a very big bluff. "Now let's talk of other things. What did you think of that Milan-Turin soccer match last week? A near riot, I heard."

And Bernard, who followed every football game on television, had a topic to keep him going on that nerve-racking walk to the *Sea Breeze*. Once he paused in his monologue—almost as they were reaching the *Monique*—to glare at a couple of young men who were about to pass and then, as they came abreast, slackened speed while they argued about some item in the newspaper one of them was opening.

"Face this way!" Tony got out in time. "Watch me!" Bernard remembered. He averted his head from the two men on his left, ignored their newspaper with its pages being turned, spread wide for consultation, and went on talking to Tony.

The *Monique* lay behind them. Tony checked a surge of relief, kept the same steady pace. Brilliant, he thought of the newspaper: Saul and Walt really knew all the tricks of the trade. They had managed to break the *Monique*'s view of Bernard and Tony, just at the crucial moment of passing; and they had made sure, too, that their own faces wouldn't be clearly photographed. Two bent heads, gesticulating arms, a flutter of turning pages: that was all Gorsky would make of them. Yes, brilliant. And essential. For the main-sail on the fishing boat was no longer of any help: it had been lowered and furled.

Tony looked at Bernard. His shoulders were squared, he held himself tall, and now that the annoyance of two young men trying to crush past him was over, he was even enjoying himself. "Careful," Tony warned. "Just another ten paces to go."

They reached the *Sea Breeze*, entered its tidied cabin. Emil was now at the ship's radio, talking with the harbor master. He broke off to say, "Got this five minutes ago," as he handed over a coded message. It was from the *Aurora*. It read, "Cargo fully loaded. Sailed on schedule."

Trust Vincent: everything done navy style. Bill and Parracini might arrive six minutes ahead of time, but the *Aurora* sailed exactly as arranged, at ten thirty.

Tony crossed over to one of the starboard windows, gently eased its heavy curtain apart. Beyond the fishing boat the *Monique* rested quietly. No sign of leaving. He kept watch, waiting for any sudden activity. Nothing. He stayed there, watching and waiting. At last he let the quarter-inch gap of curtain close. He was smiling broadly. "They couldn't follow the *Aurora* now. She's well away."

"We did it!" Emil said, and slapped Bernard on the back.

"Easy, easy, take it easy," Tony said, restraining his laughter and theirs. "Don't forget that an important conference, with four very serious people, is beginning in this cabin. And you are one of them," he told Bernard. "Don't look out. Don't open the door. Keep the curtains closed." He was removing the blond wig, reversing the jacket back to work-worn denim. The cap he would need; glasses and mustache expendable. "Get rid of the fancy dress," he urged Bernard. "Make yourself comfortable."

Bernard peeled off his dark mustache and wig. "Where are we going?"

"For a pleasure cruise."

"I just sit here? Stay inside? What about you?"

"We're the crew," Emil said impatiently. "And we'll be busy on deck until we clear the harbor. We cast off at eleven. Prompt." He turned to Tony. "I checked the harbor master about that. No delay, he said: there's another boat pulling out at eleven ten." Emil's grin was wide. "Guess who?"

So Gorsky was giving them a ten-minute start. Mighty generous of him, considering the *Monique* could raise almost thirty-five miles an hour while the *Sea Breeze,* under power, could manage eleven and a half. Their thirty knots, thought Tony, against our ten: he will be right on our tail from the word go.

"Also," Emil was saying, "I told the harbor master we probably wouldn't head in here tonight. Possibly returning tomorrow."

"You did, did you?" Tony sounded nettled.

Bernard interrupted them both. "I've got to get back by this afternoon. Brigitte doesn't know where I am. She's expecting me—"

"She'll wait," said Emil brusquely. And to Tony, "I thought it was a good idea. The *Monique* is bound to be listening for any communication between us and the shore." He paused, guessed the reason for Tony's silence. "Of course I didn't mention Nice. Did you think that I was fool enough to steer them in *that* direction?"

Tony relaxed. We're all getting too sharp-set, he thought. "Then it was a very good idea." It would certainly jolt Gorsky: what overnight trip for the *Sea Breeze,* and where? Not according to plan. And why wasn't Parracini's watch functioning? Why was nothing being received right now from the *Sea Breeze* cabin? Yes, Tony answered himself, the watch is functioning, but it has been too far away for any monitoring. Far, far away, Gorsky, and getting farther by the minute. "One thing is certain," Tony predicted, "Gorsky won't let us out of his sight."

"And then?" asked Emil, very quietly.

"It depends on Gorsky, doesn't it?"

"He could try to board us—there are five of them, don't forget. Or he could ram us."

"Oh, come on, Emil. Cool it. Worrying is my business, not yours."

Bernard stared at them. "There's still danger?"

"It's only beginning," said Emil.

"Oh," said Bernard. His face brightened. He forgot about Brigitte and cream cakes for tea. "Well, I'm not going to stay in here doing nothing. How can I help?"

"By staying in here," Tony told him. "Don't look out, don't be seen. That's the most important thing right now."

"And later?"

"Later, we'll call on you. If necessary." Tony checked his watch for the third time, and stepped onto the deck. He passed quickly to the port side of the boat, where the cabin would shield him from the *Monique*'s view. There he could wait for the next two minutes and time to cast off. He would be seen then, of course, no way to avoid it. But with his collar hunched up, and his knitted cap down over his brow, his head bent, his face averted, he

might just postpone identification until the right moment. And that wasn't
here, at this dock, at three seconds to eleven.

"Okay," he sang out for Emil's benefit, and moved toward the lines.
"Let go."

Twenty-seven

BLUE SKY AND white clouds, steady breeze and rippling waves, it was the
Saturday sailors' delight. Small craft dotted Garavan Bay, everything from
rowing boats with outboard engines to light yachts under sail. The *Sea Breeze*
headed east as though she were bound for Italy. She was taking it easy, traveling only at half speed so that she'd be less than a mile away from the harbor when the *Monique* emerged.

"There she is," said Emil, "and they've seen us."

"Good," said Tony.

The *Monique* skirted the off-shore craft, only began to put on speed as
the *Sea Breeze* passed the high promontory of cliffs that formed the end of
the bay, and was lost to her sight. Temporarily. The *Monique*, under full
power, reached the cliffs, came sweeping round them to enter Italian
waters. She found herself almost faced with the *Sea Breeze*, which had turned
and was now heading back under full power toward Garavan Bay.

Once there, the *Sea Breeze* reduced speed and sailed on, past the harbor,
past Menton's west bay, rounded Cap Martin and again dropped out of sight.
Again, the *Monique* gave chase, soon reached Cap Martin, only to find herself
head on to the *Sea Breeze* as she turned east once more.

And that was the way it went for the next twenty minutes. The *Monique*,
baffled and angry, retreated to a less ridiculous position, where—a couple of
miles out to sea—she could heave to and watch the *Sea Breeze* from a distance.

"She should have done that in the first place," Emil said. "Whoever is
giving the orders isn't much of a sailor. He's more accustomed to tailing
his quarry through city streets."

Bernard, dressed in a heavy ill-fitting sweater borrowed from Emil's locker,
clung on tightly to the rail and said, "If he isn't much of a sailor, then he's
feeling like me." He was cheerful, but pale of face. He averted his eyes from
the waves that seemed to him to be growing bigger. It was colder, too.

"Go below," Emil advised. The clouds were moving, the breeze had
strengthened into a wind from the southeast. Not too much force as yet,
but it was blowing up.

Bernard shook his head, clung on. Bright sun and blue sky should surely
mean that there was nothing to worry about. "I like it here." They were far
out in Garavan Bay now. He could see the whole of Menton.

Emil's bout of sharp temper, back in the harbor, had left him. It was the
waiting that had irritated him, that and the unnecessary ballast they had been
forced to carry in the shape of Bernard. Now, he clapped Bernard's shoul-

der before he moved inside to the radio. The message from the *Aurora* was due any minute.

Tony was at the wheel, and enjoying himself immensely. He had zigzagged across both the bays, sometimes heading out to sea as though he were actually making for the *Monique*. Then, before he got too close to her, he had steered a wide curve back toward land. In a light breeze, this had been simple enough to maneuver, but with the wind strengthening—well, thought Tony, it won't be too pleasant for them sitting out there: they'll have to use more power, keep themselves steady, not let the *Monique* get out of control.

Emil called to him, "Still thumbing your nose at Gorsky? He's got the message by this time."

"But we've lost our advantage," Tony reminded him. Back in the harbor, and even for the first five minutes of this erratic voyage, the *Monique* had been unaware that the *Sea Breeze* knew all about her. The *Monique* had been the watcher, the calculator, the chaser. She hadn't realized that she had been watched, calculated against, and then led into a senseless chase. But now Gorsky knew. The *Sea Breeze* was going no place.

"Well, we've given him a couple of real problems," Emil said. "Is there anyone important on board? Has he been duped all the way?"

"And," Tony added, "how much has his own security been endangered? That is what really hurts."

"Just a moment!" Emil pressed his left hand against his earphone, noting down the message as he listened. "Received. Over and out," he said at its end. He brought the slip of paper to Tony. "How's that?" he asked with a wide and happy smile.

The *Aurora*'s message was succinct. *Cargo unloaded. Easy transfer made. Already airborne. Instructing escort return full speed Menton, ETA noon. Will cover your position.*

"An escort?" Emil said. "We could use it."

"If it arrives in time. I think we'll make our move right away. In another twenty minutes that sea is going to be rough. And what d'you make of that, Emil?" Tony pointed to a motor launch, traveling at full speed, sending spray flying high as it cut and bumped over the waves. "It left the harbor eight minutes ago, has been circling widely around us."

Emil picked up his binoculars. "Looks official to me. Harbor police? They don't like the way you handle a boat."

"I doubt if harbor police would be as wild and erratic as that."

"They're crazy," Emil agreed. "But it must be fun too. I'll go on deck, have a clearer look."

"No. Take the helm. Head her straight out." Tony was pulling all the curtains apart, leaving a glass-enclosed cabin. Conference over, he thought with a smile.

"Toward the *Monique*?"

"That's right. Get within hailing distance."

"Too close."

"All right. Within clear sighting distance. That's all Gorsky will need. His binoculars are as good as ours."

"That's still within pistol range."

"In this rising sea? They couldn't hit an elephant."

"They'll have rifles," Emil warned. But Tony was already stepping out on deck, binoculars ready for a quick look at the motor launch.

Bernard had retreated to the mast, one arm hooked around it. His hair blew wildly around his eyes. But there was still a smile, small but determined, to greet Tony. "No, I'm not going inside," Bernard said. "I prefer to be sick out here."

"So do I," Tony told him. "A useful tip. Stay relaxed. Keep your knees slightly bent. Sway as the boat sways."

"What's that ship? I think it has been following us."

"That brown boat? A motor launch. And I think you're right."

"It's like a sheep dog, moving round and round."

And we are the sheep to be herded? Tony raised his glasses. The launch didn't show any official pennant. Two figures, keeping well down. But not clearly visible, with the spray flying over their heads. Was this some reinforcement that Gorsky had ordered up? Or— "I think you're right again," Tony said. "That's our sheep dog." But who? Those two crazy maniacs? He kept staring at the launch. Its circling became tighter as it drew protectivly nearer. Protective, thought Tony, that's the exact word. They are giving us support. He waved both arms.

Emil was bringing the *Sea Breeze* around. And there, across a short stretch of rough water, was the *Monique*. Clear sighting distance, thought Tony: our empty cabin will be easily seen—Gorsky has his glasses trained on it. He pulled off his cap, said to Bernard, "You take it, keep your ears warm. And stay behind the mast." Then he stepped forward to the rail.

He faced into the wind, his hair blown straight back, revealing his face clearly as he confronted the *Monique*. He could almost feel Gorsky's binoculars boring into him. So there goes my cover, he thought: identity established. But there'll be no rough stuff, no rifle bullet between my eyes. Tempting, though, at this moment, when I'm an easy target. Would Gorsky risk it, with that motor launch watching? I doubt it. Gorsky likes things neat and natural, all evidence concealed.

Suddenly, the *Monique* moved ahead. Rough stuff after all, thought Tony: she's going to ram our bow, witness or no witness. "Hold on!" he yelled at Bernard.

But within seconds the *Monique* had passed clear, leaving the *Sea Breeze* rearing and bucking in the cross-waves from her wake. Tony picked himself up from the deck, held on to a safety line. He was soaked through. So was Bernard, but he was still in place, both arms tight around the mast.

In the motor launch Saul said to Walt, "Did you see that?" He stared after the *Monique*. "A real bastard, could have clipped them."

"His last word?" suggested Walt. "All right, let's head for the beach. This storm is really building up now."

The *Sea Breeze* had the same idea. "She'll make it," Saul said. "That kind of old tub usually does."

"Old tub? She looks smooth enough."

"But snub-nosed."

"Which was lucky for her."

They fell silent, partly because of the rising sea. The *Monique* was still in sight, on a westerly course, under full power, keeping well clear of the land.

"She'll make it, too," Walt said as they entered Garavan Bay. "Pity that tail wind doesn't catch her stern, tip her bows into—" He stopped short, staring, wiping spray out of his eyes.

For at that moment, the *Monique* had exploded. "My God," said Walt.

And then a second explosion, bigger, louder, flashing a ball of flame.

"My God," echoed Saul. "She had ammunition on board." He looked back at the *Sea Breeze*. But she was still ploughing her steady course toward Menton harbor.

Twenty-eight

BY SUNDAY MORNING, the storm had blown itself out, the bitter wind and chilling air had gone as quickly as they had come. The promenade was no longer an empty stretch of writhing palm trees lashed by spray, or a target for pebbles picked up from the beach and thrown by angry waves. Once again people were walking and talking, or sitting at outside café tables. All had returned to normal.

Except Nicole. She was still partly under shock, Tony noted as he entered under the yellow-striped awning and saw her seated at her usual window table. Her dark hair was as smooth and gleaming as ever, and her clothes as smart. But her pale face, perfect in its shape, was even whiter; her large brown eyes still larger. There was no smile on her lips. Her morning paper had been pushed aside, coffee was untouched, three half-smoked cigarettes lay in the ash tray.

"Are you early or am I late?" Tony asked as he took the chair opposite her.

"I couldn't sleep, couldn't stay in the house. I've been driving around." She tried to smile, and failed. "But thank you for coming, Tony. It is safe to meet here now, isn't it?"

"Well," he said, "the opposition is in slight disarray. Meanwhile. But let's keep our voices down—until my coffee arrives, at least." He covered her hand with his, and pressed it. "Are you all packed? Ready to leave? I've got a car waiting at the garage—"

"First," she said, drew her hand away, "first I must tell you something." She fell silent, not meeting his eyes, until the waitress brought his coffee and left. Then she looked at him, her voice low but determined. "I'm leaving, Tony. Permanently. I am going to send in my resignation."

"There's no need for that," he said quietly.

"I want out."

"Why?"

"Because I've lost confidence. I was of no help to you. I might even have endangered the whole—"

"On the contrary, you helped a great deal."

"Tony, I don't want excuses and I don't want sympathy. I failed you. I failed everyone."

He glanced around the room, empty except for the waitress and counter-man, who were having a discussion of their own in this lull before lunch-time. "You helped," he insisted. "You made that house up on Garavan Hill a very pleasant place for him."

Yes, she thought in anguish, Parracini had found it very pleasant indeed, far easier than he had ever expected. "And so he became too sure of himself?" she asked bitterly. "He thought I was a simple-minded idiot, and Bill was an easy-going American, and Bernard and Brigitte were just part of the furniture."

"Well, he's disillusioned about all that now."

"About Bill—yes."

"It all worked out, you know," Tony tried.

"With no help from me."

"You're really determined to ruin my day, aren't you?" Tony asked half-jokingly.

"Sorry. You should be celebrating, instead of—sorry, Tony. At least you got your sleep, I see." He looked a different man, in his well-cut jacket, excellent shirt and tie, from the one who had driven up to the house yesterday along with Bernard, two disheveled figures in borrowed clothes, incongruous in a Mercedes. He had stayed only long enough to tell her about Parracini.

"Twelve solid hours."

"At the Alexandre?"

He shook his head and smiled. He was thinking of the waiter who had been scared witless. It had seemed the easiest solution to have Saul pay his bill and collect his belongings.

"See?" she asked, and sighed unhappily.

"See what?"

"You don't trust me, Tony."

He said nothing to that. What's behind all this? he wondered.

"You could have told me more when we met here on Friday. You could have drawn me into the action. You used to do that. We worked well together, once."

"I hadn't anything to tell you on Friday."

She stared, incredulous. "You mean, you didn't know about—about his real identity?"

"As much as we all knew, you included."

"Then why did you come to Menton?"

"A simple tour of inspection. That was all."

"But you sensed something, didn't you?"

Again he said nothing.

"You thought I liked him too much. You thought—"

"Let's say you were too uncritical of him." Tony's anger was sudden, sur-prising even him. He regained his calm. "You didn't keep him in check. But what worried me most, on Friday morning, was that he was endanger-ing himself." Tony shook his head over that stupidity. "We were all fooled, at least part of the way. So shut up, will you, darling? You aren't the only one who's hiding a blistered ego under his celebration shirt."

"Except," she said slowly, "I didn't even earn a celebration shirt. Not this time. And so I'm backing out. If this could happen once, it could hap-pen again."

"All you need is some rest and recreation. I'm driving to Paris, a nice slow trip, regular meals, no wet sea, no telephones. Will you join me?" The question was casual, the invitation not.

She smiled, but she shook her head. "You have plenty of girls, Tony. They'll be at every stop along the way on that nice slow trip." The smile vanished, her eyes left his, her voice seemed strangled. "I liked him, Tony." She looked up, then. "I really liked him."

So that's it, thought Tony. She fell in love with Parracini.

"And you're still in love—" he began, and stopped, his lips compressed.

Nicole saw his face tighten. She gathered up her handbag and left so swiftly that he was only halfway to his feet as she touched his hand and was gone.

"Nicole—"

She was out on the sidewalk, walking steadfastly away, the skirt of her loose white coat swinging above her red leather boots.

She made the choice, he thought, and sat down again. His coffee tasted bitter. He reached for the abandoned newspaper, if only to stop thinking about Nicole.

Front-page prominence was given to the two explosions yesterday on board a luxury cabin cruiser, and to a lot of wild speculation. The only factual item was that a naval patrol boat, arriving just after the *Monique* had disintegrated, had searched for survivors, an impossible task due to the heavy seas prevailing at that time. None had been found.

But on an inside page, tucked away at the bottom of a column, was a small report on a suicide at Shandon Villa. Tony rose, went over to the telephone, searched for some *jetons,* and dialed the Kelsos' number.

It was Dorothea who answered. "Tony—we wondered where you were. Why didn't you call us yesterday?"

"I was pretty well tied up. But what about lunch today?"

"Oh, Tony—we can't possibly. I'm in the middle of packing. We leave tomorrow. Tom is down in Menton now, making all the final arrangements. About Chuck. He's—he's going home too."

"Did you see that Shandon made today's paper?"

"Oh, that! It didn't tell you anything. But I've got the inside story!"

"From whom?"

"Remember that nice young policeman, the one who came up to the house on Friday night to get our statement about the burglary?"

"Louis?"

"He came back yesterday to ask more questions."

That was Louis. Definitely.

"He had been down at Shandon Villa—"

"When?" Tony asked, his interest quickening.

"Around breakfast time. Just after Rick Nealey shot himself. Incredible, wasn't it?"

The only thing that had astonished Tony was the quickness of it all. He'd have given Nealey three or four more days, perhaps a week. What had happened that had made Gorsky move so fast?

Dorothea said, "It *was* suicide, Tony. He was found in his bedroom, with the gun in one hand and a letter in the other."

"Typed?"

"No. It was in Nealey's own writing." She laughed as she added, "You really are a very suspicious man, Tony. Nealey had been overworked; and depressed. As I think he should have been."

Tony restrained a sudden attack of sarcasm. Not to Dorothea, not to dear sweet trusting believing Dorothea. Had she forgotten the fakery of Chuck's accident? "Yes," he agreed. "But who else had been wandering in and out of that bedroom?" One of Gorsky's electricians, or the little redhead . . .

"You don't think it was—" Dorothea began slowly.

"No need to think anything. It's all past tense now."

"Yes," she said. "Yes." Then she roused herself. "Tom's going to be disappointed he missed you. Can you drop in this evening?"

"No, I'm leaving too. I'm on my way, in fact."

"Then we'll see you in Washington. When are you coming to America again?"

"Can't say exactly. But we'll meet."

"Yes. We really must have dinner together. And talk." She sounded vague, as if she were already thousands of miles away.

"Better get back to your packing."

She laughed. "You should see the complete chaos around me. Everything seems to have multiplied."

But that was all she had to worry about now: where to put what in which suitcase. "Give Tom my best. How is he?"

"Fine, just fine," she said happily. "Our thanks, Tony. And my love. See you sometime." She ended the call.

"Good-by, beautiful," he said into the silent phone. Sometime . . . That was how it went.

He paid the check and moved quickly out of the café, felt a strange depression as he stood there, among brightly checked tablecloths under a yellow-striped awning. Now the garage, he thought, and a car with luggage in place, ready to go. But he still stood, undecided. Out of habit he scanned the faces that passed him, the cars that were parked along the curb. And suddenly, just ahead of him, there was a car he recognized. A small red Opel. He began walking.

Nicole hadn't seen him. She was seated at the wheel, her smooth dark head bent, her shoulders drooping, her eyes on her hands lying inert on her lap. She was a girl crying out for help.

Tony opened the car door. She looked up, her cheeks tear-stained, her large eyes despairing. "Move over," he said. And she did.

He got in and started the engine, glancing round at her suitcases piled into the back seat. "Where?"

"I don't know," she said, barely audible. She dried her cheeks, and tried to laugh at herself. She broke down once more. "Oh, Tony—I thought I'd never see you again."

He wondered, then, if her tears might have been for him, and not for Parracini. For a moment he stared at her. "You don't lose me as easily as that," he told her. His old smile was back, his spirits rising. He edged out into the traffic and headed for the garage.

The
Hidden Target

To
Sir William Stephenson

—a man well named Intrepid—
with admiration and affection

One

THE CHURCH LAY in the heart of the city. It was old, a thousand years old, his fellow workers at the bookstore had told him. And kept telling him, as if to impress the newcomer that Essen wasn't merely a West German town surrounded by coal mines: no more blast furnaces or steelworks since the war; modern factories, fine shops, a handsome art gallery, pleasant suburbs. Yes, they had assured him, he would find life agreeable here. In turn, he had assured them it would be most agreeable. How easy it was to be accepted, he thought as he approached the main entrance of the church, if you smiled and nodded. Criticism jarred, rousing animosities, even curiosity about any offbeat character who didn't fit in. If there was one success in the eight months he had spent in this industrial town, it was that he had fitted in. To his acquaintances, he was simply Kurt Leitner, a quiet, unassuming, undemanding young man, totally unremarkable. Dull? He hoped so. It had spared him from parties and overfriendly interest.

Leitner stepped into the church, cold gray dimness towering around him, glitter from the far-off altar to lighten the gloom, stillness broken by the slow shuffle of tourists' feet now entering the Gothic hall that formed the nave. Their guide's hushed voice droned on: that part tenth century, this part thirteenth, this built by so-and-so, that added by whoosis; notice the pulpit, the chancel, the narthex; all tributes of centuries past. The monotone faded into a murmur; the shuffles merged into silence. Leitner's eyes, accustomed now to the shadows, were fixed on the third massive pillar to the right of the nave. Slowly, with total unconcern, he moved into the aisle and approached the carved stone column. Theo wasn't visible from this angle, but Theo would be there. As usual, Theo would have arrived early and given himself time for a leisurely stroll around the church, studying the people in prayer or contemplation before the altar, checking the group gathered at a side chapel for some remembrance. Theo was thorough. Caution and care were his professional mark.

And Theo was there, a prosperous bourgeois in his dark suit blending with the pillar against which one shoulder rested. A man in his fifties perhaps, of medium height, with brindled hair cut short and a smooth white face. He glanced at Leitner, and gave an almost imperceptible nod of approval, not only for Leitner's casual approach, but also for his somber gray jacket and dark shirt. Then the two men, vague shadows in this unlit area of the church, faced the pillar ahead of them: two strangers lost in quiet reverence.

Leitner waited. Theo would set the pace. This was an emergency. No doubt about that. The signal for it had been simple, planned long in advance. "If ever I call you—before you leave for work—about your family in Munich," Theo had said when Leitner was being installed in Essen, "that will be the sign. We'll meet in the Minster seven minutes after the bookstore shuts down for lunch. When is that?" Leitner had answered, "Twelve-thirty. But I could be delayed. I'm the junior clerk." There could be a dilatory customer to ease out of the shop before he closed it. "Then," Theo had replied, "we'll make it twelve-forty-five—the third pillar to your right as you enter. One early-morning phone call and you'll be there." The call had come this morning. A brief, innocent talk with "Uncle Ernst" about Leitner's mythical father in Munich, who had slipped and broken his thigh. Simple. That was the way Theo liked it. Ultraclever voice codes or notes that had to be deciphered were something that could arouse suspicion if they were overheard or intercepted. Keep it natural, was his dictum.

Now, he stayed silent for a full minute: two strangers didn't start talking as soon as they had met. And then, as if making a remark about the church, even gesturing briefly toward a distant sculpture on which his eyes were fixed, he said in his low voice, "You do not travel to Frankfurt next week. You do not fly to London as planned. Instead, you leave tonight. Nine o'clock. By truck. From Leopold's."

Leitner nodded. He knew the place. It was one of the smaller machine shops on the outskirts of town. There was worry in his eyes. What had gone wrong? He did not pose the question. Theo would tell him—if he needed to know.

"You'll travel light. The night dispatcher at Leopold's is reliable. Leave your motorcycle and extra baggage with him. We'll have them picked up within the hour. The driver of the truck will give us no trouble. It will be a safe journey. And short. You will be dropped off the truck at Duisburg."

Shock stiffened Leitner's spine, but his brief stare at the placid face beside him was its only evidence. Duisburg, on the Rhine, the largest inland port in Europe, with its twenty basins, vast stretches of silos and warehouses, oil storage tanks; Duisburg, the target his people had been aiming at for more than a year, long before they drifted quietly into Essen. It was a convenient half hour away by car or motorbike. Careful infiltration, well-directed sabotage, and the storage tanks, with their one hundred and seventy-eight million gallons of oil, could add considerable color to the background of red smoke from the Ruhr's blazing blast furnaces. "Tonight in Duisburg," he reminded Theo, his voice equally low, "we had planned some fireworks."

"We've postponed them."

This time Leitner's stare was long-lasting, challenging. All those preparations, all that work we put into the plan, the risks, the dangers . . . "I've got Section Two all set up in Duisburg. Section One in Essen is ready. They cooperate well. They—"

'We have an informer among us." Theo's face was expressionless.

"In Section Two?"

"No."

"Section One?" The section I organized and led for the last five years . . . Leitner's disbelief turned to alarm, even into a moment of panic. Quickly, with an effort, he repressed all emotion. "It's definite?"

"Quite definite. The police raided the Friederikenstrasse apartment at midnight and arrested Ferdi and Willy, your radio experts. They also found weapons. Amalie wasn't there, or Berthe."

"They had dates last night, picking up some information from a couple of army sergeants. Who is the—"

Theo signaled for silence, moved aside.

Leitner waited, head bowed. The disaster wasn't complete: the communications unit was destroyed, but they could be replaced. Not like Marco, with his assistant, Karl, installed in the Rüttenscheid area: Marco was the specialist, the expert in demolition. The other three members of Section One, with part-time jobs as hairdresser, drugstore clerk, bus driver, shared quarters in Töpferstrasse. He, himself, had his own place, a rented room within walking distance of the bookstore. None of the others, not even Marco, had visited it, or even knew where it was or where he worked. To them, old comrade Marco excepted, he was Erik, possibly a courier, a trusted go-between. His instructions were conveyed by public phone; meetings, only when necessary, took the form of a beer party in the apartment on Töpferstrasse. And there he had guarded himself by staying in the background, appearing to be a minor cog in this well-designed machine, listening to Marco giving out the orders Leitner had passed to him on the previous evening when they had met in the anonymity of Gruga Park.

As for Theo, their bankroll, their supplier of forged papers—passports, identity cards, licenses—their arranger of reservations on planes, their adviser and controller, none of the others, not even Marco, had ever seen him; and only Marco knew the code name Theo. But even with Marco, Kurt Leitner had kept silent about his secret encounters with Theo. He didn't allow himself too much speculation, either, about Theo. Yet some things were fairly obvious if you thought hard about them. Theo must run a tourist agency, hence his expertise in travel arrangements. His office could be in neighboring Düsseldorf. (He had, quite abruptly, refused Leitner's plan for an operation in that city, tempting as it was as the financial and administrative center of the major Ruhr industries.) But where Theo's supply of money came from, or what vast intelligence source supported him with world-wide information and contacts, these were matters best left unquestioned. They existed. That was enough.

Theo was still a few paces away, seemingly studying the nave of the church. He had been quick to notice the three wandering visitors who were exploring this aisle. But they had found nothing of interest in its unlighted alcoves and walked on, paying little attention to the young man in the shadows, his head bowed, his eyes covered by his hand as if in prayer. Theo returned to stand close again, and Leitner could drop both his hand and his far-ranging thoughts. He asked the question that had been bottled up for those last three interminable minutes. "Who is the informer?"

"Amalie."

"Amalie?" Recruited by Willy in Milan where she had headed out of West Berlin when the remnants of the Baader-Meinhof group were scattering. She had been one of its minor members, but dedicated and intense. At first, she had been doubtful about returning to West Germany, but Willy had persuaded her. Checked and double-checked, her credentials were good. And Willy kept her close to him. "That little whore—" began Leitner, and was silenced by a restraining hand on his arm. Checked and double-checked. By Theo, too. Nothing escaped his oversight. Except this bitch.

"We'll take care of her. And of Willy," Theo said grimly.

Leitner nodded. He had liked Willy, trustworthy, indefatigable, always willing. Too willing, as it had turned out, with a pretty little blonde called Amalie. "Who is she working for? The CIA?"

Theo was smiling as he shook his head. "Forget the CIA. Its throat is cut. Bleeding and paralyzed." He liked that picture. "She isn't with the British or French, either. But we'll find out. She had no direct contact with the Essen police; her information was usually passed to them through some Western intelligence unit. Just as well for us that she never was familiar with police headquarters, or she might have stumbled on my informant there." Theo paused, his eyes watching the nave. "Yes," he went on, "that's how I learned this early morning about the midnight arrests."

"Then you had time to warn Töpferstrasse," Leitner said with relief. "But Marco and Karl are already in Duisburg."

"Marco is on his way to Hamburg. Karl is in hiding. Time enough to warn the others when you and Marco are safely out of Germany."

"Time enough? The police could be moving in on them right now."

"No, no. The police are keeping the arrests quiet—no publicity for thirty-six hours. That way, they hope you will all be unsuspecting and gather as arranged for tomorrow night's meeting in the Töpferstrasse apartment. Then a mass arrest."

Yes, tomorrow night was to have been the celebration party for the Duisburg blowup. A surprise party for most of them—only Marco and Erik and Section Two had known the exact timing of that project. So that was one defeat for Amalie. At the last general meeting in Töpferstrasse, Marco had mentioned the end of next week as zero hour. Leitner's idea: security, security . . . And it had paid off. Partly, at least; for the police must be watching those oil and propane-gas storage areas even if they expected the attack to come ten days away.

Theo seemed to guess Leitner's worry. "The police won't cover the entire waterfront. They'll be nowhere near the Hafentreppen."

Duisburg's quays stretched almost thirty miles along the Rhine. The Hafentreppen, a seamen's bar, was close to the docks but far from the target area. "I contact Sophie?" She worked there regularly; a raddled, blowzy blonde with a quick ear and sharp eyes, one of Theo's prized undercover agents.

Theo nodded. "She'll have one of her clients take you to his ship. It's loading right now. A coastal freighter. Sailing at midnight."

Half an hour to Duisburg, a ten-minute walk to the Hafentreppen, another half hour making careful contact with Sophie, ten minutes or so before he could follow her seaman out of the bar; and how much distance to the freighter? He hoped it was short. "Do I stow away or stay topside?"

"You'll stay in the hold. Quite safely. The first mate needs money. It was easy to arrange that—easier than getting you seaman's papers at such little notice. Besides, your hands would have given you away."

"Sailing at midnight . . . down the Rhine to where?"

"Rotterdam should suit you."

"And there—the usual place?" A safe house, all necessities provided, from money and clothes to the American passport for his new identity. There would be a careful life history worked out for him, too.

Theo answered with a nod, drew a thick envelope from an inner pocket, slipped it into Leitner's hand. "For the journey as far as Rotterdam. Pay the seaman. The mate has had his in advance, but he could need a sweetener. There may be others, too, who'll look aside—with their hands out. That covers everything, I think." Theo glanced at his watch. He didn't need to ask if Leitner had memorized the details of the long journey in the months ahead of him. They had been over all that in their lengthy meetings in the woods beside the onetime estate of the Krupp dynasty. An excellent place for quiet conversations: visitors to the Krupp museum were constantly arriving and departing, so access was safely covered. And the visitors spent their time in the mansion or its vast gardens, had little energy left to explore the wild woods. "You'll arrive in London by next week. Good luck, Erik."

The code name had slipped out. Or a mark of confidence? Leitner wished he were as sure of the London assignment. It was unnecessary, an addition to the original mission. "The girl worries me. Do we really need her?"

"Yes—an opportunity in a million."

"I know little about her. I'll need information, background—"

"You'll get everything from Greta. She's been in London for almost a year, scouting for talent. It was Greta who discovered the girl."

And added several headaches, possibly serious complications. Leitner shook his head. "Frankly, I'm wary about this. Didn't you tell me that Greta decided against recruiting her?"

"But not," Theo said sharply, "against using her. She's important to your mission, ultimately important. Once we heard who her father was—well, the decision was made at the highest levels. Not by Greta." He paused, added softly, "And certainly not by you." His white round face was set, all its usual amiable softness banished.

It's still a crazy idea, thought Leitner. "How do you know she'll even like me?" He tightened his lips, again shook his head. "Without that, there is no trust. Without trust—I'll never get her beyond Amsterdam."

"If you sense danger, then back away—drop her—continue your assignment as originally planned. But I insist you meet her—make your own assessment. Keep remembering that we consider her to be of the utmost importance to our future plans. Never forget that." The hidden command ended. Theo's voice lightened. "There's one small change in your itinerary. After Bombay, fly direct to Indonesia. Omit Malaysia, Singapore. You will reach Bali by early November. You and the girl leave Bali on the seventh of that month—by the cruise ship *Princess Royal*. You will have space reserved for part of that world trip—not unusual—I am taking a segment of the cruise myself. We shall have a very safe opportunity to meet for your last briefing before America." Theo's smile became almost angelic. "I'll join the ship one stage ahead of you—at Singapore—and leave it one stage later than you do. You and the girl disembark at Hong Kong."

"Why the diversion to Bali?"

"It will be a suitable place to leave your travel companions behind."

"Except the girl. If she is still with us."

"Except the girl. And she will be with you. I've never known you to fail with women, Erik. This time, no personal involvement for you, remember! The girl is an assignment, more important than you can guess. Blowing up oil tanks will seem a child's game compared to what I plan for America."

I plan? Not we plan? But it made a good exit line, thought Leitner as Theo pulled out a pair of heavy-rimmed glasses and walked into the nave. A good moment, too, to choose: Theo would have excellent cover all the way into the street. A straggling party of tourists was passing Leitner now, heading for the church door. Theo merged with them, wasn't even noticed.

Leitner waited for five minutes before he started up the aisle. Just what is planned for America? he couldn't help wondering. He and Marco would be working with local talent there. Perhaps they were being selected right now and sent to South Yemen, or to North Korea where he had been given specialized training almost ten years ago. But would they be as efficient as Section One? Marco, of course, would still be with him. The others—where? Regrouped or assigned to Section Two in Duisburg? Perhaps scattered, sent underground? Lying low for how long? Six months? A year? How would they feel tomorrow when Theo gave them the warning signal to clear out? As I am feeling, Leitner knew: enraged to the point of blowing up all of Duisburg, not just setting off a chain reaction of explosions in an oil-storage area. Section One was not dead—after America, he'd be back to give it life again—but it was badly mangled. Last week, it had been the most effective operational unit of the People's Revolutionary Force for Direct Action.

He came into the busy street, the June sunlight strong after the gloom of the church. For a brief moment he paused, lighting a cigarette. Anyone loitering around, waiting to follow him? Just a normal crowd, he decided, and stepped into the stream of people. Intense anger was controlled. Now he was planning his exit from Essen.

First, the bookstore and his pay collected. (What good German boy would disappear without the money he had earned?) Second, Frau Zimmermann, his elderly and inquisitive landlady. (What good German boy would leave by night without rent fully rendered until the end of the week?) In both cases, he would rely on the same story: a father in traction, hospitalized for months; mother ailing; Uncle Ernst needing urgent help with the family's butcher shop in Munich. Bloch, his boss at the bookstore, would let him leave early (half a day's pay, of course). Zimmermann would shake her head over the crisis that forced a young man back to a business he had never wanted—and would he be able to finish the book he was writing? So much work, so much reading he had done for it . . . He could guess the phrases, have brief replies ready, back away gracefully. But he had at least silenced the questions of eight months ago, by giving her just enough in the way of answers so that she, in turn, could answer the questions of her friends. It was a neighborhood of small gossip. Dangerous? Not if you kept your story straight, leaving Zimmermann's romantic imagination to supply an unhappy love affair. Besides, what police spy would think that anyone hiding something important would choose to live in the Zimmermann house?

Everything went according to expectations—except for one surprise punch delivered by Bloch. As he busied himself with Leitner's work papers, he looked up from his desk, cluttered with catalogues. "Have you returned all the books you took out?" Then he went on signing.

Leitner's face tightened. Briefly. "Yes, sir," he said, his eyes fixed on Bloch's bald head, as smooth and gleaming as an ostrich egg. "I brought back the last two books this morning. They were all from the secondhand shelves. I was careful with them, didn't harm them."

"Interested in travel, I see. You'd have found a wider selection in the public library."

And have my name noted along with the subject matter? Leitner looked apologetic and said, "I did try that, but it is difficult to get there when it's open. I'm sorry if I—"

Bloch waved a large expressive hand. "It's over. Forget it. No damage done to the books, but you should have asked permission. So you've got to go back to Munich and give up your travel plans."

"Plans? Oh, no. Nothing immediate. Not for some years yet. First, I read and gather background material. Next, I write. And if my book is success-ful—then I can start traveling."

"A writer, eh?" Bloch pushed his heavy glasses up over his domed head and studied this young optimist—a handsome fellow with steady blue-gray eyes, a beard and mustache and a thatch of brown hair that Bloch could envy. "Better stick to selling books. You'd eat regularly, at least." He dismissed Leitner with "I hope your father recovers" and a clap on the shoulders.

No bad feeling there, Leitner thought with relief as he hurried back to his room. But that was a surprise punch right to my jaw. Who'd have thought the old boy could notice so much through those thick lenses? Did he also notice the pattern of travel that interested me? Western to Eastern Europe, Asia Minor to India, the Far East . . . But I was careful not to take the books in order, and I added several old chestnuts—early journeys of the eighteenth and nineteenth centuries—just to keep my interest looking gen-eral. I underestimated Bloch: a sharp reminder to take nothing for granted, to remember that the smallest mistake might be the big one. Like Willy falling for Amalie's shy smile. Damn them both to everlasting hell.

There was no problem at all with Frau Zimmermann. In her best flow-ered print, she was preparing to leave for early supper and a game of bingo.

That should hold her until nine o'clock, at least. He could pack without interruptions.

He did not need to burn any documents; anything important was well disguised. Such as his cryptic descriptions, no definite place names, of the camping grounds outside the towns and cities he was scheduled to visit in the coming months—all part of the folder boldly headed "Notes for a novel." There was also a page of scrawled first names, some scored out for the sake of realism, above which he had written "Suggested characters." And on another sheet of paper he had made out a list of ages for his proposed characters, giving date and place of birth. The places were entirely a random choice, meaningless. So were the years. But the days and the months were to be remembered. On them, precisely, he would make the arranged contact with the small terrorist factions of the various countries he would visit.

As he placed the folder carefully in his duffel bag, he reassured himself again that these dates appeared quite innocent. He needed that list. He had easily memorized the names of the localities where meetings would be held, but the dates were tricky. Theo had given him a quantity of them, and he couldn't risk any mistiming. Could there be so many groups of would-be guerrillas? Well, he would soon judge, once he met with them, listened to them, studied their leaders, decided whether they were worth taking seriously or not. His reports would go back to Theo, harmlessly phrased about the state of the weather—good, promising, disappointing—and on them the future of the local terrorists depended. Either they'd be found wanting and left to continue their holdups and wild shoot-outs like a lot of cheap gangsters, or they'd be accepted as potentially valuable. In which case they'd become, once their natural leaders had been given specialized training, members of the New International—Direct Action United. They would be ready and waiting for their assignments by the time Leitner was established in America.

Once more he found himself wondering at the cost of all this, at the months of preparation. But no important project came off the drawing board in a week or went into full production within a year. Revolutionary patience, he thought, and smiled. The marriage of opposites. Yet natural complements. Like love and hate. Like destruction and creation . . .

He finished clearing the room of all traces of his existence. Good-bye to Essen; and in Rotterdam, farewell to Kurt Leitner. And to Erik? No. He would always keep Erik, his one constant identity.

Two

Eʀɪᴋ ᴀʀʀɪᴠᴇᴅ ᴀᴛ London's Heathrow Airport, his American passport (new to him, well used in appearance) stating he was James Kiley, born in Oakland, California, on October 10, 1952. This made him two years younger than he actually was, but he looked it with his beard and mustache shaved off, his mid-brown hair shorter and more controlled. It was, he had to admit, quite a transformation. American nationality was no problem: his accent was good, his vocabulary excellent; after all, he had spent a year in Berkeley after his return from North Korea. And one thing he could rely on: his future activities in the United States would certainly not be in the San Francisco area, where he might—a long chance, but still an added worry—be recognized.

As for his real identity—Ramón Olivar, born in Caracas, Venezuela, in 1950—that was past history. Like his parents. Father, a Spanish lawyer from Barcelona, with intense Anarcho-Syndicalist opinions that made him a professional exile; mother, a medical student from Sweden, with Marxist-Leninist views that were in constant argument with her husband's politics, each trying to convert the other. Ludicrous people. But they had taken him to Mexico when they escaped there. Ramón Olivar's name had last been used at the university in Mexico City (1967-69) and in 1970 for his trip along with forty-nine other socialist-minded students to Lumumba University in Moscow. A new name and passport for the concealed journey to North Korea. For the journey back to Mexico, another passport. Yet another, Dutch this time, for the flight into California once the Mexican police had started questioning the 1970 crop of Lumumba graduates (two of them, idiots, had been caught with dynamite all set and ready to explode). And still another passport when he was ordered to proceed to West Germany.

The only constant in all these travels had been the cover name Erik, his own invention. Chosen, unconsciously perhaps, because of his mother? Just as, like her, his hair was light, his eyes blue-gray? He certainly did not look Spanish. There his mother had won out over his dark-haired, dark-eyed father. But not in politics. (He was now far to the left of his father, much farther to the left than his mother.) He hadn't seen either of them since 1970. His father had escaped from Mexico and ended—literally—in Chile. His mother was still alive, and suitably in Cuba.

Other times, other places . . . All distant, all shut away in tight mental compartments. Now he was James Kiley, a footloose American. He had his history at tongue tip: California born, moved from Oakland with his parents to Illinois; and when they were killed in an automobile crash, became a ward of his well-to-do uncle in Illinois who owned a wire and sheet company—gold and silver, in other words, necessary for jewelry manufacture. No brothers, no sisters, no other relatives, no marriages, no complications . . . He looked the part he was playing: a young man traveling, with some ambitions to be a roving correspondent, looking for wider horizons than his uncle's factory in Chicago.

He passed through Heathrow's arrival formalities, no trouble at all, and walked briskly to the main entrance. Greta, Theo's devoted talent scout, would be waiting for him. And she was. A red-and-white-checked suit, a red purse over her left arm, as prescribed, so that his eye could pick her out even before he saw the familiar face. She gave no hint of recognition, either. As he drew near, she left. At a leisurely pace, he followed the red-and-white-checked suit until she had stepped into her dark-red car. Then, with his one bag heaved into its small back seat, he slipped in beside her and they were on their way. For the next hour, Greta would be responsible for his safety.

They hadn't met since Berlin, almost five years ago, but Greta, close up, hadn't changed much: the same slight figure, rusty-brown hair, eyes so light in color that their blue was almost colorless, a white skin that never tanned, pale lips, a furrow between her eyebrows that made her look helpless and anxious, and a smile that was deceptively sweet. He knew neither her real name nor anything about her origins, although his guess was that she came from the Berlin area itself—the accent was there when she spoke German in her brusque voice, and she had shown an intimate knowledge of its streets and shops that one didn't find in a guidebook. She had been well-educated, obviously; a medical research scientist, registered for a course on tropical diseases at London's University College. She had entered England almost a year ago and was now established there as Dr. Ilsa Schlott from Stockholm.

"We are taking the quickest way into London," she told him. "Route A4. Then the Great West Road." Having announced that, she seemed to be concentrating on driving, but two brief side glances showed she was studying his new appearance. "If Theo hadn't told me to look for a light-green jacket and dark-red tie, I'd have taken longer to spot you. The beard always did make you look older than you were."

"That was the idea."

"You'd pass for twenty-six or -seven now."

That was also the idea. He said, "How are our prospects?"

"Fairly good. I've got them thinking about traveling."

Them? More than one girl? "How did you meet them?"

"They live where I live—at the Women's Residence for University College. It houses a lot of foreign students."

"How well do you know them?"

"Enough. I never force the pace. I sit near them at breakfast—long tables shared with other students. I have a weekly game of tennis with Nina O'Connell. In fact, that's how I managed to become her friend."

"Who wins?" Greta had been an excellent tennis player.

A smile parted the pale tight lips. "Somehow, she always manages to beat me in the third set."

"Nina O'Connell. Main target?"

Greta nodded. "The other is Madge Westerman. Two Americans meeting at college in London, bolstering each other in a strange new world. A peculiar thing about Americans: once the novelty of a different life wears off, they get homesick. Won't admit it, of course. But you'll find them grouping together, lusting after hamburgers."

"Attend the same classes?"

"No. O'Connell persuaded her father to let her come to study at the Slade School of Fine Art. She is just completing her first year there—still as unsettled as when she arrived. In America, Vassar and then Berkeley—one term only at each. Her father remarried two years ago, and that could be the key to her behavior. Westerman is the overseas scholarship girl, every penny budgeted. She's in escape from a middle-class home in Scranton. Her year is almost over—English literature, the history of the English novel, that's her field. At present, she's in a state of gloom. But so is the poor little rich girl. She doesn't like facing a year alone at the Women's Residence. She only landed there, in the first place, because it was either a room in that safe location or staying with friends of her father. That was his stipulation."

"Then he supervises her carefully?" And that could be a major difficulty.

"Actually, he's lax. And indulgent. He's like all busy and famous men. Every now and again they remember their fatherly duties and lay down a rule, and feel they've done a good job by insisting it be followed. Then they feel they might have been too strict and relax the reins again. Besides, Francis O'Connell is also learning to be married once more after being widowed for so many years. He was stationed in India when his first wife fell ill— some infection that never did get cured. She was sent back to Washington with Nina, aged four; she was in and out of hospitals for three years, and then died. Nina lived with her aunt and uncle while her father was stationed in various places abroad. Eight years ago he returned permanently to Washington, and Nina joined him there. Any trips abroad, after that, were always high-level conferences in Europe, where his daughter wouldn't catch a wasting disease like her mother in India. So from 1972 until 1977, Nina went with him, acted as hostess."

"Heady stuff for a teen-ager."

"She wasn't a gawky child, always seemed older than she was. From what I could find out, she was bright and self-possessed. Quite sophisticated, even between the ages of fourteen and nineteen. And then"—Greta was smiling again—"her father married. Nina was packed off to college; and I've told you the rest. Reach over into the back seat, Erik, and you'll find an old *Time* with the story of Francis O'Connell. He is being groomed for something important. The new Secretary of State? Or foreign affairs adviser to the President? And pick up that day-old *International Herald Tribune,* too; it's interesting. Or perhaps you've read it?"

"I've been busy," he said curtly. Four days in Rotterdam, holed up in a room with cassettes of American voices for company to get his ear tuned back in, with recent editions of New York and Washington papers to let him see what were America's current problems. He had read the columns, political as well as personal, and even studied the sports pages. From his set of new clothes, with Chicago labels sewn into place, to his accent and vocabulary and grasp of current events, he could face most real Americans.

"This," Greta said, her annoyance showing, "has all been a very great nuisance. I have other work to do." And she was not referring to a cram course in tropical diseases.

"A nuisance for all of us." He was studying the *Time* article on O'Connell. New wife given a nice play, too: a most successful Washington hostess. No reference to Nina—possibly the new wife had seen to that.

"What *is* Theo's idea behind this?" Greta asked suddenly, showing her own importance by dropping his name.

"He didn't say."

"Could it be to apply pressure—threat of scandal, important government official's daughter consorting with hippies and drug addicts? Possibly with Communists, too?"

"Would Theo risk blowing Marco's cover and mine?"

"If he comes to believe you are still anarchists, he will ditch you and Marco when he pleases," Greta said with a small laugh. But there was a jab of truth in her half-joking words.

Not as long as we are useful to him. And we'll put up with his Marxism-Leninism as long as Theo is useful to us. He said, "What gave you the idea that we were anarchists?" He pretended considerable amusement. Careful, he warned himself: Greta's ideas are cut from Theo's cloth, and everything I say will be reported back to him. "Because we use plastic and dynamite? When did Lenin ever ban them?"

"Marco talks too much about the absolute freedom of the individual. That means no obedience except to himself, doesn't it?"

"He was probably testing you to see if you had anarchist sympathies."

"I?" She was indignant enough to drop her sweet smile. She almost missed a traffic signal.

"If I remember you, five years ago, it was as the wildest bomb-thrower in Berlin. I had to straighten you out."

"And had me removed from your group?" It still rankled.

"That was Theo. He needed you elsewhere—for more important work than aiming a machine pistol. Any nitwit can do that. By the way, when did you see Marco?"

"He was here five days ago."

"Here?" Then Marco had been quick out of Hamburg.

"He's on his way to Amsterdam now. With a handsome caravan—"

"Caravan? Oh, you mean camper."

"Just right, he says, but too new looking. He hopes it will develop some scars on the car ferry across the Channel."

"British registration and plate?"

"All set, along with Tony Shawfield's British driving license and passport."

"Tony Shawfield? What part of Britain does he come from? Manchester?" Marco had lived there when Erik had been in the States, before they joined up again in Berlin.

"What does it matter? His papers are good, so is his accent. You've been together a long time, haven't you?"

Ever since we trained in North Korea. "Off and on." He unfolded the *Tribune*. "What page?"

"Three. But leave that until later—you can read it in your room. Where do I drop you?"

"Regent Street."

"Which end?"

"Wherever I can find a taxi."

"Cautious as ever, Erik."

And fishing as always, dear Greta. "Just following Theo's instructions." To mollify her, he added, "I'll let him know what an excellent job you did on O'Connell—you really got her talking."

"No no. Too obvious. Westerman was useful," she said abruptly. She became absorbed in the problem of traffic, now increasingly complicated by pedestrians and buses and unexpected side streets.

London's maze always baffled him. He knew they had approached it from the west, but he had paid little attention to the initial stretches of suburbia, followed by warehouses, apartment houses, offices, pubs—he wasn't using this route for his exit; no use cluttering up his mind with unneeded details. Now he was beginning to recognize street names from the map he had studied. Soon they would be reaching streets that were recognizable by appearance as well as by name. A large green park on his left gave him a clue. Kensington—or Knightsbridge? Greta was heading in the right direction, anyway. Thoughtfully, he said, "Westerman . . . has she any final lectures to attend this week?"

"A couple I hear."

He might be able to audit one of these. A visit to O'Connell's art class would be hard to explain: not within his competence. So he had better concentrate on Westerman first, although ten minutes ago he had almost decided to separate her from O'Connell, leave her out of this project as unnecessary baggage. "How close are they?"

"Like sisters. That's one of their jokes. Might pass, too. Except for O'Connell's blue eyes. Westerman has brown."

Then Westerman wasn't so unnecessary after all. One probably would help persuade the other. . . . "Does Marco know I'm bringing two girls to join us in Amsterdam?"

"I told him. He didn't like it. He's the recruiter for your trip."

James Kiley thought back to Amalie and Willy. "He'd better make sure we take no informants along with us," he said grimly.

Greta nodded. "That's the reason he didn't stay here any longer than it took to pick up the caravan—everyone he recruits in Amsterdam will be checked."

"Triple-checked. Theo's friends can start using their computers."

Greta dropped all her defenses, became the ingenuous girl who had enlisted in Berlin. "Do you actually know who Theo's friends are?"

"No. But we can guess. Who else had us trained?"

"They certainly have the power."

"And the money." In the last couple of years, there had been plenty of that.

"Changed days from the time you and Marco founded the People's Revolutionary Force for Direct Action. When I first joined—"

"I remember."

"That manifesto you and Marco wrote—do you still believe all you declared in it? Destroy to build. The insurrectionary act is the best propaganda."

Suddenly, he was alert. Was this how she had edged Marco into his talk about absolute freedom? And get the quotations right, he told her silently. He curbed his irritation, laughed, made his own small attack. "Don't knock that manifesto. It brought you running to join us." He looked around him with interest. "Piccadilly, I see. Now I'm beginning to know where I am."

"You always do, Erik," she said quietly. She drew an envelope from her pocket. "Here's a ticket for the concert at Wigmore Hall tonight. I was supposed to be going there—with O'Connell and Westerman. I'll let them know I can't manage it, that I'm turning in the ticket at the box office. It won't be a good seat—students' rates—but you'll be sitting beside them. And then it's up to you. By the way, if you want to attend that lecture on the English novel, it's tomorrow morning. University College. Eleven o'clock." She was eyeing the traffic ahead of them. "I'll drop you near Fortnum & Mason's—that's close enough to Regent Street," she decided. She selected a vacant slot near the curb and drew up. He was as quick as she was: he had the door open as he reached for his bag. "If you need help," she said, "you know the telephone service that will take your message. I check with them each morning. But where can I reach you?"

"At that number. Same procedure. And thanks, Greta. Many thanks."

A nod for good-bye and she was driving off. He went searching for a taxi, resisted hailing one that was just passing. Greta might have seen him enter it, and followed out of sheer curiosity. She had plenty of that. Which made her a damned good undercover agent. Certainly she had done a superlative job on O'Connell and Westerman.

Five minutes of loitering and he found a taxi, directed it to a small hotel off Russell Square. It had been carefully chosen: the Women's Residence was nearby; University College, in Gower Street, was not much farther away. As for this evening, with the concert ticket in his pocket and English pounds in his wallet, he was equally well prepared. Wigmore Street was easily reached. No problem at all. But what would he have to sit through in Wigmore Hall? He had no interest in music whatsoever. Just grin and bear it, he told himself, and opened the *International Herald Tribune* at page three.

It contained a news item from Essen, headed CAPTURE OF FOUR TERRORISTS. Two men arrested in an apartment on Friederikenstrasse; two women taken into custody on their return to the building. Arms and sophisticated radio equipment discovered, along with maps and documents. One of the women, known only as "Amalie," had collapsed with severe chest pains and was taken to the prison hospital. The real names of all four terrorists were yet uncertain, but Berlin police were hopeful of identifying them. They were thought to belong to a terrorist organization known as the People's Revolutionary Force for Direct Action, which had been responsible for at least four major bomb explosions (five dead, thirty-seven injured) and three assassinations in the last two years. Their activities had centered around West

Berlin and Frankfurt. Their main objective in the Essen area seemed to be the storage tanks in Duisburg. Thanks to the vigilance of the police . . . "Et cetera, et cetera," said James Kiley. So Amalie had chosen a hospital room for her means of escape. All very neatly arranged.

But not so neatly, he discovered as he saw a small paragraph, a later report. Amalie's body had been found in her heavily guarded hospital room. Death seemed from natural causes.

Seemed . . . Theo's ways and means were highly efficient. And just as Kiley was relaxing, scanning the rest of the page, he found a stop-press item. Three more Essen terrorists belonging to Direct Action, residing at Töpferstrasse, had been identified in Duisburg. Arrests were imminent.

Fools, thought Kiley, making their way to join Section Two in Duisburg, endangering its members and sympathizers. What was Theo's idea? Keep the police concentrating on that area? Keep them from tracing Marco to Hamburg, or me to Rotterdam? It could be. He could find no mention of either Marco or Erik—and Amalie had known these two names. No mention at all. Somehow, that worried him.

He was in a grim mood when the taxi deposited him at the sedate entrance to the Russell Arms. Carefully, he counted out the strange money— but he would soon get used to Britain's present system, changed from the £.s.d. he had once known—and calculated a ten percent tip. The driver gave him a hard look, refrained from saying what he thought, but his face spoke adequately. Kiley added three more pence, coldly received, but he couldn't stand here adding coins to an outstretched palm like some yokel from a hick town. He strode into the hotel, grim mood replaced by annoyance. In Rotterdam he had studied guidebooks, maps, but not one item on tipping. Small things can trip you up, he warned himself; that cabbie is going to remember your face and where you are staying. And then, as he looked at the paneled lobby and saw the mixture of ordinary tourists and small businessmen, annoyance with his own stupidity changed to a strange uncertainty.

It was a long time since he had walked into a reputable hotel and openly claimed his reservation; or crossed a lobby without pausing behind that large flower vase, for instance, just to note if anyone seemed interested. A long long time since he had shared a lift to his floor without getting out at the one above and walking down to his room by the back stairs; or entered a room such as this, where he'd come and go for two weeks (three weeks, if things moved slowly), curtains wide open and only to be closed when the lights were turned on, a window at the front of the hotel and not facing a blank wall in a back alley. Yes, it had been years since he had lived as an ordinary civilian. He had forgotten how this kind of life felt. Disturbing, somehow.

He tipped the boy who had insisted on carrying his bag and opening the room door, on showing him closet space and bathroom and the bedside radio. This time he must have calculated correctly, perhaps even too generously. But that was more in keeping with his American clothes and voice. The boy left, a happy grin added to his thanks, blissfully unaware of Kiley's opinion of him: a human being debased by gratuities, living on perpetual handouts; a typical example of the serfdom that capitalism had imposed.

When the people had established a true social order, there would be no need
for tips that lowered the worth of a man, turned him into a leech sucking
other men's blood.

Kiley looked around his room, at an untapped telephone, at walls that
hid no microphones or concealed cameras. Pure luxury, he thought, and
began unpacking his bag: three weeks ahead of him, three weeks of leading
the ordinary life of an ordinary man. For a moment, he felt a surge of
elation. And then crushed it down, replaced it with a touch of guilt for that
brief, inexplicable betrayal. The ordinary man, he reminded himself, was
enslaved by a system that was long overdue for destruction.

As he stripped and showered in bourgeois comfort, he was quoting
Anarchist Bakunin to a steam-fogged mirror: "There will be a qualitative transformation, a new living life-giving revelation, a new heaven and a new earth, a
young and mighty world in which all our present dissonances will be resolved
into a harmonious whole." Yes, you had to destroy to build. Bakunin had said
that, too: "The passion for destruction is also a creative passion."

If he felt any exhilaration now, as he dressed and left for the concert, it
was only from the challenge ahead of him. No time for dinner, but that
was of little account—the assignment was all that mattered. I'll begin carefully, he decided, take things slowly, coolly. Yes, that was the angle needed
for a first encounter.

Three

THE ENCOUNTER WENT as planned. Except for the first five minutes after Kiley
had arrived at Wigmore Hall. In the lobby, like most of the crowd who had
gathered there, he walked slowly around, putting in time before he went
searching for his seat. His eyes, traveling over the small groups, the couples
with pink and glassy faces, the standers and the strollers, were in quest
of two blonde girls. They'd be easy to find—look-alikes who probably
thought it amusing to carry the effect still further by matching clothes. He
couldn't see them, had a sharp attack of worry over a no-show possibility,
tried to reassure himself: either they were already seated in the concert hall
or they were late.

There were a few blondes, mostly faded, but all attached to intellectual
types with long gray hair and glasses. Was this what Bach did to you? (He
was well out of luck in the music tonight: a chamber concert, of all damn
things; not one trumpet or drum to keep him awake.) There was a drift of
people, a thinning of the crowd near the staircase. Standing to one side of
it, keeping out of the traffic's way, was a solitary blonde, not at all flustered
by waiting alone. Her light-gold hair was shoulder length, brushed smooth,

falling free. Medium height. Excellent figure. That he could see from this distance, and a perfect profile. He continued his stroll, passed in front of her.

She turned her head to look at him, observed his glance. Their eyes met. And held. Dazzling blue eyes, brilliant against the honey tan of her skin, edged by curves of dark lashes. Involuntarily he caught his breath, his pace slowed, hesitated, almost halted. Then he came to his senses and walked on. He was still stunned by that moment when everything had seemed to stop, a strange weird moment that now angered him. What the hell had come over him?

It was then he saw the second girl with shoulder-length fair hair, hurrying from the cloakroom, busy fumbling with the low shoulder line of her blouse. "It would happen, wouldn't it?" she was asking as she joined her blue-eyed friend. "These darned shoulder straps . . ." He halted this time, watched them ascend the stairs, deep in talk. He didn't need the sound of their American voices to know who they were. He followed slowly.

His seat was on the aisle. He slipped into it, paying the two girls little attention. Nina O'Connell was next to him. He read the program, then kept his eyes directly ahead. She was sitting as still as he was, each sensing the nearness of the other, each ignoring it. He was actually grateful when the music began.

At the intermission, he let the girls out first, as if he were undecided whether to stay or to leave. His foot edged out just enough as Madge Westerman passed him so that her heel came down on his toe.

"Oh, I'm sorry! Please—"

"That's okay," he told her. "I'll live." Brown eyes looked contrite as he gave a reassuring smile. Enough for now, he told himself, and waited until they were well ahead of him before he followed. He didn't join them in the foyer, just studied the crowd in his role as tourist, looking (he hoped) both remote and lonely. He succeeded.

"Don't you think we should take pity on him?" Madge Westerman asked.

"Why should we?"

"Well—he's an American, and alone in London."

"So are a hundred other men."

"I must have hurt him. My heel came down—"

"Not your night, it seems."

"I ought to make a proper apology." I really don't go around tramping on other people's feet, Madge thought.

"Don't worry. He will be over any time now to collect it. I know that type." Handsome and self-contained, although I did shake him for one brief moment, Nina decided. And I was shaken, too, she admitted. It was that look he gave me, the same look when I first met— Oh, ridiculous, stupid. Geneva was six years ago—how do you remember the way a man looked at you six years ago?

"Something wrong, Nina?"

"Nothing."

Annoyed about nothing? Madge wondered. "All right, I'll omit the apology and leave him alone and loitering."

"I'm just tired of strange men trying to pick us up."

"But he didn't—"

"He has looked twice this way." Nina began to study her program notes. A tantalizing man. Should she cut him or talk with him?

Madge said with a laugh, "Forget it. He has no designs on us. He's leaving."

Nina, to her credit, said, "I guess I was wrong. Oh, well . . . Is the intermission over? But let's move in slowly. I'll step on his foot this time." If he can lip-read, she thought, I'll be really embarrassed sitting beside him.

She needn't have worried. When they arrived at their seats, his was vacant. "What discouraged him? The music or us?" And now they were both laughing.

Satisfactory, James Kiley was thinking as he left Wigmore Hall: one small, ludicrous move—a high heel coming smartly down on his foot—and the scene was set for tomorrow. They wouldn't forget him, these two. Just as well to teach Miss O'Connell that a man could gawk at her like an idiot when she caught him for a split second off balance, but that didn't mean she had made another little conquest. She had had too many, too easily. As for Madge Westerman—less sure of herself, a simpler character. She would be no problem.

No problem at all. Next morning, at eleven o'clock, he was seated at the back of a somber lecture hall with rows of dutiful heads in front of him. Madge Westerman was among them. She hadn't noticed him, too busy with frantic note-taking. Conscientious type, worried about failure in the coming exams. Inclined to be a loser, just as O'Connell clearly considered herself a winner. Attraction of opposites?

The lecture ended five minutes short of noon. So much useless knowledge, he thought, a meaningless parade of names who had never made any impact on the world except as producers of imaginary plots and characters. Reality would have scared them witless. Slowly, he made his exit in a stream of a hundred or more students, some young, some aging, with few thoughts now in their heads but a midday meal. I could have given them a lecture, he thought, that would have stiffened their spines, sent them into the streets without those grins on their faces. He was watching Westerman's blonde hair, and marked time until she was near the door. He was there just as she reached it and stared at her in surprise. Would she, or wouldn't she? But of course she did.

"Hi!" she exclaimed, brown eyes staring back at him.

"And hi to you!" He looked equally astonished, and then grinned. "How was the rest of the concert?"

"You were wise to miss it. They substituted a—" They were bumped aside by someone trying to meet someone else. He steadied her, caught the slipping books that had been cradled in her arm.

"Let me carry these until we get rid of this mob scene."

She laughed then. Really a very pretty girl, he decided, if not quite as spectacular as her blue-eyed friend. "No one has carried my books since school."

"What's happening to higher education?"

She laughed again, lost most of her nervousness. "About last night—I'm really sorry—I hope I didn't hurt you too badly."

"Oh, that! Forget it."

"But I don't make a habit of—"

"Of course you don't. Are you enrolled in this class? What's it like? I mean, what did you get out of the course? I was auditing it, trying to see whether I should think of taking it next year."

"What courses have you been taking?"

"None so far. I only reached London two days ago. I'm just in the process of trying to decide."

"Decide what?" She was definitely interested.

They had come into the open, a square patch of ground with a broad walk leading into Gower Street. A batch of white-coated medical students, two with stethoscopes proudly displayed from bulging breast pockets, swept past. "Everyone seems to know where he's going—except me," he said with a rueful smile. "That's my problem. Do I hang around London, take a summer course? Or wait for the fall? Come on, I need your advice. Say—why don't you have lunch with me?"

She looked regretful. "Sorry—I'm meeting a friend."

"I'm sorry, too. Perhaps another time?" He paused at the entrance to Gower Street. "Tell me one thing: where's a good place to eat?" Nothing here but gray houses and college buildings.

"Good in food, or good in price?"

"I can't get both? Okay, okay. Someplace cheap, but clean. Is it too much to hope for a real hamburger?"

"Would spaghetti do? Or a BLT?"

What the hell's that? he wondered. "Either," he told her.

She considered for a fraction of a second. He's really alone, she thought as she remembered her first week, when she had been overwhelmed by the strangeness of everything. "Don't you know London at all?" He looked so self-possessed; it was a relief to find he was as naïve as she had been.

He shook his head. "But I have a good map in my pocket."

"Why don't you join us for lunch?" she asked impulsively.

"No. I don't want to impose—"

"You wouldn't. My friend and I see each other every day. Come on." She began walking down Gower Street.

"He'd object perhaps to—"

"Not a he. It's a she. Oh, there will be men around. There always are. But it's no big deal—just a café near Charlotte Street, half Italian, half American, and filled with students. The hamburgers are awful—the beef is ground into paste. But the bacon, lettuce, and tomato sandwich is for real. By the way, I'm Madge Westerman."

"And I'm James Kiley."

"From where?"

"Chicago four weeks ago, arrived in London from Paris, Brussels, Amsterdam."

"Paris?" She was impressed. "I'm envious."

"It isn't too far off, nowadays " he reminded her.

"I know, I know. But . . ." She sighed. "It's maddening. Here I am, about to end a year in London. And just across that little bit of water there's the rest of Europe—Paris and Rome and Venice. Maddening because *when* will I ever get so near to them again?"

"Surely you could—"

"No," she said abruptly, "I can't." She pushed aside a heavy strand of hair from her brow. "I'm here on a scholarship. It ends next month." Then she pretended to laugh. "Back to the coal mines. Scranton—that's where my people live."

"Why don't you get a job in England, save up, fly over for a week in Paris? It's worth it. Expensive, though, as I found out. It was a relief, in a way, to get to Holland and stop figuring what the dollar had sunk to."

"Holland—what's in Holland except tulips and dikes and windmills?"

"More than you think. I had a pretty good time there."

"Well, I'll even have to pass up Holland. Because I'm a foreign student in London, can't take a job here unless it contributes to my studies. That's the law. I can't see myself applying for a job to teach a British family how to speak English, can you?" She was laughing again. Then she turned serious, remembering his first approach to her. "If you are thinking of taking a course on the history of the English novel because you'd like to be a writer, forget it. It will only depress you: hundreds and hundreds of novelists in the last three centuries, and only half a dozen remembered." She corrected herself. "Well, only half a dozen are read. All the rest—just names to be memorized for examinations."

"Did you ever think of writing a novel?"

"Who doesn't? How about you?"

"Oh, I'd settle for some articles being published."

"So you *are* a writer?"

"Not yet." He hesitated, then sounded as if the admission was dragged out of him. "Actually, I'd like to be a free-lance journalist who writes about international incidents. That's one way of traveling and seeing the world, isn't it?"

"Yes," she said, and sighed again. "What kind of incidents—" But they had come to the door of Matteoti's Café; yellow curtains over its windows rippled by an electric fan, warning of a small interior packed with people. At one table near a wall he saw Nina O'Connell. Her eyes looked at him in disbelief, and then she recovered herself.

What's it to be? he wondered. Freezing temperature or mildly sunny? Easy does it, he warned himself. So far, all goes well. Keep it going, Kiley.

He shook hands—slightly freezing temperature, he noted, as she merely nodded a how d'you do—and pulled out a cane chair and looked around the room. "I'm overdressed," he said with a grin. Flannels and tweed jacket, clean shirt and tie, were definitely out of style this season. "Ought to have remembered myself as a student."

"Where?" asked Nina, curiosity beginning to melt the ice.

"Berkeley."

"Oh! I was there, too. In 1977."

"After my time," he said regretfully. And smiled. It was a warm, generous smile that had won him approval before now. It had its usual effect.

The ice melted rapidly. There was an answering smile, small but friendly. "Let's order. I'm starved," said Nina.

I have been accepted, he thought. Tentatively, at least. Keep conversation light and general. Let Madge tell her all about me later. She will.

The two girls walked slowly down Gower Street. "You liked him, didn't you?" Madge asked, eager for reassurance. James Kiley had been fun to meet. She wished he had arrived nine months earlier.

"As far as we got to know him," Nina conceded, and then relented. "Yes—he's better than I thought." Not the usual pattern of young men who had been hanging around her this year. "At least he didn't dog our footsteps for the rest of the afternoon." It had been a long lunch, with extra coffees and *tortelloni* being ordered just to keep the table.

"Well, he did want to get to the Admissions Office and find out about courses and costs. If he does decide to enroll, you'll be seeing him next term, Nina."

"If I'm here."

"Why shouldn't you be?"

"I've just about had it with the Women's Residence."

"You'll feel differently after the summer."

"What summer? Three weeks at a time with four of father's old friends? Oh—I just hate feeling I'm all packaged and delivered."

"And I'll be looking for a job in Scranton," Madge reminded her.

"Why not cut out for California?"

"I don't know anyone there."

"You soon will."

But there were always those three, four, five weeks when you wondered if you'd stay lost and lonely forever.

Nina was laughing. "Just look at the way you picked up a strange man today."

"I didn't!"

"He picked you up?" Nina's laughter had faded.

"No, no. It was just accidental." And Madge plunged into a full description of what had happened.

Nina relaxed. She was two months younger than Madge, but somehow she always had to do the protecting. "He's almost as unsettled as we are," she said, and felt sympathy for a fellow sufferer. "But I think he'll do something about it. Not like us, who talk and talk and stay undecided."

"Well," Madge said, tactfully avoiding any mention of Nina's adequate allowance, "he does have the means to travel. I wonder if I inherited money when I was twenty-seven, would I have the courage to blow it all in one year?" Just a small inheritance, James Kiley had said, nicely embarrassed when the subject of cash flow and life style had somehow risen: enough to let him do what he wanted to do for twelve months.

"You know what? I don't think he will be here next year. I think he's deciding right now to take off like a bird. And why not?" Nina ended gloomily. "He's free. Free to do what he likes."

"That mad friend of his—Tony Something or other—"

"Shawfield."

"Well, if I were James I'd take Shawfield up on his offer. Imagine—around the world in eighty days in a camper. Isn't that something?" Madge's eyes were filled with dreams.

"Yes," said Nina, "it's wild."

"So why isn't he jumping at the chance?"

"Because he has more sense than we have. You heard him: he'd have to find out what kind of camper, what kind of route, what kind of arrangements, what kind of people his friend was corralling for a trip like that."

"You take the fun out of traveling."

"Well," Nina said, the expert on foreign countries, "you just don't step on a flying carpet and away you go. There are visas and inoculations and officials at frontiers."

"But you loved every moment of it, didn't you?"

Yes, thought Nina, I loved every moment of it. Geneva, Paris, Rome, Venice . . . But you can't go traveling alone. What's the fun in that? "Look—don't get angry—you always do, you know, but not this time, Madge. I've got some spare cash, so let me lend you—"

"No." Madge's voice was sharp.

"But I can't go traveling by myself. The two of us would have a wonderful time. You know we always laugh at the same things. And it's only a loan."

"No." Madge's voice was less on edge. "I get my bank statement tomorrow. I hope. Or the next day. Then I'll know how I stand." Probably cut off at the knees, she thought. Still I might juggle something around. I could sell my books; and my winter coat—that would save me packing it home. "Tomorrow, he said he'd meet us for lunch if we didn't mind. Do you?"

"No."

"But will you be there?"

"Perhaps. Will you?"

"Yes," Madge said. "I like him. He's different." Then, as they turned the corner away from the busy street and headed toward a quiet green square, she remembered to ask, "Are you keeping that date with Barry and Jack tonight?" Nina had been undecided at breakfast.

"I think I will. You're included, you know."

"Can't possibly." Madge hefted the books in her arms. "I'll be cramming all the rest of this day—and every day for the rest of this week."

"Except for lunch, of course," Nina suggested. She might smile, but she was feeling that elder-sister attitude worrying her again. She didn't like the role yet someone had to look after Madge, the perpetual innocent. Not that James Kiley was any real danger: he'd take one look at student life, recall his Berkeley days, and be off to wider horizons. Wider horizons . . . She looked around her, everything neat and quiet, buildings solid and asleep, iron railings. An attack of summer fever, she thought as she repressed a sigh.

In silence, the two girls climbed the steps into the hall of the Women's Residence. "Irish stew," Nina said as the smell of cooking hit them. "If it boils for so many hours, why is there always so much water in the gravy?"

They fell into silence again and climbed to the second floor. Nina halted at her door. "I'm going to start packing."

"A bit early, aren't you?" Madge called over her shoulder.

Nina shrugged, went into her room, four walls which she had tried to brighten with her posters, a back-view window blocked from sunlight by the opposite houses. "Couldn't be too soon," she answered both Madge and herself. But of course it wasn't possible to start packing: trunk and suitcases would have to be hauled up from some lower depths. Even gestures were thwarted, she thought as she stared at herself in the small looking glass. Could be worse: her eyes could squint, her front teeth could be broken, her hair could be thin and falling out in patches.

Then she looked down at the letter from home that had come this morning and lay unopened on the dressing table. It was addressed in Beryl's writing—a stepmother just nine years older than she was. ("That's the good thing," Francis O'Connell had said cheerfully. "You two can be really close friends.") Slowly, Nina opened the envelope. Beryl and Francis were leaving for a summer at the Maryland shore. Time to get out of hot Washington. All well. Much love. Hoped to see Nina in September when Francis and Beryl would be in London for a few days. Ever, Beryl. And a postscript from Daddy: See you in September, kitten. Have a splendid summer. Keep us posted. All love always.

The Maryland shore, easy commuting distance for Francis O'Connell, pleasant house parties for Beryl to arrange. And, thought Nina, not even the smallest hint of an invitation for her. She could hear Beryl saying, "Francis, darling, you know it would be useless. Nina is having much too good a time. We really can't drag her home just to please us." At least she hoped her father had to be persuaded about that. She wasn't sure any more. She tore the letter into small pieces. Would she have gone to Maryland? Perhaps not, to be absolutely honest. But it would have been nice to have been asked.

Oh, well—tonight could be amusing. She'd better call Barry and warn him to find another girl, unless the prospect of a threesome didn't bore him and Jack. It wouldn't. She never had any trouble with two beaux to her string. Safer that way, actually. Less satisfactory for them perhaps, but a respite for her.

At the small bar in the Russell Arms, James Kiley sat over a beer and thought about today's encounter. It had gone well. Tomorrow, a third meeting. And after that, a stepped-up schedule concentrating on Nina O'Connell who had no examinations to keep her occupied: dinners as well as lunches, a movie, a theater, sightseeing (he was the stranger, wasn't he?) at Hampton Court or the Tower or what have you; and of course an exchange of life stories, of future hopes as well as of past disappointments. All of it laying a strong foundation for friendship and trust. That's what she wanted now, he was sure of it: she had too many men chasing after her, too many macho types obsessed by sex. So he'd play the opposite, keep her interested, let her think she made the decisions. It wouldn't be too difficult. The opportunities were there for him to take; all he was doing was to make the most of them. She liked him. He was sure of that. There was an attraction between them that was hard to explain. But it was there.

He left the bar, paying scant attention to the clutter of strangers around him. Foolhardy? Scarcely. German Intelligence, far less the Essen police, didn't know he was in London. His escape had been clean. Amalie had certainly given them the name Erik as well as his description, but now he was unrecognizable: no need to look over his shoulder as he reached the street, no need to avoid brightly lit thoroughfares or crowded restaurants. Even so, he warned himself, don't let your guard be too far lowered. It's enough to stay alert, without acting the conspirator. This whole assignment was turning out to be easier, more enjoyable, than he had foreseen. He had even stopped brooding about the Duisburg fiasco. If it ever could be resurrected, that was Theo's responsibility. His responsibility, too, to have his lawyers win the release of those who had been arrested.

Theo . . . Was Theo having him watched right now? Probably, he admitted, and felt a slight chill. It passed. Theo would receive only reports that James Kiley had merged nicely into the London scene. A beginning had been made, no suspicions aroused, progress favorable. Just give me three weeks, perhaps less, he told Theo, and I'll have these two girls in Amsterdam.

Four

IT WAS A cheerful morning, bright and sparkling, spreading its smile over the waterways of Amsterdam. Robert Renwick had allowed himself an extra hour in his early-morning drive from Brussels—in July there were thousands of tourists and hundreds of sightseeing buses as well as the usual trucks to cope with, not to mention some unexpected delay at the frontier. Today, there had been no complications at all. He had an hour and a half on his hands before he met Crefeld. Purposely, he chose a garage near Central Station: it lay on the far side of the old town from Crefeld's discreet office. Not his official office; that was in The Hague with the rest of the government buildings. Because Crefeld, in his scrambled call to Renwick yesterday, had suggested Amsterdam for their meeting, there must be a piece of highly important business to discuss. Crefeld, of Dutch Intelligence, attached to the North Atlantic Treaty Organization until two years ago, was not inclined to suggest a face-to-face meeting unless the information he had was both urgent and vital. Renwick's response had been quick. He had dropped the work that had piled up on his desk during his absence in Germany last week, and headed in a nicely anonymous rented car for Amsterdam.

An hour and a half . . . Well, a walk would stretch his legs. He set out at a leisurely pace, in keeping with his civilian clothes—tweed jacket and flannels, nothing flamboyant, just old favorites that made him feel comfortable. The man-made island on which Central Station lay was well behind him. He headed south, then slightly to the west to escape the main thoroughfares and their jam of traffic. Here, in the close huddle of streets, medieval houses edging ancient canals, pointed gables, brick, and sandstone decorated with elaborately trimmed cornices, walking was almost pleasant: still too much traffic, torrents of flying Dutchmen on their bicycles. So he changed direction again, traveling a little to the east to reach the long narrow stretch of Kalverstraat, where traffic was banned and pedestrians could walk without any nervous glances over their shoulders. Too many shops here, for his taste, but you couldn't have everything. And most of Amsterdam, the tourists, too, seemed to be window gazing.

It was the usual problem, he was thinking, of an old city trying to cope with the twentieth century. From a bird's-eye view, central Amsterdam would seem to be a completely geometric layout, a concentric sweep of straight-running canals and parallel streets suddenly twisting, but neatly, carefully, in true Dutch fashion, to let canals and streets run as straight and parallel as ever until the next sharp turn. On a map, the pattern would be logical and easy; on foot, especially a stranger's foot, it could be mystifying. It had taken him several visits to Amsterdam to master short cuts.

Ahead of him were two of the mystified, pausing in the stream of pedestrians, hesitating about their direction. Two newly arrived lemmings— Renwick's word for the trek of backpackers swarming off the trains for a week or two of reclining on grass, cozily squashed together, unperturbed by the mixtures of music from a hundred radios or by the polite policemen trying to separate heroin users from the dreamers on hashish. But these two girls weren't bent under backpacks: their shoulder bags were large but smart. Striped shirts were tucked into tight blue jeans that didn't have a quarter inch to spare over neat buttocks. Their blonde hair, shoulder length and no doubt parted in the center to swing free, was gleaming clean. Two most attractive lemmings, he thought as he noted the slender waists and thighs, the well-proportioned legs poured into skin-tight trousers. From this rear view at least, he added to that. Then one of them obliged his curiosity by turning to face him. Good God, he was now thinking, it can't be, it couldn't be—but it was.

Nina O'Connell's casual glance turned to wide-eyed astonishment. "Robert Renwick—Bob!" She came running toward him, arms outstretched. He had been about to shake hands. Instead, he was caught in a tight hug. Laughing, he hugged right back. She hadn't changed much in six years. She had been fifteen then, against his thirty-three. Hopeless from the start, he reminded himself as he felt the soft touch of her cheek against his. Then just as quickly, she released him, suddenly remembering she wasn't fifteen years old any more. But she was still beautiful, a glowing girl, with the same direct glance he remembered only too well. "Madge," she told her friend, "this is Bob Renwick. Bob—Madge Westerman. Oh, Lord—I got that all the wrong way round, didn't I?" She was slightly flustered, perhaps embarrassed by that spontaneous hug.

"Let's forget protocol," Renwick said with a grin. No, she hadn't changed much. He shook hands with Madge; gentle brown eyes, he noted, with warmth and a lurking smile. "And I don't need to ask what you are doing here. On your way to Paris or points south?"

"Much farther," Nina told him. She glanced at Madge and laughed.

Madge said, the smile spreading to her lips, "It's a chance we couldn't refuse."

"It isn't a joke, Bob." Nina had been watching his face. "We really *are* traveling. We decided this morning."

"Just like that?"

"The same annoying man as ever! You never take me seriously. But why are you here? Or shouldn't I ask?"

She remembers too damn much, Renwick thought. Better get it over with, quickly, and hear more about this far journey. They're in earnest, both of them. Two innocents abroad. "I'm considering a change in jobs." Which was true enough.

"What? Are you leaving NATO?" Nina was astounded. She turned to Madge. "He's a disarmament expert—"

"Oh, come on, Nina," he interjected.

"Well, you were at that disarmament conference in Geneva—"

"A minor flunky," he informed Madge. "I opened doors for the generals and saw that the pencils on the conference table were properly sharpened. What about getting out of this foot traffic? An early lunch?" And a fast one. He had only an hour to spare.

"Can't possibly," Nina said with real regret. "We're meeting our friends in"—she glanced at her watch—"forty minutes. How far is the university from here?"

"Which one?"

"The one near the palace."

"Ten minutes away, perhaps less. What about some coffee? There's a café in that alley." He pointed to its sign.

"Indonesian?"

"Why not? Java, after all."

Madge laughed. "A cup of Java—but of course!"

"All right," Nina said, starting toward the alley. She was a little annoyed she had been slow to catch his small joke. "And afterward, will you point us in the right direction?"

"I'll deliver you there in five minutes—if you can walk as quickly as you once could."

They entered the café, barely ten feet wide, with miniature, closely packed tables along one wall. "Cozy," Renwick said, "but the coffee smells just right." One good thing: they had friends; they weren't traveling alone. Stupid of him to worry. They were two competent young women. He noted the unobtrusive way they placed the large handbags between their feet, their ankles guarding against any expert snatch from a quick-fingered thief. "The floor is clean," he reassured them.

"You notice *everything*." Nina shook her head.

"All your valuables?" he teased.

"Well, it's the safest way to carry them. We're traveling light, you know. A duffel bag for our clothes; they roll up easily, don't crush, drip dry."

So this was no usual tour, he thought. "Where are you staying now?"

"In a small hotel near the waterfront. The Alba. Perfectly respectable and clean, although it isn't much to look at."

"You're lucky to find a room at this time of year."

"A friend in London—she's a Swedish doctor, knows all about tropical diseases—she recommended it. And we were lucky. There were two cancellations on the day we arrived."

"You see," Madge said, "we delayed leaving London until the last minute. So many things to be done. And I—well, I really had to be sure I had enough money for a week here." He looked a little puzzled, so she rushed on. "I'm cashing in my return ticket to New York, so that helps me get around the world." And I'll pay back the Scholarship Foundation later. They were accustomed to that, James Kiley had said.

"Around the world?" Renwick asked. On a shoestring? "How are you traveling?" On a freighter, possibly. Even so . . .

"In a camper," Nina said. "And it's a beauty. It's really a minibus. Plenty of room. All the comforts of home. Air conditioning. A refrigerator—"

"Four-wheel drive," broke in Madge, "and an eight-cylinder engine. Tony has even got an extra gas tank installed, and there's storage for canned food and space to sleep at least three. The men will be outside in sleeping bags, of course, and—"

"Hold on," Renwick said with a wide smile. "You're traveling way ahead of me. How many are going?"

"Eight. Three girls and five boys, with two guitars, one cassette player, and of course there's a very special radio. James and Tony were getting that installed this morning, making sure it really will keep us in touch with the world."

He kept his voice casual, amused. "And where are you going?"

"Across Europe first of all, but we are still deciding about Asia. Tony will have the last say, of course. It's his camper, and he does know the best routes."

"Oh?" He didn't need to do more prompting. Now that the world tour had come into the open, the two girls were explaining how this magic opportunity had come about. Tony Shawfield was English, a car buff who knew all about engines; this trip he was planning was a test run for a firm that had supplied all the special equipment—a kind of promotion job. James Kiley was an American they had met at college in London; he was hoping to get some stories that could give him a short cut into free-lance journalism. The others who were going—well, Tony had to choose from fifty students clamoring to join him. Once the news was out about the trip, he had been besieged. James hadn't made up *his* mind about going until a few days ago: he wanted to be sure about the camper, about travel companions.

"He sounds sensible," Renwick conceded. He kept trying to think back to himself aged twenty-one. Would he have jumped at the chance of such a trip? Yes, he damned well would have. "How old are James and Tony?"

"Twenty-seven, I think" Nina said. "Much more practical than we are. It's really all right, Bob." She sensed some reservation on his part. "James is a good friend. I trust him. He really is reliable."

"And the others?"

"Near our age, I'd guess. There's a French girl, Marie-Louise, married to a nice Dane. And a Dutch law student—at least, he's going into law after he gets back from this trip. And a friend of his from Italy. But we won't have much trouble with languages. Tony insisted that anyone traveling with him had to speak English."

"That figures."

"He *isn't* your typical Englishman," Nina protested. "It's just that he's the captain of the bus, as it were."

"He will have to know more languages than English to let him pilot it through all these foreign countries—"

"But he does speak three languages. James knows even more—not well, but enough. And Marie-Louise knows some Syrian—she was born there. And Sven Dissen, her husband, who is in medicine, has been working with Pakistani students in Paris. Guido Lambrese was in Greece and Turkey last summer—he's an archaeologist. And Henryk Tromp—he's Dutch, from Leyden—can speak Spanish. They all know English, of course. Madge knows French. So do I—and a little German, too. We'll manage."

It was certainly a well-arranged travel group. "What's your route?"

"Oh, we're still arguing about that," Madge said. "We've all got ideas, but Tony says we've got to be sure they are possible."

"And James says he wants to avoid Communist countries," Nina added.

That, thought Renwick, with the way things are going might not be so easy nowadays. "Just keep out of the trouble spots."

Nina laughed. "You sound like Father."

I suppose I do, Renwick thought. It wasn't a role he fancied. Damn it all, I'm thirty-nine, he told himself, not Francis O'Connell approaching sixty. "What does he think about all this? No, don't tell me—I can imagine." He expected Nina to join in his amusement. She didn't. "He doesn't know?"

"Not yet. I'm writing him tonight."

"And when do you leave? Tomorrow?" he asked jokingly.

"Tomorrow."

"You know, I'll be seeing your father when I'm in New York next week. Any messages?"

"You do get around, Bob."

"Just visiting my friends before I settle back in Europe."

"You're taking a job in Europe? I think it's sad that you're leaving NATO. Why, really?"

"I'm still making up my mind about a change. Advancing years, you know." His smile was infectious.

Madge thought, he isn't old. But of course NATO never made any man rich.

"What will you do?" Nina asked.

"At the moment, if I don't hurry you out, we'll have to run all the way." He was counting the money for the coffee, adding a lavish tip with some guidance from the smooth-faced waiter in his Indonesian turban. "I like their headgear. Natty. That twist of cloth sticking out in front—" But he wasn't to be let off so easily.

"What *will* you do, Bob?" Nina insisted, reaching for her bag, leading quickly to the door. There, she turned in the wrong direction.

He caught her arm, steered her to the left. She winced sharply. Behind them, Madge said, "We don't need to go all the way to the university—just toward it. We're meeting the others near there, where Rokin Street meets something called Spui."

"That saves us three minutes." He slackened his pace slightly, caught Madge's hand and pulled her alongside. She winced, too.

"Can't you talk about your new job?" Nina asked.

"Well, I'm undecided. Which would you choose—an oil company in Amsterdam or an import-export firm in London?"

"Oil would bring money," Madge said reflectively.

"But the other job offers more travel. I think I'll settle for London."

"I'll be back in London by Christmas," Nina said. "I'll miss the first term of the year at the Slade, but they don't seem to mind. Actually, I'll learn more about decorative art on our travels than I'd get from any old lectures."

"And where will Madge be at Christmas? In London, too?"

Madge shook her head. "Scranton, probably. I'll be dropped off in America. The first to leave," she added slowly.

"What if you want to leave before then? Either of you."

The two girls looked at each other, then laughed.

"I'm serious. You could get bored—a camper is a pretty confined space for that length of travel. Or fall ill."

"We won't get bored," Nina said. "We'll be lapping up enough memories to last us a lifetime. And we won't catch smallpox, typhoid, paratyphoid, cholera, or anything. We've come prepared. We've even had booster tetanus shots."

Shots? So that was why they had winced. "You've had a busy morning. I hope the doctor was—"

"No, no," Nina said. "We didn't get them here. We had the inoculations in London before we left."

Something didn't quite match. They had only decided to go on this trip around the world yesterday. "And you thought you needed a cholera shot for Amsterdam," he said. He looked around at the healthy Dutch faces filing past and shook his head.

"Ilsa advised it. So many refugees and foreign laborers from faraway places. They are a time bomb, she says, medically speaking."

"Ilsa?" That helpful Swedish friend again.

"Ilsa Schlott. She's a doctor, you know. Tropical diseases. She's taking a course on them at University College."

"She could be useful on your world tour."

"She doesn't know about that," Madge said. She turned to Nina. "Won't she be astounded when we send her a postcard of the Blue Mosque?"

"She'll start worrying that you didn't get yellow fever shots, too," Renwick predicted.

"Oh, she did tell us to get them. But I don't think it's necessary," Nina said. "Or is it?"

"If I knew what places you were visiting—"

"Don't worry. James will make sure we get these shots if we must have them. I hope we don't need them, though. They sound ghastly."

"Is he in charge of you?" Then I hope he is as sensible as Nina said.

"He's taking care of the details. Visas and that kind of stuff. That's why we're meeting him—to have a lot of pictures taken, regulation size. Isn't it an awful fuss? James knows a photographer who is guaranteed *not* to make us look like scared rabbits."

"Then after that," Madge said, "we'll pack into the camper—it's in the garage, right next door to the camera place—and we'll have a little test drive out to Haarlem for lunch." She giggled. "Or, as Tony says, he will take us for a spin."

Nina had a small fit of amusement, too. "One good laugh a day," she agreed. Then her smile was directed at Renwick. "And you thought we might get bored," she chided him gently.

He took it with good grace, just wished that with all this merriment and general jollity he wasn't nagged by his own private doubts. Am I really getting old? he wondered. "Well, in case you break a leg or get run over by a camel, just remember there's always an American embassy or consulate. They'll cable your father, and he'll have you whisked back to Washington in no time. By the way, when I see him, shall I drop a tactful hint where he can send your next allowance?"

Nina considered. "Why not? We'll be in Istanbul by the beginning of September. Ask him to send it to American Express."

"It's called Turk Express in that part of the world." And if they were reaching Turkey only in September, they'd never be back in London by Christmas; not at that rate of travel.

They had come to the end of the long narrow street, but not long enough for the questions he'd like to ask. Although, Renwick reminded himself, this was really none of his business. The girls were healthy and happy, confident and determined, foot loose and ready to go. He knew that feeling well. "Here is where I turn you over to your friends. Are they visible?" One helluva place to choose for a rendezvous, he thought, looking at Spui, broad and busy with traffic as it met crowded Rokin.

Nina's eyes searched the other side of Rokin. "They should be near the bridge, just across the street. Yes, there's James." She raised an arm to wave, let it drop. "He's too busy listening to Tony."

Renwick glanced over at the two men. The one who seemed to be doing all the talking was tall and thin, dark-haired. The listener was of medium height, medium build, brown-haired. Blue jeans, checked shirts. From this distance, that was all that could be seen. Tony finished his speech. James clapped him on the shoulder. Good friends, Renwick judged by the way they laughed. Then they consulted their watches, looked across the street, caught sight of Nina and Madge. They started over, misjudged the traffic, were halted by its sudden swoop.

"Good-bye," Nina was saying. "This was wonderful, Bob." She reached up and kissed his cheek. "See you in London?" And then, as if surprised by her question, her cheeks colored and she averted her eyes.

"I'll see you," he promised. He shook hands with Madge, and turned away.

Somehow, he didn't feel like meeting the young men now plowing through a stream of pedestrians.

Nina said softly, "He was the first man I ever loved."

Most of the old Geneva story had been told to Madge, but this was something new. "And how did he feel about that?"

"If I had been three years older, I might have learned."

"He still likes you a lot. At least, he was worried about you."

"Why should he? I was surprised he even remembered me." But he had.

"He must be your type. Didn't you notice that James looks something like him?" Except for the smile and the thoughtful eyes.

Nina was startled for a moment, and then recovered enough to say, "Nonsense." She became absorbed in the decorated barrel organ now being wheeled past them. It halted and blocked James and Tony as they were about to reach the sidewalk. Now why is Tony so mad? she wondered. It can't be us: we weren't late. "He's cursing out the barrel organ," she told Madge, and they both laughed.

Five

Yᴇs, Sʜᴀᴡғɪᴇʟᴅ ʜᴀᴅ cursed the barrel organ, something to vent his anger on as they had to change course and found they were now blocked by a car. Kiley said, "Ease off, Tony. Hold it down." (The names Erik and Marco had been laid aside; so was their knowledge of German, even when they spoke in private: a precaution against a slip in security.) For the last five minutes, as they waited near the bridge, Tony's worry had spilled out in a stream of angry advice: ditch the two girls now, and to hell with Theo: tell him they're unpredictable, dangerous—no discipline at all. Our first and only concern is to make contacts with revolutionary elements, judge their possibilities. "I know, I know," Kiley had said, "but O'Connell is of more importance than you think." Then he had added, "It could be worse than having them along. We could have had someone like Ilsa Schlott." That had raised a reluctant laugh, and he had clapped Tony's shoulder.

But as they started to cross Rokin, Tony's mood sharpened again. He stared at the stranger on the opposite sidewalk. "Who's that? She kissed him. Did you see?" A sudden rush of bicycles forced them back to wait some more. Yes, Kiley had seen.

"Well, well," he said as they reached the girls at last, "you collect friends everywhere, Nina."

"Oh—just a friend of Father's."

"Does he live here?"

"No." She seemed more interested in the barrel organ with a string of paper flowers draped around it. "Hideous colors. But should he be parking it right up on the sidewalk?" For the organ-grinder, small and lithe but obviously well muscled, had eased its wheels over the curb and then brought it to rest in front of a store's busy entrance.

"He knows where he can draw a crowd," Madge observed.

"Let's move," Tony said impatiently. "We haven't all day to hang around barrel organs." They were part of Amsterdam's street music, like the carillons from the churches. For a city that had been run by socialists and Communists for so many years, it had too many bloody churches, he thought; a fine bunch of Marxists, they were.

Kiley said, "Why didn't you ask your friend to spend the rest of the day with us? He probably was counting on having lunch with you when he arranged to meet you."

"We met by accident—just ran into him on Kalverstraat. Is that enough information for you?" Nina noticed the sudden flush on his cheeks, and relented. "I knew him years ago. He taught me how to volley and play a good net game. That's all."

The four of them began to walk toward the corner, but slowly in spite of Tony's urging. Madge looked back at the barrel organ. "No music? He won't make much money that way. And I think he did choose the wrong place." Two policemen, young and tall, long hair jutting out from the back of their caps, were making a leisurely approach, half curious, half amused. "He probably doesn't know the regulations. He certainly isn't Dutch by the look of him."

"Come on!" Tony said, catching Madge by the wrist. He glared back at the policemen, saw the little man dart off, one officer starting to give chase, the other still standing at the barrel organ. Tony's spine stiffened. As the explosion burst out, he was already dropping flat on his face with Madge pulled down beside him. In the same split second, Kiley acted, shoving Nina onto the ground, falling partly over her with a protecting arm around the back of her head.

There were screams, shouts, traffic screeching to a halt, children crying, a woman moaning near them. The two men picked themselves up, helped Nina and Madge to their feet. "Okay?" Kiley asked.

Nina nodded. Apart from the sudden fall, jarring every bone in her body, and street dust clinging to her shirt and jeans, she was all right. Breathless and dazed, but all right. So was Madge.

But it had been close. Near her, two women were bleeding, a man was covering his wounded eye, children had been knocked to the ground; and over by the twisted remains of the barrel organ, the policeman lay still.

"Let's get out of here," Kiley said. Soon there would be more police, and ambulances, and possibly a TV news camera.

"I agree." Tony was shaking his head. "To think," he added in a low voice, "you and I might have been put in a hospital for six months by some home-grown terrorists. Imbeciles! What did they accomplish?"

A splinter group working on a small scale, thought Kiley: a half-baked operation, ludicrous. "Not German, at any rate," he said thankfully. That would have brought West German Intelligence onto the Amsterdam scene. The sooner we get out of here, the better.

"Indonesians?" Tony suggested. He couldn't repress a laugh. South Moluccans putting him and Kiley out of business, the bloody fools.

"Don't think so." So far the Moluccans' protest against Indonesia had limited itself to occupying a train and holding its passengers as hostages, or secreting arms in their housing developments, or talking, talking, talking.

Madge was still staring around her in horror. But Nina had recovered a little. She had heard that last interchange. "Indonesians?" she repeated. "Why should they do this?"

"Let's move," Kiley said. He slipped an arm through Nina's, steadying her. He set a slow pace. Both girls were obviously shaken.

"They've been independent for thirty years," Nina said. Shock was giving way to indignation and anger.

"Some Indonesians want to be free from Indonesia," Tony snapped.

"Then why don't they bomb Indonesia?"

"Because," said Kiley patiently, "they now live in Holland."

"Refugees? And so they take it out on the Dutch?" She shook off Kiley's guiding arm. Her voice was more decisive than it had ever been. "Terrorist logic," she said scathingly. "Cowards, too. All of them! They leave a bomb and run. Oh, no, they don't get killed or mutilated. They'll telephone the newspapers later, claiming they were responsible. How very brave—how noble!" She laughed unsteadily. Tears were approaching. "Don't terrorists ever think of people?"

"They are fighting for the people," Kiley suggested, his tone mild.

"So they kill them?"

"We can get a drink in here," Kiley said, and led the way.

Nina said, "We ought to have stayed and helped," but she followed him inside the restaurant. She suddenly noticed his arm had been bleeding.

"Nothing," he told her. It wasn't much, actually—a glancing blow from a splinter of wood: it could have been a shard of glass from the store's window. But the small wound was effective. Both girls became silent.

Then, "Thank you," Nina said to James Kiley; and Madge looked at Tony Shawfield, smiled shyly, and thanked him, too.

"You were so *quick*," Madge told him. "If I had been alone, I would have been caught standing up. Like that woman with the blood pouring over her face . . . Oh, God!" She saw Tony frown. In sympathy, she guessed.

But what worried him was the thought that some trained eye might have seen the way he and Kiley had dropped to the ground just as the bomb was about to explode.

Kiley ordered Scotch for everyone. No expense spared: it was the quickest restorer, raising them all back to normal again. "We'll lunch here before we get the photographs taken. We'll cut out the jaunt to Haarlem. Instead, we'll leave this afternoon. How's that? You don't want to stay much longer in Amsterdam, do you?"

After what had happened? Nina shook her head. "Just one thing, though. It has been bothering me for some time."

He waited, suddenly tense. Tony was sitting very still.

Nina said, "I just can't go on calling you James. It's too—too—" She laughed. "It doesn't sound natural. Too formal for a real American. What shall it be? Jim or Jimmy?"

"Jim will do." So I made a small mistake, he thought: I insisted on James. *Too formal for a real American* . . . Real? He looked at her sharply, but she was quite oblivious of the scare she had given him. "So we leave today," he said. "You are ready, Tony?"

"Any time you say."

Nina was looking at the stains on her shirt. Madge needed a change, too. "Let's not bother about the photographs. We can have them taken later. We don't need visas right away, do we?"

"We'll keep to the arrangements," Kiley said. The photographer could be trusted: a loyal comrade, knowing what was needed, following instructions and keeping his mouth shut. "Besides, the others are having their pictures taken at this very moment."

Tony rose. "I'd better get over there and tell them about the change in plans. They have gear to collect and stow on board." He was already halfway to the door.

"What about his drink?" Madge asked.

"I guess he didn't need it," Kiley said. Tony's blood pressure must already be high enough. He'll have to remember to tolerate all the damn silly thoughts about clothes that women find natural. The more they chatter about nitwit topics, the less they'll discuss anything serious. As for Nina's outburst against terrorists, that couldn't be better cover for Tony and me. Who'd expect Nina's friends to be anything except political dolts like her?

"We have our own gear to pick up," Nina remembered. "The bags are at the Alba. That's nowhere near the garage. So what do we do? Take a taxi?"

A taxi? With some sharp-eyed driver linking two blondes, the Alba, and the garage? In spite of his own advice to Tony, Kiley drew a long breath to steady his voice. "No. We can stop and pick up your bags on our way out of Amsterdam. Or have you got to pack?" That wouldn't do at all. The camper waiting, waiting; Tony's fury unleashed in some savage though apt phrases.

"A couple of minutes," Nina assured him. "Just toothbrushes and soap. That's all."

"There's the bill—" began Madge.

"I'll settle it," Kiley said.

"We paid six days in advance. So they owe us for two."

God give me strength, he thought, and then realized he had called on the name of a deity in whom he didn't believe. For Christ's sake . . . He took a deep draught of the Scotch, newly arrived, and choked with sudden laughter. Very American: God and Christ, and two pretty blondes trying to understand and failing. Real enough, Miss Nina?

"Let's eat," he said. "We haven't time to waste." And we'll be out of Amsterdam before the police search reaches garages and courtyards and workshops near the university area. For that barrel organ couldn't have been pushed for any great distance—too cumbersome. And that little man hadn't been running blindly. He was headed for his escape route, must have had a car parked safely out of sight. In our garage? Kiley wondered. Always a possibility, considering it's owner's sympathies. Not that a camper, all prepared for a long trip, couldn't be satisfactorily explained. Even so, police made notes in little books. "What will you have?" he asked Nina. Whatever she'd choose, Madge would choose.

"I'm not really hungry."

"Then we'll order the *Koffietafel*. It's always ready to serve." He finished his drink and signaled to their waitress.

"I don't think—"

"You'll eat," he told her. "Your next meal will be in Belgium." He lifted Tony's glass. "To our travels."

"To our travels," Nina echoed.

"Far and wide," Madge ended, and smiled happily.

Six

BRUNA IMPORTS, READ the restrained legend above the doorway of one of the restored houses on the Prinsengracht. There were other commercial establishments, too, on this Old Amsterdam street, including expensive restaurants and a luxury hotel, so that the firm of Bruna was not remarkable, tucked away as it was in the middle of a row of ancient gables. Crefeld's office was on the top floor, reached by a very small private elevator installed years ago for someone's heart ailment: it could hold two people if they were thin enough and pressed in a tight embrace. Renwick touched an ivory button to signal Crefeld. The elevator door was released, and he could ride up in solitary state, avoiding the staircase that would have taken him through the busy second and third floors, where imports of coffee and pepper were actually marketed. Bruna was authentic, not a false front for mysterious activities. But how Jake Crefeld—Jacobus van Crefeld, to give his full name; Brigadier-General to give him his equivalent rank—had ever managed to secure an office in this building was something that aroused Renwick's admiration. Knowing Jake's diplomacy, he wasn't astounded.

The corridor was short and narrow. Crefeld's door, as old and heavy as all the other carved woodwork in this building, had a faded sign, small and difficult to read: J. SCHLEE / RARE BOOKS / BY APPOINTMENT ONLY. The door swung open as Renwick was about to knock, and Crefeld was there with his broad smile and firm handshake to welcome him inside. "Had a peephole installed, Jake?" Renwick asked, studying the carved upper panel of the door as it was closed and bolted behind him. The small cutout was centered in a wooden rosette, part of the door's decoration both outside and in, not noticeable except by close scrutiny.

"And necessary," Crefeld said. "Such are these times, Bob." His large round face tried to look sad and failed. He was a big man in every way, in voice and laugh as well as in body and heart. The surprising thing was his light footstep, his quick movement. Nothing heavy or lumbering. Now he was at his desk, pulling a chair in place for Renwick. "I am sorry to bring you all the way from Brussels, but I thought it wise if we weren't seen together there. Den Haag was also out of the question for the same reason."

"I guessed that. No trouble at all. I enjoyed getting away from the office." This one was still the same as when Renwick had last visited it: dark paneled walls enclosing a square room, with a large desk, two comfortable chairs, a filing cabinet, and three telephones. There was one powerful lamp for evening work; by day, light beamed through the diamond panes of two windows, narrow and tall, which stood close to the desk. Everything was well in reach of Crefeld's long arm. Now, he was lifting a large attaché case onto his lap. Renwick waited, wondering if the business that had brought him here necessitated so many documents. Then he smiled: he had forgotten that Jake never let business interfere with regular mealtimes.

"We'll lunch first," Crefeld was saying as he opened the attaché case, "and talk of this and that. I heard a rumor that you were resigning. Are you?" He swept blotting pad and letters aside, and in the cleared space spread out a checked napkin which had covered the food. Next came a plastic box containing cold cuts and cheese, a smaller box with cherries, a sliced loaf, two mugs, two plastic glasses, two paper plates, a Thermos of coffee, and a flask of gin.

"Negative. Only a rumor." In fascination, Renwick watched the deft way in which Crefeld's massive hands arranged the items in logical order. "Just a nice little piece of camouflage."

"Because of your new project?" Crefeld poured gin into the two glasses. "That's wise. No useful purpose in spilling the—What *do* you Americans spill?" He frowned at the glass he held out to Renwick. He prided himself on his command of colloquial English, acquired over his years of service with NATO.

"Beans." Renwick smothered his grin. It was years since he had heard that phrase.

Crefeld inclined his head in acknowledgment. As usual, a strand of fair hair—now graying and thinning, Renwick noted—fell over his high forehead. He pushed it aside, a temporary victory, and studied his glass. "Glad it was only a rumor. You've still got twenty years ahead of you before you reach my age."

If any of us are still functioning by that time, thought Renwick. Or alive. He raised his glass. "To survival."

"To the project," Crefeld said. They both drank to that. "Have you got a name for it yet?"

"The choice seems to lie between Counter-Terrorism Intelligence and International Intelligence against Terrorism. Pretty heavy. Any suggestions?"

"Well, your idea is based on something after the style of Interpol. Find something short and snappy like that."

"Interintell?" Renwick's grin was broad.

"Why not?"

"Sounds like a cable address."

"So does Interpol. Few people know it as the International Criminal Police Organization that began in Vienna."

Renwick added tactfully, "Nineteen-twenty-three," and ended a short discourse on the history of the international crime-chasers before Crefeld could deliver it.

"Interintell," Crefeld said reflectively. "I like it."

"So you really have decided to join us?" Renwick kept his tone light, but he waited anxiously. Crefeld would be excellent as the head of Interintell's main office. Larsen, in Oslo, and Lademan, in Copenhagen, were his close friends. Add to that trio Richard Diehl, in West Germany, who was already co-operating: his country, after all, had more than its share of terrorists who sought refuge abroad when the heat became too great. (Only a few months ago, one of the Baader-Meinhof gang had been arrested as she tried to cross into the United States from Canada.) Then there was Ronald Gilman, in London—also definite. So was Tim MacEwan, in Ottawa. And Pierre Claudel, in Paris, had been enthusiastic from the start. All were old friends, had worked together in NATO, and now were back with their own intelligence services. A real blockbuster, reflected Renwick: brains and guts, and clout to match.

Crefeld was watching the younger man with a smile. "Of course. Did you ever doubt it? Who else has been rounded up?"

Renwick, with relief undisguised, gave him the names. "Next week, I'll be in Washington and talk with Frank Cooper."

"He has retired out of everything, hasn't he? He's on the old side, I'd say."

Not as old as you, Jake, thought Renwick. "He's still a good man."

"What is he doing now?"

"International law. New York firm with a branch in Washington."

"Ah—that could be useful. Well, you've made an excellent start. And I must say it is a first-rate idea."

"But borrowed, as you said, from Interpol," Renwick added.

"With considerable differences. They go after international crime. We go after international terrorists. But we face one difficulty."

Only one? thought Renwick.

"Police forces of a hundred countries co-operate with Interpol. Will intelligence agencies do the same for us?" Crefeld shook his head. "They keep their records to themselves."

"We aren't asking them to open their files. All we ask is any information they have collected on terrorists, and in return we'll give them all the evidence we've developed. We'll act as a kind of clearinghouse for them. It's much needed. Terrorism is international."

"Terrorism . . . And that is a second difficulty. Whom do we call terrorists? We shall have to be quite clear about that, or else we'll be in trouble. Some more gin?"

"No thanks. Breakfast is a long time away. I think I'll make myself a sandwich." Renwick selected a slice of ham, a slice of cheese and cushioned them between two thick slices of bread. "We'll make the definition as clear as we can. Easiest done, perhaps, by stating what terrorism is not. It is not, for instance, resistance to alien forces that have invaded a country—against the will of the majority of its people: resistance fighters are not terrorists. Again, revolutionaries are not terrorists when they represent the will of the majority of their people."

"The will of the majority," Crefeld said. "That's your measure?"

"That's the way votes are counted, Jake."

"In a free country," Crefeld reminded him.

Renwick nodded agreement.

"But what if resistance fighters or revolutionaries find they don't have a majority of the people behind them? Are they then terrorists?"

"If they use bullets and bombs to gain power over a majority that wants none of their ideas—yes, that's what they have become: terrorists. Amateurs, of course, compared to the hardcore activists who think of power in terms of world revolution. Poor old world—whether it wants it or not, it's to have anarchy thrust down its throat, for its own eventual good."

Crefeld was helping himself to two of everything for a hefty sandwich. "When I was a boy, an anarchist was something left over from the nineteenth century. Bakunin—"

"'The passion for destruction,'" quoted Renwick, "'is also a creative passion.' Or Malatesta declaring that 'the insurrectionary deed is the most efficacious means for propaganda.' Or Kropotkin cloaking the total overthrow of the state as it exists—and all the chaos that would bring—by preaching that anarchism is a moral and social doctrine before it is a political one. That has its appeal, you know. Freedom from the tyranny of national and corporate giantism. Everyone equalized and co-operating; under anarchist control of course. But where is freedom then? Somehow, no anarchist seems to face that problem. Or is their control good, and all other control bad?" Renwick shook his head, his lips tight.

"The simplifiers," Crefeld said. "Terrible and terrifying. Not too many of them around, though."

"Not as yet. Wait until the neo-Nazis start using them as shock troops."

"But they belong to the left—the far left at that."

"If the Communists can use them to create a revolutionary situation, so can other totalitarians. It's the old delusion: you use me but I'm really using you; I'll deal with you when the revolution is won. Where else do you think the anarchists get their money and training right now? Their ordinary sympathizers don't carry that kind of clout. So they use their future enemy, and intend to get the final jump on them. The old delusion," Renwick repeated, "and a mountain of trouble for the rest of the world."

Crefeld studied his friend. "Why this interest in the anarchists? Have you found some evidence that they are actually in alliance with the Communists? You know their opinion of Soviet Russia—a betrayer of the revolution, curtailer of freedom."

"But the Soviets are still socialists who could be set on the correct track again. And if there's a choice between socialism and nonsocialism, the anarchists will make it on the side of the far left. Or the far right. The Nazis called themselves socialists, remember? As for actual evidence of an alliance with hard-line Communists—yes, I think we've found something."

"Was that why you visited Essen two weeks ago?"

The quiet question jolted Renwick. Then he laughed. "You've got ears and eyes everywhere, Jake. Yes, I was in Essen. Following another lead, and found something else, too."

"What kind of lead?" There was more than curiosity in Crefeld's question, a definite interest. He had finished his outsize sandwich and was now onto dessert.

Renwick poured himself some coffee, lit a cigarette, measured his thoughts. Keep them crisp and clear, he warned himself, for it was a long story, beginning two years ago. "Remember my report on Vienna? Uncovering one source of the money that was subsidizing terrorists?"

Crefeld nodded. "Deposited in a numbered bank account in Geneva."

"With a million and a half dollars already paid out before we tracked down that account. So we started tracing the people who had been sent that money. Three names, in three separate cities—in France, Italy, Denmark. But before we caught up with their bank accounts, transfers had been made to three more names: customers of three banks in different cities, but all in Germany this time."

"Half a million dollars in each account?"

"Yes. That was careless of the man who was laundering the money—made a difficult search a little easier for us. But I guess he was in a hurry, or had a mania for keeping things as simple as possible."

"Did you trace him?"

"We had to wait until all the money was eventually transferred to the firm where he works. Ostensibly, he's only second-in-command there—it's a travel agency in Dusseldorf—but his boss delegates a lot of responsibility to Otto Remp."

"Remp, Otto Remp," Crefeld searched his memory, then shook his head.

"It baffled us, too. Nothing on Remp. A stalwart citizen, quiet in manner, pleasant, popular in the firm. With some trouble we managed to get one decent photograph after fifty failures, and a set of his fingerprints."

"Surely he couldn't explain a windfall of one and a half million dollars. Wouldn't that have been enough to uncover him?"

"But if the money disappeared into the many financial transactions of Western Travel Incorporated? Soon to develop as West-East Travel? They are expanding beyond Europe. They have begun arrangements for branch offices in Istanbul, Bombay, Singapore, Hong Kong, Honolulu, Los Angeles."

"And you say the head of this agency, Western Travel, is mostly a figurehead?"

"He enjoys his leisure. And his income. No complaints."

"A fool."

"All of that."

"And this Otto Remp—" Crefeld paused, then smiled. "What did you find from his photograph and fingerprints?"

"Your old friend Herman Kroll. Remember him? You did a pretty good report on him ten years ago when he was head of Special Operations in East Germany. Our photograph doesn't quite match the one your agents took: basically, it's similar, but he has altered his appearance enough to deceive most people. The fingerprints, however, are identical with your sample. That was quite a file you kept on East German Intelligence."

"And their KGB advisers," Crefeld said softly. Then, "Good God—Herman Kroll! So Theo is alive and well."

"Theo?"

"A code name he used in earlier days when he was an agent in the field. He dropped it when he was promoted to an office and two secretaries. The last I heard of him was five years ago, when he was reported killed in a helicopter crash." There was a pause, and then a sudden question. "How long has he been in Dusseldorf?"

"Five years."

Crefeld laughed. "Theo wastes no time. You're keeping him under surveillance?"

"Yes. We watch and wait. The old routine."

"No results?"

"Three visits to Essen in the last eight months. He's elusive. Remembers his past as an agent in the field."

"You mean you lost him in Essen?"

"Twice. On his last visit he was less alert—perhaps deeply worried. He had cause to be. Three terrorists had been arrested that morning, along with the girl Amalie. Who was she working for, Jake?" Renwick ended blandly. His own guess had been based on deduction. Now he waited, hoping for a confirmation. He got it.

"For us. But I didn't send her in. That happened a few years ago when I was still in Brussels. West German terrorists had been using Holland—they were responsible for two murders and a brutal kidnapping, so Amalie went into West Berlin, attending its Free University, and started from there. She had an independent hand, no direction except to act through the local police in an extreme emergency, and to send brief reports of progress back to The Hague—to me, in fact, since my return there. She was a good agent—just a slip of a girl." Crefeld's eyebrows knitted. "Why the hell do we have to employ women, Bob?" he burst out.

"Because they are often better than a lot of men." Renwick thought of his own loss, back in Austria. Almost two years now. Avril Hoffman . . . No, he couldn't forget her. But *I never sent her to infiltrate,* he told himself, as if to help remove the burden of guilt, the sense of responsibility, an emotion Jake obviously shared. Avril was liaison between me and— He cut off his memories. Avril was dead. "Also," he went on, "they volunteer. They want a mission that will mean something. Just try keeping women out of intelligence work, Jake, and you'll be picketed from here to Greenland." That eased the tension, but Crefeld had backed away from the subject of Amalie. Renwick let it drop. For now. Amalie's reports on the Essen terrorists could be vital.

"So on the day of the arrests in Essen," Crefeld continued, "you managed to follow Theo."

"Not all the way. As far as the center of the city, near the Minster. Just over half an hour later we picked up his trail again—as he was coming out of the church. Alone: We didn't see whom he met there. Another failure," he admitted wearily. Then Renwick brightened. "He went to a suburban bank, withdrew his account—it was under a false name, of course. A considerable sum, almost twelve thousand dollars. No doubt it was there for the expenses of Amalie's terrorist friends in Direct Action. Isn't that what they call themselves now?"

Crefeld nodded. "Section One of Direct Action, to be exact. But go on!"

"With Richard Diehl's help we found out who had been cashing checks drawn on that account, which originally had amounted to forty thousand dollars. Always a man, young and bearded, of medium height, brown hair, grayish eyes, pleasant manner. Name of Kurt Leitner. We traced him to his rented room. But he had left on the previous night—right after Theo's visit to Essen. Then we traced his motor bicycle—it had been left at a warehouse. But all we could learn was a vague story about a bearded young man whose motorbike had broken down and who asked for a lift in a truck. He was dropped, the driver said when the police started questioning, near the Duisburg docks. Anyway, Kurt Leitner has vanished. We have a composite drawing of him, with his employer—a bookstore owner—and his landlady obliging. But we needed Amalie to identify him. It wasn't heart failure that killed her, was it?"

"No. Possibly cyanide. A gas pistol disguised as a fountain pen. Theo would know her hospital room number—from the same informer at police headquarters who gave him the warning about the police raid. Amalie hadn't, of course, submitted any full report to the police on Direct Action—just identified herself, as instructed, and told them of the addresses and names she knew, and of the imminent attack on Duisburg. It would have been a disaster. Not just the oil destroyed, but fire sweeping part of the town. Untold deaths."

"Who was the leader of Section One? Kurt Leitner?"

"She never reported that name. She did emphasize that two of that gang were known only as Erik and Marco, definitely the leaders."

"Any descriptions?"

"Both had beards at that time. Both dressed in the same style—wool hats pulled well down on their brows. Hair hidden, even indoors. Erik wore dark glasses. She couldn't risk any photographs. Marco seemed to be in charge. But they were both important, she felt."

"She was right. They were the ones who got away. An early warning by Theo? The others he left to take their chances. As if—" Renwick was now thinking aloud—"as if he wanted them safely out of Essen before the others started scattering. Yes. They're important, all right." It was an ominous thought. He rose. "Well, if that's all the business on hand, I'll start Richard Diehl on a search for Marco and Erik. They could be named in the Berlin police records of five years ago when Direct Action was robbing banks to finance its operations. A rash of bank robberies, in fact: a warning signal of trouble to come." And then, he thought, Direct Action stopped its robberies and holdups. But not its operations. Five years ago . . . Just when Theo came on the West German scene.

Crefeld waved him back to his chair. "Sit down, Bob. We haven't finished all the business. Here's an item I thought might interest you. It ties in, perhaps, with your findings in Essen." Crefeld pushed aside the remains of their picnic, lifted a thin briefcase onto the desk. He took out a slim folder, extracted three typed pages, glancing at them as he talked. "A coastal freighter sailed from Duisburg on the night Kurt Leitner disappeared. It docked at Rotterdam to discharge a cargo of cereal. Fifteen minutes after its arrival, a roughly dressed man, bearded, appeared at a house close to the docks. He was immediately admitted and taken upstairs to a room. The woman who owns that house is Cuban, pro-Castro Cuban. She spoke sharply to the newcomer in Spanish, telling him he should have waited until it was dark. He asked her in rapid Spanish whether she wanted him to hang around the docks until it was dark enough to please her.

"Our informant is a police undercover man. He works at that house, sweeping and cleaning and emptying the garbage. He was assigned there because the Rotterdam police suspected drug smuggling. But, from his reports, visitors who arrive and depart are not dealing in drugs. They arrive on some freighter, stay inside the house for a few days, get a change of clothes, leave."

"A safe house?"

"Exactly."

"The man spoke Spanish?"

"Fluently. Too quick for our informant to catch everything."

"Then if this was Kurt Leitner—" Renwick broke off. Fluent Spanish?

"Whoever he is, he's a linguist. Our informant was given a heavy bundle to take up to the stranger's room. Before this parcel was left outside the door as instructed, our man had a look inside its brown paper cover. American newspapers. A mass of them. Another time, he left a tray outside the door and knocked. As the door opened, he was waved away, couldn't look inside. But he heard an American voice, on a radio or from a cassette player."

"An English lesson? Or was he learning an American accent?"

"And the newspapers?" Crefeld asked. "Studying present-day problems?" He paused. "I don't like it, Bob."

"Nor I."

"There is not much more to add. Except that the man had arrived with a dark beard and mustache."

"That could be Leitner. His hair was lighter—mid-brown?"

"Couldn't be seen. He was wearing a close-fitting knitted cap. Also an old leather jacket and heavy glasses. Four days later, he left—June 14, 8:15 exactly. Our informant caught only a glimpse of him. No face description possible except that there was no beard. Black hair, heavy and thick. Good shoes, gray flannel trousers, jacket hidden under a raincoat. He was unrecognizable. In fact, it was only when our informant was sent upstairs to sweep out the emptied room that he could confirm his suspicion."

Renwick said slowly, "There must have been a car waiting for him. And there had to be a tailor involved—or someone who could make expert alterations on store-bought clothes."

Crefeld laughed. "The Rotterdam police are attending to those problems. They had the house under outside surveillance."

"No luggage?"

"One large but lightweight bag."

"Air travel?"

"Perhaps. Perhaps not. Again, we've asked the police to—" He was cut short by the ringing of one of the telephones. Unerringly, he picked up the right one.

Possibly identified by its bell tone. All different? Jake, thought Renwick, is a well-organized man. A pleasure to work with him.

"Excuse me," Crefeld said hurriedly. "This may be a fuller report on that bombing today in Rokin Street." He was listening now, speaking in his turn in Dutch, listening, speaking, listening. With his hand over the receiver, he made a quick aside in English for Renwick's enlightenment. "From my office at The Hague. Johan Vroom."

Vroom was Crefeld's assistant, reliable and competent and a little long-winded. Renwick waited patiently, his thoughts on the Rokin bombing. He had been only a short distance away when the explosion had swallowed up all street noises. He had halted, turned, started to run back. Nina, he was thinking, Nina. . . . But she was all right he could see as he reached the fringe of a gathering crowd; so was Madge. Judging from the way they lay on the ground, their two friends had shoved or pushed them down, then fallen on their faces, too. And saved the four of them from flying debris. Near and around them, other people hadn't reacted in time. They had paid for it. The policeman had had no chance whatsoever.

Renwick, once he saw the girls being helped to their feet and dusted off, backed away. They weren't hurt, except for bruised egos. As for the men—attractive-looking types, he had to admit—they seemed fit and healthy, and they were certainly capable. Must have had military training, he decided as he looked at his watch, remembered Crefeld, and began a brisk walk to the Prinsengracht: they had certainly shown a proper respect for explosives. Sensible types, too. So that was a relief. He could stop worrying about Nina.

Or can I? Renwick asked himself now, waiting for Vroom's long call to end. She's so damned independent, thinks she can take on the world and come out winning. But you don't win all the time, Nina. Not all the time. You're the same vulnerable, romantic girl I met six years ago; in spite of your grown-up airs, you're still just that. Why the hell did I have to meet you today, start remembering—

"What?" yelled Crefeld into the phone, and Renwick's memories ended abruptly. "What?" Crefeld repeated in a quieter voice. "You are sure? I'll be back this evening. Call me if you hear more." He clamped down the receiver, swung around to face Renwick, and broke into English again. "You know who the man was? The one who wheeled the bomb into position? A Japanese. A Japanese, for God's sake."

There was a brief silence. Crefeld went on, "A member of some terrorist

group called the Red Banner. Came here from Tokyo to arouse the conscience
of the workers against the fascist government that is persecuting their Moluccan
comrades. Persecuting, for God's sake? We took them in when they left Indonesia. And a Japanese, of all things . . ." He was outraged. Then, "If there
weren't people wounded and one man killed, I would laugh." Another pause.
"Ironic note: he was caught by three workers on bicycles. They ran him down,
breaking his leg, and held him firmly until the police arrived."

Lucky about that leg, thought Renwick, or else he would have karate-
chopped their necks and high-kicked their jaws and left three more injured
Dutchmen on the pavement. "There must have been a backup man in a
car, an escape route planned."

Crefeld agreed. "The police have begun checking all cars parked in that
area."

"What about garages? Or the small warehouses? The barrel organ must
have been prepared some place nearby."

"Everything will be checked. But first, there are questions to be put to
the people who live in that district. Information. A lead. That could save a
lot of searching. You agree?"

"I'm not sure," Renwick admitted frankly.

"But you are sure about a barrel organ? How did you learn that, my
friend?"

"I was there."

"You just happened to be there?" Crefeld was now highly amused. Did
Renwick attract trouble or did trouble attract Renwick? Crefeld had often
wondered about that.

"Not exactly." Renwick gave a three-sentence explanation of meeting Nina
O'Connell and her friend, escorting them to Rokin, leaving them there for
Kiley and Shawfield to take over. "They're planning a trip around the world.
No, I mean it, Jake. In a camper. With some other students."

"I thought you looked worried when you arrived here. In a camper?"

"It sounds as if it were a custom-built job. So that's possibly safe. And
Kiley and Shawfield are not college students: older. In their late twenties,
I'd guess."

"Couldn't you persuade your young friend—"

"Nina? She has reached the point of no argument. Besides, I'm not her
father. He is Francis O'Connell, by the way."

Crefeld was impressed. "I can see why you might be worried."

About Francis O'Connell? That self-centered career-artist? "What is nagging away at me is this: the girls arrive in an Amsterdam packed with tourists, no reservations of course, go to a recommended hotel called the Alba,
find that two cancellations have just occurred. Lucky girls, Jake. Too lucky?"

Crefeld's lips were pursed. "The Alba? Don't know it. Who recommended
it?"

"A friend in London, a Swedish doctor, name of Ilsa Schlott. She also
recommended inoculations for an Amsterdam visit. The works—cholera
included. Nina balked at the yellow fever shots, though. Schlott knows something about tropical diseases. She knows Amsterdam, too, obviously. So why
suggest these inoculations for a visit here?"

"She possibly heard of this world tour."

"She knows nothing about it—according to Madge Westerman. That's Nina's friend."

"Cholera and yellow fever?" Crefeld was bemused. "For Amsterdam?" He repressed a laugh. In a desk drawer, he found a sheet of paper and began noting: "Alba—Dr. Ilsa Schlott—Madge Westerman—Nina O'Connell." He looked up to ask, "Any other names you can give me?"

Suddenly embarrassed, Renwick said, "Look, Jake, perhaps I've been exaggerating the problem." Personal interest could distort judgment. "No need for any—"

"You've aroused my curiosity," Crefeld said. "Cholera and yellow fever in Amsterdam?" He laughed openly this time and then tapped his pencil on his notes. "I just like things complete. You know that, Bob. Who owns this camper?"

"Tony Shawfield, English. His friend is James Kiley, American. Then there's a Sven Dissen and his wife—Marie-Louise. Two others: Lambrese, and Henryk Tromp from Leyden."

"Tromp? There's a Henryk Tromp at The Hague. A lawyer. Friend of mine. He has a son, Henryk too, who was a student at Leyden. He hopes young Henryk will join the firm someday. "

"Possibly a father-son relationship. Young Tromp is going to law school when he gets back from this trip."

"Well," Crefeld said, "if the others on this trip are like Henryk, you needn't worry about your friends. Doesn't that reassure you?" He didn't destroy his notes, though, but slipped them into the desk drawer. "I'll get word to you about any more reports from Rotterdam. Quite a useful exchange of information we've had. A successful launching of Interintell, wouldn't you say? Let me know further developments. You'll be arranging for others to join us—Italy, Greece, Turkey?"

"I'll keep you informed," Renwick said as they shook hands at the door.

"The sooner the better," Crefeld suggested.

Another handshake on that, and the door closed behind Renwick. Almost four o'clock, he noted with surprise, as he reached the street and began walking along the canal side. Yes, quite a useful exchange of information, and possibly more to come from Rotterdam. Just where was Kurt Leitner bound for, with his nice new clothes and his traveling bag? One thing we do know for a certainty, Renwick decided: he left the name Kurt Leitner along with his leather jacket in that house by the docks.

Renwick chose the Breda road for his return to Belgium. Traffic was mixed in the late afternoon, fewer trucks but more sightseeing buses and small cars loaded to the gunwales with holiday baggage. Outrageous gas prices were having little effect on vacationers southward bound. At the border, there was a general slow-up, unusual in the Benelux countries, where goods and people flowed easily across frontiers. But the bombing in Amsterdam was having its effect: closer scrutiny than usual of all vehicles leaving Holland.

Renwick eased his Citroën's speed and joined the line of cars that edged their way forward, stopped, moved forward again. A Europa bus was released and sent on. One more car behind it, then a minibus, two more cars, and Renwick's turn would come. That wouldn't take too long. He would make good speed on the road bypassing Antwerp, be able to wash up at his apartment before he went out to dinner at his favorite restaurant, where he could meet a couple of his friends.

Then as he looked along the road ahead of him, he noticed there was a small group, a half-dozen people or so, gathered close to the minibus. Or camper, he decided. Green, well-built body, tarpaulin strapped securely over the baggage on its roof. Would they have to open that up? he wondered in dismay, glancing at his watch. Just in case a Japanese terrorist was hidden topside? Kids, he thought now, as he heard the small group break into laughter, saw some light-hearted horseplay between two of the young men. A couple, affectionate, holding on to each other. Two girls; shoulder-length golden hair, slender, medium height, outsize shoulder bags. He looked again, amazed. Nina. And friend Madge.

He recovered from his surprise. Where were the remaining two, Shawfield and Kiley? Still inside the camper talking with the Dutch officials? But all was in order, for the group was called together, climbed back into the camper. It moved off, quickly gathering speed. The two cars ahead of him, now getting into position for identification, blocked Renwick's view of the plate above the camper's rear bumper. When he could see the camper again, it was too distant to note its number. An automatic reflex, he thought, excusing his curiosity. Anyway they were off, with a clean bill of health: no Japanese stowaway—that hadn't worried him—and no evidence of drugs being smuggled or used, and thank God for that. He could smile and shake his head at that brief touch of suspicion. They were safely off, a day ahead of schedule. There would be no Dear Daddy letter written to Francis O'Connell tonight: he'd be lucky if he got a postcard from Brussels.

Seven

CREFELD HAD ALLOWED fifteen minutes, after Renwick's departure from his office, before he left. The remnants of their luncheon, gathered up inside the checked napkin, had been thrust back into the attaché case. The letters on his desk—addressed to J. Schlee, Rare Books—could be locked away in his cabinet. He'd attend to them on his next visit, nothing urgent, nothing important. But the slim briefcase was. With it tucked securely under one arm, his hand holding the attaché case—a nuisance, but useful, letting him avoid restaurants and crowds whenever a special meeting had to be arranged, and where else but in this office could secret reports be handled securely?— he doubled-locked the door behind him.

He had already summoned the elevator, so it was waiting for him. Its stately descent always reminded him of his maternal grandfather, the last Bruna to use that top-floor room when he wanted to stay overnight in the city. Crefeld had often wondered about the elevator: no heart weaknesses in the Bruna clan; possibly a lady visiting who found stairs hard to climb in her tight-corseted waist. The days of whalebone, he thought, and was smiling broadly as he stepped into the dimly lit hall. Apart from a telephone operator at her switchboard, kept neatly out of sight, built under the curved flight of staircase, the hall was empty. From the floor overhead came the sound of a typewriter clacking away, making good time before closing hours.

The hall wasn't empty. A man was standing in one corner near the front door, leaning on his rolled umbrella, his neat dark suit blending into the mahogany wood paneling of the walls. His hair, cut short, was gray—prematurely gray, for his thin face was unlined. He smiled shyly. "No receptionist here?" he asked. "How do I get in touch with the accountant's office?"

So he had just entered, wasn't waiting as I first thought, Crefeld decided. His suspicion leveled off, but he still kept a distance from the stranger. "Try the telephone girl—you'll find her just around that curve of staircase."

"Thank you." The stranger came forward, but he was giving Crefeld ample room to pass him.

"Not at all," said Crefeld as he averted his face and made for the front door.

Suddenly, the stranger raised his umbrella, its ferrule pointed at Crefeld's thigh.

Crefeld felt a sting, hot and sharp. He stared at the man, then at the umbrella. He raised his voice to shout and gave a strangled croak. He had no strength in his body at all. His legs were beginning to buckle. The man hit him sharply over his hand that held the briefcase. Crefeld's grip was loosened; the briefcase was pulled away from his arm. He saw only a blur as the dark suit turned and hurried to the front entrance; he heard only a faint noise as the heavy door was closed.

Crefeld fell backward to the ground, the attaché case clattering beside him on the wooden floor. He tried to shout again, knew it was useless. Only his brain seemed to be working. He made an effort to reach into his jacket pocket, take hold of the card he always kept there in case of emergency. He could feel it, even gripped it, but he couldn't pull it out.

"What's wrong? What's wrong?" It was the telephone girl, kneeling beside him, looking in horror at the man who lay staring up at her. She screamed and kept screaming until heels came running down the staircase.

"He's alive," a man's voice said. "Get an ambulance."

"I thought I heard the door close. Then I heard a crash." The telephone girl pointed to the attaché case. "And another crash. Together almost. He's trying to speak." She lowered her ear to his lips.

"He's Schlee, the book collector. Saw him one day—"

"Get an ambulance!" The telephone operator was yanked to her feet. "Call now!"

"What's in his pocket?"

"His hand!"

"But why?"

Crefeld's hand was pulled out gently.

"A card. Emergency, it says. A telephone number. A name: Jake. Here," the man's voice said, "call this number, too. First, the ambulance; then the card. Quick, quick!"

High heels retreated. "She's always so damn slow," said the man's voice. "Hurry!" he yelled after her. Then, as an afterthought, "What did he say? Could he speak?"

"Didn't make sense," the girl called back. "Sounded like umbrella."

"Stupid as well as slow," the man told the rest of the small crowd. Umbrella. Schlee wasn't carrying any umbrella. "Heart attack. Don't move him. Keep back. Give him air."

Somberly, helplessly, they watched the man whose eyes stared up at the vaulted ceiling. His lips no longer moved.

Eight

By THE TIME Renwick had crossed the Dutch frontier into Belgium, the green camper was well ahead of him, mostly out of sight except as a distant blob when the road ran straight. Here, the long flat stretches of well-tilled fields and windmills had given way to a gentle rise and fall of land. Blue canals, reflecting the color of the summer sky, were replaced by streams edged by woods. By the outskirts of Antwerp, the camper had disappeared from view completely, probably taken some turnoff to a picnic ground or park on the perimeter of the city. Good luck to you, Nina of the sparkling blue eyes and golden hair and warm, ready smile. Good luck to you. But why Antwerp? Why not Brussels?

He kept his speed steady, like the other travelers on the road, fore and aft, all dutiful citizens. It made for pleasant driving: no zigzagging in and out like a demented hornet, no one tailgating and forcing the pace. He could relax, thinking now only of Essen and Rotterdam, of Theo and the monies paid out to Kurt Leitner; but mostly of Theo.

Should he try to suggest that the West German authorities pick Theo up? Or should he still go along with their decision—standard practice, he had to admit—to keep watch on Theo's movements and contacts? He hadn't much choice: his pet project, International Intelligence against Terrorism, would have no powers to detain or arrest. Like Interpol, it could only track down, gather the evidence, and ask the participating countries to make the arrest. Or get them to demand extradition if that was necessary. But, he reflected, have we sufficient proof to set things in motion? The answer was a definite no. The evidence was circumstantial. As yet, he promised Otto

Remp presently of Dusseldorf, Herman Kroll late of Leipzig, Theo. As yet . . .

When he entered the busy streets of Brussels he noted a small white Fiat, which had chosen the same route as he had, following him still more closely. He hadn't noticed it until he was just south of the frontier, and from there it had kept its place in line, like all the others on the road, staying four cars behind him. Someone tailing him? Had someone picked him up as he left Crefeld's office on the Prinsengracht? Kept him in sight all the way to the garage near Central Station? All the way to the Breda road? Damn me, he thought, for an idiot, too occupied with Nina and her friends, with Crefeld and his information about Rotterdam, with Theo, to notice anyone following. If surveillance had occurred, it was pretty skillful. Expert job, involving two or three men passing him one to the other. He would have noticed one man dogging his heels through the streets of Amsterdam. Yes, an expert job. If it had occurred.

He tested that, now, by heading for the crowded center of the city, without too many twists and turns to betray the fact that he had been alerted. In spite of the heavy traffic, the white Fiat hung on, at a safe but definite distance. So he didn't drive to his office or his apartment, or make for the garage where his rented car had been delivered that morning, but left it in the parking area of the Dove, a thriving and expensive restaurant. The Fiat decided to park there, too. No one got out. Perhaps the prices had scared him off, or—more seriously—the man at the Fiat's wheel was alone and now debating whether to follow or wait. Always a mistake, thought Renwick, to put one man alone on a tail. He could have radio contact, though, and be calling for a backup at this very moment. So be quick, Renwick, quick but casual.

He made a leisurely entry into the Dove. Once inside its fashionable gloom, he headed for the bar. He ordered a short drink, paid for it, gave himself just enough time to make sure that the man he had briefly glimpsed wasn't following him after all, and then left for the men's room. If his memory of this place was accurate, there was an adjacent service door. His departure was speedy. Into a passageway dodging a waiter with a loaded tray, passing the clatter and heat of a busy kitchen, taking a back entrance into a small courtyard, another exit from there that led into a short stretch of cobbled alley. No one in sight. No one waiting at the other end of the alley, either, or in the narrow street that brought him into the Grand' Place. There, in the huge square dominated by seventeenth-century façades, he could ease his pace, blend into the constant movement of people, pass the outdoor cafés, flower stalls, elegant restaurants, and reach a street where taxis could be found.

Within a minute, he was being driven to the air terminal, a short haul, where he had left his own car that morning. Five more minutes—he was counting each one—and he was in his Volkswagen of nondescript gray, joining the stream of cars leaving the city. Twenty minutes at most, and he would be in his office. No one was following.

First, he must call Jake Crefeld, who would be back in The Hague by this time, warn him that the House of Bruna on the Prinsengracht must be under observation. Because of Jake or because of me? he wondered. Who had led to whom? Always a baffling question, but one that needed answering.

Renwick, in his private office mostly occupied by a wall of filing cabinets, a desk with two telephones (one line to the general switchboard downstairs, another for direct outside calls), and a couple of hard chairs that kept visitors alert and attentive, wasted no time. He dialed Crefeld's own special number. If Jake wasn't in his office, he'd have to try Crefeld's home, something he disliked doing: no scrambler available there.

His call was answered promptly on its first ring. But it wasn't Jake at his desk. Nor Johan Vroom, Jake's assistant. The voice was recognizable: Luisa, Jake's faithful secretary, who, like Vroom, had gone back to The Hague from Brussels along with her boss.

"Working late, Luisa?" Renwick asked, his voice light, his manner easy. When she hesitated, he added, "Renwick speaking."

"Oh, Major Renwick—I mean Colonel—"

"Half colonel," he corrected her.

"I was putting my desk in order; so much to clear up at the end of the day." She sounded flustered. But then, he had caught her at Jake's desk, not at her own in the outer office. That didn't surprise Renwick, though. Luisa was not only efficient but also officious, the perfect factotum who would drive him crazy. Her command of English was perfect, thank heaven. That saved Renwick from floundering around in his meager Dutch. "Is the Brigadier available?"

"No."

"Do you expect him soon? Or has he gone home?"

"He said he would come here first, on his return from Amsterdam."

"Is Major Vroom there?"

"No. He hasn't returned."

"Oh?"

"He left about half past four. It was—some kind of emergency, he said."

There were always emergencies, thought Renwick. "Leave word for the boss, will you? Ask him to telephone me."

"Your number?"

"He knows it," Renwick said. "Good night, Luisa. Don't work too hard."

He went scouting in the small refrigerator next door, where there was also a cot, a closet with his tennis and running gear and change of clothes, an adjacent bathroom. He found some cheese and hard-crusted rolls, apples, a bottle of white wine, and drinkable milk—the remains of yesterday's lunch. He chose the milk rather than the wine: it would settle the tension building up in his stomach. The cheese was a mild Edam, the rolls still fresh. It was all the supper he needed at this moment. He ate it slowly, worrying about Jake: what had delayed him? Then he went over today's mail and the morning newspapers. And waited.

At nine-fifty, the call came on his private line. It wasn't Jake. It was Johan Vroom, his voice easily identified by the American accent he had brought back, along with a Virginian wife, from two years at Georgetown University, but his initial words were too quick, too emotional to be fully understood.

"Take it easy," Renwick advised, his own tension rising. He could see Vroom's face, thin and sharp, with its dark brows knitted.

Vroom sounded hoarse. "I've just got back from Amsterdam. Crefeld is dead." His voice was unsteady, then he mastered himself, went on. "I got the word at sixteen hours twenty-five. I—"

"Dead?" Renwick repeated blankly. "Dead?"

"Heart attack, they say." Vroom was bitter, almost savage. "But I think—"

"Hold on, hold on. Get the scrambler working." Renwick reached for his own, adjusted it to receive. He drew a deep, long breath, steadied his own emotions.

"Okay," Vroom said. "Can you hear clearly?"

"Clear enough. So you got the word at twenty-five past four?" *Just over half an hour after I said good-bye to Jake, fit and strong, vitality bursting out all over him.*

"Yes. From the Bruna building—that's where he was found. In the hall, halfway to the front door."

"Was he already dead?"

"Not then. Paralyzed. He was taken to the hospital, and I went directly there. But too late. Then I went to his office—just to make sure that nothing else had been stolen. You see—in the hall—all that had been found was an attaché case lying beside him. But he had had a briefcase, too. I saw it this morning as he left for Amsterdam. Valuable papers inside it, Bob. A police report—highly confidential. Sorry I can't say more. He said he would be seeing someone who would be interested in it."

Renwick hesitated. Then, as a precaution, he asked, "Only one person?"

"Must have been. Luisa was told to pack lunch for two—have it ready early this morning."

"When was she told?"

Vroom was mystified. "Yesterday, of course. She always prepares the attaché case for his Amsterdam meetings."

"When did Jake receive that highly confidential report?"

"Yesterday. It came by special messenger. He read it, then showed it to me. We have been working together on—well, on a problem connected with—well, the report was a possible addition to the solution of that problem. About one of our undercover agents."

About Amalie possibly, thought Renwick. *Not about Theo, thank God.* Vroom knew only a tenth of the problem, perhaps not even that. "And after Jake showed the report to you?"

"He put it in his briefcase."

"Not in his safe?" Renwick was surprised.

"That was later. First, Luisa brought us our coffee, and he made a special call to someone—don't know who."

To me, thought Renwick. "Then he told Luisa to pack lunch for two people—for the following day?"

"Right. And he put the briefcase in the safe once Luisa had left the room."

"Who knew of his visit to Amsterdam?"

"No one except Luisa and me."

"Don't forget the man who had lunch with him."

"He worries me. He's in danger, too—he knows the contents of that report."

"What if he was followed from the Bruna building but managed to shake the tail?"

"He's still in danger—if he talks about that visit."

"You're in danger also. Jake discussed that report with you."

"With the door closed and no one in the outer office."

"Not even Luisa?"

"She was in the pantry at the end of the hall, making us that cup of coffee."

"Who, besides Jake, had access to the safe?"

"Only I had access." Vroom's anxiety sharpened. "Security is tight. Day and night guards in the corridor, alarm signals—"

"Take it easy, Johan. Access to the safe may have been unnecessary. All that was needed was someone in your antiterrorist section to be alerted to watch for any special delivery from—a certain quarter." From Rotterdam.

"Someone here? Alerted?"

"And saw the document arrive; then made an outside call to his contact, who'd pass on the word to someone who could arrange the theft."

"And Crefeld's death."

"And had me followed from the Prinsengracht." But at least I know now, thought Renwick, I didn't lead the killers to Jake. It was the Rotterdam report that focused interest on the Bruna building. Whoever planned all this was well informed. Recent information, too: the Bruna building was secure until today.

Vroom said sharply, "You took your time telling me."

"Just like you. We've both been circling around each other." Renwick's voice hardened. "So give me the details. Who found Jake? Was he able to speak? Who telephoned you?"

"The telephone girl—from the Bruna switchboard. There was a card in Jake's pocket marked *Emergency: Call at once*—with my number on it."

"Who found him?" Renwick insisted.

Vroom plunged into the telephone girl's description of the scene in the hall. "She swears it's true, she didn't invent it. He tried to speak, could only say one word. He said it twice. Umbrella." There was a pause. "Everyone else in the hall thought she was crazy."

Renwick said softly, "Not so crazy. Tell me, Johan—there's an autopsy going on right now?"

"Yes. I've sent one of our medical men to attend it."

"Call him. Tell him to look for a small, a very small puncture of the skin—not a needle mark, not a hypodermic. Not a deep puncture, either; that wouldn't be necessary. And it's probably some place that could be overlooked, some place seemingly protected by clothing. So have Jake's suit examined for a neat little hole that would overlie the puncture—shoulder, back, thigh, wherever the point of an umbrella could have been easily aimed as the trigger in its handle was pulled."

Vroom was silent. Then he burst out, "The Bulgarian refugees—the writers who were working for Radio Free Europe!"

"That's right." There had been one, perhaps two mystery deaths of Bulgarian intellectuals in London, from a raging fever that ended, after four days, in heart failure. Then another intended victim, in Paris, had dodged a full attack and lived to tell about the incredible weapon: an umbrella. It had been a sensation in the newspapers for almost two days. *Vive détente*, Renwick thought. "Let me know what your doctor discovers. Whatever poison was used in Jake's case, it was something damned speedy. Not the usual four-day fever."

Vroom was hesitant. "But the umbrella was always used logically—in a crowded street or subway. Why now, in an empty hall?"

"In Jake's case, a briefcase had to be snatched. He would have hung on to it if a delayed poison had been used."

"I get it. Instant paralysis, and no one around to notice the briefcase being stolen? Yes—" Vroom's deep breath was noticeable—"that's possible. But why not a cyanide pen? Much simpler."

"Jake would be watching for that, wouldn't he?" I bet he was keeping as much distance as possible from the man in the hall, averting his face, holding his breath, ready to raise the heavy attaché case as a shield. Jake, thought Renwick, had known of too many cyanide attacks. "One thing is certain: the report from the Rotterdam police must have been dynamite. It wasn't complete, though. They were still checking on the possible destination of that man who came off the Duisburg freighter. So hurry them up, if you can, and let me know—"

"Oh, God," said Vroom, "how do you tell them you've lost their confidential file? It was a special favor from the inspector to Crefeld."

"Do you know the inspector?" More important, does he know you well enough to grant *you* a favor? Renwick wondered. For that matter, do I really know Vroom well enough to ask him to replace Jake on the Interintell Committee? One thing is definite: I had better contact all its members, tell them to recruit replacements. Jake's death has proven that necessary. Jake . . . I'm going to miss him, I'm going to miss that man.

Vroom was talking about his knowledge of the Rotterdam police inspector who had recognized a safe house when he saw it in an undercover report about suspected drug smuggling. "Bright lad," Vroom finished.

"Young?" Renwick liked that idea.

"Yes. About our age."

In spite of the weight of depression in Renwick's heart, he almost smiled. Vroom was thirty-seven, two years junior to Renwick. "Only people over forty call that young."

"I feel eighty tonight."

"You'll be taking Jake's place, of course?"

"I'll fill in. Until they find someone . . ." Vroom sighed.

"Who is eighty?"

"Oh, well, I've had no experience in the field. I'm a desk man. Analysis and—"

"Stick to that." You've a pretty little wife, Renwick told him silently. "Leave the action to unmarried types."

"No guarantee that I'll live. Look at what happened to Crefeld."

"It happens. Listen, Johan, when you are finding out about Jake's office—who had access, who drifted in and out—just remember one thing."

"To trust no one?"

"Play it safe. No open phone calls to Rotterdam, or to me."

"You think we have a mole in our department?"

"All the best people have that nowadays," Renwick said bitterly. "But perhaps not a fully trained mole—just a small mouse picking up crumbs of information."

"We must meet—"

"Carefully, carefully."

"Carefully," Vroom agreed. "I'll keep you informed. About the umbrella. About Rotterdam. About my search for the mouse."

"I'll be here around six every evening. Until next Friday. Then I leave for ten days' vacation." A visit to his own country would be a vacation, Renwick hoped, even if it was coupled with a little business. Suddenly, he felt tired and sad and drained of words. "Good night, Johan. A bad day for all of us." He switched off, went into the small room next door, flung himself down on the cot, stared up at the ceiling.

Half an hour later, Renwick rose and went back to his desk. Not to work. No more work tonight. He picked up his telephone and called Thérèse. She was long in answering, and his hopes faded. Then he heard her voice clear and light, "*Ici* Madame Colbert." His heart rose.

"Hello, Tessa," he answered. "What about seeing—"

"Bob—I've been trying to reach you all day. The party is off tomorrow night."

"Forget tomorrow. I want to see you tonight."

"Tonight? It's eleven o'clock. I'm just getting ready for bed. Oh, really, Bob, why didn't you call me earlier?"

"I'll be with you in twenty minutes."

"But you can't come here. Not tonight. Mother has just arrived from Bruges—she's staying with me for a few days."

He broke into English. "Tessa, I need you."

Thérèse hesitated. "She's asleep in the spare room. At least I think she's asleep."

"Lock her in," he suggested, and heard a ripple of laughter.

"I believe you would," Thérèse said. "But no, Bob, we can't risk it."

"Then what about my place? I'll be outside your door in twenty minutes in my little Volkswagen. Just pull a coat on. No need to dress."

"And how would I look tomorrow morning, leaving your apartment in nothing but some black lace with a coat pulled over it?"

"In twenty minutes," he said.

Luck held. At this time of night, traffic through the approaches to the city had eased. Renwick reached Tessa's apartment with three minutes to spare. She was waiting, and watching: he saw the light in her living room flick off. He found he was smiling. Tessa, never forgetting her upbringing by that old battle-axe from Bruges, switched off lamps, went marketing in the mornings and counted her change, turned down the heat when she wasn't indoors, didn't leave the radio or television playing, and yet looked like a girl on the front cover of *Elle*. She dressed like it, too: a combination of much taste and some money. That came from her interior decorating business, certainly not from her late husband, who had provided her only with eight years of miserable marriage. Now she was free, and staying free by choice; a convert, through sad experience, to complete independence. Which suited Renwick's own life style. He'd marry someday, once he was content to stay with a desk job and concentrate on analysis and evaluation. But now—well, you served where you felt you were useful. In his line of business, that could mean unexpected absences, indefinite hours, friendships and secrets that couldn't be shared even with a wife. Nor could danger be shared, ever-present danger making her vulnerable, a hostage to fortune. Perhaps some men could carry that load of worry around in their minds; he couldn't.

And there was Tessa at last, her smooth dark hair highlighted by the bright door lamps, a white coat covering what she was or wasn't wearing, coming decorously forward. Then her pace quickened as she neared the car's opened door, and she was beside him, eyes smiling, lips soft and inviting.

Nine

In the week that followed, the work piled up on Renwick's desk, and he was on the point of deciding to postpone his visit to New York. Another four days, what did it matter? But suddenly it did matter. A report came in from Richard Diehl, of West German Intelligence: Herr Otto Remp, of Western Travel Incorporated, had left Dusseldorf and was now said to be in the United States. Diehl had contacted both the CIA and the FBI, but no confirmation of Remp's movements was available.

Diehl's inquiries at Western Travel Incorporated had been discreet, but produced no further information. Remp's sudden departure was considered normal: he was now making a world-wide tour in connection with the firm's expansion into West-East Travel. He would set up financial arrangements and oversee the selection of qualified staff to begin operations early next year. Such things took time, various employees of Western Travel had stated. They were more interested in the promised increase in their pay, once West-East Travel was established. As for Remp's itinerary, the same list of place names was supplied; but when he would visit these countries, or how long he would stay, depended on any difficulties he might encounter. He would overcome them, an assistant manager had said emphatically: Herr Remp was a seasoned and successful negotiator.

Indeed he was, Renwick thought as he read the report. A very successful con man might be closer to the truth. Shipped out, had he? Yet Renwick couldn't blame the West Germans for that. This was no sudden exit by Theo: it was long planned, carefully arranged. Once out of Germany, he was free: no extradition possible unless there was evidence of a crime. If the Germans had even one piece of real evidence against him, they would have arrested him four weeks ago.

So all we can do, Renwick decided, is to watch him. Where? *Now said to be in the United States* . . . If this was accurate, then it seemed as if Theo had started his travels in the opposite direction from his listed itinerary. It had begun with Istanbul, gone on to Bombay, Singapore, Hong Kong, Honolulu, and ended in Los Angeles. Or can we even be sure he will take that list in order? Why not Los Angeles, then jump to Bombay, just to keep us guessing? Difficult to follow him in any strength: two of the countries concerned were outside of NATO, while Hong Kong and Honolulu thought more of the Pacific than they did of either Atlantic or Mediterranean problems.

If only, Renwick's mind raced on, if only we had Interintell all set up and ready to go. With luck, it would be in good working order in another two months. Two months . . . And where will Theo be then? What will he have already accomplished? The places listed were possibly accurate. Possibly? More than possible. Theo as Otto Remp, big wheel in an expanding travel agency, would have to give his company a true list, for the simple reason that he would indeed be expected to open branch offices in these cities; and if he didn't—if he switched to other locations—he'd rouse so many questions back in Düsseldorf that his entire job would be at stake. Which meant he would have blown, all by himself, a most useful cover. No, no, Theo wasn't stupid. Remember, too, that Theo had no way of knowing that he had been traced to Essen, far less to East Germany. If he had known, he wouldn't be setting out on this long business trip; he'd be in East Berlin, heading for Leipzig at this moment.

Thank God, thought Renwick, that no one did try to stop him leaving Düsseldorf. He'd have got away, in any case, either by a sudden maneuver or by the help of his lawyers. And he'd have known we were onto him. End of the trail for us. Reappearance of Theo a year, two years later: just a slight deferment in plans. His agents, gone to ground, would be there to carry them out. They never give up, these bastards, thought Renwick; they'll take one big step backward if that lets them jump two forward.

He rose and went into the bathroom. He pulled wide the open neck of his shirt, splashed the cold water over his face. Then he stared at himself in the small mirror. He looked normal, not like a man under the worst attack of anxiety he had experienced in a long time. He smoothed down his rumpled hair. If you were Theo, he asked himself, in what country would you begin? Wherever you had most to do, to arrange. You'd make sure of all that before you moved on to less important places on your list.

So, Renwick decided, no postponement of New York. He'd leave tomorrow. There was a full afternoon and part of the evening ahead of him before he packed and saw Thérèse.

He began reading a folder that dealt with three thousand fully equipped

Soviet troops now in Cuba. When does Washington admit this? one report ended bitterly. (Six weeks later, to keep the record straight, Washington admitted it.) Renwick just shook his head, and moved on to a bulkier file dealing with a Soviet breakthrough in thermonuclear fusion. Renwick was no armaments expert, but he knew enough to be able to maintain a credible cover. Three hours, four reports, and one final staff meeting later, he could consider he was actually ahead of schedule. Except for one thing: news from Vroom at The Hague. He had heard nothing at all, either about the confirmation of the use of an umbrella in Jake's death or about Rotterdam's additional information on the travels of a man once known as Kurt Leitner. Or about the mole in Crefeld's section. Which could mean nothing at all had been discovered. There must be something, Renwick thought irritably. Vroom knows I'm off on my own travels tomorrow. So what's delaying him? It's five o'clock now. Do I just hang around here hoping for a call from The Hague?

Ten minutes later, as he was packing his tennis gear (part of the vacation myth), his telephone did ring, a call from the lobby downstairs. A special messenger had arrived from The Hague with a sealed envelope to be delivered to Renwick. "We've checked it," the sergeant on duty was saying. "No booby trap. The messenger's credentials are in order, too."

"Then have it sent up."

"That's the trouble, sir. The messenger has instructions not to hand over the envelope to anyone except you. Shall I have him escorted up to your office?"

Vroom is really taking no chances, Renwick thought. But I don't have any messenger, however reliable, coming up into this department. "Tell him the house rules."

"I've tried that, sir. He insists he must see you. He has a verbal message to deliver."

"I'll come down," Renwick said. He reached for his tie, pulled his shirt sleeves into place and buttoned the cuffs, found his jacket, and left.

The lobby was crowded and bustling at this time of day. Between forty and fifty people, some in uniform, some in civilian clothes, were in constant movement in and out of the building. The sergeant and two guards were at the desk near the entrance. No sign of any messenger. "Where is he?" Renwick asked.

"Over there, sir, standing by the bulletin board. Gray hair, dark-blue suit, and a cane."

"I see him." The man was holding the large envelope tightly against his breast. "Doesn't trust anyone, does he?" Renwick asked as he started toward the somber-faced messenger: a man who took his duties seriously, Renwick thought as the stranger caught sight of him and, after a moment's hesitation, came to meet him. The man moved slowly; his left leg limped heavily. And then Renwick noticed that the cane was held in the wrong hand—the left hand. No proper balance for any injured left leg. He's faking it, Renwick thought, suddenly alert. A crowded lobby, a press of people, a walking stick instead of an umbrella? He halted abruptly, let the man approach. What now?

The maneuver was subtle. The envelope slipped from the messenger's free arm, fell to the floor. The man tried to pick it up, but his left hip appeared to make that painful. "Sorry," he said. "Could you?"

So I bend down for the envelope, and the tip of the cane just happens to strike me? Renwick said with a smile, "Sorry, too. I've a slipped disc." He kept his eyes on the walking stick, took a step backward. "We'll call the guard, shall we?"

The man's face froze; he made an attempt to reach down, stumbled slightly. The cane seemed to skid on the waxed floor, came pointing up toward Renwick's thigh in a sharp angle. Renwick caught it midway on its shaft, held fast. He could feel the full strength of the man's arm trying to direct the cane at its target. "Easy, easy," Renwick said, twisting the cane suddenly to slacken the man's grip. "Or do you want to lose an eye?" The man stared at him, let go, ran for the entrance.

"Stop him!" Renwick shouted, and the two guards came to life. The man never reached the front steps. "Detain him for questioning," Renwick told a startled sergeant. "Make sure he doesn't escape," he added grimly. "Get highest security onto this."

The envelope contained only two sheets of typed paper giving this week's weather reports for western Europe. Renwick left it in the sergeant's charge as evidence of an attempt at false entry. The walking stick he trusted to no one but carried it carefully upstairs, not even risking the elevator with its jostle of people. He'd let the laboratory boys experiment with it. Pressure on the handle at a certain spot that ejected a miniature pellet coated with poison? And then a raging fever that would begin to work on him halfway across the Atlantic?

Down in the lobby, the brief sensation had subsided. Few had even been aware of it. "Another kook?" someone asked, and got a shrug for an answer as the man, now subdued and under heavy guard, was led away.

Renwick reached his office, placed the cane carefully along the center of his desk, its tip turned well away from him. He telephoned Security, just to make sure they'd fully understand the possible importance of this prisoner, and then called Evans in the lab. He explained, quietly and succinctly, what was needed. "Is this one of your jokes, Bob?" he was asked. So he lost his temper and let a few curses burn up the wire. Within ten minutes, Evans and an assistant were carrying away the cane, handling it with the proper respect.

Strange, thought Renwick, that it takes a string of oaths and a voice raised like a drill sergeant's to make people listen. As for the fact that he would look like a bloody fool if the cane turned out to be harmless—well, he'd just have to sweat that one out.

He poured himself a Scotch and settled down to wait for Evans's report. The grip of his right hand was still painful, a sharp reminder of that short desperate struggle in the lobby. The man had recognized him, had come forward to meet him without waiting for a signal from Renwick. The man had known in which building he'd find Renwick's office—and in the huge complex of NATO's sprawl, that was quite an achievement. Especially when

Renwick's office was in no official listing, and when his name was in no directory. But what really perturbed Renwick now was the feeling that he had seen that man before. Just once. Fleetingly. Yet in circumstances that had stamped the solemn face—gray hair, tight lips, pointed jaw line, high-bridged nose—on Renwick's memory.

His phone rang. It wasn't Evans. It was Millbank, whose office lay at the other end of the hall. "I've got Vroom here," Millbank said. "He's down from The Hague arranging a memorial service for Crefeld. You knew Crefeld didn't you?"

"Yes."

"Then I'll bring Vroom along to meet you. Okay?"

"Okay."

'We'll be with you in three minutes flat."

"Okay."

But nothing was okay at this moment. Delayed shock, Renwick told himself. The attack had shaken him more than he had been willing to admit: a near thing. Much too near. Much too quickly arranged. Someone—and who the hell was someone?—had wanted to deal with him before he left for America, make sure he'd never return. One moment more and he might have lost that battle if the assailant's will power hadn't suddenly weakened and let his grip loosen. That was all it would have taken, one moment, in a crowded lobby with only two or three bystanders even noticing—and not understanding a damned thing.

The door opened and closed. "Are you all right?" Vroom was asking as he waited for Renwick's greeting. It wasn't given. Vroom noted the untouched drink, the half-packed bag, and drew up a free chair to face Renwick. He might have congratulated me, Vroom was thinking, on the way I managed to see him—no attention drawn to this particular visit, buried as it was among all the other interviews I've been conducting in the last two hours. "Sorry I couldn't contact you before this. But I do have some results to give you. First, about Crefeld's death."

That captured Renwick's attention.

"It was murder. A close examination of Crefeld's body and clothing showed a matching puncture on both. A miniature pellet no bigger than a pinhead was found under his skin."

"What poison, this time?"

"No definite opinion, as yet. Does that matter so much?"

It didn't. Dead was dead.

"Secondly," Vroom went on, "about the Rotterdam report. It was easier to approach the police inspector than I had thought: their files on the safe house near the docks are missing, too. The Narcotics Squad is blaming the antiterrorist section, and they in turn are blaming Narcotics. But what isn't missing is the final report on the escape route of that man who came off the freighter from Duisburg. For the simple reason that no report has yet been drawn up. There are just pieces of information from the detectives who were trying to follow his trail from the house in Rotterdam."

"Trying to? They didn't succeed?"

"Not altogether. Again we had the conflict between two different departments: the antiterrorist section taking over midway—almost at the end of the trail, in fact. Which was at Schiphol Airport, in Amsterdam."

"An international flight? To the United States?"

"No. At the time he disappeared, there was only one flight scheduled to leave—for London. En route to New York, possibly. That could be. . . . Why else did he study so much about the United States in that safe house in Rotterdam?"

Renwick nodded a tentative agreement. "But how the hell did he manage to dodge the cops at Schiphol?"

"By the way of the men's room. It had only one entrance, no window. He was only one minute there. Walked out with a couple of strangers. No longer wearing a raincoat or his black wig. They were found later, stuffed into a cistern. And he had help. Someone ran interference for him—collapsed against the cop just as he was about to enter. A gray-haired man who seemed to have lost his balance." Vroom paused, frowned. He was getting ahead of himself. Further information about the gray-haired man belonged in the next segment of his story. He liked things in their proper order, neat and clear. He was saved from his indecision by the telephone.

Renwick reached for it at once. "This should be Evans—I hope. Pour yourself a drink, Johan," he said quickly, and gave his full attention to the message. "Better contact Security," he told Evans. "Make sure that they don't release that man, and they don't spread the word around about assault with a deadly weapon. Once you've tracked down that substance, the charge could be attempted murder. Meanwhile, tell them to keep it quiet, will you? Also, you'd better get in touch with New Scotland Yard's antiterrorist squad. The poison their scientists found in a similar pellet was ricin." Renwick replaced the receiver, looked at Vroom's startled face. "So I wasn't a damned fool, just damned lucky." He picked up his glass and drank deeply. "Go on. He took a flight to London?"

Vroom recovered from his bewilderment. Murder? Whose murder had been attempted? He said, "That was the deduction, once he couldn't be found anywhere in the airport."

"Any attempt to check the passenger list of that flight?"

"Not until later. Much later," Vroom conceded unhappily. "I made my own inquiries, but remember that all this happened five—almost six weeks ago. And the carrier was British Airways. We should have any further checking done in London."

"What about immigration?"

"I checked with them, too. They have a record of eleven American citizens traveling to London that day from Amsterdam. No names."

"They had no warning to keep a watch for any American?"

"The man wasn't *known* to be an American. And the policeman who was watching the passengers loading had a different description in mind. Not just clothes and hair, but also the wrong age. When he was wearing a raincoat, the man had seemed middle-aged—hunched shoulders, slow movements, heavy around the waistline."

Renwick nodded. "An adept performance." More than police routine had been necessary. If only Crefeld's department had been alerted five weeks earlier . . . Well, it hadn't been. "I'll see what help Gilman can give us in London," he said, but without much hope. The trail was cold by this time. And yet—Renwick's thoughtful gray eyes studied Vroom's unhappy face. He said, "There may be one link, one connection. Someone tried to eliminate me today. He was using a cane, not an umbrella."

"The gray-haired man in the lobby?" Vroom burst out. "Attempted murder? Was that the one? My God, I never realized. . . . Just saw him being taken away by the guards. I was coming in with Millbank, stopped at the desk for identification—" Vroom broke off, shook his head. "I thought— we all thought—it was someone trying to gain unauthorized entry. Kept it quiet, didn't you?" Then Vroom's thin dark face broke into a wide grin. "I think we've got that link. Two, in fact."

"Two?" The obvious one was quite enough, thought Renwick: the identity of the man who had been followed from Rotterdam to Schiphol Airport had to be protected at all costs. Crefeld had known of his importance; I could know; so, get rid of us both along with any existing copies of that police report.

"Two," Vroom insisted, now enjoying himself. "And that gray-haired man is both of them. Attempted murder today; running interference at Schiphol five weeks ago. It's the same man, Bob. What do you think I was doing at the Rotterdam police station a couple of days ago? Studying a composite drawing of the man's face, reading his description. Gray hair, sharp jaw line, narrow lips, thin, high-bridged nose."

That could be the man, all right. Renwick stared at Vroom. "Why didn't you tell me—"

"I was just coming to that. He is part of our investigation on the informer in our department." There was no disguising the triumph in Vroom's voice.

"So you've traced him."

"Her."

"Luisa?" Jake's devoted secretary? It was hard to believe.

"Not too difficult to uncover, once I started thinking the unthinkable and delved into Luisa's private life. Her first reaction to Crefeld's death was embarrassing—that was the night I returned from Amsterdam with the news and told her I was convinced it was murder." Vroom was thinking of that scene. Luisa waiting in Crefeld's office, hours later than her usual routine allowed, her face contorted with the shock, her abnormal protest, a voice rising into hysteria: "But why—why? They didn't have to kill him, they didn't have to kill him!" Vroom shook his head. "She went to pieces. Excessive anguish. Yet the news about the stolen briefcase had left her quite unmoved."

"You told her a lot." Renwick's quiet voice held a touch of reprimand.

"I trusted her," Vroom said simply. "But after that hysterical reaction— well, we started investigating. Hard. Intensively. She's been living secretly with a man called Maartens. Younger than she is. Handsome. Ardent. Most flattering for a woman over forty who isn't particularly attractive."

"Was she aware she was being investigated?"

"We made sure she was aware. And we got results. She asked for sick leave, pleaded doctor's orders, a visit to a clinic in Switzerland. But we caught her yesterday at the German border, on a train for Berlin."

"You've had a busy week," Renwick observed wryly.

"Unpleasant," Vroom admitted. "Most unpleasant. Except that Maartens is an important discovery. We had his telephone tapped. He has been very busy in these last eight days since Crefeld was murdered. He has connections here in Brussels as well as his little love nest in The Hague. He works on women, and through them." Vroom drew a snapshot from his pocket, handed it over to Renwick. "Ever come across him?"

The photograph was poor—hazy background of café tables—but the fair-haired man, face turned for a quick moment toward the hidden camera, was clear enough. I've seen him, Renwick thought: I've seen that face. Once. Briefly. With the gray-haired man? Renwick kept his voice normal. "Works on women, does he?"

Careful now, Vroom warned himself. He said, "That's his specialty. Some through sex. Some—" he hesitated slightly, avoided Renwick's eyes—"through money. Subsidizes a failing business, brings it new clients and success."

Renwick's face was unreadable. "Any connection with the gray-haired man?"

"Luisa admitted she had seen him once, when he paid a late-night visit to Maartens. She never learned his name, but her identification of him—we showed her a copy of the composite drawing made by the Rotterdam police artist—was definite."

"So that's how he got directions to this building? From Maartens, by way of Luisa?"

Vroom shook his head. "Not through Luisa. She didn't know where you worked. That information must have come from—from someone in Brussels." His voice was hesitant. He almost spoke again, and then cut himself off.

Renwick looked at him sharply. Vroom was the voluble man, quick-witted, with phrases to match that often covered his nervousness. Tonight he had been showing a new assurance—perhaps the prospect of promotion, a sense of accomplishment, had added to his confidence. So why all this backing and filling now? "Did Maartens telephone Brussels?"

Vroom nodded. "He wanted information about you. His call—" again there was that agonizing hesitation—"was to an interior decorator here. To a business he subsidized eighteen months ago."

And suddenly the long-buried memory of those two men rose to the surface. A cold bitter evening in November just after he had met Thérèse Colbert—a visit to her apartment an hour earlier than intended—two strangers stepping out of Thérèse's door into the elevator, brushing past Renwick as they pulled on their overcoats. Gray hair, blond hair; one with a sharp beak of a nose, a pointed chin; the other, smooth-skinned, even-featured. Clients, Thérèse had told him without any prompting, two men who were in the hotel business giving her a contract as their decorator.

Vroom was saying, "The name of that firm is . . ." Again the tactful hesitation.

"Colbert et Cie," Renwick said.

"Of course, Madame Colbert would have no idea what his real purpose was. He'd ask information about your office, your movements, in a round-about way."

"Of course." Renwick rose abruptly. And there, in Thérèse's apartment, Maartens would have made sure of a photograph for his files. Together with a photograph taken as Renwick left Crefeld's building, his identification had been easy. Small wonder the gray-haired man could recognize him on sight. Renwick drew a deep breath, slowly poured out two more drinks. "One for the road," he said as he handed Vroom his glass.

Vroom took the hint, got to his feet, spoke hurriedly. "Yes, we've spent too much time together. But I'd like to question the gray-haired man. Can that be arranged?" He finished his drink quickly. "I'll see you on your return from America. There is still a lot to clear up."

"A lot," Renwick agreed. "Can I keep this photograph of Maartens? You've other copies?"

"Of course. And one thing more—" Vroom remembered as he reached the door—"did you ever come across the name Herman Kroll? This man Maartens was one of his young men. That was some time ago—in East Germany—before Kroll was killed in a helicopter crash." With that, Vroom was out of the door, leaving Renwick to stare after him.

Kroll—Otto Remp—Theo; and the man Maartens. Renwick set aside his glass. In that last second, Vroom had given the most important piece of information of all. Unwittingly. Didn't he know Kroll's death had been faked? That Theo was alive and functioning? Of course he couldn't have known: talk of Kroll had been only between Crefeld and Renwick, and Crefeld had never lived to take Vroom into his confidence. I was too slow, too damned stupefied, Renwick thought, too shocked by Vroom's information on Thérèse. . . . I ought to have told him about Theo. I ought to have warned him. And why didn't I even get around to telling him about Interintell? Or asking him to take Jake Crefeld's place? I was just too damned stupefied.

He still was. The agony of betrayal was hitting him hard. His fist clenched and struck his desk a heavy blow, as if physical pain could be a substitute for what he felt.

Then he thought, I can either sit here and get soaking drunk. Or I can take a good look at myself and start reshaping my life. Too much desk work in these last eighteen months. Apart from my visits to Essen and Amsterdam, I have been Brussels-bound, tied by responsibilities. That came from my promotion, of course: paperwork and conferences, committees and decisions. Too much of that by day. And by night? Smooth white arms, blue eyes wide with sympathy, and wild embraces . . .

Forget her, he told himself. You can't even allow your vanity the luxury of doubting Vroom's word. Vroom had been too sure of his facts. A man intent on becoming Crefeld's replacement was not going to jeopardize his promotion by wild statements or half-cocked deductions. Vroom had more information than he had divulged. Out of friendship—or at least a desire for friendship? Or perhaps give him credit for believing this could happen to any of us. As it had done to Crefeld, with his complete trust in an invaluable secretary. Except in your case, you goddamned fool Renwick, you weren't deceived by a woman's efficiency. You fell for the oldest game in this sorry world.

All right, he told himself now. Make out your report of today's events, deliver it along with your resignation. This was as good a time as any to turn the rumors—a nice little piece of camouflage, he had told Jake—into something that could be believed by the opposition. But he would have to make two things clear in that report: he had no interest in Kurt Leitner or Maartens. As for Thérèse Colbert—no connection with Maartens, just a woman on the make.

Quickly, he uncovered his small typewriter, began batting out the reasons for his tendered resignation. There were two of them, compressed into one page—the Big Man upstairs liked all urgent business condensed to a quickly readable statement. First, the assassination attempt in this building (briefly described) proved Renwick was under close scrutiny: all future work, based here, was now rendered difficult and ineffective. Second, Thérèse and his stupidity (no punches pulled there) made this resignation obligatory.

Yes, he decided as he read his brief report: this would be believed by men like Theo. The acceptance of his resignation would also be believed. (And, he reminded himself, any more mistakes like Thérèse and his resignation would indeed be accepted. How could he have been so easily gulled—as if he were a naïve twenty-one-year-old, filled with trust in sincere blue eyes?)

The office upstairs would still be open. The Big Man worked late, never left his desk until eight o'clock at the earliest. It was now almost seven. Renwick reached for the telephone and made a request for an emergency meeting. His luck, grim today, had turned: his request was granted.

What if, he wondered wryly as he took the elevator upstairs, I lose this gambit? What if I have my resignation actually accepted? Then no backing for any future work—no base for operations, no files to be called on, no computers to help, no pool of information, no agents working under my control. Without all that, a project like Interintell would be dead, and Theo's man, so carefully groomed for future stardom in America, could slip away from us as adeptly as he had left Essen, Rotterdam, Schiphol Airport.

His luck held. He won his gambit: Theo, and the file Renwick had collected on Mr. Otto Remp of Düsseldorf, won it for him.

By nine o'clock he was back in his office, finishing his last job of clearing up. He made one final telephone call. To Thérèse.

She sounded slightly rushed, a little flustered. "Oh, darling—I'm so glad you called. I've been trying to reach you for the last hour. Tonight's impossible. I'm just leaving. Mother isn't well—I've got to go to her."

"At this hour?"

"It isn't so late—a short drive to Bruges."

"How long will you be there?"

"Overnight. We'll leave tomorrow for Switzerland. Mother's doctor says she ought to visit a clinic."

"Sounds dull for you. Where is it?"

"Near Lausanne. It depends on Mother's health how long we'll stay.

August is soon here, the shop will be closed for the vacation, so I'm free to be with her. You do understand?"

"Of course."

"What about you? When do you get back here?"

"I don't. I'm looking for a job."

There was a marked silence. "Where? What kind of job?"

"I'm still deciding. I've had two offers—London or Paris."

"You are really resigning? No more Brussels?"

"I handed in my resignation tonight."

"Oh, Bob! . . . There's the doorbell. It must be my driver to tell me the car is waiting. Good-bye darling." And the line went dead.

Good-bye, darling. Just like that? He replaced the receiver, shaking his head. He had heard no doorbell ringing, although her telephone was on the table in the small hall only six feet away from its entrance. And that long silence— a hand covering the mouth of the receiver? There had been no sound whatsoever—a complete clamp-down. Who had been with her? he wondered. Who had shared the call, prompted her to ask what kind of job and where?

Or perhaps he was overreacting. What had he wanted to hear from her, anyway? Words that would reassure him she hadn't known what she had done. A voice that recalled memories of nights past. Goddamned fool, he told himself. The verdict is in but you want it miraculously reversed. Quickly, cutting off all sentiment, he seized his bag, locked the door of his office suite, dropped the keys with Millbank's office.

Millbank, the complete diplomat, had been waiting to make a formal good-bye. He was still a little stunned, but secretly delighted, with his sudden promotion. "I'll take care of your office," he reassured Renwick as they walked together to the elevator.

He would, thought Renwick: he was a capable man. "Couldn't be in better hands."

Millbank dropped his voice. "How long?"

"Indefinitely."

"Oh?"

"But I'll keep in touch."

"Yes. Any time we can help—"

"I'll lean on you," Renwick said. "See about renting my apartment, will you?"

"I've got a secretary who's already putting in her bid."

"News does get around."

"We'll have your things stored for you."

"There isn't much that's valuable. But have the place gone over thoroughly, will you? We don't want your secretary having her love life bugged."

That startled Millbank. "You think someone had your place wired for sound?"

"Shouldn't be surprised. But don't let that bother you. I never talked business there."

"Careful fellow," Millbank said.

"Not careful enough." There was no smile now in Renwick's voice or eyes. But his final handshake was warm. "Take care of the shop." He will, thought Renwick; otherwise I couldn't be leaving with this feeling of freedom.

"Good luck, Bob."

"And to you." With committees and conferences and files upon files. Poor old Millbank, he didn't know what he was getting into. But it was possible Millbank was the type to enjoy it all.

"One thing—" Millbank had suddenly remembered—"I had your travel arrangements changed as you asked. You'll have a—"

"Yes. Thanks for that," Renwick cut in. He would have a stopover in London to have a quiet session with Ronald Gilman. Agenda, in order of importance: Theo; the "American" from Rotterdam, traveling to London on June 14; the tropical-disease expert, Dr. Ilsa Schlott. The last two items were difficult, might be impossible to trace. But Ronald Gilman had the resources, and the brains and the tenacity. Interintell was no longer an idea; it was now being put to work. "Thanks again," Renwick said, as the elevator arrived at last.

"Just watch out for men carrying walking sticks," was Millbank's parting advice to the elevator's closing door.

Yes, Renwick thought, news does get around. But in this instance he had no objections. He couldn't help wondering what kind of reputation would be left him, once speculation had done its work: an attempt on his life, so he picked up and ran. Just part of the picture, Theo. You haven't much of an adversary, have you? You can forget about me. You've more important enemies to worry about.

Ten

"So," NINA O'CONNELL said, "this is Greece." She shook her head. In the dusk, the empty sands and the curve of gray-dark waters looked desolate. More desolate still were the half-dozen blacked-out houses edging the shore. Even the lights in the adjoining café, the one sign of possible life on the beach, were dismal. Madge came stumbling out of the camper, stiff from the long jolting ride, over the Yugoslav border and down through the mountains to this stretch of flat land. She halted abruptly. "Where are we?" she asked in dismay.

Guido Lambrese said, "It isn't Athens, certainly. Or Sounion. Or Delphi." Then he added a quick phrase in Italian that sounded far from complimentary. His friend Henryk came to stand beside him. "Perhaps it will look better by daylight," Henryk suggested.

Nina glanced at the Dutchman, the perpetual optimist, but tonight his constant smile had vanished. Nothing will look better in the morning, she thought; this place can never look better at any time. She eased her tired shoulders, tossed her long fall of hair back from her brow, said nothing.

Marie-Louise and Sven Dissen joined the silent group. The French girl, small and plump, dark eyes flashing indignantly, said, "But this isn't a camp-site! Where do we get water, where do we—"

"At the café," James Kiley said as he reached them. Tony Shawfield was still in the camper. Fussing as usual, Nina thought, checking all his equip-ment before he locked everything tight. "We can get food there, too. We won't need to do any cooking for the next few days. Come on, let's get moving." His arm went around Nina's waist, and he drew her toward the café. The others straggled behind them.

Sven looked back at the far-stretching sea, halted briefly as he pointed over the darkening waters. "Isn't that the Gulf of Salonika?" He was the avid studier of maps and guidebooks. Not, thought Nina, that all his infor-mation has done any of us much good except to remind us of the capital cities we've bypassed. Europe had become a series of campsites, she decided angrily, with long stretches of scenery in between. Jim had always, of course, his day in the nearest town—collecting the cash that he had waiting for him at Basel, Innsbruck, Zagreb. And Tony, guarding the camper and fiddling with his radio while Jim was absent, would have his day in town as soon as Jim had returned—there always seemed to be some piece of equipment he needed to have checked or replaced. Of course, she had to admit, all of the campsites had been adequate; some of them attractive. And there were the necessary chores to take up time: laundry—my God, she thought, at the end of this trip I'll never want to drip-dry a shirt again—the buying of food, the cooking of meals, the cleanup jobs to keep litter from gathering; details that no one had thought about back in the comforts of Amsterdam.

"Or," Sven was saying, forever the purist, "should we say Thessalonica?"

Guido, the expert on Greece and archaeological remains, set him right. "It's the Thermaic Gulf. At the head of it—to the north"—he waved a hand up the coastline—"we have Thessalonica. Or Salonika. What does it mat-ter? It is still only a northeast corner of Greece."

Madge ventured, "How far away is Salonika, Jim?"

"About twenty miles. Thirty-two kilometers, or thereabouts." Kiley sounded vague.

"And to the south of us?"

"Katerini."

Sven said, pleased with his memory, "And across the gulf, there are three peninsulas with hotels, bathing beaches, rich Greeks—"

"Too crowded, too expensive," Kiley said and forestalled any questions about why hadn't they headed in that direction. He went on easily, "The beach here is just the same kind of sand. We can catch up on our sun tans without bankrupting our budget." And that silenced them completely: com-pared to Shawfield's expenses with gas and oil and camping-site fees, and Kiley's expenditures on basic foods, they hadn't spent much. It was practi-cally a free ride. Who could grumble at that?

Kiley's arm tightened around Nina's waist. Her silence worried him. "Are you all right?"

She nodded, her eyes studying the six miserable cottages they were now passing. They were deserted. No sign of life at all.

Kiley spoke hurriedly. "This is a fishing village, but in summer the fishermen move down the coast, nearer Katerini. There's a better market for their fish. In winter, they come back here—this part of the bay is more sheltered."

Nina looked at the thin trees sparsely scattered, the bushes that bunched in clusters where the sand ended and the rough road began. To think that only a hundred yards away there was the main highway, down which they had speeded this evening, down which they could have traveled all the way to Athens. "What made you choose this place?"

"Tony phoned ahead from the frontier and found that the camping sites near Salonika were all full. It's August, the European vacation month. A campsite manager told him about this beach." He didn't need to invent any more excuses. Nina's attention was now on the Café Thermaica, which they were entering. Simple but clean, he noted with relief: scrubbed wooden floor, oilcloth covers on the long tables carefully washed, a charcoal fire against the back wall glowing and ready to broil the fresh fish piled on a small serving counter. He ignored the two men, roughly dressed, who sat in the darkest corner of the room, just as they were ignoring him and the group of hot and crumpled people who came straggling behind him.

The woman who owned the place ("Can be trusted," Kiley had been told; "widow of a faithful party member who died fighting the fascists") switched on an extra light bulb along with a brief smile of welcome that softened her usually intense, haggard face. Beside her, a very young girl and an even younger boy ("niece and nephew, orphaned, negligible" had been the report on them) hesitated nervously, dark eyes fixed in wonder as they stared at the foreigners. Then at a string of sharp commands from their aunt, they hurried forward to serve.

They were so anxious, so willing, so pathetic, that Nina's resistance eroded. To please them, she even drank the *retsinata* wine that tasted of turpentine, tried a mouthful of cold rice wrapped in cooked vine leaves, ate—with enjoyment—the crusted black bread. And the fish, when it came to the table at long last, was excellent.

Kiley relaxed. Exhaustion and hunger had been the trouble. Now, everyone around the long table was in a more docile mood. But we nearly had a mutiny on our hands, he told himself. He rose, saying, "I'd better find Tony before we eat his dinner." And then to Nina, "Okay now? Hardly the Ritz, I know." He left, glancing briefly at the two men in the corner, who were making a glass of wine last all through their evening. I'll be with you, he told them silently, once I get this crowd bedded down for the night.

Shawfield had finished receiving the latest instructions and was locking the thin metal doors that protected his special equipment. "Coming, coming," he called to Kiley as he slid into place a screen of medical supplies and canned foods—all tightly secure on narrow, deep-lipped shelves backed by a wooden panel—that covered the metal doors exactly. A neat job, he thought—as he always did each time he used his radio transmitter—a pleasure to work with: so carefully set into the side of the camper that no customs official yet had noticed the depth of the shelves was less than the total depth of the supply cupboard. He closed its wooden doors and locked them, too. All complete.

He let Kiley enter. "No Istanbul," he reported. "It's canceled."

"Why?"

"Turkish Intelligence is snooping around Istanbul. Something has stirred them up."

"So we go directly to Bursa," Kiley reflected.

"That's where our meetings are scheduled, anyway. So no problem."

"But that could cause us more trouble. We nearly had a mutiny tonight," Kiley said as they left the camper.

Shawfield locked its door, turned to stare at Kiley. "Now what reason could they—"

"This beach is the reason. No Salonika. Before that, no Dalmatian coast, no Belgrade, no Venice, no Vienna."

"This beach suits you and me. You gave them a good explanation about why we had to come here. They accepted it."

"And what about my absence tomorrow—for three days and nights? And your three to follow?" A long stretch, thought Kiley worriedly. Usually, his one-day disappearances had a standard explanation: someone to be interviewed, a place visited for a future story, a finished article to be mailed to a Paris agency that handled free-lance material. All that, and the collection of money waiting for him at prearranged banks or travel agencies, took care of a busy day with no time for ordinary sightseeing. Marco's standard excuse had also worked: the firm subsidizing his trip had sent various spare parts ahead to be picked up in certain places; wanted tests to be made and radio reports on the results. "It's a long absence this time. They're just in the mood to start questioning—"

"Bloody hell, we can't arrange our schedules to suit their whims. You've heard them: six different ideas on what they want to see at every discussion session."

That was true enough: everyone with his own demands, his own interests to satisfy. "Democracy, it's called," Kiley said with a laugh, and turned Shawfield's anger into a smile.

Shawfield said, "You'll find an additional excuse to shut them up. Tell them you've got an old college friend who married a Greek girl, and they're living on her father's farm not far from here. Can't refuse their invitation, can you?"

"It might work. If Nina were persuaded, Madge would listen. Possibly the others, too." Nina, surprisingly, had more will power than all the rest added together. "A strong-headed girl."

"A spoiled little bitch."

"No. I thought that at first. She's just too damned independent, that's all."

"You know how to handle her."

"Look, you told me to ease up." Kiley's lips tightened. "In Innsbruck—"

"Only as far as you were concerned. Keep her tied to you, but no real involvement on your part. Wasn't that your plan?"

Kiley was silent.

"You aren't in love with her?" Shawfield asked sharply.

In love? Perhaps I've been in love since I first caught sight of her standing at the foot of a staircase in Wigmore Hall. Kiley drew a long breath,
said, "Don't be a damn fool, Tony. I have other things on my mind. Being
in love is no part of them." He pretended some amusement, changed the
subject back to the six days ahead of them. "What excuse will you give for
your absence?"

"I'll find one. The engine needs extra special attention after all these
mountain passes, don't you think? I can take the camper to Katerini and
have it checked there—a three-day job." Then Shawfield glanced at his
friend. "Or perhaps I should start giving them pills for malaria?" He slapped
Kiley's shoulder, led the way into the café.

The air was bland, still warm from the intense heat of the day. There was
no sound except the gentle lapping of the sea. A night with little moon,
but the sky was free of clouds and the stars were brilliant. Nina sat alone
near the water's edge, her arms folded around her knees, her head tilted
sideways with her blonde hair falling unchecked over her brow. *Hardly the
Ritz* . . . Jim's parting shot had rankled. I don't and never did expect the
Ritz, she told the ripple of dark water; dammit I've only been in the Ritz
once in my life, when Father took me to that reception in Paris. For a
moment, she had an attack of nostalgia: life had seemed so much simpler
then. Now, she was completely and thoroughly confused. About Jim Kiley.
And because of Jim Kiley.

What had she done to change him? He had been in love with her—she
knew that. Then something had happened—but what? Her fault? He was
still friendly, still affectionate, but different, too. Ever since Innsbruck, all
through Austria and that mad dash through Yugoslavia, he was changed. It
was her vanity, she tried to tell herself: she had always been the one to push
a man aside; no one had ever pushed her. Except—the long-past memory
quickened—except Robert Renwick . . . But not this way; and now that she
was no longer a girl of fifteen, she could understand what Bob must have
felt. A silly romantic, she chided herself, embarrassing the hell out of a man
who liked you. Liked you a lot. More than liked you. If only you had been—
well, you weren't. . . . God, how you cried your eyes out after he left Geneva
so suddenly, went back to Brussels. . . . And then she realized that this was
the first time she had ever thought about Renwick's feelings instead of
remembering her own. Perhaps, she thought in surprise, perhaps I'm growing up at last. Perhaps—

She heard the light footsteps only as they reached her. One hand caught
her shoulder, another laid its fingers across her lips as they opened to cry
out. "Let's not wake the others," Jim Kiley said as he knelt beside her. "All
asleep." Except Shawfield, who was again back at the café, deep in quiet
talk with two hard-bitten characters. Kiley's fingers moved from her mouth
to caress her cheek, trace the line of her neck down into her loosely buttoned blouse. He dropped back on the sand, pulling her with him. She tried

to speak, make one small protest, but his arms were tightly around her and his lips silenced hers with a kiss that was as vehement and hard as his body.

She tried to free herself, but he caught a long strand of hair and pulled her back. Nina cried out in pain. He eased his grip but still held her captive. Now his kisses were soft, smothering. At last he released her. "Is that what you want? You just want to play at love. Is that it, Nina?"

She sat up slowly, tried to fasten her blouse. "I just want to be sure of love," she said. She was close to tears.

He noticed her trembling. Wrong tactics, he told himself. "Did I scare you?" he asked gently, his hand caressing her hair, fondling her cheek.

Three times, she thought. First, the silent approach. Then the sudden attack—as if I had no say at all, just a puppet that danced when he pulled the strings. And now—this sudden change to tenderness, all passion turned off in one short moment. It was this change that upset her most of all. Yes, he scared her.

"Nina . . ." He sat up beside her, slipping an arm around her waist. "You've got to understand. These last weeks have been pure hell for me—close to you, watching you. I'm sorry if I scared you."

Her smile was nervous, uncertain. "You shouldn't slip up behind me in the dark. I didn't know who it was."

He relaxed a little. "Stupid of me. But you looked so tempting, sitting there, lost in dreams."

"If I had been an enemy sentry," she said, confidence returning as her voice steadied, "you could have slit my throat. Where on earth did you learn that trick, Jim? In the army?"

He turned that aside with a laugh. There had been no army listed in James Kiley's history. "In the Boy Scouts." That was safe enough; untraceable. He had got her laughing, too. So he kissed her again. "A pity to waste the starlight." Then he said, "You are right, you know. We can't let emotions run away with us, not when we're crowded into a camper, and six other people are noticing every look we exchange. And at the campsites, there are just too many strangers around, children everywhere, no privacy. Not like this beach. It's the first time we could get away from everyone. Do you realize that, Nina?"

She nodded, staring out at the quiet sea.

"So you forgive me?"

She nodded again.

"Once we get rid of the others—"

She turned to look at him.

He cursed himself for that slip. Nina had scattered his wits. "Perhaps in America," he said, "we'll get away from them."

"Aren't we going back to London?"

"First, we have to travel through America, don't we? I'd like you to meet my uncle. He'd certainly want to see me. And you."

This really startled her. She had been thinking so much about Asia and the Far East that she had forgotten about America. "No doubt my father will expect to see me, too. He'd be hurt if I didn't make an effort to get in touch."

"Then I can meet him?" Would Theo approve of this suggestion? he wondered. It could do no harm at the moment; later, if Theo had other plans, it could be canceled. Excuses came in the hundreds. It was only necessary to choose the most acceptable and make it believable.

Her amazement grew. "Jim—do you really want to meet him?"

"I'd like his approval."

Nina waited. But nothing was added. What was he trying to say? That he wanted to marry her? "You're the strangest man, Jim Kiley."

"Then we make a very good pair." He drew her close again and kissed her. She's so damned beautiful, he thought.

And Nina, looking at the handsome face, the tender eyes, felt a surge of emotion. "Jim—what do you really want?" she asked. He made no reply to that except to kiss her and pull her—gently, he warned himself—down onto the sand beside him.

"Almost midnight," Kiley announced, so suddenly that Nina, still under the spell of bright stars, could only look at him in surprise. "I've an early start tomorrow." She sat up slowly, staring at him. He gave her three kisses, lightly, one on each eye, one on her lips. "That's for the days I'll be away."

"Three days?"

A visit to an old college friend, Kiley explained: he had married a Greek girl, was now helping her father run his tobacco plantation just west of Salonika. A couple of days with him, and a day in Salonika for a visit to the bank, and he would be back here to join her on the beach.

"And then Tony has his three days?" she asked bitterly. "What about us?" Six days in this place . . .

"You'll all catch up on your sun tans, swim, relax. The next stage of this journey won't take you near any seashore. It will be a long haul until we reach Bombay." As for Tony, he went on explaining, he'd need three full days to get the camper thoroughly overhauled. He was worried about the front axle; had to make sure everything was in good condition for some of the mountain passes through Iran, Afghanistan. Sure, there were trouble spots there, but she wasn't to worry. In Salonika, Kiley would arrange for local guides to meet them and ease their way, help steer them clear of the fighting. There was a definite highway all the way into India—didn't she remember the two campers they had met at the site where they had stopped after crossing the Yugoslav frontier at Ljubljana? A German teacher, wife, and two young children in one, an Englishman with wife and three children in the other? They were taking the same route; it was practically becoming a main thoroughfare nowadays. "I'll make sure it's safe," he ended, watching her reactions warily.

"Of course you will." He always did. "So we are here until Saturday." She frowned.

"For rest and recreation," he said, smiling.

"Then we'll reach Istanbul by next Tuesday at latest?" That would be the fourth of September, she calculated, and time enough to collect the money that would be waiting for her at Turk Express. She had written her father about that from Basel, weeks ago—just in case Robert Renwick had forgotten her message.

"We'll cross the Bosporus into Asia by ferry from Istanbul, and make our main stop at Bursa. It's the old Turkish capital; you'll find it interesting. You could even make a visit to Troy from there. You'd like that, wouldn't you?"

"No stop at Istanbul?" she asked in dismay. "What about Topkapi, Saint Sophia, the Blue Mosque, the Bazaar? Oh, Jim—we *can't* miss them!"

"The good campsites are already booked full. August, you know—the holiday month in Europe. We'll be better off in Asia. Bursa is old Turkey, authentic. No hordes of tourists from France and Germany and—"

"Jim! We must have two days at least in Istanbul."

"Come on," he said, raising her to her feet, "my bus leaves for Salonika at six in the morning."

"Leaves from where?"

"On the main highway, just as the road to the café branches off."

That was only a short distance away. She remembered the sudden cutoff they had taken that evening, and the large modern hotel that stood well back from the highway at that point. Its gay blue and yellow wall decorations had caught her eye: Mondrian design, Matisse colors. "Why didn't we park at the hotel?" she asked suddenly. "We might have had hot baths there." I'd give anything for a long hot tub, she thought, brushing her shoulders and hips free of sand. Her hair, too, was filled with fine grains. She'd never sleep tonight, even if she combed her hair for an hour.

"It's a motel, government-run," he said curtly. "Doesn't allow stray campers. Come on, Nina, come on." He was already starting over the beach.

She gave one last look at the quiet, dark waters. The salt wouldn't help her hair, she decided, even if the sand was washed out. She caught up with him, saying, "I'm going to the café." It hadn't closed as yet: meager lights still showed.

"Why?" he asked, worrying now about Shawfield. He must still be there.

"To get a bath. They have a tub, surely."

"Zinc, no doubt. And three inches of cold water."

Remembering her horrified retreat from the café's one toilet, the size of a telephone booth, stone floor with a hole in the center, overpowering smell of chloride of lime, no window, a hundred flies, she admitted that Jim could be right. "Okay," she said in resignation. "I'll have a swim even if it leaves my hair sticky and dull." She halted, began loosening her blouse, unfastening her jeans.

"Nina!" He pointed to the four sleeping bodies sprawled near the caravan.

"Dead to the world," she told him. "Coming?"

He turned away, began walking toward the road.

Where was he headed? The café? Okay, damn you, she told him, stripping completely, and ran into the tepid waters. She had almost a hundred yards to wade before her waist was covered. No swimming possible but she could float, letting her hair spread around her head like a silver halo under the stars.

Quietly, Nina slipped into the camper, decided against switching on its light and wakening Madge, fumbled her way toward her narrow bed. This must be the way you lived on a submarine, she thought as she reached into her overhead locker and groped for a towel: every foot of space accounted for, and not one inch wasted. Comfortable enough, once you remembered what to avoid and spared yourself some sharp bumps. All these windows would be useful now that the camper was heading into hot weather, although their thin curtains, even if they gave privacy, weren't any protection from being awakened by early-morning light. A long sleep, a real bath, that was all she asked for. So far, she had taken everything as it came—except for six days stuck on this beach with all the rest of Greece beckoning. And Istanbul? We'll see about that, she decided as she finished drying her hair. Jim could be persuaded. If he loved her, he could be persuaded.

"Nina?" Madge's voice was half asleep. "Turn on the light. Where were you?"

"Having a swim."

"Alone?"

"Yes. Jim balked."

"Why on earth?" Madge wakened enough to raise herself on one elbow. "Too romantic for him?" She was speaking slowly, softly.

"He's a mystery to me." There was a long silence. "What about going into Salonika tomorrow? There's a six o'clock bus."

"In the *morning*?" Madge shook her head. Her weak laugh turned into a yawn.

"We'll all be awake by then with that damned sun."

"Not me. I'll be sleeping until noon." Madge sank back on the pillow. "Another time, Nina," she said dreamily, totally at peace with the world.

"Are you all right?" She's been on edge all day, thought Nina. Why this sudden bliss? The bunk wasn't as comfortable as all that.

Madge's answer was another small laugh, another yawn.

"We'll be here six days, Madge."

That roused no response.

Nina said, "We may not even stay in Istanbul—just a quick ride to the ferry."

There was a brief response. "No Istanbul?" But there was no indignation, no outburst. Instead, Madge was suddenly asleep.

Nina laid out a fresh shirt for tomorrow. She'd ride with Jim into Salonika, borrow some drachmas from him until she could change dollars in a bank. Then she'd leave Jim, wander around, see the Byzantine churches and their decorations, and then—oh, well, when she felt good and ready, she'd find her way to the bus stop. Or even take a taxi back here. She checked her wallet and counted her traveler's checks, packed sketchbook and pencils into her large shoulder bag. All set.

Her rising spirits declined sharply when she discovered Madge had drunk most of the water in the carafe beside the collapsible basin, leaving her a couple of sips. No washing of her face, no brushing of her teeth tonight. She'd have to rise at five tomorrow and get to the café and scrounge some water from the Dragon Lady. Those poor kids, she thought as she slipped under the sheet: that awful woman with the harsh voice that sent the two children scurrying. Remembering their thin faces, their large eyes watching the foreigners leave so much on their overheaped plates, she wondered what she had to grumble about.

It was going to be a restless and brief night. She threw off the sheet, let the gentle breath of air from the wide-opened windows glance over her body. It was easy to rise when her watch told her it was almost five o'clock.

She left Madge deeply asleep. Outside, in the pale light of a new day, the others were asleep, too. Tony Shawfield was among the scattering of living corpses. No Jim. Was he having breakfast at the café? But he wasn't there, either. The small boy was already up and around, sweeping out the earth floor. Her English was beyond him, so she unwrapped her facecloth and showed him her toothbrush and soap and did some sign language which amused them both. With teeth cleaned and face washed at the kitchen sink, and a quick visit to the obnoxious toilet—the bushes might be better in future, she decided; oh, the joys of carefree travel—she waved a cheerful good-bye and took a short cut over the rough grass to the highway. She'd have breakfast in Salonika while she studied her guidebook.

As she reached an outcrop of rock just above a short line of trees along the highway, she saw the bus approaching. It was headed north—the right direction, but its timing was wrong. Barely half past five, her watch told her. Either it was slow or the Greek buses ran ahead of schedule. She saw Jim rising from his seat on the grass, but he didn't move forward, didn't signal. The bus trundled past, its top covered with string-tied suitcases, baskets, cartons. She halted in astonishment, hesitated, and then—as a car approached from the south and Jim stepped out—she retreated behind a meager bush, as if it could hide her confusion. So he's hitchhiking to Salonika, she reassured herself; probably the bus is too crowded with local people market-bound.

She was about to call out, wave, start toward the highway. Jim was too quick for her. The car was too quick. It barely stopped, a door wide open to let him step inside before it sped on. She dropped onto the grass beside the bush, her shoulders sagging along with all her plans. Then she heard the car again. It had made a turn at the driveway to the Mondrian-Matisse motel and was coming back. For a brief moment she felt a surge of hope. Jim had seen her in spite of all the scraggy bushes around her. He was coming back to get her.

But he didn't. The car was traveling at high speed toward the south.

For many forlorn minutes, she sat watching the empty highway, the lonely stretches of dry grass and gray-green scrub. Then she raised her eyes to the background of hills, of far-off mountain ranges etched against a sky that was turning a clear light blue. She rose, her plans still vague but beginning to have shape like those distant peaks on the horizon, and started toward the motel. I'll damned well show him, she told herself.

The motel was a recent addition to the landscape. New, its bright colors and bleak design proclaimed: give me another twelve months, add some condominiums and cafés, a shopping center, a pool and tennis courts—then my three stories jutting high over this empty plain won't seem so lonely. Certainly, thought Nina, the large parking space set to one side of the building showed that expectations were high for the future, although now there were only a dozen cars or so waiting for their owners to awaken and have breakfast. There was also a solitary bus, a large glossy model, the type that toured Europe and supplied package deals. Apart from a gardener watering the young trees and plots of geraniums, and a man hosing down the bus while he chatted with a girl perkily dressed like an airline stewardess, the motel seemed deserted.

Better and better, thought Nina: anyone in charge would have leisure to talk, give advice, even help. How would she begin? Transportation, first: there must be a taxi or a car for hire. Or—she studied the bus: traveling where? And after transportation had been arranged—she'd even settle for any nearby railway station and a slow train to Athens—she'd get help with a phone call all the way to the Maryland shore. It would still be Sunday there; midnight, possibly; perhaps later, if the call to her father took a little time to go through. But, once he got over his annoyance about being hauled out of bed, he'd listen. And then, finally, information about inexpensive hotels in Athens. Elated by her three-point program, hoping for the best, she called a cheerful good morning to the bus driver and the girl, answered their surprised stare with a friendly wave, and entered the lobby.

Empty; except for a boy mopping the floor, a middle-aged woman absorbed with passports behind a cluttered desk, and a tall young man, impeccable in a neat black suit, with carefully brushed hair and a melancholy Greek face. Its normally impassive expression gave way to a look of astonishment as he stared at the newcomer. She had a moment of nervousness; then she smiled. "Good morning. I need your advice. Would you be so kind as to help me?"

The young man's dark eyes scanned her expertly. Clean and crisp blouse, neat-fitting jeans—and who would quibble with them since the Jacqueline Onassis era?—expensive shoulder bag and shoes, a charming voice, quiet manners, and, above all—he ceased staring—a figure and face that were remarkable. "Yes," he told her in excellent English, "how may I help you?" He left the desk, came forward to welcome her.

This may just work, thought Nina, her blue eyes sparkling.

By half past seven, she was back at the camper pulling a dazed Madge out of bed. "Rise and shine! Come on, come on! Pack and get ready to move out. The bus starts loading within the hour."

"Bus?"

"For Athens."

That wakened Madge completely. "But how—"

"Tell you later when we're squashed into two back seats." Traveler's checks, obligingly cashed by the motel manager, had helped to secure that space. Impossible, the bus attendant had said in halting English, impossible to sell any seats: this was a private tour. Yes, there were four vacancies in the back row, the girl admitted sadly, but impossible to sell. The emphasis was slight but definite—a timid hint? Nina had taken it. "Then don't *sell* them," Nina had suggested. "Just let two be occupied? This is what I intended to pay for a car to take us to Athens," and quickly she slipped fifty dollars into the driver's unrefusing hand. (He had been shaking his head all along, over wasted space and agency regulations.) She then had clinched the arrangement by assuring them that she and her American friend, a girl just like herself, wouldn't bring much luggage, would find their own lunch, keep to themselves, be practically invisible, cause no trouble at all. The little conference broke up in smiles and handshakes. Nina's budget was sorely dented, but it was a long journey to Athens, and a hired car—if one had been available—would have cost twice fifty dollars and bankrupted her completely. She eased her attack of conscience by noting the clean but fraying cuffs on the driver's shirt; both he and the thin-faced, harried attendant were obviously overworked and underpaid. Tips from a busload of package-deal tourists being steered through the wonders of Greece couldn't be overly generous.

"But how—" repeated Madge.

"Wear your best shirt," Nina advised. "If we hurry, you'll have time to brush your teeth in a real bathroom."

"What about breakfast?"

"We'll get coffee and a croissant at the motel, too."

"Motel?"

"Shut up, darling. I'm thinking." Nina had drawn out her sketchbook, torn off a page, and was writing. "A message for Jim," she explained. "I didn't see Tony around, so I'll leave it with Guido. He seems the only one who's half awake." Nothing but comatose bodies outside. The dead and the dying. What was wrong with them? "How much wine did you drink last night?"

"Two sips for politeness."

"You slept as if you had been hit on the head."

"Exhausted." Or, thought Madge, it might have been that malaria pill handed out by Tony. Perhaps that was the way it acted. Pleasant, anyway: relaxing. "Didn't you take your pill?"

"What pill?"

"For malaria. Tony left one on the washbasin for you. You were down on the beach and—"

"Didn't see it. Malaria? But there are no mosquitoes around here?" There wasn't a pool or a stream or a stagnant puddle in this bone-dry piece of real estate.

"We should start taking them in advance, Tony says." Madge knotted the cord of her canvas bag. "Ready to leave."

Nina handed her the note to Jim. "Will that do?"

It was brief. *Taking our R and R in Athens and points east. Meet us in Istanbul, four o'clock, September 4th, Hilton Hotel. See you then, Nina.*

"He won't like it," Madge said.

"Why not? It says all that needs to be said." Nina took the note, folded it—no envelope, but let them all read it—and picked up her tightly packed bag.

"He will be worried sick."

"Good."

"Points east?" Madge asked, puzzled.

"The Aegean. We may not have much time to land on any of the islands, but we can see them, can't we?"

"We're crazy."

"Yes, aren't we?"

With light hearts, they stepped down into the strong sunlight. There wasn't one cloud in that bright-blue sky.

Eleven

RENWICK'S EXIT FROM Brussels by way of London paid major dividends. They didn't mature, of course, until a full month later but—even without foresight of information to come—the brief meeting with Ronald Gilman was encouraging.

Renwick was then at the stage of taking extreme precautions: if a man called Maartens, linked to Theo and East German Intelligence, had been given instructions to eliminate him, there could be a second attempt on his life. It was only when he was considered to be out of the game, showed no interest in anyone or anything connected with Theo, that he might be regarded as possibly negligible and left in uneasy peace.

He would now be under surveillance, of course. That would last until the reports on his movements became dull, repetitious, boring, and he would make them all of that. So his first twenty-four hours as a man who had quit his job at NATO—even Theo's agents would have little suspicion that his intelligence-gathering wasn't strictly on Soviet military maneuvers—were a very tricky period indeed. Yet he had to meet with Gilman, that quiet self-effacing man who had dodged suspicion for his fifteen years of highly classified work. This was not the time for Renwick to draw Gilman to anyone's attention, far less Theo's.

So there had been precautions for his visit to London. First, he changed his flight and hoped he had complicated others' arrangements. Next, he made a brief call to London from the Brussels airport, a couple of unremarkable sentences that let Gilman know he was on his way. Then it was a matter of following their previously set plans: baggage left at Heathrow until the early-evening flight to New York, a long stretch of empty hours ahead of him; why not visit the city, drop into a movie house near the Strand? The place was less than half filled, ill-lighted, and noisy with the bangs and booms from a World War II film. Gilman was already seated in the empty back row, a thin tall figure slouching in his unobtrusive way; no one within listening distance even with any hearing device—the noise of the sound track would take care of that. Renwick slipped into an adjacent seat. He sat in silence for several minutes, making sure he hadn't been followed. But no one entered the cinema, and they could talk.

There was a succinct briefing of Gilman on Theo; Essen—Kurt Leitner and Section One of the Direct Action terrorists, his tie-up with Theo, his well-arranged escape, his transformation in Rotterdam into an American, his departure for London. "Any possibility about tracing him at this date? Through the airline record of reserved seats, handled by a travel agency that buys them en bloc and pays for them months later? An airline is bound to keep records of what is owed them. Certainly, Leitner wouldn't risk any delay in buying space at the airport. He must have been booked in advance."

"June fourteenth, afternoon flight from Schiphol to Heathrow." Gilman's face was imperturbable, as usual, but his voice was far from optimistic.

"Then there is another puzzle, smaller, less important perhaps. Ilsa Schlott." Renwick told what he knew.

"That's simpler—if she is a student at University College. Anything else?"

"Yes. Now that Crefeld is dead, I'd like you to head Interintell. Any problems about getting an office, a place for files and communications?"

"Not if I can suggest to my boss that the French would like to have the Interintell headquarters in Paris."

"They're trying hard. But they already have Interpol in Paris, so they can hardly argue against London having its fair share."

"Why not in Washington? Why not Frank Cooper in charge?"

"Frank would be the first to agree with me: no security possible with this right-to-know kick they're on." What foreign intelligence agencies would trust their secret files on terrorism, their classified information on the doubtful activities of American citizens, to Washington? "That really would dry up our sources of information." He paused. "How quickly can you set up headquarters? It's urgent."

"We'll make it most urgent. Give us a month." Gilman already had an office selected, a skeleton staff in mind. "I'll be on a quick visit to New York at the end of August."

"See you then. Meanwhile, get the word about Theo to Oslo and Copenhagen. I've already briefed Claudel, in Paris, and Diehl, in Germany. And what about Vlakos, in Athens? And we need someone in Ankara."

"I have a good friend there." Gilman's quiet smile lightened his calm face. "It seems that Interintell is really on its way."

With a file on Theo as its first case. Most fitting, thought Renwick: Crefeld's death would not be meaningless. "Would you meet with Vroom? Brief him on Interintell, get him to replace Crefeld—if you think he fits in."

"Don't you?"

"I'm not sure." Or, wondered Renwick, is my bruised ego still smarting? "He's making himself too visible for my taste. Could be a danger—to himself, to us."

"Justifying his promotion? That may wear off. What other choice do we have?"

"Not much. I was betting everything on Crefeld." He could sense Ron Gilman's empathy. It was a good moment to leave. Renwick rose, walking unhurriedly to the nearest fire exit for a quick but safe route back to Heathrow.

Precautions, precautions . . . They seemed comic, an unnecessary waste of time and energy. Until you remembered a man approaching you in a crowded lobby with a highly sophisticated weapon disguised as a simple walking stick.

Arrival in New York was the usual confusion when several major flights descended on Kennedy. It was natural, perhaps, that the attractive young woman who was traveling alone should look so helpless and harried as she waited for her luggage to appear on the roundabout. She had stuck close to Renwick on most of the long journey from the landing area. They had gone through immigration together, so she was American—or at least traveling on an American passport. Customs had separated them temporarily, but here she was beside him again in the main hall with the late-evening sun streaming in from the street outside. The odd thing was that, in all this time, she hadn't given him one small glance: most of the transatlantic passengers had noticed each other, exchanging the usual cursory look as they angled for the best position to grab their suitcases or compete for the attention of a porter if one did deign to arrive. For someone who was now standing at his elbow, it was strange that she seemed totally unaware of his existence. Their luggage should be arriving any moment now. Would she ask his help, delay him enough to let them leave together? And would she take a taxi to follow his?

Renwick lit a cigarette as she faced his direction briefly. His lighter missed twice, flamed on his third try. He had just time for a couple of drags before he saw his bag near two dark-blue suitcases, a matched set varying only in size, come circling slowly toward them.

"Oh!" she said, pointing to the larger of these cases, which lay far up on the conveyor and needed a long arm to be reached.

Renwick extracted his bag and her smaller case, a nice excuse to let the larger one go majestically on its way. He placed it at her feet. "Don't worry," he told her. "The other will come around again." In four or five minutes. And with an encouraging smile that was met by a look of complete frustration, he left for the door. No porters available, either, he thought with some satisfaction.

Outside was turmoil complete, taxis and buses and a row of limousines with drivers at their wheels. People on the sidewalk, people darting into the roadway to get hold of a cab. It took him several minutes to secure one, and as he threw his baggage inside to stake his claim, he noticed one limousine in particular. Its driver, impatient, stood by its opened door, scanning the crowded sidewalk. As he caught sight of Renwick about to enter a taxi, he slipped back into his seat. But his way out into the turgid stream of traffic was blocked by a tourist bus that halted, no apologies, in the middle of the road to load a group of Japanese businessmen. Renwick's last glance at the sidewalk showed him the young woman emerging, her large suitcase abandoned in her desperate haste. So was her diffidence as she saw Renwick's taxi ease through a narrow space and then speed off. Now there were two frustrated people left behind him. How nice for them if she could have emerged on his heels, stepped into the limousine with no bus to complicate the easy following of his taxi. Renwick's smile was broad. He made sure his lighter was safe in his pocket. He could take photographs, too.

He might have judged the woman on a hunch, but there had been no guesswork on the man. Fair hair, thick and waved; smooth handsome face, the type that some women, such as poor middle-aging Luisa, found irresistible. Maartens, definitely, but no longer pretending to be an embassy employee in The Hague, no longer the big hotel man throwing business in the way of an interior decorator in Brussels. Had Thérèse found him irresistible, too?

Renwick's smile was wiped from his face. "Grand Central," he told his driver, "by way of the Queensboro Bridge and down Lexington to Forty-second Street." And having established the fact that he knew his way around this town, he relaxed and didn't have to worry about the meter.

He would find another cab at Grand Central Station and drive to the Stafford, a busy hotel in the East Fifties where he could get his thoughts in order before Frank Cooper paid him a quiet visit for intensive briefing on both sides, and a discussion of tactics. (Strategy would come later, when Frank Cooper had gathered information and put the search for Theo into motion.) And that would be all Renwick would see of Frank, for the time being. Discretion was the better part of safety.

Tomorrow, he was heading for Vermont and a visit to his parents' summer cottage on Caspian Lake. (Scattered farms, groves of sugar maples burgeoning for tapping at winter's end; browsing deer by day, bobcats screaming over the hills by night, skunks dodging under the woodpiles, an occasional bear wandering down from the Canadian border.) Two weeks later, he would jaunt to San Diego for an eight-day stay in nearby La Jolla with his young sister and her husband. (Tennis and scuba diving, flowers for all seasons, people from everywhere.) After that, the mountains of Wyoming for a week with his older brother, wife, seven children, five horses, three dogs. Then a return to the East. August would be almost over. Ron Gilman would be arriving from London with full reports. Frank Cooper's news-gathering should be producing results. And Maartens, with his interest fixed on Renwick, might even be discouraged: what intelligence officer could be taken as a threat when he spent four crucial weeks in holiday pleasures with no communication, no contacts that were in any way connected with his work?

The end of August . . . It couldn't come too soon. Suddenly, his mind was jolted out of all those neatly planned prospects as he remembered his promise to Nina O'Connell for the beginning of September: a message to Daddy for money money money, ready and waiting at Türk Express in Istanbul. Hell and damnation, he thought, how do I put in a call to Francis O'Connell at the Bureau of Political-Economic Affairs in Washington when I'm practicing nonexistence in New York? It's the last thing I need, making a call to a State Department number, identifying myself by name to O'Connell's secretary, being questioned by him about Amsterdam, of all goddamn places.

Then, as the taxi drew up at Grand Central Station and he was hauling
his luggage onto the sidewalk, he knew one solution: he'd unload Nina's
message onto Frank Cooper's broad shoulders. Frank knew O'Connell well.
No problem there. Nina, Nina, Renwick was thinking, you do complicate
people's lives in your own sweet little way. In a moment, he had a spasm of
sympathy for Francis O'Connell, quickly dissipated as he began wrestling
with more practical matters such as counting out the dollars and calculating a sizable tip. No audible thanks, either. I'm home, he thought as he
hefted his luggage out of the pedestrians' way, and waited for another taxi.

A month might not seem adequate enough for a view of America, but on
Renwick it had acted like a tonic. No need to judge his country by the
headlines any more; now he had a wider frame of reference—people in all
their variety, with all their opinions and beliefs and pride in their jobs. Sure
there were some weaknesses here and there, even some rents and tears,
worrying self-indulgences, but the main fabric was still strong. A good place
to live, and worth a good fight. Renwick's return to New York was definitely upbeat.

"Raring to go," he told Frank Cooper over the phone. "I'll be leaving
by the end of this week. What about having a drink with me? Or lunch? I
know you're a busy lawyer, but . . ." He left the suggestion hanging. If anyone were listening in to this call, its vacuity might make it seem negligible.

"Just let me have a look at my calendar. Let me see . . ." Cooper's deep,
rumbling voice hesitated, as if he were really consulting his engagement book.
"Washington tomorrow, dammit. A prospective client. That could take until
Thursday. Then Friday is the start of the Labor Day weekend. Why not join
us in East Hampton? The kids and their friends will be there before they go
back to school. A full house. But we'll always find room for you."

Renwick had to smile. Frank's summer cottage had only three bedrooms,
a giant living room where stereo played well into the night, and Frank's
sacrosanct den with everything from trophies to gun rack struggling for space
among bookshelves. He took the concealed hint. "I'd like that, but my new
job in London begins with September. They don't allow for Labor Day over
there, you know."

"What about tonight? There's a cocktail party at my place. We've just
won a major decision, so I thought I'd have a celebration for my staff and
our happy clients."

"Tonight is pretty well planned—dinner and theater."

"Drop in, if you can manage it. It will be a madhouse; you know how
these things multiply. Too bad you didn't let me know when you were planning to pass through New York."

"I really wasn't sure myself. Next time, I'll—"

"The party begins at six. But no one will be there before six-thirty, I hope.
I've got an emergency meeting midtown at four-thirty—a couple of important clients."

"Then you'd better hang up. It's almost four now."

"So it is, dammit. Hope to see you at my place—it's the old stand on
Sixty-first Street. Remember? Good to hear from you."

Renwick replaced the telephone on his side table and stretched out on his bed. An emergency meeting at four-thirty . . . Cooper would just make it from his Wall Street office to his suite at the Stafford, kept for the benefit of out-of-town clients and his own private meetings. Renwick's room (booked by one of Cooper's friends) was on the floor below, but the fire staircase near Cooper's suite had its uses. And Ronald Gilman, who must have arrived from London by this time, would have had similar arrangements made for him. Frank Cooper was a believer in easy access: friends all together under one roof, no visible coming and going.

Four-thirty exactly. The door to Frank Cooper's suite had its lock released, ready for Renwick's arrival.

"You look well," Cooper told him, studying the younger man, lean and trim, sun-tanned, as he reactivated the lock and closed the door. There was a warm handshake, and then a quick embrace with two hefty pats on Renwick's shoulders. "Good to see you, Bob. Pick a chair. Sorry about the decor. I take what the hotel offers, but the wives of my South American clients seem to like it."

"You still make a good telephone call," Renwick told him as he chose one corner of a spindle-legged sofa, glanced around the green-and-gold room, and took his turn at studying Cooper, now pouring a couple of Scotches at an elaborate serving tray. Cooper was a large bear of a man, big and deliberate; he had lost weight in recent years, and his face—large and craggy—showed permanent furrows. His hair, thick and heavy, was now almost white. His fine dark eyes were more serious, almost sad in expression. His clothes hadn't changed, though they hung more loosely on his big frame: thin dark-gray suit worn carelessly, and slightly crumpled—enough to drive his custom tailor into a nervous breakdown.

"Well," Cooper was saying, "you know what's expected of the typical New Yorker. He has the best intentions but he's always too damned busy to spend much time with his friends."

"Your phone is tapped?"

"Let's say that someone likes to listen to my conversations. A recent development."

"Because of me?"

"Perhaps. Or perhaps it is just someone trying to get inside information on one of our legal battles." Cooper's face relaxed as he handed Renwick his drink and then lowered himself into an opposite chair. He stretched out his long legs, raised his glass in salute. "Don't worry, Bob. We'll find him. Or her. But it's wiser, at the moment, to play along with them, give them no hint of suspicion aroused." He glanced at his watch. "Quickly, any new ideas on Theo? What's his plan, do you think?"

"It isn't clear yet. Could be aimed at America. That's my hunch. Just a gut feeling, mostly. Didn't Gilman have any more details on Theo?"

"He passed on all he knew when I saw him in London two weeks ago. Including something you didn't mention in our last meeting: the attack on you. That wasn't pretty, not pretty at all, Bob."

"It only proves that Theo's plan must be damned big."

"Any signs of interest in you recently?"

"Not in the last four weeks."

"Then any interest in me must be the result of the inquiries I was making in Los Angeles about Herr Otto Remp and his new West-East Travel bureau." Cooper pursed his lips, shook his head. "And I thought I was being careful."

"What did you find out?"

"That Theo is one smart operator. He slipped into Los Angeles, made the necessary appearance, with his lawyer and real-estate agent and his new manager in charge of the West-East office, to sign all the papers at a local bank. Also a hefty check for his newly acquired property. He had to use his Otto Remp identity, of course, to keep everything legal for that brief interlude. Then he departed as quietly as he had arrived, the office left in charge of his manager. Impossible to trace, so far—we've no idea of the name he used to enter the country or travel around in it."

"When did he make that visit to Los Angeles?"

"Damn quick. It must have been within a couple of days after he arrived here from Germany."

Before any of us knew he had disappeared from Düsseldorf. "So all arrangements for the purchase of an L. A. office must have been made while he was still in Germany. Who handled them? The manager?"

"No. The manager is a stalwart citizen. So are the real-estate agent and the bankers and the lawyer. It's the assistant manager who is not quite what he seems to be. He's the real boss of the Los Angeles branch of West-East Travel, affiliate of Western Travel in Düsseldorf. Theo's contact man, in fact. Handles the finances."

"You found out a lot," Renwick said, recovering from his initial disappointment. Of course Theo would act as quickly as possible, before any alert about his movements could be given.

"Not enough. We don't know if he is still somewhere in America; or has he left us? We've quietly circulated his description, of course, but there are a hundred ways of leaving this country without presenting a passport—even a false one."

Circulated his description . . . "You've put yourself in some danger, Frank."

"Well—like you—the more I studied Theo's case, the greater my gut feeling that this man is worth stopping. Whatever it costs us." Cooper laughed off his touch of drama, but his eyes held something of the old zest. He glanced at his watch, pulled himself out of his chair, lumbered toward the door and unlocked it.

Gilman, guessed Renwick: arrivals spaced twenty minutes apart? Frank and his experience—OSS agent dropping into unfriendly territory, CIA analyst in its early years, National Security adviser, and now a corporation lawyer on the international scale—might just discourage Theo's recent interest in him. Renwick couldn't be sure, though: the inquiries around Los Angeles must have been extensive even if discreet. And the innocent civilian was often an ignorant one, too: he never knew when to keep his trap shut, not indulge in a little gossip to enlarge his self-esteem. Some people just couldn't resist confiding.

"He's late," Cooper said, glancing once more at his watch.

"Is he staying in the hotel?"

"Sure. He has brought Gemma with him."

Gemma was Gilman's wife. "Cozy," said Renwick.

"Nice and normal. Probably they've gone shopping."

Or something, thought Renwick.

"Maggie used to try to drag me around the stores when we were abroad." Cooper's voice had softened at the mention of his wife. Even if she had been dead for eight years, her memory was still alive.

Quickly, Renwick drew him away from the past by saying, "About Theo—isn't it possible he would have invested in a furnished house somewhere in Southern California? A safe house, where his agents could stay and be subsidized by payments through his travel bureau in Los Angeles? I mean, why else would he have chosen L. A. if it weren't convenient for the payment of his people's expenses? That was the pattern he set up in Essen."

"Somewhere in Southern California," Cooper said thoughtfully. "That covers a lot of territory."

"Somewhere within easy driving distance of L. A.—two or three hours away." A hundred miles, as Renwick had discovered on his visit to La Jolla, was considered an acceptable distance to drive out for dinner. "He'd have negotiated that deal, of course, well in advance—like finding the premises for his West-East Travel branch."

"Using the assistant manager?" Cooper's interest had quickened. "Who would, perhaps, employ the same real-estate agent? But the house wouldn't be bought under Herr Otto Remp's name."

"Nor under the assistant manager's name. He'd choose something mythical: his cousin or a good friend from the East needs a winter home in sunny California."

"Could be. We'll start some checking."

And be careful, thought Renwick. Tactfully, he didn't offer Cooper that advice. Instead, he took out two snapshots. "You should look out for these, Frank. The man is definitely one of Theo's. Maartens by name. The girl? Possibly working with Maartens. They were both in New York on the day I arrived from London."

Cooper studied the photographs: the blond man sat at a café table; the girl's picture was clearer, taken close up. "I've seen—" he began. But at that moment the door opened quietly and Gilman slipped inside. "Put that lock to work, Ron. And welcome!"

"Four minutes late. Unforgivable." Gilman was definitely annoyed with himself. "But Gemma went shopping and brought back two dresses. She had to try them on for my approval. You know how it is."

"Don't look at me," Renwick said with a grin. I like Ron's style, he thought: no false excuses about waiting on a back staircase until the corridor cleared of people. Gilman's equanimity returned. He was, as usual, immaculate; tall, thin, his pleasant face made solemn by horn-rimmed glasses, and not one blond hair out of place. The perfect picture of a quiet civil servant in one of Her Majesty's less glamorous departments. Renwick rose and joined in the general handshaking.

"Hope I didn't hold up the proceedings," Gilman said, noting the snapshots in Cooper's hand, ignoring them politely.

"Just discussing Theo and Los Angeles," Cooper said. He had briefed Gilman in London about them.

"And as you were saying, Frank"—Renwick pointed to the snapshots—"you've seen one of them? Which?"

"I've seen both. Last weekend." Cooper handed over the photographs to Gilman. "Of all the damned impudence! They came visiting my house. At East Hampton. I had gone down to the beach for my daily walk. But the rain came—it's been one hell of an August for weather—and so I jogged back. They were at my front door, trying to talk their way past Libby—that's my oldest girl. Their story? The woman said she was a real-estate agent, heard our house was for sale; there has been a lot of selling and buying around us. The man with her, exceptionally polite, handsome, almost convinced Libby I had put our house on the market. I've talked about that, vaguely, in these last few months. Once the kids are off on their own—and that's coming; I can see it—why the hell do I need a place in the country?" He took possession of the photographs once more. "Do you need these?" he asked Renwick. "I'd like to have copies made. Two more for your rogues' gallery," he promised Gilman.

Trying to get inside Frank's cottage, a polite look-around? Brief enough not to be annoying, but sufficient time to plant a bugging device? Renwick looked at Cooper worriedly and dropped all tact. "Be careful, Frank."

"I was in the business of being careful before those two were born. Or you, either. Okay, Ron—what news from London?"

"Promising, I think. The office is ready—a nice old house, narrow, four stories high—in a small side street. Top floor has my cubbyhole; and communications to keep us all in touch. Below that, two rooms of maps, reference items, filing cabinets waiting to be filled. Then there's a floor for our borrowed computer, deciphering machine, and other miracle devices. Staff selected. Some foreign contacts already established. The first floor, above the main hall, is for genuine business, with a couple of expert surveyors dealing with any actual requests for our services. The entrance hall is for reception—and security."

"Surveyors?"

"Just part of our firm," Gilman continued smoothly. "Actually, here's the full scope." He drew out two small cards from his waistcoat pocket and handed one each to Renwick and Cooper. "For the benefit of our representatives who travel in foreign parts."

In restrained type, the card's legend read:

J. P. Merriman & Co.
Consultant Engineers
Advisers on Construction Abroad. Surveys Made.

"Not bad," Cooper said. "In fact, damned good. There's a hell of a lot of construction going on all around the world. Your first-floor experts, Ron,

may even make some money for you. You'll end up as a successful businessman yet."

"Not my line."

"But who's paying for all the initial expenses?"

Gilman looked bland. "Oh, there's always a little extra money available
when a state sees a threat to its security. As the free countries are linked
now, like it or not, danger to one is danger to all. I think they'll find that
Interintell is the best investment they can make." Then he studied Renwick.
"Any objections to being one of our traveling representatives, Bob?"

Renwick shook his head. "I was just going over their backgrounds in my
mind." He, himself, had earned an MIT engineering degree before he went
into the army. Claudel? Yes, the Frenchman had worked in aerospace
dynamics before his stint with NATO. MacEwan, the Canadian, had worked
in mining. Larsen and Diehl had been sappers. "Engineers? I suppose so.
But we're stretching it a bit, aren't we?"

"It's the one common denominator you had in civilian life. Not much,
but enough. What else would seem feasible for all you ex-NATO types?
Certainly not interior decoration or textiles and ceramics." Gilman was
ruffled. "I thought you'd be comfortable with—"

"I am, I am," Renwick cut in. "We'll have ample cover." If no one starts
questioning us too closely. But then, that's part of our job: avoid the questions. Certainly, I'll be able to move around a foreign country, meet officials more interested in terrorists than in bridges, dams, or new hotels. "It
gives me enough traveling room, anyway." And Gilman had planned well.
For that all-important cover, export-import was now suspect; so were tea
or wine merchants, wandering reporters, news photographers, moviemakers,
lecturers—you name it, they've tried it. "Original," he conceded, and brought
relief to Gilman's watchful eyes. "Do I have some backup?"

"You can choose your team. Two or three. Don't you think?"

I do think, old boy. That's the way I like to work. The lone eagle looks
damned foolish when one of his pinions is torn off. Renwick said, "Okay.
That's that."

"You'll be in London soon? You'll find Merriman & Co. at 7 Grace
Street—between the Strand and the Embankment."

Cooper had a question. "And what about some aids and comforts for your
agents? Or do they just rely on karate and smoke signals?"

"Gadgets will be provided. But from another building in another location. That should baffle any of the opposition who might come prowling
around. All the technology we have on the premises could be used by any
modern-minded business firm. Okay with you, Bob?"

"You're the right man for the job, Ron."

"I agree," said Cooper, and he meant it. "I couldn't have handled it, not
with legal cases piling up." He hesitated, and then added, "And not with
the climate of opinion that's fogged everything over here—I don't know
if we're coming or going. Am I depressed? You bet I am." Then he tried
to laugh that off. "There's one man more depressed than I am. Francis
O'Connell. Telephoned me this morning, a long spiel about his daughter,

Nina." He began pouring another round of drinks. "Have to watch my time. That damned cocktail party. Never could stand them. A hundred guests milling around; and that allows you one minute per person. How's that for hospitality?"

Renwick said, "What's this about Nina?" Frank, he was thinking, is not only overworked and depressed, he's also beginning to digress. He ought to take a vacation, travel across his own country for a change, lose some of his pessimism, come back to New York and Washington with his old sense of purpose restored. "Nina," he repeated firmly. "What has she done now?"

"Got her father out of bed last night with a call from some place in northern Greece. She needed her money to be delivered at the American Express office in Athens instead of Istanbul. Seemingly she decided to leave the camper."

"Good," said Renwick.

"Not permanently," Cooper corrected him. "She and her friend Madge wanted to see Athens and the islands. The camper is parked on a beach on the Salonika gulf—it's staying there for six days."

"Six days?" Gilman asked. He knew that part of the world. "Why six whole days?"

"Poor old O'Connell," said Cooper. "Never got a postcard or letter from her all across Europe." Thank God for my girls, he was thinking. "Her aunt Eunice—she looked after Nina for years, you know—never got a postcard, either. But here's the strange part: Nina told him she had written him from Basel and postcarded Aunt Eunice from Dijon and Innsbruck. Of course, she might have been trying to pacify him. He's had friends at the various embassies keeping a watchful eye for any blonde American girls traveling in a camper, but with no luck."

"But have they been passing through any capital cities?" Renwick asked. Neither Dijon nor Basel nor Innsbruck qualified for embassies.

"It seems not. He couldn't find out too much. Her call was brief—not enough cash to spare, she told him. She had spent a lot on a bus ride to Athens."

"And after the Greek islands?"

"Istanbul. She's rejoining her camping friends there by September fourth." Cooper glanced at his watch. "My God, look at the time!" He picked up a heavy briefcase on his way to the door. "Sorry about the party, Bob. Next visit, we'll spend a couple of evenings together."

"Watch out for the uninvited guest."

"A gate-crasher? Expecting you to be there?"

"And perhaps wondering if we are using the mob scene to retreat to your study for a little talk."

Cooper was suddenly smiling. "Could be an interesting party after all." Then to Gilman, "See you in London on the tenth." With that, and a wave of his hand, he left.

Twenty minutes' clearance before one of us starts leaving, Renwick reminded himself as he rose and made sure the door had locked automatically. He checked his watch. Gilman was doing the same thing.

Gilman said, "Why did Francis O'Connell phone him? Not just looking for sympathy, surely."

"Probably he wanted Frank to get in touch with any friends in Istanbul, find out what they can about this damned camper. I suppose O'Connell is trying to handle everything quietly: no publicity. Everything done on the discreet old-boy level."

"Afraid of drugs?" That wouldn't make a pretty story if it started spreading around Washington. And what about the inevitable leaks to the press? Francis O'Connell's daughter, no less: *the* Francis O'Connell.

"Nina isn't the type." But Renwick was worried. He changed the unpleasant subject. "What about those two people I asked you to check on—any luck?"

"A lot of luck with Ilsa Schlott—but it came sideways, not through our efforts. We did verify that she is a foreign medical student, postgraduate research in tropical diseases at University College. She lives at the Women's Residence, where she met Nina and her friend Madge Westerman. Schlott attended a lot of rallies and demonstrations, seemed to be merely an interested observer studying the London scene. That was all we found out until I had a meeting with a friend in New Scotland Yard's antiterrorist squad. The subject of the meeting was actually those bloody umbrellas and their high-velocity pellets. After we talked about Crefeld—and you, too, old boy— I branched onto the subject of terrorists. Had my friend seen signs in London of anything being plotted on a wide international scale? Nothing so far, he assured me. Unless recruitment of terrorists could be the beginning of an international plot. And after I promised an exchange of future information between his department and Interintell—You've no objection?" Gilman asked, interrupting himself.

"It makes sense. Go on—recruitment, you were saying. In London?"

"Yes. Last April, four young men had been quietly selected as suitable material and, after six weeks of indoctrination and testing, were about to travel abroad—to a hard-training camp for terrorists in South Yemen. One of them—a Trotskyite—had a change of mind. He managed to break his ankle on his motorbike just in time to evade the trip. His recruiter didn't altogether believe his story, and he became scared. Scared enough to make contact with my friend of the antiterrorist squad and ask for protection. In exchange, he told all he knew. Including the name of the person who first approached him. It was a code name, of course: Greta. He described her, gave details about their meeting places. And with some hard-working detectives on the trail of Greta, they uncovered her identity: Ilsa Schlott. How does that grab you, my friend?"

Renwick recovered, said, "It grabs all right. Good God, Ron—"

"That's not the end of the Ilsa Schlott story. She was put—still is—under tight surveillance. And so she was observed meeting a flight from Amsterdam on June fourteenth. She made eye contact only: she knew the man, and he knew her. Then she walked some distance to her car. He followed, got in. She drove skillfully, used every bus and truck to blot her car from sight. She managed that, too, when she skirted a bad holdup in traffic just before it became a complete snarl."

"So they lost him," Renwick said, curbing his bitter annoyance. Schlott didn't matter: the police knew where to find her. But the new arrival—that was something else.

"He is recorded as being five feet ten or eleven, medium weight, good-looking sort—brown hair, clean-shaven—wearing a green tweed jacket and flannels. He was photographed, too. Here!" Gilman reached into a pocket, produced an envelope. "And the detective who took the photograph made immediate inquiries about the passenger list of that plane. You'll find a copy of it along with the snapshot. I've marked the Americans—eleven of them; but canceling out three children, four women, two elderly men, we have only two names really to consider."

Renwick opened the envelope. The snapshot was that of a half-turned face, as if its owner had sensed danger. The shape of the head, the cheekbone, chin, were vaguely familiar. Not familiar, exactly: just glimpsed once . . . Renwick's lips tightened. Quickly he glanced at the listed names, two of them underscored in red: Wilbur Jones; James Kiley. "Kiley," he said, his eyes once more on the photograph. "Yes. James Kiley."

Gilman was startled. "You know him?"

"He's conducting that camper tour."

"Nina O'Connell?"

"Her good friend."

"My God . . ."

They looked at each other. "I agree," said Renwick. My God—James Kiley. "Which is he—Erik or Marco? Theo made sure they both got safely out of Essen."

"There was another man," Gilman said, recovering himself. "He was in England just a week before Kiley arrived. Met Ilsa Schlott briefly, and then disappeared. He was six feet, dark-haired, thin. No photograph of him, I'm afraid. Could he be connected with Kiley?"

Tall, dark, thin . . . Again Renwick's mind went back to the bombing in Amsterdam, to two men helping Nina and Madge to rise to their feet. Tall, dark, thin. "Is he a car buff, by any chance?"

"He vanished too quickly for anyone to notice his hobbies."

"Check out the name Tony Shawfield, will you? Says he is English."

"Shawfield." Gilman spelled it out, memorizing it carefully.

"Right. Could have taken possession of a green camper, custom-built probably, British registration definitely, and then had it ferried over to Holland. It might have been ordered well in advance from Ilsa Schlott's favorite garage."

"We'll check," Gilman said tersely. He rose. "Have to go, Bob. Gemma will be ready and waiting. We're taking in a show tonight."

"I'll give you ten minutes and then leave, too."

"What are your plans?"

"First flight I can get for London, so let Merriman & Co. know I'll soon be on their doorstep. I'll need some help, a lot of help. Including a trace put on two young blondes, who look almost like sisters, arriving on some crummy ship—a freighter, possibly—in Istanbul. Around the beginning of September."

"Why a freighter?"

"You don't find many Greek interisland boats sailing into Istanbul, do you? Besides, Nina will be watching expenses. So flying is out. Also cruise ships."

Gilman said reflectively, "But what small cargo vessels sail from any Greek island to Turkey? Coastal steamers from the Levant or Egypt?"

"Lesbos," said Renwick. "They used to call in there, didn't they?" As far as he could remember, it was the only island that did have that link with Istanbul.

Gilman nodded. Lesbos, in the northeast Aegean, a few miles from the Turkish shore, was on the trade route from the Levant to Istanbul. "Could be that your blondes will head for Lesbos—if they have any sense. Or else they'll find themselves retracing their journey to Athens."

"Why not call Vlakos in Athens and get him to steer Nina in the right direction? She's collecting her allowance at the American Express office tomorrow," Renwick suggested.

"You want her in Lesbos?"

"I want her in Istanbul before her friends arrive. Can't go chasing through the Aegean after her. Nina wouldn't appreciate that."

"Kahraman is in Istanbul. He can help—"

"I'll get in touch with him from Merriman's."

"Will you be able to persuade her to leave her friends?"

"I can try."

"And if she won't listen?"

Renwick said nothing.

"If she were dependable enough," Gilman said, "she might travel along, co-operate—"

"No." Renwick was definite. He quieted his voice. "Too dangerous." He thought of Amalie in Essen, of Avril in Austria two years ago. "No. Not that," he ended.

"A pity. She could be useful."

"You're going to be late for dinner," Renwick said.

"We can have supper after the theater. I'll call Vlakos right away."

"And perhaps see if he could send someone over to Lesbos?"

"Just to make sure the coastal steamer isn't in the whiteslave traffic?"

"Can Vlakos send someone?" Renwick persisted.

"With luck and good friends in the right places."

They shook hands quickly, firmly. Yes, thought Renwick as the door closed behind Ronald Gilman, that's what it took: good friends in the right places. And a large dose of luck.

Twelve

THERE HAD BEEN a fresh breeze turning into a cool wind when the sun came up, light still weak, the Turkish coastline as yet a vague white line edging a flat stretch of land. It can't be Gallipoli, that was before we reached the Dardanelles, thought Nina as she stood by the rail and watched the struggle of waves and current; we must now be in the Sea of Marmara. Twenty-four hours on this decrepit little freighter, but we are lucky to be here, and with no strain or stress. Yesterday, on the Lesbos quay, the crew had looked like Hollywood's idea for a pirate movie. All they had needed was a knife held between their broken teeth to complete the picture. They might have stared but they had kept to themselves. The captain, equally in need of a bath and a dentist, had seen to that. And possibly that most amiable Greek, Mr. Christopoulos, who had befriended the girls in their little waterfront hotel in Lesbos—he was a teacher from Athens on holiday and spoke perfect English, thank heaven—and even came down to the wharf to see them safely off, might just have smoothed the way in his talk with the captain in some incomprehensible language. Certainly, Mr. Christopoulos had bargained for the small price of their trip, paid from Nina's dwindling store of Greek drachmas, and advised them to keep dollar bills out of sight. Not much in the way of food, he had warned them—but the coffee would be good. He was right about that. A very nice man indeed, Nina thought, and in the last excitement of boarding he forgot to give us his address. Now I can't send him a postcard to thank him.

The light was strengthening. Nina turned away from the rail, looked at the deck behind her where Madge was still trying to sleep, head pillowed on her duffel bag, a windbreak formed by the loosely roped sacks and olive oil drums that had been dumped on board at Lesbos. Forward, at the ship's prow, two goats were tethered. The rest of the passengers—three shabbily dressed men and two women swathed in black cotton, from head scarf down to shapeless trousers partly covered by equally shapeless tunics—were below in the cabins. Dirty gray blankets on thin straw mattresses hadn't deterred them from a good night's rest.

At last, Madge gave up her pretense and rose stiffly, drawing her cardigan more closely around her shoulders. "You didn't sleep much."

"Trying to think things out."

"Still mad at Jim?"

"Just puzzled. That's all." Keep off the subject of Jim Kiley, Nina's tone of voice said.

Madge took the hint. "Where's Istanbul?"

"Somewhere toward the sun."

She doesn't have to get cross with me, thought Madge. What on earth is worrying her about Jim? He's a perfectly normal guy; in fact, I like him. I like him a lot. "So you are going on with the trip?" In Athens, Nina had talked of spending a week there, a week in the Aegean, and the hell with Jim Kiley.

"Yes," Nina said.

"I'm glad." Even if I'm feeling miserable now, I'm glad. She shivered, looked wanly over the rail at the strong current battling the small waves. The boat was steady enough. It was she who was definitely shaky.

Nina said, "What about some hot coffee? That should warm us up."

"Coffee . . ." Madge shuddered at the word.

"Are you all right?"

"Just a little upset. That last meal in Lesbos . . ." Madge didn't finish, shuddered again.

"You shouldn't have eaten that camel stew. Mr. Christopoulos did try to steer you away from it." But Madge had been stubborn. Poor Madge, thought Nina, the world-wide traveler who wanted to be part of the local scene.

At the mention of camel stew, Madge said, "Don't!" And as one of the crew, the least prepossessing in that motley bunch, appeared with two mugs of coffee, she averted her head.

Nina took the mug with no cracks apparent around its rim. "Wonderful," she told the man. He didn't understand her, but he caught her meaning. His sudden toothless smile changed hard brown eyes into a friendly beam. "For you," Nina said, pointing to the torn undershirt exposing a hairy chest, waving the second mug away from Madge. He understood after some more pantomime gestures, and with nods and a spreading grin, he drank the coffee as he stalked off. "Just an upstanding citizen," Nina said. "He's got a wife and ten children back in Alexandria."

"And another ten in Tyre," Madge said, almost coming to life.

"You'll be all right." But Nina was worried. This could really complicate things. "You only need a decent bed and some sleep."

"Where will we stay?"

Not so easy to choose now. "We'll find something. We've done pretty well so far, haven't we?" But this time I'd like a bathroom of our own. What wouldn't I give to soak in a hot tub without the door handle being rattled every three minutes by some stranger in the corridor!

"How long will we have in Istanbul—only a day and a half?"

"Just about that." Tomorrow was Tuesday, the fourth. "Perhaps the others will be delayed and give us an extra night."

"Will I see anything of Istanbul at all?" Madge asked, misery increasing.

"You can have a look at it, anyway." Nina pointed ahead. On a promontory that jutted out from Europe's last stretch of land rose the domes and minarets of mosques and palaces, close-packed on a sloping hill. Walls encircled the Sultan's old domain, a city within a city, to reach the water's edge. There, a low white mist drifted upward, thinned, disappeared, setting stone columns and rounded roofs afloat on a gossamer veil.

They had passed the Golden Horn, crowded even at this hour with small craft, and entered the Bosporus. "Thank heaven we're on the European side," Nina said as they gathered their belongings and headed for a shaky gangway. Docking on the Asiatic shore of Istanbul might have been more than she could have handled. Madge was pale under that rosy tan they had both collected on Mykonos. And the sun was coming up, hot and strong, with all mist vanquished. "This shouldn't take too long," she reassured Madge as they crossed the quay toward a wooden shed. Not many passengers disembarked at this section of the Galata quays, just goats and black-swathed women with stocky husbands wearing old tweed caps.

Nina hesitated at the wide doors of the shed. It was small, low-roofed, and bare: two long tables, two serious-faced men in uniform gray jackets, an opposite door firmly closed, a host of notices around its wooden walls. And nothing I can understand, thought Nina. She heard Madge gasp as she, too, stared at the notices. Nina held out her passport, waited for further directions. "Do you speak English?" she asked in her politest voice, adding a friendly smile to sweeten the atmosphere. Two pairs of dark eyes stared at her, then at Madge. Solemnly, the passports were studied. Solemnly, the expressionless eyes looked at the girls, looked back at the passports. Trouble? Nina wondered. Yet the officials must understand English, for they could decipher the passports. Or couldn't they? They were talking together now, in a burst of vowels and consonants that left Nina more depressed. Culture shock, she was thinking. How do we, a couple of idiots who can't understand a word, manage to cope with this place? Then one of the men, Nina's passport still in his hand, moved to a telephone. Definitely trouble, Nina decided. She looked at Madge, resting her weight against a table, white-faced and mournful, and said nothing.

There was a long wait, their small baggage examined briefly, most of the time spent watching their five fellow travelers being thoroughly questioned while innumerable parcels and baskets spilled out on the tables. Hotter by the minute, Nina thought, and wished that the opposite door could be opened for a through draft of air.

It did open. From the street, a man entered briskly, well dressed in silver-gray, carefully groomed, dark-haired, dark-eyed, dark mustache, middle-aged, authoritative. A sharp glance at the wilting girls, a brief look at their passports, a voluble exchange of words with the official who had telephoned. Then the stranger came forward, spoke in excellent English, his smile friendly. "Everything is solved now," he reassured Nina. "Your friend is ill?"

"Not really." No communicable diseases being smuggled into Turkey. "Just the heat—and exhaustion, I think. She'll be all right once we get to our hotel and she can rest for a few hours."

"What hotel?"

"I thought we could get advice from a tourist bureau. Is there one near this dock?"

"Not here. Do you speak any Turkish?"

Nina shook her head. "Perhaps the tourist police could direct us—"

The man brushed that aside. "You should have a guide and interpreter. Not expensive," he added quickly. "How long do you stay here?"

"Until tomorrow."

"One night? Then you should consider one of the large hotels where English is spoken. For one night, not too expensive."

He knows who we are, Nina was thinking. What is he? Someone high up in the tourist police? Or what? I bet, I bet this is Father's doing: somehow he has arranged all this. "Not the Hilton," she said firmly: that would be her father's choice. She drew from her shoulder bag the small secondhand guide to Istanbul she had bought in Athens. Ten years out of date, but streets stayed the same although hotels might change. She consulted the list she had marked. "I thought this hotel might be suitable."

The man shook his head, shrugged, signaled to the door, which he had left open. A much younger man entered. Turkish, Nina decided—these same dark brows and solemn eyes; but in dress and manner he could have passed for an American student. He stood still, smiling and pleasant, while his long name was rattled off in a quick introduction. Nina could only catch part of it: Suleyman, she thought. "Most reliable," the man in the silver-gray suit told her, and turned away for a brief word with the immigration official who saluted. Actually saluted, Nina thought in amazement. Then as quickly as he had appeared, he departed.

Suleyman said, "It is all right now. You can leave. I shall bring a taxi. Wait there!" He pointed to the doorway to the street. A street of low buildings and a maze of traffic; movement and noise and complete chaos.

Madge roused herself. "We'll wait. Thank you." And to Nina, as he hurried away, she said, "We need him."

I guess we do, thought Nina. They left the shed, the officials too busy shaking out every tightly rolled piece of clothing even to notice their departure.

Suleyman was polite, efficient, and at three dollars a day—his frankly stated price—not expensive. He even directed the taxi, without comment, to the hotel Nina had selected. Built of wood, one bathroom to a floor, lethargic ceiling fans, no dining room, no English spoken in spite of its advertisement: otherwise possible enough for a grade-B establishment, although the floors needed scrubbing and the lopsided curtains had a year's dust ingrained in them. Nina, guidebook opened at "Accommodations," had another hotel to suggest. Outlying district, Suleyman said, very nice but sixteen kilometers away. Ten miles? I give up, thought Nina. "What do you advise?"

"A hotel near Taksim Square. It is the center. Taxis, buses—"

"What hotel?" And I know his answer.

"Perhaps the Hilton?"

"Too expensive."

"Not all rooms are so expensive. I can arrange something. I am guide and interpreter for many guests."

Madge said, "We're wasting more money on this taxi ride than we'll spend in one night at the Hilton."

Hardly, thought Nina. But she still had much of her allowance money intact, and she was too hot and damp and tired and bewildered to argue. "All right. We'll try it. At least I can get my traveler's checks cashed there. Will the taxi driver take dollar bills?" She had hoped, naïvely it now appeared, that there would have been a money exchange at the pier.

"I can change your dollars now." Suleyman took a wad of large Turkish notes from an inner pocket. "Very good rates."

"I'm sure. Are you a student, Suleyman?"

"Some of the time," he said, with his bright smile.

"And what are you going to be?" Surely not just a guide forever, Nina thought, as she watched him deftly counting out the right monies.

"A poet," he said.

Completely bemused, Nina asked no more questions for the rest of the journey.

Suleyman made his call from the Hilton lobby. His voice was cheerful. "All is settled. I directed them to the place you wished. This afternoon early, we sightsee. One only. The other is not well."

"Which one?"

"The brown eyes."

"Serious? Does she need a doctor?"

"No, no. A little rest, that is all."

Sightseeing, thought Renwick. It would have to be Topkapi; tomorrow, as on all Tuesdays, the palace would be closed. And if he knew Nina, the Sultans' seraglio would be at the top of her visiting list. "There will be a lot of walking, many courtyards," he suggested, to give Suleyman a clue to the place he had in mind for a meeting.

Suleyman caught it. "In the third courtyard? Ladies like to see the—"

Quickly, Renwick cut off the identifying word: "harem." "The second is better. Near its entrance gate. About four o'clock?"

"Later, perhaps."

If Nina began her sightseeing early (the seraglio opened at one), she'd be collapsing by five o'clock closing time. "Not much later," Renwick said firmly, and hung up.

He turned to Pierre Claudel, seated in the bedroom's one lopsided armchair, which he had angled as much as possible under the ceiling's fan. "You heard most of it. Topkapi Palace around four. The Divan courtyard."

"Who's ill?"

"Madge. Nothing serious. I hope."

"Then you won't need me to take her off your hands?"

"I'd like you to stick around, just see if Nina is all right."

"Trail after her and Suleyman? Deliver her safely to you?"

"Might be an idea." Claudel wouldn't be noticeable: dark-haired, dark-eyed, dark-mustached, he could be taken easily for one of the young Turks who sat around the cafés talking politics and poetry. In addition, his Turkish was excellent, thanks to eighteen months in Ankara a few years ago. Renwick grinned. "I may need you as a guide and interpreter once Suleyman bows out."

"You're doing not so badly by yourself."

"Don't kid me, Pierre." His previous visit to Turkey, when Greeks and Turks had been forgetting their NATO alliance in the heat of the battle over Cyprus, had lasted only five weeks: enough time to get him interested in the language, but to give him only a minimal grasp. It was this feeling of inadequacy, the struggle to understand and be understood (he managed better than he imagined) that had prompted him to steer Nina and Madge toward an English-speaking hotel. Not that Nina would thank him for it, if she knew. "How the hell do I persuade the girls to leave that goddamned camper?"

Claudel's bright eyes looked at him in astonishment. "I thought you had that worked out. Dangerous terrain ahead. And that's the bloody truth. Haven't they been listening to the radio? Nothing but revolts and armed attacks all the way down through Iran into Afghanistan. Or perhaps the Soviet advisers there will give Mr. Kiley and his party a safe-conduct guarantee."

Renwick said nothing. Once into India the camper would be safe. But after that? Bangladesh again in turmoil, Burma, Malaysia and brigands, Indochina with all its vicious politics and millions of helpless victims. Surely Kiley must be planning to have the camper ferried from India to Hong Kong—the land route was now a death trap. "I wonder if anyone, except Kiley and Shawfield, has been paying much attention to the news."

"Then you might have to let Nina know, that—well, that Kiley is not exactly what he seems."

"And how do I do that without blowing the whistle for all to hear?" Including Theo. Particularly Theo. His new branch office of West-East Travel was now open and flourishing in Istanbul. "Kiley . . ." Renwick paused, shook his head. "If we only had the whole picture."

"We've got enough evidence on him."

"There's still a gap. Two, in fact. No one actually witnessed him boarding the coastal freighter in Duisburg. The captain and crew swear they saw nothing. And we haven't heard yet from the Rotterdam police about that blocking of the men's-room doorway at Schiphol Airport. Three men came out, the cop noted. Later, he discovered the suspect must have been one of them. He must have made a report on what he could remember about them: rough details, certainly."

"Such as a green tweed jacket? Yes, that would tie Kiley to Heathrow and Amsterdam's Schiphol Airport. One gap closed, at least. But Duisburg? We know all we'll ever know about that: a man called Kurt Leitner, from Essen, definitely important in Section One of the People's Revolutionary Force for Direct Action, traveled by truck to the Duisburg docks and vanished completely just before a coastal freighter, called the *Maritza,* sailed. What more do you need, Bob?"

"Something that one of Theo's clever lawyers won't twist around in court. Give them three inches of a loophole and they'll stretch it to twelve feet."

"So that's why you aren't asking the Turkish police to detain Kiley here, and have the Germans request his extradition to Essen. It's tempting, I must say: it could end Theo's plan before it achieved anything."

"It would end only Kiley's part in his plan. Theo would lose one man, but he'd wait, do some reorganizing, and try again for another angle. The ground is too well prepared; there's been too big an effort, too much thought and money invested, for everything to be discarded along with Kiley. Whatever that plan is, it's a shocker, Pierre."

Claudel nodded. "Then our best chance of uncovering it is to let Kiley go on his way, stirring up trouble wherever the camper stops—possibly organizing or recruiting terrorists. And, of course, get Nina O'Connell safely out—without breaking our security. Will you manage it, Bob?"

"I'll make a damned good try. And we'll find out Kiley's stops, tip off the governments involved—if they'll listen."

"But if Nina won't listen?"

"God knows," Renwick said wearily. He looked at his watch. Ten past eleven. "Time to separate. I'll see you in the distance around four o'clock. Okay?"

"In the second courtyard, the place of the Divan. A good choice." It was spacious, filled with numerous trees, pleasant cover on a hot afternoon. Cooler than this chair, thought Claudel as he rose and pulled his shirt free from his back.

"It's the closest to the seraglio's entrance gate—making sure I don't get lost," Renwick said with a smile.

"Meanwhile, I'll take a little drive with my friend Fahri around the outskirts and visit another camping site, see if any advance reservations have been made. Do you know how many camping grounds Turkey has? Hundreds. Incredible."

"The old caravanserai spirit, perhaps."

Claudel cocked his head to one side. "Now why didn't I think of that?"

"You will, Pierre. You will."

With a laugh and a nod, Claudel closed the door behind him.

Renwick sat on the edge of the bed, reached for the telephone. With some care, and the help of his little book *Useful Phrases,* he asked for Kahraman's number. Extraordinary language, he thought as he waited for the call to go through. Where else would one two three be *Bir Iki Üç?*

Kahraman came on the line, as crisp and confident as ever. His impeccable silver-gray suit wouldn't dare sport a crush even in this weather. He rushed into conversation in his usual way, answered everything before it was asked. All had gone well at the quay this morning. Fortunate that he was there. Renwick's delightful friends might have had just a little trouble. Because of the companions they had on their journey. Three men, two women. Smuggling. Definitely. Sticks of dynamite inside tightly rolled bits and pieces of clothing. Could not be too careful nowadays, could one? And what about lunch? And a long talk between old friends?

"A short lunch, I'm afraid," said Renwick. "Only two and a half hours." But time enough to get Kahraman's help to communicate with London. Claudel's remark about "recruiting terrorists for training" had sparked another train of thought about Dr. Ilsa Schlott.

"No time for a little drive?" Kahraman was audibly disappointed.

"Some place central," Renwick insisted, remembering Kahraman's favorite haunt up the Bosporus for four hours of good food and good talk. "I remember an excellent meal we enjoyed on my last visit. At the Grand Bazaar?" It was a small place near the pepper market, and easy to reach.

Kahraman was delighted he had remembered it, and pleased enough to forgive his American friend for being the first to suggest it. "At the same time as on your last visit?"

"Perfect," said Renwick. Twelve-thirty would be just right.

He prepared to leave, now thinking about Ilsa Schlott and his message to Merriman's. Gilman must contact Diehl in Berlin, immediately. Some hard probing might uncover Schlott's connection there—if she had had one—with the People's Revolutionary Force for Direct Action, founded by Erik and Marco. Then any story she was concocting would fall to pieces.

What would it be? She had been meeting James Kiley at Heathrow simply because he was someone she had known, and liked, on a visit last year to Chicago? Or in New York? Or wherever? Theo would make the fabrication seem plausible. But a direct connection with Erik and Marco—well, that was something to baffle even Theo's ingenuity. Let his well-paid lawyers wrestle with that evidence.

Still not enough to pin down Erik or Marco. Schlott wouldn't identify them; she'd go to jail with a smirk of triumph on her face. There could be another way, though. Get Diehl to explore that item recorded by a Dutch undercover agent about the man who had arrived on a coastal freighter from Duisburg: extraordinary expertise in Spanish. Which of them—Marco or Erik—had any Spanish-language background? And then we would know which of these men was the one that left the safe house in Rotterdam as James Kiley. That's vital if he comes to trial. How would it sound to a jury if we could only testify, "He may be Erik, he may be Marco"?

He dropped all thought of terrorists as he reached the street and concentrated on finding a taxi. A walk would have been enjoyable, down the broad avenue, over the bridge at the Golden Horn, into the old town, but he hadn't the time. The taxi would allow him half an hour of wandering inside the Grand Bazaar before he met Kahraman.

He chose one small area of the walled and covered market, four thousand little shops jam-packed along narrow, twisting, bewildering streets. Noise and confusion everywhere, the usual bedlam of bargaining; Turks and foreigners as crowded together and as varied as the objects on display. Easy to lose anyone who might be interested in his movements; too easy to get himself lost as well. So he limited his choice of routes and paid attention to the direction he followed rather than let his mind be sidetracked by antiques, clothes, carpets, amethysts, lamps, furniture, gold bracelets, slippers, everything and anything imaginable. He came safely out of the gate near the pepper-market area just as Kahraman entered the restaurant ahead of him.

Renwick loitered among the crowd, made reasonably sure that Kahraman hadn't been tailed, either, and then followed him inside. The room hadn't changed: blue-and-yellow patterned tiles over the walls, overhead fans, a display of cold dishes, the smell of well-seasoned food; and alcoves. Discreet and comfortable alcoves.

"A good morning?" Kahraman inquired politely.

"A very good morning," Renwick said as they bowed and shook hands. He could only hope that the afternoon would be as successful.

Thirteen

THEY WERE ALMOST on time, a mere ten minutes late, which was probably a record in punctuality for Suleyman. Renwick, who had been exploring the seraglio's second courtyard, always keeping a watchful eye on the area around its giant gate, suddenly saw the two figures coming his way through the plane trees. Suleyman he recognized immediately. The girl needed a second look. Today, Nina had abandoned blue jeans for a wide-skirted dress. Fair hair was swept up from her neck, pinned high on her head, a few tendrils escaping. Dark glasses and earrings added to the change. She was tired, tripping once on the cobblestones in spite of her sandals' low heels. Suleyman, as enthusiastic as ever, was doing all the talking. He was so engrossed that he had never noticed the quiet, compact man, dark-mustached, who had followed them at a comfortable distance. Claudel looked the part of the tourist, a guidebook opened in his hand, stopping to consult its map whenever he needed to slow down, merging with other visitors when that was prudent. He noticed Renwick before the engrossed Suleyman did, began closing his map. Renwick judged the right distance between Nina and himself, went forward to meet her with a wave of his hand to attract her attention.

She stopped abruptly. Disbelief spread over her face.

"Hello, Nina," he said, taking both her hands. "I thought it was you—couldn't be sure at first. Is this a permanent change?" He stood back to look at her, smiling wholeheartedly, not even trying to conceal his pleasure.

"It's cooler." She laughed delightedly as she recovered from her surprise. "But, Bob—what on earth are you doing here?"

"The same as you. Dipping into a spot of history."

"If you are just arriving, you won't have time to see everything. I didn't. And I've been here for three hours. Oh, this is Suleyman." She turned to the boy, who had backed off a little and was now waiting for a signal from Renwick.

"Perhaps Suleyman could scout around for a taxi?" Renwick suggested.

"Where will we find you?"

"By the Bab-i-Hümayan Gate. At the esplanade. You know where to go? Shall I show you?" Suleyman asked hopefully.

"We won't get lost." Once they left here, there was only a stretch of the first courtyard's almost empty space to cover before they reached the entrance gate at the street.

Suleyman left regretfully. It had been a splendid afternoon, and now it was over. Judging by the way the American had caught her hands, held them, looked at her, there would be no evening ahead for Suleyman, either.

"But I need him to get me back to the hotel," Nina said. "He's my guide."

"I'll get you back. Perhaps not as efficiently as Suleyman, but we'll manage. I know a café where the seats are comfortable."

"That's tempting. But I don't want to drag you away from here."

"I've seen enough for one day. I believe in taking museums in small slices. Remember?" He was thinking back to Geneva, six years ago.

She remembered. She looked quickly away, but barely noticed the trail of tourists now passing by. Claudel, walking leisurely, didn't even exchange a glance with Renwick. "Today," Nina was saying as she and Renwick began following the slow exodus, "I hadn't the time for small slices. I only had one afternoon. Poor Madge couldn't even have that. She's in bed. She ate some camel stew."

"Adventuresome. And where are your other friends? Or did they also eat some camel stew?"

And that led, naturally, into explanations—vague about the reason for her sudden rebellion at the Thermaic Gulf, more expansive about her travels through Greece—which lasted well into the wasteland of the first courtyard. In its center, she halted, looked around. "Whatever happened here?"

"A lot of churches were razed when the Sultans started building their seraglio. Then the Janissaries were stationed in this courtyard, outside the main palaces, of course—a fierce bunch of fighting men. Originally, for a couple of hundred years, they were tribute children. Fair-haired boys from Greece in great demand."

"Tribute children?"

"Recruited by force. Taught to be savages. They terrorized Europe, including their homeland."

"Didn't they remember anything about Greece?" Nina asked in horror. "How old were they when they were taken as tribute?"

"Practically kindergarten age. By the time they were fourteen and trained to fight, the whole world outside these walls had become their enemy." Renwick turned bitter. "Complete and thorough indoctrination."

"Was it really possible?" Nina's voice faltered.

"It was." *And still is. How else could today's hard-core terrorists be willing killers of their own people?*

"It's so empty, so peaceful now. No sign of any buildings."

"Blown to pieces by the Sultan's artillery when the Janissaries became too much of a threat to their masters. Those who survived the bombardment were executed." *A hundred thousand dead. A quick end to a brutalized force, to four hundred years of complete terror.* "Come on, Nina. Suleyman will think we've really lost our way." He took her arm, urged her toward the street gateway ahead of them. He hoped she wouldn't notice the large nails on either side where decapitated heads had once been hung as a reminder of the Sultan's displeasure.

But she was more interested in him. "What *are* you doing in Istanbul, Bob?"

So he talked, briefly, about Merriman & Co. His explanation, much to his relief, seemed to be acceptable.

"Of course," she said thoughtfully, "you did get an engineering degree at MIT. And then the army. Artillery, wasn't it? Then you went into NATO and attended disarmament conferences. And now you are a consultant. Very impressive, Bob."

"You remember a lot." He was both surprised and pleased. "But I'm not a consultant—just one of the firm's representatives abroad. There's a lot of building being planned around the world."

"Exciting. How long will you be here?"

"Well, I arrived three days ago. Another four days might be necessary."

"And then?"

"Wherever a client needs some practical advice."

"Well, I hope your travel expenses let you stay in the best hotels. You know, Madge and I landed in the Hilton. All Father's arrangement, I am sure," she said ruefully, and then laughed. "But I did have the most wonderful bath. We're really pampered, aren't we? Americans always have a longing for good plumbing. Tony calls me a complete bourgeoise, but he wouldn't have thought so if he had seen us arriving this morning. The dock was kept for grade-C traffic, I think. We got out fairly easily—thanks to Father again. That disguised colonel or general didn't arrive by accident. Father probably phoned someone in Ankara to watch out for his helpless little daughter at the Galata quays."

"How would he know?" Nina was quick, thought Renwick: what had prompted her idea that Kahraman, in his silver-gray suit, was a man of authority? He could only hope that she had been as quick to notice strange details in her journey across Europe.

"Because I called him from Greece, told him we'd be here around the beginning of September. Actually, the Hilton couldn't be more suitable. That's where we're meeting Jim tomorrow. At four o'clock. Unless, of course, he's so mad at me he won't turn up."

"He will."

Something amused her. "Now Tony will just *have* to find a space for his camper near Istanbul and let the others have at least a little time here. You see, we weren't going to stop in Istanbul at all. Jim said the campsite was all booked up—he always likes to arrange everything in advance, you know."

"Only one campsite near here?" Renwick was smiling.

Sharply, she looked at him. "Are there more?"

"So I've heard."

She frowned, halted at the gate, turned to stare back at the far walls of the seraglio.

What the hell did I say? he wondered. He said, "If not Istanbul, where were you going to stop?"

"Bursa."

"Bursa?"

She nodded, fell silent, became engrossed by her last view of Topkapi: towers and cupolas, palaces and gardens, courtyards and terraces, all guarded by the vast encircling wall. "Riches and treasures . . ." Then her eyes traveled over the courtyard of the Janissaries. Her voice stifled. "Poor children." She turned toward the gate.

He had taken her arm. Suddenly, he kissed her cheek.

"For what?" she asked, a smile coming back to her lips.

For hearing the cries of pain. Not many did. They'd marvel at history as it was laid out before them, wonder how much money it had taken to build this or furnish that. Eyes were bewildered by incredible treasures. Ears were deaf. He said, leading her through Bab-i-Hümayan into the esplanade, "I wanted to. That's all."

"Bob, did you see those huge nails? In that black-and-white marble gate?"

"More history, I guess. Where's Suleyman the Magnificent?"

He was there, gesticulating from the other side of the street, urging them to hurry. So they did. Either the taxi driver was impatient or there were rules and regulations to be obeyed. Their departure was equally speedy, Suleyman looking after them with regret but partially consoled by Renwick's tip, tactfully concealed in a warm handshake.

"I have to pay him," Nina said, rousing herself, looking back in dismay.

"Taken care of."

"And I'll need him tomorrow morning. Madge and I will be visiting—"

"He'll be at the hotel tomorrow, waiting for you."

"You arranged that? I didn't hear."

"You told him your plans, didn't you?"

"Well, I did mention the Bazaar and the Blue Mosque."

"Then he'll be at the hotel tomorrow. Now, let's see . . ." Renwick fished a map from his pocket, and began reinforcing his directions to the Café Alhamra.

The café delighted Nina. It was small, set down in a public garden on a twisting hill road, with a terrace and flowerpots to mark its allotted space. From here, she could see the Bosporus and the coast of Asia. "How far?" she asked, eyeing the stretch of water and its busy traffic.

Renwick studied it. "More than a mile, perhaps a mile and a half. The port for the car ferry is just below this hill. That's where you'll be crossing over on Wednesday morning. I don't imagine you'll start out for Asia late tomorrow and risk traveling in darkness to Bursa. The roads over there can be tricky."

She studied her glass. "This tea is marvelous." As in all cafés in Islamic territory, only coffee or tea or fruit juice was served. "The best I've ever tasted. Where do the Turks get it?"

So we're slipping away from the topic of Bursa, he thought. "It's home-grown. Once they had orange groves. Then there was a stretch of bad frosts. So they planted tea instead. But over on the Asiatic side, winters must be warmer. That's where the fruit orchards are. You'll pass through miles of them on your way to Bursa."

"Have you been there? What's it like?"

"I've never seen it. But I hear it has a lot of charm—purely Turkish, of course. Not many foreigners around. You'll like it." He studied her eyes. Thank God she had taken off the dark sunglasses. Now he could really see the Nina he knew. "Don't you want to go to Bursa?"

"I'd like more time in Istanbul."

"Well, can't you manage that? Don't any of you have a say in the selection of major stops? The ones where you spend several nights?"

"Oh, we talk and plan and talk. But everyone has his own idea of where he wants to go. Someone just has to take charge and decide."

"Who does?"

"Tony and Jim, usually. It makes sense. Tony has certain routes to follow—he is making a sort of test run, you know, for the manufacturers in England who want to know how their camper behaves. And Jim—well, he's paying more than his share of the expenses as well as coping with all the documents and details."

"What about sightseeing when you have several days to kill? Do you scatter, or does Jim shepherd you around?"

"Heavens, no. Jim—he's writing some pieces for a newspaper, you know—goes off to meet people who can give him details for a story. And there's money to be collected at a bank, and our mail to be weighed and sent off at a post office. Things like that," she ended lamely. She was frowning.

"Don't," Renwick said, and reached out his hand, gently smoothed her brow. He could guess what had troubled her: a letter and two postcards that never had reached America.

She tried to smile, rushed on with talk about Tony, who guarded the camper while Jim was away, and, once Jim returned to take charge of it, took a day off himself to have something replaced or checked or repaired. "He ought to have been a mechanic. He's always tinkering around his machine, always fussing over his radio equipment."

"You don't like him too much, do you?"

"How did you guess?"

By the tightness in your voice, he said silently. By the cloud that's still hanging over those beautiful eyes. "I just feel something is troubling you. What's wrong?"

"Nothing."

"Oh, Nina—come on."

She was silent, stared unhappily at the view which had so delighted her fifteen minutes ago. "I really ought to phone Madge. She may be worrying—"

"She's probably asleep. In any case, the Hilton is near—just at the top of this hill—and I'll have you back there by half past six." That is, if our taxi driver returns here at six-twenty, as he promised. "Then you can have another wonderful bath, and rest, and I'll be waiting in the lobby at eight-thirty. We'll drive up the Bosporus—not too far—and have a leisurely dinner. How's that?"

"I'd love it. But Madge—"

"If she feels up to it, bring her along," he suggested without much enthusiasm. He didn't want to wish Madge ill but he hoped she couldn't face a Turkish dinner, not tonight. If she could? Then there would be no quiet meeting for two, no possible chance to persuade. Perhaps he'd better start the persuading now. My God, he thought as he looked at Nina, she can't go with Kiley; she's got to be eased out of his grasp. But how do I begin?

"Now you're the one who's looking worried," Nina challenged him.

"I am. I'm thinking about that journey ahead of you. It's the wrong time for it, Nina. Haven't you been reading the news? Listening to the radio? There is trouble all along the line; if not war, then armed revolts and—"

"Jim says we can bypass the danger points."

"I suppose he's arranged in advance for the fighting to stop as you approach?"

"Now, Bob! The main routes must still be safe. We've met other campers, with wives and children on board, who are traveling to India."

Wrong tactics. Swallow your bitterness. "All right. But that doesn't mean they'll be safe from a raiding party or a bunch of guerrillas who mistake them for the enemy." That had happened last week: a German schoolteacher, wife, two children, shot dead in Afghanistan, mistaken by the rebels for one of its hated government's equally hated Soviet advisers. "I just don't want to see you running these risks."

Nina's eyes softened. "You really *are* worried. Oh, Bob—we won't be near the danger spots. Do you think Tony is going to have his precious bus shot up?" she asked lightly.

"Nina—how well do you know these two men?"

She glanced away at the other tables. So many foreigners, even in this small space, so many different kinds of people.

"Nina," Renwick pleaded, and brought her back to him.

"How well do we know anyone?" she asked. "How well do I even know myself?" She shook her head, tried to smile, said sadly, "Perhaps I'm the one who is at fault. Perhaps I fall in love with a man and then—just as suddenly—start falling out for no reason at all. At least, no real reason that makes any sense."

"In love with Kiley?" Renwick's lips were tight, his voice almost inaudible.

"I thought I was. Why not?" She was on the defensive now. "He's attractive, very attractive. And he's in love with me." Suddenly, she was miserable. "He has never actually said it. But—but—"

"But what?"

"Oh, this is all so difficult, so stupid. You don't want to listen to my—" She broke off, then said, "It's just that I have no one to talk to. Madge— no, that's difficult—she was ready to fall in love with Jim herself. But you, Bob—you know how men feel. If you *were* in love, would you never even say 'I love you,' never even mention marriage, and yet tell her that you want her to meet your uncle and that you want to meet her father?"

"To meet your father?" Renwick was startled. "When?"

"Around Thanksgiving—we'll be passing through America then. But what does that mean, Bob? Marriage?" She shook her head, sighed. "He isn't shy. He isn't one of those awkward, tongue-tied men. What does it mean?"

He could guess what it meant: instructions. Get the girl to fall for you; it will make sure she'll go along with you on this trip. But don't let your emotions run away with you; keep your mind in control.

"Bob?" She was watching him anxiously, almost regretting her confidences.

"If you were in love with me, Nina, I'd be telling all the world. Kiley's either a goddamned fool or a trickster."

"Trickster?" She was indignant. "He couldn't be more honest." And then she frowned. "Not altogether," she admitted. "Oh, how I hate lies! They make you feel used—as if you were some idiot who'd believe any story. Am I an idiot, Bob?"

He shook his head. "Only if you insist on going around the world with Kiley."

"But I want to go."

"Why? You aren't in love with him now."

His words had been sharp, almost angry. Surprised, she let his eyes hold hers, felt uncertainty, bewilderment.

"He isn't the man for you, Nina."

And who is? "How do you know so much about him?" she demanded. Annoyance increased the color in her cheeks, brightened her eyes. "You just don't want me to make this trip. Why? Did Father send you here, ask you to—"

"I never saw your father. I wasn't near Washington."

"No?"

"No." He eased his voice, added, "And that's not a lie, either." He glanced at his watch, signaled to the waiter. In a brisk five minutes, with silence complete from Nina, they were out of the café, into the taxi.

Her silence still held for another long minute. And then, contritely, she said, "Bob—I'm sorry."

"I'm sorry, too."

"About what?" I was the one to blame, she thought.

"That you won't listen to me."

"Perhaps I did. In my own way." She paused. "If I don't rejoin the camper, where do I go? Maryland, for Beryl's dinners and parties? Or England again, to make my apologies for being late in arriving at Lower Wallop?"

"What about Paris? I have a friend there with an apartment on the Left Bank. He would lend it to me for September, and I'd lend it to you. That's better than Lower Wallop or Upper Twistleton."

"Pronounced Twitton?"

But in spite of the lightened mood, Renwick's worry deepened. Was she or wasn't she leaving with Kiley? If that guy could make love as well as he talked, Nina was lost.

"You look so serious," she told him as they entered the hotel. "Am I such a responsibility?" Not yours, surely.

"Think about Paris. And let me know this evening. Will you?"

"But I must go on this trip, Bob. Because I'm curious."

He didn't quite understand, looked at her questioningly as they waited at the desk for her key.

"Exactly half past six," she said delightedly. "Bob, you're wonderful. No, don't come any farther. Look at the crowd around us, all speaking English. I won't get lost." Suddenly, she reached up and kissed him gently. "Just wanted to. That's all," she quoted.

He caught her hand. "Nina—because you're curious? About what?"

"About Jim. If he isn't in love with me, why does he pretend? Why so eager to have me along on this trip? I didn't force myself on him, you know."

"I know," Renwick said, releasing her hand. He watched her enter the elevator. Then he turned toward the bar, where Western rules prevailed and he could have a non-Islamic drink. Pierre Claudel had already found a table and ordered two tall glasses of Scotch and soda.

"How did it go?" Claudel asked.

"She's a hard girl to convince." Apart from that, it had been a good afternoon—one of the best in a long time. She was easy to be with. Too damn easy, thought Renwick. And too unsettling.

"No large green camper with British registration and plate has yet crossed the frontier from Greece. And at the campsites, no inquiries have been made in Shawfield's name or in Kiley's."

"Then they are late." Nina might have her extra day in Istanbul after all. "That will give them something to worry about. They'll have to juggle their timetable in Bursa."

"Bursa?"

"That's their main stopover. Not Istanbul."

"What scared them away? The police arrests?"

"Could be." In the last three weeks the Turkish authorities had been exceedingly active: the large political demonstration scheduled for this Sunday near the stadium was not, if the police could help it, going to have terrorists inciting a riot. This summer, politics were at boiling point, and both parties—the Republican socialists and the Justice conservatives—had their bands of wild extremists eager for bloody action. Renwick glanced around the placid bar, well filled with well-dressed people—some businessmen still worrying over contracts; some tourists relaxing after a hard day's pleasure. "Drink up," he told Claudel. "We'd better get Kahraman to switch his attention from Istanbul to Bursa."

"Damned annoying. He had it all nicely planned here."

Renwick nodded. Kahraman might also have a more recent report from the Greek frontier.

Claudel drained his glass. "Meet you back at our hotel. Kahraman will be there at seven-fifteen."

"I'll have to leave before eight-thirty." Their hotel, Kahraman's choice, was a bare five minutes' walk along Cumhurijet Avenue from the Hilton. "Help me disentangle by a quarter past eight." Kahraman, brisk when he dealt with something that was already decided upon, could become painstaking and explorative when new tactics were being discussed. Bursa would mean an entire reshaping of his plans.

Claudel, quick in thought, quick in action, could sympathize. "I'll do my best." He was master of the sudden but polite departure. He nodded as he rose, and left.

Five minutes more and Renwick could leave, too. *Why does he pretend? Why so eager to have me along?* Nina's questions lingered in his mind. They were only the first of more to follow: they were bound to arise, Nina being Nina. And questions demanded answers: she'd search for them, too. Bright, intelligent Nina was something Kiley hadn't bargained for. Nor Theo . . . She was placing herself in extreme jeopardy: one question too many, one sign that she had found an answer, and she became a danger to Theo's plans. She would be dumped out, abandoned in the wilds of Afghanistan—if she lasted that long.

Grim-faced, Renwick passed through the huge lobby, with its swirling currents of voice and movement. Outside, the light was golden, the glow of sunset spreading warmly over the wide avenue that lay beyond the hotel's driveway. But the first hint of coolness was in the air, a first touch of night lay in the far horizons. Goddamn it, he told Nina, you just don't *know* what could happen to you; you just don't know, goddamn it.

Fourteen

EVERYTHING WAS NORMAL. The DO NOT DISTURB notice still dangled; the door to their bedroom was locked, as it should be. After a small struggle with the cumbersome key—an ideal shape to prevent forgetful tourists from walking away with it—Nina could enter. She went in, smiles and cheerful words ready for Madge. The invalid was recovering. She was sitting on her bed, dressed in shirt and jeans.

"Feeling better?" Nina asked. "Better enough to go out for dinner? But change into your dress. We're driving up the Bosporus to one of those restaurants that—"

"Going out for dinner?" a man's voice asked, and James Kiley stepped out of the bathroom.

Madge said quickly, "When we heard your key in the lock, Jim wanted to surprise you."

And when, Nina wondered, did he get here? How did he find us? She stared at him unbelievingly.

"I hope it was a nice surprise," Kiley said, coming forward to remove her bag from her shoulder and throw it on her bed. He looked into her eyes. "Not the kind you gave me. Oh, Nina, Nina!" His arms slid around her and drew her close. "Don't do that ever again! Don't do that to me, Nina." He kissed her hard; then suddenly letting go, he turned to glance at Madge.

"Don't let me stop you," Madge told him, but he walked over to the window, stood looking out, his back to the room. Madge shrugged her shoulders, said to Nina, "How was it?"

From silence, Nina broke into a rush of words. "Fabulous. I wish you could have made it, Madge. And tomorrow, Topkapi is closed. But Suleyman will take us to the Bazaar and the Blue Mosque. He's an excellent guide. And I think he really is a poet. Flights of phrases." She eyed Jim's back.

Am I supposed to go over to him and say I'm sorry? Or is he really so upset that he doesn't want to face us? "As we were leaving the second courtyard, the one where the kitchens have miles of shelving with all the Ming dinnerware displayed . . ." She didn't end the sentence, cutting off any reference to Bob Renwick. She could hear Madge saying, but how wonderful, how is he, was that why you were late in getting back here, what did you talk about? And if she replied that Bob had been persuading her to leave? No thank you, she decided: Jim was in a bad enough mood right now. Her fault, too, she had to admit. So she rushed on, "I was so tired and hot that I decided I wanted a seat at a café and something to drink. Tea was all I got. But it was marvelous."

"So that's where you and Suleyman were," Madge said. She spoke to Jim's back. "See, I told you Nina was perfectly safe. There was nothing to worry about."

Kiley swung around to face Nina. "Wasn't there?" he asked quietly. "First, you scare the daylights out of me when you took off in Greece. Next, you spend hours with some little tout who picked you up at the docks."

Madge cut in. "I told you all about that, and he isn't a tout. I told you all about our travel in Greece, too, so you don't have to keep worrying about Nina. You might think a little about me. I'm the one who fell ill." Then she tried to laugh, said to Nina, "He's been here for the last hour—almost—and nearly drove me back to bed with all his questions."

Kiley said, "I had every right to be anxious. Nina can't go wandering off by herself like that in a strange city."

Let's end this, Nina thought. "I'm sorry, Jim. But I really didn't expect you here until tomorrow afternoon. Did you cut your visit short in Greece?"

"Oh, they drove like mad all yesterday," Madge said, "and crossed the frontier last night. No wonder he's in a bad mood."

Nina was surprised. "Why all the rush, Jim?"

He said, "No rush, actually. Just trying to get back on schedule."

"And where is everyone now?"

"We found an inn on the outskirts of the city, nice little place with a courtyard. There are some gypsies around—local color, you know—so Tony's keeping an eye on the camper."

"And how is our Jolly Green Giant?"

Kiley stared at her.

Don't tell me he has to have that little joke explained, thought Nina.

Madge was smiling. "Don't you ever watch TV commercials, Jim?"

"Rarely."

"Our Jolly Green Giant is now dark brown," Madge told Nina. "It had an accident and the paint got scarred. Nothing serious, otherwise. But *you* know Tony. He had to have it looking perfect."

"But why not keep it green? I rather liked it."

Kiley said, "There was only a light green available. It would have taken three coats of spraying to cover the damage."

Nina dropped down on her bed. "I really am tired. We must have covered miles and miles. All I want now is a hot bath and then—"

Madge said, "You'll have to hurry. Jim has a car waiting for us."

"The innkeeper's son drove me in," Jim explained. "He'll drive us back."

"We're leaving, Nina," Madge said. "No dinner on the Bosporus. But there's one at the inn—all arranged—gypsies and music and dancing."

"Leaving?"

"Yes," said Jim, "and we are late as it is."

Nina sat bolt upright. "Look, Jim, I'm not leaving tonight. I'm going to have—" She halted abruptly.

"Have dinner with a guide? A young kid who just happened to appear at the docks this morning. Who sent him?"

"Jim—"

"Some story he laid on you! What's his name—his full name?"

"Jim—I wasn't going to have dinner with Suleyman. Madge and I were going to—"

"What's his name?"

"I didn't catch all of it. Did you, Madge?"

Madge shook her head. "He *is* a guide and interpreter, Jim. And we needed one. Without him, we wouldn't even have found a hotel where I could be sick in comfort."

"So he steered you here? I think I'll get the police onto this."

"And get him into trouble for doing nothing wrong?" Nina demanded. "You ought to thank him for making your job easy."

He looked at her sharply.

"For helping you to track us down," Nina said patiently. "There are a lot of hotels in Istanbul."

"And I must have phoned half of them."

"Come on, Jim. How many, really?" She was thinking, he really was worried about me.

"Three," he admitted and laughed and took her hands to draw her to her feet. "All those where Americans are sure to be found. Now, have a quick bath if you must—five minutes? Madge can pack for you." His arms were around her. "My God, anything could have happened to you today. I'm sorry if I was uptight. But—"

"Pack?"

"We're leaving. Madge told you."

Nina struggled free from his embrace. "Look," she said angrily, "I'll go to the inn for dinner. But I'm coming back here to sleep in that bed. It's mine and I haven't—"

"There's a bed at the inn, if that's what you want. Now hurry, or you won't even have time for that bath."

"But we have this room. Why waste the money?"

"Counting your dollars?" he teased her.

"Why can't we stay here tonight?"

"Because we leave at the crack of dawn for Bursa."

"What? We don't even have one more morning in Istanbul?"

"We've got to be in Bursa by tomorrow. That is, if you want the others to have time on the following day for that side trip to Troy. Or have you forgotten about them, Nina?"

I'll scream, she thought, if he reminds me that Troy is one place I've always wanted to see. But he didn't. He gave her a gentle push toward the bath-room. "Five minutes," he said.

She reached for her bag.

"Going to wash that, too?"

"My make-up," she told him and left for the quickest of showers. "Madge," she called back, "hand me my shirt and jeans, will you?"

And what about Bob? she was thinking as she slipped out of her Greek dress. I just can't leave without an apology, some explanation why I cut his date. I can't do that, not to Bob. . . . From her bag she took out her small sketchbook and pen. She tore off a page, carefully leaving intact the ones already filled with her copies of decorations and designs. Her message had to be brief: the shower, now running, was ready; minutes were vanishing. She finished writing, folded her note, slipped it into her wallet.

"Seven minutes," Jim told her when she came back into the room carry-ing her folded dress to pack into her duffel bag. He was at ease, tension and worry banished. "Changed your hair back to normal? I prefer it. But I liked that dress. You looked good in it. When will you wear it for me?"

"Whenever we can get dressed up for dinner. Not much chance of that for a long time. I've been looking at a map, Jim. We're really going to be traveling through some wild places. I think you should buy three black bed sheets. Then Marie-Louis, Madge, and I could wrap ourselves up like cocoons, and no one would give us a second look."

"You'll be safe. All the way into India. I'll buy you a sari there. How's that?"

"In New Delhi?" She had been trying to persuade him toward there for a major stop—after all, he knew she had spent two years in New Delhi with her parents. "I wonder how much I remember of it. I was four years old when I was sent home with Mother."

"You were too young to remember anything. It's always a disappoint-ment to go back."

"Then where do we make a major stop? Calcutta—oh, no!"

"What about Bombay?"

"And before that?"

"Curious, aren't you?"

She concentrated on repacking the top items of her duffel bag, said, "We just like to know what we are going to see. Don't we, Madge?"

Madge nodded. "Something to look forward to. No more dead ends, Jim—like that awful café on that empty beach in Greece. Six days there? I ask you."

"We'll stop at plenty of interesting towns and villages," he assured them. "Even the wildest places will be safe." He was amused. He began walking around the room, making sure nothing had been left.

"What about languages, road signs?" Nina asked. After today's experi-ences, her confidence was shaken. "Tony may be good at following maps, but what about food and shelter?"

"We'll manage," Jim said. "We've got an interpreter for each country where language is a difficulty. We have one for Turkey right now. He met us at the frontier last night."

"But how?" She was knotting the duffel bag's cord, securely but slowly, wondering now about her note to Bob: would Jim find an excuse to read it when she left it at the desk?

"Advance booking. Simple. There's a tourist agency that handles these things."

"Such efficiency!" Madge exclaimed. "But what extravagance."

"Not much. You pay a little and you get a lot."

"Oh, heavens!" Nina was horrified. "Three dollars a day. Madge, we forgot all about that!"

Kiley stared at them in turn.

"Suleyman's fee," Madge said.

Nina moved to the writing table. "I'll leave him a message canceling tomorrow."

"There's no paper left, just envelopes," Madge said. "I used it to write my mother and Beth Jenson and Herb Galway and—"

"Letters?" Kiley asked. "I'll mail them downstairs while you check out. The time you waste, you two! Come on, come on."

Nina found an envelope. "I'll put the money in this and leave it at the desk."

"Marked for Suleyman? Some hope that he'll ever get it."

"At least I tried." That would make a nice epitaph for her tombstone, she thought as she scrawled Suleyman's name on the envelope. She took out her wallet and removed three dollars from her American-money section. Her note to Bob was among them. She had a brief pang of guilt as Jim, with Madge's bag in his hand, came to pick up hers. "I'll leave Suleyman's envelope downstairs with our room key," she said, and wondered at her calm voice. Not really a lie, she told herself: I didn't tell the facts, but who asked me for them? A lie is the opposite of truth, and that's a different matter. I wasn't the one to say I was going by bus to Salonika and then took a car in quite another direction.

Still troubled by that memory—but now she knew somehow that she'd never challenge Jim on that story—she followed him into the corridor.

In the lobby, Madge said, "There's Suleyman!" He was standing by one of the decorative plants, talking amiably with a bellboy. But his eyes were alert. He had seen the girls and the stranger. No astonishment showed on his face. He looked completely unconcerned, and totally innocent of the stranger's sharp scrutiny.

A seventeen- or eighteen-year-old kid, thought Kiley; nothing to worry about there. "I'll get the right stamps for your letters," he told Madge. "Shove them in my pocket. And you tell the desk you're checking out. I'll pay the bill when it's ready."

Nina said, "I'll do that, Jim. But first—Suleyman."

"Keep it short."

"I will," she called back, already on her way. "Suleyman—your fee," she told him, handing him the envelope. "With our thanks."

"You are leaving?"

"Yes. And inside the envelope you will find a note. Please give it to my friend—the man who met us today at Topkapi. He will be here at half past eight."

"I will give it to him."

"And tell him not to worry. We are having interpreters and guides all the way to India."

"To India?"

"Yes." She smiled. "They speak English there. We will have no need for an interpreter in Bombay."

"Bombay," he repeated.

"Yes."

"I will tell him all that," Suleyman assured her solemnly.

"Thank you, Suleyman."

He pocketed the envelope, bowing politely, thanking her with a flow of charming phrases. Suddenly, he was aware that the stranger now buying stamps at the porter's desk had a keen eye directed at him. So, with another small bow, he quickly turned away to resume his conversation with the bellboy.

Abrupt, thought Nina, as she joined Madge. But she was more puzzled by herself: why mention Bombay at all? The name had slipped out. Purposefully? Just a need for a little insurance—in case the letters she'd write in Bursa to her father and Aunt Eunice would go astray like the rest of her mail? Her suspicion distressed her, stabbed at her conscience. She glanced over at Jim, now posting Madge's envelopes. At least he was standing in front of the letter box going through the right motions, although her view of them was partially blocked. Really, she asked herself, why shouldn't our mail arrive home? You're ridiculous, she told herself. Just because two postcards and a letter, sent on three different dates from three different places, never arrived. They could have been delayed by a coincidence of strikes or a slowdown in services; such things happened nowadays. She clung to that hope as she saw Jim coming to meet her. There was a warm smile on his lips, pleasure in his eyes, and admiration, too. He'd never hurt me, not Jim. And if he lied about Salonika? There could be an explanation for that. She hoped so.

"All set?" Jim was asking. "Then let's not keep the gypsies waiting."

Suleyman seemed unnoticing of their departure, but his chat with the bellboy was over. Slowly, he moved around the lobby. Then, reassured, he headed for a public telephone.

Robert Renwick glanced at his watch: fifteen more minutes and he would have to leave. Claudel and Kahraman had now finished with the problem of Bursa and were discussing the green camper. Kahraman's verdict was that it must cross the frontier by early tomorrow morning. Otherwise, their four o'clock appointment with Miss O'Connell would not be kept. "You are quite sure it will be kept?" he asked Renwick.

"I'm sure. If not tomorrow at four, then certainly as soon as they arrive."

"Then what puzzles you, my friend?"

"That six-day stay south of Salonika."

"Twice the length of any other major stopover," Claudel agreed. "According to Gilman, that is." Merriman & Co. had been making inquiries, with excellent results. The intermediate stops of the camper were unknown as yet, but Dijon, Basel, Innsbruck, Ljubljana had been verified: three nights in each place.

Kahraman said, "They perhaps had twice as much business in northern Greece." He smiled benevolently.

"Vlakos won't like that idea," Claudel said. Nor had Vlakos liked the report of two agents sent up to the gulf to scout around its quieter beaches. After a careful search—difficult, because they couldn't question too noticeably and arouse suspicion—they had found a neglected stretch of sand, with four young foreigners in a state of happy daze. Spaced out, obviously. But no camper. No Englishman who owned it. No American called Kiley. From the woman who ran the solitary café, there had been only a blank stare and a harsh curse for the four foreigners who had invaded her beach yesterday. As for the foreigners, they had lost all sense of time, could give no sensible reply, no verification or denial of the woman's date. The agents had left to continue their search, returned two days later. The foreigners had gone. Transportation? Probably a bus, the café owner had said, and good riddance to them and their pills. "Drugs . . ." Claudel shook his head. "Surely they can't be so stupid as to get into that scene?"

"At the border we will search the camper," Kahraman said. "That might be a quick solution to all our problems."

And the end of any lead to Theo's plan, thought Renwick. "Kiley isn't so stupid," he told Claudel. "There will be no drugs carried across frontiers. If they are being used—" he corrected that—"if they are being administered, it will be well inside a country."

"Administered?"

"To begin with. Once the habit is started, then there will be dependence."

"And control," Claudel said. "No rebellions, no defections. Kiley wants them to stay together. Why? Cover for his own trip?"

Kahraman nodded. "Excellent cover. All innocent young people, you tell me. None with any connections to terrorists or agitators or lawbreakers. A very excellent cover for—"

The telephone rang. Kahraman took the call. It was brief, his reply equally so. He looked grave as he faced the two men. "That was from my office. My nephew just phoned to leave a message for me. Very urgent. He is on his way there now to give us the details." Kahraman was, in a surprisingly quick movement, already at the door, beginning to open it.

Renwick said, "I've got an appointment to keep."

"She will not keep it, my friend." The door closed quietly.

Renwick and Claudel stared at each other. "Five minutes?" Claudel suggested.

"Three." That was long enough to wait. Even three were an agony.

Claudel said, "I'll take the short route to Kahraman's office."

A back alley from this hotel, two courtyards, a covered passage. "We'll go together, waste no more time," Renwick said. It was dark now, and there wouldn't be many lights strung along that short distance: little danger of being seen. He kept his eyes on his watch. "Okay," he said quietly and fell silent again, his sense of failure increasing with each passing moment.

They left the radio playing, the two meager lamps glowing feebly. Cautiously, they took the service stairs, reached the ill-lit hall that would lead to the alley. There, in its heavy shadows, their pace increased. "Identification?" Claudel asked worriedly as they came to the end of the covered passage. But Kahraman, sharp-minded as always, had guessed their route: the man stationed at the back door to his office was Claudel's old friend Fahri. Claudel relaxed into a small laugh, sheathed the knife he had been carrying since he had stepped into the alley.

The rear of this three-story building might seem decrepit, but its front put quite a new face on it. Its imposing entrance near a busy avenue had a number of firms identified at its doorway—all of them dealers in rugs, handwoven and expensive, Turkish, Persian, Afghan, Indian, Chinese. Kahraman's name was among them, nestling unobtrusively in the middle of the list, his business inherited from his family when he had retired from the army. His private office was the one both Renwick and Claudel knew. The rest of his suite—four rooms strung along a winding corridor on the top floor— was a mystery. At least one of them must be devoted to import and export; the others, to Kahraman's particular interests. They were extensive. It was impossible, thought Renwick, not to be impressed by Kahraman's ingenuity and energy.

The office was medium in size, furnished with only the necessities: a desk, four chairs, two tray-topped coffee tables, but their Turkish workmanship was both intricate and perfect. The carpet was a treasure of Persian design. A prayer rug was spread near one bare white wall; a copy of the Koran lay on an elaborately carved stool. In contrast to this, the overhead lighting was a glaring monstrosity. But Kahraman would see every expression on any visitor's face: no change in a smile, no drop of the eyes would be hidden by any silk-shaded lamps.

He was seated at the desk, impatient to begin. Suleyman, at one of the brass-topped tables, was pouring three small cups of coffee. With those safely delivered, he stood aside and waited while the coffee was sipped down to its halfway level. Then, at a wave of his uncle's hand, he began his report. It was concise and clear, ending with the delivery of the note to Renwick.

"Well?" demanded Claudel as Renwick read the slip of paper.

Renwick, for politeness' sake, passed the note to Kahraman as he quoted its contents to Claudel. "Jim is here. The camper crossed the frontier last night—waiting for us at an inn on the outskirts—leaving at dawn tomorrow for the early ferry. So tonight is impossible. Truly sorry. Always, Nina."

Kahraman's composure vanished. "Crossed the frontier last night?"

Some poor devil of a border guard will have to pay for that, thought Renwick. He said, "They've changed the color of the camper."

"That long stopover in Greece . . ." Claudel said. "But of course! What about the camper's registration? They must have had a faked copy all prepared, giving the new color."

"New plates, too, probably. Shawfield's name would be kept—because of his passport. His signature is possibly an illegible scrawl, anyway."

Kahraman controlled his anger. "We will watch the ferries tomorrow morning. Impossible to find that inn on the outskirts—a hundred or more.

And in which direction from the city? Our best chance is with the car ferries. We do not know the new color of this camper, but we shall look for eight young people, two of them girls with fair hair. We will follow them into Asia and see if they indeed go to Bursa. I do not trust these men." He shook his head sadly.

"I'd like to—" Claudel began, fell silent as he noted Kahraman's small gesture: a hand raised delicately for one brief moment.

"You did well," Kahraman said to his nephew. "The young lady was definite when she spoke about interpreters and guides? Not just one interpreter and guide?"

"Interpreters and guides. All the way to India. In Bombay there would be no need for them. That is what she said."

"Thank you, Suleyman." Kahraman smiled a dismissal. As the door closed behind the boy, Kahraman could not resist saying in his most offhand manner, "Fortunate that I had him posted in the Hilton lobby."

"Most fortunate," Claudel said. Thank God, Renwick was thinking as he nodded his agreement.

"And what would you like?" Kahraman asked Claudel. "To go on that car ferry tomorrow morning? Follow the camper to Bursa?"

"With Fahri, if that doesn't inconvenience you."

"Go with Fahri, certainly. But not to Bursa. I shall arrange surveillance of the camper. It would be best if you and Fahri were not visible immediately. Later . . ." Kahraman paused and considered for almost a minute. "We have so many frontiers. Greece and Bulgaria we no longer need consider. But Russia, Iran, Iraq, Syria—which border will the camper cross on its way to Afghanistan?" This was developing into a widescale operation. Kahraman's eyes gleamed with pleasure at the difficulties facing him.

Renwick said, "In Amsterdam, Nina said that Kiley was avoiding Communist countries. There's no work for him there—no rebels to be encouraged and organized. Definitely not allowed."

Claudel laughed. "He traveled through Yugoslavia. That shows his opinion of its politics."

"Syria, Iraq, Iran." Kahraman was thoughtful. "There's unrest in Iran. Trouble will come in another month or two. But if Kiley makes haste, and if he has the right guide, he will pass through quite easily by following the main route east. Iran has a frontier with Afghanistan. Syria and Iraq do not. But we shall see, as we follow his direction from Turkey. And you," he said to Claudel, "will be informed in time to cross whatever frontier the camper uses. You will need Turkish papers—was that what you would also like? And Fahri will, of course, be with you. He speaks several dialects, he knows Parsee. He has traveled much through these regions—all the way to India. Carpets and rugs. They take many months, sometimes a year, to make. Naturally, Fahri, as my firm's representative, visits the makers of these rugs to place another order. Yes, I think it is a possible mission."

"A car big enough to let us sleep in it?" Claudel asked. There were stretches of desert and wastelands with no inns.

Kahraman nodded. "Changes of cars may be necessary. It will be arranged."

"Communications?" Renwick asked. I'm out of all this, he thought unhappily. My Turkish isn't adequate, I don't look like a Turk. And yet, and yet . . .

"Continual communication," Kahraman assured him, but gave no details. "It is customary practice. We are not only interested in buying extraordinary rugs. We also must try to learn what our neighbors are doing. Their political changes can affect us, too."

Renwick nodded. But his depression grew. "Will Pierre and Fahri be enough surveillance? Two cars, perhaps?"

"And you in the second one?" Claudel broke in. "No, Bob. Fahri and I can handle this assignment. Neither of us will be recognized by the O'Connell girl or her friend Westerman. What explanation could you give them if you met in some unlikely place? Your Nina might have enough sense to keep quiet about such a meeting. But Westerman? Too much risk, Bob. Better wait until Bombay. You can take over then."

As usual, Claudel made good sense. Renwick's lips tightened, but he said nothing.

Kahraman studied him. "No need for further discussion my friend. You are needed in America. A message from Gilman, in London, came here just as I returned to this office. It is decoded." He opened an embossed leather folder on his desk, drew out a sheet of paper. "For you," he said, handing it to Renwick.

The message was brief. "Frank Cooper advises you see him in Washington soonest. Interesting developments need immediate study." Renwick passed the sheet to Claudel.

"Developments?" Claudel speculated.

Renwick shrugged. "Could be anything." It was certainly urgent. And important enough to be sent as a carefully coded message. He rose. "I'll leave tomorrow. Early. Or," he asked Kahraman, "is there a late flight tonight?"

"For Paris, perhaps, by way of Rome. I shall check and telephone you at your hotel. Next visit"—Kahraman rose from the nest of red silk cushions in his carved armchair—"we shall see each other more often." There was an affectionate embrace and wishes for a safe and good journey.

Claudel was also on his feet, uncertain whether he should go or stay.

Kahraman decided for him. "We have much to discuss. Fahri will join us. Your strategy must be well planned."

"Then it's good-bye," Claudel said to Renwick, walking with him to the door. "Until Bombay?"

"I wish you better luck than I had on this trip. Keep in touch if you can."

"I'll keep you briefed, when possible."

"If you feel—sense—some crisis, some danger—"

"I'll make contact with Nina, show her she has friends."

"Get her out!" Renwick's voice was sharp.

"Kidnap her?" Claudel was smiling. "Fahri is just the man for that." Then he turned serious. "Stop worrying about those spaced-out kids on that beach. Kiley wouldn't risk drugs with Nina. He wants to meet her father, doesn't he?"

"Tell Nina I gave you this." On impulse Renwick reached into his jacket for Merriman & Co.'s card. In pencil he wrote: *Courtyard of the Janissaries.* Claudel read the message, raised an eyebrow. "Adequate introduction?"

"If you need more, remind her how she pitied the tribute children."

Claudel looked at his friend curiously, pocketed the card in silence. They shook hands in a tight grip. Then Renwick left, with a last salute and a word of warm thanks to Kahraman—an imposing figure standing erect beside his massive desk, not one crease in the silver-gray jacket, not one hair escaping from its brilliantine hold, not one furrow on that smooth benign face.

"Now," said Kahraman, "I arrange for transport to Paris. Then to business, Pierre." He seated himself on the red silk cushions, switched on intercommunications, began giving orders.

Fifteen

AT DULLES AIRPORT, Frank Cooper was in the car that met Renwick. Cooper, large frame and long legs occupying most of the rear seat, white hair almost hidden by his battered felt hat, well-tailored suit worn uncaringly, had the look of repressed excitement in his broad grin of welcome. At the wheel, Salvatore Marini also showed pleasure, with a smile of white teeth all the brighter by contrast with his olive complexion. His thick hair was still dark although he was almost of Cooper's vintage—they had worked as a team in their OSS visits to occupied territory some thirty-five years ago: Cooper, the lieutenant in charge; Marini, his sergeant and radio expert.

Renwick dropped his bag into the front seat with a "Hi, Sal!" before he slid into a corner of space beside Cooper. Controls were pressed to lock the doors and raise the glass partition. Not even Sal, now guardian and general factotum to Cooper for the past thirty years, needed to hear all the details of his boss's business. Sal understood: the less he knew, the safer he—and the information—would stay.

Cooper was studying Renwick. "A bad journey?"

"Delays. At Rome. And at De Gaulle. Sorry if I'm behind schedule."

"Not at all. You're on time. How was Istanbul?"

"It's fine. But I wasn't. I missed. Badly."

"Not your fault. A matter of luck. Sometimes it's with us; other times, against."

"You've heard from Kahraman?"

"At six this morning. Nina and her friends are about to leave Bursa. The camper is brown, by the way."

"That was a short stay." Renwick tried to calculate it exactly, but the long flight and time changes had left his mind soggy.

"Two nights. But productive from Kahraman's point of view. No details, of course. I'll hear more when I visit Gilman in London on Monday."

That's where I'd like to be right now, thought Renwick, on top of all the reports coming in. Of course, they might not: there could be long gaps when I'd sit staring at a map.

"I've just bought you a house."

Renwick's exhaustion left him.

"Rather, I've leased you a house with a view to buying it. Your hunch about Mr. Otto Remp's interest in real estate near Los Angeles was on the right track."

"Theo has got himself a safe house in Southern California?"

"I thought that would revive you," Cooper said.

"And you've rented a place near him?"

"About five miles away by road. Half of that distance by a climb over rough terrain. Let me explain." Cooper took out a map of the area. "Theo, as well as purchasing an office for his West-East Travel bureau, used the same agent to find a house for his friend from New York, a Mr. Walter Gunter. Gunter took possession about a month ago. It's a large property, several buildings, many acres, called Rancho San Carlos. The house where you'll be staying for a couple of weeks is much smaller—just room for you and Sal and Tim MacEwan. Mac is flying to San Diego today from Montreal. Sal will leave tonight to join him. They'll pick up the keys and have the house opened and ready for your arrival. You'll go in by Los Angeles, reaching there by Friday."

Today was Thursday. Or wasn't it? Renwick asked himself. "And do I just waste today in Washington?"

"Catching up on your sleep and getting mealtimes back to normal," Cooper suggested. "Sorry to have brought you here on such short notice, but this is urgent business. Something is going on at Rancho San Carlos. All we could learn from our real-estate firm—don't worry, we didn't use Theo's agent: we got our little house through a San Diego outfit—is that Rancho San Carlos needs a lot of improvement and the new owner has brought in his own work crew to do the job. Who are these workers, Bob? Who is Walter Gunter? We had inquiries made in Los Angeles, where he seemingly put in an appearance at the real-estate office. From the description, he comes close to the photograph you gave me—taken at a café in The Hague."

"Maartens." Renwick caught his breath.

"Could be. We'd like to know, wouldn't we? And what's the purpose of Rancho San Carlos?"

"It might be a training camp, or a briefing station," Renwick suggested.

"Something's being cooked up. One hell of a brew." Cooper spread out the map and pointed. "There's Sawyer Springs—just over seventy miles southeast of Los Angeles, about fifty miles northeast of San Diego, and some forty miles from the Pacific. Your place is three miles east of the little town— fewer than eight hundred inhabitants, a gas station, agricultural implements, a general store, not much else. You'll find the house easily: its name, Buena Vista, is well marked. All clear?"

Renwick nodded. "I rent a car at Los Angeles?"

"One has been booked for you. Name of Roger Black."

"What's my line of work?"

"You're a writer—natural history."

"The open-air life?" A good excuse for wandering around rough terrain.

"That's it. Mac is your secretary. Sal is cook and bottle washer, chauffeur and buyer of supplies."

"At least we won't starve." Sal was a master at cooking as well as an expert in electronics. "But can you spare Sal?"

"He's all set to go with you. Like an old war-horse, he senses action ahead. Wish I could be there, too, but I'll have a couple of quiet days at East Hampton to get my thoughts ready for London on Monday. After that, it's Rome with a team of lawyers, and then over to Algiers. I'll be in New York by the time you get back. Well, here's your motel, Mr. Black. I hope your room is comfortable." Cooper pushed an envelope into Renwick's hand. "Driver's license and ticket for tomorrow morning's flight to Los Angeles. You board the plane at Dulles. I thought this place would be a handy location."

The car drew up; the glass partition was lowered. "Good hunting," Cooper said softly. "Sal will bring you some equipment and heavier clothes. Hope they fit." Then he remembered one last piece of news, small but amusing. "About that cocktail party I gave on your last evening in New York—just as well you didn't appear. We had gate-crashers. One came with a young man from the State Department: beautiful woman, brunette, an interior decorator from Brussels."

Renwick, reaching for his bag, looked back sharply at Cooper, who went on, "She's now living in Washington. She asked me how you were." Cooper laughed, shaking his head. "She was so sorry you weren't at the party."

"Still using her own name?"

"Thérèse Colbert? Of course. She thinks she is in the clear, that no one suspects. Cool customer. But damned attractive."

"She's all of that," Renwick said, tight-lipped. He opened the car door and stepped out. "Be seeing you," he told Sal. By the time Renwick reached the motel entrance, the car was already on its way to Cooper's branch office in Washington.

California's multiple-lane highways brought Renwick halfway to Sawyer Springs. The rest of the journey from Los Angeles was then on narrow roads, well surfaced against all weathers, nicely cambered for any twists or turns as the route began a long ascent. The fruit ranches, with their orange groves drinking in the hot September sun to nurture their fruit for next January, gave way to the avocado farms, acre after acre of neatly spaced trees, richly green against the red soil of the gentle slopes. Then, as the incline increased, there were rough fields with wild flowers of blue and bright yellow, with scattered boulders and outcrops of rock, with groupings of trees. To the east, farther than he would travel but near enough for the dark green of bristling pines to be marked, were the forest-covered reaches of Mount Palomar, with its observatory on the crest of six thousand-odd feet. But this was hardly the time for stargazing, Renwick thought regretfully. Bird-watching, and of some ugly specimens at that, would keep him well occupied for the next two weeks.

Sawyer Springs was like the rest of the isolated small towns—villages? settlements?—he had passed: a stretch of two-story houses along a lethargic main street. If there was a church, it was well disguised; probably hidden, spireless, in the background of eucalyptus trees. One small motel, no cars visible; a post office adjoining the general store; no police station; a volunteer fire truck near a repair shop for tractors, only one evident; a small café; a gas station, which seemed to be the one flourishing place of business—it, at least, had been given a recent coat of paint. There were few people visible at this time of day, and only two dogs asleep under the tractor. This was a town, thought Renwick, with its life ebbing.

Beyond Sawyer Springs were more fields and a gentle slope away of land on the right-hand side of the road. To his left, there were a few houses, well separated, each with considerable acreage. Buena Vista was the third one, shielded like the others by trees and its own spread of ground. The short driveway was of hard-packed earth, no longer red but grayish brown, a color matched by the weathered wood of the two-story building. There was an adjacent garage, a large chimney of rough-hacked stone, a garden that had been abandoned, window boxes unplanted. The door was wide open, and Sal was standing there: one encouraging note, thought Renwick as he got out of the car. He looked back at the road. Buena Vista lived up to its name: there was a clear view of the southern hills, rolling limitlessly to the east and west. Space and peace, a feeling that nothing had been touched by man.

Sal stood beside him, eyeing his clothes. "You'll need something warmer for this part of the world. We're three thousand feet high."

"Above snake level?" Renwick smiled. In Wyoming, that was the safety limit, he had been told. Only a month since he had been there? Scarcely two months since he had met Crefeld in Amsterdam? How much learned, how much planned since then, how much still to do. He turned to the house. "Where's MacEwan?"

"Mixing the drinks. Snakes—what kind of snakes?"

"Probably not here," Renwick reassured him. "Nearer the coast, you get rattlers in the canyons. Climb up into people's back yards."

Sal didn't believe him. "You notice the drop in temperature? Twenty degrees cooler, at least. And no humidity." Thinking of Washington and New York, his smile was back to normal.

They entered directly into the main room, medium-sized, furnished with odds and ends—a makeshift for renters, no polished surfaces to be marred or scarred, no carpets to be spotted by stains or burns. But there was a fireplace and logs at its side; three armchairs and a deep-cushioned couch; tables, one large and strong, two small and rickety; a shelf of paperbacks, a radio, and a TV set.

"They work," Mac said, bringing over a Scotch-and-soda. "Everything works. Miss Gladstone tested it all. Good to see you, Bob."

"Good to see you here, Mac." Renwick took a long drink. He pointed to the flowers in a vase on the mantelpiece, then at a basket of fruit centered on the large table. "Miss Gladstone?" The woman's touch, he thought. "Who the hell is Gladstone?"

"Works for the San Diego real-estate office. She was waiting for us there when we picked up the keys, led the way here to make sure we didn't get lost. Actually," MacEwan went on in his serious Canadian voice, tinged with Scots, "she was very helpful. Stopped at Escondido—that's a fair-sized town about twenty miles from here—and showed Sal the biggest supermarket. He bought enough food to feed us for the next week."

"And some light bulbs," Sal called from the kitchen, which was almost a part of the room. He came back with his can of beer. "Yes, she went around this place, switching on and off lights, turning on faucets, flushing the toilet, checking the refrigerator, stove—everything."

"Too helpful?" Renwick asked.

"Just a nice warm-hearted woman," Mac judged. Then his thoughtful face cracked into a smile. "When she left, Sal went around this place. With his useful little gadget. Found no bugs, no nasty surprises."

"Changed the light bulbs, too," Sal said cheerfully.

"Relax, Bob," Mac told Renwick. "Have a seat."

"I've been sitting for the better part of three days." Renwick paced around the room, looked out of its windows—two faced south, toward the road, three faced west toward a field bordered by a few old trees. Very few.

"Well, I'm resting my legs. Sal and I've been unpacking for the last two hours—got all his paraphernalia set up in his room. That's on the ground floor."

"Lets me keep an eye on the doors," Sal said. "There's a big TV aerial; we'll have no trouble disguising our own. You want to see upstairs?"

"Later, Sal."

Mac said, "Our rooms are up there. A lot of windows. View at the back of the house is mostly of hill, and of burned trees. There was a big fire in this region a few years back. So Miss Gladstone says. I tell you, Bob, she was very helpful. She was born near here, lives in Escondido, still keeps in touch with Sawyer Springs. That's why, I guess, she was miffed by the sale of Rancho San Carlos through a Los Angeles real-estate firm: she had it on her list, and L.A. shouldn't have horned in."

"You actually asked about San Carlos?" Renwick's step had halted. He stared at MacEwan in astonishment. Mac was a careful man; definitely cautious. That was the reason, Renwick supposed, why Gilman had sent him here—to act as a brake on Renwick's hunches. That reason, as well as the fact that Mac and Renwick were solid friends, a good team dating back to five years ago.

Mac's blue eyes, strong in color against the contrast of his reddish fair hair and pink cheeks, were amused. "I just asked about our neighbors in the next house up the road. They are a retired couple, quiet, live there year-round. But that led to a complete tour of the district: the house after that one belongs to some Hollywood character who's seldom here. Then the road starts turning to the north, passes San Carlos. All that, and more, came out unsolicited."

"Talkative, isn't she?"

Sal said, "And big. Must be five feet ten, a hundred and fifty pounds, in a pink pants suit." Sal, who was close to five feet six, preferred smaller European types, nicely rounded, who wore black silk dresses.

Mac said, "She was just hoping we'd like it here—enough to buy this place. So she wanted to make us feel it was peaceful, just right for a naturalist. We are not to let the excavating at Rancho San Carlos bother us—a few bangs now and again, but soon it will be over. The workmen keep to themselves, sleep up there in the old stable—the horses left years ago."

Sal finished his beer. He had heard all this. "Time to get dinner on the stove," he said and headed for the kitchen, closing its wide double doors carefully behind him.

Quietly, Mac said, "The workmen don't come into Sawyer Springs, not even on a Saturday night. They are driven down to Escondido in a minibus. But some people in Sawyer Springs have sharp eyes: no beards went out last Saturday to Escondido; two beards traveled back on Sunday afternoon. Gladstone thought the workmen were coming in relays to speed up the work. She offered that little item as part of her not-to-worry theme: soon all the bustle would be over, and peace would be everywhere."

Renwick relaxed, poured himself another drink, sat down. "My belated apologies to Miss Gladstone," he said. "They're coming in relays, certainly. But what kind of work? How many at a time? Or did Sawyer Springs' sharp eyes miss on that?"

"I've the impression they miss very little. And why not? They've been given no employment by Rancho San Carlos; no custom, either. They've told Miss Gladstone—she's one of them, went to school here when there was a school—that if Gunter had any sense, he'd have hired locally, got the work done just as well, instead of bringing in five or six at a time."

"And what does Sawyer Springs have to say about those big bangs?"

"There are cottages to be built. The workmen ran into rock, so they have to level the ground by some blasting."

"Gunter is expecting a lot of guests?"

"He's planning a Foundation for Ecological Studies—with seminars. Miss Gladstone thought you'd like to meet him, since your interests coincide." Mac was enjoying himself immensely. "But not this weekend. He left yesterday, told the post office to hold all mail until Monday."

If Gunter is Maartens, why would he leave for a weekend when a new group of workmen was due? Renwick wondered. "Frank Cooper thinks he may be Maartens. He was the one who directed Crefeld's assassin, you know."

Mac's smile had vanished. And almost had you murdered too, he was thinking.

Renwick said, his voice flat and emotionless, "He also controls Thérèse Colbert. She's operating in Washington, I hear."

"Are you sure—that she's one of his agents? She could have been just another innocent caught up in—"

"I hoped for that. I kept hoping. But no innocent makes a calculated move. She turned up at one of Frank's parties, expecting me to be there—

possibly thinking we might start where we left off. She could only have known I'd be at that party through a telephone call from Frank's office."

"Cooper's office phone was bugged?"

"Must have been."

Mac said angrily, "Where was Sal? Doesn't Cooper have him check all phones?"

"At home, yes. But bring Sal continuously into the office? Difficult."

"Cooper takes chances." Mac shook his head.

"Let's trust he didn't have anyone connected with his law firm rent this house."

"We're in the clear, I hope. Cooper had someone in San Diego do the renting."

"Thank heavens for that." Frank did take chances, though. He must have made a lot of inquiries in Los Angeles about Mr. Otto Remp and his new branch of West-East Travel—how else had he found out so much in so short a time? Why else the tap on his phone? "You know, I think we ought to advise him to cancel his visit to Merriman & Co. Postpone it until Theo's interest in him fades a little." Suddenly, surprising Mac by his speed of movement, he was opening the kitchen doors. "Sal—can you contact the boss at East Hampton?"

Sal looked astonished. "At East Hampton? No. In his New York house, yes. But we can always reach him by phone at the cottage."

Not from this place. "It would have to be a call from Escondido." Even that was unsatisfactory, when you were trying to argue Frank out of a visit he was all set to make.

Mac echoed Renwick's thoughts. "You'll never persuade him unless you can give details. And that's impossible. What details, anyway, Bob? You're overworrying. Come on, let's get some fresh air before the sun starts setting. The view from the back porch will interest you. Once it's dark, we could take a stroll up the hill. Sal's brought you some rough clothes, and I've some thick-soled sneakers you can borrow. We take the same size in shoes, remember?"

Renwick nodded, repressed a smile. Mac wasn't a tall man, but he always—perhaps to make himself feel closer to five foot ten rather than three inches shorter—wore shoes that were too big, and filled up the extra space with heavy wool socks.

Mac led the way out of the back door onto the porch. A small terrace faced them (patio, it was called in this part of the world), ending in a stretch of grass bounded by a few trees that had survived the forest fire. A change in the wind perhaps? Fires played strange tricks. Beyond the trees the hill slope steepened, a place of sad reminders in the blackened trunks and leafless boughs, yet a place of new promises, too: man-size saplings, thick bushes, grass, even wild flowers, had replaced burned-out ashes.

"That," Mac said, looking at the hill, "is our quick route to the back of Rancho San Carlos. The distance, if my map is accurate, is less than two miles. By road, it's between four and five. That's because the road—once it's past the retired couple and the Hollywood guy—takes a sharp curve north, leaving our immediate neighbors in a kind of peninsula. We'll cut across its neck, won't even have to cross their land—get the idea?"

"I've got it." The saplings and undergrowth should afford sufficient cover. "Tomorrow, we'll spend the day bird-watching—see the general layout, note who is prowling around. By night, we could have a closer look."

"Enter the grounds? My God—you move fast."

The workmen, so-called, would be in Escondido; replacements not due until Sunday. There would be a caretaker and a couple of guards, but Gunter himself would be absent. "This Saturday might be the best chance we could have," said Renwick.

Sixteen

THAT NIGHT, RENWICK and MacEwan explored the hill behind Buena Vista, testing the terrain and the cover it afforded. The sky was clear; the moon in its last quarter was at half strength. Once they were over the crest, they could sit, catch their breath, and study whatever lights they could see at Rancho San Carlos. There were few of them. But at least, thought Renwick, we know the position of the place; we see the kind of ground over which we'll travel; we can even calculate the time it will take for a closer approach, much closer than this. In daylight, with field glasses and telescope, we'll try for a front-row view.

"Enough?" he asked. Mac nodded. Carefully, they worked their way back to the top of the hill. All was quiet; nothing stirred around them: a peaceful scene, and an eerie one. Moonlight turned grass to pewter gray, bushes and saplings into islands of dark shadow, burned trees into black telephone poles—scarce and scattered—that pointed to the stars.

In half an hour, they reached Buena Vista, welcoming them with lights and warmth. Sal had had his own job to do under cover of night: extending the long wire, which would act as the antenna for his transmitter, right up the outside wall from his bedroom window. Safely attached, he told them, to the base of the existing television mast. His transmitter was small but powerful; so was his short-wave radio. He could reach London with ease. Seven thousand miles were no difficulty at all. "Just encode the words and I'll send them." He smiled, his dark eyes amused. "I even had time for a little drive past the front of Rancho San Carlos. Nothing much to see. Just dark windows and a light over the door, a garden with a wall and a big iron gate, a driveway. How was its rear view?"

"Quiet. But that's where the buildings are. Tomorrow night we'll need you."

"So?" Sal's eyes beamed with pleasure. Then he went to check locked doors and downstairs windows, and there was a general drift toward bed.

Next morning, Renwick and Mac took a normal stroll around Buena Vista's acres. By ten o'clock, with a sideways approach, they had started climbing the hill. Movements became cautious: they were no longer two nature lovers out on a bird-watching spree. In long-sleeved shirts and jeans, both dark blue like their heavy-soled sneakers, they were not obtrusive. Mac had covered his fair skin with an antisun lotion that gave him a banana tan—better, he stated, than a third-degree burn. By day, September could be blistering hot in this high country, even if night was shivering cool.

They reached the crest, went over it at a low crouch. Carefully, they selected their way downhill, headed for a spot that seemed promising, keeping shoulders bent and their heads well below the height of the bushes and saplings. They halted. But they could see only part of the buildings that were grouped around a wide field stretching almost to the base of this hillside. "Not close enough," Renwick murmured. Mac nodded. They would have to go much farther down, until the bushes began to thin out. At present, from this nice safe cover, a complete view was broken by clusters of shrubbery.

Progress was slow, and painful on the hips. The incline was not steep, but definite enough to make them descend half-sitting, half-slipping. Give me a belly crawl any day, thought Renwick. But he'd have that, too, on his way back. The bushes became scarcer, thinning into a broken line. Over to his left, some distance away, the hillside was bare except for boulders and crags. He rejected that direction, aimed for a large bush not far from one of the burned trees. It seemed perfect: its branches didn't hug the ground, giving Mac and himself about eighteen inches of clearance as they lay prone under its leaves.

"Careful," Renwick whispered, pointing upward.

Mac nodded. As he raised himself on his elbows for a clear view of the compound below them, he could sense the branches were only a few inches away from his raised head. One careless movement would send leaves swaying. Slowly he adjusted his minitelescope, took out his pad and pen from one breast pocket. The other one bulged with a flask of water. It was going to be a long morning.

Now let's see what we face tonight, Renwick thought, and brought his field glasses into focus.

In the foreground was the field—short grass, but rough—bounded by a tall chain-link fence, new-looking, no sign of weathering. In the background there was a two-story house, not as large as expected but still dominant: yellow stucco in Spanish style with a ripple of red tiles on a low-pitched roof; tall, narrow windows on the second floor with wrought-iron balconies; on the first floor, fewer and smaller windows with total protection in their elaborate screens; a door that led onto a small paved terrace with a large wooden table and two benches. No driveway around the house from the road, so all deliveries must be carried into those back premises from some service door at the front of the house. Cumbersome but effective as far as security went: no curious eyes would have a chance to see the extent of the compound.

To the left of the main house, adjoining it at right angles, was a one-story building, whitewashed, undecorated; windows small, one door. A mess hall perhaps? At the moment, with no activity visible, it was impossible to judge.

The old stable was easier to identify. In Californian custom it was situated some distance from the main house; a long building, solid, that—like the possible mess hall which it faced across the open ground—ran at right angles from the line of the main building. Near it was the barn, with its huge door closed and small windows boarded over. Abandoned? It looked that way. Yet there were vents under its high roof equally spaced. Air-conditioning units? One thing was definite: it was part of the compound, enclosed by the fence that ran from the right-hand side of the main house to the stable and barn, then swept in a wide semicircle around the grass to reach the rear wall of the mess hall.

Garage? It must lie to the front of the house, near that driveway Sal had noted last night, with easy access to the road. He could check on that later. Now it was this rear view that interested him. The fence in particular. Where was the gate? Possibly close to the right-hand corner of the house. Only one? His eyes searched the fence, section by section. Right in the center of its long sweep around the field, situated immediately below him, was a narrower section of fencing—perhaps three feet wide. Definitely a gate, edged by heavier supports. He tapped Mac's shoulder and borrowed the telescope.

Adjusting it carefully, Renwick could bring the gate right up to him, almost as if he were standing six feet away. It was secured by a lock, a solid-looking piece of metal, with a dark spot in its smooth surface. A keyhole? So that the gate could be unlocked from either side? Logical enough: anyone who came out onto the hill would need to get back into the compound, unless he wanted a long walk around the property to the front of the main house.

Renwick's eyes traveled up the height of the gate, about eight feet, he guessed. Well above the lock he saw something that blocked the edge of daylight between the gate and the fence. Small, neat, its color white. A circuit connector for an alarm system? Yes: two white-covered wires were attached, carefully strung through the heavy mesh, one running around the left of the fence, the other crossing the gate to pass its upper hinge and continue around the right side of the fence. A very complete alarm system, probably switched on from the main house. Renwick drew a long breath. But problems were to be expected.

He angled the telescope lower, studying the base of the fence. Then he noticed something resembling a path, a track made by footsteps, that led from the gate straight to the hillside. Anyone following it might pass near this spot. Too near, perhaps, for any comfort. Renwick tapped Mac's shoulder, returned the telescope, and gestured to a bush farther off to their right.

Mac wasn't enthusiastic about any change; he was nicely settled where he was. But Renwick was already on the move, flat on his belly, propelling himself by elbow power across the sloping hill. Mac pocketed pad and pencil and telescope, and followed. At least, he was thinking, he had made some preliminary sketches of the layout. His forebodings were correct: the new hiding place might be secure but it was hellishly uncomfortable. The large

bush Renwick had chosen had low-sweeping branches so that they had practically to fight their way into the middle of its tangle. But the view, Mac
had to admit, was good.

Renwick said, almost inaudibly, "Do you see lights around the fence?"

Mac shook his head. "Could be well hidden. Floods perhaps. Turned on
by a master switch?"

Renwick nodded. No floods were visible, but they must be somewhere,
ready to beam over every inch of ground at the first alarm. It seemed as if
Gunter preferred to leave his place looking as natural as possible: a nightly
blaze of lights would set the sky aglow and Sawyer Springs wondering.

Suddenly, peace ended. The house door was flung open, a voice commanded, two large Dobermans came bounding out. They made directly for
the mess hall. A man—black-haired, early thirties possibly, broad-shouldered,
dressed in jeans and sweat shirt—followed them as far as the terrace, stood
watching them as they reached the end of the building and began a patrol
of the entire fence. As they approached the barn, the man gave a whistle,
fingers at his mouth. The dogs halted abruptly, raced back to their handler,
stood on either side of him as the barn door opened. Six men trooped out,
dressed in work clothes. Young men, Renwick saw; early twenties, he guessed.
A heavy-built man, older, half-bald, was the last to leave the barn. He closed
and padlocked the door, started after the others, shouting directions. There
was a babble of replies, some laughter, and the troop of six jogged over to
the mess hall and disappeared inside.

Eleven-thirty, Renwick noted. A bit early for a midday meal. If mess hall
it was.

It wasn't. The six men came straggling out. Two carried automatic rifles;
two were joking about the grenades they had strung over their shoulders;
one carried a small box, carefully; his mate, with a canvas bag on his back,
was horsing around with something he tossed in the air and caught (much
laughter) before it reached the ground. A yell from their instructor, waiting
near the fence, ended the fun and games. The group joined him, drawing
together as the dog handler, with his two Dobermans now leashed, came
slowly down center field to unlock the gate and swing it inward. The six
armed men and the baldheaded supervisor passed through. The Dobermans,
never a bark or a whine, walked back to the terrace with their master. There,
he sat down on the corner of a bench, the dogs resting beside him. Peace
returned.

Not for long, Renwick was thinking. It had been plastic that was tossed
in the air. The small wooden box held blasting caps. No spool of wire had
been visible, so the canvas bag carried the means for detonating the caps by
remote control.

"God," said MacEwan as he heard footsteps on the path. "Plastic. Here?"

"Keep praying." Renwick rolled over on his side to watch for the armed
men. Now he knew why he had seen no signs of any demolition down in
the compound. The practice ground was on this hillside.

The voices drew nearer. Too near. American voices. They were a talkative bunch, but the phrases overlapped and Renwick could pick up nothing of importance. Except the names—that could be their supervisor who

was calling them out as he posted the men to their positions on the hillside. First names or nicknames, not much help at all. Renwick exchanged a glance with Mac and received a look of equal frustration. There was a scramble of feet. (Receding, Renwick judged thankfully.) Then silence, a long silence, broken only by the heavy tread of someone approaching where they lay. The footsteps halted. Slowly, Renwick's hand parted a cluster of leaves. The baldheaded man was clearly in sight, barely five yards away, his face turned to the hillside, his arm upraised, waiting.

The arm dropped. There was an eruption of violent sounds. They came almost simultaneously: the swift blast of automatic fire, the explosion of plastic, the burst of a grenade. The bullets had been aimed at the blackened trunk of a burned-out tree, close enough to let Renwick see the wood splinter. The plastic had been used in a rock crevice farther along the hill, with only a few shreds of stone visible as they shot into the air. The grenades—and these men had taken a big chance; they must have held them alive in their hands while they waited for the signal—left a small cloud of dust farther uphill.

Renwick glanced again at Mac. He, too, had found a viewing space between the leaves and was staring at the settling dust. Then he looked at Renwick, shook his head partly in surprise, partly in admiration. It had been a neat maneuver, three separate operations to sound as one. Sawyer Springs would hear only a distant bang and say, "There goes more demolition."

Instructions were shouted. The maneuver was repeated. And again. That seemed to be the allotment, possibly for the town's sake: not enough to arouse curiosity, just enough to give the men practice. They were good, too damned good, thought Renwick. They weren't beginners. This morning's exercise was a matter of keeping their hand in. Or of learning teamwork? That idea depressed him still more.

The instructor was slow to leave the hill. First, he inspected the blasted tree, its trunk now split in two. He moved out of Renwick's sight, but his heavy boots could be heard as he scrambled along the slope toward the small boulders where the plastic had been detonated. Then he returned nearer to the path and had a look where the grenades had landed, presumably checking how close they had come to some marked target. At last he was satisfied, and hurried down to the fence where his men were waiting for him. They weren't a silent crew: talk, jokes, laughter rose up the hillside. A merry romp, Renwick thought bitterly: is that all it is to them? No sense of responsibility, no thought about the deadliness of the weapons entrusted to them? Nothing but the feeling of power—exciting, exhilarating? He nodded to Mac, and once more they were lying prone, raised on their elbows, field glasses and telescope trained on the compound.

"Close," said Mac.

"Too damned close."

The group eased back through the fence gate, kept well apart from the handler with his two Dobermans as he came toward them, then hurried to deposit their equipment in the armory.

"Careless," was Renwick's comment. "He left that gate unlocked while they were on the hill."

"Or too confident." The man was taking his own good time in securing the gate. Perhaps his movements would be brisker if Gunter was around to watch him from an upstairs window.

"Comes to the same thing." Renwick was watching a middle-aged man coming out of the main house, carrying onto the terrace a heavily loaded tray. He dumped it on the table, returned to the house for a second load. No one else in the kitchen to help him? He was the cook, apparently: a large white apron was tied around his bulging waistline. Again he lumbered back into the house, brought out a third tray. Once it was set on the table, he left without a glance at the seven men who were reaching the terrace. The handler paid no attention to them, either. With the leashed Dobermans closely at heel, he followed the cook into the house.

Two things probable, thought Renwick: the kitchen—judging from the speed of the tray deliveries—was close to the door; and there was no socializing between staff and terrorists. Security reasons? The less the exchange between the two groups, the greater the anonymity of identities and backgrounds. There was a third thing to be noted, and this was definite: not even terrorists trusted those Dobermans. That was marked: the group had kept silent, even motionless, as the dogs had been led across the terrace.

Now, with the door closed, food was set out and talk began. Voices were low. The instructor began a monologue, perhaps a post-mortem on this morning's exercises. The others ate, listened intently. It was a long meal. Mac drew out his flask of water and handed it to Renwick with a smile.

The meal was over. The talk went on. And then it ended. Renwick gave a sigh of relief, stretched his back and rubbed his neck and shoulders. Mac finished his last sketches, jotted down the scant names he had heard—Joe, Bill, Shorty, Tiny, Hal, Walt—and buttoned his pad and pencil securely into his breast pocket. "Dispersal?" he asked, looking back at the group.

It seemed like it. The six men were on their feet, began walking slowly toward the stable. The instructor, still on the terrace, called after them, "Leave nothing behind. Be ready to move—sixteen-thirty out front. Don't keep me waiting!" With that reminder, he went into the main house.

Moving out by bus at half past four? Renwick and Mac looked at their watches: three-quarters of an hour to go.

"Need we stay?" Mac asked.

Renwick didn't answer. A cook, a watchman with a couple of Dobermans, an instructor—all of them seemed to live in the main house. Was that all? Gunter might have taken someone with him to act as driver and bodyguard. Understaffed, and yet—come to think of it—these were no ordinary men. Carefully selected, politically reliable from Gunter's point of view. A larger number would have attracted attention from Sawyer Springs, where no help was kept. For a house the size of Rancho San Carlos? Perhaps a couple. The neighbors would accept that as a normal extravagance.

"Do we?" Mac insisted as the six men filed into their dormitory.

He was answered by the door of the main house opening to let the two dogs run free into the field. This time their handler didn't stop on the terrace but followed them as they dashed for the fence and stood there, heads turned to watch his deliberate progress, bodies taut as they waited for him to come unlock the gate and let them loose on the hillside.

"Let's get the hell out," said Renwick.

Once they were safely over the brow of the hill, they could straighten their spines and descend almost at a half-run. They reached Buena Vista with six minutes to spare before the bus would leave Rancho San Carlos. Sal had heard it coming up from the town ten minutes ago, watched it pass. Only a driver, no one else, he reported. Also, no message had arrived from Merriman & Co.; nothing from Frank Cooper, either; and food was ready and waiting anytime they wanted it.

"Later," Renwick said. First, he and Mac would toss to see who was first for a hot shower, the loser posting himself as near the road as was safely possible. He lost, and barely made it to a cluster of trees and bushes before he heard the bus traveling downhill. The six men were inside, work clothes discarded, dressed normally like their instructor who accompanied them. Was he responsible for seeing them each scatter in the cars that waited for them at Escondido? Responsible, too, for the new group arriving one by one—collecting them, escorting them safely here tomorrow night, keeping their arrival circumspect? Altogether a low-key operation, Renwick reflected as he made his way back to the house, but organized and deadly.

In the kitchen, he sat down heavily, still covered with dust, his shirt streaked with dried sweat, and began briefing Sal. "It's more than either Frank or any of us bargained for," he ended. "We can't handle a nest of conspirators being trained for terrorist operations in this country. It's the FBI who should be taking over—it's their job."

"The boss will pass the word to them. If he thinks there's enough evidence to bring them in."

"*If?*"

Sal looked curiously at Renwick's taut face. "What's the plan for tonight?"

"We'll gather that evidence."

"We are going in?"

"We'll make a try."

"We may find nothing. You are risking a lot."

"I'd just like to complete our report to Frank, make his warning to Washington as strong as possible."

"Two Dobermans?" Sal was reflective. "They'll be loose in the compound by night. Well, we can pacify them. I expected dogs. What about their handler?"

"He relies too much on them. They're highly trained." And why patrol the compound for endless hours when you had two Dobermans on the loose? "At least," Renwick admitted with a wry smile, "I'm counting on that." The handler had been careless today, taken security for granted.

"Just the cook and the handler? That's all? You're sure?"

"It's a quiet Saturday night with Gunter absent. No sign of trouble in these last three weeks, none expected now." And I am not sure of anything. Deductions and hunches—that's all I've got.

"One lock. One padlock at the barn. That shouldn't be too difficult. But this alarm system . . ." Sal was frowning. "If it's what I think it is, we'll use wire and clamps. When do we go in?"

"Around nine o'clock. When prime-time television is on."

Sal smiled broadly. "The baseball season is just coming to the play-offs. Wanted to watch the Dodgers tonight, myself."

Mac came downstairs, his yellowed face restored to its usual pink health, his movements once more brisk. "I'm famished!" he warned Renwick.

"Won't be too long," Renwick promised him. He left Sal going over Mac's sketches and diagrams. Sal was efficient, knowledgeable, a welcome surprise. He's as good as either of us for this kind of work, Renwick thought as he slowly mounted the staircase. Perhaps better.

Seventeen

THEY ATE AT five o'clock, still talking over their plans. By half past eight, well prepared, they were on their way. The hillside and its easier routes to Rancho San Carlos were becoming familiar. The half-moon was strong enough, the stars brilliant. Once their eyes became accustomed to the eerie shadows that played over the rough ground whenever a white cloud drifted across the sky, they found it a simple matter of putting one foot in front of the other. Renwick and Mac led the way. Sal, pockets bulging with equipment, a spool of wire dangling from his belt, followed their footsteps precisely.

As they came over the brow of the hill, they crouched low, but—provided they didn't clatter or stumble—they could even speed up their approach to this morning's vantage point. At the path to the fence, they halted; now Sal could see the layout of the place for himself. No one spoke. Dark-blue sweaters, the color of night, were pulled over their dark shirts. Mac's reddish fair hair, brightly silvered in moonlight, was covered by a navy-blue wool cap. Faces and hands were made less noticeable by a deep nut-brown tan out of a bottle.

There were lights behind the curtains of two downstairs windows near the doors onto the terrace. Three more lights, isolated, shone bleakly over the entrance to the armory (some mess hall, Renwick thought with a smile at himself), the side of the barn door, the corner of the stable-dormitory. The fence was left unlit, attracting little attention, making the gate unnoticeable. Sal stared down at the compound, then nodded. He was ready.

Renwick waited. It was an innocent scene; a house half asleep, three buildings abandoned. But the dogs were there, a pair of dark shadows moving constantly and in unison, prowling slowly around the compound's perimeter, alert, silent, their path undeviating.

Watching the rate of their patrol, Renwick calculated quickly. A near approach to the gate should be made when the dogs had reached the barn. From there, they'd pass the stable; then the main house; then the armory and the beginning of the fence; then the sweep of the fence itself. When they reached the gate, that was the moment to face them. On this round he let them continue on their appointed way. Just making sure they followed their training to the last detail, he told himself grimly. As they passed the gate for the second time and headed toward the barn, he signaled and moved forward. Mac and Sal followed, equally cautious in their movements. They knelt down, stayed low, waited for the dogs' long patrol around the compound to come their way again.

Sal was already prepared for work. Around his head he had slipped a broad elastic band with its attached shaded flashlight over his brow ready to be switched on. He had uncoiled a length of insulated wire from the spool at his belt and was now feeling the small, high-pressure spring clamps at either end of the wire as if to make sure they were secure. If he had misjudged Renwick's description of the alarm system in use, tonight's operation would end before it had even begun. But Sal would have had a close look at the circuit connection, would have seen how it could be put out of action. After that, all that could be done was to retreat to Buena Vista, prepare for another attempt next weekend when the dormitory was empty again. In one breast pocket he carried keys; in the other, delicate probes if the keys proved useless. He had a small transmitter in his hip pocket, a sheathed throwing knife down the back of his neck.

Renwick and Mac also had transmitters in their pockets. In their hands were the pacifiers—dart pistols loaded with just enough sleeping power to put the Dobermans out of commission for one hour. ("No longer than that," Renwick had warned Sal as he prepared the dosage. "We want the dogs on their feet again before anyone sees they are doped." And what if the handler came out before the hour was over? Mac had wanted to know. Sal had grunted and said he'd take care of that.)

The dogs were nearing the gate, heads down as if they were following some scent—and perhaps they were, thought Renwick: was that the secret of their well-trained patrol? He signaled; the three men rose, moved swiftly. Renwick was praying he could rest the pacifier on the mesh of the fence and have a steady shot at the dog on the left. Mac would take the one on the right. "Chest," Sal had advised, and Mac had said bitterly, "Yes, they jump and go for your throat." A Doberman wasn't his favorite animal.

Abruptly, the Dobermans halted, heads lifting to the gate at the first sign of danger, teeth showing, muscles tightening as they began an instinctive leap. Renwick and Mac pulled the triggers. The pistols were soundless. Renwick even wondered if his had misfired. But the dogs' leap ended in a weak fall back to the ground. "Quick-acting," Sal had said. And the drug was certainly that. Their weak struggles to rise were soon over, ended in complete collapse and sudden sleep.

Sal hadn't waited for the pistols to be fired. With his flashlight switched on, he was examining the alarm system. Yes, it was a single-wire circuit with a make-or-break connector of two contacts linking the current that ran through them when the gate stood shut. Break that circuit by opening the gate, and the alarm would sound.

Sal nodded to Renwick. This job was his: the tallest of the three, he had a better chance of reaching the connector at its seven-foot height from the ground. But it wouldn't be easy, reaching up, keeping arms steady, making sure that the teeth of the two clamps—sharp as razor blades—would bite into the wire on either side of the connector at the same split second. Timing was everything.

Renwick shoved the pistol into a pocket, grasped a clamp in each hand. Sal held the wire that joined them, kept its length from twisting into a tangle—he had allowed double what they'd need for entering a half-open gate, but he never could tell how far the gate might swing with its heavy weight. He angled his flashlight upward to let its small beam shine on the circuit connector.

Renwick braced himself, slowly lifted the clamps, kept them parallel as he forced the small jaws open against the pressure of their springs. Briefly he hesitated, made sure he was aiming the teeth of each of them to bite cleanly into the wires. He took a deep breath. Then—at the same exact moment—he released the clamps, let them grip. No alarm sounded.

He stood back, arms dropping to his sides, hands suddenly weak, and stared up at the clamps. The long loop of wire, through which the circuit now ran, curved out like a balloon.

Sal redirected his flashlight, began working on the lock. It gave him an unexpected problem: the first key, useless, almost stuck. Two minutes passed, with seconds ticking away on Renwick's watch. One hundred and twenty-four seconds now, and more to come. They could only sweat it out while Sal eased and coaxed the recalcitrant key. Suddenly, it came free. Sal tried another one; it wouldn't go into the keyhole. The third fitted and turned. Gently, Renwick pushed the gate inward while Mac and Sal eyed the circuit connectors. The clamps were working.

Sal was the first through, running toward the barn. Renwick drew the gate closed as they entered the compound. Then Mac and Renwick, one dog apiece, had the heavy task—a nerve-racking one, too—of dragging the animals as far from the gate as necessary. Almost at the gable end of the armory, they judged the jut of the building would block any view of this spot from the terrace, and dropped their burdens. For a brief moment, regaining their breath, they looked down at the slumped bodies. Mac still couldn't believe it: he had hauled a Doberman over a stretch of ground and hadn't been mauled. Then, with a grin, he was racing toward the barn.

Renwick let him reach it and began a full-speed run. Rubber soles were soundless on grass, thank God. And praise be that the barn door faced the hill and was out of sight from the main house. He reached its safety with his heart beating wildly. Sal's work was finished there. The padlock had been easy. He had the door open and waiting. Renwick and Mac, stepping over the threshold into darkness, brought out their penlights.

Sal closed the door. With equal care, he started making his way along the side of the barn; from there to the stable that served as a dormitory when school was in progress; and at last, to a chosen patch of ground near the right-hand side of the terrace. It was deep in shadow—the lighted windows lay to the left of the door—with a small tree and some shrubs to reassure him. He got rid of his equipment in pockets that he buttoned securely, pulled out his small transmitter and held it close to his ear. The barn was the objective, and the objective had been reached. Halfway home: he'd feel better when they were safely out of this damnable place. If lights had been strung along the top of its fence, it would have looked like a prisoner-of-war camp. His thoughts flickered back to one he had known. Along with Frank Cooper. A joint escape that made them friends for life.

He waited patiently, scanning each building in turn. "No need to waste time on the armory," Renwick had said. "We can guess what we'd find there. And we know what to expect in the stable. But in the barn? A classroom with maps—books left for the next batch of pupils? Thirty minutes, Sal. Just give us thirty minutes inside that barn. Perhaps less." Sal checked his watch once more: eleven still to go. They must have found something, or else they'd have left before this. It was a comforting thought to help him through the last minutes: they were always the worst.

The door onto the terrace opened. Sal drew himself against the tree's thin trunk, reached for the back of his neck to grip the handle of his knife. Then he stood motionless, eyeing the light that streamed over the central flag-stones, listening to the outpouring of sound from a distant TV set. A sports commentator's voice was raised, a roar from the crowd burst out.

At his left ear, he heard Renwick's quiet voice. "Leaving. Okay?"

He risked a whispered reply as the roar from thousands of throats rose to a crescendo. "No! Wait!"

The door closed as unexpectedly as it had opened: this was an inning not to be missed. "Okay now. Hurry!" he told Renwick as he left the shelter of the tree. How near was the inning to its end? After that would come commercials and time to have a beer and look outside. Sal sprinted for the barn.

Renwick had already snapped its padlock in place. At a wild run, he and Mac—with Sal at their heels—headed for the gate. They were through, out, safe. "Quick, quick!" Sal told them as he locked the gate while Renwick released the clamps simultaneously and withdrew them at exactly the same instant. Some muffled curses from Sal as the wire almost snarled when he was winding it around the spool. Then they were scrambling up the path, all caution abandoned for speed until they reached the fringe of bushes. There, in good cover, they dropped to the ground. Slowly, breath returned to normal.

Mac pointed to the empty compound. "Look!" Two dark shapes were coming slowly out of the armory's shadow, still unsteady, still unsure of what had happened to them. "My God, Sal, an hour you said. Like hell it was."

Sal raised a hand for silence, his eyes on the main house. "Don't move yet," he whispered.

Renwick and Mac exchanged a puzzled glance, but they stayed where they were. The door to the terrace opened, a path of bright light spread halfway toward the fence. The silhouette of a man stood at the threshold, took three-dimensional shape as he crossed the flagstones. He halted again, looked around the compound as if puzzled. Then his hands went to his lips. The whistle cut through the night. The Dobermans heard it. They came slowly around the armory's end wall, hesitated. A second whistle, and they were out of their dream world. Obediently, they began their patrol. "Don't play tricks with me," the man yelled at them. He turned to go inside, met the small fat cook. "Lazy sons of bitches," he was saying, "thought they'd take it easy for . . ." The voice dwindled to nothing as the door was shut behind the two men.

Who's the lazy son of a bitch? Renwick was thinking. He rose and led the way. Mac made an effort and smothered his fit of laughter. Sal was grinning widely. "Wonder who's winning that game," he said softly.

They were over the top of the hill. Their pace increased on the home slope, the lights of Buena Vista welcoming them from behind carefully drawn curtains. Just as we left it, thought Renwick as they reached the back porch and heard the radio playing. First, we'll unload our gear: next, food and drink; then questions and answers. He could sense Sal's impatience. "Yes," he said to hold him meanwhile, "we got something. Enough, I think, to make Washington's eyes pop."

"Then it was worth it?" Sal asked.

"It was worth it."

Mac had a sudden fit of laughter. "Those dogs—" His laughter choked his words. "Groggy. A couple of old soaks—" The laughter increased.

Sal looked at the usually solemn MacEwan in amazement.

"He has these attacks," Renwick said. "Just be thankful he didn't let one explode on the hillside. Come on, let's heat up that soup. I'm starved." Strange ways we all have, he thought. After tension and fear are over, I get hungry. Mac goes into uncontrollable laughter. And Sal? Renwick studied him as he got rid of his tools, placing them carefully in a neat group on a counter top. There was much more to Sal than he, or Mac, had ever surmised. Chauffeur, cook, guardian angel? Not on your life, Renwick told himself. Without him we'd have accomplished little. He watched Sal unfasten the light harness that held the throwing knife between his shoulder blades. "Thank God you didn't have to use that," Renwick said.

Sal only smiled.

Supper was quickly eaten. The windows were firmly closed, the radio turned on once more. The three men still sat at the table, plates pushed aside.

"So here's what we learned from the barn," Renwick said. "It looks abandoned, shuttered tight. But it *is* a classroom, with desks and chairs and good lighting. Air conditioning, too. The blackboard behind a lectern had been rubbed clean—except for some faint chalk marks on one low corner. They didn't mean much at first, until we began examining the big maps fixed on the wall. I took photographs of them—directed the strong light on the lectern at them, hoped they'll be clear enough. Three maps. One of them covered the southeastern states with red circles near certain small towns, but not on highways or roads. The circles were on railway lines. That was Mac's discovery: freight routes for inflammable material, dangerous chemicals."

Mac turned modest. "I just noticed one of the circles was crossed off, and remembered the name of the town. A bad derailment near there three weeks ago: town evacuated; two deaths; everything blamed on faulty equipment."

Renwick went on. "The next map showed the United States—not the usual relief map. Just a large stretch of white paper with the states outlined, and across them a spider web of black lines: heavy for main highways, thinner for first-class roads. Only certain towns were named. Near them, or within reach by road, were small red squares. We recognized some of these locations—major storage facilities for oil. At first we wondered if the markings meant atomic energy plants, but these can be dealt with by someone on the inside who forgets to turn a little wheel, or turns the wrong one. You don't need a squad of trained terrorists for that job."

"The third map was a real puzzler," Mac said. "It was a city, streets and buildings clearly plotted but unnamed. However, the layout—if you knew Washington—became recognizable."

"Washington?" Sal asked. "And where were the red markings this time? The White House, the Cap—"

"No. Not the White House. Not the Capitol. Not the busy center of the city, either. They were—most of them—in a row along one street. Bob's guess was—foreign embassies."

"Embassies?" Sal was incredulous.

Renwick said, "Seize them, blackmail their governments, prevent them from helping America when she's under attack."

Sal stared at them in open disbelief. "Listen you two—" he said, suddenly breaking into a broad smile—"railroads, oil and gas storage, embassies. And all that taken care of by six young bastards with a week's training behind them?"

"Six young bastards each week," Renwick reminded him. "Rancho San Carlos has already been in operation for three weeks at least. Give it free rein until the end of the year. How many trained terrorists by then? A hundred and fourteen. All ready to command their own groups of men."

"Could be even more," Mac said somberly. "Once Gunter establishes that Foundation for Ecological Studies, he'll extend the numbers. Demolition, of course, would have to stop—unless he adds field trips out into the desert areas."

"But how good is their training?" Sal persisted.

Renwick said, "It's a refresher course. These guys aren't novices. It's just possible they've been brought here to learn how to operate as a team. Perhaps," he added with a pointed look at Sal, "we won't have one hundred and fourteen expert terrorists on call by the end of the year. We'll have nineteen well-functioning squads, capable of instructing others in close teamwork."

"Not funny," Sal said slowly. His dark eyes narrowed as he stared at the fireplace and its dying embers. "Equipment—how do you rate it?"

"Simple but effective. It can be just as deadly as more sophisticated hardware. And it's easier to procure."

"What's their purpose? Complete anarchy?"

"It could end that way." And that was more than Theo and his friends had been aiming for. Break down a dam, release a flood of water that would serve their needs; but what if it reached the strength of a tidal wave? They'd be swept away along with the rest of us. Poor comfort, thought Renwick.

There was a brief silence. Renwick's quiet voice continued. "We didn't find much in the desks. Just some textbooks on explosives. Elementary stuff but good for hard basic training. Also several mimeographed sheets dealing with urban guerrillas, treatment for tanks and armored cars in city areas. I filched a specimen." He went into his hip pocket and produced a folded sheet, handed it over to Sal.

Mac said, "There was a communications setup in one corner of the barn. Nothing too elaborate, just enough to teach them some electronic facts."

"What about the chalk marks on the blackboard?" Sal handed back the mimeographed sheet to Renwick.

Mac pulled out his notebook, opened it to the page with his copy of the marks. "Juncture of railroad tracks. A neat place for dynamite, I presume."

For a long minute, Sal sat glaring down at the table. He pushed aside his coffee cup and rose. "Yes," he said to Renwick, "the sooner the FBI gets into this, the better. I'll contact the boss late tomorrow afternoon—Sunday. He should be back in New York by then. He leaves for London that night."

"I'll contact London, too. They'll get in touch with Washington." We need someone at the highest level to start pushing the right buttons, Renwick decided. "I don't want our report, with copies of our photographs and that mimeographed sheet, to be dropped into an in-tray and left lying on someone's desk while he makes up his blasted mind whether to risk his promotion. I don't want someone, either, who'll read it and go shrieking the news to the outer office. Or someone who likes to leak hints to reporters, just to show his importance. None of that. We need someone who can start the action, and keep his own lip buttoned as well as all his agents' lips. They'll want time to observe, to follow the terrorists when they scatter from Escondido. Not too much time, I hope. If it were left to me, I'd gut out that suppurating sore next week."

"But we don't," Mac said regretfully. "We discover the facts, make our report, and fade away." He pulled himself onto his feet. "I'm fading right now, upstairs, into a sweet, soft bed. Call it a day, Bob."

"Shortly." Renwick listened to their heavy footsteps slowly making their way to their rooms. We're all dropping with fatigue, he thought. But we did the job. We did it; and left no trace. What remains to be done? Tomorrow, an urgent message for Merriman & Co., full report to follow next week; and a look, if possible, at the busload of new arrivals. On Monday—Gunter. How do I manage to see him? He could identify me, too. If he is Maartens. Maartens and Amsterdam and a green camper changed to brown, and Theo behind it all.

He knew this stage of exhaustion well. The mind was lost in a maze of possibilities and every solution ended in blank depression. They should have been celebrating their small victory tonight. Instead, all three of them could only think of the grim threat they had uncovered. To America. To the rest of the free world, too. Why else the foreign embassies? Blackmailed by terror into inaction? Allies split apart?

He roused himself, rose and switched off the radio, the lights, opened the front door. He stood there breathing the clean cool air, looking at the darkened mass of endless hills and valleys, listening to the deep silence of a sleeping land. At last he turned back and locked the door. A sleeping land, but with hidden strength, too. Remembering that, he felt better. He went upstairs ready to face tomorrow.

Eighteen

ON SUNDAY MORNING, the message went out to Merriman's listening station in Grace Street. Renwick kept it brief: he'd take the full report to London himself and, with luck, that could be in a few days' time. It was enough now to give Gilman the essential facts about Rancho San Carlos and let him contact Washington for an immediate response—if not action, then certainly containment. Renwick also appended advice about Frank Cooper: on his arrival Monday, get him to postpone his visit to Grace Street—not only for its security but also for his own safety; tell him to stick to the law business until Theo's interest in him has cooled off. Frank wouldn't like the suggestion, but he would listen.

The message was received and acknowledged. Two hours later, Gilman sent a terse answer: *Will co-operate fully.* Renwick relaxed and began planning some way of slowing up the minibus later that afternoon. Keep it simple, he warned himself: all you need are photographs, a head count, a check on the bald instructor. Was he a regular, a permanent part of the training program?

So just before noon Sal paid a visit to Sawyer Springs in search of a Sunday paper and stayed for a chat with a couple of old-timers who sat on a bench outside the General Store and watched the passing traffic. There were three cars in twenty minutes by Sal's count, one of them stopping for directions to Palomar. "They're always getting lost," he was told as the car left. "Should have kept on the highway instead of coming around here."

"This road rejoins the highway, doesn't it?"

"About seven miles past the last house. A bad stretch of road, too. They'll be turning back. Just wait and see."

"The last house? Where's that?"

"Eight miles up the road. Used to be a big ranch. Horses."

"Oh, the San Carlos place? Miss Gladstone was telling us about it. A lot of new money. That should be good for business."

"Haven't seen it." A look was cast in the direction of the gas station. "Stan was expecting some. Didn't get it."

"I'd have thought there would have been a lot of gas sold. It's a big establishment, Miss Gladstone said."

"They don't go driving around. Don't keep many cars anyway."

Only a jeep, Sal learned, and Mr. Gunter's Mercedes-Benz. A beauty. Silver gray and fast, held the road, didn't need to slow down for the turns. Serviced in Escondido. Understandable, it was admitted: no spare parts for it here. The workmen didn't bring their cars. A small bus was provided for them by the contractor. Saved energy, it might be said; this gas shortage and all; was there an oil shortage? Never knew what these big companies were up to.

Sal got the drifting talk back to its moorings. "A bus can use a lot of energy, too. That is, if it makes many trips back and forth."

It didn't do that; Saturdays to Escondido, Sundays back here. He could see for himself if he just waited around until four-thirty. He'd see the truck, too. Brought in supplies for the week. Nothing too good for these boys.

"A truck? They must eat a lot." And need constant supplies of ammunition and explosives. Sal, leaving a couple of laughs behind him, waved good day and went back to Buena Vista empty-handed. There had been no newspaper to buy: all copies spoken for.

By quarter past four, Mac was driving the Chevrolet into the service station at Sawyer Springs. "Can you spare a few gallons? My tank is half empty." The owner and sole attendant (Stan, if Sal was correct) was glad to oblige, glad to talk with someone new. "Pretty quiet around here," Mac said as he got out of the car. He didn't have to add anything more. Sure it was quiet: few Sunday drivers, scared they'd run out of gas, what did you expect with all the odd-and-even-day rules, and the rising prices and that OPEC and those oil companies? The surmises and opinions lasted a full ten minutes. Then water and oil were checked while Mac strolled around the car and listened sympathetically to Stan's woes as a small businessman.

Mac halted, turning his back to the road as he heard a heavy engine coming uphill into Main Street. He raised his hand to his lips, kept watching. Quietly, he spoke into the small transmitter hidden in his palm. "Small truck. Passing now."

"Who found the goddamned oil wells anyway?" Stan was asking as he polished the windshield. "If I had my way . . ." He broke off, stood hands on hips, looking at the bus now traveling into sight.

"Bus. About to pass," Mac told his transmitter. He shut it off as he slipped it back into his pocket, took out a cigarette. "Have one?" he asked Stan. Not one head in the bus was turned in their direction.

"Don't even give us a good-day," Stan said, staring after them. He noticed the offered cigarette, shook his head. "Gave up the habit when I bought this place, started working the pump."

"Who was Sawyer?" Mac asked, getting into the car.

"Who?"

"Sawyer."

"Oh, him. Been dead for ninety years."

"Where are the springs?"

"They dried up."

Like everything else around here, thought Mac. He reached for his wallet. "What's the damage?"

He paid, talked some more. There was no need to hurry. Up at Buena Vista, a traffic jam should be in progress.

Sal let the truck pass. Then, as he received Mac's message signaling the approach of the bus, he began backing the station wagon out of Buena Vista's driveway. He turned the wheel just enough to put the big Dodge at an angle athwart the road. There, he stalled the engine, kept trying to restart it. All he created was a series of rasping sounds and a strong smell of gasoline.

Perfect, thought Renwick. He was well hidden by bushes, his favorite camera ready. The bus ought to come around the curve of road below the driveway and stop. There would be plenty of curses and genuine confusion until Sal could get the ignition started again and angle the station wagon around to face downhill. Even that last maneuver would take time: the Dodge was long, the road narrow.

The bus came around the turn, groaned to a halt. Renwick was barely fifteen feet away from it. He didn't expect a clear view of faces through glass windows, but he did hope to get—if curiosity and surprise were strong enough—several heads stuck out of the windows to see what the hell was going on. His hopes weren't disappointed. He began photographing. Six newcomers, he counted. And the baldheaded instructor.

They stayed inside the bus, let their driver get out to yell at Sal. "You're flooding it! Let your foot off the pedal. Stop pumping, goddamn it!" There were accompanying calls from the bus, far from complimentary. Sal pressed the pedal firmly to the floor, held it there, gauged when he could turn the ignition, and got the motor running. Now it was a matter of straightening the car. The bus driver shook his head, walked back, yelling now at his passengers to shut up. Renwick managed two pictures of him before he climbed into his seat. A good one, too, of old Baldy coming to the door to talk with him. And one, of course, of the rear registration plate of the bus as, at last, it started moving. Once past the station wagon, it picked up speed and soon was out of sight.

Mac returned from his visit to the gas station and found Renwick and Sal with broad smiles on their faces. "So it worked," he said with relief. He had had his doubts. They went indoors to have a quiet drink to celebrate.

Sal had one ludicrous note to impart. "The funny thing was the way that busload passed me: no more leaning out of windows; no more catcalls; all faces turned away from me." His amusement ended. "Foul-mouthed little bastards. There was a moment when I felt like getting out of the car and ramming those twelve-letter words right down their throats."

So Sunday's operation was over, thought Mac, and successfully. As a man who was devoted to the sophisticated device, he was still astonished by the simplicity of Renwick's approach. "What about tomorrow, Bob? Got another bright idea?"

"We'll think of something." A view of Gunter may not be so easy to arrange. We know he must either come through the town or make a detour by way of the Palomar highway. But there is a bad stretch of road linking up with that highway; that much we've learned. Can we take a chance Gunter won't risk his silver-gray Mercedes there? He'd have to slow down to a crawl, which would make it easier for me to see him—if there was any cover nearby. But we haven't enough men. If I'm stationed near the worst patch of road near the Palomar highway, will my transmitter carry all the way back to Buena Vista or Sawyer Springs, where Mac and Sal would be waiting? The distance could be beyond its range: we'd be left out of contact, floundering around; not know what was happening at the other end. "We'll take the chance that Gunter will choose the regular route. But we can't stage anything near our driveway again. We'll keep the action closer to Sawyer Springs." There was a long pause. Then suddenly Renwick was smiling. "How many bottles can you produce, Sal?"

On Monday their vigil began at daybreak. "We haven't a clue when he will arrive," Renwick had said as they finished a hasty cup of coffee in the kitchen. "So it's a fourteen-hour stint for us. Perhaps longer."

"And if he doesn't show?" Mac wanted to know.

"There's tomorrow. And tomorrow. And tomorrow."

"After four days—what? If he doesn't appear—"

"Then he risked using the other route, and we'll be facing another close-up view of Rancho San Carlos. How does that suit you, Mac?"

"Not much," Mac said and headed for the Chevrolet. He'd be stationed three miles below the start of Sawyer Springs' Main Street.

Sal and Renwick, carrying their load in two knapsacks, walked at an even pace down toward the town. On its outskirts, at a carefully chosen bend in the road after it had left Main Street, they halted and took shelter beside some trees with heavy undergrowth. They eased the packs off their backs, settled down to wait. It was now five o'clock. By ten o'clock, as the air warmed up, they had pulled off their sweaters. At eleven, they ate a chocolate bar, drank some water from Sal's flask. A garbage truck growled uphill. A bronze-colored, two-door Cadillac came down. An elderly man was at its wheel, a blue-haired lady sitting beside him: next-door neighbors going shopping in Escondido, or farther afield for a luncheon date. The garbage truck (unnamed, but Renwick had already caught its license number) returned, traveling at considerable speed. It made the curve safely. Well calculated, thought Renwick: the man knew this route, must be the regular driver for Rancho San Carlos. It was ten minutes to twelve.

September heat was rising. There was shelter in the shade of the bushes under which they lay, but the sun now beamed full strength at the road in front of them. On its other side, the far vista of open countryside lost its sharp outlines and lay peacefully drowsing in a warm haze.

At twenty minutes past twelve, Mac's signal came through. "Silver-gray Mercedes now passing. Estimated speed seventy."

Renwick and Sal were on their feet and out of the bushes, knapsacks in hand. In haste, they unfastened the buckles, opened the sacks and spilled out the contents across the road. Jagged fragments of broken glass lay gleaming in the bright sun. They kicked a few pieces into a better position, didn't waste any of them near the road's left-hand ditch or the fallaway of land on its right side. Renwick stood back for a second, eyeing the bits and pieces of glass. They didn't look carefully placed or too purposely set. Well worth the sacrifice of all their soda water, which had been poured down the kitchen sink, of their beer, of the jam and pickles and olives now in bowls; and of two large vases which could never have been anyone's delight.

Sal was already across the ditch and onto the low bank where their section of trees and heavy bushes lay. He waved frantically, relaxed as Renwick followed at high speed. They dropped on their faces, rested elbows on knapsacks, risked less than three inches of viewing space between the leaves. They wouldn't have long to wait: seventy miles an hour must have slackened for the run through Main Street, and then back to seventy for the surge uphill, with another slowdown for the bend in the road. If the driver was paying any attention, he'd see the glint of broken glass. He'd have time to slam on the brakes, bring the car to a halt. Just in front of us, thought Renwick as he reached for the camera in his hip pocket.

His hand had scarcely grasped it when the car came swiftly around the corner. He heard it, couldn't see it, daren't risk lifting himself on his elbow and twisting his head to his right for a better view. The shriek of brakes told him enough. He could almost feel the jolt of the car as it stopped dead, its hood no more than twelve feet away from him. Sal's body had stiffened, too. They lay absolutely still, waiting for the curses to end and the driver to step onto the road.

He wore a thin blue suit and a chauffeur's cap well pulled down to cover his hair. His face was rigid with anger, his jaw clenched, his chin and nose prominent as they pointed at the spill of broken glass. He walked quickly toward it. Renwick, his eyes still on the car, could hear him kicking the larger fragments aside.

"Clear it all!" a voice shouted from the car, and a man stepped out on its other side. He was tall enough for shoulders and head to be visible; the rest of his body was hidden by the Mercedes. His hair was fair and neatly cut, but that was all Renwick could see; the man was facing out toward the fine view of hills and valleys, but not in admiration. His head turned slowly as he scanned the sloping fields below him, looking for a movement, one sign of someone hiding down there. Then he swung around to look at the opposite side of the road with the same careful intensity. Renwick held his breath, didn't even risk an arm upraised to get his camera into position. There wasn't much need for it anyway. Gunter was Maartens.

The chauffeur shouted, "Can't clear it all. Not the smaller pieces. We need a broom."

"Use your cap and sweep them away," Maartens called impatiently, and studied the view once more. Now Renwick could angle his head, look up the road to catch a glimpse of the chauffeur's back as he swept the last remnants of glass aside. The man straightened up, turned toward the Mercedes, dusting off his cap against his thigh. Gray hair, cut short. Prematurely gray, for his face was that of a fairly young man with a sharp jaw line and a beak of a nose.

It can't be, Renwick thought, it can't be. . . . For a moment shock gripped him. Then as the man reached the car, saying, "You might have given me a hand," Renwick took his photograph, with Maartens in the background.

"Now, Hans," Maartens said, his bad temper subsiding as his worry and suspicion died away, "you've got your job, I have mine." One last look around him, and he stepped into the car.

Hans settled his cap firmly down over his gray hair, slid into the driver's seat. The Mercedes gently passed over the small glass particles still clinging to the road and gathered speed.

Renwick got up. "We better waste no time. They could send a couple of their yahoos down here to beat around these bushes, see if any trace was left." It can't be, he was still thinking, but it is. "We'll keep to the rough ground, circle to the back of the house. Come on, Sal, come on."

Sal straightened a clump of grass, swept his knapsack across the shorter blades where they had lain, adjusted a branch. "No traces," he said. He looked curiously at Renwick, but kept his silence until they were well away from the road. "Well?" he asked at last.

"That was Maartens. Now calling himself Gunter."

"And the other—you recognized him, too, didn't you?"

"He's a killer."

"The gray-haired fellow?" Sal shook his head. "You never can tell. He looked the spitting image of a math teacher I once had. What's his job at San Carlos—classes in assassination?" His amusement faded as he noticed Renwick's anger.

"How the hell," Renwick burst out, "did he escape custody? That's the guy who tried to kill me. How did he get loose, goddamn him?"

"Where was he being held?"

"Near Brussels."

In silence, they reached the house. Mac had just parked the Chevrolet in the garage. He looked at the two unsmiling faces. "Okay?" he asked anxiously.

"Okay. Very much okay," Renwick assured him.

Sal said, "I'll contact London. Gilman ought to know about this."

Renwick nodded. "I'll encode the message." And then he turned to Mac, clapped his shoulder. "Come on, I'll explain later. Now I need a drink." He led the way into the living room, still thinking about Hans, and found the one bottle of Scotch that hadn't been sacrificed. As he lifted it, he came out of his memory of a bad dream, his thoughts now on the scattered fragments of glass gleaming in sunlight. He began to laugh. "It worked. It actually worked."

"No suspicions?"

"At first, yes. Maartens lives on a diet of suspicions."

"He could have an attack of second doubts."

"We'll pack tonight, leave early tomorrow." Renwick frowned. "That real-estate girl—Gladstone?—yes, I think we owe her an explanation. Just can't walk out on her cold."

"We owe her," Mac agreed. "But what explanation?"

Renwick studied his drink. "Have you noticed many birds around here?"

Forest fire and blackened trees . . . "Not too many." Mac began to smile. "Most discouraging for a naturalist."

"I'll call her this evening," said Renwick. His spirits lifted: we are leaving; our job here is finished; and ten days ahead of time. Frank Cooper had allowed them two weeks. "I'll get that message off to London," he said, "and then I'll tell you about Hans."

Sal joined them, his eyes worried, his lips tight. "Got through to London and had an instant reply. Here!" He handed over Gilman's message to Renwick, who read it aloud. It consisted of three words: *Where is Frank?*

"He hasn't arrived?" Mac was unbelieving.

"Delayed," said Sal. "I'll contact his New York house." But he knew, as the others did, that Frank Cooper ought to have let Gilman know if there had been a delay.

There was no response from Cooper's place on East Sixty-first.

"What about his office?" Renwick asked. "Anyone there you know, Sal?"

"Wallace Rosen and Chet Danford."

"How many partners are there?"

"Forty-eight."

Two out of forty-eight . . . Possibly they were Frank's close friends. Renwick said, "You'd better drive down to Escondido, Sal. Telephone from there."

Sal nodded. "I'll try East Hampton first. If there's no answer, I'll try the office." He glanced at his watch. "One-thirty. Four-thirty New York." And it would take him half an hour or more to reach a telephone in Escondido. "I may just catch them," he said, already at the door.

"Let's hope Rosen and Danford are working late," Renwick said as he heard the Chevrolet being driven out of the garage.

"Are they part of Frank's brain trust?" Then as Mac watched Renwick, now walking restlessly around the room, he said, "Bob—stop that, will you? Frank's a wily old bird. He will outlast us both. Come on, lunch is on me: bread and cheese and a gallon of coffee. Then we can start packing some of Sal's gear. Three heavy suitcases, and a fourth for the clothes."

"How did he get that hardware through airport security?"

"He didn't. He borrowed most of it from a friend in San Diego." That, at least, got a laugh out of Renwick. Much better, thought Mac, as they went into the kitchen.

"Sal and his friends," Renwick was saying in wonder, and shook his head.

Sal was late. It was almost six o'clock before he returned. His face was set, his eyes expressionless.

"Didn't you reach them?" Mac asked.

Renwick said nothing, just kept watching Sal.

"I spoke with Rosen. Danford was down in East Hampton. Identifying the body. Frank is dead."

"What?" Mac burst out.

"He was found by the cleaning woman this morning. In his den. The police think it was suicide."

With a vehemence that startled even Mac, Renwick said, "No! Not Frank. No!"

"He has been depressed. Overworked. That's what the office is saying."

Renwick made an effort, controlled his emotion. "When?"

"Saturday." Sal's voice was unnaturally quiet.

"How?"

"A bullet through the head. With his .38. The pistol was beside him. The bullet was found."

Mac said, "I can't believe it. Frank?" The color had drained from his cheeks. "Any sign of intruders, Sal? Anything burglarized?"

"Rosen said nothing was disturbed. The back door was locked, the front door, all windows. The keys were on the hall table. He was sitting at his . . ." Sal couldn't finish, turned away, walked stiffly to his room.

There was a long silence. Then Renwick said, "I don't see Frank sitting at his desk with all the windows closed. In September?"

"You're telling me it was murder? Good God, Bob—the doors were secured. No forcible entry. He might have locked the windows to keep the sound of a bullet—"

"He would certainly have locked doors and windows if he were taking a walk. Frank wouldn't leave the house open—there were legal papers he was working on; his collection of guns and pistols was in his den." Renwick frowned, his eyes half closed as he tried to recall his memories of the cottage. "There's a lot of ground, left rough and natural, trees. No neighbors within sight. Yes, they could have jumped him on that driveway to the road."

"You're saying he might have been knocked unconscious and carried back into the house? You're supposing they'd find the door key in his pocket. Then they placed him at his desk, took the revolver from his collection, shot him in cold blood. God in heaven, Bob—you can't believe that! And what about the door? It was locked. The keys were on the table."

Renwick's eyes studied Mac. "I remember that door. It shut me out one afternoon. It locks automatically." Frank had thought it a very great joke: Bob Renwick forgetting to push a button and keep a door from locking. No kind of joke, any more . . . He looked up quickly as he heard a footstep behind him. How long had Sal been there? How much had he heard? I hope nothing, Renwick thought. But Sal was in control again; almost too controlled, too emotionless. This wasn't the Sal he had known. "We'd better send out word to London," Renwick said, rising to find paper and pencil.

He completed the message after several attempts. In the end, he simply wrote: *Frank died Saturday. Will give details Wednesday.* He signed it with his old code name, *Bush*. And suddenly his thoughts flashed back to a message he had to send almost two years ago; a message to Brussels with the exact same wording, days and all. Except the name wasn't *Frank*. It had been *April*. Oh, God, he thought, the more it changes, the more it's the same bloody thing. In silence, he handed the slip of paper to Sal.

"Uncoded?" Sal asked.

Mac had been watching Renwick. *Old Bob has been worse hit than I* thought: first, Jake Crefeld; now, Frank Cooper. "I'll do that, Sal. And then I'll call the airports at San Diego and Los Angeles, book the first flights out of there for all of us. We'll leave as soon as possible. The more distance we put between us and Pretty Boy Maartens and Killer Hans, the easier I'll be. Bob, you're heading for London. Right? Sal's for New York, and I'm for Montreal."

Sal was suddenly himself again. "We could leave tonight, stay in San Diego if necessary," he said to Mac. "We'll split up, of course. Go as we came. I've got some things to leave with a friend in San Diego; probably won't fly out until late tomorrow. Okay?"

"Fine. Can you drop off the house keys at the real-estate office? Make our excuses to Miss Gladstone—we won't have time to phone her tonight. Come on, let's move it." At the door to Sal's room, he halted to call back. "Did you hear what we're planning? Any improvements to suggest?"

Renwick said, "Don't forget the outside antenna."

He has recovered, Mac thought with a surge of relief. As he followed Sal into his room, he began explaining about forest fires and lack of birds—something that wouldn't hurt Gladstone's feelings and would raise no wonder in Sawyer Springs.

Mac was right: keep busy. Renwick went upstairs, started emptying their rooms of small items and clothes, making sure that not even a matchbook was left behind. For a few last moments, he stood at the window, looked at the rise and fall of hills stretching far to the south. The sun had set; the light was fading. But another day would follow tonight, take him to London and reports from Claudel and his friend the rug buyer. Istanbul must have had some messages from them: by this time they'd be following the camper out of Turkey. If all went well, they'd be following.

He carried the two suitcases downstairs. "Ready when you are," he told Mac.

One hour later, they were leaving. For their final minute together in the darkened driveway, all talk ended. In silence, they shook hands. In silence, they got into their cars. Mac and Sal were the first to go. Ten minutes later, Renwick followed. Sawyer Springs seemed already asleep, didn't even notice their departure.

Nineteen

THEY CROSSED THE Turkish-Iranian frontier in late afternoon, a small cavalcade of four cars and one brown camper, all heading for the nearest town before dusk set in. Tony Shawfield was in a thoroughly bad mood, partly due to the long delay at the border when Turkish officials were intent on how much money was being taken out of their country and Iranian officials were scrutinizing passports with heavy frowns. One Englishman, three Americans, one Frenchwoman, one Dane, one Italian, one Dutchman, was a total that baffled them; or perhaps it was three young women traveling with five young men, and only one couple married. But at last, with no drugs found and the pills in Shawfield's medical kit—all bottles clearly marked as aspirin or malaria or dysentery or digestive—briefly inspected, the campers were free to leave. Selim, their Turkish guide, who was accompanying them as far as Tabriz—this district spoke a Turkish dialect—hadn't been much help. The Iranian border officials were not of this province, he was explaining now to Shawfield and Kiley; they came from Tehran. "Religious fascists," he ended. "But we'll—"

"Shut up," Shawfield said. Kiley laughed and the rest of the group joined in. Except Nina. There was nothing funny about Selim's perpetual excuses to cover his failures; nothing funny, either, about the way all the others would laugh so easily without even knowing why they were laughing. But, thought Nina, I'm beginning to guess why, and I hope I am wrong.

"Are you all right?" Kiley asked, coming to sit beside her.

"Just tired and hungry."

"Well, it won't take long now. Selim recommends a small hotel on the outskirts of Tabriz. I thought we could all use proper beds tonight."

Nina stared out at the rolling plain and hills, at the backdrop of mountains. "That's Russia over there—to our left?"

Kiley nodded. "And to our right, the Kurds. We're giving them a wide berth—a lot of fighting, I hear." He spoke conversationally; he always did when politics came up. None of his business, there were other things in life, let's all be sane and sensible—and tolerant of people like Selim.

"What would Selim call them? Nationalist pigs?" That was a phrase he had used of the Armenians, of the government in Ankara, of both Turks and Greeks in Cyprus. "I wonder if he approves of anyone," Nina added with a smile. "His idea of politics seems to be hatred for everything: tear it all down, destroy, destroy. He belongs to Genghis Khan and a pyramid of skulls."

"He just likes to speak. Too much rhetoric. It's endemic in this part of the world." Kiley slipped an arm around her shoulder, drew her closer. The gesture, like his voice, was gentle, reassuring. Then he was talking about the field they were passing: a lot of cultivation around here, good grazing land, too; markets, plenty of markets in Tabriz—tomorrow she and Madge could go exploring them. "What are you going to buy?" he teased her. "Another skirt?"

"If I can get some money changed. Perhaps at this hotel—"

"I can get better rates for you tomorrow. I'll be going into town." He turned the conversation back to safer channels. "It was a good move to pack your jeans away. A pity, though. They suited you."

"If Madge and I had been wearing tight pants, I wonder how much longer we'd have been delayed at the frontier." She laughed. "We might even have been refused entry. Then Tony would really have had something to make him mad. Why does he get so uptight?"

"Selim gets on his nerves." And will I have a bad report to make on that loose-mouthed idiot, thought Kiley grimly: a playacting revolutionary who can't resist driving home the obvious. Not that the Dutchman Tromp or his good and dear friend Lambrese paid much attention to anything outside of archaeological remains, photography, and themselves. The French girl and her stolid Dane were lost in their world of music. Madge—a small problem at first—had stopped concentrating on him and now found some consolation in Tony Shawfield and his magic pills. If the Iranian border guards had taken five blood samples or listened to the confident voices and fits of laughter, they would have examined Tony's medicine chest with real interest. Nina was the holdout. ("I hate pills," she had said; "won't even take aspirin unless I have a hundred-and-three-degree fever.") And Nina was the one who noticed everything. But he could manage her. At this moment, he felt her body relax against him. "Also," he went on, "Tony hates driving with a pack of cars at his heel."

"He could slow up and let them pass."

"Tony?" That amused Kiley. "He wants to reach our sleeping place—I guess it's an Iranian version of a motel—before it's dark." And the four cars following might have the same idea, thought Kiley. Still, they had seemed fairly innocent. During the delay at the frontier he had drifted back, chatted with the drivers, made a genial exchange of small talk. The Mercedes immediately behind the camper had three Germans in the oil business. Next was the gray Fiat with a couple of Turkish carpet buyers. Then came a station wagon with a Swedish newspaperman, wife, and three children on their way to India. The last car was a rakish red Ferrari with two Australians bound for northern Pakistan. A race against weather, they had said; the newly completed highway over the top of the world, from Pakistan to China, could be closed by heavy snows in another six weeks. "In any case, no one passes Tony on the road. Or haven't you noticed?"

"Who are they—did you find out?"

Yes, Nina notices, Kiley thought. Not that it mattered in this instance. So he could give a humorous account of the people traveling behind them. "They'll never make it," he ended his description of the Australians. Brawn but no brain, he decided. Certainly not undercover men. No intelligence agent would travel in anything so noticeable as a red Ferrari.

But Nina's interest was caught by something else. "Carpets—Persian carpets? Oh, Jim, can you persuade Tony to take us to one of the towns where they are made? Not to the factories—to the places where families still spend years on one carpet. The designs—"

Kiley laughed, shook his head. "Oh, yes—designs again." Careful, he warned himself: don't imitate Selim and give a lecture on impoverished families being exploited by a few rich people who wanted an expensive rag to throw over a floor. "Why don't you ask Tony yourself? All right, all right— I'll do it," he agreed, watching the fleeting expression on her face. It seemed a good moment to probe. "What have you got against Tony anyway?" he joked.

Nina shrugged her shoulders.

"He isn't a tyrant, you know. He's easy to get along with."

"For you, yes. For the rest of us?"

"Madge seems to think he's okay. He talks a lot with her, doesn't he?" Kiley had made sure of that, even if Shawfield had at first resisted the idea: stupid little blonde, Shawfield had said. Kiley had insisted: Madge was Nina's confidante and a sure way at getting to Nina's private thoughts. She had them, thought Kiley as he looked at Nina, yet I never feel she tells me anything that really matters. Was that reserve part of her nature and nothing to worry about?

Yes, Nina was thinking, Tony talks and laughs with Madge now. Now. Not before our little trip through Greece, though. Only since Istanbul. It isn't the kind of thing I can even mention to Madge: she's convinced she has made a conquest. Perhaps she has. I'm only certain of one thing: Madge and I don't talk any more—not the way we did in London. What has happened to all of us? We've changed: Henryk and Guido, always sharing their own private jokes; Marie-Louise and her Sven, polite and amiable but remote somehow, impossible to talk with them except with pleasant little remarks that only skate over the surface. And everyone except me—and Jim and Tony—worrying about nothing, accepting everything, wild attacks of laughter and giggles followed by stranger fits of lethargy and vacant stares. They look but they don't see. They aren't on heroin—there are no punctures on their arms. What is it, then? This isn't just my imagination, she told herself. Or is it?

Kiley said, "And were all these thoughts for Tony? I'm envious."

She pointed to a background mountain. "What is it—a volcanic cone? We've seen so many of them all day."

Was this just a way of changing the subject away from Tony? But Nina did notice scenery. "You're a puzzle, Nina. What's in a view? Just another collection of hills."

"But not like those we saw in Greece, or in Yugoslavia, or in Switzerland or Austria. All those were different from each other, too. Just like the people who live among them."

"People are people. They're all the same. It's their economic environment that makes them seem different. And these are the differences that can be changed." Changed with a revolution that would end the differences, the inequalities, the barbarities of privilege.

"Changed by force? By proclamations and edicts? Social engineering, my father would call it. He'd give you a good argument against that, Jim."

"I'd probably agree with him," he said lightly. "Who talked about force or edicts anyway?"

"Then how do you change people into all the same pattern? First, you'd have to destroy all their values, all their achievements, everything that didn't agree with your ideas of how people should live. Then you'd have to get them to accept all your laws and regulations, change them into—"

"My ideas? My laws? Oh, come on, Nina." He was laughing now.

"Not *yours,* Jim. You know what I mean. It's a manner of speech." Suddenly she smiled. "My father would agree with you there. He never uses 'you,' always 'one.' One does this, one doesn't do that."

"What is your father exactly?" Kiley knew quite well what Francis O'Connell's function was: he headed the Bureau of Political-Economic

Affairs in Washington and was about to be given that peculiarly American position of ambassador-at-large. He would be jetting around the world mending political fences, shoring up breaks in economic dams, Mr. Almighty in International Affairs, Pinhead Supreme.

"Economics and politics, that's his thing," Nina said.

"You don't sound impressed."

"But I am. I just don't like impressing other people."

"Did he talk with you at all? Or was he too busy?"

Nina was angry. "We talked. We traveled together. At one time." Then she recovered, said, "He taught me a lot, actually. I'd put forward my ideas, and he'd argue them out. But patiently. I remember once—I was fifteen at the time—I wanted everything in the world to be equalized." Nina shook her head, laughing at herself.

"But he didn't believe in equality?"

"Before the law, yes. In civil rights, too. But how on earth, Jim, do you keep people equalized in what they do or what they want? I mean, you may force everyone—if you are ruthless enough—to be equal in earnings and in possessions, but how do you *keep* them equalized? I don't see how you can make a program of behavior for the whole world and expect it to stay the way you want it to be."

There was a brief silence. Thoroughly indoctrinated, Kiley thought, as he looked at the girl beside him. He raised a hand and pushed back a lock of her hair behind her ear. "There's that 'you' problem again," he said, and won a smile. "You're so beautiful, darling. Why do you bother your pretty little head with all that political talk?"

Bother your pretty little head . . . "I wasn't talking politics. I was talking about people."

"Of course," he said soothingly. "I think I'd better spell Tony at the wheel. He's just about had it with Selim chattering in his ear."

Whispering would be a better word for Selim, seated up front with Shawfield. "He looks like a conspirator out of a grade-B movie."

For a second, Kiley stared at her blankly.

"Selim," she explained. "Who else?"

Drawing his arm away from her shoulder, Kiley prepared to rise. "We'll soon reach our stopping place. Selim says the food is good there—plentiful, at least." With a brief touch of his hand on her cheek, he went forward. Seemingly, however, there was no need for him to take the wheel. He stayed beside Shawfield after elbowing Selim aside, cutting him out of their quiet conversation. Nina watched them for a few moments. Now we've got two conspirators, she joked with herself. Then her eyes turned to the gray landscape, a high plateau of dusty green surrounded by hills. As fields gave way to trees sheltering small cubes of houses built of earth-toned brick, she reached across the narrow aisle to shake Madge awake. "We are here."

"Where?" Madge straightened up, looked out the window.

"At the oasis."

"Oasis?" Madge's wits were slow in gathering. "Oh, you mean the town?"

"The outskirts." Always the outskirts, thought Nina. But tomorrow, somehow, I'll get into the center of this city, find the bazaar and a skirt to change with the one I'm wearing, find a bookstore and look for a map, newspapers, and magazines (will there be any in English?), and get malaria pills at a drugstore or chemist's or whatever it's called. "Madge," she said softly, "don't take any more pills from Tony. I think they're some drug."

"What's wrong with them? They are harmless, make you feel wonderful."

"They may not be harmless. They may lead—"

"It will soon be dark," Madge said curtly. The long road ahead, tree-lined, was unlit and already slipping into night shadows. To her relief, the camper slowed down before a flat-roofed building of virulent pink, one-storied, with a small gas station at one side. At the other side, where the camper was now following a rough driveway into a rear courtyard, was a café with its name in bold lettering of dashes, dots, and curlicues sprawled above a bleakly illuminated door.

They drew up in the courtyard, a large square of packed earth surrounded by trees on three sides. Other cars were following them, but there was room—and space to spare—for everyone. Shawfield still sat at the wheel as his crowd followed Selim out of the camper; he was ready to angle it into another corner of the yard if some cars were parked too near him. But they settled for the garage side of the inn. He noted them carefully: the Fiat with the Turks; the station wagon with the Swedes; even the red Ferrari and the Australians. Only the Germans in the Mercedes had preferred to go on their way with a more expensive lodging in mind. As his crowd straggled slowly across the yard to the entrance of the building, Kiley joined him. "We'll get them asleep by midnight," Kiley said. "Does that give you time?"

"That should do it. You'd better give O'Connell a pill tonight, make sure she's as stretched out as the rest of them."

"She's tired enough."

"Don't chance it," Shawfield warned him. "Hey, what is she doing now?"

Kiley looked across the yard to the small group halted outside the inn's central doorway. He swore, jumped out of the camper, then checked his pace to a saunter. Nina was talking with one of the Turks. The other was listening in rapt attention. So was Madge. And the Swedish couple. "Hello, hello," Kiley said genially as he reached them. "Quite a traffic block we've got here."

"I'm getting some names," Nina told him, excitement and success bringing her face to life. "Names of places where the best carpets are made." She turned back to the Turk, a handsome man with large dark eyes and a sweeping black mustache. "Would you repeat them again, please?" And then to Kiley, "Jim, can you note them down for me?"

"We may not be anywhere near these places," he warned her.

The Swedish newspaperman had his notebook out, ready for dictation.

"There are a few places in Tabriz," Nina was saying, "and some on the outskirts of Tehran."

"Ab 'Ali," prompted the Turkish carpet dealer. "Good as Isfahan. Ver' good at Shiraz. Also Kerman ver' good."

"I've got them," said the Swede, scribbling hard. "I'll give you a copy," he told Nina. "Tomorrow morning? I will draw you a little map, too."

"Wonderful."

"Very educational," he remarked to his wife as they left in search of the children.

"Thank you," Nina said to the carpet experts. They bowed gravely, spoke a phrase in Turkish as polite good-bye, and entered the inn.

"Their Turkish sounds better than their English," Kiley said, letting the Swedes pass inside. "Must be Eastern mind readers, too. How did they know you wanted to see carpets?"

"I asked them," Nina said. "It was simple."

Madge was laughing. "You know Nina. She just goes up to a stranger with her best smile and asks him if he speaks English. He looked a little astounded, I must say. Then he answered, 'Ver' good English.' But it did take him a few moments to understand her questions."

"Ver' simple," Nina said.

Kiley took her arm, led her indoors. "We'll have some music tonight. Marie-Louise tells me she has mastered two of the gypsy tunes that she heard in Istanbul. That was a good night, wasn't it?"

On the outskirts of Istanbul, Nina thought. But that had been a good night. In spite of her anger and almost-revolt on leaving the Hilton, she had enjoyed herself. Negative emotions had ebbed away, leaving only a touch of guilt: Jim was thoughtful, Jim was kind, and what was she? "Marie-Louise says one of these songs was brought from India by the gypsies. It's one of the ragas that are played there. She's hoping to trace it—"

"Ragas? We're getting fancy, aren't we?"

"Well, that's their name."

"How do you pick up all these little pieces of information?" He half turned to the entrance, where Shawfield and Madge had appeared. "I know—you go up to a stranger, stun him with a smile, and ask if he speaks English. That's how she does it, Tony. Got the names of carpet towns from our Turkish traders. Everything okay outside?"

"Locked up and secure." Shawfield looked around the small hall suffocated with large posters above its side counter, where Selim was superintending their registration. Ahead of him, through a wide doorway, he could see a dining room. Sparse lighting, but plenty of space. It looked clean even if it was overdressed with garlands of bright-colored paper flowers decorating cracks in newly plastered walls. Posters there, too: religious leaders in black turbans, the cult of personality, brooding over several large tables. At least, he thought, we won't be packed together with a mish-mash of strangers. "Could be worse," he said and relaxed.

Selim was triumphant. "We have three rooms. The Australians have one. The Turks have one. The Swedes have one. But I have obtained three."

"All together?" Shawfield asked.

"Impossible. Only three bedrooms on each side of this hall. The biggest one was required for the Swedish family. We have one on either side of them." He pointed to a corridor on his left.

"That will do." The three girls in one of them: Tromp, Lambrese, and Dissen in the second. "Kiley and I will take the room on the other side of the hall."

Selim's eyes were pleading. "And me?"

Nina said, "You could sleep in the camper. Couldn't he, Tony?"

Tony gave her a look that chilled her bones. "No one sleeps in the camper. It stays locked for the night."

Hastily, Selim said, "I'll sleep in the dining room. Okay? Now I need your passports."

"I'll collect them," Kiley said. Then to Nina, "Let's find your room and see if you'll be comfortable."

"Where are the bathrooms?" Madge wanted to know.

"One bathroom. Very nice," Selim assured her. "Next the kitchen." He pointed to his right. "Very new."

The kitchen would be easy to find: women's voices were loud and the smell of food was rich. Madge started in its direction.

"But much engaged," Selim called after her. "Everyone standing in good line."

Kiley led Nina along a narrow hall to its farthest room. "All right?" he asked anxiously.

"Fine." It was small, with three narrow cots, two wooden chairs, one window, and a row of pegs on one wall. "And we do have a bathroom even if we must stand in good line. Poor Selim—must he sleep in the dining room?"

"Do you think we want him bending our ear all through the night?" Kiley looked around the room again. The window, covered by a straight hanging curtain, was barred. "All right?" he asked again.

"Of course it is!" Nina handed him her passport. "I'll need that back by tomorrow morning. I'm going into town, and I'd better carry some identification, don't you think?"

"Why not wait until the next day? I'll take you into Tabriz then."

"Tomorrow you'll be busy?"

"Bank—a travel bureau to meet our new guide—a visit to the university to see a professor of English, an old friend from Chicago. Yes, I guess you could say I'll be busy. Everything takes time in this part of the world. I'll leave fairly early in the morning. Around eight. You just rest up or explore the food markets nearby. You'll see a lot of new types there." Again he looked anxiously at her. "All right?" he asked for the third time.

"Yes." Her voice softened, a smile came into her eyes. "I do notice the trouble you've taken. I'm not ungrateful, really I am not."

He caught her in his arms, kissed her long and hard, would have kissed her again but the door opened and Madge came in.

Almost three o'clock in the morning and wide awake. Nina turned over again on her cot. Its mattress was thin, with a middle depression. Silence everywhere outside, making Marie-Louise's snores seem louder than they were. Madge lay still, gently breathing. Both had fallen into deep sleep by midnight. I'm tired, yet I can't sleep, Nina thought: it's this small room and the window closed, securely locked. What are the owners of this inn afraid of? Prowlers or night air? I'm suffocating.

She rose, drew on her dark-blue robe—practical in weight and color for traveling—and found the pen flashlight in its pocket. She switched it on to search for her sandals, and then played its weak small beam across the floor to lead her safely to the door. Quietly, she turned the key. "Keep this door locked," Jim had said as he kissed her good night. So she drew the key out, closed the door and locked it, slipping the key deep into her pocket as she started along the corridor. Dark and silent, with deep breathing from the Swedes' room, with steady snores from Sven, Guido, and Henryk next door. She switched off her flashlight before she reached the entrance hall, where one small bulb had been left burning. The counter that served as a reception desk was empty. The owner of the inn must be in bed and asleep, lucky man. But voices were coming from the dining room. One meager light there—such extravagance, she thought with a smile, recognizing Selim's voice. The other talker? It could be the owner's son, who had bustled around the dining tables, directing the waiters—four small boys, thirteen or fourteen years old, anxious and willing and overworked. She looked at the front door, wondering if Selim and his friend would hear the turning of its heavy key. It might be better if she told them that she was only wanting ten minutes of cool sweet air. But she knew what would happen: Selim would come with her, talk and talk. No, she decided, not that. She'd be driven inside within four minutes flat.

She reached the door. The key in its lock was massive. It wouldn't turn. Then she realized it wouldn't budge because it was already in the unlocked position. Some security, she thought: windows shut and covered with iron screens, and an entrance door left open for anyone to enter. She stepped out into the yard, pulling the door closed behind her to cut off the insistent murmur of voices from the dining room.

There was only a sliver of moon, but the stars were clear and beautiful. She drew long deep breaths, welcoming the cold air. Dawn was still some time away. No wind, not even a breeze to stir the surrounding trees. The parked cars, three neatly placed shadows, their color eaten up by the night, were at one side of the yard. The camper, curtains drawn, stood aloof like some proud beauty. And its lines were good, she admitted. Custom-built, outside as well as in. It must have cost Tony all of his savings; no wonder he guarded it so constantly. Then, as she studied it, she saw a faint almost imperceptible glow spreading into the darkness from the ventilation window on its roof. Careless of Tony, she thought at first: he left one of the small lights turned on. Or has someone broken into the camper?

She hesitated, looked at the door behind her. No, she had better make certain the camper really had been entered before she alerted Selim. A false alarm and she would be apologizing all tomorrow for waking up everyone: Selim wouldn't handle this quietly; of that she was sure.

Cautiously, she approached the camper. Its hood pointed toward a line of trees, its rear end—with its door—stretched into the center of the courtyard. If anyone is inside, she told herself, I'm not risking that back door: it could be opened at any moment. The side of the camper was safer; its curtained windows, slightly opened at the top to air it thoroughly, should let her hear the sounds of anyone moving around. She reached it and steadied herself against its smooth surface, her legs suddenly weak. She was more nervous than she had realized. Nervous? She was terrified.

She calmed down. There was no movement inside the camper. Tony had been careless about the light, that was all. With relief, she was about to turn away. And then she heard a voice raised in a sudden burst of anger. Jim's voice. Good old American swearwords, she thought, and smiled. And stopped smiling as he broke into German. Another voice answered him, speaking German, too. Tony's? The pitch was Tony's—that short bitter laugh was Tony's—but in German? Neither of them knew much German, had never been in Germany, had called on Sven Dissen for help in being understood when they were in Basel, in Innsbruck.

Disbelief and shock seemed to paralyze her body. Unable to move, she stood with her hand resting on the camper's side. She couldn't hear much, now that the voices had quietened. In any case, their fluent exchange was too quick for her, far beyond the German she had learned at school. Something about "a change," "arrangements canceled," "new arrangements made." The word "Afghanistan" was repeated twice. So was the phrase "absolutely necessary."

And then Tony's voice became clearer—he must have moved close to the window near where she stood. "They will call us again. At twelve noon. What is your message?"

Jim's reply was less audible, but it sounded authoritative.

Tony said, "Okay. I will tell them."

There was a brief silence. Suddenly, she heard the rear door open. Nina took an uncertain step away, abandoned her hope of reaching the inn. Instinctively she edged toward the front of the camper, feeling some protection from its solid body. They were talking as they closed and locked the door, their voices sounding so near that she was unnerved. Quickly, she moved to the nearest tree, only six paces away. She drew behind its trunk, her heart beating wildly, her eyes on the two men as they started a slow walk to the inn. From behind her, an arm went around her waist, a hand went over her mouth.

"Don't scream," a voice whispered in her ear. "Please don't scream. And how could we explain this situation to Mr. James Kiley?" Her struggles ceased. The hand left her lips. "Sorry. There was no other way." The arm was still firm around her waist, supporting her now. She needed it. "I'm a friend," the whispering voice said. "Your Turkish adviser on Persian carpets."

Nina turned her head to look. It was too dark to see anything clearly beyond black hair, black mustache, and a wide smile. "Your English has improved."

"Sh!" he told her, his eyes on the courtyard. He drew his left arm away from her waist to let him raise the small object he had been gripping in that hand to his ear.

Nina heard a faint murmur of voices, stared at the small object. A radio? No—something else, picking up the sounds of talk in the courtyard. "You're eavesdropping!"

"Weren't you?" He pulled her closer, so that she could listen, too.

"They're speaking English now," she said in astonishment.

"Someone at a bedroom window might hear them. Wiser to get back into character, don't you think?"

She stared at him.

He remained silent, listening, until Kiley and Shawfield had entered the inn. Then he clicked off his receiver and slipped it into his pocket. "Did you get any of that?" he asked.

"Not much. I stopped listening," Nina said unhappily.

"It was of little importance." Nothing compared to what had been already discussed in the camper, Pierre Claudel thought. "Merely their projects for tomorrow. Shawfield will have extra work to do—he will study maps, plan a new route. Kiley leaves at four o'clock to meet his friends."

"At four? No, he said. . ." Eight o'clock, she remembered, and closed her eyes.

Claudel glanced at his watch. "Thirty-five minutes before he leaves. I think you had better remain here until then. He might be having breakfast in the dining room."

Nina nodded, bit her lip, fought back a sudden attack of tears.

"I'll stay with you. Bob Renwick would insist on that."

"Bob Renwick?"

"Yes," Claudel said mildly. "We are good friends. I saw him in Istanbul before I left. When he heard I was traveling this way, he asked me to keep an eye open—speak with you—find out if you were all right."

This is a trick, Nina thought. This pleasant, frank-spoken man could be lying—just as Jim Kiley has lied. She said, "I don't believe you."

"Bob thought you probably wouldn't. So he gave me this." Claudel reached for his wallet and handed her a card. Then he pulled out a thin pen, flashed on its small light, shielding it with his cupped hand as he turned his back to the yard.

Nina read: J. P. *Merriman & Co., Consultant Engineers. Advisers on Construction Abroad. Surveys made.*

"Look at the back," Claudel urged.

Courtyard of the Janissaries. Nina looked up in amazement, held Claudel's eyes with hers. Then her face hardened. "You could have been there—seen us together."

"Yes." He switched off his flashlight. "But I couldn't have heard how you pitied the tribute children." He heard her sharp intake of breath. She kept staring at him.

"Not even with that listening device?" she asked.

"By the time you were talking about janissaries, I was far away, too far for even the—that device to reach. It has its limits even with all its latest improvements." That reminded him of something. He said, "Wait here. I'll only take five minutes. I'll come back. I promise you. Will you wait?"

She looked toward the inn. Jim Kiley might be in his room; again, he might not. She nodded. "I'll stay."

Claudel took the card from her hand. "It's safer with me," he told her. It went back into his wallet. He touched her hand encouragingly. "My God, you're freezing!" So the wallet went into a trouser pocket as his jacket came off and was placed around her shoulders. "Five minutes," he said and left.

He didn't go directly to the camper, although it was only a short distance away. Instead, he used the trees on his left to circle partway around the yard until he found a spot where the camper's bulk would block his approach if anyone was looking out a bedroom window. Then, as he judged it safe enough, he darted forward. Nina could see him, barely twenty feet away from her, reach the side of the camper that was not visible from the inn. His hand was raised, touching something on one of the windows, pulling it away. Then his hand was lowered and he pocketed whatever he had removed, and he was retracing his steps exactly. She watched his dark shadow merge into the row of trees, lost him completely as he worked his way back to where she stood. What had he taken from the window? Another gadget, something to let him listen clearly to any sounds inside the camper? She could only guess. And guess at this man's interest. It wasn't with her—it was with Jim Kiley and Tony Shawfield. Why? But I'm interested in them, too, she thought bitterly. I've been used. All of us have been used, manipulated. The rest of our group still don't realize it, never will. And I never would have if Bob hadn't sent his friend—Where has he gone? She panicked for a moment, and then relaxed as he left the neighboring tree and stood beside her.

"Okay," he said softly. He fell silent, his eyes on the inn.

That was all he was going to say, Nina realized. But she had questions. "Who are you? You are not Turkish, are you?"

He dodged that neatly. "My mother was French. I went to school in England." Both statements were true.

So that explained his accent: idiomatic English with a hint, every now and again, of French. "What shall I call you?"

"My mother chose Pierre," he said briefly. Again, true.

She looked at the inn. "Are they German?"

"I don't know. They aren't strangers to the language, that's certain."

"Why use it?"

"They may have received a message in German, just continued talking in it."

"May have? Didn't you hear it?"

He hesitated. "It doesn't work that way. They received a message, yes. In code. They decoded it from German and continued talking in German."

"Received a message . . . But how? On our camper radio?"

He repressed a smile. "No. Something more sophisticated than that."

"Hidden. Where?"

He shrugged his shoulders. He had noted its antenna, the long wire that ran cleverly under the edge of the camper's roof. "It could be anywhere inside the camper."

"I'll find it."

"No," he said sharply. "What you have to concentrate on now is—escape. Leave tomorrow. With me. I'll see you onto a plane to Tehran. You'll fly to Rome. Renwick will meet you there. I'll let him know."

She said slowly, "So that's why Bob wanted you to meet me. . . . This was his idea, wasn't it?"

"Yes. But not exactly this kind of meeting, at this time, in this place. He wants you out. He's counting on that."

"What about Madge? We're together." More or less. Without Madge I'd never have joined the camper. I wanted the world trip, yes. It seemed a dream for the taking. But I'd never have come alone. "I can't walk out on her. I'd have to tell her."

Claudel shook his head to that idea. "Ask her—in a general way—if she's had enough. Suggest leaving, but give no details. Don't mention tonight, or this talk. If she's willing, bring her along. If she says no, then you'll feel free to leave. Would that work?"

"No. Madge would wonder, be alarmed. She'd talk. Shawfield has become her friend. It's too dangerous, Pierre. For you as well as for me. Shawfield would have you arrested at the Tehran airport for kidnapping."

Nothing quite so official as that, Claudel thought. Shawfield's type of friends in Tehran would do a little kidnapping of its own: two bodies found in some back alley. Silently, he cursed Madge and the problem she presented. "Leave," he urged. "Get out of this mess. Why do you think I told you so much, let you see so much? Goddamn it to bloody hell, I've—" He broke off in frustration.

"I know," she said. "You risked everything in order to shock me into leaving. You did shock me. But I can't leave. Not yet." She reached for his arm, pressed it reassuringly. "I won't go running to Shawfield. Or to James Kiley. Or anyone."

He stared at her in disbelief. "You really think you can go on, never let them know, never give your real feelings away? No, no. Now that you've learned so much, you're in double danger."

"On the contrary. Now that I know—and it isn't so much, either—I'm on guard."

"Not so much?" My God, he thought, when Renwick hears how I broke the rules tonight, he'll—no, perhaps Renwick wouldn't. He can guess what I'm dealing with here; he warned me about Nina. And I thought I could handle her.

"No," Nina was saying. "You didn't tell me who sent Kiley's instructions tonight."

His quick French wits failed him for a moment. He searched for an answer, found none.

"Are Kiley and Shawfield working for the Russians?" she asked.

"Indirectly," he hedged.

"What on earth does that mean? The Russians are in charge?"

"From a safe distance."

"Then who is—"

"Sh!" he said. Their voices had been kept to a murmur all through their talk, but now complete silence was needed. He pointed to the inn. Its door had opened. And simultaneously, from around the far corner of the inn where the gas station lay, a farm truck, small in size, loaded with baskets, drove quietly into the yard. It barely stopped at the inn's door—less than a minute to let Kiley emerge and climb on board. Then it left, easing its way into the rough driveway, and turned right as it reached the main road. It looked like any truck heading for one of the early markets in Tabriz. Claudel glanced at Nina. Yes, she had seen it all.

She slipped off his jacket, handed it to him. "It will soon be daylight. When do we meet again?"

"You won't leave with me tomorrow?"

"No. But couldn't we meet—"

"Not here. You'll be taking the southern highway out of Iran—into Baluchistan, then Pakistan."

"No Afghanistan. Why? There's been some trouble, I know, but we were to have an escort. Jim said it would be safe."

"No longer. Eight foreigners killed last week, one on a tourist bus. There's more than trouble there. It's war. Atrocities on both sides. Soviet troops, Soviet tanks are massing at the border, and Muslim rebels are massacring anyone who looks like a Russian."

"Then why did we ever plan to go through Afghanistan?"

"Because the planning must have been done months ago. You don't imagine, surely, that this trip was arranged in a few weeks? That camper you're traveling in—it wasn't custom-built in less than three or four months. History just caught up with them: their plans had to be changed. So, as there are only two decent roads leading east out of Iran, one through Afghanistan, one through Baluchistan, I know which one you'll be taking. I can't tail you. Too many bare stretches. But I'll meet you. Somewhere. Possibly near Kerman. Remember that name."

"The carpet place."

"Have you got a map?"

"No." She thought of the kindly Swede. "But I can get one. Safely."

He was beginning to see the expressions on her face. Daylight was coming up. "Back to the inn," he urged her. "They've left the door open. You may find a woman sweeping out the hall. They rise early here."

"I'll think of some excuse. And thank you. And don't worry. Tell Bob—" Her voice faltered. "Thank him." She slipped away, quickly reached the camper and then slowed her pace to a normal walk.

Claudel watched her enter the inn. So I failed, he thought, and the admission was bitter. But he'd have another try at Kerman. And this time he would have a plan prepared. Beyond Kerman, at Zahidan, not far from the Baluchistan frontier, there was a crossroads where the road to the east met the road coming down from the north. It had been built by the Soviets, in one of their agreements with the ex-Shah, to run south to the Persian Gulf. That could be our escape route, he thought. If she will come. What is holding her back? It's just possible she has done what Renwick didn't want to do: she has recruited herself. She doesn't know it yet, but that's what she has done.

The inn remained quiet, undisturbed. Nina must have made it safely to her room. With relief, he began making his way along the rows of trees that edged the yard, aiming to reach the inn from an angle that was the opposite of Nina's approach. And there *was* a woman, smothered in black, who was washing the floor of the dining room. Selim's voice, speaking in Turkish dialect, was listing his complaints about an uncomfortable night. The woman was dutifully silent, just moved on her knees to the next part of floor to be washed. Claudel slipped silently down the dark passage to his room.

Fahri was awake and waiting. "Well?" he demanded.

Claudel repressed his excitement. "We have big news to send out."

"Anything about Turkish terrorists?"

"Yes. They were discussed. They are not inclined for united action, insist on continuing assassination as their best means at present. But they took Kiley's money, listened to his proposals. If Shawfield can guarantee shipment of weapons—they gave him a list—they'll use them as he directs." Claudel took out his receiver. Nina, he thought, would have opened her blue eyes even wider if she had known it could record as well as listen. "The little miracles of modern technology," he said with a laugh. He kissed the receiver and set it gently on top of his suitcase. "It's all in there—discussions about Bursa and more. Much more. Okay, let's start it talking to us, and we'll condense its news." Tomorrow, somewhere on an empty stretch of road, they'd send the completed report to Kahraman in Istanbul. From there, it would be transmitted to London. Another report would go to London, too: for Renwick, about his Nina.

"Now?" Fahri asked. "Do you need no sleep?"

"I'll catnap while you drive."

"We are leaving? Is one day here enough?"

"Quite enough. Let's get to work."

Fahri was listening. The stillness outside was broken by a distant voice calling from the peak of a minaret, chanting its summons to the faithful. Fahri rose, unrolled his prayer rug.

So night is over, Claudel thought, and the new day begins. He stretched out on his cot, closed his eyes. He'd snatch twenty minutes of deep, delicious sleep.

Twenty

BY THE LAST week of September, they were on their way out of Iran. It had been a start at daybreak from Kerman. "Not much more than two hundred miles to the frontier," Kiley said as encouragement to his shivering flock as they sat in bleak silence, sweaters and jackets around hunched shoulders, and stared out at less and less foliage, more and more sand. "In another couple of hours you'll start complaining that you're being roasted." He's sharp-set this morning, Nina thought as she heard the edge in his voice: what is worrying him? It can't be our Iranian guide and interpreter—Ahmad isn't a continual talker like Selim.

Ahmad and Shawfield were tense, too, their eyes on the road ahead. It was empty enough: one car, occasionally visible when the road straightened and the small hills—sand dunes, actually—no longer interfered with the view. For once, Tony Shawfield wasn't trying to pass the car in front of them: he let it draw well away, eventually be lost from sight. Ahmad looked at his watch, spoke to Tony, who nodded and put on his usual speed, and began watching the wind-molded desert on the left-hand side of the road.

"There are cars behind us," Kiley warned. "I make out two."

"How far behind?"

"Difficult to judge. These damned sand hills—" He broke off, noticing Nina's strange mixture of interest and dejection. "You don't look too happy, Nina. Didn't you see enough carpets at Kerman?" he teased.

She nodded. But in our two days there, I saw no sign of my Turkish friend who had a French mother and an English education. Near Kerman, he had said. "It's all this emptiness," she told Kiley. "No one lives here. Not one real village."

"Only caravan routes. Actually, this road used to be one of them. We're in luck, the north wind—the Wind of a Hundred and Twenty Days, as Ahmad calls it—has blown itself out." That diverted her attention, as he had guessed it would.

"Is it the wind that causes all this erosion?"

"Lifts sand out of one place, builds it up in another. It can be violent. So we're in luck," he repeated. Good management, he told himself, and waited for her to notice that. But the barren land had silenced her completely. A signal from Ahmad caught his attention. At last, he thought with a surge of relief: this shouldn't take long—not much talk to be exchanged, just a packet of money. He would be glad when he had got rid of the bulky envelope strapped to his waist. This country was too lonely for a feeling of safety.

"Look!" called out Guido Lambrese, and had Henryk Tromp reaching for his camera.

"What is it? A fort?" Sven Dissen suggested.

"It looks empty," Madge said. "Couldn't we stop?"

All of them were too startled by the sudden appearance of the solid, strong, unembellished building, rising squarely from a stretch of flat sand, to notice that Shawfield had already slackened speed. The camper came to a halt. There was a rush to get out. "Hold it!" Kiley warned them. "Let's make sure it's deserted. Safety first."

"Safety? What's dangerous in an old fort?" Madge asked.

"It may not be deserted," said Nina. There were fresh tire marks leading from the road toward the silent building. Cars might be parked out of sight behind the towering bulk of hewn stone. "What *is* it, Jim?"

Ahmad said, "A caravanserai. A place where caravans stopped for the night. Their camels and donkeys went inside also, and slept beside the women. The men protected them from any attack."

"How?" Madge asked. "Through those slits in the walls?" There were no windows.

Ahmad, as was his way, didn't answer the obvious. With his usual disdain for all foreigners' ignorance, he descended onto the road and waited impatiently.

Damn him for a know-it-all, thought Kiley: he has said the one thing that will make them determined to get inside the place. Its vast door, high enough for a fully loaded camel to enter, was wide open to show gaping darkness. An invitation to explore. He cursed under his breath. "It may not be empty. So we'd better find out who is inside before we walk into something we can't handle. Tony—you come with me. And we'll need Ahmad to speak the language and get us out of there—if we meet any sign of trouble."

"Trouble?" Madge was excited.

"You want to lose that little Kodak of yours?" he joked, and dampened her enthusiasm. It also ended Tromp's. His Japanese camera had cost eight hundred American dollars. "Wait here," Kiley told them. "Guard the camper. Don't leave it, remember! We'll signal you if we find only a couple of camel drivers having a midmorning rest."

"Where are the camels?" Madge asked.

"Inside with the women and children," Nina said. "Watch out for those slits, Jim. There's a homemade rifle pointing at you right now."

He looked at her sharply, and then laughed.

"A funny sense of humor that girl has," Shawfield said sourly as he walked off with Kiley and Ahmad. The distance ahead of them was short, barely a hundred yards.

At the camper, the group gathered together. Lambrese studied the uncompromising shape of the caravanserai. "Pathetic," he said. His taste ran to the Parthenon, or at least Doric pillars.

Tromp said, "It was built for defense, Guido."

"Even so—just think what the Knights of Rhodes could have made of it."

"Grim," Dissen agreed. "What's that lying outside its threshold?"

"It doesn't move," Marie-Louise said. "Something dead?" She took a step forward. Then another. Her husband followed her, so did Lambrese and Tromp. All four were soon walking slowly toward the caravanserai. They halted as Kiley looked round, waved them back.

Nina watched them, Madge still indefinite about staying beside her or joining the others. We aren't meant to see inside that place, Nina thought. Jim and Tony and Ahmad were now skirting the motionless object to step into the yawning blackness beyond the entrance.

Curiosity drew the others another twenty yards nearer the caravanserai. Again they halted. "It's a dead donkey," Marie-Louise cried out. "*Affreux!*"

At that moment, a car from Kerman passed the camper, traveling rapidly. Behind it came another—a gray Fiat. It slowed down, stopped. "Have you trouble?" a man called in halting English. "We help, perhaps?" Pierre got out, raised his eyebrows. "Ah, the young lady who wish to see carpets. You like them?"

"Damn!" said Madge, looking at the rest of the group, who were now halfway to the caravanserai. Henryk was busy photographing. "We're missing all the fun."

"I'll guard everything here. Go ahead."

Madge needed no urging. Kodak in hand, she left at a run.

Quickly, Pierre came forward, took cover at the side of the camper, placing its body between him and the caravanserai, beckoning to Nina to follow. She watched in astonishment as he bent to feel something underneath its rear fender. Whatever he had checked there pleased him. He gave a broad smile and a forefinger salute to Fahri, who sat at the Fiat's wheel, then began speaking rapidly. "You'll stop at Zahidan for lunch. I'll be watching for you. Make some excuse; leave them, and follow me. To a car—not this Fiat; it goes on to Pakistan. We'll drive back into Iran and then head south for the Hormuz Strait. We'll get a boat easily and sail—"

"No." That whole terrain was a wasteland. The map the kindly Swedish couple had given her in Tabriz showed only hundreds of miles of nothingness. "I am not leaving. There's no need. I'm safe enough."

"Your friend? Is she still—"

"Still determined to stay. Besides, there's too much risk for you. You're putting yourself in danger."

He could agree with that, but it was worth a try. "Who, me?"

"You," she said firmly. "I can't leave. Later—"

"It would have to be much later. In Bombay." He shook his head.

"Another month. The last week in October—so Jim Kiley told me. I think it was the truth. This time."

The date agreed with the one he had overheard in the Tabriz courtyard. He stared at her. She was obdurate. "Do you know Bombay? Have you a map of it?" There was a quick shake of her head, a look of momentary fear in those blue eyes. "One of the big hotels—they're close together, central; you'll find them easily; any taxi driver can get you there—is the Malabar. You'll see its name—in big letters." He had taken out a small pad and pencil, was jotting down some figures. "Ask for Mr. Roy—A. K. Roy. Give your name: Nina. That will be enough." He tore off the sheet of paper and handed it to her. "That's his private number."

"Roy," she repeated. "The Malabar Hotel. Is he English?"

"Indian. Someone at that number will take your message and arrange a meeting at the hotel with me or with—" He stopped short of saying Bob Renwick. Why promise what might not be? "With someone you can trust. We'll get you safely out of Bombay. I can't risk meeting you before then, but don't be surprised if you see two Australians around. The red Ferrari—remember it?—well, it needs repairs. So if you've learned about any further stops on your journey, tell them. If you sense danger to yourself, tell them. They will improvise. And remember—" Fahri had a fit of coughing. Pierre moved toward the Fiat. "Destroy that number" were his parting words. He stepped into the car. It left.

For a moment, Nina wished she hadn't been so firm in her refusal. She slipped the piece of paper into the deep pocket of her wide skirt. Later, she'd memorize its numbers and then drop it, in a dozen small pieces, down the horrible hole in the floor of some abominable bathroom. Now, she must walk around the camper and face the caravanserai. Kiley and Shawfield were in view, their heads turned to watch the departing Fiat. Ahmad was shouting at the Dutchman, who had taken a photograph of the donkey just as the three men had emerged. The others were protesting: why couldn't they go inside—they wouldn't take long—just a quick look? But they listened to Kiley, as they always did, and he shepherded his flock of straggling sheep back to the road.

He repeated his explanation to Nina. "There are a couple of men inside there, ugly-looking types. Ahmad had to do a lot of fast talking to get us out. They looked as if they'd slit our throats for our shirts and shoes."

"Couldn't we risk a crowd of us going in?" she asked.

"They're armed. We are not."

"I wish I could have seen it." That seemed the expected remark.

"Not much to see. An empty space with a well in the center—silted up. It's dark—has a roof over it, probably to keep the sandstorms out."

"Was that all?"

"There's a stone staircase—no guard rail—leading to a small gallery around the walls. They must be four feet thick. Once that place was as strong as a fortress. Now—just piles of refuse. And the smell! The dead donkey was no help. Its belly was swollen, bloated—enormous. I thought it would explode any minute."

She looked at him in horror. "Just left to die . . . Oh, Jim, let's get away from here."

"I agree. Sorry to leave you by yourself. The others shouldn't have deserted you. You weren't feeling lonely, were you?"

"I was," she admitted. "Then a car stopped—they thought we might need help—had run out of gas or something."

"That was the gray Fiat?" he questioned.

He recognized the car, she realized: he knows who was inside it. She managed a smile. "Yes. Our ver' good Turkish friend—remember? At the inn near Tabriz? We talked carpets until his English ran out."

"Absorbing topic," Madge said as she brushed past Nina to climb into the camper. "Never mention 'carpet' to me again. I've had it."

So have I, thought Nina, aware of Shawfield's sharp glance, first at her, then at the camper's interior, as he held out a hand to pull her up its steep step. At this moment, she again wished she had listened to Pierre, gone with him, left Shawfield's constant scrutiny. He frightened her: there was something hard, unbending in his expression. He just didn't like people—he was too absorbed by mechanics and his own efficiency. See, Tony, she told him silently, nothing has been disturbed: I guarded the camper well. She mustered a steady hand as he helped her mount the step. Unusual gallantry: did he think he could feel her nervousness? "Lunch at Zahidan?" she asked, her voice as steady as her hand had been.

"No. We'll wait until we reach the Baluchistan frontier. There may be a wait for customs and inspection. The Pakistanis worry about arms; the Iranians worry about drugs. The Baluchis on both sides of the border live on smuggling."

"Drugs?" Lambrese asked, exchanging a covert glance with his friend Tromp.

"Sure. The stuff is manufactured in Pakistan—something halfway between opium and heroin." That should catch their attention, thought Shawfield.

"Morphine sulfate tablets," Sven Dissen informed them all. His friendship with Pakistani medical students in Paris made him an authority on the subject. He needed no urging to enlighten everyone. He did so at length as they settled in their seats and the camper started forward. The poppies grew in northern Pakistan, but the tablets were manufactured all over the

place. Now, the old Turkish-Marseilles connection had become interested:
they were organizing the drug trade from Pakistan to Amsterdam, Zurich,
Copenhagen, Frankfurt.

"But never to Russia," Nina murmured.

Kiley heard that small remark. He said, "Perhaps your Turkish friends
aren't so interested in carpets after all." As she stared blankly at him, he
added with a smile, "If they meet us again, better keep clear of them. Which
reminds me—" he raised his voice for all to hear—"no smuggling from
Pakistan across the Indian frontier. Prisons in this part of the world are no
health resorts. So don't try smuggling, anyone. Remember!"

Lambrese and Tromp exchanged a second glance. "No one is interested
in smuggling, James," Lambrese assured him with perfect truth.

Just in pleasant dreams between frontiers, thought Shawfield. "Traffic is
increasing," he called, and pointed to a slow file of five heavily laden camels, three overloaded donkeys, four men and two boys wrapped in odds and
ends of old clothes. Bulky head scarves were wound loosely around their
heads to form rakish turbans, then twisted around their necks to cover half
of their faces. "Baluchis, I think."

"Stop!" Henryk Tromp called out. "Just five minutes for a photograph."

"No time," Shawfield told him. "You'll see plenty of caravans in the next
three weeks. Caravanserai, too." Under his breath he said to Ahmad, "That
bloody camera."

"Do not worry," Ahmad told him quietly. No one took photographs of
Ahmad coming out of that caravanserai. His brows came down, his lips tightened, his heavy mustache bristled. He looked at the passing Baluchis with
contempt.

Shawfield nodded. "You deal with it." He glanced over his shoulder. Kiley
was talking with O'Connell, had started her laughing. Everything was
under control. The gray Fiat was not even in sight on the longest stretch of
this goddamned road.

"Well?" Fahri wanted to know as the Fiat picked up speed. "Will she go
with you?"

Claudel shook his head.

"I am glad. A crazy idea."

"The only one possible at this time."

"No towns to hide in, no safe house to—"

"Okay, okay. Slow up, Fahri. We're getting too far ahead of them."

Fahri slackened speed but not his criticism. "They saw the car. You took
a risk."

"Less risk than we would have to take at Zahidan. Remember how she
was guarded at Kerman." And how they slipped away, a day earlier than
they had told their innkeeper. If it hadn't been for Fahri's early prayers,
Claudel might not have seen the camper being readied for departure. (Now,
apparently, the idea of sleeping bags in open country had been discarded
for the overnight safety of a town and a small inn. The campers were finding out that what had been romantic fun in Europe was becoming increasingly difficult in stranger lands. Just wait, thought Claudel, until they start

down through central India: leopards, a tiger perhaps, certainly packs of wild dogs.)

"They saw the car," Fahri repeated. "That was your second contact with the girl. We must not risk a third at Quetta or a fourth at Lahore."

"I'll wait until Bombay."

"That is good." Fahri relaxed, his teeth a brilliant white in contrast with his olive skin and black mustache. He glanced at the small speaker on the dashboard, its beeps now sounding steady and true. "We've got contact. They are catching up." He increased his speed.

"We can switch it off. We don't need to track them now."

"Just testing it. You are sure your Australian friends have the right receiving device?"

"I'm sure," Claudel said with a brief smile. "They are already outside Quetta, waiting for the camper to appear." There was only one road reliable enough for motor traffic coming down from the Baluchistan plateau. Shawfield wouldn't risk the weight and size of a camper on anything less than a solid surface. "They'll pick up its signal easily."

"A long wait for them. Seven, eight days."

"That's part of the job, isn't it? Waiting." Claudel thought of Nina. She would have the longest wait of all. "That girl has courage. Underneath, she is frightened. But what is courage without fear? Blind stupidity," he answered himself.

"Will she survive?" Fahri had his doubts. "One little innocent against a pack of wolves? No place for a woman. They should stay where they belong."

There was a moment's silence. "Tonight," Claudel said, "we'll send our report to London."

"We send a report to Istanbul, too?"

"Kahraman has no interest in the girl."

"Just ask if I may go south with you to Bombay." That was where the real action could be. Fahri's dark eyes gleamed at the prospect.

"You've got business in the north where carpets are made and refugees come over the mountains from Afghanistan," Claudel reminded him. It was better that Fahri should leave him once they reached India, let him travel alone. From now on, he thought, we are a marked pair.

Twenty-one

J. P. Merriman & Co. was becoming—to Ronald Gilman's surprise and Bob Renwick's amusement—a successful business. Its downstairs department found its advisers on construction abroad in demand and its surveyors actually at work: their services were seemingly what was needed by hotel chains with an eye on expansion into romanticized areas for well-heeled tourists, such as Tahiti, Bali, Fiji, Kashmir. "It was your idea," Renwick told Gilman, "so why be astonished? It will pay the rent, keep a roof over our heads."

"Your idea has been expanding, too," Gilman said, not to be outdone in generosity. "It's working."

"Slowly."

"That's always the way. Slow but sure. And then—the end is in sight. Suddenly, one more file can be closed."

"One way or the other," Renwick said. It may have been the cold October drizzle outside, or the lack of heat in Gilman's attic room—the small electric fire looked better than it felt—but Renwick's usual optimism was chilled. Too much inaction, too many reports analyzed and broken down and reassembled in different ways to give new leads and clearer assessments.

Gilman said, "Don't tell me you are depressed by the way Interintell is growing. It had to increase its scope, Bob. Couldn't be confined to NATO. Terrorism doesn't belong only to the North Atlantic areas. We've got three additional investigations running at this moment, and two countries outside NATO are concerned enough to ask for our help."

"I know, I know. Expansion is necessary, but it might just be happening too soon." With expansion, there would come—inevitably—publicity. And at this moment, any publicity might give Theo warning of a new force moving against him. "Theo—" began Renwick, and stopped. Theo had been his investigation from the beginning. "So much seems to be hanging fire. Perhaps it's time to give Theo a jolt, make him feel that the best-laid plans may need a change here or an alteration there, set him a little off balance. But let's avoid publicity—if we can. Keep Interintell's name out of it, Ron. For now."

"And take no credit for nailing Theo?"

"Whoever got credit for keeping the peace—except the politicians?" Renwick drew his chair closer to the fire.

Gilman smiled. "Just think of Bombay and temperatures around ninety degrees. Are you really leaving tomorrow? You'll be a week ahead of the camper's arrival."

"Its scheduled arrival," Renwick said pointedly.

"They've still more than seven hundred miles to travel, and none of them easy." The camper, on reaching Pakistan, had traveled south, still keeping in Pakistan, to reach Hyderabad and some students at its Sind University. From there, heading for India at last, it had been faced with the Great Desert. That had been skirted more or less, but even after that success the camper's direction was convoluted, turning north before it swept around to the south again. "One hell of a route they chose."

"Chosen for them," Renwick said. Then he actually laughed. "So Theo does make miscalculations. When he decided on that route, he must have been trying to have the camper avoid any heavy monsoon rains—these last from June until October, usually. But this year the monsoons have failed. There's drought instead of floods."

"That was his second miscalculation," Gilman observed. The Afghanistan scene hadn't seemed to need Soviet military intervention when the camper's route had been initially planned, but the invasion forces were already beginning to group along the frontier.

"Otherwise," Renwick reminded him, "he has done too damned well. He has now set up offices for West-East Travel in Honolulu and Hong Kong." The pattern established in Los Angeles and Istanbul had been repeated: Theo, with a supply of false passports and changes in his appearance to match their photographs and descriptions, had entered foreign countries with the greatest of ease. Once there, he had only needed a couple of hours to appear as Mr. Otto Remp from Düsseldorf in order to sign the final documents—and to keep his home office convinced that their Herr Remp was doing exactly what they had sent him traveling to do. "Two offices still to be arranged," said Renwick thoughtfully.

"Singapore. Bombay. Where will he appear first?"

"I'm betting on Bombay. James Kiley will need a hefty dollop of hard cash when he arrives there." The last place where he had picked up a quantity of money had been in Hyderabad—at a small private bank where an account had been established in Kiley's name. "Theo must have an army of agents scattered around."

"Well, he has pretty strong backing. We may not have their army of agents, but we're doing not so badly." At least Claudel and Fahri had delivered the camper over to Mahoney and Benson, the two Australians, who were old friends of Renwick's. They had managed to stage a breakdown of their Ferrari at Quetta, given themselves the excuse that their trip over the Himalayas to India was out of the question until next summer, and had succeeded—by an exchange of cars—in following the camper as far as Hyderabad. After that they had noted its direction for the Indian frontier, notified A. K. Roy in time for his two agents to pick up the trail. "Roy is a formidable type," Gilman said. They had been good friends since their Oxford days. "I've known him for twenty years, and one thing is certain: he is not going to let Mr. Otto Remp set up a front for espionage right in his own backyard. He comes from Maharashtra, you know, and that's the province where Bombay lies."

So that, thought Renwick, is why Gilman, who had several strong contacts in India, had chosen Roy for this operation. "I hope he has been investigating any recent foreign interest in Bombay real estate." For once we might learn in advance where Theo-in-disguise reverts to Otto Remp for the final transactions.

"Roy is doing that right now," Gilman said. "When do you want to meet him?"

"As soon as I arrive in Bombay." Renwick's depression had lifted. He was already seeing several possibilities of getting close to Theo at last. "Theo—" He smiled. "What about giving him a real shock in time for his Bombay appearance?"

"Shake him up," Gilman agreed. "But how?"

"Ilsa Schlott." Yesterday she had been arrested by New Scotland Yard's antiterrorist squad, but quietly: nothing had yet appeared in the newspapers. "Would your inspector friend consider a little publicity?"

"How much?"

"Nothing to damage any of his continuing investigations into her contacts here in London. The news of her arrest will have to be made public,
you know. Why not now? We'll use the information that we got from Diehl
last week to flesh out the bald details that Scotland Yard will give to the
press." Richard Diehl, in West Germany, had done a mammoth job at digging deep into the past history of the People's Revolutionary Force for Direct
Action—enough to send Erik and Marco, its founders, and Theo, their
adopted counselor and friend, into convulsions. "Your contact at Scotland
Yard wouldn't object to that, would he?"

Gilman took off his glasses, polished them thoughtfully. "It might be a
boost for his section. Only he'd have to see a copy of Diehl's report—just
in case the politicians came asking too many questions."

"We'll give him a copy of one part of Diehl's report—the one that we
are willing to have published. That should bolster any answers he has to
give."

"He'll give the minimum. What shall he call Diehl—a reliable source of
information?"

"Should be enough for the moment. Later your friend can be more exact.
He understands that, doesn't he?"

"He's more security-minded than even you are." Gilman replaced his
glasses and rose. "Eleven o'clock. I'll make us a cup of tea. Gemma bought
me this electrical gadget to boil water. Let's see if it works. And you can
get your thoughts into shape for a press release."

"How much will be reported—before we add our contribution?"

"Ilsa Schlott arrested in a Camberwell garage—charged with recruitment
of terrorists for a training period abroad. Two terrorists returning to London last week, their training complete, also arrested. So were the owner of
the garage and his chief mechanic; three employees detained for questioning—and two are talking—regarding cars altered to suit Miss Schlott's specifications. Two of these cars have been identified: used for the transport of
weapons. Miss Schlott, enrolled at University College as a medical research
student, has been resident in London since September 1978. On a false
passport. Name and nationality are both invented."

"She was actually caught on a visit to that garage? That was pretty neat
timing by your friend," Renwick said admiringly.

"It seemed a good opportunity to nab her. Flagrante delicto. Stands up
nicely in court. You know—" Gilman broke off in exasperation—"I don't
think this bloody thing is going to work, dammit."

Renwick let him struggle with Gemma's brainchild, and concentrated on
the garage in Camberwell. "No mention of a green camper?"

"Actually, yes. But I wasn't sure you'd want that publicized."

"When did the garage start working on that camper?"

"In early February. Finished the job by May. There was a good deal of
work needed. Including the services of an electronics expert whose shop just
happens to be next to the garage. He and his electrician are in custody, too.
Altogether, a nice haul."

"No records kept, of course, on Schlott's special orders."

"None. But the two talking employees saw the camper, knew it was some-

thing special although they weren't allowed to work on it. One of them—
he's an odd-job man—was in the garage when a thin dark stranger, young,
six feet tall, took possession of the camper in June. Arrived with Ilsa Schlott,
said nothing; just got into the camper and drove off. The quickest exit our
odd-job man had ever seen." Gilman gave up his battle with tea-making.
"I'll ring for Liz to bring us some of her brew."

"I'd rather talk." No interruptions wanted, thought Renwick. "Ron—why
don't we use the camper? Or would your inspector be against that?"

"No. Because the green camper cost a lot of money. Because Ilsa Schlott
pretends to be a student on scholarship. That would make the press and
the public realize there is ample justification for these arrests."

"Then let's give Theo a real jolt."

"You think it out. And I'm having that cup of tea." Gilman pressed the
button twice to warn Liz. "She'll be here in five minutes." He sat down
behind his small desk in the little office he had walled off from the main
floor of the communications section, reflecting how much of a contrast it
was to his regular office a few streets away. Here, everything was scaled down,
built in, made of metal and plastic: there, his panel room had a real desk, a
fireplace, and armchairs that sagged in the right places. Renwick seemed
oblivious to the discomforts of this hygienic setup. He had even lost his
early-morning depression. "I see you've hit on something. Let's hear it."

"Let's wait for that blasted tea to arrive," Renwick said.

"Would you rather have coffee?"

Renwick shook his head: Liz made coffee out of some concentrate in a
bottle. She arrived within the next minute, bringing not only a tray with a
brown teapot, two cups, milk and sugar, a plate of digestive biscuits, but
also a folder tucked under one arm. "The latest reports, just arrived," she
said in her high, fluting voice, and placed them in the last free foot of desk
space. A pretty girl, thought Renwick, who plays beauty down: neatly competent in tweed suit and flat-heeled shoes. No frills about her manner, either.
She left at once, with a friendly nod for Gilman's "Thank you, Liz," and a
shy smile in Renwick's direction.

Gilman noted it and shook his head: I get the nods, Renwick gets the
smiles. It never failed. He opened the folder, saw the message came from
Richard Diehl, in West Berlin, glimpsed James Kiley's name. He said, "We'll
deal with this later. First, let's finish that press release." He poured the strong
black tea, adding milk and sugar generously. Renwick, who wanted neither,
took his cup without comment. "Well?" Gilman asked.

"Just after the mention of the two cars that were used for the transport
of weapons, we could insert a brief description of a camper, green in color,
that was collected in June by a friend of Ilsa Schlott's." Renwick paused.
"And then we insert more about Schlott, just after that bit about her residence in London since 1978."

"Such as?"

"Informed sources state that Ilsa Schlott had been known to the West
German police as 'Greta,' a member of the People's Revolutionary Force
for Direct Action, which, over the last five years, has claimed responsibility
for bombings that resulted in deaths and many injuries. The two founders

of this terrorist group are of the extreme left and are now being sought for their part in the attempted destruction of the Duisburg waterfront in June. Reliable sources have identified them as 'Erik' and 'Marco.' Although their joint manifesto for Direct Action preached the philosophy of nineteenth-century anarchism, it is now believed they are working for the more ortho-dox left-wing forces—temporarily, at least." Renwick smiled. "That should throw a few fits around Theo's circle."

"It's too long. The newspapers will print only half of it. A pity." Gilman poured himself another cup of tea.

"Well, even if there's only space for half of it, enough will get through. And I'm hoping some intelligent reporter will pick up on the anarchist angle. For that's the key to the extreme left of today, the red-hot activists. They want no bosses, no leaders, no organization in government, and down with all systems. Everything is to be done by committee, by joint consultation. All decisions unanimous—in the name of the people." They forgot, appar-ently, that even a large-size committee became a boss over those who obeyed it; that within a committee, a leader emerged when one of them produced better ideas, better plans. "In theory, it has a noble ring: pure equality for all in each and everything. In practice, it's either chaos or the bloodiest-minded approach to power."

"The new dark ages."

For a moment there was silence. Then Renwick returned to the business on hand. "Before we give out the names of Erik and Marco in that press release, we had better clear them with Diehl. The West Germans might not want them broadcast until they've—"

"They won't object." Gilman opened the folder, extracted a flimsy sheet of paper, gave it a quick scan. He handed over the message from Diehl. "West Germany is asking India for the extradition of Erik and Marco, now traveling under the names James Kiley and Antony Shawfield respectively. Wanted for arson, bombings, murders, in Berlin and Frankfurt."

So Kiley *is* Erik, thought Renwick, and read the details. Diehl had ap-pended his own report, giving the facts uncovered. Erik and Marco attended Lumumba University in Moscow—met at North Korean training camp for urban guerrillas—Erik sent to the United States, Marco to England—met again in West Berlin and founded the People's Revolutionary Force for Direct Action. Three members of that group had defected, had been in hiding from reprisals for the last four years. Now, with the arrest of Erik and Marco a real possibility, they had given a full physical description of the two men. Additional help had come from the Rotterdam police—physical description of man who had evaded them at Schiphol Airport tallied with description of Erik previously obtained from three ex-terrorists: height, coloring, fea-tures. Also, description fitted young student from Mexico University (Ramón Olivar, born Venezuela of Swedish mother and exiled Spanish father) who traveled to Lumumba University, never returned under that name. Olivar had also been known as Jan Andersen, Henrique Mendes, Kurt Leitner, James Kiley. Former members of the terrorist group knew him only as Erik.

Renwick handed back the sheet of paper to Gilman. "It's worth reading—all of it."

"Later. You're the one, in any case, who wanted the evidence as clear as possible. Satisfied now?"

Renwick nodded. "Diehl did a first-rate job."

With you forever sending messages to suggest some new approach. Bob would drive us crazy, Gilman was thinking, except that his ideas pay off ninety percent of the time, and that's a better average than most. "What do you make of this? We've had three unsigned messages from America."

"Using what wavelength?" Renwick asked quickly.

"The one you had for your Sawyer Springs transmissions. But the messages come from New York, we think."

"Could be Salvatore Marini—Frank Cooper's man."

"You didn't recruit him?"

"He was an expert at his job. I liked Sal. But I didn't recruit him. He doesn't even know how to reach us here, except by that wavelength."

Gilman unlocked a file and removed a folder, studied three sheets of paper. "Two messages were brief. The first one states that Maartens and his friend Hans took a flight to New York from Los Angeles on Friday, September 7."

"That's all?"

"All."

Sal must have delayed his own departure from San Diego, checked both there and in Los Angeles while memories were fresh and records easily available. But why hide that from us? Renwick's face was grave. "And the next message?"

"It states that Maartens and Hans hired a small plane under the names Jones and Brown to travel on Saturday, September 8, to East Hampton. A car waited for them at the airfield. They returned to New York on another plane that night."

Sal, thought Renwick, is telling us that Maartens and Hans are guilty of Frank Cooper's death. "Has he gone to the FBI?"

"No mention of that in his third message. It came yesterday—four weeks later than the others. It is—apparently—a word-for-word transcription of a San Diego newspaper report. Have a look, Bob."

Renwick took the sheet of paper. The news date was of last Monday, October 15. The headline read: TRAGIC ACCIDENT AT SAWYER SPRINGS. Renwick looked up at Gilman, and then went on reading. "A fire occurred on Saturday night in the garage of Rancho San Carlos, the residence of Mr. Walter Gunter. The local volunteer fire fighters of Sawyer Springs responded as soon as they received a call for assistance. It appears that Mr. Gunter and his guest, Mr. Hans Smith, were preparing to drive out of the garage. The caretaker reports that he heard the car backfire. Then flames swept the garage, where several cans of gasoline were stored because of the present shortages. Mr. Gunter and Mr. Smith were trapped inside the car with fatal results. The firemen said there had been a delay in calling them, but they managed to save most of the house. Mr. Gunter's caretaker and cook were the only other occupants of the establishment at that time."

Saturday night, carefully chosen. Renwick shook his head. "For Gunter read Maartens," he reminded Gilman.

"Marini is a lunatic! It was he, wasn't it?"

"Yes."

"Thank God he isn't tied in with us. Just acted on his own. Like that. Avenging Frank—" Gilman broke off. "You're taking this pretty calmly, Bob. If Marini had been our man, we'd have had an agent out of control."

"But he wasn't our man. He was Frank's—to the end." Without knowing it, he had avenged Jake Crefeld, too.

"I am not shedding any tears over Maartens and that murderer of his, but an eye for an eye isn't the best intelligence work. Is it?"

"No. But it must have given Theo a bigger jolt than we've administered— so far. Why don't you try to get our press release timed for the end of next week?"

"Just as the camper is arriving in Bombay?" Gilman was thoughtful. Then he nodded his agreement.

"Well," Renwick said, rising from his tubular plastic chair, "time to push off. Not a bad morning's work. We've dealt with Schlott, and Kiley and Shawfield, too. When will the extradition process begin?"

"It usually takes a little time. But with some special effort, it could be in ten days or two weeks. In Bombay." He studied Renwick's face. "Bob," he said gently, "I know you want to get Nina O'Connell safely out. But you have to remember that our first priority is—"

"Theo," Renwick said. He hesitated, then added, "No extradition for Theo?"

"On what charges? The use of false passports, changes of identity?" Gilman shook his head. "He's deep into conspiracy, but he has covered his contacts. That house in Sawyer Springs wasn't bought in his name."

Renwick was frowning. "There's something he hasn't covered, and that's worrying him. A little. Not much. But enough to keep him from traveling openly as Otto Remp of Düsseldorf."

"He must have other business on this world trip—"

"I know, I know. Other business, other contacts, and none of them to be connected with Otto Remp's name." Then Renwick's impatience ended. "Essen! He set up an account in an Essen bank. And the only person who cashed checks on that account was Erik. There's your connection, Ron: Remp with Erik."

"The account was under a false name," Gilman reminded Renwick.

"Yes. But was Remp using a disguise, then? Banks take photographs nowadays—automatic surveillance—definite records."

"They could be destroyed by this time."

"We'll leave that for Diehl to find out. He knows the date of the last withdrawal of money from that Essen account. Twelve thousand dollars. Done in a great hurry—to pass some of it to Erik and Marco for their escape."

"And you think Theo used no disguise?" Gilman asked slowly.

"If he didn't bother to use one when he deposited the money originally— didn't see any need for it, no sense of danger, enough protection from a false name—then he had to look more or less like the same man when he withdrew such a large sum."

Gilman smoothed back a thinning strand of fair hair, adjusted his glasses more securely. "It's a long shot, but you've talked me into it. Poor old Diehl, you give him no rest."

"You'll contact him at once?"

"Right away."

With that reassurance, Renwick left. A long shot, he echoed Gilman's phrase, but worth a try: the one small mistake that Theo had made—if he had made it. Yet, last November, when he had opened an account for a substantial amount, there had been no alarms, no crises. Everything had been going very much in Theo's favor. A false name, false identity cards might have seemed ample protection.

But what, Renwick wondered as he reached the street, what if the Essen bank didn't have any system for filming its daily business? Then—a still longer shot—there might be a good memory of a client's face, height, weight. After all, small banks did note large deposits and speedy withdrawals. Particularly withdrawals of twelve thousand dollars that closed an account for good.

The drizzling rain had stopped, but there was a chill that struck upward from the damp pavement. A gray overcast saddened rooftops and lent a sameness to all these stone walls of tall houses converted into business establishments. It may have been the weather, it may have been a return of his depression, but when he thought of Theo being comfortably flown back for trial in West Germany, he could empathize with Sal.

Twenty-two

THE ROOM WAS dimly lit: not much sun came through the diamond pattern of the wooden trellis that covered its window and protected it from the street outside. It was airless, too, in spite of the door on the opposite wall that lay open onto a verandah, narrow and covered, that ran around all four sides of the building's inner courtyard.

A strange mixture, Nina decided, studying the carved wooden ceiling, a single bulb dangling from sagging wires that ran exposed to a plaster wall, the decorative tiles on the floor, the stone window seat, the low wooden platform—complete with thin mattress and bulky cushions—filling a large corner of the room.

Madge, seated on the bed with her back resting against the wall, glanced up from her diary. "Stop prowling around. You make me nervous."

"And you'll ruin your eyes."

"Well, I've got to start filling up the gaps." Madge picked up her pen. *Bombay,* she wrote. "What day did you say this was? Friday?"

Too many gaps; Madge had scarcely opened her diary in the last month. Even now it was only a half-hearted attempt. In another ten minutes she'd be asleep. Like Marie-Louise and Sven next door, like Guido and Henryk. The five now alternated between euphoria—excited talk, wild plans, high laughter—and complete lethargy. I don't know which scares me the more, thought Nina, and began emptying her bulging duffel bag onto the window seat. She picked out the Greek dress—she hadn't worn it since Istanbul. It was clean, but it could use some pressing. She shook it, hung it carefully on one of the wooden pegs driven into the once-white wall, and hoped that Bombay's humid air might work wonders. Then she found her two shirts.

Inside each neckband she had inked—as if it were a laundry mark—three numbers in sequence. The blue striped shirt, her favorite, had the first three numbers Pierre had given her five weeks ago for that telephone call to Mr. Roy. The green striped shirt had the next three. A simple idea, but it made sure she wouldn't mix up their order. Now, holding the shirts close to the light from a diamond-shaped space in the trellis, she went over the numbers again and again until she knew she wouldn't forget them.

Money . . . She searched in her wallet. She had only a few rupees as well as her two remaining traveler's checks. She would need to cash one of them. But where? Kneeling on the window seat, she looked through a space in the trellis. Two floors below her was a busy street with workaday traffic. No shops, no taxis, no tourists visible. This was no luxury quarter of the enormous city. It was somewhere near the harbor: beyond the flat roofs on the other side of the street, she could see a crane, the tip of a distant mast, and the smokestack of some ship, hear a tug's sharp blast. Not much encouragement: Bombay's waterfront must be vast, with busy quays and warehouses at one end and, at the other, a place where hotels could have pleasant views. She stared out at the block of apartments across the street, with the morning's wash hung out unevenly over every wooden balcony and window sill. It was a sad display: bits and pieces of clothing, not one recognizable as shirt or trousers, and all needing more hot water and soap than had been available.

She went back to unpacking: nothing inside her canvas bag that she needed except a thin scarf to cover the bare neckline of the low-cut dress. She began changing her clothes. It was almost two o'clock. Jim Kiley had already left. (He was collecting mail and money—he expected both at the American Express office. He was sorry, terribly sorry, but after that he had an important interview with a local politician—set up for him by Gopal, the guide who had met the camper at the Indian frontier and was still with them. But he would be back by late afternoon, and this evening they'd go out to dinner and see the town, and wouldn't Nina like that?) Tony Shawfield was absent, too; he was attending the camper at some garage over on the other side of the city. The camper was in bad shape, Jim had told her to excuse their strange arrival in Bombay. Tony would probably have to sell it—if he got a good price for it.

Strange arrival . . . Surely Madge must have noticed it. "Wasn't it odd this morning—" began Nina. "Madge, *please* don't fall asleep. I have to talk with you."

Madge roused herself. "It's so hot. Don't you feel it?"

"Yes. But I have to talk with you."

"About what?"

"About our arrival this morning."

"Well we got here, didn't we?"

"Four days late. And after spending one day in a village right outside Bombay. Why didn't we drive in yesterday? Why did we wait for this morning at six o'clock, and stop at a restaurant on the edge of the city for breakfast, and not have breakfast?" They had left the camper outside the small restaurant, with Tony staying inside it—well inside it; hadn't he wanted to be seen?—and then walked through a front room into a courtyard. Jim Kiley hadn't liked the look of either place, so he had led them through the courtyard's back gate, out into another street, where two Fiats were waiting. And that way they had driven southward to follow a wide curving bay and crossed handsome streets with skyscrapers and new buildings; and old buildings; and older buildings sardine-packed on narrowing and still more crowded thoroughfares.

"We got breakfast here," Madge reminded her. "Stop grumbling, Nina!" She went back to her travel diary.

"What about the camper? Tony is thinking of selling it. Madge—please listen. Tony is selling the camper. How do you travel then?"

"Tony is going to put the money he gets for it into our expenses. A plane across the Pacific makes more sense than a set of wheels." Madge giggled faintly at the idea of a camper with water wings.

"And before you reach the Pacific?"

"We'll go on a freighter and stop off at all kinds of interesting places." Madge's patience ended. "Ask Tony. He can tell you all about it."

"Where is he? Or is he spending all day at the garage?"

"Making travel arrangements. He will be here soon—no later than three o'clock. He's taking me up to Nehru Park. We passed it this morning, remember?" Madge giggled again. "Did you see that marina?"

Nina was wasting no more time. She pulled on her dress, combed her hair again, fastened her earrings in place, picked up her scarf and shoulder bag. Then she remembered her toothbrush, almost laughed as she found it and her precious cake of soap, and added them to her bag.

"The one that Tony pointed out to us? 'Swimming Baths and Sailboat Club.'" Then Nina's change of clothes at last caught Madge's attention. She sat up on the bed, said slowly, "And where are you going, Nina O'Connell?"

"Away. Will you come with me? Last chance, Madge."

"Leaving—actually leaving? Where will you go?"

"I'll manage. I managed in Greece. And I have friends—" Nina halted. "Just get yourself together. And be quick! Leave everything except your shoulder bag. *And* your passport."

"Nina!"

"While you get ready, I'll have a word with Shahna—is that her name?" The girl, no more than twelve years old, was sitting on the verandah just outside their room door. "Our little watchdog," Nina added. "But she does speak English, and she can get us to a telephone. Madge—please hurry. I can't leave you alone here."

"I am not alone. And I'm not leaving." Madge's face was set. "Do you think I'd give up this trip? Easy for you—you'll just cash a few checks and travel where and when you like."

Nina reached the door, hesitated. "Madge—"

"No." The word was definite. Madge's head was bent over her diary.

Nina stepped outside. Shahna looked up at her with a shy smile, and rose to her feet, shaking her long cotton skirt free from the verandah's dust. She was slender-boned and fine-featured, a smooth little face with large dark eyes faintly shadowed. Her gleaming black hair was brushed tightly off her brow, caught into a heavy plait. Small gold studs of pin-head size decorated two pierced ears and one nostril. Nina said, "I don't see Gopal. Where is he?"

"He left. He will come later."

Good. "Has the Englishman arrived? Mr. Shawfield?"

Shahna shook her head.

Good again. "I need to telephone. Is there a place near here where I can find a phone?" If there was one in this house, which was doubtful, Nina had decided to avoid it. Gopal had recommended this place, and his relatives and friends were all around. Even now, eight men of various ages—some old, some mere boys—were sitting in the shaded side of the courtyard, talking, as they had done all morning. The women were out of sight, but audible even at this distance from the kitchen on the ground floor: voices drifted up along with the lingering smells of cooked spices. Not a word was understandable to Nina—among themselves, the clan of closely knit families who occupied this collection of rooms spoke Maharathi. English was kept, so Kiley had said, as a kind of lingua franca, useful for other Indians in Bombay who spoke quite different languages. Lucky for me, thought Nina as she waited patiently for Shahna's reply: lucky, too, that all the shops and street signs she had seen on the drive through the city this morning had been in English. She drew out her wallet, selected one rupee but held it in her hand.

Shahna began walking along the verandah, lithe and graceful. She kept close to the house wall, as far from the railing as possible. But with its overhanging laundry, it would be difficult for anyone in the courtyard—if he could spare a moment from talking—to see what was happening on the third-floor verandah. At the narrow staircase, Nina stopped, looked back. Madge had come to their room door. Nina beckoned. Madge shook her head. But she waved. Nina waved, too, and with a lighter heart she followed Shahna down the enclosed staircase. They reached the entrance to the courtyard and turned toward the street.

Hot, narrow, bustling with traffic, filled with people. Nina halted in dismay.

"This way. It is near," Shahna said. She looked at Nina's dress, touched it lightly with her thin fingers. "Pretty."

"Are there taxis?" Nina could see none. Plenty of cars, a bus, trucks, small carts. She began walking quickly.

Shahna shrugged. "Sometimes from the pier." She gestured vaguely along the street. "Ballard Pier. Very big. Very nice ships."

"How far is it to the waterfront where the big hotels are?"

"What hotel?" Shahna's eyes gleamed. "I'll come, too. I'll show you."

"In what direction are they?"

"Back there." Shahna pointed behind them.

"How far? One mile, two miles?"

"Two miles, maybe three." She was charmingly vague.

She's probably never been there, thought Nina. So how do I calculate how long it takes to walk from here to the Malabar Hotel?

Shahna stopped, pointed to a wide doorway.

"A money exchange?" The room inside was cavernous, without windows, dependent on light from its wall opening onto the street. Nina hesitated.

"Much business. Sailors come here from the ships. It has a telephone."

I bet it has, thought Nina, which is more than can be said for that side street we have just passed: a local market of crowded stalls with strips of canvas overhead and a mass of people moving around. "Thank you, Shahna." Tactfully, she slipped the rupee into the delicate little hand. "Now you must go back." The girl looked at her reproachfully. "Thank you," Nina said again.

The decision was made for them both by the man standing at the side of the door. He was young, alert, and much on guard. He raised his voice to Shahna, lifted the back of his hand: clear out, he must have said; no beggars allowed here. Shahna was accustomed to this apparently, for she retreated quickly out of his reach, gave Nina a bright smile to retrieve her dignity, and walked away with her hips swinging and her head held high. The man nodded to Nina, stood politely out of her path.

Nina halted at the threshold. The place was bare and clean, its one counter securely caged, a man behind it, two customers with red perspiring faces, fair hair, and bright Hawaiian shirts. Three other men—one a venerable figure in white tunic and narrow trousers; two young and strong, dressed like the guard at the door in European clothes—sat along the opposite wall. And there was the telephone, strangely encased in a plexiglass stall—privacy?—only four paces away from the door. She looked at the old man, who scarcely seemed to have noticed her. "May I use your telephone?" Everyone lost interest in her, except the two sailors.

"How much?" Nina asked.

One of the younger men rose, came forward, saying in excellent English, "Twelve rupees. You pay me, and I shall dial your number."

"Five rupees. It is a local call. And short."

"Eight rupees." The tone of voice was polite; the smooth face—fine-boned, light-skinned—broke into a persuasive smile.

"Five rupees." Nina was definite. There was a slight pause. She shrugged, looked toward the street, seemed about to leave.

"Five," he agreed, and held out his hand. He had a handsome wristwatch, a heavy gold ring. Like the other young men, he wore a cream silk shirt and well-cut gabardine trousers. "The number?"

"I can manage." Nina gave him five rupees and stepped into the plexiglass enclosure—no door, just two transparent side walls. The telephone was a dial model, much the same as she had used in London. The young man stood close, perhaps curious to see the number or hear her conversation. There was nothing she could do about that, except turn her back to him, try to hide the dial from his interested eyes, and keep her voice low. For one blank moment she almost forgot the figures she had memorized; and then, her nervous fingers began turning them in careful sequence. A distant voice said "Malabar Gift Shop."

I have the wrong number, she thought. "Mr. A. K. Roy?" she tried timidly. Oh, God, I've got the wrong number—what now?

"Who is speaking?" The voice was clearer. "Who is there?"

"Pierre?" In her overpowering relief, she was almost incoherent. "Nina. I'm near the Ballard Pier. I think. I'll need perhaps an hour to reach you."

"I'll come and get you."

"No. Not here. I can't wait here. It's a money-changing place. And the street outside—impossible."

"Then meet me in the hotel's bookstore. It is in the arcade—next to the gift shop."

"Yes. Yes."

"Are you all right?"

"I am now. I'll see you—" she consulted her watch—"at half past three. Perhaps later. I can't judge."

"Don't worry. I'll wait. Your old friend is in Bombay—the Courtyard of the Janissaries—remember? He'll be glad to see you again."

Bob Renwick? She said, her voice suddenly unsteady, "I'll be more than glad." She hung up the receiver.

The young man stopped lounging against the plexiglass partition, followed her to the door. "The streets are very crowded. It is very difficult to walk alone." He was summing up her dress, the silk scarf that covered her shoulders, her earrings. But most of all, it was her manner that impressed him: she did not belong in this quarter. "Too many beggars ready to follow you. They give no peace. Perhaps you should take a taxi."

"Is there one?" Nina glanced along the street.

"My cousin's car is there." He pointed to a vintage Chevrolet standing by the curb just ahead of them.

"How much?"

"To where?"

"Oh—" she floundered a little, recovered enough to say—"to the waterfront near the big hotels."

"Which hotel? There are several of them."

"How much?"

"Twenty rupees."

"What?" She was scandalized. "Impossible." She began walking.

He caught up with her. "Fifteen."

"Twelve."

"The price of petrol is high," he said sadly.

"Twelve," she repeated. "Not twenty, not fifteen. Twelve."

With his gentle smile, he led the way to the Chevrolet. His cousin could have been his twin, but he spoke little English. The two of them had a quick conversation, unintelligible to Nina.

It was a long long street lying ahead of her, and how many other long streets after that? "It's a short distance," she said, trying to appear as if she knew her way around Bombay.

"If you would pay me now," her mentor suggested.

First, she got into the car, making sure it wouldn't drive away without her. Then she counted out the last of her rupees. He accepted them gracefully, handed over three of them to his cousin, and bade her a polite goodday. Now I know, she thought as she nodded her thanks, why the cousin wears a cotton sports shirt and a cheap wristwatch. It was a wild ride, and speedy. She reached the approach to the Malabar International Hotel with fully thirty minutes to spare.

She entered the vast lobby and was greeted by ice-cold air. Shimmering lights cascaded from the vaulted ceiling, marble floors and walls gleamed, trees—twice her height—had ornamental shapes to match the flowers around their feet. People everywhere; and from everywhere: many well-fed and well-groomed Indians, Japanese, Singapore Chinese, all in well-tailored business suits. Europeans and Americans were noticeable by less expensive clothes—sports shirts and linen jackets. Their women in limp drip-dry dresses were quite silenced by the bright-colored saris that floated past them.

Nina recovered, looked around for the arcade. It must be at the other end of the lobby, perhaps at the back of this incredible palace. But she saw a large travel desk, a counter where Thomas Cook and American Express had staked their claims. She'd have time to cash one of her checks; then she'd stop being destitute. It had been a horrible feeling, all through the journey here, to realize she had nothing spendable in her wallet. At least I'll be able to visit the powder room, she thought as she took her place at the counter. And I'll find out where the arcade is, and I can buy a paper or a magazine in the bookstore if I have to wait for Pierre. Her fear and terrors were leaving her. She began to feel normal again.

She looked normal, too. Her eyes were bright with interest, lipstick and powder and freshly combed hair perfect, as she left the ladies' room. She passed a bank of elevators and the clearly printed English signs that directed people to the Coromandel Bar, the Victoria Grill, the Ajanta Room, the Gateway to India Restaurant. At last she found the arcade, open on one side to a lavish garden; on its other side, a series of elegant displays of gold and silver and ivory. She reached the gift shop, with a window of gossamer silks and rich brocades that would entice the last rupee out of a tourist's pocket. Next door was the bookstore.

She halted at the entrance, beside a tall rack of newspapers, both local and foreign, quickly scanning the people inside the shop. Tables with books piled on top, shelves packed ceiling-high with more books. Was Pierre there? Bob? A clerk was near her, looking at her intently, so she pretended interest in the newspapers, glancing at a headline just at her shoulder level, and stood transfixed. GREEN CAMPER MYSTERY—SPY ARRESTED. And the opening line of the newspaper report was: *Ilsa Schlott, a recruiter for terrorist*—That was all she could see. As her hand went out to pick up the paper, a man's grip, strong and painful, encircled her wrist. Tony Shawfield said quietly, "So you thought you would run off and leave us."

Nina tried to pull her wrist free. Gopal was behind Shawfield; another Indian, too.

Shawfield's voice hardened. "You came to meet someone. Who?" To Gopal's friend, he said, "Get the car. Side entrance." Then again to Nina, "Who? Who is meeting you here?"

"No one."

"You telephoned." Shawfield's grip tightened.

"Let go! I'm buying a paper and—" She caught sight of Pierre stepping forward. No, she thought frantically: stay back, Pierre—you'll be recognized.

The clerk was approaching. Shawfield had doubled his hold on her: one hand on her wrist, the other on her elbow, forcing her into the arcade.

She went unresisting. Three of them, and Pierre alone—no, this wasn't the place for any confrontation. Her steps lagged, delaying as much as she could. Pierre would follow. She hoped. But I'm not endangering his real mission, whatever it is, and it's not me.

"Whom did you call?" Shawfield was insisting.

"The American Consul. That was all."

"The truth, Nina! I'm no fool. You were to meet someone at that bookstore. And he was late or you were early."

"No. There was no one." She sounded desolate, bewildered. And she was. They had reached a street, crowded with people. Shawfield was pulling her toward a car that was just drawing up in front of him. Pierre will never be able to follow, not here, she thought in sudden panic. She glanced back but could see only strange faces; she tried to break free, run. But Shawfield forced her through the car's open door, into its back seat, followed her. Gopal jumped in beside the driver, the doors were locked, the car moved. Only then, as it edged its way out of the jumble of traffic and tried to pick up speed, did Shawfield's grasp ease on Nina's wrist.

Gopal was worried. "That clerk followed us out. Another man, too, I think."

Shawfield's head jerked round to look back. Too many people, too many cars: impossible to see if anyone was attempting to tail them. He gave up and studied Nina instead. He had a feeling that Gopal's words had jarred her. Encouraged her? She needed discipline, this girl. Jim had been too easy with her. "We'll lose them," he told Gopal. And teach Milady a little lesson. "Falkland Road," he said.

The driver and Gopal exchanged a startled glance.

"Falkland Road," Shawfield repeated. To Nina he said "So you thought you'd leave us. Why?"

"I was bored with sitting in that room."

"And you headed for the Malabar? Why?"

"It was some place I could change a traveler's check—buy a magazine, a guide to the city. I wanted to see Bombay."

"And so you shall." His voice had eased. He could relax a little: he had found her. A wild search, not a moment wasted after he had returned (and that was luck—arriving earlier than he had planned) to find Madge alone. "She has left," Madge told him, "left with Shahna." And Shahna had talked, of telephones and hotels; had even led him to the money exchange nearby. There, it took only five rupees to loosen a man's tongue: the blonde had hired a car; it had just returned from the Malabar Hotel. There, it hadn't been so easy: fifteen minutes of searching, of inquiries, of growing anger and desperation. Then quick-eyed Gopal had seen her, vanishing into the arcade. Did she think she could outwit me? Just wait until Jim gets back from his meeting with Theo and hears what could have happened. But it didn't. Who planned her moves anyway? Shawfield reached for her bag, pulled it out of her hands.

He found no slip of paper with a name or address or a telephone number. The wallet held a quantity of rupees: some large bills, some coins. They went into his trousers pocket along with her remaining traveler's check. "Much safer. You could have them stolen. I'll keep them for you."

Nina stared out at a broad square, an enormous stretch of ground where traffic circled around a statue of Queen Victoria on her lofty pedestal and streets branched off in every direction. This was far from the waterfront, from anything she knew. Her hopelessness increased with her sense of isolation. No one could follow this car, she thought as it entered a narrow thoroughfare, not Pierre, not even Bob. I know now what I should have done outside the bookstore: kicked and screamed and brought people running to help me. But would they have run? Any of them? Or would they have drawn back, avoided an unpleasant scene? Only Pierre would have come; and been recognized. . . . How did Shawfield find me anyway? Surely Madge hadn't . . . Yes, perhaps she had. Perhaps she led him to Shahna, and Shahna to the money exchange. . . . I don't want to believe that, Nina told herself, but despair seized her heart. "Where are you taking me?" she asked.

"Sightseeing."

In silence, the strange journey continued.

Twenty-three

THAT AFTERNOON IT had been Pierre Claudel's turn to wait near the telephone in A. K. Roy's most private office. It was a neat setup, spacious, comfortable, secluded, lying behind the accounting department of the Malabar Gift Shop, with a second door into the adjoining bookstore, and a third door into the arcade itself.

He was alone except for one of Roy's men, a silent restful type, in charge of Roy's communications. Roy and Bob Renwick had left only a few minutes ago, allowing themselves ample time to get into position. Soon, they would be searching the busy street where Mr. Otto Remp was scheduled to visit, at half past three, one of the small banking establishments that offered its expert and discreet services to substantial depositors. There, in a quiet room, the banker would welcome Mr. Remp, along with the senior partner of a real-estate firm *and* its legal representatives *and* the new manager of the equally new Bombay office of West-East Travel. The final transactions would be completed: signatures here, a large check there, witnesses recorded, all in order, polite bows, good-byes. And then—Claudel smiled, wished he could see that scene.

Roy was to be congratulated. Renwick, too. For the last week they had gone through the list of real-estate agents who dealt in expensive properties and foreign buyers. While Roy ran thorough checks on their finances, personnel, business records, Renwick visited their establishments as a likely prospect—he was interested in acquiring a branch office for his London firm, specializing in construction problems. Were they accustomed to handling requests from abroad? What caliber of sales to reputable clients? His firm insisted on dealing only with the best agents, they must understand; ones who had been successful in satisfying important customers. They understood and offered their most recent triumphs in the selling of real estate. "A highly respected firm from Düsseldorf" had been one testimonial.

Then Roy had zeroed in, concentrating on the small law firm that handled contracts for the real-estate agency with Düsseldorf connections, securing their co-operation and sworn silence. And so today, one of Roy's agents would be among the legal representatives attending the meeting in the bank. Two plain-clothes policemen would be posted at its side entrance. Two others would move forward toward its front door as soon as Otto Remp stepped inside. One of Roy's best agents would attend to the limousine that brought Remp there, making sure its driver sent no warning message. And Roy and Renwick would be waiting in a radio car a short distance away.

Roy was making sure this time, Claudel thought with wry amusement. The disappearance of Kiley's little band of travelers early this morning from some insignificant restaurant with a miserable courtyard had roused the equable A. K. Roy to fury. The camper itself had also evaded his two undercover agents: a well-planned maneuver that increased his rage. But at least he was now convinced he was dealing with a mastermind directing two very clever young men. Worthy opponents. That thought had calmed his anger, redoubled his efforts. The extradition of Otto Remp, Kiley, Shawfield, was no longer a politeness from one democracy to another: it was an imperative. As Roy said, once more bland in manner, "There is enough trouble in our countries without such men adding to it." It was particularly gratifying that Remp had been linked with Kiley through an Essen bank, drawing him into the extradition net, too.

Well, thought Claudel, we are almost sure of one of them: Remp would be caught in the bank. He would be out of disguise, of course, for that appearance, playing the authentic Düsseldorf businessman for the benefit of his firm back home. Renwick had made a bet before he left with Roy this afternoon: Theo will get into his car wearing a wig and other removable transformations, and, as he is driven to the bank, he'll take them off, change his jacket, march in as Otto Remp. On leaving he intends to put on the disguise again, reappear at the house or hotel where he's staying under his fancy new name. What d'you bet, Pierre? No takers, Claudel had said.

But what about the other two? Although Kiley and Shawfield and their wandered students had faded from sight, they were in Bombay. Somewhere. The two highways out of the city, as well as the main airport at Santa Cruz, the central railway station, even the docks where coastal freighters were loaded, were now on the watch for eight young Westerners loaded down with duffel bags. The sleeping bags had been found in the abandoned camper four hours after it had slipped away from the restaurant, so they must be staying in some small hotel, some lodging house. Somewhere, Claudel thought again.

He studied the large-scale map of Bombay that he had spread over Roy's six-by-four-foot desk, lightly tracing in pencil the streets he and two of Roy's agents had checked this morning. All these cruddy little hotels—have you seen, have you heard, do you know of anyone who has seen, heard? He began memorizing the streets of the next likely section. That would be tomorrow's task, and Renwick would have his turn sitting at this desk while he waited for any possible call from Nina. They had agreed that one of them must be ready to answer the telephone, reassure Nina that she wasn't among strangers in a strange city. A. K. Roy had merely raised a well-marked eyebrow at such concern; he was more perturbed by the fact that Claudel had given one of his private telephone numbers to a young girl. "It was the only Bombay number I had," Claudel had protested. "What else could I do? She's important. She could lead us to Kiley." That had clinched the argument. The difficult moment was over. In any case, thought Claudel now, Roy would have that number changed once Nina made contact.

Would she? Or—and this was Renwick's worry—could she?

An unpleasant question. If Nina didn't, couldn't, call, then they would have to find her by searching. Claudel concentrated on his map, memorizing the directions and names of the streets in the poorer sections of the city. It wasn't likely the campers, now looking like a troupe of gypsies, would be living in a luxury hotel, or in a skyscraper apartment in the business district, or in a mansion in the green hills overlooking Bombay.

The telephone rang. It was Nina.

The call ended. Roy's communications expert had been listening, too. "Got all that?" Claudel asked him. "Then make contact with Mr. Roy's car. Give the American all the details—every word. I am going to the bookstore. If there is any reply, any message, you'll find me there."

Half past three, she had said. But if she took a taxi she could be here much earlier. Would she enter by the main lobby of the hotel? Or, if the driver saw she had no luggage, he might give her the choice of lobby or arcade. It had its own entrance on a side street and was frequently used by shoppers from outside the hotel. Better to stay in the bookstore, Claudel decided, keep to the arrangement, and be available for any message from Renwick. Besides—if Nina couldn't find a cab—he might have to wait longer than half past three. The bookstore was the safest place: people loitered there quite naturally. But he still wished he could meet her as she got out of a taxi or came walking up the long approach to the hotel. And then? Renwick had arranged it with A. K. Roy: a pleasant room adjacent to Roy's own suite in this hotel; well guarded, discreet, servants all tested and true, not one whisper to give away Nina's presence. And it might be for only a day or two—until all danger was over. What could be a better hiding place than a large hotel with four hundred rooms?

Claudel had skimmed through two magazines, concentration broken continuously as he verified the time or glanced toward the door of the bookstore. There was only one of Roy's younger assistants on duty here—the Theo assignment had depleted the ranks—and Claudel had stationed him, as a clerk, in the front of the shop. Lavji was his name, and eagerness was his manner. Almost too quick: he had already signaled the entrance of three various blondes, none beautiful. Or perhaps in Lavji's eyes, all blondes looked the same.

The monotony and tension, strange mixture, were broken by a message from Renwick. Claudel took it on his transceiver, retreating to a rear table piled with books where its use wouldn't be noticeable and he could still see Lavji. "No go," Renwick said. "Illness prevented our boy's appearance. He has rescheduled the signing for Tuesday. By which time he will be out of Bombay."

"But why? Give up his West-East office?"

"Something has made him change his plans, and change them damn quick. Something more than the news from London about the camper—he got rid of it this morning. His apologies arrived at the bank only ten minutes ago—by telephone. Our legal representative was chatting with the receptionist when the call came through—swears it was from some phone with distant voices and recurrent chimes in the background."

"Recurrent chimes—used for paging people in a hotel lobby?"

"That's the system used at the Malabar. Of course, he could have been lunching there, or passing through. But we'll start checking on its recent arrivals. He might just possibly be staying there." Renwick didn't sound optimistic.

"And how is Roy taking that?" Staying at A. K. Roy's hotel? A bitter joke.

"Furious. As I am, damn it to hell. A week's work down the drain. We're on our way back to you now. Let us know—"

Claudel said quickly, "Signing off. Lavji has spotted a blonde." He switched off the transceiver, shoved it in his pocket as he started forward, hoping that Lavji—this time was giving no false alarm. He wasn't. Nina was there. As yet, she hadn't entered the store, was standing at the door with three men grouped around her. Shawfield. Shawfield was one of them. He had a grip on her wrist. And suddenly, as she saw Claudel, she turned and left—Shawfield firmly holding one arm, leading her toward the side-street entrance of the arcade. Left willingly, it seemed. Claudel stared at the empty doorway, signaled Lavji to get on their tail as he pulled out his transceiver and sent the message to Renwick and Roy: "Nina intercepted by Shawfield. Am following. Will keep in touch." Then he, too, was heading toward the side street, a busy street, lined with cars, crowded with people. There was no sign of Nina.

"She's in that gray Fiat," Lavji said. "We'll take this car." He was already inside the dark-blue Citroën that was always parked there—on Roy's orders—for any emergency. "They haven't traveled far. We shall soon catch up."

"Not too closely," Claudel warned.

Lavji only smiled for such a naïve assumption. Wasn't he as expert as any Frenchman in following a car through heavy traffic?

Claudel flicked on his transceiver again, made contact with Renwick and Roy, began identifying streets and directions.

"We'll join up with you," Renwick said. "And Roy is calling in some backup. Keep sending."

Gradually, as Lavji kept the Fiat in sight, Claudel's emotions calmed. His thoughts, too. No, she hadn't left willingly or stupidly. She must have resisted walking quickly along that short stretch of arcade to the street, slowed their pace enough to let Lavji keep them in sight. So what did you think you were doing, Nina? Trying to protect me and my cover? He almost smiled, shook his head in wonder.

He kept sending directions to Roy's car, somewhere across the city in the big-business belt. Ahead of him, the gray Fiat left the Victorian Gothic buildings of red brick, chose a modest street of three-story houses and shops. No new skyscrapers here, but small businesses; men in shirt sleeves, with ever-present briefcases; women in saris of cotton instead of silk but still attractive and constantly smiling. Caste-conscious, too. They avoided a poorly dressed man and his young son, untouchables, who were sweeping a sidewalk with a straw broom near Gandhi's house.

Streets and more streets to be identified . . . Suddenly, the names and signs above the small shops changed, no longer in English but in Arabic. "Now reaching the Muslim quarter," he told Renwick. "Quiet here, shops closed, traffic light. Friday, of course—their Sabbath."

"We'll soon be with you." Renwick paused. "Are they skirting the Muslim quarter?" There was worry in his voice

"No. Looks as if they're heading straight through. Odd direction. They'll run up against six square blocks of—" Claudel cut off the sentence. Tactless. Renwick knew what adjoined this Muslim section: he had studied the map of Bombay, too. "Turning left into a small lopsided square. Muslim quarter ending. They are slowing down—about to stop—yes, they've stopped. At the beginning of Falkland Road."

There was only silence from Renwick. Roy's voice took over. "Stay back! Don't intercept. Keep in your car. We'll soon be there. A backup car, too. Wait!"

Lavji eased the Citroën to a halt at one side of the little square, the Fiat nicely in sight. There was only very light traffic at this time of day. By dusk—that would be a different matter. Claudel mastered his flare of temper. "Wait?" he asked bitterly as he watched the Fiat's door open. Shawfield was stepping out, his hand grasping Nina's wrist, pulling her to stand beside him. "What in hell . . ." Claudel began, staring at Shawfield, who was now at the entrance to Falkland Road.

Nina wrenched her arm free, began running, taking the road that lay in front of her. Shawfield seemed unperturbed, let her run, followed at walking pace.

"The cages!" Claudel exclaimed, got out of the car. Roy's Mercedes came into the square, stopped beside him. "He's heading her into the cages!"

Roy stared at him, said "Wait!" to Renwick. But Renwick was already out of the Mercedes and running. Roy shook his head. "Now we may lose Shawfield."

"I'll give Bob a hand," Claudel said, and started after him, leaving Roy to give brisk orders to his driver and Lavji—secure the Fiat, hold the two men inside it, let neither escape.

Nina had felt Shawfield's grip slacken on her wrist. She broke free, ran into the road that stretched in front of her. It was empty of traffic. People crowded one sidewalk to her left, the shadowed side of the narrow street: men, poorly dressed, lying asleep against a house wall, loitering aimlessly or squatting near small braziers where they were cooking food; a few gaping entrances of dark cavelike shops wide open onto the pavement—a carpenter in one of them stared out at her. The other sidewalk, in sunlight, was empty, quite empty. But its long line of three-story houses was crowded. Crowded with women, packed into every story, standing at the huge glassless windows that stretched from floor to ceiling. They were eyeing her, laughing, calling out in a babble of languages.

She halted in confusion, staring at the women behind the widely spaced wooden bars that decorated the open ground floors. Women of every age—from nine or ten to fifty, sixty. Slender and fat, fair and dark, samples of beauty from everywhere, all of them barely covered by transparent silks, all of them with heavy make-up carefully applied even to the exposed breasts.

She looked at the long stretch of houses, never-ending; across from them, the crowded sidewalk with men in ragged and stained clothes, thin dark faces with unreadable eyes. Those awake were watching her with a silence that terrified her. She hesitated, fighting back her panic. No escape, she thought in despair; not this way. Or could she force herself to run on—reach another street with luck, another street that was normal? Or would it be the same as this? She froze, paralyzed with fear. Shawfield's hand gripped her wrist. "We'll walk on," he said, and dragged her farther along the street.

He kept talking. "Educational. See what can happen to a girl who is stupid enough to run away from her friends in a strange city. Look!" He gestured to the windows, seemed a little nonplused by the inviting gestures and voices that now concentrated on him. "Some are sold by their families, some drift in, and some were like you today—they thought they could take care of themselves." He may have been too absorbed in his lecture or by the street scene around him, but he didn't notice the lightly running footsteps until they almost reached him. He swung around, dropping Nina's hand, and faced the stranger.

Renwick caught him by the collar of his shirt and smashed his left fist at the startled jaw. Shawfield staggered, regained his balance; his hand went to the cuff of his sleeve, pulled out his weapon. Renwick was ready, struck Shawfield's wrist a short and savage blow that gave no time for the trigger to be pressed; the cyanide pistol that looked like a fountain pen dropped onto the road.

Claudel reached them, in time to catch Shawfield's arm in a locking grip and twist it behind his back. "I'll take care of him," he said grimly, increased his pressure, and forced Shawfield toward the cars.

Renwick picked up the cyanide pistol, shoved it into his pocket out of harm's way: too many eyes from the sidewalk were fixed upon it. "Nina," he said, holding out his hand.

She had been standing motionless, her face rigid. She looked neither at him nor at the offered hand.

"Nina," he said softly.

She came to life, began walking slowly, averting her face, ignoring any help. He fell into step beside her, said nothing more. At this moment, Renwick thought, she is hating all men. He looked at the cages, at a slender child with kohl-darkened eyes and scarlet lips. At this moment, he could agree.

Roy was at his efficient best. The backup car—a Renault—had arrived, now giving him a total of five men available. The number was enough to quell any resistance from Gopal. His friend, the driver of the gray Fiat, had bolted—been allowed to run, more accurately—and had been picked up by the police car parked out of sight. Gopal was now sitting in the Renault, his show of righteous indignation to no avail, waiting for Shawfield to join him. Lavji and the Mercedes driver were guarding its doors, but Roy had briefed them quickly and they—like the other three—knew what was expected of them.

Then, as Claudel marched Shawfield back to the cars with a firm and painful grip on Shawfield's twisted arm, Roy motioned two of his men to take charge. Quickly they relieved Claudel, handcuffed Shawfield, brought him to face Roy.

Shawfield recovered his dignity, drew himself up to his full height. "What authority have you for this outrage?" he demanded.

Roy's heavy-lidded eyes studied the young man; then he flashed a smile along with an identification card. "The authority to take you to the police station and have you charged with attempted kidnapping. Put him with the other," he directed one of his men.

Shawfield stood his ground. "There was no kidnapping." He nodded in Nina's direction. "We are tourists. She wanted to see Falkland Road. So we came to see it." He looked at Renwick, who was leading Nina to the Mercedes. "I charge that man with assault. He struck me."

"Not hard enough," Renwick said.

Nina halted, aware of the puzzled glances in her direction from the Indians who stood near Shawfield. He was saying indignantly, "She asked me to bring her here. Is that kidnapping?"

Nina drew closer to Renwick. He said quickly, "No one believes that, Nina. No one."

She stood there, uncertainly. In a low voice she said, "He took all my money. It is in his pocket. I didn't ask him to bring me here, Bob, I didn't ask—" She broke down.

Renwick called out, "Have his pockets searched. He took her money."

Then, with a hand on her elbow—no more resistance to his touch, thank God—he drew her to the car. Inside, away from the curious faces, she wept bitterly. This was a Nina he had never seen before, distraught, shaken. He put an arm gently around her, let her cry her anguish away. "Safe now, darling, you're safe," he said, smoothing her hair back from her brow. He fought the impulse to take her in his arms, hold her close, kiss the tears from her cheeks, kiss her eyes, kiss her lips. "Safe," he repeated. It seemed to be the magic word.

Outside, the scene had changed. A slight interruption to my plan, thought Roy, but a brief one. Shawfield's pockets had been searched. A wad of new rupee notes had been found, quite separate from the money in his own wallet. There was also a traveler's check in Nina O'Connell's name. "She gave them to me for safekeeping," protested Shawfield. "She was leaving her bag in the car, so she asked me to carry the money."

"But she left her passport in her bag," Roy said. "Is money more valuable than a passport?" Yes, he thought as he watched Shawfield: I won that round. "Get him into the Renault," he told his men. To Claudel, who had been standing apart, his back turned as he watched a small group of curious Muslims gathered on the far side of the square, he called, "Let us talk with the young lady. I am interested in her story." They fell into step. Very quietly, Roy asked, "Did he identify you?"

"I tried hard to avoid it," Claudel said. He was worried by the way the cars had been parked. The Renault was too far from the Mercedes and the Citroën, too near the empty Fiat. "The man held in the Renault—he isn't handcuffed."

"He heard me say I had only one pair. So I was reserving them for the one who needed them most."

Claudel looked sharply at Roy; then wisely said nothing. At the door to the Mercedes, he glanced back at the Renault. Shawfield was being forced inside. The door beside him was closed and locked. One man guarded it. Only one? On the other side of the car, Lavji should have been on guard, but he was now advancing on the crowd that had gathered, ordering it to stay back, keep away, go home. Roy seemed not in the least perturbed by this, or by his three remaining agents, who were walking slowly away from the Renault, their duty done, their prisoner secured. Wondering, Claudel followed Roy into the front seat of the Mercedes.

Nina's body tightened; she looked quickly at Renwick. "A friend," he assured her. "It's all right, it's all right, Nina."

Roy handed her the bag and scarf she had left in the Fiat. "Yes, everything is all right. Your money, too." He inclined his head. "My name is Roy."

Renwick said, "Did you mention extradition?"

"Not a word. A nice little surprise to come. But now—please!" Roy put a finger to his lips for silence, switched on the car's radio. The voices came in, quiet but clear. It was Shawfield speaking, Shawfield and Gopal.

Shawfield was asking, ". . . the car keys?"

"I have them. Did you think I'd leave them?"

"Where are we being taken?"

"The central office, I heard. They talked with themselves, not with me."

"Where's that?"

"I've never been there—how can I know? Police headquarters perhaps. But what can they arrest me for? I told them I didn't know where we were going, I didn't—"

"Listen! Your hands and ankles are free. There is no guard outside your door. It isn't locked. Get to the Fiat—it's near—no one watching it. Drive straight ahead, down that street, lose yourself in the city. Then telephone. Call the Malabar Hotel. Ask for Suite 12A. Give this message and only this message. Don't add any words!"

"Suite 12A. Malabar Hotel. And the message?"

"Marco was arrested at four-forty-five on false charges of kidnapping. Will be taken to central office—perhaps police headquarters."

"That is all?"

"All. After the phone call, get back to your house. You'll find Kiley there. Tell him to get everyone out—all five. He knows where I planned to take them—he will instruct you—you'll be in charge of them. And above all—ditch that Fiat. It's hot."

"Money—I'll need money."

"He will give you plenty. Get going—quick—quick—now!"

There was silence, scarcely broken by the opening of a door. Gopal's movements weren't audible. But he must have stepped outside: quietly, the door clicked shut.

Roy switched off the radio, rolled down a window, listened. The view of Gopal's escape was blocked by the Citroën, but the Citroën would also block Shawfield's clear view of the Mercedes. Roy smiled. His favorite game was chess. "Gopal won't get far. There is a police car waiting out of sight—near the end of the street that Gopal must take, the street that faces the Fiat. The other exit from this place—" Roy's smile increased—"we are blocking it. Ah, there he goes now!"

There were shouts of general confusion as the Fiat shot recklessly into the narrow street straight ahead. Lavji was in his Citroën, trying to get it started. The Fiat was out of sight before he could begin to follow.

Roy watched the scene with a look of triumph on his usually placid face. He stepped outside the Mercedes to get a better view of his driver, posted near the Renault, who had now come out of his daydream and swung around—belatedly—to face his prisoner. "Good show," Roy said approvingly. "Not one smile, not one laugh. Very good." He signaled to his driver to return as the other three agents reached Shawfield in the Renault. Within a minute, it was driving away, heading for the exit that had been barred to Gopal.

"Damned neat!" Renwick said. Claudel was laughing, shaking his head. And Roy, tactfully avoiding any near approach to the white-faced girl who was still tense, still bewildered, squeezed into the front seat beside the driver (now grinning widely) and Claudel. The Mercedes left, too, with a cluster of curious diehards, obvious Muslims with heads covered by turbans or caps, staring after it in wonder, or perhaps with the increasing conviction that all infidels, whether Hindu or Christian, were crazy. That opinion would have

been reinforced if they could have seen Roy pick up a phone and reach his
office, miles away behind the Malabar Gift Shop, to start inquiries about
Suite 12A. He had dropped his Oxford-accented English to speak volubly
in a language that was strange even to his driver. "We'll soon know," he
told Renwick when the call was over. "Before we reach the hotel, we will
know."

"I've one serious reservation," Renwick said. "In fact, it's more than that.
Nina—well, I don't want her staying at that hotel." And, his tone of voice
said, that was final.

"There's no time to make other arrangements," Roy objected. "Your
hotel, Robert, is neither so comfortable nor so well protected. She would
be alone there: you have much business to finish."

Renwick needed no reminder of that. "I have two friends who are on call
for any emergency. They'll guard Nina until Pierre or I can take over." He
looked at Nina. We've frozen her out of this conversation, he thought as
he noticed she was uncertain and troubled once more. He drew her into it,
said, "Remember the two Australians in the red Ferrari?"

She nodded.

"They'll have you on a plane as soon as it's safe enough. But not alone,"
he added quickly. "There will be someone with you all the way home."

"You?"

"If that is possible," he could only say. If I'm still alive, he was thinking.
He tightened his hand on hers, felt a small response. I'll damned well make
it possible: I'm not going to lose her this time.

Suddenly she was relaxed. Her voice was almost normal as she said to
Roy, "I'm sorry to be such a complication. I'll stay at Bob's hotel."

A most unnecessary complication, thought Roy, but at least she realizes
that. It seemed a good moment to press an urgent question. "Before you
reach there, would you help us? Can you describe the district where you
stayed? The street—do you know its name? The house—had it a number?"

"I didn't notice—didn't see any names. . . ." She shook her head, felt
stupid.

"Somewhere near Ballard Pier," Claudel prompted her. "Wasn't that where
you telephoned, Nina? From a money exchange in the harbor area?"

"Yes." She tried to focus her thoughts, bring back a memory she wanted
to dismiss forever. She made an effort. "If I saw it again, I'd recognize it.
The house—" so many of these houses looked alike—"wasn't far away. Quite
near. Have you time to—"

"Time? You could save us hours of searching," Roy said, forgiving her
completely for having upset his plans. "It will take only a few extra minutes," he told Renwick, countering any objection from him. "And," he
clinched the matter, "we'll drive past the house; we won't stop."

Before they entered the harbor area, the return phone call from the Malabar
came through. Roy had his information: Dr. Frederick Weber, an antique
dealer from London, occupied Suite 12A. He had registered last Tuesday
for a five-day visit, along with his secretary and his valet, who occupied
the same accommodations. "All is well," Roy reported. "He travels in
style." Later, his eyes told Renwick and Claudel, I'll give you the details

later. He glanced at his watch. Almost five o'clock. Just over two hours ago there had been nothing but apparent failure. He beamed happily at Nina.

"Travels in style, does he?" Claudel murmured. "Some expense account!"

Yes, thought Renwick, that's Theo.

Twenty-four

THEO'S INSTRUCTIONS, SENT in code to the camper before it had entered Bombay, were precise. Kiley was to meet him at two o'clock in the Malabar Hotel. Kiley was to be circumspectly dressed. Kiley was to avoid the four large elevators (attended) and make sure that one of the smaller elevators (self-service) was empty before he used it. Kiley was to get out at the twelfth floor. Kiley would be met by a red-haired man who would greet him in Italian: "This is warmer than Rome in August." Kiley would reply in Dutch: "And as hot as Jakarta." Kiley would then be conducted to Theo's rooms, pausing—if anyone should appear in the corridor—to chat with his guide until they judged it was safe to enter.

In spite of a sense of urgency—why else had such an unexpected meeting been arranged?—Kiley felt real amusement as he stepped into Suite 12A. Tony would blame that on Nina's bad influence, he thought; and perhaps it was. Back in Essen, he wouldn't have seen anything comic in the contrast between a secretive approach and an open rendezvous. For what else would you call a meeting in a luxury hotel? No shadowed Gothic pillars this time for Theo, no slipping into the aisles of the Minster.

His escort entered a room on the left, where Kiley glimpsed a blond, thin-shouldered man at a table with elaborate equipment. The door closed. Kiley waited, looking at the elegance around him. The last comfortable hotel room he had seen—the only one, in fact, he had ever occupied—had been at Russell Square in London, and it looked like a hen house compared to all this. Then his critical study of Theo's living quarters ended as the door to his right opened, and Theo appeared. The three minutes' delay had been calculated, thought Kiley. He overcame his surprise at Theo's appearance—apart from his height and weight, he was difficult to recognize. He was now a white-haired man without glasses, a white mustache on his short upper lip, slow in movement and dressed in a dark-gray silk suit.

But Theo's voice was as crisp as ever as he greeted Kiley in German. His gray eyes had the same strange alternation of bland innocence and calm scrutiny. "Four months since we met," he said, shaking hands briefly. "You look well, Erik. They have agreed with you. Not too unpleasant a journey? Sit down, sit down. We have much to discuss without wasting time. I must leave here no later than three o'clock—an important meeting at three-thirty."

He pointed to a low chair on one side of a small gilded table, and selected the one (firmer, higher, more commanding) opposite.

"I sent regular reports—" Kiley began, slightly on the defensive.

"Read with much interest. A successful trip on the whole. You had a tendency, however, to give more importance to the revolutionaries of the extreme left than to members of the Communist groups. In Iran, for instance, you saw only two of the Tudeh—"

"I spoke with them."

"So the Soviet Embassy informed me."

It would, thought Kiley: it had agents and spies everywhere, the biggest intelligence network in all of Iran. "I found the Tudeh people waited too much for instructions. The militant revolutionaries may be more extreme, but they'll take action on their own whenever they see the chance."

"And that appeals to you." Theo shook his head. "Are you still unwilling to admit that anarchists won't succeed—in the long run? That is what counts, Erik. Not today's quick victories but tomorrow's permanent success." Theo smiled. "You'll come around to seeing it yet." He dismissed the topic with a wave of his hand. His mood turned solemn. "I have had some disquieting news. We have to alter our original plan."

"Which one?"

Theo's eyebrows were raised.

"We had three objectives, hadn't we?" As Theo kept a watchful silence, Kiley went on. "First: Marco and I were to drop out of sight completely, leave the West Germans baffled. Second: we were to recruit and encourage while we traveled, select the most promising material. Third: I was to gain acceptance into the O'Connell household, possibly as a future son-in-law."

There was a brief silence. The third objective had never been detailed. Erik was smart, thought Theo, sometimes too smart. "Have you actually asked the girl to marry you?"

"Not exactly. Hinted at it. It seemed wiser to—"

"Are you lovers?"

"Not yet. I planned that for Bali." Kiley was embarrassed. "Just making sure of the last stages in our journey to Washington."

"Too bad that we must cancel your visit to Bali."

Incredulous, Kiley stared at him. "What? *Cancel?*"

"You will go directly from here to America—to a training camp I have established in Southern California. One of my best agents was in charge, but he died—along with his chief assistant. I need two capable men to replace him: you and Marco. It's an important assignment—the final training of students who have graduated from camps abroad, preparing them for specialized work in the United States."

Angrily, Kiley said, "What about the O'Connell project? You told me, back in Essen, that it was of top priority. You said it had approval and backing at the 'highest levels'—wasn't that what you said?"

How much does he need to know to be kept in line? Theo wondered. "Yes," he said smoothly, "my first suggestion was very well received at the highest levels. It was, quite simply, the idea that you would be a very useful son-in-law—for us—when Francis O'Connell becomes Secretary of State.

He is in line for that; and, in fact, if his new wife has her way, he may even run for President."

"That's not my kind of future, and you know it, Theo."

"Yes, I know it. And so, once I was given a small department of my own—necessary to prevent any leaks, any information about such a project being whispered around—I emended that original idea, added more action for you and Marco."

"Such as?"

"A more explosive situation, shall we say?"

"And is it approved by the highest levels?"

Theo side-stepped that question. "I've been given full charge of this project."

"Of the original idea," Kiley corrected him, and then frowned. "Very clever of them. They thought they'd keep me hanging around Washington for years. And who'd be leading Direct Action in Europe, then? One of their stooges, I bet." Or one of yours, he added silently.

"Relax, Erik. I changed all that."

"Do they know?"

"Time enough for them to know when my plan succeeds. It will be far more devastating than having access to a future Secretary of State."

"O'Connell might learn he's being used."

"What could he do? Let the world know that his daughter is married to a terrorist—of *your* reputation and importance, Erik?"

Kiley wasn't to be silenced by that compliment. "I don't see why you have to ditch me now. If there's some action ahead, I can handle it." The target must be big, bigger than O'Connell himself. In rising excitement, he added, "Don't cut me out, Theo. You owe me—"

"Arrangements have already been made," Theo said. That was final. "The O'Connell assignment has been given to another agent."

"Are you sure that agent knows enough about explosives? You did mention an explosive situation, didn't you?"

Theo regretted his joke. "The agent will not have to deal with explosives. We have found other specialists for that job. All my agent will have to do is—substitute. Scarcely an assignment worthy of your talents, Erik." And that should end his interest.

Kiley almost laughed. Even if Theo believed in simple means backed by elaborate stratagems, a substitution was too damned simple. No use arguing that. Theo would answer that simple means were the hardest to detect: anything normal aroused no suspicion.

"Yes?" Theo had noticed the fleeting amusement in Kiley's eyes.

Something normal, arousing no suspicion . . . Kiley's quick mind made a stab at several possibilities. "Just speculating on what you've chosen to hold your bomb. Something portable, I'd imagine—unless you intend to blow O'Connell's house to pieces. But that would be hardly worth the effort. Nothing of importance there."

"Really?" Theo was on guard. "And what would you use to conceal your explosives—something portable, you said?"

"Well—" Kiley hesitated, spoke half-jokingly—"something like a brief-

case. It's just simple-minded enough to succeed—if the right man was carrying it into the right place."

"Amusing idea." Theo managed a thin smile. "But forget it. A briefcase
did not work with Hitler." And that, he thought, ends all discussion.

"I imagine—" Kiley ventured a touch of sarcasm—"there have been a few
slight improvements in explosives since Hitler's day."

"So I've heard," Theo said coldly.

"I could rig a briefcase with enough power to blast not only a large room
apart but also every adjacent room and corridor." Kiley's confidence was
returning. Yes, he thought, I'll show him that Marco and I are as good a
team as he could find for any O'Connell assignment. "How to set off the
explosives? We could use a timer or remote control."

The best way to stop all speculation, thought Theo, may be to give him
full rein, and then pull him up to a sudden and sharp halt. "Which would
you choose? Supposing, that is, you were planning to use this hypothetical
briefcase?"

"Not a timer," Kiley decided. "A meeting in a conference room could
be delayed, or ended sooner than expected. Remote control is surer—with
someone in a corridor nearby to see when everyone has entered the room.
We'd need advance information, of course, to make certain the meeting was
important and would be well attended."

"Of course," Theo echoed, all innocence. "You'd have your sources for
that information, I presume."

"Right. And that makes it a sure thing. Give the room twenty minutes or
more—perhaps half an hour—to settle down. Then press the button."

"The man—or woman—in the corridor would be killed, too."

"He—or she—wouldn't know that."

Theo studied his hands. "A well-trained intelligence officer might have a
better solution."

Kiley's lips tightened.

"Your hypothetical briefcase could be installed with a miniature transmitter—give notice to someone a safe distance away to press the button." Judging from the chagrin on Kiley's face, Theo had pulled him up to a very sharp
halt. "But your idea is interesting. You might even use it someday. With
your ingenuity, it's a pity I had to take you off the O'Connell assignment."

"But why? Why change—"

"Because James Kiley can no longer exist. Nor can Tony Shawfield."

"What?" Kiley's stare passed from amazement to incredulity. "*What?*"

"Tonight you will leave for the United States, using new names, new
identities, and Canadian passports. You will travel separately, of course, taking
different directions. You will meet at Rancho San Carlos in Sawyer Springs,
California. It is easily reached from either Los Angeles or San Diego. Marco
already has these orders. I saw him an hour ago."

He actually met Theo? Actually saw him? That was a first. And he heard the
orders before I did? I am being disciplined, Kiley realized. He said nothing.

"It was a brief meeting," Theo said, as if he had guessed Kiley's thoughts.
"Minimal but necessary information, along with his instructions for tonight.
He is to take his five charges to the cargo area of the airport—there is a

plane arriving at nine, unloading some pilgrims returning from Mecca while others continue their flight home to Indonesia. He will dangle the prospect of Bali before their eyes, get them on board, and once he loses them in Indonesia—and I mean *lose* them—he can leave for America. You'll see him later this afternoon and give him the money for all these expenses along with his Canadian passport. Quite clear?"

I'm still in command, Kiley thought. Five of the group to be bundled off, abandoned, lost for good . . . "What about Nina?"

"Your problem. A major one." Theo was suddenly angry. He hadn't liked the use of "Nina" in just that tone of voice: O'Connell was enough. "Do you think these changes in plans are a whim on my part?" He rose, crossed over to a bureau, removed several items from a drawer—a thin folder, a thick envelope, traveler's checks, and a newspaper. "Today's," he said curtly, thrusting it into Kiley's hand. "I had the information last Monday. Why do you think I ordered you to make a complicated arrival in Bombay, ditch the camper, lose any possible tail on you? Oh, yes, there was one." He dropped the envelope packed with dollars and the traveler's checks at Kiley's elbow. "Read, read! The headlines are big enough."

Kiley read. About Ilsa Schlott—"Greta"—the green camper—recruitment of terrorists for South Yemen training camps—her past association with the People's Revolutionary Force for Direct Action . . .

He said, "She won't talk. She'll never mention Erik or Marco." So why all this uproar? This news report was bad, but it could have been worse. Theo was losing his grip.

"She won't need to talk. Read column two on page nine."

Kiley found it. It was a close analysis of the "philosophy behind terrorism." Some historical patterns were given, brief excerpts from the anarchist writings of the nineteenth century—Bakunin, Kropotkin, Malatesta—leading into the People's Revolutionary Force for Direct Action, founded by two militant terrorists known as Erik and Marco. Past activities were listed: bombings, robberies, kidnapping, and murders. The column ended with Essen, the attempt on Duisburg—discovered in time to prevent half the town from being wiped out in a fire storm generated by the huge propane tanks on the docks—and the expert disappearance of Erik and Marco.

Kiley reread the column, paid little attention to the red-haired man who had moved quietly in from the room next door and handed Theo two slips of paper. "That one," the man said, "was in code. This one is a report we picked up from United Press only a minute ago."

Kiley looked up as Theo waved the man back to his room. "Who is responsible—" Kiley began. But Theo was engrossed by the two small sheets of paper.

Suddenly, Theo's smooth white face went rigid, carved out of marble. For a full minute he stood motionless. Then he shouted, "Klaus!" and the red-haired man reappeared.

Theo glanced at his watch: five past three. "Telephone the bank," he told Klaus. "Say I am ill, unable to attend the meeting. We will rearrange it for—" he paused—"for Tuesday. My sincere regrets." As Klaus started toward the telephone on the desk at the window, Theo yelled, "Not there!

Downstairs! A public phone in the lobby. And waste no time!" He stood glaring after Klaus. Then he dropped into his chair, glaring now at Kiley, yet not seeing him, not seeing anything.

At last Theo said, his voice almost normal, his face unreadable, "The press report comes from California—from Sawyer Springs. There was an explosion at Rancho San Carlos—one building totally destroyed. The FBI were immediately on the scene. Several men, asleep in a dormitory at the time of the explosion, have been arrested. A barn was searched; its contents removed. The main house was partly destroyed. Three men living there were injured; one seriously. All three are arrested, too."

"Who did it?" Kiley was aghast. "Were there no guards posted?" Damn those Americans, always asleep on the job.

"The fence alarm was bypassed. Two guard dogs were drugged. The body of an unknown man was found near the explosion. Unidentifiable."

"One man alone?"

We may never know, thought Theo. One thing we do know: the FBI had San Carlos under observation. How else could they arrive so quickly unless they were stationed in the village? "We will have to find you and Marco a safer house. In New York. We need you in America. No delay in leaving here tonight. No delay, you understand?" He glanced at the decoded message: *Reliable source identifies new arrivals at West German Embassy New Delhi as security police preparing to escort terrorists back to Essen. Extradition.* That information stays with me, Theo decided. Mention extradition and those two might not even wait for tonight—they could leave immediately. Stop to dispose of O'Connell and get rid of those five young fools? No, I don't think Erik or Marco would waste any time on that. Extradition was a powerful word. He struck a match, pulled a large jade ashtray in front of him, and set the slips of paper burning over it.

Kiley folded the newspaper, laid it on the table. "Who informed?" he asked bitterly. "Greta?"

"It took more than informers to piece all that material together."

"CIA—MI6—NATO?"

"It could be a new intelligence unit. I've had two reports based on rumors, nothing substantive as yet. But I think I know one man who may be connected with it." And I wrote him off: his resignation from NATO seemed entirely probable—it had been rumored for weeks, and its timing fitted in with that death scare and the stupid affair in Brussels which could have ended his career anyway. "He never seemed to be too important. He just happened to be on the scene of any action." Such as in Vienna, over two years ago. "Always with a reasonable excuse for being there." Such as in Essen, which he visited on his way back from observing NATO maneuvers in West Germany.

"What makes you suspect him now?"

"His friends—who have been interested in your recent movements. Two carpet dealers—"

"I reported on them," Kiley said quickly.

"And we investigated. One works for Turkish Intelligence. The other is French, once connected with NATO, a friend of—"

"We dealt with these two," Kiley interjected. "They are out of the picture."

"Indeed? The Turk is now in Srinigar on his carpet business. The Frenchman was reported to be traveling south from Delhi. To Bombay?"

"But we had hashish planted in their car at Quetta. Well hidden. And we warned the Indian customs—"

"By the time they reached the frontier, no hashish was found. So no arrest, no prison sentence. With whom did you think you were dealing? Amateurs?"

Kiley bridled, decided to make little of that jibe. It wasn't the first time that Theo had emphasized the differences between the training of a terrorist and that of an intelligence agent. "Why Bombay?" he asked. "India is a continent in itself. South of New Delhi there are hundreds of towns, thousands of villages—"

"You and Marco are in Bombay. Nina O'Connell is in Bombay."

Kiley stared at the placid face, had the wisdom to keep silent.

Theo said, "The Frenchman is following the girl. She leads him to you. That is his plan. Obviously."

If he *is* in Bombay, thought Kiley. He could not resist saying, "And I lead him to you, Theo?"

"I do not think that will be likely."

"You certainly risked a lot in bringing me—and Marco—to this room."

"I've had many visitors—some quite legitimate," Theo said sharply. "What is better cover than a large hotel with a busy lobby and five entrances? Four hundred double rooms—with seven hundred guests at least? How many outside visitors to the restaurants, grill, bar? To the arcade for its shops and bargains? To the barbershop and the massage room, and the travel bureaus? A hotel such as this is safer than any private house, provided—" he added with amusement—"you have a man permanently in your rooms who will watch the hotel maid or service waiter."

Kiley seemed convinced. But one thing puzzled him. If Theo felt so secure, why had he not kept his appointment for half past three?

"Yes?" asked Theo, quick to notice.

Kiley shrugged.

"Yes?" Theo's voice had sharpened. "You have something to add?"

"Why cancel your business at the bank? It wasn't connected with me, or with Nina."

"Too many storm signals," Theo said abruptly. Until I find out what they mean, I do not risk a public appearance as Otto Remp from Düsseldorf. Could Renwick have traced any connection between Remp and Essen? I was careful there; used a false name and address for that bank account from which Erik drew his monthly allotments. And there was no other obvious connection with Erik: our meetings were rare and well-disguised.

"The Frenchman won't be in Bombay alone," Kiley said thoughtfully. "I could recognize him—if I had a close look." Unless he's wearing a white wig and mustache. "What is his name?"

"Claudel. Major Claudel." Theo opened the folder. It contained a page of information, very little by Theo's usual standards. There was also an envelope marked "Negatives" with a small photograph clipped to it. Theo removed the photograph, passed it to Kiley. "Have you seen that man anywhere on your travels?"

The snapshot was of two people: a man, young-looking, handsome, laughing; a brunette beauty, with a smile on her face. Judging from the background, the bedroom belonged to a woman with taste and money. "No. Never. Who is he?"

"Claudel's friend. If my informant is correct, he could be the originator of that intelligence unit I mentioned. It is called Interintell, according to Johan Vroom, the new chief of one intelligence section at The Hague."

"He's your man?" Kiley was impressed.

"No. He is just too eager to silence his colleagues—he is younger than they are, so he asserts his importance by parading his knowledge. You can keep that photograph. I have the negative."

"Interintell . . . What the hell does that mean?"

"International Intelligence. To be used against international terrorism. A good idea—from Renwick's point of view."

"Renwick." Kiley looked at the photograph again, memorizing features and the build of the shoulders.

"About your height. Your color of hair. Gray eyes. Age—late thirties. Keeps himself in good shape."

"I can see that. Also his good taste in women. Who is she? Someone who installed a camera in her bedroom?"

"We had it installed. With her knowledge, of course."

"A little more action here—" Kiley tapped the photograph—"and you could have blackmailed him nicely."

"I have other negatives," Theo said with a small smile. "But blackmail? And risk exposure for our agent? Destroy her future value?" Theo was thoughtful. "And I don't know if blackmail would work with Lieutenant Colonel Renwick. But someday we might try."

"Lieutenant Colonel?"

"Ex-Lieutenant Colonel, I should have said. He resigned from military intelligence. Actually, I think—" Theo looked sharply at the door to his suite as a gentle knock, repeated twice, sounded on its panel. It opened, and Klaus returned, pocketing his key. "You are late!"

"I walked around some streets after I telephoned. I thought that was better than returning here direct."

"We have been waiting for these passports! And the histories to go with them? Are they complete?"

"Almost ready. A few minutes." Klaus hurried into the room he shared with the radio-transmitter expert.

Theo was impatient, Theo was glancing at his watch again, Theo was restless. He rose, went to the room where Klaus was typing a last line on a sheet of paper. "That will do, that will do," Theo said and dropped his voice as he gave further instructions. Then he came back with two passports and two sheets of paper. "Here you are. Brief histories. They will carry you and Marco safely enough to New York. There you will receive other passports and much more detailed legends. Call the Soviet Consulate as soon as you arrive. Now I think that's about all. Safe journey, Erik."

Kiley glanced at the sheets of paper. "Shouldn't I memorize them here—they're short—destroy them before I leave? I'd rather not carry them around."

"Of course, of course," Theo agreed, but not too willingly. "Would you excuse me? I have much to do. Let me know when you leave." He picked up the folder from the table, pointed to the envelope and bundle of traveler's checks, and went into his room. The door closed.

He is packing up, thought Kiley, clearing out. Movements from the room next door were careful, subdued, but that sound might be said to belong to a drawer creaking open. Certainly, from the other bedroom, the activity wasn't disguised. But why conceal his departure from me? Kiley wondered. It could be that Theo's "storm signals" were of hurricane strength; perhaps he hid the worst from me in case Marco and I cleared out, too, and the hell with Bali and our five idiots. But what about Nina? Your problem, Theo had said. Not enough; he'd better be more precise than that. Quickly, Kiley began memorizing the two new histories. Graduate students returning from a year's study abroad; Marco came from Quebec, Kiley from Toronto, et cetera, et cetera . . .

In ten minutes, he was sure of place names and dates. Brief legends, compared to others he had learned in the past, but enough to skate through an entry into New York. It would have been a different matter if Marco and he had to face Quebec or Toronto. Changes, changes, he thought as he set the pages alight over the ashtray and watched them turn to black quivering leaves.

Yet change was the essence of his beliefs: spontaneity in action, flexibility in thought—he had praised them in his manifesto, had attacked stability and the status quo as enemies of true progress. As they were. So welcome change, he told himself, and stilled a qualm of regret for the end of four months that had been a pleasant interlude, could have been more. . . . But there had been successes in recruitment: that was one achievement that couldn't be halted—the tide was running his way. And Nina? He could have won her, but he had followed Theo's plan—no personal involvement for him—and whatever he had hoped for the future, in his return to America with Nina, was now ended.

He pocketed the checks and the money and knocked on Theo's door. "I'm leaving. Everything taken care of. Except . . ." He waited until the door opened.

"Except what?" Theo's tone was sharp. He was in shirt sleeves. The white wig and mustache were gone. Suitcases were on the bed. "What?"

"Marco takes five of them to Bali. Where do I take Nina?"

"Nowhere. She can identify every stop you made on your journey. Get rid of her."

"Kill her?" Kiley asked. His face was tense.

"What else?" Theo stared at him unbelievingly. "Do I need to tell *you* how to make it look natural? No gun. Use your cyanide pistol. Or an overdose. She isn't one of your addicts, but who is to know that?"

Abruptly, Kiley turned to leave.

"It is possible," Theo said, "she has duped you completely. She may be one of Renwick's agents. As you said, he has good taste in women. He knew O'Connell—very well indeed, I heard."

Kiley left. In the corridor, he paused. A lie, he thought, a lie to make sure I'd deal with Nina. Because if she's one of Renwick's agents, then the stupidity in sending her on the world trip belongs to Theo. He selected her; I didn't. And before he ever chose her to accompany me, he had checked her background: no intelligence training of any kind. It was a lie. Nina and Renwick? Ludicrous. He pulled out Renwick's photograph, tore it into shreds, thrust them deep into the sand of a giant ashtray.

He walked on, almost forgot to take one of the small self-service elevators, found himself, still arguing with Theo. Then, about to pass through the lobby to its huge front door, he came to his cool calm senses again and switched directions. Five entrances, Theo had said. Kiley chose one that led out of the bar onto a side street. He'd take the usual evasionary tactics, allow himself a spell of wandering around, catching a taxi here, another taxi there, before he headed for the house near the docks. He had told Nina he'd return by four o'clock. His watch said it was now past that hour. For a second he was tempted to go back directly, but habit and training prevailed. He began his tortuous, seemingly purposeless journey. No one followed.

Twenty-five

KILEY'S ROUNDABOUT ROUTE was long enough to bring him back to normal, to a sense of reality. No matter how he felt about Nina, she was a danger. The sooner he dealt with that problem, the safer for him, for Marco. His pace increased as the houses on the harbor road came in sight. Joined together to form a continuous line, they seemed so similar that he might have passed Gopal's place had he not spied Madge—Madge and the little Indian girl—loitering in front of its entrance. What the devil were they doing there? he wondered, his mood changing into sharp annoyance.

Madge saw him. Like the idiot she was, she came running to greet him right there in the open street. "I'm worried about Tony," she began. "Have you seen him?"

"Let's get inside." He pulled her into the cover of the entrance almost as far as the foot of the verandah stairs but out of sight from the courtyard. A murmur of distant voices told him that the men still sat there.

The Indian girl followed them, saying, "She is gone, she is gone. The Englishman went looking. Gopal, too. And Gopal's friend who drives the car." Her words, spilling out in her excitement, were scarcely understandable.

Kiley stared at her. "What the hell is she talking about? Nina?" Nina gone? Gone? He mastered his rage.

Madge, almost as incoherent, tried to explain. It was Tony's absence that worried her. Two, almost three hours since he went searching for Nina. Yes, Nina had left. That's the way she wanted it, so let her go. But Tony—

"Yes. You need Tony," Kiley interrupted harshly. Tony and some more hashish to meet the evening ahead. He looked at Madge with contempt: gaunt face, vacant eyes, drooping lips; she had become a caricature of herself. In anger, he turned on the little Indian, who was still babbling away about a phone call and the American in her pretty dress and a taxi ride. "Shut up and listen! Is Gopal's cousin here—the man with the scar on his cheek? Bring him to me. At once!"

Storm signals, Theo had said. Kiley was sensing them now, and taking their warning. "Madge, you'll all have to leave. This place will be raided for drugs. You've got to get out, all of you. Get the others together. Tell them to pack. Gopal's cousin will take you to a plane. It leaves tonight. For Bali."

"Bali?" Her sudden smile of delight faded. "But what about Tony?"

"He will join you at the airport. He's making the arrangements now. And if he is delayed—don't worry. Gopal's cousin will travel all the way to Bali with you, keep you safe. Tony will join you there. Now hurry—don't waste a moment! Get the others down here in ten minutes—five, if you can manage it."

Madge started toward the staircase. "How long did Tony search for Nina? Really, she caused so much trouble. But he shouldn't have worried. No need."

Something is behind these words, Kiley thought. Carefully, he said, "Tony had travel arrangements to make. He has more on his mind than Nina."

"Just as well. She met her friends. I saw them. They drove past here."

"When?"

"Oh, just before you came back. Shahna and I had gone walking to the market. I was—I was restless after Nina left. Trust Nina to travel in style—a Mercedes!" She giggled nervously. "And with Robert Renwick. Did she ever tell you about him?"

"Often." He even smiled. "Now, get the others. Quick! Make them understand you could all be arrested."

"I haven't any drugs." But she was climbing the staircase.

Gopal's cousin was interested in the fee for his services—half paid now, the rest in Bali. Certainly he could find the runway where the cargo planes loaded. Certainly he could arrange for transport among the returning Muslims. Certainly he would see everyone safe—as far as Bali. His sharp brown eyes glistened at the prospect. They were a little dashed when Kiley handed over the money, for fares and food and his fee's second installment, to the tall Dane, who came downstairs with his French wife and her guitar, followed by the Dutchman and the Italian and the American girl.

"What about transportation to the airfield?" Sven Dissen wanted to know, stowing the wad of notes inside Marie-Louise's handbag, which he'd carry under his arm.

"The cars that brought us here this morning," Kiley answered. Yes, he had been right to make Dissen the treasurer.

"There's only one left," Gopal's cousin said. "The Englishman took the other along with—"

"Then get the one that is left," Kiley said sharply. "It's parked in the courtyard next door."

"There will be a payment necessary."

"Yes, yes," Kiley said, and handed out more money. "Now get to it!"

There was a short wait. To Kiley it seemed interminable. No one around him had much to say: they were all a little dazed, but no objections were voiced. There was the usual lament from Henryk Tromp about his stolen camera—and now he was going to Bali, where he'd need it more than ever. "I'll lend you my Kodak," Madge told him. "Just don't talk about your camera any more. Or the film that disappeared with it." She looked around her, said, "This place is really crummy. I'll be glad to leave." She led the way to the street, where the Fiat had drawn up at the curb. Then she noticed Kiley wasn't following. She turned and waved, "See you in Bali, too?"

He nodded.

They settled into the Fiat with squeals and laughs at the tight pack, everything forgotten except the excitement of the journey ahead. The car moved off. Twenty minutes to six, he saw by his watch. Time to start leaving.

Ignoring the men sitting in the courtyard, he ran up the stairs to the room he was to have shared with Shawfield. Both their duffel bags were padlocked. He opened his own, extracted the cyanide pistol and some extra pellets. The knife he strapped above his ankle. His .32 was anchored in his belt. His movements were brisk, precise. Soon he was ready.

In haste, he checked the rooms to make sure those clowns hadn't left any identifications behind. Strange how quickly they had moved at the threat of a narcotics raid, although they pretended they never took drugs, never began squirreling them away as soon as they were safely across a frontier. Hooked on hashish—and heroin, too: Lambrese and Tromp had graduated to that along with the gold chains around their necks. Well, they could sell these for food when the money ran out in Bali. And after that? If they had any willpower left, and that was improbable, they might find a way to leave. Perhaps Sven Dissen could manage that, unless he was kept paralyzed by his Marie-Louise. As for Madge—he could see nothing for her. But no one had forced hashish or morphine sulphate tablets down their throats. It had been their own free choice, and their stupidity.

In Nina's room he halted. Her canvas bag lay on the window seat: two shirts unfolded and abandoned. The blue one matched her eyes, he remembered, and then choked off that treacherous thought. A movement from the entrance to the room caught his ear: the little Indian girl was there, looking at the shirts and the open bag.

"Take them," he told her. "But don't let the police see them."

She shook her head. She ran forward, swept up the bag and shirts in her thin arms, hurried to the door. "Wait!" he called, stopping her at the threshold. She looked at him fearfully, brown eyes pleading, while she clutched her new possessions more tightly to her chest. "Take this, too." He tossed over Shawfield's bag, watched her drag it away with her other arm still full of Nina's clothes. Like a little pack rat, he thought. "Remember," he called to her, "tell the police nothing. Nothing! Or you'll get arrested for stealing."

Out of fright, she almost dropped her load, but gripped it again, and vanished from sight. The last of Antony Shawfield . . . The last of James Kiley, too, as soon as a brazier or a kitchen oven could be found on the ground floor, and a passport could be destroyed.

He gave a final glance at the window seat where the blue striped shirt had lain, his lips tight, his jaw clenched. Suddenly, he felt a surge of relief: he didn't have to face Nina, deciding—even as he smiled and talked—how she would die. She'd stay alive. And Theo couldn't blame him.

And that reminded him: he must find the nearest telephone, call Theo, tell him what had happened. The news about Renwick would send him flying out of Bombay. That should be easy for Theo: he was already preparing to leave.

He hoisted his duffel bag over his shoulder, stepped out onto the verandah. And where do I go? he wondered. To New York? Hide there, inactive, waiting for Theo's orders while someone else takes over my Washington assignment? But damned if I know why Theo canceled me because of Greta and a onetime green camper and a column on Erik. There was no identification of Erik with Kiley or of Marco with Shawfield. So why was I ordered to drop out after all the work I've put into this mission? To hell with New York: I'm not a puppet, jerking at the end of a string.

He heard a movement from the room just ahead of him, its door flung wide open for air. He halted, waited until the footsteps had ceased, made sure that no one would emerge. Marco, he was thinking, Marco wouldn't be in New York, either. Once he gets back here—what the hell has detained him?—and finds we have all cleared out, he will get the message. He will head for Germany and our friends there. That's where our connections are. Ours. Not Theo's.

The movements in the room ceased. Carefully, he slipped past the open door. Yes, he decided, we'll reactivate Direct Action. We'll move; in our way, not in Theo's. We'll scare him witless, him and his Leninist friends. We'll show them what revolution really means. And if his plan in Washington succeeds—all the better for us. Devastating, he had said. America to be paralyzed, unable to act—even temporarily? For that, Theo, thank you.

Kiley reached the end of the verandah. Suddenly, the courtyard erupted in noise: protests, shrill cries, authoritative voices. He halted, took one look over the balustrade, drew back. Police. Three in uniform, two in plain clothes.

Beside him was the last room on the verandah, its door gaping wide. He threw his duffel bag across its threshold and started down the narrow staircase. His .32 was in his right hand, held close to his thigh, unnoticeable. His left hand concealed the bogus fountain pen. As yet he hadn't been seen from the courtyard. Walk normally, he told himself; don't hurry, don't rush, don't look as if you were escaping. Keep cool, Erik. This isn't the first time you have strolled out of a tight spot.

He reached the last flight of stairs. One man had been posted at the foot of the steps and was watching the courtyard scene with amusement. "They've all left, they've all left," the little Indian girl was screaming, "all left in a car." Forever the center of attention, Kiley thought. She throve on drama, that girl; and on a gift of clothes.

He continued down the stairs. The guard turned his head to look up at him. Kiley smiled easily, said, "What's happening out there? A family fight or something?"

The policeman studied him. "Stay there, please!"

"Of course," Kiley said pleasantly. He took three more casual steps and halted only a few feet away from the upturned face. He took a long deep breath and held it. He raised his left arm.

"What's that in your—" The man's question was never completed. Kiley pressed the release on the cyanide pistol, aiming it directly at the opened mouth. The man groped for support, began sliding to the ground.

Kiley stepped around the crumpled body, kept on walking, released his breath. The man would be dead before Kiley reached the street. But even policemen could have heart attacks, he thought as he slipped the pen into one pocket of his jacket, the .32 into the other. He kept firm hold of it, straightened his tie with his free hand, and ignored three cars drawn up in a phalanx before the entrance to the house.

Automatically, he turned to his left—away from the city's center and toward the docks—and mingled with the crowd.

"Stop!" came a yell behind him.

He walked calmly on, people around him on every side. Then as another "Stop!" was yelled, his pace increased. He was ready to break into a run, but he reached a side street, jammed with people and stalls and happy disorder. Well into this excellent cover, he slipped off his jacket, removed his tie as he stopped at a cart where morsels of food were being cooked. He chose two of the small brown objects, highly spiced, and enjoyed them while he sat on a narrow sidewalk beside a group of men and listened to the fading sounds of alarm from the main street.

He sat there amid dirt and debris taking stock of his resources. Money, yes. Three passports: two Canadian, one of them now unnecessary; one American, now dangerous. Three weapons.

At last, he felt he could risk walking slowly out of the market with his tie out of sight and the jacket tucked under his arm. The approach of early night was a help, too. So was the closing of the stalls: under a load of curling green vegetables, he slipped the French-Canadian passport. It would lead the police nowhere. The Kiley passport, however, would have to be destroyed, not abandoned. As soon as he reached the docks he would tear up its inside pages, drop the whole thing into the filthy waters. A sad ending for James Kiley.

And a new beginning for Louis Krimmon, graduate student traveling abroad, Toronto-born and raised, now in need of a berth on a freighter, any honest job to help him work his passage home. No luggage? Stolen. Everything lost except what he carried. Innocent Canadian deceived . . . Yes, that was the angle.

He had gone barely fifty yards along a street seething with people when he reached the lights of a money exchange still open for business. He saw a telephone just inside its wide door. Call Theo? Warn him of Renwick? Hell no; Theo was saving his own hide, right this minute. More important now was the group of seamen at the exchange entrance. Foreigners, all of them. This was his chance: choose an American, if possible—someone who'd be free with advice, if not help. His eyes were so busy searching out a likely soft mark that he didn't notice a slight small figure tugging at a man's sleeve.

Shahna said to Roy's man, Lavji, "That's him."

Lavji signed to the two men who had been waiting behind him for almost an hour. All three reached Kiley, took firm hold. They disarmed him there and then: a .32 in his jacket pocket, a knife strapped above his ankle, a thick fountain pen and pellets. Their car was waiting, drove off before a curious crowd could start gathering.

As Roy had said when he had learned of the escape, of the death of a policeman, "He will telephone a warning. As soon as it grows dark, he will come out of his hiding place—it can't be far from that house—he disappeared too quickly. So where is the nearest public telephone? Where?"

And Shahna had obliged.

Twenty-six

"SEVEN O'CLOCK AND all's well," Claudel said.

"So far," Renwick added to that. Nina was safely asleep nowhere near the Malabar; his friends Mahoney and Benson, the Australians whose room was opposite Renwick's, were taking turns at guard duty.

Roy, relaxing at his desk in the office behind the gift shop, was entitled to some self-congratulation: the report from Lavji had just come through; Kiley had been taken, too surprised to offer much resistance. "Two down," he told Renwick.

"And the biggest one to go."

"Well, he's still in his suite. When Lavji and the others return, we'll pay 12A a little visit. Meanwhile . . ." Roy shrugged and smiled. He had installed a floor waiter to keep watch and a chambermaid who had even entered the suite ten minutes ago with a batch of fresh towels. True, she hadn't got beyond the central living room, been dismissed by the red-haired valet; but she had glimpsed suitcases packed, ready and waiting.

"And when Theo leaves," Renwick said, "he won't be Dr. Frederick Weber with white hair, white mustache, and slow movements." That was all the information on Weber that the hotel desk could provide; that, and the fact that he had been a normal guest—sometimes visiting the bar, sometimes eating in the grill, and sometimes taxiing out for dinner. His

announced visitors had been businessmen—antique dealers—which was to
be expected.

"We know his height, his approximate weight," Roy said. "That won't
be altered."

Probably not, thought Renwick: this climate made added girth unpleasant; heavy padding around Theo's waist would have him sweating like a pig.
"I think I'll take a walk around the elevators," he said.

"Again?" Roy was amused, slightly annoyed, too. "I have men posted
there: one on each elevator along with its operator. Anyone descending from
the twelfth floor whom the operators haven't seen before will be detained.
We'll hear about it as soon as it happens. Time enough then to have our
confrontation. The elevators are only a minute away—less—from the accountants' room next door to us. And don't worry about the self-service elevators. They are out of commission."

Renwick stayed where he was, even if unwillingly: Roy was in charge; he
had co-operated fully and well. That's the hell of it, Renwick was thinking:
you take assistance, and you're in a subsidiary role. No matter that all Roy's
information about Theo had come from Claudel or himself: Roy was in
control at this moment and, with two successes already claimed, he was in
no mood to have his excellent arrangements questioned.

Claudel said tactfully, "Extraordinary news we received from London,
Bob." Gilman had given it when Renwick had contacted him about Marco's
arrest and Nina's safety. "Have any idea who blew up that San Carlos
ammunition dump? He did more than that: he has the FBI swarming all
over the place."

And died, too. It could only have been Sal. He knew the way to enter
that compound, silence the dogs, approach the armory. "I didn't arrange
it—wish I had," said Renwick.

"He was working alone?"

"Must have been."

"Someone with a grudge?"

"Or his own sense of justice."

"That can be dangerous."

"It was—for him." But Sal would have thought the price well worth it.

"How important was Rancho San—?"

Roy's telephone rang. It was a message from the hotel desk. "Did you
announce him? He was expected? I see. What's his description?" The call
ended and Roy could turn to Renwick and Claudel. "A visitor for Dr.
Frederick Weber. Introduced himself as Schmidt, an antique dealer. Said
he had an appointment for quarter past seven. The desk cleared that with
Weber's suite. Schmidt is now on his way up to 12A."

"Inconvenient timing," Claudel said. "Unless Dr. Weber isn't planning
to leave tonight." That had been Renwick's hunch: Theo would clear out
of Bombay as soon as possible; Theo was running scared—why else cancel
that vital meeting in the bank, and at such short notice? "Oh, I know,"
Claudel went on, catching a sharp glance from Renwick, "his suitcases are
ready to go. But some people do pack on the night before an early-morning start."

Renwick said, "What description did you get, Roy?"

"Cream-colored suit. About fifty years old, wears heavy glasses, has dark-brown hair—worn long but well brushed, carries a Panama hat. Very presentable." Roy frowned. "Sounds possible. All open and above board, wouldn't you say?"

"Height? Weight?" Renwick asked quietly.

Roy stared at Renwick, but he picked up the receiver again and—after some delay—got the information. "Medium height and weight and a deeply tanned face. Anything more, Robert?" he asked with a touch of sarcasm.

"Check with the twelfth floor. When did Schmidt enter the suite?"

"The floor waiter will report when there is anything to report," Roy said. "See!" he added, pointing to his expert over by a proud battery of radios and powerful transmitters who was receiving a message by means of a humble transceiver. It came from the twelfth floor. A visitor in a cream-colored suit, dark-haired, had been admitted to 12A eight minutes ago. He was just leaving now.

"The old shell game," Renwick said softly.

Claudel and Roy exchanged puzzled glances.

"He stayed just long enough for an exchange of suit and tie, an adjustment in make-up if needed." Renwick was on his feet, halfway to the door. "Let's move! Come on, you two, come on!" He left.

Claudel recovered, followed quickly.

"I'll warn the elevators," Roy said and began trying to contact their operators.

Renwick's run through a startled accounting department brought him into a short stretch of narrow hall. He checked his pace to a brisk walk as he entered the hotel lobby. A bank of four elevators faced him: two doors open, waiting for customers; one door closed, its indicator showing an ascent; the last door, also closed, its indicator beginning its descent from the upper floors.

Renwick nodded to Claudel, who had joined him, looked around for one of Roy's agents. Yes, there was the Mercedes' driver, trying to appear inconspicuous.

Claudel said, "I see Lavji arriving—he looks a very happy man. Promotion assured."

"Does he see us?"

"Yes."

"Good." So had Roy's driver. He folded his newspaper and walked slowly forward. "Keep your eyes on that elevator," Renwick told him. "Look for a cream-colored suit." And then Renwick stared at the indicator. "It has stopped." Stopped at the second floor.

"Not for long," Claudel said as the elevator started down again.

It reached the lobby. Its doors slid open. Several people emerged. Nine altogether. And not one light-colored suit among them.

"Goddamn it—" began Renwick. Then to Roy's agent, "Where's the staircase?"

"The main staircase or the fire staircase?"

"Where are they?" Renwick's voice was urgent.

"There—near the hotel desk—that's the main staircase. The fire exit . . ." He was pointing now to the rear of the lobby, close to the arcade, where a handsome door had a small orange light glowing overhead. "There are other fire exits, too," he said helpfully. "In all quarters of this building . . ."

"Any of them near these elevators?" Renwick cut in.

"That one!" He pointed again to the orange light.

Quickly, Renwick said to Claudel, "Take the front entrance. Lavji, too. I'll watch the arcade with helpful Harry. Keep in touch, Pierre." He had pulled out his mini-transceiver, small enough to be concealed in his hand: not much range but good enough for the lobby's long stretch. Pierre nodded, moved off with his transceiver ready.

Renwick signed to Roy's driver to follow, left for the lobby's exit to the arcade. The bar and restaurants lay that way, each with an entrance from the lobby, each with its door onto the arcade's covered walk. Theo would have plenty of choices for an escape if he used the fire stairs. Renwick kept his eyes on that door with the subdued orange light, expecting it to open any moment. Wish to God I had my Biretta, he thought: a courtesy to Roy, who had forbidden the carrying of any gun in crowded places; Renwick's role was to identify Theo and leave Roy's men to deal with him.

Renwick glanced around for his backup; but the man wasn't following. He was explaining everything to Roy, who had just appeared. For God's sake, thought Renwick—and then froze. Beyond where Roy was standing, the main staircase swept down into the lobby, its balustrades banked by flowers. A man in an ice-cream suit was descending at a leisurely pace, his shoulders visible, his Panama hat being donned over his dark hair as he prepared to step down into the lobby and join the flow of people.

Renwick swung around, retraced his steps, resisted breaking into a run: haste would attract Theo's attention—he had been studying the lobby, gauging its safety in his measured progress downstairs. You blasted fool, you damned idiot, Renwick told himself: you were wrong, you were wrong—he's going to stroll out by the front entrance into a nice dark night. But why? Not just because of a grand exit—not Theo: he'd take the surest way to certain escape. Through a crowded lobby where he couldn't hurry? Then Renwick guessed the answer. As he reached Roy, saying quickly, "He is in the lobby, just passing the hotel desk," he raised his transceiver and pressed its signal for Claudel's attention. "Pierre—he is taking the main entrance. Schmidt's car and driver—they could be waiting at the front steps. Best get him there—away from the lobby. Check outside. Take Lavji and whoever is with him."

"Will do. He's now in view—partially. Just glimpsed him—walking slowly—using a cane. We'll move out ahead of him."

A cane . . . "Look out, Pierre! Warn Lavji! That cane could be dangerous."

Slight pause. "*That* kind of walking stick?" Pierre asked with an attempt at nonchalance.

"We'll be close on his heels." Renwick signed off, looked at Roy. "We can risk hurrying. Theo will be keeping his eyes on the entrance."

Roy, without a sign that he objected to having his men ordered around by anyone but himself, fell into quick step with Renwick, his driver following closely.

"A cane?" Roy asked, his eyes searching past the islands of ornamental trees and clusters of people. "Lavji is trained to deal with that. No, I don't think it's too dangerous a weapon. Look—there he is!" Roy had caught sight of the cream-colored suit and the Panama hat. Theo had joined a small group of people: two more light suits beside him—almost indistinguishable from Theo's. There was also another Panama hat visible, but below it was a gray suit. "He merges well. A clever man," Roy said.

"And cautious." Renwick's hand grasped Roy's arm, slowing their rapid pace. Theo's group had drifted away from him to the porter's desk, and so now he had drawn close to a decorative tree, appeared to be studying the flowers around its base as he looked back along the lobby. Renwick's face was averted. He seemed to be deep in conversation with Roy, who kept a smile on his lips and his eyes now entirely on Renwick.

Renwick was asking, "How many men with Lavji?"

"Two." Roy's smile widened. "Enough to take care of that very dangerous cane."

"It's lethal. As lethal as that fountain pen James Kiley used."

The smile was gone. "You are sure?"

"Why is he carrying it? Schmidt didn't."

"He has started moving again," Roy said.

They quickened their pace, pressed through the last fringe of people standing just inside the entrance. Theo was already outside.

He was waiting on the steps, looking for his car, speaking angrily to the puzzled doorman. "It should have been here. Where is it? A black Lancia—"

"There it is now, sir!" It came slowly out of the darkness, reached the brilliant lights of the hotel's entrance.

Theo brushed the doorman aside and went ahead of him down the steps, quickly reached the car. The driver was not in uniform. Two men were in the rear seat, opening the door, coming out at him. He backed two steps, turned as he heard footsteps behind him, gripped his cane. He saw an Indian, tall, immaculately dressed, and with him a younger man, European or American, of medium height, watchful, alert. Theo stared.

"Yes, Theo," the American said, "I am Renwick."

Theo's cane was raised. His eyes flickered toward the trees and flower beds on his right, gently illuminated, partly shadowed.

Roy said, "Otto Remp, I am placing you under arrest for extradition to—"

Theo moved, a sudden dash toward the trees, lunging at Renwick as he passed. Renwick caught the cane, deflecting its aim, wrenched it free from Theo's grip. Theo tried to run on, but Claudel and Lavji had closed in, grasped his arms and forced them behind his back. Deftly, Lavji handcuffed his wrist to Theo's.

Roy, his Oxford English still more noticeable, said, "Otto Remp, I am placing you under arrest for extradition to West Germany. You will now be taken to police headquarters, where you will be questioned. That may delay your extradition for a few days." His voice became cold, his eyes hard. "But we, too, as well as West Germany, have questions to ask you about certain projects you are planning." Roy nodded to Lavji, and Theo was led to the car. His face was composed. Not one protest, not one comment. An old hand, thought Renwick, a real professional.

Claudel said, "Here, Bob, let me hold that piece of evidence." He tried to take the walking stick from Renwick's fingers, found it was too tightly gripped. Renwick relaxed, attempted a laugh, slowly released his grasp. Damn me, he thought, noticing a tremble in his hand, and stuck it deep into his pocket.

Roy eyed the cane with distaste. "Leave it in my office—you will have a report to send to London. I shall join you there. At nine o'clock." He looked toward the Lancia. "I am taking that one in myself. A tricky customer." Roy shook his head. "Canes and fountain pens that can kill and—"

"I forgot," Renwick said. "This belonged to Shawfield. He had it with him today—at Falkland Road."

Roy took the small cyanide pistol. It was similar to the empty one that had been found on James Kiley. It could be a useful piece of evidence—destroy Kiley's protest that it was only a fountain pen. "Is this one loaded?"

"Yes. He didn't manage a shot."

Roy pocketed the imitation pen gingerly. "And you've been carrying it around?" he asked with marked disapproval.

"I forgot," Renwick said again, and smiled.

Roy studied him, decided to forget this lapse of memory. "We talk too long. I must leave—"

"The longer we talk," Renwick suggested, "the more Theo will worry. And there is a little information you could use. He has many names. But you could shake him by dropping his real one—Herman Kroll, of East Germany."

"Herman Kroll," repeated Roy. "An East German?"

"KGB-trained. He arranged his own accidental death, came back into the world as a new man. He thinks Herman Kroll's file is closed, if not forgotten."

"A little name-dropping? Yes, that is always useful."

"Also a little word dropped into Theo's ear—about the kind of questions he will be facing."

"Concerning his future projects here in India? Yes, he has several—why else did Kiley and Shawfield have secret meetings with certain Communist students?"

"Mention Washington, too. I have a strong feeling that's a major project. Oh, just a feeling—but he was sending James Kiley there on a special mission."

"What mission?"

"That is what we would like to uncover."

Roy was thoughtful. "He will not talk, that man."

"No. But if he believes we know about this project—he will send out word from prison by way of his lawyer. Perhaps the project would be postponed—until we are all assuming it has been canceled. Theo's people don't act unless they have a good chance of success."

"If this project were postponed, then you might uncover it?" Roy asked slowly.

"We'd make a pretty good try. But we need time."

"You don't think the project could be canceled altogether?"

Renwick shook his head. "There's been too much preparation, too much careful planning."

Roy nodded. Thoughtfully, he turned away.

As the car moved off, Claudel asked, "Will it work? Will Theo believe that his Washington project is blown?"

"A few of his other plans have disintegrated recently. He's shaken." The attempted flight from Bombay was proof of that. "Let's walk a little—ten minutes of fresh air to clear our minds." Renwick chose the path that led into the garden. Soft perfumes stirred by the night, soft lights bringing out the bright pinks and purples of the flowers. The spaced trees were smooth-barked, as light and graceful as ballet dancers with the lift and droop of their arms.

Claudel was thinking of Theo. "You were expecting him to bolt."

"I was watching his eyes." Renwick tried to make a joke of that. "Always notice the front wheels of an approaching car, then you'll know when to dodge."

"A clever effort. He couldn't escape. He knew it, but he made it look like a real attempt. When he pointed that cane, it seemed as if he was just fending you off—a natural movement." And who would have known what caused Bob's death if he hadn't warned us the cane was a weapon? "How long does this take to kill?" Claudel held up the walking stick.

"Depends what is used. The Bulgarian method was a matter of four days and a raging fever. The one used against Jake Crefeld—" Renwick paused, said abruptly, "Paralysis. Death in thirty minutes. And for God's sake, Pierre, stop brandishing that damned thing around."

"Sorry, sorry."

Renwick calmed his voice. "Let's see if it was loaded." He took the cane, advanced near a floodlight. Then he examined the handle and found a small button that could be released sideways. He took aim at the tree beside him, pressed the button. There was no sound. Only an indent so small that Claudel had to use his cigarette lighter, holding it close to the smooth bark before they could see a pinhead hole. "I guess it was," said Renwick.

"Roy won't like missing the demonstration."

"Better that than having Roy play around with it and shooting himself in the foot."

"Risky business we're in," Claudel said with a wide grin. And I might have shot myself in the foot, he was thinking as he remembered the casual way he had handled that cane. "Time you got out of it, Bob—out of field work at least. Why not? You're a split personality. You've got ideas and you put them to work: that's one part of you. The other is that you hate being stuck in an office: you want to see what the big bad world is doing."

"And it's doing plenty."

"Well, fight it with ideas. You've got them, Bob."

"And sit at a desk, signing memos?"

"You don't have to sit at a desk. Sit in an armchair with a telephone on the floor beside you, prop your feet up, take a clipboard with paper and pencil, and let the little secretaries sign the memos. Ideas and plans come just as easily that way. You'll have to rise now and again, of course, to study maps, or go into the hush-hush room to see how your boys in the field are coming along." At least, Claudel thought, I've got him laughing. But his luck can't run forever, and he knows it. It must have been hell for him tonight, waiting for that bloody cane to come within a few inches of his body, a replay of what nearly happened before.

"I'm trying to imagine an antiseptic office in Merriman's with a chaise lounge for the weary brain," Renwick said. "You forgot the pink and purple velvet cushions, Pierre."

"I'm serious. I'm also serious about something else. Why don't you marry the girl? You would if you'd stay in your think tank in London. People who work there don't leave young widows behind."

Renwick said nothing.

"If you don't marry her, I will."

Renwick halted, looked at Claudel.

"I mean that. I've meant everything I've said." Claudel's usual bright smile returned. "Now, come on—let's make Gilman happy."

Their report to London was barely ended when the telephone rang in Roy's office. Renwick answered it. It was Roy himself. "Get the scrambler working," he said.

The untalkative communications expert obliged. "Something important," Renwick told Claudel and brought him over to the desk to listen, too. "Ready," he said to Roy.

"He killed himself."

"What?"

"He killed himself."

"How? Where?"

"In the car. He had one hand free. He was fingering his tie, pulled off one of his shirt buttons, bit into it. One minute—less—that was all."

"Why?" asked Renwick.

"Difficult to say. He was silent, didn't seem worried when I mentioned he would have to answer many questions. Just sat with a small smile on his lips. And so I dropped the name Herman Kroll, and he stopped smiling. But he was still silent—even when I mentioned his Washington project and said he would have to answer more questions about that. And then—suddenly—as quick as a snap of the fingers—he bit into the poison. Cyanide." Roy paused. "There will be inquiries about this. My critics will be delighted."

"I don't think so," Renwick said quickly. "Not when they hear you saved Bombay from a new tourist agency that was geared to make travel arrangements for your terrorists—and supply them with expense money under the counter. That should shut up any of your critics. Besides, what have they done for Bombay?"

Roy's gloom gave way to laughter. "You have a point there, Robert. I'll see you tomorrow before you leave—won't manage an office visit tonight." He paused, added, "Too bad about Theo: he told us nothing. Not that I expected it. Ah, well—good night. It has been quite a day, wouldn't you say?"

Renwick replaced the receiver. Theo, he was thinking, told us a great deal. Something was most definitely planned against Washington. Something so big, so important that he wouldn't risk being questioned. Surely he didn't expect Roy's people to use the brutal methods that he knew from his early KGB days—God knows, Theo had enough practice. But he did know what clever interrogation can do with hypnosis or truth serum or the new wonder drugs that can drag the facts out of any man. Questions about this Washington project? He made sure they'd have no answers. Not from him.

Claudel asked, "Are you thinking what I'm thinking, Bob?"

"Probably. Let's discuss it on our way home." A strange slip: home? A small hotel run by a retired British sergeant and his Pondicherry wife? But Nina was there. Safe in his room. That was home enough for him.

Twenty-seven

THE GUARD WAS still posted at the end of Renwick's corridor, and he was staying there—that was obvious by the way he smiled politely, vaguely, when Renwick suggested the alert was over—until Roy himself countermanded the order. The Australians' room had its door wide open: Mahoney sat just inside, with a clear view of Renwick's room opposite, while Benson had been doing his stint of watching down in the Back Bay Hotel's lobby among its wicker chairs and potted palms.

Mahoney rose briskly. He looked at Renwick and said, "So it's going well?"

"Two arrested. One dead: Herr Otto Remp—Theo, no less."

"Who got him?" Mahoney lowered his voice to a whisper as Renwick had done.

"Himself."

"Well, I'll be—"

"How's everything here?" Renwick glanced over at his room. The door was slightly ajar.

"She wanted it that way," Mahoney said quickly, "so that I could hear her. She slept. Then she woke, and I had Madame smuggle up a tray of food. She didn't eat much, but she's recovering rapidly. What happened?"

"Claudel will brief you. He's in the dining room. Benson is joining him. Why don't you?"

"You don't expect trouble?"

"Not here. The Bombay assignment is over."

"So we push off—"

"Claudel will brief you," Renwick repeated. "See you later. And thanks, Mahoney."

"Anytime." Mahoney pulled his room door shut. "It was a pleasure," he said and left for one of Madame's hot curries.

Renwick hesitated. Then he knocked lightly to warn Nina if she were awake. There was no answer. He pushed the door quietly open, closed and locked it behind him. She was asleep.

He went over to the bed, looked down at her. She had been reading a newspaper, its pages slipping over the sheet that barely covered her. Her hair lay loose and tangled on the pillow, her cheeks were flushed like a child's, her arms stretched out for coolness. Smooth firm arms, smooth and firm as her shoulders and breasts.

He folded the pages of newspaper, placed them on the table beside her. Carefully, he drew up the sheet, left her shoulders bare for the breath of air that came through the heavily screened window. He didn't switch off the light—let her see him when she opened her eyes and not have a wild moment of panic in a strange dark room. Then he dropped into the high-backed wicker chair facing the bed, pulled off his tie, pulled off his jacket, and let them fall beside him. He listened to the soft whirring of the fan overhead, to the gentle play of water from the small fountain in the court-yard below. Peace. Peace and thankfulness.

He opened his eyes. Nina was propped up in bed, watching him with a smile. "How long have I been asleep?" Incredulous, he looked at his watch. Almost eleven o'clock.

"I wouldn't know—I only woke up five minutes ago."

"Why didn't you wake me, too?"

"I hadn't the heart to do that. You were so completely out of this world."

With one hand she pushed back the sweep of hair that had fallen over her brow; with the other, she clasped the bed sheet over her breast. Above the white linen, her sun-tanned skin was the color of golden honey. Renwick steadied his voice. "I was," he admitted. "Just slipped away without know-ing it." And that's a first, he thought: I've never fallen asleep in a chair with someone else in the room; my guard was really down. "Fine watchdog I make," he added with a smile. "Just as well the door was locked."

"I know." She was laughing now. "I went to look—make sure we were safe." Then the laughter vanished. Blue eyes were anxious, questioning. "Are we?"

"Yes." He was still watching her.

"Then you—your business is all over?"

"In Bombay, yes." He rose, took the few steps that separated them; then he halted, unsure, uncertain, as she looked abruptly away.

"I have so many things to ask." About Madge and the others, and Jim Kiley. And Tony Shawfield . . . Her voice became low, strained. "I thought he was going to leave me there. In that street. He nearly did. As a lesson. Educational, he said."

"Don't, Nina. That's all over." All over, Renwick told himself, too. He crushed down the memory: his hand outstretched, Nina turning away.

"But it *was* educational. In this room when I was awake, I lay and thought and—" She broke off. Then her voice strengthened. "I know more about myself than I ever did. I know that I—" She raised her head, let her eyes meet his. I know that I love you, she ended silently. "Oh, Bob—" She held out her hand.

He grasped it, took both her hands, held them tightly, felt her draw him nearer. His arms went around her, and he kissed her mouth, her eyes, her cheeks, her slender neck, her mouth again—long deep kisses lingering on yielding lips. Her arms encircled him, pressed him closer.

Nothing else matters, he thought, nothing else in this whole wide world.

He had showered and shaved, pulled on trousers and shirt to let him bring in the two breakfast trays he had ordered before he woke Nina with gentle kisses to draw her slowly out of sleep. "Yes, it's early, I know," he told her, "but there's some business to be finished before we leave." Pleasant business: thanks and good-bye to Roy; last messages from Merriman's to be collected; warm clothes to be bought for Nina to let her face an October arrival in London. "Now come and have breakfast. It's waiting and ready."

"When do we leave?" She slipped out of bed, headed for the little bathroom, as lithe and graceful and unconcerned as a nymph on a Greek frieze.

"Today if possible." There was an Air India direct flight at nine o'clock this evening. Before, he hoped, any of Theo's agents in Bombay came out of shock, tried to put things together. "We'll go to London first. I have some things to clear up at the office." Mostly a matter of sending inquiries to Washington, of trying to find any possible clues to the question that kept nagging him: why was Francis O'Connell so important to Theo's plan? O'Connell's job was not so sensitive as all that. If he had been in defense or intelligence, that would have made sense. But for Theo—and Kiley—to have taken such infinite trouble to reach O'Connell, that was a real puzzler. Or was Kiley to have been a long-term infiltrator, a mole burrowing his way into O'Connell's circle? That didn't feel right to Renwick: Theo's sudden suicide didn't match with something that could wait for a year, two years, before it was put into effect. No, thought Renwick, that doesn't feel right: there's a reason beyond anything I can latch onto. I'm just stuck with this goddamned hunch—no more than that, but it's biting deep.

Nina had washed the sleep out of her eyes and was now combing her hair as she came back into the bedroom. She watched him curiously. So serious now—how many men is he? It would take a lifetime with him to find out. A long long life, she prayed, and then laughed with the joy of it. But did Bob feel that way? The thought ended her laughter.

He noticed her change of mood. "What is it, honey?"

"I hate leaving so soon." She looked around the little room. "I wish we could stay here forever."

"Leaving it won't end what we've begun," he said softly, and kissed her. "I'm not going to let you get away from me, ever. Ever," he repeated, and kissed her again. "So don't try."

The laughter was back in her eyes. "Or else you'll put all of Merriman's bloodhounds on my trail?"

For a moment he was startled, and then amused. "That's one job I'll do entirely by myself. And I'd find you," he warned her. "More easily than I found you this time." He kissed her again, ruffled her newly combed hair. "Now come and have breakfast before the omelette turns to cotton wool."

"Omelette?" Nina picked up a sheet from the bed to wrap around her, sarong style. "However did you manage that?"

"Madame did. She's Pondicherry French."

Nina went over to the table at the window and looked at the heaped little dishes that almost overflowed two trays.

"*Parathas,*" Renwick identified the whole-wheat bread. "And these are *jalebis*—doughnuts to you." The omelettes, flecked with parsley, had been well covered and still looked edible. "I don't know what the rest of this stuff is. But we'll soon find out."

"Actually," Nina said, "I'm famished. I could even eat cotton wool—if I had some of that jam over it. What is it? Marmalade, for heaven's sake!"

"That's the ex-sergeant's touch of home."

"I really didn't eat much yesterday. Did you?"

"Not much." Nothing since yesterday's breakfast, in fact. Quite a day, as Roy had said. Quite a day.

"Now tell me about Madge," Nina reminded him as the last plate was emptied. "Where is she? And the others? Did Mr. Roy get them out of that place, put them up at his hotel? He owns one, doesn't he?"

"I shouldn't be surprised." Renwick poured the last of the coffee into Nina's cup.

"Not fair," she said, and emptied half of the coffee back into his cup. "Madge must have been terribly upset when she heard about Tony Shawfield's arrest."

"She hasn't heard. None of them have. They left before the police arrived at the house. That was just about the time I was bringing you here."

"But where—" Nina began in horror.

"We don't know. All that Roy could learn was that the five of them drove away in a Fiat—one of the two cars that brought you into Bombay yesterday. The police are searching. Perhaps we'll hear something this afternoon."

"And if we don't, Bob? If they have left Bombay?"

"They'd need money for that. Have they any?"

She shook her head. "I think they've spent most of what they had." Drugs, those damnable drugs, she thought. "Shawfield was going to buy their fares." No, Shawfield had never returned. "Jim Kiley always had a lot of extra money after we arrived at certain places. That's the first thing he did: cash checks or something. Was Jim at the house? He might have sent them all away. But why?"

Because of orders, Renwick thought: new orders, obviously. "He could have. He was there." Renwick hesitated, then said, "The police came to arrest him. He escaped, left a dead policeman behind him, and was caught later. He may face a murder charge here—if the weapon he used can be proven to have killed—but in any case, after that, he will be extradited to West Germany. Like Shawfield." Renwick caught her hand. "I'm sorry, Nina. But you'd learn the truth sometime."

"Extradited—for what? For spying? Was that what they were—agents?" She remembered a courtyard near Tabriz, the voices in German, and Pierre listening. . . . "Against whom?" Her hand had tightened under his. Her voice had risen.

"Against most of the world," Renwick said very quietly. "They are terrorists. They are being extradited for bombings, arson, murders, and a brutal kidnapping." There it's out, he thought unhappily. He raised her hand to his lips.

For a long moment she stared at him. "I could believe that of Tony," she said slowly. "But Jim? . . . Oh, I knew he could lie—he had an explanation for everything. Yet, I had to like him. He was kind. He looked after me— he really did. He was thoughtful. Bob—he was *gentle*." Except once, she remembered. But that was my fault perhaps—I was uncertain, indefinite. "Oh, I don't know," she said helplessly. "It's just hard to believe."

"Have you ever heard of the People's Revolutionary Force for Direct Action?"

"But of course! It was in all the newspapers last winter. They kidnapped and killed—"

"Kiley is Erik. Shawfield is Marco. Erik was the leader. Marco was second-in-command."

"Oh, no!" She turned to point at the bedside table where yesterday's folded newspaper still lay: Ilsa Schlott, known as Greta; once a member of Direct Action; connected with Erik and Marco—terrorists; a green camper delivered in a Camberwell garage. "Ilsa Schlott invited Madge and me to a concert," Nina began. Then Ilsa had backed out at the last moment. And her seat was taken by James Kiley. "That's how we met," she said. "At that concert." Her eyes met his, her lips trembled. "Oh, God!" she said. "What an idiot! What a complete and total idiot I was."

He caught her around her waist, pulled her onto his lap, held her close. "We have all been idiots at one time or other. It's the human condition, my love." He smoothed back her hair.

"Not you, Bob. Never you."

"Oh, yes, me, too." He kissed her ear.

"When?"

He hesitated. "For months on end, my sweet. Not just for a few weeks."

"Was she beautiful?" Nina tried to laugh.

Well, he was into it now, right up to his neck. "Yes." When Nina said nothing more, he went on. "She was a widow, lived in Brussels, ran an interior decorating business."

"She sounds entrancing," Nina said with a most definite lack of enthusiasm.

Renwick threw back his head and laughed.

In spite of herself, Nina joined in.

"As entrancing, it turned out, as a black widow spider," he said and drew Nina closer. My God, I'm actually laughing about Thérèse Colbert, he thought; talking about her and laughing. "You're good for me, darling— good in every way." His hand slid over her thigh, gently caressed her. "Nina—will you marry me?"

Her face turned toward him. Her eyes searched his.

"Will you?" His voice had tightened.

"Yes and yes." She threw her arms around him. "And yes."

"Look, darling," Renwick said, "it's almost ten. We'd better get organized around here." Quickly he began dressing again.

"Oh, Bob—"

"I mean it, love. There are a few things I *must* do before we leave. I want you to stay here—"

"But why?"

"Because you'll be safe. There's a plain-clothes policeman still on duty at the end of the corridor. I don't want you to be seen walking through Bombay."

"I thought the danger was over," she said slowly. "I mean, Tony Shawfield isn't around any more. Or Jim Kiley."

"I'm just making sure there's no more danger. I'm taking no chances with you. Trust me, honey."

She nodded. "I'll shower and wash my hair and wait for you." Then she remembered her muslin dress, hanging on the back of the bathroom door, and thought of London in late October. "And you know what? I haven't a thing to wear." That sent her into a fit of giggles. *I'm already sounding like a married woman,* she thought.

"You'd be a smashing success at Heathrow. But I'll get something for you—a skirt, shirt, sweater, coat? In shades of blue, if possible. It won't take long." Roy's gift shop had a variety of departments and helpful assistants.

"But the fit—" she began doubtfully.

"I've got your sizes—approximately." He grinned and added, "Don't worry about the styles. Claudel has a sharp eye for women's fashions."

"Claudel?"

"Pierre."

"Then he *is* French?"

"As Parisian as they come."

"Is he an engineer, too?"

"Sure."

"And these nice Australians? Or are they Australians?"

He evaded the last question by answering the first. "They are pretty good engineers." Mahoney knew a lot about planes; Benson had once helped design submarines.

"Are they all flying back to London with us?"

"Claudel will be there. But separate. So don't speak to him, or even look at him."

"Not the tiniest smile?" she teased. "Oh, Bob—before you go—would you help me put a call through to Father? I really should let him know."

"Yes, I suppose so." Not through Merriman's—Gilman wouldn't want the firm to be connected openly with Francis O'Connell. Not through A. K. Roy's gift shop, either: the Washington problem wasn't in Roy's field of inquiry; there had been no need to spread Renwick's interest—the less known about it, the better.

She noted his hesitation. "Would it be so difficult?"

"We may have to place a call, wait a little. And there's the time element, too. A rough guess—" He calculated quickly, checked his watch again. "I'd say it is now half past eleven yesterday in Washington." *Phone from this room? Well, we should be out of here before any interested party starts trying to trace any calls.* "Where would we find your father near midnight? I've got his new number somewhere." Renwick went over to the chair that held his jacket, found his small book of innocuous addresses. "They've just moved into a house in Georgetown."

A new house? What was wrong with the old one? And how does Bob know its number—has he been in touch with Father? Yes, it was Father who sent him chasing after me. Her eyes lost their smile, her lips were strained. "He may be at home, perhaps even gone to bed. Oh, it doesn't matter. And you haven't got the time to waste on a call. Let's forget it."

Watching her, Renwick made up his mind. He hadn't the time, but he couldn't leave her looking dejected like this. "We can try," he said, picking up the phone, enlisting the help of the ex-sergeant. No problem at all, he was firmly assured: he'd have a Washington line in a matter of minutes. "Now we wait," he told Nina as he replaced the receiver. He looked at it thought-fully. "Dammit, my brains are really scrambled this morning. Look, honey— if your father wants to know how you found his new number, just tell him you had telephone-operator assistance."

"Didn't he give you that number?"

"No." Renwick looked at her in surprise.

"He didn't send you?"

"He doesn't even know I am here. No one sent me looking for you. No one." My God, he thought, if she only knew how everyone kept prodding me to think of that damned camper first and put her second. He lightened his voice. "There wasn't any camper in Lesbos, was there? Or in Istanbul when we met?"

"You arranged all that?" Her eyes brightened.

"You bet I did. All I wanted was to get you out—away from Kiley and Shawfield."

"And I wouldn't listen."

"You've got a pretty strong mind of your own."

"I'm sorry—"

"No, no. I love it. It may be hell at times—have you any idea what you put me through?—but you've got spirit, darling. Did you think I just adored you for the way you look? Oh, there's that, too." He thought of last night, this morning. "Very much so," he said, and watched a blush spread deli-cately over her cheeks. "God, you are the most beautiful girl. How many men have wanted to marry you, Nina?"

"I never said yes to any of them. And I never—" She halted in embar-rassment. "You're the first man I've ever been—who's ever made real love to me."

"And you're the first woman I've ever asked to marry me."

"The very first?" Her heart lifted.

"The first. And the last."

"Oh, darling—"

The telephone rang. "We've got through." He handed her the receiver. "Keep me out of it."

Of course, she thought, no one knows he is here. With a smile in her voice, she began speaking "Daddy? Yes, it's me. In Bombay . . . Why yes, I'm fine—wonderful, in fact. . . . Look, I can't talk long—this call is cost-ing the earth. But I'll be home soon. Next week probably. I'll phone you from London, let you know." Then she looked over at Renwick, gestured helplessly as the phone call went on and on. "Please, Beryl—don't worry about my new room. . . . Yes, I'll be home next week, but don't worry. . . . I'm sure it will be beautiful. . . . Yes, yes . . . My love to both of you." With a decided bang, Nina put down the receiver.

Renwick tightened the knot on his tie, reached for his jacket.

"She means well. But it's really comic. Father doesn't know a thing about anything: he is so glad I had such a splendid time, but wishes I had sent more than one postcard. I sent four, actually, and two letters. Then Beryl cut in. All she's worried about is that my new room isn't ready, but Madame Colbert will have the painters start on it at once."

Renwick had been drawing on his jacket. He stopped for a moment, then jammed his arm into one sleeve. "Colbert?"

"Some interior decorator—French or Belgian, Beryl said, with marvelous taste. A pink-and-blue bedroom for me. That's where I ended the phone call."

So James Kiley hadn't won entry to the O'Connell household, but Thérèse Colbert had. Renwick settled his jacket comfortably on his shoulders, eased his shirt collar slightly. "I'll be back by one o'clock. No—" he looked at his watch—"make that one-thirty." I'll have to warn Gilman to get in touch with Washington immediately and prepare the way for some FBI collaboration: Colbert to be put under discreet but complete surveillance. And what is security like at O'Connell's home? Check workmen, all visitors. Any bugs installed? Any phone taps? Gilman can make a start on that before I reach Washington—without delay, critical. Yes, he thought, critical. "No goodbye kiss, Miss O'Connell?"

She came running over to him. He caught her, kissed her, said, "We'll have lunch here in the room." And four hours at least to wait before leaving for the airport. "Lock the door behind me. Don't let anyone enter."

"I'll be safe. Don't worry about me."

"I always will," he said softly. "My pleasure."

"Bob—" She looked around the edge of the door as he stepped into the corridor, keeping her body out of sight from the rooms opposite. "About Madge—"

"I'll find out what I can." He looked at her anxious face, kissed the tip of her nose, started her smiling as he pulled the door shut, waited until he heard the lock turn. Then briskly he took the stairs—quicker than the elevator—and ran lightly down. For a man who had had less than a couple of hours' sleep, he felt wonderful.

Twenty-eight

It was the last day of October. Nina and Renwick had spent the four nights since their arrival from Bombay in the Gilmans' London flat. By day, Nina—with Gemma Gilman's help—had rescued her trunk from storage and selected some suitable clothes for November in Washington. The rest went back into the trunk for further storage until she and Bob returned to live in London. When that would be, she didn't know: Bob had said simply, "It depends." Depends on what? She didn't ask: she was learning quickly.

Gemma was a help there, too. "Why ask questions if they can't be answered?" she said in her quiet, competent way. A pretty woman of forty—even that age didn't disturb her—with dark hair and eyes, and almost as tall as her husband's six feet.

"Doesn't Ron tell you anything about his work?"

"Whatever can be told, sweetie." Gemma smiled encouragingly at Nina's thoughtful face.

"You must trust him a lot."

"Why not? He trusts me."

"I know. He must," Nina said quickly. The Gilmans were happy; and close friends, too. That was evident as soon as you saw them together. "It's just that truth is part of trust, isn't it? I mean—" She halted, sighed helplessly.

"Bob will give you the truth if it can be given. If not—then he won't answer you at all. That's your signal to ask no more questions. Inquisitive people aren't really very attractive, are they?"

"No," Nina agreed with a smile.

"Truth and confidences," Gemma mused. "Oh, you'll have plenty of them, don't worry. Provided you don't gossip. And you don't. It's a very private kind of life, actually. Rather nice, too: it draws you closely together. It has to. Or else it would all fly apart."

A very private kind of life . . . "A lot must depend on the woman, doesn't it?" Nina asked hesitantly.

"Of course. And very flattering it is," Gemma said cheerfully. "Now, what about that call to your father to let him know you'll be home tomorrow? It's eight in the morning, Washington time. You'll catch him just before he leaves for the office."

"Yes. I'd better tell him. But this has to be a collect call, Gemma. Really, it must! If Beryl comes on the phone, she'll talk and talk."

"No telephone sense at all?"

"Not much. She's never had to worry about money. Oh, well—" Nina's smile was real—"Beryl keeps Father happy—he doesn't even have time to worry much about me any more. And that, frankly, is a relief. I'm free and can choose my own life." And have Bob to worry about me, she thought. "A very private kind of life," she added softly, and went into the hall to telephone.

Renwick and Gilman spent a long day at J. P. Merriman & Co. collecting last reports and pieces of information about Francis O'Connell's house, habits, and job in Washington. There wasn't much to establish any kind of purpose behind Thérèse Colbert's interest in O'Connell.

"Let's see what we've got," Renwick said at last. They were seated, facing each other, at Gilman's desk. Renwick's office would be ready for his return to London, with the antiseptic furnishings removed: all he wanted was one large table with one telephone, some maps on the wall, good lighting, a small safe, a radio for some music, and a leather armchair with a leg rest. (The file room was next door, the typist pool was at the end of the hall, the communications setup was within easy reach. What more did he need?) "Take it from the beginning, Ron."

"Washington listened to us and was receptive. They are studying Colbert carefully; she is now under close surveillance. So far, they've found nothing derogatory in her past. She arrived from Switzerland in July, had some helpful friends to establish her in Washington, where she has been a success—both socially and as an interior decorator."

"Nothing derogatory." Renwick shook his head. "Didn't Belgian security spread the word?"

"Seemingly not. Perhaps they couldn't find much against her. You didn't spread the word, either," Gilman reminded him.

"And let Theo know I was still functioning?" If I had been the one to pass the word to Belgian security, Theo's listening post would have picked that up. I'd have had more to worry about than getting Interintell working, Renwick thought. Still, that had been a door left unlocked—my fault, even with good reasons—and Thérèse Colbert had slipped through.

"You hadn't much choice," Gilman agreed. "Anyway, Colbert is moving around the best circles quite easily. They like her charm and her French accent. She has become Beryl O'Connell's friend as well as her adviser on colors and wallpapers. So far, her telephone conversations have been blameless. She doesn't take circuitous routes to appointments. She has had no meetings with anyone outside her own circle of acquaintances."

"During the last five days." Before then? When she wasn't under surveillance? Perhaps, thought Renwick, the warning about Colbert has gone out too late. "So she seems totally harmless. Yet we know she was working for the late Mr. Maartens, who worked for Theo. We know Kiley worked for Theo, and Kiley was heading for the O'Connell house. She headed for the O'Connell house, too. Were they to work together? Is she now adding his assignment to hers?"

"Is she capable of that? Could she carry out this assignment by herself?"

"If it's intricate, no. She'd need outside help. What's the security like at O'Connell's place?"

"He's against it. The Secret Service insisted on the usual two guards, but all he wants them to do is to drive him around. He can't conceive of anything happening to him right in his own home."

"Frankly, I don't think anyone will take a pot shot at him even in the streets or at his office. Kidnapping? I'd rule against it. It's not money that Theo was after. Top-secret papers to be stolen or photographed?"

"The FBI says he keeps them in the safe at his office. He's not known for breaking the rules. He brings no highly classified material home."

"And the FBI reports they found no bugs," Renwick said, frowning. They had sent in two men to check the telephones on Monday. Yesterday, they had had an agent appear as an inspector of all the new electrical wiring. "Nothing."

"A lot of workmen have been in and out of that house in the last six weeks. But no doubt they are being checked right now. I must say, Bob, Washington did take our warning seriously. I just hope . . ." Gilman sighed. "Well, it would be rather a sour joke on us, wouldn't it, if no warning was needed?"

"But it is."

Gilman said nothing.

"Kiley used Nina to be accepted by O'Connell." Renwick ran his hands through his hair, rose, walked over to the electric fire, stood staring down at it. "What if—" he paused—"what if Kiley was then going to use O'Connell?"

"Use him?" Gilman was suddenly interested. "For an introduction higher up? Could be, could very well be."

"Except," Renwick said, "that would have to be a long-term project. Kiley gets the entrance into high circles of government, but he'd need time to insinuate himself even with all his powers of persuasion. Theo didn't die to protect some project in the distant future. What's more, Kiley was trained as a terrorist, not as a diplomat."

"He could have been aiming at assassination."

Renwick nodded. "Use O'Connell to get him into some place where Kiley could get off one shot—" He stopped, reconsidered. "That could mean Kiley's death, too. I don't think he would be in favor of that," Renwick said with a brief smile. "He's a man with a mission: Direct Action. He was following Theo's plan because it would help the cause—his cause. His death wouldn't help it one bit. In fact, as its leader, he'd intend to stay alive."

"Hold it, hold it!" Gilman exclaimed. "You've got something there, Bob! He was following Theo's plan because it would help his cause—Direct Action. And what is that but anarchy?"

"Theo would have got more than he bargained for."

"Always the danger when you play along with terrorists."

"But," said Renwick, beginning to walk slowly around the room, his head bent, his hands in his pockets, "Theo might have been aiming at a temporary anarchy—just enough confusion and disaster to throw America into panic. The Western world, too. Make them helpless, unable to move if aggression took place—" He halted his pacing, stared at Gilman. There were three danger spots in this world right now, ripe for aggression. Last night, he and Gilman had discussed them at length and ruined a perfectly good chess game. First, turmoil; and then aggression; and propaganda to wrap it all up.

"Throw us into confusion and panic," Gilman repeated. "An attack on your White House—kill the President? Kiley was to use O'Connell in order to reach the President?"

Renwick thought quickly over the report they had received on O'Connell's duties beyond his daily office routine. Special advisory sessions at the White House—but others were present, too. Breakfast last week at the White House—but with others there, too. A National Security meeting last month—full attendance. "He never sees the President alone."

"Then," Gilman said, "Theo may have planned something bigger than we thought. What was he aiming for—the National Security Council?" It was intended as a joke.

"A full house," Renwick said slowly.

"Look—we might just be allowing ourselves to get carried away." That was always the danger with thinking out loud. But he still brooded over

Renwick's wild and outrageous idea. "They couldn't possibly turn poor old O'Connell into some bomb. Wire him for an explosion?" He began to laugh, choked off his amusement. "Would it really be possible to have some explosive device on O'Connell without him knowing it? In his watch—in the heels of his shoes?"

"Nothing that would be powerful enough except to blow him to pieces. If he carried some reference book to back up any statement he wanted to make—"

"It would be examined by security, before he ever reached the council table."

"Yes. Any briefcase, too. He does carry a briefcase, doesn't he? Now that could pack a real blast."

"As you said, it would be opened and examined, wouldn't it?"

"I hope to God it would be." Dead end, thought Renwick. He stopped pacing around, dropped back into his chair. "Theo's target," he said softly. "Hidden. With extreme care and cunning."

"And how the devil do you hit a hidden target?"

"You can damn well think your way toward it. And then be ready—for one small glimpse. Just one quick sight, that's all we'll need."

"Perhaps a little pressure on Madame Colbert?" Gilman suggested.

"Yes. I think that's what we'll try. Shock tactics. They worked on Theo. Damn it all, Ron, we keep talking of that man as if he were still alive. Who's in charge of Colbert now, I wonder? It could be Boris or Kolman or—what the hell. Let's call them the opposition."

"What kind of shock tactics on dear Thérèse?"

"Sudden confrontation. Inform her that I know she's one of their agents. That might shake her. But then, the opposition might try shaking me."

"How?"

"Blackmail. They must have taken photographs in her Brussels apartment. How else did Maartens' killer recognize me so quickly when he came at me with that damned walking stick?"

"Blackmail." Yes, that was always a possibility, thought Gilman. "What would be your reaction?"

"Publish and be damned."

"But now there's Nina."

Renwick said nothing.

"Would she stand by you?"

Still Renwick was silent.

Gilman studied his friend. "I'm sure she will, Bob." Then he rose quickly. "I think I'll get in touch with my friend A. K. Roy. We had a long chat yesterday. But there's something I'd like to ask him. Shan't be long."

"It's probably early in the morning Bombay time," Renwick reminded him.

"Then I'll be certain of reaching him at his home," Gilman said briskly and left Renwick to his own thoughts.

They weren't pleasant.

But I'll be damned if I'm taking myself off this case now. I've been with it since Vienna—uncovered that terrorist bank account—found it in Geneva, one and a half million dollars already paid out. And I traced them, even if they had been carefully laundered, to Düsseldorf and Herr Otto Remp. Then there was Essen, and Erik and Marco bowing in. And Otto Remp, once Herman Kroll—nicely dead in some helicopter accident, now Theo again. We got him; we got Erik and Marco. I'll be damned if I take myself off this case.

And Nina? I've told her about Brussels, thank God for that. . . . At least, the shock won't be so vicious if she finds photographs with an anonymous letter in the mail some morning. That's how Theo would have worked it: no press release, just a quiet threat using Nina.

Who is succeeding him? More important, who is in Washington directing Colbert? She has a control, possibly a resident well disguised in their embassy: the harmless chauffeur, the quiet press attaché. Well, if we move quickly enough, I'll nail Colbert and get her out of the picture. Who takes over for her, then? That could delay Theo's plan, set it back some weeks, some months, before a new operative could insinuate himself into O'Connell's household.

And whatever that plan is—Renwick began from the beginning again. Kiley, Nina, O'Connell. And from there? Renwick ended with the same deductions: O'Connell's importance was only as an intermediary, leading to—leading to what? "Just can't get my mind to take any other direction," he told Gilman when he returned. "About O'Connell," he added. Not about Nina. That was a torment that no thought could resolve. He loved her, would always love her. Nina? He could only hope and trust. "Did you have to haul friend Roy out of bed?"

"He didn't object. He's on top of the world. That was a big haul he pulled in—at Theo's suite. Theo was traveling light, remember? He, himself, was carrying only a new passport, an automatic, and a wad of money. All his baggage was to be taken out by his two men and that joker wearing Theo's white wig and mustache. Yes, quite a haul for Roy, a lot of valuable stuff there." Gilman paused, then added in his most offhand manner. "I'll leave for Bombay tomorrow morning."

Renwick said, "That's a quick decision, isn't it?"

"I'd like to see what Theo left behind—before it all gets listed and dispersed."

"Roy has no objections?"

"None whatsoever." In fact, the visit to Bombay had been Roy's suggestion. "Shan't stay around too long. Quick in, quick out. I'll be back here in three days—let's say by Sunday, November the fourth. Claudel will take any messages you send from Washington."

"I'd have liked to have had him with me."

"Better keep separate. You were in Bombay together."

"Who'll be my backup then?"

"Why not Tim MacEwan?"

"Mac?"

"He's in Ottawa at the moment. But he does know his way around Washington."

"He's good. But does he have any helpful contacts in Washington?"

"He has been working with the FBI. Gave them as much as possible on the layout of Rancho San Carlos, the weapons, the drill, the faces and builds of the men. Neat sketches. He has the sharp eye for that kind of detail."

"That he has." Renwick grinned. "You should have seen him crawling on his belly, his face covered with antisun lotion, having his first close-up view of terrorists in training. Later that night . . ." Renwick's smile faded as he remembered Sal. "Well, we'll keep Dobermans out of Mac's way in Washington. Now what about getting back to your flat? I'll take a bus and walk the rest."

"It would be safe enough to give you a lift if you'll join me on the side street."

"No, thanks, Ron. I'd like to walk." He left first.

Gilman waited to make arrangements for his three-day absence. He, too, was thinking about Nina.

It was almost nine when Gilman reached home. "Bob is taking a walk," he told Nina, and kissed his wife. "Anything to eat, Gemma?"

"You haven't had dinner?"

"Not so far. A busy day. By the way, I'll have to leave tomorrow morning. I'll be home by Sunday."

"Did Bob have dinner?"

"No. Better make a double helping of sandwiches."

Nothing can be wrong, Nina thought: Ron isn't worried; his voice and smile are easy, natural. "I'll help," she offered.

"No need," Gemma told her. "Ronnie and I have a system. And no more than two people can crowd into our kitchen anyway. Open the door for Bob when he rings, won't you?"

The ring came soon. Renwick entered to be met with Nina's arms around him and a happy laugh. The best welcome a man could get, he thought as he tightened his grip around her waist and kissed her upturned face. They stood there in the small dark hall holding each other.

At last Gemma's voice from the sitting room called them back to reality. "The sandwiches are getting cold, Bob." She shook her head at her husband, who'd have left them alone for another ten minutes. "They can't stand there forever," she murmured.

"Didn't we?" he asked.

Gemma smiled. Two thin shirts and a lightweight suit, he had told her in the kitchen. For some place hot and humid, she guessed. She'd hear about it when Ronnie got back. Perhaps. Certainly this trip must be important, highly important. He was giving up *Cosi fan Tutte* tomorrow night, and he had been looking forward to it for weeks. "When do you leave?"

"Just after breakfast." He rose to his feet as Nina and Renwick came to join the picnic at the coffee table. He glanced at Renwick. All's well, he thought with relief: whatever he decided on that walk, all is well. Then they sat down and relaxed. It was a very merry party.

Gemma was talking about her morning with Nina—a visit to Harrods nearby for some last-minute shopping. "And when we got back, Nina called home."

"Collect," Nina said.

"Now I understand why. How long did that call last? Must have been ten, fifteen minutes." Gemma poured more beer for the men, another cup of tea for Nina and herself. "Beryl must be so accustomed to money that she never asks the cost of anything."

"Beryl," said Nina, "is filthy rich. But that isn't the reason Father married her. It isn't, Bob!"

"Okay, okay, honey. I didn't say a thing."

Gilman looked over at his wife. "Now wouldn't it be nice if you were filthy rich, darling?"

"Indeed it would be. I could have breakfast in bed—like Beryl. Was that why she talked endlessly? All cozily wrapped in a satin quilt?"

"Was your father there?" Renwick asked Nina.

"For two minutes. He was dashing out—a breakfast meeting. Yes, one of those. He was a little on edge, in fact definitely cross, until he realized it was me on the phone. Then he became normal, started arranging my arrival. But I told him not to worry: I was taking the same flight as a friend, so I would have company all the way."

Renwick looked at her, a smile spreading over his face.

Taking the same flight as a friend, Gilman noted. "Not bad, not bad at all," he said, exchanging a glance with Renwick.

"Then Beryl came on from the phone in their room." Nina was amused. "She seems to listen in, doesn't she?" It had happened in Bombay, too.

"What did she have to say?" Renwick asked. "Is your new bedroom ready? I hope it isn't."

"I'm afraid it is." And we'll be separated, Nina thought. "But Beryl hardly mentioned it. She was too busy persuading me that Father's bad temper had nothing to do with her."

"Probably couldn't find a cuff link, or his shoelace had snapped and there wasn't a spare one around. Nice picture: economics expert entering the White House tied together with string."

"Oh, Bob!" She laughed and shook her head. "It was his attaché case that spoiled his morning. It's his favorite, uses it all the time. I gave it to him for Christmas two years—Something wrong?"

"Not at all," Gilman said quickly. "Unless he had important papers in it. When was it stolen?"

"It wasn't. And his papers weren't in it—they were in his safe. It just got ruined."

"Ruined?" Renwick asked, avoiding Gilman's eyes.

"Well, not ruined exactly. That was Beryl's word. It was badly stained—acid got spilled on it—some kind of paint remover that was being used in Father's study. You see, the painter almost dropped the can and some of the remover splashed on one side of the desk and on the attaché case. The whole house was thrown into an uproar. Madame Colbert was furious—Beryl said it really was appalling how she screamed at the poor painter. But in a way, it was her fault for hurrying everyone with their jobs. Father wasn't there at the time. Didn't know his attaché case was missing until this morning."

"Missing?" Gilman asked.

"Oh, he will get it back in a day or two. Madame Colbert took it to one of her 'little men' to have the stains removed and the leather restored. There's a furniture polisher working on the desk now. And Father went off to breakfast with an old leather envelope holding his papers. Much ado about nothing."

"Much ado, certainly." Gilman took off his glasses, polished them, looked at Renwick, who was equally thoughtful.

Renwick said, "Stains removed in a day or two? From leather? Not likely. Nina, I'm afraid your father is going to have a well-marked attaché case to carry around. Hasn't he others?"

"Bulky briefcases, which he hates."

"Spoils the silhouette," Renwick agreed. O'Connell was a careful dresser, neat and dapper. "He will just have to buy a new attaché case; that's simple enough."

"Beryl wanted to do that, but Madame Colbert wouldn't hear of it. Said it was quite an unnecessary expense."

"I like that," Renwick said, suddenly smiling, "considering the thousands of dollars she's charging for color schemes and wallpapers." Yes, he thought, I like that last touch: unnecessary expense—any quick excuse to keep Beryl from buying a new attaché case; a different-looking case. Why was dear Thérèse so intent on keeping the old one in use?

"Why don't I buy Father an attaché case?" Nina asked. "His birthday is next month. Bob—wouldn't that be a good idea? Sort of a peace offering for all the postcards he didn't receive?"

Renwick's smile broadened. "A peace offering for bringing me into the family?"

"Bob! He likes you—he told me in Geneva you were the brightest young man he knew."

"Except?" he teased.

"Except that you were a soldier," Nina admitted. "But you aren't a soldier now, are you?"

"Would it matter?"

She shook her head. "I thought you looked *wonderful,* but wonderful, in uniform."

"And when was all this?" Gemma asked. She had never seen Renwick in anything but civilian clothes.

"In Geneva. Six years ago," Nina said.

Gemma looked slightly bewildered. "When you were fifteen?"

"Yes," Nina said.

"Oh," said Gemma.

Renwick rose, catching Nina's hand. "We'd better finish packing." He pulled Nina to her feet. "An early start tomorrow."

"Not so early," Gemma suggested. She was enjoying herself. "Tomorrow, if you leave here by half past nine, you'll be in plenty of time—" Ronnie, she suddenly noticed, was giving her that fixed look, one of his specialties. "I've really got to do some packing myself. Ronnie, will two shirts be enough?" She let herself glance after Renwick and Nina as they entered the corridor to the guest room. "Fifteen," she asked in a hushed voice. "Do you think he—"

"No, I don't think," Gilman said. "You're an incorrigible romantic, my love."

"After all," Gemma said as she gathered plates and teacups, "Juliet was only fourteen. Would you bring those glasses, darling?"

They were about to leave. Renwick made a last quick check of the guest room. "All clear, I think." He looked at Nina, radiant and ready for travel. She was wearing the coat he had bought for her in Bombay, and that pleased him. "One moment, Nina." He caught her hands. "I've been thinking about this—a matter of security. We can't talk about it in the taxi or on the plane. But listen, darling, will you? I'll leave you at your father's house, see you safely inside. But don't mention—not for a few days—anything about our marriage. Don't mention we are in love. Please, Nina. Just keep those pretty lips closed." He kissed them lightly. "Also, honey, don't talk about Bombay—about Erik or Marco. Never mention these names in your house: Kiley and Shawfield will be enough. For a few days, anyway. I'll explain everything, then."

She was startled, puzzled, too, but she nodded.

"And don't tell anyone that we met in Istanbul. Or that you ever saw Pierre. Or how we met in Bombay."

"Nothing about you at all? Not even that we met in Amsterdam?"

"Nothing. Not yet. I'll telephone you night and morning; and then, in a few days, I'll call at your house—a friendly visit. That's all. And after that . . ." He didn't finish.

"It will be difficult to hide what I feel," she said unhappily. "Bob—must it be this way?"

"It has to be this way. But it won't last long." I hope to God it won't.

"Am I endangering you? Is that why—?"

"No, darling. You've got it the wrong way around. I could endanger you."

"But how?"

He hesitated. One last warning was needed. "Keep Thérèse Colbert at a distance. Be careful. Very careful. Remember the interior decorator in Brussels? I told you about her and—"

"The black widow spider? Yes, I remember." Then she caught her breath. "Thérèse Colbert?"

"Yes. She's an enemy agent."

She stared at him. "In Father's house?"

"In your father's house. He knows nothing. Nor does Beryl. Just you—and I. Will you keep that secret, honey? Be on guard?" He caught her in his arms, held her close. "I've told you more than I should have. But I couldn't leave you in that house without—"

"I'll take care," she said. Her hand touched his cheek. She had never seen him so serious, not even in Istanbul when he had listened to her with eyes grave and worried. "Darling, I'll take every care." She kissed him. "I needed to know. It will keep me safe." And you, too, she thought. I could stamp on that black widow, stamp her to death.

He picked up the suitcases, and they entered the corridor. "One thing I know, Bob Renwick," Nina said. "Life isn't going to be dull with you."

Nor with you, he thought, nor with you.

Twenty-nine

A COOL AFTERNOON made pleasant walking around the sweep of Potomac waters called the Tidal Basin. Unpoetic name, thought Renwick, for a romantic spot. The encircling cherry trees, even when touched by early November, had delicacy and grace. Yellowed leaves loosened their hold on black branches, drifted gently to the grass below. Soon, bare slender arms would stretch to a winter sky, wait patiently for spring to come and cover them in sleeves of white-petaled silk. Lincoln had his Reflecting Pool, Washington his Mall, why not give Jefferson a lake? Tidal Basin . . . Was that the best we could do for a man who named his home Monticello?

Renwick glanced at his watch: three-forty-five. Tim MacEwan should be coming into sight any moment now. Midway between Lincoln and Jefferson, Renwick had suggested yesterday evening when they had arranged today's encounter. He wondered now if Mac had had time enough to find the answers to all his questions. "I'll keep out of the picture, let you meet with your federal friends," Renwick had said. "But these questions are vital, Mac."

Mac had nodded his agreement, and in his own Scots way qualified his chances of success. "Not much time to find the right answers." Renwick had reminded him grimly, "Not much time for anything, Mac."

There he was now, reviewing the cherry trees at a brisk march, high color in his cheeks, red hair mostly covered by his tweed hat. "Hello, how are you?" Mac said, stopping to shake hands with a friend met by chance. A few sentences, and Renwick seemed persuaded to change his direction to walk alongside. There were several couples as well as singles taking an afternoon stroll. Renwick and MacEwan looked completely in place as they walked and talked. Nothing—apparently—serious; just a pleasant chat.

"Did you get the answers?" Renwick asked.

"Yes. First, that type of stain on leather is not easily or quickly removed. Wood can be scraped and refinished, but leather is a problem—usually permanently blemished."

"Okay."

"Next: there was no complaint made by Madame Colbert to the firm that employs the painter."

A show of temper, of real anger over a careless job, and no follow-up? "I see," said Renwick.

"He came to work for the firm last week. He left of his own accord yesterday. No explanation. My friends at the Bureau are having him traced, if possible."

"Good."

"Colbert was followed to the shop of that 'little man' who does special leather repairs for her. But when we went in to see him this morning with a suitcase that needed attention, we were told he did no work on damaged leather, just stitching or reinforcing corners."

"So he is now being watched, too."

"Yes. My friends—Joe and Bill—" Mac smiled. "Simpler to keep it Joe, Bill, and Mac. Anyway, their interest is now aroused. At first, they were just politely helpful—they owed me that from the case we had in Canada last winter: two Berlin activists using Toronto to slip over the border into the States."

"How far does their interest reach?"

"Far enough to have a couple of workmen in O'Connell's house adjusting the burglar-alarm system, checking all the wiring. One window's circuit was somehow broken yesterday—" Mac smiled again—"so the whole system went out. Work is going on there today—and tomorrow."

"Tomorrow's Saturday," Renwick reminded him.

"They'll work time and a half. O'Connell agreed. Burglar alarms have got to be in order."

So there would be two FBI agents in the house through Saturday. "Who is covering Sunday?"

"Joe and Bill are planning that now. Might even tip off the two Secret Service agents to loiter around. By the way, Bill has a question for you. That briefcase was bought here in Washington, wasn't it?"

"Yes. At Burke and Evans. Just before Christmas, 1977."

"Burke and Evans carry the same basic line, don't they? There are some suit and attaché cases that are always in stock."

"Yes. Nina is probably shopping there right now—she wants to give her father a birthday present of an attaché case."

"Similar to the damaged one?"

"As close as possible. He liked it a lot."

"Then Bill's question makes sense: if a duplicate could be bought at Burke and Evans, wouldn't it be used for the substitution?"

"That worried me, too. But it could mean too difficult a job to line a case with some explosive device and have it absolutely perfect with no sign of any tampering. And—" Renwick paused for emphasis—"with no alteration of the inside space for O'Connell's papers. So my guess is that the substituted case will be custom-made."

"You mean," Mac said thoughtfully, "the outside dimensions might have to be increased a little to hold the explosives? So that the inside measurements would stay the same?"

Renwick nodded. "Who notices if his attaché case is a bit longer or deeper? But he damn well notices if he finds his papers curled up at the edges instead of lying smoothly in place. Does that answer Bill's question?"

"I guess it does. Theo really thought of every detail, didn't he?"

"Right to the end."

"Well, that's about all. Have you met Colbert yet?"

"I decided to keep our little confrontation for the right moment. I'm depending on Bill and Joe for that."

"Oh, they'll know when Colbert carries a case back into the O'Connell house. She is being tailed."

"And they'll send me the message? No delay."

"You'll receive it on that communicator Bill supplied." It was a small beeper, the type that gave the warning to call headquarters at once. In Renwick's case, he wouldn't need to telephone. One small signal, and he'd know what that meant and he'd be on his way. Since his arrival with Nina yesterday afternoon, he had never traveled far from the area. This meeting place today was within direct reach, and his hotel on Wisconsin was only a few blocks from O'Connell's house on Dumbarton Road. "I think it's all pretty well arranged," Mac went on. "How long do you think we'll have to wait?"

"I don't know. But I think that accident to O'Connell's case could have been the beginning of the action."

"There could be a delay in returning it—with the excuse it needed a lot of repairing."

"Yes. But too much delay and O'Connell will get impatient. He will buy himself a new one. Wouldn't you?"

And Mac, who was neither extravagant nor impatient, agreed completely. "How's Miss O'Connell holding up?"

Renwick smiled. "Pretty good, I think." He had called her this morning—as old friend Jack. Tonight he'd phone again, as Tommy. Tomorrow it would be Ed and Steve. Nina and he had agreed on this idea on the flight across the Atlantic. And if she managed to find the right attaché case, she'd just say, "Sorry I couldn't meet you for lunch. I had a birthday present to buy." Any mention of the present, and Renwick would know it was now wrapped up as a gift and waiting in her closet.

"She doesn't know we expect an attaché case to be substituted?" Mac asked.

"No. Nor what it could contain. Nor how it might be used. I just told her to be careful answering questions about her trip; and extra careful with Thérèse Colbert."

"I suppose you had to warn her about all that," Mac said.

"You're damn right."

"A tricky situation. What if she panics, thinks she is in some danger?"

Renwick's face tightened. "I gave her a number to telephone." And I'll be at Dumbarton Road within six minutes.

"Not *your* number?" Mac was horrified.

Renwick didn't answer that. "By the way, who has Colbert been calling? Any particular friends?"

My God, thought Mac, still staring at Renwick. Renwick was taking too many chances, and all for Nina's sake. Gallantry and security didn't mix, that was for damned sure. "She has two. One is State Department. The other is a French journalist."

"Any contact with the Soviet Embassy?"

"Apparently not."

"Doesn't the journalist have meetings with any press attaché there?"

"He is covering the White House at present, concentrates on that. Joe says he is young and pleasant and well liked. He is constantly around—attends briefing sessions. He's accepted."

"Qualifications?"

"The best. He is deputizing for *Le Temps*'s correspondent, who is back in Paris for a couple of weeks."

"Bill and Joe—"

"Are checking him out," Mac answered Renwick's question before it was asked. "Also Colbert's friend at State. He has been introducing her around. That's how she met Beryl O'Connell—at one of his parties."

"I don't like that particularly."

"Too many bloody moles everywhere," Mac agreed. "But you know what's worrying Bill, Joe, and me? You, Bob. Colbert hasn't seen you yet, but she probably heard you brought Nina home. Who was there when you both arrived?"

"Beryl O'Connell."

"See what I mean?" Taking chances again. Like staying at a hotel instead of a safe address, just to be close to O'Connell's place.

"I didn't even enter the house. She didn't remember who I was." An old friend of Father's, Nina had explained briefly. "All very casual."

"Even so," Mac began doubtfully. "The fact that you're here in Washington could send Colbert running to the phone."

"In that case, the Bill-Joe team certainly overheard that message."

"Not if she telephoned from a drugstore."

"Well, whom did she meet after that call?"

He's got a point there, thought Mac: a possible lead to her control, who might in turn lead to the resident agent who is in over-all command? But I'm still worried about Bob. "You are the one guy who can name her for what she is," Mac insisted.

"She may think I'm just an easy mark." She must have been testing that out in New York last August when she arrived with her State Department friend at Frank Cooper's cocktail party and hoped to find me there. "Or," Renwick went on calmly, "she may think she can have me blackmailed and made impotent." Then he laughed. "I don't turn impotent so easily."

No, he wouldn't, thought Mac. He said, "I'll be moving into your hotel tonight."

"Oh, who set you up as my baby-sitter? Billy-Joe?"

Mac extended his hand, said, "Good-bye, old scout. Be seeing you in the distance. I'm your backup, goddamn it."

"Good-bye. Nice meeting you." And Renwick meant that. They separated with a casual wave, MacEwan to pay a short but elusive visit to the Smithsonian, Renwick making for a taxi and—eventually—Wisconsin Avenue.

There was no signal from the alarm in his pocket.

Before six-thirty, when Beryl O'Connell might be in her predinner bathtub and safely out of the way, Renwick called Nina. No, she couldn't really make any appointment for tomorrow, and she was sorry she hadn't been able to lunch with him today: she had been shopping for a birthday present and hadn't found what she wanted until two o'clock. Next week, she would have much more free time—the first days home were really hectic. "Next week," he said, "we'll take in a movie and have late supper. I'll call you on Monday. Okay, Nina?"

He would have something to eat himself. Then he'd read. Then a long lonely night. But at least she sounded fine—a laugh in her voice that reassured him. So far, she was safe.

He decided on one of the nearby restaurants—there was a string of them along this busy part of Wisconsin—and chose one where he could have a rare steak and a real Idaho potato. That was one thing about European cooking, even in the best of places: no idea of how a baked potato should look or taste. With a tankard of nicely chilled beer, he had a pleasant meal. Quick service, too. He had little time to read the newspaper he had brought with him as insurance against a long wait. But the front page had two items of interest.

One dismayed him: the ex-Shah of Iran was in New York Hospital, and the loud demonstrations had begun in front of it. But what did politicians and diplomats expect? God in heaven, Renwick thought, don't they see more than six inches in front of their noses? And why the hell couldn't the Shah have had treatment in Mexico? The doctors there were good. If American doctors had to butt in, why hadn't they flown down there? They had traveled to plenty of places all over the world—Saudi Arabia, the Dominican Republic, among others—in order to advise or operate. These thoughts nearly ruined his appetite, but the second news item restored it: Erik and Marco, leaders of the Direct Action gang (the newspaper's word, not Renwick's) which had terrorized West Germany for the last five years, had been held in Bombay for extradition. Marco was already on his way; Erik was now under indictment for the murder of a Bombay security officer.

That charge may not stick, Renwick thought: what court had ever dealt with a cyanide pen as a murder weapon even if refills for the little pistol had been in Kiley's pocket? But Roy's anger demanded justice: a long sentence in an Indian prison; and then extradition. Kiley's record as Erik would weigh heavily against him. Too bad for him now that the People's Revolutionary Force for Direct Action had always been so quick to claim proud responsibility for all their deeds. Out of their own mouths they had condemned Erik.

Was Thérèse Colbert reading that paragraph, too? She possibly didn't understand its significance—Kiley was Kiley to her—but the agent who was in control might. And if he, too, were ignorant about James Kiley's true identity, then the resident—the central spider in the web of espionage agents woven around Washington—should know.

Unless, Renwick thought as he finished his coffee, Theo had kept his agents entirely under his complete management, had not put them under any usual control or resident, had instituted his own branch of espionage for his own purpose. With approval of one or two at the highest level, of course. He would never have had so much power, so many resources, if they hadn't given assent to his plan. Indeed, they could very well have let him avoid the usual chain of command, bend the rules, in order to serve their own purpose: if he succeeded, excellent; if he failed, they had nothing to do with it.

In which case, Renwick decided as he paid the check, there could be one very ignorant resident in the Washington area tonight. Ignorant . . . How much was known even by those who directed the KGB? Known of Theo's actual plan? He was inviting World War III, and why should the Soviets risk that—at a time when everything was going their way? He had been given immense power, certainly, and complete backing, but he could have added Theo's own touch to his initial assignment. It couldn't be that Theo had gone out of control, taking his own section or department with him?

The question halted Renwick abruptly at the restaurant's door. Now you're really going off half-cocked, he told himself. The KGB wouldn't let any agent, far less the head of a department, get out of control without pretty heavy retribution to be paid. Yet, if Theo's purpose was achieved, if he really produced a result that would send the world reeling, that would win World War III before it even began—well, the Soviets would live with that situation quite comfortably.

Renwick came out into the bright lights of Wisconsin Avenue. There was only one thing he could be sure of: Theo's death must have shaken those who did know about his Washington project. Would they back out? Or push forward their timetable?

Suddenly, he was aware he was being followed. Two men in loose overcoats, bareheaded, had left the restaurant almost on his heels. Presentable types, young, keeping a respectful distance. Too obvious. Was this Mac's idea, or his friends at the Bureau? *Worried about you,* Mac had said. Hell, I don't need baby-sitters, Renwick thought angrily.

He paused on the sidewalk opposite his hotel, glanced over his shoulder as he lit a cigarette. The men were no longer behind him—not in clear view, at least. They might have dodged into one of those doorways. Renwick's eyes narrowed, but he fought down the impulse to walk back and confront them. If they were Bill-and-Joe's agents, they'd have a cold wait out there. He was going straight to the warmth of his room. And if they weren't Bill-and-Joe's agents? So Beryl had talked about Bob Renwick to her dear Thérèse, and Thérèse had gone running for advice, and her adviser had decided on action.

Well, he thought as he waited to cross the avenue, I may not carry cyanide or a knife or a walking stick, but I'm damned glad to feel the weight of my little Biretta right here in my pocket. Then, glancing over at the hotel, he saw that the window of his room on the second floor was lit. The curtains were drawn, but they were not heavy enough to darken the light completely. It hadn't been burning there when he left.

He crossed the busy thoroughfare, entered the lobby, and took the stairs to his floor—a more silent approach than the elevator allowed. The maid had turned the sofa into a bed just before he had telephoned Nina. Fresh towels, too, had been placed in the bathroom. His room required no more attention tonight, but someone thought it needed company. Hadn't the intruder expected him back so early? Watched him leave for dinner, calculated on his absence for an hour and a half at least? If so, the man was wrong by thirty-five minutes.

About to enter his corridor, Renwick drew back. A woman was standing at the door to his room, watching the elevator. She was dressed in black as if she were one of the maids, but no apron, no sensible shoes. All this floor had been serviced—there were no maids around. No one in the pantry, either—everyone was out to dinner.

He slipped off his coat, dropped it on the stairs' bannister, walked into the corridor, his right hand in his jacket pocket. The woman turned her head to look at him, stared, rattled the door handle as she brushed past it on her way to the elevator. Neat, thought Renwick: a complete picture of innocence; but I'll know you again, Milady.

He reached the door. The woman was waiting impatiently for an elevator that was slow to respond. No weapon there, he decided: a warning and a quick retreat were her tactics. But why the delay from inside the room? What's waiting inside? He drew the Biretta, threw the door open, sidestepped quickly as he entered.

Two men faced him. Young. One tall and fair, one short and dark. Both powerful. They had been preparing for him—room in disorder, apparently burglarized—the tall man had a silencer already fitted into place on his revolver.

There was a brief second of no movement, no sound. Then a knife flashed across the room, missing Renwick by inches as he swerved his body. He dropped to one knee, his eye on the man with the revolver, and fired first. He caught the man's right shoulder, deflecting the aim of the bullet, which plunged into the wall behind him. The small man leaped forward, a straight-legged kick aimed at Renwick's chin, and ran.

"Far enough," said Mac's voice. He had a firm half nelson on the struggling man. "All yours," he told one of the two agents who were just behind him, and relinquished his hold. The baby-sitters. Renwick would have laughed if his damned jaw hadn't hurt: he had jerked back instinctively from that lethal karate kick, but some of it had grazed him. Nothing much, he told himself, considering what it could have been.

The tall man was no problem: a shoulder wound was painful and discouraged further action.

"Saw the light in your window," one of the agents said. "Just wondered."

"Thank you," said Renwick and rose to his feet.

The other agent looked around. "A setup."

"I guess."

"Don't touch anything; we'll want—"

"I know." The bullet embedded in the wall; the knife there, too, deep and holding. Mac was looking at them, his lips pursed.

As the prisoners were handcuffed, Mac said, "I'll help see them safely housed. Be with you later, Bob. You okay? Need anything?"

"Ice. A bucketful of ice."

Mac repressed a smile. "Will do." He followed the handcuffed prisoners into the corridor and closed the door, partly blotting out the rising voices now gathered outside. An agent was speaking with complete reassurance: nothing to worry about, everything was all right. The voices diminished. Soon there was silence complete.

One thing is definite, Renwick decided as he wrapped a towel around a handful of ice cubes, I cannot have it both ways. Either I take Claudel's advice entirely—no excuses, no halfway dodges to get into the field again—and stay in my nice new office with its inspirational armchair, or I don't marry Nina. I can't put her through this kind of thing.

Sure, a man can die crossing a road, a man can break his neck in his bathtub, a man can fall from his roof fixing a chimney. A coward dies a hundred deaths before he meets the real one. So what?

I'm not giving up Nina.

And what am I giving up, anyway? It isn't as if I were action-crazy. I like problems, bits and pieces of information to fit into something understandable. I like outthinking the opposition. When they challenge us, I damn well enjoy doing the greatest harm where it will do the most good. Fight their ideas with better ideas—or, at least, try. And all of that, I don't give up.

I won't stop traveling, either. There will be visits to various places abroad, exchanges of information. Interintell is growing—at last count we had twelve of the NATO countries and two other democracies, all interested and co-operating. Yes, there will be travel and old friends to meet. And Nina with me. In the field—impossible; not just for security's sake, not just for rules and regulations, but for her safety, too.

He studied his jaw in the mirror. It could have been worse. That kick could have snapped his neck.

Just remember, Renwick, you may have swerved from a knife, avoided a bullet, but you almost didn't dodge a kick. One hell of a way to learn that Pierre Claudel had been right: move over and let the men in their twenties do their stint. He took another handful of ice, wrapped it in the towel, felt his jaw go numb with its chill. If it took another five hours, he'd have this damned face back to normal.

He settled down to wait for Mac's return with any news he had gathered about the two thugs. Bought with money? Or trained in another Rancho San Carlos? One thing he did know: whoever was now in charge of Theo's plan was pushing forward the timetable—hard.

Thirty

SATURDAY MORNING, EXCEPT for Renwick's phone call to Nina, was uneventful—just a part of the waiting game.

"Ed here. Thought you might like to drive out to Mount Vernon. Would you come?"

"Oh, Ed, I'm sorry. I really am. But this afternoon, Beryl's interior decorator wants me to choose the curtains for my room. She is bringing samples of material, and I've got to look through them."

"Couldn't she postpone that until Monday?"

"I tried. But she's borrowing the samples from some wholesale house, and she has got to return them by Monday morning."

"Samples—you mean small scraps of cloth? That shouldn't take you too long. Just flip through them."

"No, no. Large samples—enough to show the repeat in the pattern." Nina was laughing. "It's a very serious business, Ed. There will be an hour of argument, I know."

"When do you expect her?"

"Sometime this afternoon—that's all she said."

"Well, why don't you give me a ring as soon as she arrives—would you, Nina?"

"Why, yes," Nina said slowly.

"We might make something yet of the afternoon. Just call me. Will you? And I'll drop in unannounced and hurry the argument along."

"I won't forget."

"See you then."

Renwick put down the receiver, looked at the blue-and-white roses climbing over the long yellow curtains at his bedroom window.

"Well?" asked MacEwan. He was lounging on the sofa bed, now back into early American shape, surrounded by sections of the *New York Times* and the *Washington Post*.

"What's a repeat in the pattern?"

Mac shrugged, and had his own question. "Do you remember the days when a newspaper came in one piece and could be carried in your coat pocket?" He watched Renwick in amazement. "What the hell are you doing with that curtain?"

"Got it!" Renwick said. "Yes, these samples could be quite large. Enough to hide an attaché case being carried into the house."

"Any case carried by Colbert will be spotted before she reaches the house."

"That's what she feared, perhaps."

"When is she expected?"

"Sometime this afternoon."

Mac pushed aside the newspapers. "Trouble brewing in Iran. I can smell it." He rose and picked up his leather jacket. "I'll contact Bill, make sure his alarm-signal boys will keep working through the afternoon."

"Tell them to stay near O'Connell's study. I'll give them the high sign when it's time to make their move. They know what to do."

"As planned. Shouldn't be difficult. You've got the tough part." Renwick had to keep Colbert in the house, prevent her from leaving or telephoning. "How will you do it?"

"Play it by ear."

"She may not bring the case back today," Mac reminded him as he opened the door.

"Then we wait for tomorrow. Or the next day. Or the next."

Mac made no comment, just nodded and left.

After lunch, Nina went upstairs to her room and chose a book and a chair at the window. From there she could see part of Dumbarton Road, and certainly any approach to the house. There was, she noticed, a heavy-looking van parked on the opposite side of the street. Probably it belonged to the workmen now tracking the burglar-alarm failure in the living room.

She couldn't concentrate on reading. Even the silence of the house seemed to increase her nervousness. Her father was at his office today, a sign of disturbing news if he stayed there on a Saturday. Beryl was in her room on the floor below. Mattie, the cook, was in her far-off quarters where no one could hear her television. Saturday afternoon—a strange time to select curtain material. Nor could Nina understand why the walls had been painted blue and the strawberry-pink carpet had been laid before the curtains had been chosen. A roundabout way of decorating, she thought. And if the Colbert woman saddled me with blue and pink, why didn't she complete the choice by herself? I'll never like this room; never. But I won't be here much longer. Whatever colors I choose in London for our flat, there certainly won't be a blue wall. Or a pink carpet.

She couldn't concentrate on a book; she couldn't concentrate on music from her record player. But at half past three, her impatience was rewarded. Madame Colbert arrived in her black Thunderbird, driven by the young man who worked in her showroom. Nina was already on the phone when two large books of samples were being hauled by him out of the car while Madame Colbert carried a lighter load of chintz and satin draped over one arm.

"Ed?" Nina asked as her call was immediately answered. "She's here."

"See you, darling." The call was over.

Darling . . . He forgot to be careful. Smiling, she combed her hair, put on fresh lipstick, took a last look in the long mirror and ran downstairs. On the second floor she slowed her steps and arrived, sedate and decorous, she hoped, in the hall. It wasn't large: it still amazed her how expensive houses in Georgetown could be so crumpled up inside. But it ran through to a garden at the back, where Beryl had chosen to place a conservatory. Poor Father, Nina thought now, this house will never be finished. At least he had his study almost complete. Beryl and the Colbert woman were there, while across the hall the two repairmen hadn't yet tracked down their problem.

Nina avoided the samples deposited near the foot of the staircase, and hesitated. She could hear the Thunderbird being driven away. The Colbert woman must be planning a long visit. Nina overcame her aversion, and entered the study.

"Nina, come and see what Thérèse has managed," Beryl said. "Isn't she wonderful? The stains have all gone, and it's just the same old case as before. Thérèse, couldn't your little man have removed the scratch on the side and that bruised look at the corner, too?"

"I thought Mr. O'Connell wanted things just as he remembers them," Thérèse Colbert remarked. However much I dislike her, thought Nina, I've got to admit she's attractive: blue eyes and dark smooth hair and a ready smile. Her taste in clothes was elegant. And expensive. Today she had chosen a white wool dress to emphasize an excellent figure, half covered it with a mink coat draped over her shoulders. She pulled it off, dropped it on a chair.

Nina came forward slowly. The attaché case had been laid with pride on the center of the desk. "It looks very nice." And what do I do with another case, all ready to give as a birthday present?

Beryl stared at her stepdaughter. "Is that all you have to say? Nice? It's a *marvelous* job. Your father will be delighted." For a moment her hazel eyes looked reprovingly at Nina. She shook her head, auburn hair falling loosely, and exchanged a tolerant smile with Madame Colbert.

Nina recovered herself, said, "I know he will be. He hates that leather envelope he has been carrying around. But how did you manage to have the stains removed? I thought that would have been impossible." That is what Bob had believed, and Ron Gilman had agreed.

"Just a little trade secret," Madame Colbert said with a light laugh. "Now, shall we go upstairs and choose your curtains? I have brought a divine toile which I know you'll adore. It's one of the loose pieces of material in the hall, so that's easy to carry. But, Beryl, we'll need help with the sample books. Do you think your workmen would oblige? Who recommended them to Mr. O'Connell?"

"It's a firm we have always used."

"You must give me its address. I don't have any adequate people to install alarm systems."

"Of course. But before we go upstairs—" Beryl walked over to the paneling that covered low cabinets under the bookshelves—"do look at this. Awful, isn't it? Francis absolutely refuses to have any more paint stripped off. No more accidents, he says. We were lucky his books weren't splashed, too. So what would you suggest, Thérèse? Dark green enamel to continue the color of the carpet?"

The doorbell rang. "I'll get it," Nina said, halfway toward the hall.

Thérèse Colbert's smiling scrutiny of Nina ended. "Very shy, isn't she?"

"Oh, don't worry about her. This house is so very new to her. She must feel a stranger, but she'll soon become accustomed to us all."

"She talks little about her world trip."

"It couldn't have been comfortable. Francis is amazed that she endured it for so long. Now, about this woodwork, Thérèse—"

Nina opened the door, stood looking at him.

"Hello, darling," Renwick said softly, and stepped inside. A repairman gave a brief glance out from the living room—one of last night's baby-sitters, Renwick saw—and withdrew with a nod. Women's voices came from another room a short distance along the hall. "Beryl and Colbert?"

"In the study. Oh, Bob—"

"What's wrong?" He took her hands, resisted putting his arms around her.

"The attaché case—it's back. Stain-free."

"Where is it?"

"On Father's desk. And what will I do now for his birthday?" My last traveler's check went on it, she thought in dismay; I even had his initials, small and neat, printed under the handle exactly as before.

"Give him the one you bought. He'd like that."

"*Two* attaché cases?"

"Always useful." He drew her close, risked a kiss. "Where's the present—in your room?"

"No. Madame Colbert has been in and out of there every afternoon. She was upstairs when I brought the attaché case home yesterday, so—it's in the coat closet." Nina nodded to a narrow door in the wall under the staircase.

Renwick let go her hands to pull off his Burberry. He hung it in the closet, looked puzzled as he saw only hats on the shelf above the rod. Quickly, he held aside the coats and glimpsed a package propped against the wall, hidden by their skirts. "Pretty good," he said with a sudden smile, and shut the closet door. Pretty damn good, in fact. The smile vanished as he glanced toward the study: the voices were drifting nearer. "Get them upstairs, out of the hall. And after that—I've got to see her, Nina. Alone." There was a moment of fear in the blue eyes that met his. He said nothing more.

Nina's face was tense, but she nodded and moved away from him as the voices grew clearer. Renwick braced himself.

Beryl was saying, "Then you think we should keep the original brown? I did want something brighter. Oh—Mr. Renwick! But how nice!" They shook hands politely. "Did you come to see Nina?"

"To see your husband, actually." His voice was easy, completely natural.

"He ought to be home soon. At least I hope it will be soon. Oh, Madame Colbert—may I present Mr. Robert Renwick?"

Always correct, thought Nina: Beryl really reads her Amy Vanderbilt. But, for once, Madame Colbert had lost her manners. She was standing as if transfixed, the usual smile quite wiped off her face.

"We have met," Renwick said.

Thérèse Colbert's composure returned. "Really?" she asked politely. "I'm afraid I—oh, yes, I remember now. Paris, wasn't it?"

"Brussels."

"You meet too many attractive men, Thérèse," Beryl said with a laugh. And to Renwick, very sweetly, "You can't expect Madame Colbert to remember all of you."

Quickly, Nina said, "I asked Bob to stay for tea—wait for Father."

"Of course." Beryl recovered from her surprise. "That would be delightful. And you'll stay, too, Thérèse. Once we choose the curtains, I'm sure you'd enjoy talking with—"

"I'm afraid I must leave before tea time. Another appointment."

"But I thought—" began Beryl. Then she stopped thinking and could only feel a drop in the hall's temperature. In her best tradition, she covered Thérèse's refusal with a spate of words. The curtains had better be chosen right now. What about those heavy sample books, so cumbersome? Mr. Renwick, would he be so kind?

Nina interrupted. "Carry those things up, and then carry them down? No need. I think I see something I like here." She lifted three loose pieces of material at random and started toward the staircase. "Coming?" she asked Beryl. "Or do you trust my taste?"

That decided it. "We'd better go," Beryl told Thérèse Colbert, who gave up her momentary hesitation with a show of good grace. "Do excuse us, Mr. Renwick. You'll find magazines in the living room."

"I'll be all right," he assured her. He waited until Beryl's inexhaustible talk dwindled into a far-off murmur. Then he moved quickly.

Inside the living room, the men had packed their gear. "Desk in the study," he told them, and left for the coat closet as one of them made his way across the hall. The other opened the front door, signaled the van standing opposite to start pulling out of its parking space. Renwick had already torn off the birthday wrappings, jamming them into the closet's farthest corner.

Altogether, two minutes. He gave one last glance at Nina's present, centered on the desk as the other attaché case had been, and left the study. The outside door was closing. A brief silence. Then he heard the van pull away from the front steps, traveling at slow speed, as he entered the living room. Now, it was a matter of waiting.

Not easy for him, but worse for the experts who were examining the attaché case, preparing to dissect it. He didn't envy them that job: finding the detonator, disarming the explosive device—but what if they found nothing, just an empty case with no deadly lining? Then Colbert could walk out that front door. She would be kept under surveillance, of course—until she vanished one fine morning, heading for Lausanne again. And I would be the prize fool, the intelligence officer whose credibility lay in a thousand pieces. Interintell, too. It would suffer.

No, he told himself, there *has* to be something in that damned attaché case: stains aren't so easily and perfectly removed. It's a substitution, it has to be. A clever piece of work, prepared well in advance, with details and measurements and photographs to make sure it was an exact reproduction. It has to be. . . . He turned away from the window as he heard a light footstep in the hall, moved quickly.

He was just in time to stop Thérèse Colbert from reaching the study.

"My coat," she explained. "I left my notebook in its pocket. I need it to mark down measurements and—"

"Of course. In here?" He entered the study before she did, picked up her mink coat while she hesitated at the door. She glanced at the desk, seemed relieved. She was quite content to leave the study with Renwick.

"Thank you," she said with one of her old smiles. "You know, Bob, I did give you—what d'you call it?"

"An out."

"That's it. Why didn't you take it? Why mention Brussels?"

"Because," he said, grasping her wrist and urging her toward the living room, "I want to talk about Brussels."

"Have the workmen gone?"

"Yes. We won't be disturbed." She knows they've gone. She heard the van drive away. That's why she came down here, to check on the attaché case. I should have expected that, he thought. His wariness increased.

"I really ought to go upstairs—"

"They'll manage without you for a few minutes."

"And I have to telephone—my next appointment—I'll be late."

"We'll talk first." He released his hold on her wrist as he got her inside the living room. He took her coat and handbag, dropped them on a settee, and closed the door. "Sit over there." He pointed to a chair, well away from the window.

Startled, she looked at him; but she crossed the room and sat down. He chose a chair close to the door, and faced her.

"This," she said with a light laugh, "is hardly the way for old friends to talk. It isn't exactly tête-à-tête. You used to do better, Bob. Let's sit on the couch and be comfortable." She made as if to rise.

"No. Stay there! I'm perfectly comfortable."

She changed her tactics. "Oh, Bob—I'm really sorry. About Brussels. Leaving you so quickly. But my mother was ill, very ill."

"Is she still in Lausanne?"

Thérèse Colbert looked at him. "Yes," she said, trying to guess how much he knew about Lausanne.

"A useful place to drop out of sight."

"Really, Bob—"

"You heard Maartens was dead, of course."

That silenced her.

"And his gray-haired friend, too," Renwick said. "And talking of death, weren't you surprised to find me alive this afternoon?"

"I had nothing—" It was a mistake. She bit her lip.

"Nothing to do with that? Just a warning call to your control here in Washington? Who is he, Thérèse?"

"You are mad, completely mad." She rose.

"You aren't leaving," he told her. "I locked the door. The key is in my pocket."

"I only wanted my cigarettes. In my bag."

He reached for her handbag, saying, "I'll get them." He found the cigarette case and a small Derringer tucked into a side pocket. "Neat little toy," he said. "I hope you don't play with it often." He examined the cigarette case—this alarmed her—so he slipped it back into her handbag. The lighter was also dubious: a concealed camera, probably. He left it where it was in its own small pocket. He held up the Derringer. "Would you really have shot me with this?"

"If necessary. It's for my protection." Her eyes were hard and cool.

So she would have fired it, he realized. And pleaded? God only knew what story she would concoct: an accident, probably. He replaced the Derringer, snapped the bag shut, and dropped the bundle of evidence beside his chair. Sadly, he thought, she's well trained: not just the pretty woman being caught by money, being blackmailed one step at a time into a deeper and deeper morass. Right from the beginning, she knew what she was doing. "Sit down," he told her, "and let's talk about Theo."

Slowly, she sat down, even forgot to cross her legs and show a nicely molded thigh at the split of her tight skirt.

"You've never seen him, of course. And now you never will. He died in Bombay. Or didn't your control tell you? Probably not. Too many deaths are disturbing."

She stared at him.

"You really ought to tell us all you know about Theo's conspiracy. That might help you."

"Conspiracy?" She made an effort and smiled. "Ridiculous—"

"Tell us how James Kiley was to join you here, and Tony Shawfield." Keep out all mention of the attaché case, he reminded himself: that would come later, and not from him. "You'd have enjoyed working with them. Too bad they've been arrested and sent back to West Germany." He paused, noted her astonishment. "Or perhaps you didn't know their real names: Erik and Marco. You read the newspapers, don't you?"

"Terrorists—anarchists. I have never had any connection with them!" she burst out angrily.

"Indeed you have. You're up to your pretty little neck in a terrorist conspiracy. So tell me about it."

"Why? To help you give evidence against me? But I don't think you will. If you do, there will be nothing left of your career—or of your life. Renwick the laughingstock! No, I don't think a man with your reputation could face that." Her voice had risen, her face was triumphant.

"Oh, those photographs," he said. "I wondered when you'd get around to trying some blackmail."

"You're a fool. They will be used."

"Well, if my stock goes down in some quarters," he said with a good show of amusement, "it will go up in others."

"I've warned you. They will be used."

"And let yourself be exposed? In every sense," he added, smiling.

She looked at him in frustration, not knowing whether to believe him or not. "If it has to be," she said slowly, "it has to be."

"All for the good of the cause? Well, well—you really are a dedicated woman. Perhaps it might be better—for you as well as me—if you burned the negatives."

"You know I don't have them."

He knew that quite well. But who did have the negatives now that Theo had abdicated?

"I don't," she protested. "Theo—everything was sent to Theo. It was his idea, his orders. I never—"

"Of course not," Renwick said wearily. "You were just the little innocent trapped by the big bad men."

"But I *am* innocent, Bob." She had turned to pleading again, her eyes soft, her lips tender. "I loved you. I thought you loved me. Didn't you? And I still love you."

"In God's name," he said, his anger suddenly breaking through. He rose, went to the window.

"Expecting someone?" She looked at the door. Had there been a key in that lock? Even if he had it now, her bag was there—easily reached, easily opened.

"Yes." He turned to face her. "And don't try it!" he warned her as she took a few steps toward her handbag. He had his Biretta in his hand. "My own small piece of protection," he said as he pocketed it again. "Sit down, Thérèse. You may as well wait in comfort. But don't make up stories. Tell the truth. It will be easier for you in the end." He went back to his own chair.

"Would you have used that—on me?" she asked.

"Not to kill. Just to delay you a little." Would Mac and his friends never arrive? Or, he thought again, nothing has been found in the attaché case. I'll get a phone call telling me to let her go. And for me—hell to pay.

In silence, he waited six agonizing minutes. Then a car drew up at the front of the house. Could be anyone, he told himself: a delivery of flowers, liquor, even O'Connell. He kept his hopes down and his eyes on Thérèse Colbert.

The door to the living room opened. Two strangers, serious-eyed, entered with Mac. Mac was grinning all over his windbeaten face.

They've found it, thought Renwick as he got to his feet and handed over Colbert's bag. "One weapon at least," he said quietly. He wasn't going to stay and hear her rights being read, or to see her being taken out handcuffed. Nodding to Mac, he turned away from the front door and walked slowly down the hall toward the back of the house.

He reached a white conservatory, barely completed, with decorative trees in giant pots, flowers in rustic boxes, all clustered in the center of the tiled floor to leave space for work-in-progress around the curving windows. Outside, the light was fading, the small remainder of a garden bleak with falling leaves. Well, he thought, that is one file we can close. Our part is done. The FBI and other security agencies can dig hard and come up with more. But for J. P. Merriman & Co., Theo's file is closed—ended along with his Washington project.

He heard a movement behind him. "Nina?" He turned quickly. But it was Mac.

"I asked her to give me two minutes with you," Mac said. "It's news from Claudel. He had a call from Bombay, just before Gilman caught his flight back to London. It's about that baggage Theo left in his suite—for his three men to bring out safely. Some safety!"

"Do we never get rid of Theo?"

"Gilman and friend A. K. Roy got rid of his negatives. Burned them. That's the message: all negatives burned. Does it make any sense to you?"

Renwick drew a long deep breath. "They found negatives?"

"Among a few special files. Theo's own small traveling office, I gather. We'll hear more from Gilman when we all get back to London. Clever bastard."

"Gilman?" A slow smile spread over Renwick's face. "Yes," he said gratefully.

"No. Theo." Mac shook his head. "You're right. He still keeps cropping up. For a man who'll never make the headlines, he's quite a personality. Which reminds me—my federal friends would like to have a little talk—just a general wrap-up, more background information."

"You could handle it."

"Sure. But don't you want some credit—share the congratulations?"

Renwick laughed. "Come on, Mac. Everything is okay. Leave it at that."

"It will be played down, of course. The newspapers will never hear of that damned attaché case. Do we tell O'Connell about it?"

Renwick shook his head. He would tell Nina. But O'Connell? Definitely no. "Not our job, Mac. We'll leave it to your friends Bill and Joe." They'd decide what should be told—or not told.

"Wonder what they'll come up with?"

"Oh—that the attaché case was damaged inside. Beyond repair."

"And that's a pretty fair description." Mac smiled at some memory. "But they'll certainly have to warn O'Connell about an enemy agent making free with his home."

"That could be enough."

"A shocker," Mac predicted. "At least he won't be carrying any high explosives into the White House. I wouldn't be surprised if there's an emergency meeting this week. Tomorrow, perhaps—when more news comes in. Iran of course. Sunday morning over there, now. Well, I'll see you in London. We'll have a celebration party. When?"

"In about ten days. I'm due some leave." Geneva, he thought: that's where we'll go.

Mac studied Renwick's face. "So you're getting married?"

"Yes."

"Saw it coming. Couldn't be any other explanation for—"

"And your two minutes are up, old boy." Renwick disengaged his hand from Mac's enthusiastic handshake, clapped his shoulder, gave him an encouraging push toward the hall.

"Best idea you ever had," Mac said over his shoulder. He half stumbled over some potted plants, swore, added, "You need some light in here." He shook his head, gave a mock salute, and was on his way.

Renwick waited. Yes, he decided, we'll fly to Zurich, drive from there to Geneva. But I'll surprise her: she'll think it's London, will never know until we are picking up our tickets at the airport.

And then he saw Nina walking down the hall toward him, walking slowly, almost hesitantly. "Nina," he called out, went forward to meet her. Suddenly she was running, joining in his laughter as his arms caught hold of her. He drew her away from the lighted doorway, into the island of trees and flowers.

Cloak of
Darkness

For Keith and Nancy
with love

One

I T WAS THE usual Monday-morning fever in Robert Renwick's office. After
a slow weekend with scarcely a report coming in, there was a deluge of cryptic
messages—most by shortwave radio, some by coded cable or Telex, and even
two by scrambled phone calls from Berlin and Rome requiring immediate
attention.

But now it was five o'clock, the working day drawing to an end, his desk
almost free of questions needing answers, of memoranda and suggestions
to be considered. The easy replies would go out tonight; the difficult problems would need more computer research and analysis, perhaps further
queries to agents in the field, certainly some scrambled phone discussions
with agencies in various capitals. The intelligence services, not only of the
NATO countries but also of those that had allied themselves with the West,
were finding the London headquarters of Interintell a useful clearing house
of information.

Interintell—or International Intelligence against Terrorism. It had been
Renwick's brain child, conceived in Brussels, set up in London, staffed by
ex-NATO intelligence men like Renwick himself. As an American, he would
have been pleased to see Washington as Interintell's headquarters for shared
information on terrorist conspiracies and connections. But he had decided
on London for several valid reasons. Western Europe had been under savage attack by organized terrorism; the United States—so far—hadn't experienced the same intensity. Then there was the matter of co-operation between intelligence services, and that came more willingly from Europeans;
they had felt the need. The United States—so far, again—had not.

But then, America had been having its own headaches: the CIA under
attack at home, in danger abroad from the exposure of its agents. Small wonder that Washington, overloaded with bureaucrats and competing agencies, had
been in a foot-dragging mood when Renwick put forward his tentative idea
almost three years ago: the necessity for pro-NATO countries to share intelligence information if terrorism was ever to be challenged successfully.

France, of course, had been interested—it was already establishing its own
counter-terrorism department. But even though Paris had its attractions, it
also had the headquarters of Interpol, the International Police Organization that tracked the criminals who once thought crossing a frontier would
solve their problems. Fair was fair, Renwick had decided, and so London
was the choice. In the two years since Interintell had been established, in a

quiet house on Grace Street with the modest plate of J. P. Merriman & Co., Consultant Engineers marking its front entrance, it had prospered. Business, alas, was booming: too many damned terrorists, Renwick was thinking as he rearranged three remaining reports on the desk in front of him.

He would read and compare them once more—they were succinct, only a page to each of them—and then go home, still brooding about them, to be ready by tomorrow morning for a conference with Gilman and Claudel. (They were reading the duplicates right now.) He glanced at the clock, looked at Nina's photograph smiling at him across the small room. "Tonight," he told her, "I'll even be home in time for dinner."

And then the telephone rang, the green one, his own private line to the outside world without benefit of the telephone switchboard downstairs. Serious business, he thought with a frown as he picked up the receiver. A man's voice asked, "Renwick?"

"Yes."

"Say a few words, will you?" The voice was strong, confident, American.

Someone who knows me, a careful type, making sure. Renwick said, "'O what a tangled web we weave when first we practice to deceive.'"

There was a pause, then a smothered laugh. "Yes, Colonel, sir. You're Renwick all right."

"And who are you?"

"That doesn't matter. What I know, does. Is this line safe?"

"It should be."

"No other connection? No one listening?" The questions were tense.

"No one." And who the hell was this? Not more than twenty people had Renwick's private number, and the voice didn't belong to any of them.

The man's brief anxiety was over. He spoke more easily now. "I'll take your word for it. Meet me at six o'clock. In your favorite pub."

"Sorry. I'm meeting a friend there for a quick drink this evening. Why not join us?" Renwick would like to see this character who had ferreted out his private number. But not alone. He would get Ronald Gilman or Pierre Claudel to accompany him.

"I'm not joining you there. Just passing by your table. I'll stop to light a cigarette—a red throwaway lighter. You'll see a heavy gold ring on my right hand. Give me five minutes—five exactly—and then follow. Alone. Take a cab. Drive to Paddington Station. I'll be waiting just inside the main entrance. Follow me again. We'll stop at a newsstand, and I'll slip you a ticket. Then trail behind me, and we'll have us a little train ride. An empty compartment is a good place for serious talk."

"If it's empty." A compartment? Did they exist any more? This must be an amateur, and a stranger to Britain, too, who had worked out his own security plans.

"Leave that to me. You just leave your friend sitting in the Red Lion. Got that?"

"Which Red Lion? There must be fifty of them." On Bridle Lane? If so, this man had been watching him. A disquieting thought.

"Come on, Renwick! Your favorite pub. Not too far from the office."

So Bridle Lane it was.

"Six o'clock. Prepare for a short stay. But your friend stays there. No one follows you outside. No one follows me. I've got your word on that?"

"No one follows us into the street."

"And no one waits for us outside, either. Agreed?"

Renwick glanced at the reports in front of him. "Agreed, but I've some work to finish. Make it seven o'clock." And what have I to lose? he thought. If I sense something wrong about this man, I don't have to walk out of the Red Lion after him. He seems to know me. I feel I've heard that voice before, can't quite place it, but if I can see him I may remember where we've met. And was that what he wanted, my recognition? So that I'd follow him, have confidence in him?

"Six o'clock. There's a train to catch. And I hold you to your promise. No one watching the Red Lion. Remember!"

Renwick restrained a surge of annoyance, kept his voice cool. "Why should I go through all these antics? I don't know who you are or your credentials, or even—"

"Three weeks ago, I met a man who had just escaped from a prison in India—sentenced for murder in Bombay, 1979."

Renwick's spine stiffened. That was Erik—it had to be. News of his escape had reached Interintell six weeks ago. Since then, silence. And it had been Interintell (chiefly Renwick and Claudel) who had tracked Erik in 1979 through Europe and the Mideast and Iran, through Pakistan and India to Bombay, where the long chase had ended. Erik, the founder and leader of a West German group of anarchists calling themselves "Direct Action." Erik, or Kurt Leitner, or James Kiley, or a dozen other identities that he had used in his ten years of dedicated terrorism . . . Renwick recovered. "You met him where?"

"I'll tell you when we meet. I'll tell you that and more important things, too." The call ended.

More important than Erik wandering free? Renwick replaced the receiver. He picked up the three sheets of paper, placed them in a folder in his safe and locked it. (Tomorrow he would come into the office before nine, finish his homework on their problem before the meeting with Gilman and Claudel at ten o'clock.) The rest of the litter on his desk was gathered into neat piles, placed methodically in a drawer with a dependable lock: nothing of much importance there. The room was orderly once more.

Antiseptic, Renwick called it. Apart from the large maps on the walls above the low bookcases, the only decoration was Nina's photograph. The one comfortable item was the black leather armchair with its footrest. Everything else was practical: desk, two chairs, three telephones, good lamps, wall safe, filing cabinet with a radio on top, an electric fire, and windows close to the ceiling with plenty of air and daylight and even more privacy than the room already possessed. Nina had suggested color for the walls, a bright carpet on the floor, but he had kept the room as plain as possible—white walls, wooden floors, nothing to distract or seduce him from the work on hand.

He called Nina on his regular outside line. "Honey—I'll be late tonight. Sorry. Terribly sorry, darling. Don't keep dinner—I'll have a sandwich. And get to bed, will you? Early?"

Nina took it well. She always did. It was as if she could sense some real urgency whenever he was forced to alter their plans. Now, she only said, "Take care, darling. Please?"

"Sure. I love you, don't I?" He was the luckiest guy, he told himself for the thousandth time.

There was no need to call Gilman on the interoffice phone. Their doors were always open to each other. He lifted his Burberry off its hook on the wall, checked his hat in its pocket, and entered the passage that led into the main house. The filing room, vast with its steadily increasing data, was still at work. Next door, the computer room had its two experts busy with their question-and-answer games. And at the end of the corridor was Ronald Gilman's office. He was the director of this establishment, elected by Renwick as much for his diplomatic connections as for his expert knowledge. It was Gilman who had arranged for the lease of this building, for the initial acquiring of equipment, and had managed to attract the unobtrusive support of his own government. The English had a quiet way in such matters.

Gilman, busy comparing the three reports, looked up in surprise. "Finished?" he asked. "Well, it looks as if you were right in your prediction two years ago." He tapped the pages in front of him. "Right-wing terrorism is now as ruthless as left-wing. Joining each other, too, in some cases. An unholy alliance."

"But I didn't foresee any right-wing terrorists being trained in Communist camps." That was what the three reports, each from a different source—France, Turkey, Lebanon—had indicated. "I'll have to finish studying the evidence tomorrow morning. Something else has come up."

Gilman looked at the American's calm face. Nothing there to show any worry or alarm: thoughtful gray eyes, brown hair slightly graying at the temples, even features, a pleasant mouth relaxing into one of his reassuring smiles. Yet Renwick's voice had been too casual, always a small storm signal. "Something interesting?"

"I don't know. It's the damnedest thing." Renwick began pacing the room, no larger than his own and just as sparingly furnished. "I had a call—my green line—" He halted, frowning at the floor, and began an accurate but brief account of that strange conversation.

Gilman was a good listener, silent, expressionless, but as Renwick ended, he said quite flatly. "I don't like it, Bob. It could be a trap."

"It could also be important."

"The man knows you?"

"Seemingly. He certainly knows my phone number. How did he get that? And where did he meet Erik? He didn't just *see* Erik. He met him. Exact word."

"Three weeks ago . . ." Gilman's glasses were off, his hair—blond, thinning on top—was ruffled and smoothed and ruffled again. "Erik will have moved on by this time."

"At least we get a direction. We don't know, now, whether Erik left India, or traveled east or north or west."

"Certainly not south," Gilman said, "unless he was taking a header into the Indian Ocean." Then he looked at his watch, began gathering the pages in front of him. "You go ahead. I'll take my car and join you in the Red Lion."

"I hoped you would. Just as well for two of us to see this man."

"He had no objection to someone meeting you?"

"No. Only to being followed."

From the pub or from the street, Gilman remembered. "He didn't mention anything about being followed at Paddington, did he?"

"No." Renwick raised an eyebrow.

"Start moving, old boy." Gilman locked up the three agents' reports. "I'll see you at six."

Renwick left, still speculating. Why should Ron choose to delay, then take his car instead of walking the short distance to the Red Lion? Renwick could guess the answer, and felt the better for it. Gilman would now be on the phone to Claudel. And Renwick wouldn't be heading out on a train, as yet unknown, to some benighted part of the country without someone nearby as a backup. Of course, if Gilman's first objections were true, then he could be trapped. A train, to quote the man on the phone, might be a good place for a serious talk, but it was also a useful place for throwing out a body.

Renwick stopped, hurried back to his office, unlocked its door. Quickly, he opened the filing cabinet, found his Biretta and its lightweight holster. Almost two years of marriage and the sweet life had turned him—what? Soft? Careless? Not altogether, he decided as he made sure the Biretta was loaded and slipped it into the holster, now under his tweed jacket. Cigarette case and lighter were in his pocket. All set. He left, using the rear staircase and avoiding the main-floor offices of J. P. Merriman & Co., whose full-time surveyors and practical engineering advice brought in, and legitimately, the profits that kept Interintell expanding.

It was raining hard.

Two

TWELVE MINUTES AT a smart pace brought Renwick in good time to the lower end of Bridle Lane. It stretched northward for a hundred yards, even less, close-packed on either side by low-storied buildings, before it was obliterated by the blare and bustle of Fleet Street. Up there, as in all the main arteries this evening, the roadway would be jammed with traffic and bad tempers, the sidewalks filled with umbrellas and sodden raincoats. The calendar might say June; today's onslaught of cold wind and rain made it feel like March. But there was no need to approach the Red Lion by an overcrowded highway; there were shortcuts if you knew this part of the city, a loose haphazard web of short and narrow streets that merged and separated and changed their names as unexpectedly as their direction. And Renwick knew this area.

Each day after lunch, usually a sandwich in his office, he seized half an hour for a couple of miles in various directions and got the tension of too much desk-sitting out of his shoulder muscles. This evening he could even take a brief detour once he left Merriman's by its inconspicuous rear exit, and still have six minutes to spare when he reached the pint-sized square where Bridle Lane began. So he slowed his step, making note of everything around him: no one loitering, no one following—the footsteps behind him hurried on, drew ahead, passed into the lane, kept hurrying. The shops and businesses, all small-scale, were closed, and if people lived up above them, then this was a night to stay indoors. The café at the corner of the square had its usual enticing suggestions on the hand-printed card displayed in its window, chief among them "Hot Peas and Vinegar." That possibly explained the empty taxi, desolate and abandoned, that had been parked in front of the café while its driver enjoyed some sausages and mashed. But it also reminded Renwick that taxis were scarce on a wet evening like this, and he wondered how—in this place, at this time of day—he would find a cab to take him to Paddington. That was one detail forgotten, perhaps not even imagined, by the man who had telephoned with such precise instructions. It was a revealing omission. The man might know the name and location of the Red Lion, but he didn't know this district. So how did he get the address? From someone who had met Renwick there? Someone who also had access to Renwick's private number? If so, decided Renwick, that narrowed down the field: few of his contacts possessed both pieces of information, very few. In grim mood, he entered the Red Lion.

From the outside, it didn't look particularly inviting: it could have used some paint and polish. If that was its method of discouraging tourists in their search for quaint old London pubs, it was highly successful. It had its own clientele, some regular, some—like Renwick—occasional. And that was another point to remember: his visits here had no fixed routine, formed no pattern. Even constant surveillance—and he hadn't seen or sensed any such thing—wouldn't have marked the Red Lion as a special meeting place. No, that information had come from someone who had been here with Renwick. A mole in our group, a real professional sent to infiltrate? Or someone greedy for money, or open to blackmail? Or just a blabbermouth, overflown with wine and insolence?

Renwick resisted a searching look around the long room, seemed to be paying all attention to shaking out his raincoat and the old, narrow-brimmed felt hat he kept for bad weather. As yet, the place was only half filled—it opened at five-thirty—but that would soon be remedied, and the smell of tobacco smoke would be added to the smell of ale that impregnated the dark woodwork of walls and tables. Casually, he noted two groups of men standing near the bar—no high stools here, no chrome or neon lighting, either—and three more groups at the central tables. He chose a high-backed wooden booth, one of a row on the opposite side of the room from the stretch of highly polished counter, hung coat and hat on a nearby hook, and sat down to face the back of the room. It was from somewhere there that the man must come in order to pass this table on his way to the door. I'll make sure of a good look at his face, Renwick thought as he ordered a beer and tried to look totally relaxed, but he felt a tightening in his diaphragm, an expectation of something unexpected, something over which he would have no control.

Even before his beer was brought by a pink-cheeked, red-haired barmaid, the room was beginning to fill: journalists in tweeds, conservatively clothed civil servants interspersed with exactingly dressed barristers, music students in leather jackets, and businessmen in three-piece suits. Renwick smoked a cigarette, seemed normally interested in the growing crowd, wondered if his man was in the group gathered around a dartboard at the far end of the bar.

"Sorry," Ronald Gilman said, ridding himself of coat and umbrella, taking a seat opposite Renwick. "I'm late—this weather." He smoothed down his hair, asked, "Seen any likely prospect?"

"No. But he's here." Renwick could feel he had been observed and studied for the last few minutes. "Where did you park your car?" Gilman hadn't walked—his raincoat was dry, his umbrella rolled.

"I didn't. Claudel dropped me at the door and then drove on."

"Oh?"

Gilman only nodded and ordered a double whiskey with water, no ice. "I'm more nervous than you are, Bob. You know, you needn't follow this blighter out. If you have the least doubt—"

"Here's someone now," Renwick warned. The man didn't pause to light a cigarette. "False alarm," Renwick said with a small laugh.

"Have you managed to place his voice?"

"I've heard it before. I think. I could be wrong." But a telephone did accentuate the characteristics of a voice—its tone, its inflections.

"Strange that he didn't disguise it. Muffle it. He didn't?"

"No. He wants to be identified, I guess. Hence the double play. There was no need to meet twice, first here and then at Paddington." Another man, could be a student from the school of music near Magpie Alley, passed their table. This one was lighting a cigarette. But no red lighter.

"One meeting with proper signals would be enough." Gilman agreed. "An odd bird. Perhaps—" He heard footsteps slowing down behind his left shoulder, barely turned his head to glimpse the man who was about to light a cigarette, went on speaking. "Perhaps this foul weather will be over before the Wimbledon finals."

"Did you get tickets?" Renwick looked down at his watch. The man continued toward the door. A red lighter, a heavy signet ring . . . And a face that was deeply tanned, fine wrinkles at the side of the brown eyes glancing briefly in Renwick's direction; hard features, thick black hair. His suit was well cut, fitted his broad shoulders, but its fabric was too light in weight for London. Passing through? Certainly the opaque plastic raincoat over one arm was easily packable.

Gilman, with a good view of the man's departure, dropped his voice. "Straight spine, strong back, about six feet tall. Did you get a full view of his face?"

Renwick's voice was now at a murmur, too. "His name is Moore. Albert, Alfred—no, Alvin Moore. He was one of the drivers at NATO—his second enlistment. First one was in Vietnam, saw a lot of action, good record. But in Belgium he got involved with a couple of sergeants who were caught selling stolen supplies to a dealer in Brussels—they drew seven years each. There was no real evidence against Moore. They used his car, that was all. He had a mania for automobiles and speeds of ninety miles an hour." Renwick kept an eye on his watch.

"Did he drive for you?" That couldn't have been very often. Renwick liked to drive himself.

"Occasionally—when I had a meeting and had to be in uniform. Staff car, driver, that kind of thing."

"Then how did you remember him?"

"When he was brought up on charges, he needed me as a character witness."

"And you appeared?"

"He was honest—as far as I knew. One time I carried a briefcase, some sealed folders, an armful of maps. I had a clip of dollars—emergency cash—in my trouser pocket. Belgian francs were in my wallet. The dollar bills slipped out. I didn't notice, didn't even remember where I had lost them. Corporal Moore was my driver that day. He returned the bills intact. Found them slipped down in the back seat of the car."

"Did your testimony clear him?"

"Every little bit helps, doesn't it? But he was transferred stateside, discharged. Joined something more to his taste—the Green Berets, I heard." Renwick glanced at his watch once more. "That was about seven years ago."

"He's the type who needs action, I think."

Renwick agreed. "His trouble at NATO was boredom." Then his voice changed. "On the phone he addressed me as colonel. Just once. Yet I was a captain when he knew me."

"Where did he get that information?" Gilman asked quickly. Renwick's promotion had been kept very quiet indeed; he never used his rank, just as the others in the Interintell group didn't use theirs. Civilians for the duration and the preservation of peace, it was to be hoped.

"That," said Renwick, "needs finding out." There were too many damned questions needing answers. His eyes left his watch. "Time to start trying. It's five minutes to the second." He rose, unhooked his coat and hat. In a voice back to a normal level, he said, "Sorry I have to leave. Be seeing you."

"See you, old boy." Gilman's eyes were troubled, but he gave one of his rare smiles, warm and real. *Just hope that Bob has been keeping up his karate sessions,* he thought as he watched Renwick pull on his Burberry and jam his rain hat well down on his brow before he stepped out into the cold world of Bridle Lane.

For a moment, Renwick hesitated on the sidewalk. Walk to Fleet Street, try to find a cab there? Or would that taxi parked outside the café still be waiting? He started down Bridle Lane toward the square, then halted. Luck was with him: the driver had finished his sausages and mashed, or was it hot peas and vinegar? The taxi was coming this way. He signaled, and it stopped. He opened the door. A man raised himself from the back seat, held out an arm covered with a thin raincoat. Renwick saw the businesslike nose of a revolver just showing from under the coat's folds. "Hop in, I'll give you a lift," said Alvin Moore.

Renwick got in. "Unnecessary," he said, looking at the pistol. The driver hadn't even noticed; he had had his instructions, for the cab started forward with not a minute lost. A rednecked man, well fed, too, he was only intent on entering Fleet Street and gauging the traffic flow. "And much too noisy," Renwick went on, controlling his anger. Moore was staring back at Bridle Lane.

"Not so noisy." Moore lifted the raincoat's fold to show a silencer was attached. "And not unnecessary. What guarantee did I have that you wouldn't use a gun to make me redirect the cabbie to your office?" He kept looking back.

"No one was there to follow us. As promised." Renwick was watching the direction the taxi was taking. So far, it seemed normal—allowing for one-way streets. They were now out of Fleet Street, driving north and then swinging west. They could be heading for Paddington Station.

Moore took the rebuke with a shrug. He was tense, though.

Preserve me from a jumpy man holding a pistol, Renwick thought. If he releases the safety catch, I'll grasp his wrist, twist it up. I could draw the Biretta in that split second, but I won't: a shoot-out in a cab is faintly ridiculous—would upset my British friends, too. Renwick eased his voice and kept a careful eye on Moore's right hand. "You've got some strange ideas about the way we carry on our business at the office. Forcing people inside is not the way we work."

"You sure don't consult or engineer."

"No?"

Moore stared. "You an engineer?" he asked, unbelieving.

"I was."

"Before the army?"

"And for the first two years of my service."

"As I heard it, you engineer more than dams and bridges now."

"You've heard a lot of things, it seems." Renwick looked pointedly at the driver's red neck. "A friend of yours? Then we can start talking about what you've heard and where you heard it."

Moore shook his head. "Don't know him. Just doing his job. And we'll need more time than we'll have in this cab. There's a lot to talk about." He was no longer on edge.

So Renwick kept the conversation innocuous, nothing to stir up any more tension in Moore. "How did you produce a taxi at the right moment? Quite a triumph."

"Easy. I took a cab to Bridle Lane, found it couldn't park there, so I settled for the square. All thirty feet of it. Some district, this."

"And you paid double the fare, promised double again if it waited for you?"

A grin broke over Moore's face. "With the cost of a hot supper thrown

in. Easy." He was back to normal, more like the corporal Renwick remembered from seven years ago. There were interesting changes, though: he
carried more weight, but that was muscle, not fat. The deep tan, the leather
skin with its creases at the eyes, and the furrows on either side of the tight
mouth indicated much time out of doors in strong sun and tropical heat.
His suit spelled city, however, some place like New York, where summer
needed thin clothing. It looked fairly new, expensive but not custom-made.
Not enough time for a tailor to measure and fit? A quick visit to America?
The crisp white shirt had a buttoned-down collar, the tie was recognizably
from Brooks Brothers. A nice picture of an affluent man. Except for the
raincoat—definitely incongruous, probably bought in an emergency this
morning when the rain had set in.

Moore noticed the quiet scrutiny. "Well?" he demanded, his eyes defensive.

"Pretty smooth. But you always did like a smart uniform." Renwick
touched the sleeve of the plastic coat. "Bought today, thrown away tomorrow. Heading for a drier climate?"

Moore's eyes widened for a moment. Then he laughed. "I came to the
right man, that's for sure." He looked long at Renwick. "Engineer!" he said,
shook his head. "Never met one yet who noticed anything except stress and
strain on a pontoon." He settled back, began watching the streets.

Again, Renwick checked the direction they were taking. It could indeed
be Paddington. Fleet Street and the Strand area were well behind them.
Piccadilly Circus, as bright and garish as Times Square, lights at full glitter
even in daylight, had led them to the curve of Regent Street. But not for
long. A quick left turn took them into quieter streets, rich and restrained,
where people didn't stand on pavements waiting for doubledecker buses.
The taxi driver knew his London: a left turn, a right turn, traveling west,
then north, then west and north again, through an area of exclusive shops,
imposing houses, and most correct hotels. This part of London always
seemed to Renwick to be floating on its own cloud nine, far above the dreams
of ordinary mortals. But soon the cab would be nearing Oxford Street and
touching reality again. Still a long way to travel. Renwick glanced covertly
at his watch. Pierre Claudel should be already at Paddington, waiting to
track him into the station. "We may miss that train," Renwick said.

It didn't seem to worry Moore. With an eye on a corner sign reading
Park Street, he stopped lounging. "Nearly forgot about this." With quick,
expert touch, he removed the silencer from the revolver, slipped them into
separate pockets of the raincoat. "When we leave the cab, you walk ahead.
I follow."

"And if I don't walk ahead? Will you reassemble that piece of artillery,
use it in front of a hundred people?" Renwick's voice was soft, his eyes hard.

"I can put it together in three seconds flat. But I don't need to use it
now."

"Why the reprieve?"

"It did its job. Got you into this cab damn quick."

Renwick remembered Moore's anxiety as they had left Bridle Lane. "You
weren't nervous only about one of my friends following us, were you?"

No answer to that. Moore watched the street ahead. "Just do as I say. If you took off, you mightn't live to regret it."

Renwick looked at him sharply, wondering if that negative had crept in by mistake.

"You might not live," Moore repeated. He saw Renwick's glance at the bulge in his plastic raincoat's pocket. "No, not that. I'm no assassin. I'm doing you a favor. I owe you one." Then he looked at the street ahead, raised his voice for the driver. "Is this it? Okay, okay. Stop at the corner. How much?" His wallet was in his hand.

Good God, thought Renwick, we're at Marble Arch.

Moore frowned at the wad of English pound notes, made a guess, began counting them. He spoke to Renwick from the side of his mouth. "Buy a ticket for Tottenham Court Road. We're taking the subway."

"Tube," Renwick corrected quietly as he opened the taxi door.

Moore halted him with another half-whispered command. "When we reach there, reverse positions. I lead. You follow. Room 412."

Renwick nodded and left Moore handing over a clutch of notes; more than enough, judging by the driver's sudden geniality. Marble Arch, he thought again, Marble Arch! Damn me for an idiot. He fooled me. I fell for Paddington. And Claudel hanging around there, watching, worrying? Pierre Claudel would do more than raise a fine French eyebrow when he waited and waited. . . . The French could produce a flow of curses that would outdo anything an Anglo-Saxon tried.

Can't even dodge into a telephone booth and warn Gilman—if I could reach him. Moore would take that as a breach of faith; he'd walk away and leave me flat, and I'd learn nothing in Room 412, wherever it was. In some hotel, obviously. In the neighborhood, again obviously, of Tottenham Court Road: no mention of another tube, or a bus, or a taxi. In Soho, perish the thought? Or in Bloomsbury? Let's hope it's a short distance. Tonight, I'm in no mood for a walk in the rain.

Three

THE DISTANCE WAS short, a two-minute walk up Tottenham Court Road, which looked even worse than usual by the gray light of a wet evening. Moore set a sharp pace, plunging through the clots of pedestrians seemingly paralyzed by weather and traffic. Although he walked at a quick march through the crowd, Renwick managed to keep Moore's black hair in sight. He almost lost him when a left turn was made into a quiet, narrow street but reached the corner in time to see Moore disappear into the Coronet's doorway. It was one of the new hotels, rising high, a flat-faced block of building with innumerable windows that was attempting to uplift the neighborhood and edge in on the tourist trade of Bloomsbury.

Its lobby was crowded, people discouraged by the weather sitting on fat couches or standing in talkative groups. A plumbers' convention, Renwick noted from the outsize announcement propped on a gilded easel. He crossed the soft mile of carpet—no expense spared—without anyone paying him the least attention and went up to the fifth floor in an elevator filled with jovial Birmingham accents and the smell of wet wool. Then he walked down one flight and in the rear of the building found Room 412.

The door was ajar. Moore turned from pouring Scotch at a table, gave his first real smile. "Take the load off. Have a drink." The atmosphere has changed, thought Renwick. He's still giving orders, but perhaps that's become natural: certainly, Moore hasn't been following them for a long time. "Later," Renwick said and went into the bathroom, pulling off his raincoat and hat, hung them up where they could drip themselves slightly dry. He glanced around—nothing unpacked here, just gleaming surfaces, cramped but clean; only the two-inch cake of soap and hand towel used, and the two glasses missing from their holders.

The bedroom was small-scale, too. No possessions on a miniature bureau. An air-travel bag, closed, lay on a bed that imitated an armless couch. Curtains were now drawn over the window, the overhead light turned on. Moore was back at the table pouring himself a second drink in one of the bathroom's missing glasses. "Sure you won't?"

"Not at the moment." Renwick chose the chair that had a dwarf table within reach, molded out of white plastic to match the few pieces of furniture; the other held Moore's coat, dripping onto the carpet. "Any music available?"

"Sweet and low. Will that do?" He reached for a knob on the radio on the nightstand. "How loud?" He let "That Old Black Magic" blare out.

"Not so loud that we can't hear each other."

"You boys slay me. Who's to know we're here? They didn't have time to plant a bug." He was confident, assured, his voice—perhaps fueled by two strong drinks—assertive.

"The walls are thin."

Moore shrugged, adjusted the sound to a reasonable level. Then a cough from next door, muted but clear enough, made him stare at Renwick and shake his head. He picked up his glass, empty once more, thought better of it, and put it down. He came over to the couch, sat on its edge to face Renwick. "Not much of a room," he said, speaking more softly. "The best we could get at short notice—a friend booked it from New York. I only got here this morning."

And out tonight, Renwick thought. A friend? But that could wait. "All right, Moore. Let's begin. I have some—"

"Cut out the Moore. Don't use it, now. Al will do," he added just to keep things friendly. He slipped off his jacket, threw it to the other end of the couch, loosened his tie, unbuttoned his collar. "How the hell do you put up with these clothes?" Then he settled back on one elbow, crossed his legs, looked relaxed, but his eyes were alert. "You have some what?"

"Some questions to ask. Then I'll listen to you." Al seemed about to object. "Not questions about you," Renwick went on. "Okay?"

"Any information about me comes from me when I'm damned ready and willing to give it. Understood?"

"Understood." He would be alarmed at how much I've learned about him since we first met, thought Renwick. "First of all, where did you see the man who escaped from an Indian prison?"

Moore, or whatever his new name was to match a false passport, brushed that aside with his hand. "Not important. He won't last long. Forget him."

"I can't."

"Oh, yes—your outfit caught him, he said."

"Tracked him down," Renwick said to keep the record straight. Incredible, he was thinking: Erik the dedicated anarchist, Erik the leader of a ruthless gang of West German terrorists, Erik dismissed as "not important." How naïve could Moore get? "He was recruiting terrorists abroad, and we followed him to India. It was the Bombay police who arrested him."

"Interintell, he called you. That was the first time I heard the name. He was teaching a class. I was standing at the back of the tent, just curious. I wasn't a part of that crowd, see?" Moore wanted to make that clear.

"A class for terrorists? Where?"

"He was giving a couple of lectures on how you dodge arrest, but if you're caught, then how you escape."

"Where did you see him?" Renwick was insistent, firm.

"South Yemen."

"At a training camp for terrorists?"

"Yes, but I wasn't—"

"Part of the scene. Just curious." And why the hell were you there? Renwick wondered. But that would keep. Moore seemed mollified at least, perhaps more ready to talk. "Why won't he last long?"

"He got the Cubans flaming mad. There were two of them—not terrorists—intelligence agents from Havana, I heard. Sent to Yemen to make sure he got to South America. As ordered."

Casually, Renwick had eased the plastic table closer to his knee, steadied its ashtray, taken out his cigarette case, pressing its hinge to activate it. "Ordered? By whom?"

"By the people who got him out of prison, helped him reach Bombay."

Renwick seemed to have forgotten his cigarette. "He actually chose Bombay?" His disbelief sounded real.

"A cool customer. No one would expect him to enter a city where he had been arrested for killing a cop. So he told the class."

"And after Bombay? Aden?"

"On a freighter as a deck hand."

"Smart customer, too. Unless, of course, he was helped all the way—by the same people who got him out of prison and need him in South America." Renwick abandoned his cigarette case beside the ashtray, shook his head. "Perhaps not so smart, after all—not if he argued with the Cubans."

"There was damn near a fight, words rattling off like a spray of machine-gun bullets. I've picked up some Spanish, other languages, too, but it's just as well not to let others know. That way, you keep your nose clean."

Renwick nodded. "What was the argument about, did you hear?"

"Not much. Too quick. But one thing is certain. He isn't going to South America. A couple of nights later, he vanished. Like that!" Moore snapped his fingers. "The Cubans were fit to be tied."

Yes, thought Renwick, he will head for West Germany, where he will reorganize his Direct Action group. He was their founder. He was their leader. He will get them moving again. To Erik, that is all that matters. "When did he disappear?"

"Ten days ago, just before I got clear of that godforsaken hole. No trace. Not at the airport, not at the docks. But he won't get far. The Cubans have money behind them. He'll never make it." Moore was suddenly restless. "Think I'll have that drink. Questions make me thirsty." He was about to get to his feet. "Keep them short."

Renwick made a fast decision as he lifted his cigarette case—couldn't leave it lying there unused, not all the time, he told himself. "I'll do better than that. I'll postpone them until you've given me your information. Okay?" Moore had been stopped in his tracks. Renwick offered a cigarette, delaying him still more.

"No, thanks. Never use them. That stuff can kill you."

But bullets and whiskey can't? Renwick smiled. So the red lighter and cigarette pack had just been props for the pub scene. Or another subterfuge, like a mustache shaved off—there was a less deep tan over Moore's upper lip—and completely different clothes? "Come on, Al. Begin! I'm listening." He took a cigarette, closed the case, laid it once more on the table top.

Moore glanced over at the bottle of Scotch. "Want me to keep a clear mind?" he asked. "Is that it?"

"That's it," Renwick said brusquely. "Let's get started." He pointed to the corner of the couch. "And keep your voice down." As Moore resumed his seat with a one-finger salute, Renwick flicked his lighter, but it didn't catch.

"Get one thing straight," Moore was saying, leaning forward, elbows on knees, his left hand fingering his heavy signet ring. "I'm no informer."

"Just a reliable source of information," Renwick assured him. The lighter failed again. Renwick dropped it into his pocket and found some matches.

"And I'm no terrorist. I'm a soldier. That's my trade and I'm good at it. That's why Exports Consolidated hired me. Ever hear of them?"

"Yes." A report on Exports Consolidated had been on Renwick's desk for the last month, part of a general survey of armaments sold by Americans and shipped abroad to Third World countries. It was a flourishing business these days, with plenty of competition from European merchants as well as from Soviet Russia and its allies. Renwick's special interest in such trafficking had been roused by one of the simple questions that, as soon as he asked it, demanded an answer: Where did today's international terrorists get their sophisticated weapons, and how? "Exports Consolidated once exported agricultural machinery, then expanded into military hardware. Nothing illegal about that. Unfortunately."

"Nothing illegal?" Moore laughed.

"You tell me," Renwick said softly.

"It began with Vietnam."

What didn't? thought Renwick but restrained himself.

"A buddy of mine—we were in the same outfit—was killed there. When I got back stateside, I went to see his wife. She was an old friend. She had been running her father's business, learning everything she could from him. Built it up, made a go of it. Agricultural machinery, can you beat that? When her father died, she owned the shop. Then Mitchell Brimmer came along—you heard of him?"

Renwick stubbed out his cigarette, compressed his lips. Brimmer was the founder and head of Exports Consolidated. He had been in Vietnam, too. Not as a soldier. Began as an agent, low grade, in the CIA; quit the Agency to become a journalist in Saigon, then businessman. Or perhaps he had been that all along. He made good contacts, helpful friends, but he seemed to have helped them, too. Legitimate business apparently: no drug smuggling, no gems, no official secrets. "Interested in agricultural machinery, wasn't he? Moved back from Saigon to the States, set up a firm there, expanded it and—"

"That he did. Took over several outlets for agricultural machinery. He made an offer to—to my friend. A good deal. She had brains, and he knew it. Paid her a fair price and offered her more money than any she could set aside for herself. So she took the job."

"Doing what?"

"Keeping the books and a chance to rise with his firm. She did, too. But that was during my second tour of duty, when I was at NATO, and after that—well, I was a couple of years with the Green Berets. Then I tried some soldiering abroad—in Africa, mostly." Moore noticed Renwick's expression. He said quickly, defensively, "I wasn't a mercenary. Sure I was paid, but I trained troops to fight. Troops." He shook his head over that memory. "A bunch of slobs when I got them, but I turned out soldiers, all right."

"Guerrillas?"

"Call them what you like, but they damn sure weren't terrorists. They meet the enemy in a fire fight, a fair skirmish. They don't infiltrate a town and pretend they're ordinary folks, and then start plotting where they'll hide the bombs to blow up civilians. That isn't war, kill or be killed. That's bloody murder."

"There's a difference," Renwick agreed, but it was a subtle one and sometimes fragile. Guerrillas on a rampage could leave a lot of innocent civilians maimed, raped, or dead. "So you're against terrorism. And assassination."

Moore looked at him sharply.

"You told me that. In the taxi," Renwick reminded him. "But you haven't finished about your wars in Africa."

"Two years were enough. In seventy-eight I came back to New York and met—met my friend. She was Brimmer's good right hand by that time. She told me I was just the man that her boss was looking for. Or one of the men—he hired three of us, all with plenty of experience. Exports Consolidated was by then into selling arms to countries that could pay for them—

or had rich friends who'd oblige. They wanted the newest and best, and instructors to show them how to use the weapons. Sure, I jumped at the job. It was big money, and travel, and I got respect, too."

Don't rush him, Renwick decided. He has got to justify himself. But even in Moore's self-explanations, the shape of something ominous was beginning to form.

"One thing I made clear to Brimmer from the start. I'd train soldiers. I'd instruct them in weapons. But I wasn't teaching a damn thing to terrorists. I wasn't running a school for assassins, either."

"He agreed to that?" What about South Yemen? Renwick wondered.

"With a joke and a slap on the back. So everything went fine. Big and bigger money. Brimmer can afford it; he's making millions. He's got business contacts everywhere. And three months ago, he joined up with another big outfit that sells arms. It's international, so my friend says. Based in Europe."

That was news to Renwick. "Their name?"

"Brimmer isn't telling. And you won't find the merger in any financial pages. Anyway, when I got back to New York—"

"Your friend"—Renwick cut in quickly—"surely she knows the name of that firm."

"It isn't important."

"Just part of the picture, Al. I must have all of it, as complete as possible, if you want my help. That's why you brought me here, isn't it? You don't need money, that's obvious."

"Wouldn't take it—" Moore began angrily.

"That's right. You are no informer. What's the firm's name?"

"Klingfeld and Sons. They don't sound like much, but she says they're high-powered. Offices in Paris, Geneva, Rome."

"Each firm is keeping its own name?" A strange merger. Stranger yet was the fact that Klingfeld & Sons was not on any list of armament traffickers that Renwick had ever seen.

"They're a silent partner in Exports Consolidated. She says it's funny: Klingfeld is bigger than Brimmer."

"Can't go on calling your girl 'she,' Al. What's her name?"

Moore's lips tightened.

Renwick's voice was sharp. "Look—how many personal and invaluable secretaries does Brimmer have? We can trace her. Easily."

"Lorna." The name, incomplete, came unwillingly.

Had dear Lorna instructed Moore not to give her name; not Klingfeld's, either? It had been like pulling teeth to extract these two small items from Moore. "I take it Lorna is a close friend of yours. Very close? Then you can believe what she tells you. You trust her completely?"

"Trust her? Lorna saved me from blowing everything when I got back to New York last week. That son of a bitch Brimmer had sent me out to South Yemen. I didn't object to that. I've been in Libya, Chad, Lebanon, Zaïre, Tanzania, the Sudan. Politics? No interest. I train soldiers, I'm worth my hire. That's that. But in Yemen—" Moore's sudden anger almost choked him. "In Yemen, I wasn't instructing a bunch of camel drivers in how to handle grenades and antitank guns. I was given a bunch of goddamned know-it-all terrorists yapping about ideals with murder in their eyes. Couldn't quit, either, unless I wanted to be found behind cargo containers at the docks with my throat slit—that's happened to one guy I knew who tried to bug out."

Renwick's spine went tense. "Where did the terrorists come from? Who paid their way?"

Moore shrugged his shoulders. "Must have come from ten, twelve, fifteen countries—Europe, South America, the Mideast—you name them, I had them. And the weapons sold by Exports Consolidated didn't come direct. Re-routed through other countries. Rockets, the newest explosives, top-secret detonators and electronic devices, army supplies we don't sell anyone."

"Illegal trafficking in weapons and military equipment," Renwick said softly. Then Brimmer must be using false or cover agreements in sales abroad; falsified accounts, too, in the purchasing of supplies, and bribery. A mess of corruption wherever Brimmer moved. "Get me a sample of one page of his business ledger—"

"That's only the half of it," Moore interrupted, either determined to tell things his way or unwilling to involve Lorna in supplying proof of Brimmer's flourishing conspiracy. He rushed on, and Renwick kept silent. "That super-secret equipment was beyond me or anyone else in Yemen. Brimmer is sending in an expert this week from California—fifty thousand dollars for him out of a two-hundred-thousand fee for Brimmer with compliments of Yemen's big friend in North Africa." Moore paused, well pleased with the effect he was producing. "So I came back from Yemen ready to tell Brimmer to go shove it. Lorna met me at Kennedy, warned me to ease off. For now. That was what she was doing, going along, arousing no suspicion in Brimmer or anyone at the office. But she had had it. Like me. Too dangerous if Brimmer thought we were backing out. We knew too much."

"What changed her? She must have known all along about the sale of illegal arms and secret payoffs. If," Renwick added, "she is as important to Brimmer as you say she is."

"She keeps the records—the private ones. Not the books that are handled by the accountants and shown to the income-tax boys. She's important, all right." He was proud of his Lorna.

"What changed her?"

"A list that Brimmer made. The Klingfeld people insisted on it, passed him some information, too. He didn't like the idea, Lorna said, but he swallowed it. Couldn't refuse his new partners, could he? He might lose more than his business."

"Did Lorna see that list?"

"Yes. Later, she made a copy—photographed it. Took a chance after office hours when Brimmer was in Washington. He has a lot of friends there. Good old Mitch Brimmer, everyone's pal."

"That list—what's it about?" If it jolted Lorna into revolt, it had to be something that scared her. And Lorna didn't sound like a woman who would be easily scared out of an oversized salary and all the comforts of New York.

"Names. Nine names. Men who are dangerous. Too interested in Exports Consolidated. Asking questions, looking for answers. They could blow Brimmer's operation sky-high."

"And what does he plan for them?" Renwick sounded cool, kept his voice detached.

"His Minus List, he calls it. That's his kind of joke. You see, he already had a Plus List—had it for the last five years."

Patience, Renwick warned himself. Moore's evasive, embarrassed. Don't rush him. "A Plus List? Men who are *not* dangerous?"

"More than that. People who help him and get well paid for it. They are hooked and they don't know it. Too busy counting up the dollars deposited for them in numbered bank accounts—the Bahamas, Switzerland, any place where they can dodge the tax man. They've got influence, can persuade a supplier to sell what shouldn't be sold, can introduce Brimmer around, vouch for him."

"So he has a list of them, too?" And that's something I want to see, thought Renwick. "Everything is recorded? An exact accounting?"

"A page to each man. Brimmer needs to know how much he has paid out, when and where. It's kept damn secret, you can bet your life on that."

A page to each man . . . "It's in book form, then. A small ledger or a diary?"

Moore's face went blank. "I didn't say that."

"Just a lot of loose leaves clipped together?" Renwick asked, openly disbelieving; but he got no rise from Moore. "If Lorna has a copy . . ." Renwick left the suggestion floating. No doubt she had, for Moore's strange small smile seemed to confirm it.

"That's not for you." Moore said. "That's for Lorna and me to deal with." He rose, started over to the bottle of Scotch. "The Minus List is yours. You can nail Brimmer with that."

So that's my function, thought Renwick: nail Brimmer and let clever Lorna and her devoted Alvin deal with corruption in high places. With Brimmer out of circulation, they'd feel safe to start a new life—new names, new country—financed, of course, by some of the dirty money now in numbered bank accounts: blackmail barefaced and simple, no matter how they justified it, and they would. Brimmer's friends had been overpaid, could well afford to transfer some of their hidden assets to those who had done the hard work. And if anyone ignored that suggestion? He'd lose more than twenty percent (or was Lorna aiming at thirty?) if Internal Revenue were to receive a copy of his page in Brimmer's little account book. Renwick shook his head. Al, he told the big man's back, you may have survived battles and bullets, but I doubt if you'll survive this.

Moore, coming back with a drink in his hand and a quick one inside him, noticed that head shake. "You're the man to deal with it. But you've got to move soon. And fast."

"We'll need real evidence. Nine names listed for what?"

"Real evidence?" Moore swallowed a gulp of Scotch as he sat down again. "Real? It's in Brimmer's own writing. Just jotted down the names at his last meeting with Klingfeld's men in Mexico—two weeks ago, Lorna said. He wouldn't even allow it out of his hands to be typed."

"Nine names listed for what?" Renwick repeated. Careers ruined, possibly, with the help of Brimmer's powerful friends.

"Assassination."

For a long moment, there was no sound or movement in the room. Then Renwick's eyes narrowed.

"It's true, believe me! You know what he wanted me to do? Pick out ten men I could trust—two squads of five men each—train them to coordinate, plan, and execute."

"And how did you handle that suggestion?" A refusal, and Moore would never have reached London with all that money in his pocket. In spite of his protestations—*I'm no assassin*—could I be facing one right now? He's nervous, on edge, increasingly worried. Why?

"I stalled. Told him the job of searching for the right men would take a couple of months, perhaps more. Training and planning needed double that time at least—if he wanted the deaths to look like accidents or suicides."

Renwick put out his hand. "The assassination list. Come on, Al. Give!"

Moore emptied his glass and dropped it on the bed. Reaching for his jacket, his eyes never leaving Renwick, he fumbled with a zipper in an inside pocket. "You'll deal with Brimmer?"

"Yes."

Moore relaxed, pulled out a folded sheet of paper. "Just making sure you'd do the job. Your word on it, that's all we wanted."

"Or else you'd have found someone else?" And I, thought Renwick, would have been the man who had been told too much. Not a happy thought.

Avoiding Renwick's eyes, Moore handed over the folded sheet as he rose and headed quickly for the Scotch, empty glass in hand. He spoke over his shoulder. "Your name is there, sir."

"What?"

"Your name is third on the list."

Renwick stared at him, then unfolded the closely written page. Yes, there it was: Robert Renwick (Col.)—Interintell—cover of Merriman & Co., Consultant Engineers, 7 Grace Street, London. His private number was given; two restaurants he favored on occasion were named; so was the Red Lion, with a cryptic note saying "special meetings." Home telephone was noted as unlisted. Residence changed in April—address to follow. . . Renwick drew a long slow breath, steadied himself.

"Gave me a bit of a shock," Moore said. He looked over at Renwick's grim face, fell silent.

Renwick scanned the list. He recognized six of the names: two inquiring reporters; a crusading editor; a United States senator who kept a sharp eye on sales of armaments abroad; two intelligence men, in Paris and Frankfurt, now investigating terrorists' weapons and their sources of supply. Two names were unknown to him: businessmen, heads of chemical firms. "What's their danger to Brimmer?" he asked, pointing them out on the list as Moore returned, bringing him a drink. This time, he didn't refuse.

"Oh, them! Government contractors. They turned him down when he tried to buy some new type of explosive. Offered big money, talked of national security, hinted at connections with the CIA. He uses that line when he's pressing hard. It has worked. Who's to know it's fourteen years since he's been with the CIA? But these two guys got together: they are making inquiries, stirring things up. It will take time before they get anything out of the CIA. You know these intelligence boys—don't talk, don't tell or explain." Then he looked quickly at Renwick, gave a brief laugh, and covered his gaffe by pointing to the list. "A bunch of unknowns. You wouldn't think they'd be important."

"Not one head of state among us," Renwick said drily.

"Strange how they've got Brimmer so damned scared."

"We're flattered. But this list won't nail Brimmer. It's useless as evidence."

"What?"

"No heading, no indication what it concerns. Brimmer will talk his way out of it. His handwriting, yes. The names? Just people he wanted to meet or entertain. He gives lavish parties, doesn't he?" One of his methods of operation, establishing his credentials with a likely prospect by having credible people around him.

Moore was aghast. The brown eyes hardened, seemed as black as his hair. "You said—"

"I must have evidence, something to stand up in court. Either Lorna or you can testify: she can verify the purpose of that list; you can bear witness about Brimmer's death squads. Or—Lorna gets hold of a record of illegal purchases in the States, of false export declarations, of deliveries abroad."

The idea of testifying, as Renwick had guessed, was rejected. Moore concentrated, as Renwick had hoped, on the record of illegal sales. "She'd have to wait until Brimmer is in Washington. That's early July." He frowned, calculating. "Doesn't give her much time. She's leaving—" He halted abruptly, concealed his lapse by adding, "Okay, okay. She'll get a copy of these records for you. One page enough? Two?"

"Illegal transactions," Renwick emphasized. "Three pages. When she has something to give me, she can send a signal to Merriman's and I'll contact her—"

"No! She can mail the records. No more contacts."

"But if I have to reach you—"

"You don't. Nobody does."

"Traveling far?"

"As far as I can get."

"Lorna, too, of course. But later." Renwick glanced at Moore's bag. Traveling light and all ready to leave. "When you call Lorna from the airport, tell her to include a statement of Brimmer's hidden profits for the last year. The income-tax boys could add fifteen years to his sentence."

"Airport? Who the hell mentioned calling—"

"But you will. She's probably sitting near a telephone right now, waiting for your report." Renwick rose, folding the sheet of paper, slipping it into an inside pocket. He picked up his cigarette case. "Now it's my turn to do you a favor. Avoid any country where there's no extradition. For that's where

Brimmer will run, if he skips bail. Also, don't forget Klingfeld and Sons. They will know you have the Plus List as soon as you start making use of it."

Moore's eyes were disbelieving. "They've never seen it. No one has."

"But they'll assume Brimmer had one—just as they must have a list of their own. Don't underestimate their interest in your disappearance. And Lorna's." Especially Lorna's.

Something amused Moore. "We'll make no move for a year. We've got enough money to tide us over until then. And by that time, who knows? You'll have nabbed Klingfeld, too." He pulled on his jacket, buttoned his collar and tie. "I leave first. Room is paid in advance. Take five minutes before you leave."

Renwick tried once more. "That Plus List is as dangerous as any nitro you've ever handled. As soon as Klingfeld starts looking for it, there will be whispers, rumors. There isn't an intelligence agency that wouldn't join the search. You'll have plenty of people on your trail."

Moore, unheeding, was drawing on his raincoat. The allusion to intelligence agencies baffled him. "Why them? Are they into blackmail? Wouldn't be surprised," he said, shaking his head.

"It's a ready-made list of men who could be manipulated or threatened into betraying their countries. They are halfway there already, poor devils."

"What would you do with the Plus List?" Moore was enjoying this moment.

"Destroy it. Saves trouble all around."

"You're crazy."

"Crazy enough to think Lorna didn't need to make a copy of that list. It's in book form, small, easily carried. How many pages, one to each name—thirty, forty? She'll bring the book out with her, complete."

That stopped Moore. Briefly. "That's wild," he said, and lifted his bag.

"It's obvious. If you were Brimmer, how would you plan an escape if you ever had to make a run for it? Destroy the secret accounts with a fire or a bomb, but take the Plus List for future use. So it's a book, small enough to be pocketed, lying right now beside a false passport and a bundle of dollar bills."

Moore had reached the door. "You know all the tricks, don't you? Too smart for your own good."

"For Brimmer's good, I hope," Renwick said, and won a brief nod from Moore. The door closed, and Renwick could safely stow away his cigarette case.

As he turned off the music, he checked the room. The almost empty bottle of Scotch was in keeping with Moore, and so was one glass. The half-smoked English cigarette was not, so he carried it into the bathroom, along with the tumbler he had used, and flushed it down the toilet. His coat was half dry, his hat still sodden. Three minutes had passed. Quite enough, he decided, allowing for his call downstairs from one of the public phones. He wondered, as he closed the door quietly behind him, if Moore had been idiot enough to use that room phone today.

The lobby was less crowded at this hour—it was nine-forty, he saw by his watch—but with enough stragglers to keep him unnoticed. He dialed his number, heard Nina's voice. "Darling," he told her "I'll be home in an hour. Yes, everything's okay. Are you all right?"

"Ron and Gemma came round to have supper with me, so I wasn't alone. And Pierre has just arrived. We're all having coffee and brandy right now. Have you eaten yet? No? Oh, Bob! I'll put one of Gemma's casseroles in the oven right away. She brought lashings of food in a picnic basket. You know Gemma." Nina's laugh was a happy one, infectious.

He found he was actually relaxed, worry and strain banished for these moments. "No casserole. Can't face it. Make a sandwich—heat up some soup, will you? I love you, darling. Be with you soon."

Outside, the rain had stopped. Wet streets and pools of water reflected the shimmer of lights from never-ending traffic in Tottenham Court Road. Moore might be taking that obvious direction, so Renwick headed into Bloomsbury. There were hotels a short distance away, and his best chance to find a cab would be near one of their doorways. (With regret, he had had to ignore a taxi at the Coronet entrance; just a minimal precaution.) His luck was good. First, a taxi to Euston Station, where he could easily find another cab after a few minutes' delay. Then, sure that no one had been interested in him, he decided to cut down the time spent in his dodging game—it was tedious, and comic, too—and head for home. His heart lifted at the thought. Nina's voice on the phone had brought him back into normal life, blotted out the obscenity of Brimmer's world.

He paid off the cab at Kensington High Street and chose one of the three streets that would lead to Essex Gardens. Once it had been a stretch of Edwardian houses; now there was a block of flats. He looked up at the third floor, saw the lights of his living room, and quickened his pace.

Four

INSIDE RENWICK'S SMALL flat—it had seemed so much bigger when they had viewed it empty in March—the living room was full of light and warmth. Still better was Nina's welcome, arms around him as they stood in the almost-privacy of the entrance hall, a six-foot-square breathing space inside the front door. He kissed her so vehemently that the breath went out of her body, and her eyes, blue and large, widened in surprise. Then they turned serious as she helped him pull off his raincoat and saw it had been drenched, now only half dry and the hat still sodden. He answered her unspoken question with another kiss and drew her into the room.

"Sandwich and soup," she told him. Very hot soup: his hands had been cold. "Are you sure that's enough?"

"Plenty." They sounded perfect compared to a casserole, his least favorite dish. Thank heaven that Nina hadn't adopted Gemma's art of cooking, a little bit of everything in a heavy sauce with a touch of whatever herbs were in favor at the moment.

Gemma's pretty but indefinite face showed obvious relief. "Now we can all stop pretending not to worry," she told him in a whisper as she dropped a light kiss on his cheek. "I'll help Nina," she said to her husband, and as Gilman gave a thankful nod, she hurried toward the kitchen. Renwick watched her—tall and thin, elegant as usual, her dark hair now showing unabashed gray—until she closed the door behind her. Then he turned to the two men. Gilman, he noticed, had been sitting close to the telephone. Pierre Claudel was pretending unconcern, lounging in the most comfortable chair, but his brown eyes—bright and clever, alive in typically French manner—held a decided question; several questions, in fact.

"I'm sorry," Renwick said. "He fooled me with that Paddington dodge. Sorry."

Gilman deserted the phone to pour a Scotch. "You look as if you needed this."

"I do."

"Well?" asked Claudel, rising to help himself to another brandy, a neat compact figure of medium height, quick in movement.

Renwick glanced at the kitchen door. "Later."

"You got something?" Claudel's English, schooled at Dowanside, was perfect, with the addition nowadays of American phrases thanks to his years of close friendship with Renwick.

"Plenty. What happened at Paddington?"

"I waited. When you arrived, I was all set to follow you into the station, find what train you were taking. But you didn't arrive."

"He was in a taxi outside the Red Lion, invited me in, with a thirty-eight and silencer pointed at my stomach. Then it was Marble Arch and the Underground to Tottenham Court Road, and then a short walk to a hotel room." Renwick glanced once more at the kitchen door. "Details later, if requested."

Gilman's tall, thin figure drooped into a chair. "We were really quite worried, Bob."

"Worried?" burst out Claudel. "I was practically having fits. Thought I had slipped up, somehow missed you. And then, with almost two hours gone and no show, I went into the station. I had a feeling that we had been tricked. I asked the information desk—a nice girl, pretty, very helpful—if the train to Oxford was modernized. Certainly. All trains from Paddington—"

The kitchen door opened, and Nina carried in a tray.

"They are doing a good job, I hear," Renwick said.

"Who?" asked Nina.

"British Railways. Thanks, darling." Renwick began his supper.

"Still haven't beaten the French records," Claudel said, "but they're on the way. For instance, in every train running out of London—except from Fenchurch Street—all old-style single compartments have had their walls ripped out and central gangways made. No more privacy." He smiled over at Renwick.

"I heard about that," Gemma volunteered. "Privacy is thought to encourage vandalism and attacks on women."

"And it did," said Gilman. "But no more having a quiet compartment to oneself. Frankly, I didn't know that *all* railway carriages had been altered."

"It only proves we don't travel in trains very much," Renwick observed. He was eating soup and sandwich in record time. So we were all misled— even Moore: his idea of British trains had probably come from the movies he had seen. Renwick shook his head.

"We may have to," Gilman said, and led the talk into a possible scarcity of petrol for cars, even with the North Sea oil pouring out by the barrel-load. Rumor had it that it was being used up too quickly: people didn't realize that it couldn't last forever.

"What does?" Claudel asked. "*Carpe diem*—seize the day."

"And seize half an hour before we start heading for bed," Renwick said. "That meeting we have scheduled for tomorrow—I think we'd better discuss its agenda right now and be prepared for any opposition we'll meet from Thomson and Flynn." He rose, the last half of his sandwich in his hand. "No, darling," he told Nina, "you stay here with Gemma. We'll move into the small room." His study, it was supposed to be; but Nina, thinking a year ahead, had been suggesting it would make a wonderful nursery. Not much of anything at the moment, except a dumping ground for the unpacked crates of bibelots and boxes of books which had so far defeated arrangement. Wall space for shelving was limited in this living room with its large windows, its mantelpiece trying to make an electric fire look natural, its radiator that produced more groans than heat, its doorways. "Gemma, you might have some ideas about bookcases. I vote we take down the pictures, except for the two painted by Nina. What do you think?" And with that he could start leading Gilman and Claudel into the temporary box room with no more delay.

In alarm, Nina said, "But there are no chairs, darling."

"Honey, they are the most nicely dusted crates we've ever sat upon."

Nina, bless her, had made curtains and installed them, bright coral stripes on white to brighten the sea-green walls. They were heavy enough to be opaque and, once they were drawn and the light switched on, no curious neighbor from the block of flats across the street could see three men choosing three of the most solid-looking boxes.

"Cozy," Claudel said.

"All eight by twelve feet," Renwick agreed. He looked at his watch. "Here's the gist. The details you'll learn tomorrow from the tape." He took out his cigarette case, laid it beside him. "Two photographs, up close," he said as he produced his lighter and added it to the case. "Moore has changed his hair color since I knew him. It was brown, brindled. Probably got bleached, living in so much strong sun. So, since he is disappearing from sight, he has dyed his hair black, eyebrows, too. These photos will at least show how he now looks."

Gilman asked, "He talked easily?"

"Incessantly. Some of it as a cover-up, a justification for his own role. But it's all informative, more than he realized. The main points are these, in order of importance to us: first, Erik. Moore did meet him. He was in South Yemen about ten days ago. Refused to follow orders from two

Cubans who had been sent to meet him there, and took off. Not by the airport and not on a freighter. Disappeared completely. Heading for West Germany, no doubt. By what route?"

Gilman said, "He would scarcely risk crossing the desert into North Yemen. The frontier is watched—an undeclared war going on. Anyone from Communist South Yemen could be shot on sight."

Claudel had a suggestion. "What about bribing his way onto a dhow? Small boats under sail don't use the docks. The dhows sneak over to Djibouti from South Yemen all the time. It's a short distance—the narrow entrance to the Red Sea—a few kilometers." Claudel ought to know: he had two agents in Djibouti, a good listening post as well as a smuggler's delight. Once it had been part—a very small part—of the French Empire in East Africa. Now it was independent, and only recently, but still with the French presence around to guard its port.

"That's an idea," Renwick said. "So why don't you leave for Djibouti tomorrow night—or the next day at latest? Erik may not be there, but your agents could have heard rumors or gossip. They sail in and out of South Yemen, don't they? Besides the news on Erik, we'd like to know if any right-wing terrorists are being trained in left-wing camps."

Claudel nodded, his quick mind already measuring the best means of transportation. "*Mon Dieu,* it will be hot. Djibouti in July?"

Gilman looked at Renwick. "Then you didn't question Moore about right-wing terrorists being trained in South Yemen?"

"Thought it better not to dwell on terrorism at all. I just let him talk about it. He could have been on a fishing expedition, trying to find out how much we have uncovered."

Gilman agreed, but with regret. "Who is he working for? The Soviets? Or other unfriendlies?"

"As far as I could find out, he's now working for himself—or, rather, for Lorna." Then, as eyebrows were raised, Renwick added, "Listen to the tape."

"Did you find out any more details about Erik?"

"Just giving a seminar on how to escape if caught. It's my guess he is trying to reach his old stomping ground. That's where his real support is— the Direct Action group, with their sympathizers and backers. Communists? He tried using them before, but they used him. He will be wary of them, of course, but if he needs their help, he will take it. On *his* terms. It seems the Cubans wanted him on their terms. It didn't work. He probably became more of an anarchist than ever in that Indian prison."

Gilman nodded. "I'll alert Richard Diehl in Frankfurt that Erik could be heading for West Germany. Other friendly intelligence agencies, too. But if somehow he reaches Libya or Algeria—"

"The Communists there don't have enough diplomacy to handle Erik. The quarrel between him and the Cubans was savage. Moore thinks Erik will never make it—the Communists will take care of him. But I wonder."

"I could wish they would," Claudel said frankly. "It would save a thousand lives. If Direct Action has Erik back to mastermind operations—they could be on a disaster scale. Like that wipe-out he planned two years ago for Duisburg." The oil and propane storage tanks on that huge stretch of docks on the Rhine would have started a fire storm. Claudel's voice turned bitter. "Don't underestimate our dear little Erik with his noble, noble ideals."

Erik's career, until he was caught in Bombay, had been ten years of violence. Born in Venezuela, educated in Mexico City, then at Lumumba University, then in a Communist training camp in North Korea, he had become the founder of Direct Action in Berlin, an anarchist group that had bombed and robbed, committed arson and murder and brutal kidnappings. As for the reason for his appearance in Bombay, he had been in flight from West Germany after his plans for Duisburg's waterfront had been discovered, traveling as an innocent American eastward across Europe, through Turkey and Iran and Pakistan, selecting extreme left-wingers for training and coordination into an international force of terrorists. Dangerous? He was lethal. We won't underestimate Erik, thought Renwick grimly. "Now, let's get to the second main point in Moore's information: Exports Consolidated, founded by Mitchell Brimmer."

Gilman spoke with distaste. "Arms trafficking."

"Illegal arms."

"What?"

"Bought with bribes and lies, shipped with false declarations, sold to foreign countries that send them on to terrorist-training areas. Brimmer is now supplying instructors to teach the use of these weapons. Also, Exports Consolidated is expanding, has merged with a European firm—Klingfeld and Sons."

Gilman and Claudel looked at each other. "Never heard of it," Gilman said. "New to me," said Claudel.

"Details in here," Renwick reminded them, tapping the cigarette case. "Third main point: Brimmer has a list of names which his sense of humor calls his 'Plus List.' People with power or in sensitive places who have been most helpful to Brimmer and now have the amounts paid to them, *and* the dates of these payments, all nicely noted under their names."

"Bribery and corruption," Gilman said slowly.

"The whole bloody mess." Claudel shook his head. "Idiots! Did they never think what they were getting into?"

"Fourth main point," Renwick pressed on, glancing at his watch. "There's another list which he calls his 'Minus List.' I was given a copy of that."

"Men who are *not* helpful to Brimmer?" Gilman asked. "Dangerous to him?"

"So he thinks. So Klingfeld and Sons think." Renwick pulled the list out of his pocket. "It's in Brimmer's writing, mostly dictated by Klingfeld. No heading. Just nine names. Men to be eliminated."

"Assassinated?" Claudel asked, lips tightening.

"Apparent accidents or suicides." Renwick passed the list over. Gilman and Claudel seized it, shared its reading. "Four Americans, five Europeans," Renwick went on. "We'll have to warn—"

"Good God!" Claudel burst out, while Gilman raised his eyes from the list to stare at Renwick. "Your name is—"

"Yes. Doesn't get so much space as the other eight. Minimal information. Does that mean only one source?"

Gilman's calm face was furrowed with worry. "Someone inside Interintell?"

"Looks like it. My telephone number was given to Brimmer—or Klingfeld—by someone who has used it. The name of the Red Lion, also given by someone who has met me there. My change of address, by someone who knew my studio, heard that I had moved but—so far—hasn't been invited to our new flat. No mention that I'm married, as yet. But Nina could be added to the list any day." Like the other wives . . . There was a long pause. "I'll get him," Renwick said, too quietly. "But now we concentrate on warning the other names on that death list. Ron—you approach your friends in D15 here and those in French and Italian Security, get them to offer some protection. I'll handle the American angle. Pierre will have plenty to do in Djibouti. All agreed?"

"Agreed," said Gilman. "We'll sleep on this information, and tomorrow morning we'll have some ideas how to deal with it."

"Without alerting Brimmer. Or else we may not get three pages of his illegal transactions. Assassination and corruption aren't in our particular field of operations. But who supplies the weapons to terrorists, who arranges for expert instructors, who receives them and where and how—that *is* Interintell's business. Let's not cause any flap in Brimmer's office. We need three samples of his secret accounts, photocopied in peace and tranquillity."

Gilman gave a nod of approval. Photocopies made hard evidence.

Claudel broke his silence. And good-bye to my own plans for tonight, he told himself. "I think I'd better take the tube straight to Blackfriars. It's an easy walk from there to Merriman's. Old Bernie never leaves before two or three. He's an owl." And a specialist in dealing with miniature tapes as well as with more sophisticated gadgets. Bernstein found late working hours provided less interruption than normal daytime, and never wandered into his basement laboratory at Merriman's until early evening. "The quicker he makes this ready for Ron's tape player tomorrow"—Claudel picked up the cigarette case—"the sooner we'll hear it. He might even be cajoled into using his back room for us." The lighter was picked up, too. "Okay?"

Renwick nodded. "And while you're there, Pierre, run off some copies of that list."

Gilman looked at the Minus List still in his hand. "Two names for D15, two for French Security, one for Rome, three for the FBI. Yes, that covers the nationalities. And Pierre—use my car. Safer. This is the pickpocket season." A mild little joke, but it eased the tension.

"We'll move up the meeting tomorrow?" Claudel asked, pocketing all three items. "Eight o'clock?"

"Seven," Renwick suggested. "A lot of discussion, a lot of decisions." Then we start moving.

Gilman said, "I'll call Bernie and tell him to expect you, Pierre. This could be one night he thinks he might knock off early for dinner at midnight. Odd bird."

"Our mad scientist," Claudel said lightly, "but what would we do without him?"

"We'll need special care on this job. Sorry about that, Pierre. Hope you didn't have a prior engagement."

Special care, tightest security. I stay with Bernie until the work is completed, Claudel thought. He will play the minitape, transfer it to a regular tape, filter it to diminish any scratch. And it will all be done behind the closed door of his soundproof closet with both of us on the outside—once he checks the voice level of the first sentence—and not a whit wiser about the words being recorded anew. That over, the two tapes will be placed in separate containers, sealed tight, and locked away in Gilman's ultra-safe safe. Then I stretch out on Gilman's emergency cot. "At seven tomorrow, first order of business, I'll be listening to that recording. So"—he said with a grin—"what's a sleepless night against that? But one thing, Bob—could the Minus List be a fake? This Moore fellow tricked us once today."

"Just another dodge to enlist our help and get Brimmer off his back? Yes, I thought about that. But he talked so damn much, let slip a lot of details that added up to a fairly complete picture. And from that I'd say that the Minus List is the logical development in Brimmer's career. You shuck your moral sense, let greed take over, and one day you are talking murder and excusing it as expedient. That list is for real, Pierre."

"Well, if a man is judged by the enemies he makes, then the list could be taken as a compliment."

"One we could do without," said Gilman. They entered the living room in silence.

It was a scene of concentration. With head bent, note pad on knee, Gemma was writing. Nina, slightly bemused, sat on the couch beside her with three slips of paper in her hand. A fourth was added as Gemma tore off a page. "There—that's the last one. I know Bob will love it." She said to Renwick with one of her ingenuous side glances, "Just giving Nina some of my casserole recipes." Then she noticed her husband waiting by the telephone. "Time to leave? I'd better collect the picnic basket. Coming, Nina?" She was already halfway to the kitchen.

Gemma, thought Renwick, after eighteen years of marriage to Ronald Gilman, had perfected the art of making a tactful retreat. And Nina? An almost imperceptible wink as she passed him, a small flutter of the eyelid, showed she was learning.

Gilman had already dialed Bernie's laboratory, began speaking as the kitchen door closed. "Gilman here. Claudel is bringing your little trinket back for some adjustments. Too delicate for us to handle. Expect him within the hour. Special care," he emphasized and ended his call.

Claudel was amused. "Little trinket?" He would hardly call the cigarette case that.

"Bernie's word for it," Renwick said wryly, remembering Bernie's disapproval. "Told me it was time to give up these old-fashioned methods, wanted me to experiment with his latest idea of using a micro-bug with a chip that could record and talk back to me, too."

Claudel had picked up his coat and was headed for the kitchen. "I'll use the rear staircase—the car is parked down there, anyway." He paused for a moment. "Did you know Bernie has made a chip to imitate a small sequin

on a lady's dress? Now all we need is a girl to wear the damned thing."
Then he was into the kitchen, saying, "Good night, fair ladies, good night.
What about dinner at my place next week?" And with a kiss for each of
them, he made his exit.

The Gilmans' leave-taking was equally short. "Dinner next week?" Gemma
asked, and then remembered that if there was one thing that irritated Ron,
usually the mildest of men, it was the protracted good-bye. So she didn't
sit down for a last five-minute chat, but let Ron drape her coat around her.
"Day and time to be arranged, I suppose. Isn't that always the way?" she
added lightly to sweeten her small criticism. "But at least we saw you tonight."

"And thank you for that." Renwick's voice said more than his words. A
hug and a kiss between the women, an answering nod from Gilman, and he
could close the door, lock it securely, and openly look at his watch. Almost
twelve.

"You know my trouble?" Nina asked him as he slipped an arm around
her waist and led her back into the living room.

"Me."

She laughed and shook her head, her soft blond hair falling over her eyes.
She brushed it away. "My trouble is that I never can guess what is really
happening."

"I tell you when I can. And as much as I can."

"I know. But only after everything is solved, another case filed away. And
not everything is told, either. It can't be, I suppose."

"You suppose right, my love." He folded his arms around her, held her
close.

"Sorry," she said quickly. "I shouldn't probe. I really don't mean to, but
the questions do rise up and won't lie down."

"Like my problems. They always seem to come in clusters."

Nina broke free, looked at him anxiously. "That kind of day?" I knew it,
she thought; I could sense it over the telephone tonight. "Not just one
problem?"

He eased his voice to reassure her. "Don't worry, pet. We'll take them as
they come." *New address to follow*—the phrase kept haunting him. Essex
Gardens could even now be reported to Brimmer. How did he get Nina
safely away until that threat was over? He looked around the room. "Yes,
this place is too small. I think we have to face another move, honey."

Nina stared at him. "Bob! We are scarcely settled! And it does get sunshine and fresh air; the windows *are* big. It's so convenient for your office,
too—no changing trains, a straight run through. And it's—" She cut that
sentence short. The flat was affordable, its rent within their budget. "I
thought you loved it," she said, all joy leaving her face. "When we moved
here in April, you—Bob, what's wrong?"

Residence changed in April . . . Who the hell gave Klingfeld that information? "I'm all right, honey. Just pooped. Come on, let's go to bed." He
pulled her close again, smoothed back a rebellious lock of hair, looked deep
into her blue eyes, brought a smile back to her lips as he kissed her chin,
her cheeks, her brow, her mouth. "I'm never too tired for that," he told her.

Afterward, he lay beside her, not moving, not wanting to disturb the deep sleep into which Nina usually drifted. His dejection had lifted, his exhaustion, too; perhaps that had only been part of the depression, the feeling of uselessness—so few of us against the hidden threats, the secret intents of a widespread power-force. Not organized crime, he judged, although crimes enough were being committed: if Brimmer or Klingfeld were backed by any kind of Mafia, they wouldn't need to search for assassination squads. They'd have their own hit men already prepared for action. Political backing, then? Klingfeld & Sons could have introduced that note. What else to think of a firm that had so much seeming power and money behind it and yet appeared to be anonymous? Neither Gilman nor Claudel had heard of it, and he was willing to bet that it was unknown, as an illegal business trafficking in forbidden exports of military equipment, to all other intelligence agencies. If its name was recognized, it would be as some family firm in the regular import-export trade.

He looked down at Nina, resting within his arm, her body soft and warm drawn close to his. Protect and comfort; for better or worse, until death—

She may have heard his small intake of breath. She opened her eyes, saying, "I'm not asleep, either." She turned sideways to face him, drew still closer, slid her arm over his body. "And I thought I had driven away your worries, darling." She laughed, the light small laugh that echoed the affection in her voice. "Bob, you were right. This flat is too small. Look at this room. The bed almost fills it."

He had to smile. King-size was what Nina had wanted. We could have done with a single bed for all the space we take up, he thought.

"But it's storage that really is the problem. Of course, when that carpenter *does* arrive and makes us some closets—I've drawn out all the plans for him, measured everything—we'll have more space. Much more, Bob." He's been so patient about that, she thought. His suits were hung on a rack near the bathroom door. "We could really be settled by July. Or August," she added, thinking of the nonappearing carpenter.

"How about the Fourth of July in Washington?"

She pulled away from him, tried to sit up and look at him in wonder.

"Don't you get homesick, Nina?"

"Yes. As you do. But I thought we were going back in September for two weeks—if you were free then."

"I'm free now. Let's make the trip when we can."

"Leave in a few days?" She was dumbfounded.

"Leave tomorrow—no, day after tomorrow. On Wednesday."

"Bob—how can we? You've got meetings." And problems, she remembered. Even one problem always meant several late nights at the office. "And I'll have to pack, and close up the flat—Why, the Fourth is on Saturday! We'd never make it."

He reached out, took firm hold of her slender waist, pulled her down where she belonged. "Remember the evening in Georgetown when I waited for you in that half-built conservatory behind your father's house, and you came running into my arms?"

"And you swung me up. Told me we were leaving the next morning to get married." Nina was smiling again.

"You didn't find it so hard to pack in a hurry then," he said gently, and kissed her.

"Then," she told him, "I was a foot-loose student. Now, I'm an old married woman."

"The difference," he said in mock wonder, "that nineteen months can make to a twenty-one-year-old!"

"Darling"—her arms were around him, her body yielding—"we'll leave day after tomorrow. I'll pack and write notes to everyone and close the flat up tight."

"No notes," he said quickly, then softened that small command by adding, "A waste of time. We'll just slip away and forget this flat. We'll leave Gemma in charge of the key." And Gemma could start looking for some other place for them. Gemma would love that: no imposition. "We may stay in America for several weeks."

"Can you manage it?" She looked at him. "Or is this a business trip?"

"Now and again," he admitted. "I'll take you to see my—" cut out the word "people"—"my sister who married an ex-Marine and lives in La Jolla." Not to see anyone with the name Renwick, not now at least. And what about the name O'Connell, if Nina's family connection was being traced? "Is your father in Washington, or has he left for the Maryland shore?" Nina's stepmother liked its cooler temperatures in the summer months for her incessant dinner parties.

"He isn't very happy in either place nowadays."

Out of a job, Renwick thought. No longer an economic adviser to the White House or attached to the State Department. A quick and total resignation—the modern way for an honorable man to put a bullet through his brain.

Nina was watching him. "He likes you, Bob."

"That's news." Why should a proud man like Francis O'Connell like anyone who knew about his stupidity? With his high-minded scorn for all security, he had almost walked into a White House meeting with an explosive device planted in his attaché case by someone he had taken on trust.

Nina was suddenly still. She said, "He told me all about it. You saved him. And a president. And all the others in that room."

"He told you?" The words were jolted out of Renwick.

"I'm glad he did. Don't try to shelter me so much, Bob."

"And you never mentioned it—"

"I was waiting for you to tell me. The obedient wife," she said, turning it into a joke.

"How obedient?" he asked, and took her into his arms again.

Five

DJIBOUTI WAS AS hot as Claudel had predicted, and more crowded than he remembered from last year's visit. It always had held half the inhabitants of this small and arid land, a sliver of scrub and desert stretching a rough hundred miles in length, even less in breadth, tightly bound both north and west by Ethiopia, in the south by Somalia, freely breathing to its east with an indented coastline that lay on the Gulf of Aden just where the Red Sea began its long stretch northward to the Suez Canal. Facing South Yemen across the Gulf, Djibouti had always been a trader's delight, but with the reopening of Suez it was once again on a major shipping lane—from India and the Far East right up into the Mediterranean. It might be a minuscule republic, a speck on the map of Africa, but it had significance. Today, it seemed to Claudel as if the town would soon hold most of the country's population and its assimilated foreigners.

He poured another cup of coffee, finished the last croissant. He was sitting on the Café-Restaurant's deep-set verandah, shaded almost to the point of darkness against the morning sun. The Café-Restaurant de l'Univers, six modest bedrooms upstairs (one of which was occupied by Claudel), owned by good friend Aristophanes Vasilikis; once of Athens, later of the Sudan, and for the last ten years a resident in Djibouti, capital of the Republic of Djibouti. Too bad, thought Claudel, that independence had ditched the old name: Territory of the Afars and Issas. That had a sound that few countries could match.

The Afars and Issas were still around, he had been glad to see, and still predominant; dark-skinned nomads, thin and tall with hawk-nosed faces, who wandered in from the barren hinterland with camels and goats, and lingered indefinitely. Muslims, of course, like the Arab traders who had modernized their act and no longer exported slaves. There were European settlers, too: venturesome small-businessmen from Greece and Italy. And, of course, the residue of French who had simply stayed on. Add to that mix the indefatigable Indian merchants, the Somali refugees, the Sudanese fishermen, the Ethiopian laborers, and you had a full house.

Watching the variety of faces and dress out in the street, people on foot going their own mysterious way, Claudel could be grateful that they made his visit easier, less noticeable. But it also meant that the elusive Erik, if he had escaped to Djibouti, had found a place where he could stay submerged until his plans were completed for the next stage of his journey toward West Germany. Yet, once here—if he were here—he would find it more difficult to leave than to reach. There were only fifty miles of paved road in the whole country, hundreds of trails and tracks. And where would they lead him? Into the desert regions of Ethiopia, or south to Somalia, now filled with starving refugees from the war with Ethiopia—hardly worthwhile trying to hire a car (scarce and difficult) or a camel (slow and stately). The railway—one railway only, connecting Addis Ababa in Ethiopia with the port at Djibouti—hauled mostly freight: import-export trade, Ethiopia's one direct outlet to the sea. And Addis Ababa, Communist, had Soviet advisers and Cuban agents in control. It was unlikely that Erik would find that an attractive prospect.

So there were two possibilities left to Erik, and Claudel in the last three days had been checking them both.

First, there was the port for Djibouti, built by the French some three miles from the town. (Or the other way around, Claudel reminded himself: the port was begun first; the town came a few years later.) It had become a complex of installations: piers, quays, docks, water reservoirs, fuel-storage tanks, even a refrigeration plant—everything that was needed for the refueling and replenishing of French naval vessels (two destroyers were there now; an aircraft carrier had just sailed). There were many paying customers, too, such as passenger ships that had docked for supplies and oil before they cruised onward, and numerous freighters at the loading and unloading piers. Yes, there was a choice for Erik in that variety of vessels. Except that the French were still in command of the port—its strategic importance higher than ever since the Soviet Union now had its friends established on the other side of the Red Sea's narrow entrance. On Claudel's arrival in Djibouti, he had visited the port to see his friend Georges Duhamel, whom he had known when they were both semi-attached (a diplomatic way of describing their function) as French Intelligence representatives to NATO. It was part of DeGaulle's ambiguity—keeping one French foot inside the Western alliance while withdrawing the other foot. Duhamel was now with French Naval Intelligence and had been sent on special assignment to assist the head of security at the port. He had been delighted to see Claudel again, and there were no false pretenses: Duhamel knew of Interintell and approved. He assured Claudel that there had been no European, no imitation Arab, trying to stow away on any freighter during the last two weeks. So, with the alarm on Erik sounded, Claudel could only return to the town and wait, and rely on Duhamel's eagle eye.

Secondly, there was the airport. Flights were limited, and checking the passenger lists for the last two weeks was fairly simple. Claudel concentrated on the flights to Egypt and France. (The others, to Mombasa and Addis Ababa, were obviously less attractive for Erik: the former because it only led Erik farther afield, farther from Germany; the latter because Ethiopia now had an influx of helpful Cubans.) But there was nothing to discover. No record or sighting of any unknown European, of any unidentified Arab. The French kept tight watch over the airport, a precaution particularly against hijackers. So, again, Claudel could only give a warning about Erik and go back to the town, and wait. And wonder if Erik had ever come to Djibouti in the first place.

But any day now, his two agents should be arriving from Aden. Husayn would sail in, land his cargo of salt and lamp oil and canned tuna at one of the pint-sized harbors some distance from the port. Shaaban would seek another anchorage, equally insignificant, for his cargo of cotton, wheat, and sesame. They would come separately, and Claudel would keep them well apart. Husayn was an Afar; Shaaban an Issa. The nomad Afars wandered in and out of Ethiopia; the Issas in and out of Somalia. That difference was, in these days of war and hate, a possible troublemaker.

Waiting and more waiting, thought Claudel as he finished breakfast. But while he did that, he could turn his attention to some legitimate business as the traveling representative of Merriman & Co., Consultant Engineers. He would visit once more the projected site for a possible hotel—if its backers received any encouragement from Merriman's—to be built on an empty stretch of coastline about two miles from the port and a mile from town. A desolate place, with a gray-sand beach, flat land broken by huge shallow pools where white herons—the only touch of beauty—stood ankle deep and picked fastidiously at the sedge-covered water. He would put in a negative report: drainage problems enormous, costs astronomical, sea view dull, background dismal with gray desert and shrubs, possible objections from the port authorities although their personnel might like a nearby luxury hotel for their families' visits, definite objections from all the sailors and seamen as well as the people in town who couldn't afford the prices charged. Also, Muslims did not drink. Also, swimming near the Red Sea was not comfortable: sharks. Also, fresh-water supply would entail a search for underground streams such as Djibouti and the port were built over. Also, the white herons would leave as the dredging operations began.

His report, of course, would be written as soon as his other business was completed. It made an adequate explanation for his appearance in Djibouti, though. Neither the Police Inspector nor his assistant, both French, had questioned it—not openly, at least, even when he had mentioned the possible need for some of their well-trained native policemen to arrest a murderer and terrorist. Erik . . . always back to Erik, although Claudel had also taken the opportunity to talk to Georges Duhamel about any freighter unloading crates from Exports Consolidated or a firm called Klingfeld & Sons—both names to be treated as highly sensitive, not to be bruited around the port. Duhamel, good security officer that he was, had promised a few tactful questions. A wild shot, Claudel thought, but every small chance was well worth taking.

"You are thoughtful this morning, my friend." Aristophanes Vasilikis, making his morning tour of the premises, stopped by Claudel's table. He was a blond Greek, now graying, with snub features and blue eyes. Of medium height and girth, he had his clothes carefully fashioned to fit by an Italian tailor: lightweight gabardine trousers that hung without a wrinkle; a cream silk shirt opened at the neck, its sleeves turned back at their broad cuffs. With a reproving frown at the wooden ceiling above him, where a fan had started a slowdown and was threatening a work stoppage, he chose the cane chair opposite Claudel's, sat down as he took out an Egyptian cigarette and fitted it into an ivory holder. He came right to the point, speaking in his fractured French, saying with an increasing frown, "Surely you do not consider giving a favorable report to those idiots who waste good money on building hotels where they are useless."

"They have built many hotels in unlikely places."

"Where?"

"Sardinia, Kota Kinabalu—"

"Oh?" Aristophanes had never heard of it, but that wasn't to be admitted.

"It's in Borneo—the Land below the Winds."

"Headhunters!"

"They've stopped the habit, I hear. In any case, Ari, don't lose sleep over any big hotel being built here. Your place won't suffer at all."

Aristophanes had had a moment of hope, dashed down by Claudel's last sentence. His restaurant was small, with wine for the French and Italians, fruit juices for the wealthier Arabs who liked to adopt European dress. The bar was enormous, with beer and spirits flowing freely for off-duty sailors, seamen from the freighters, the traders who were Christians, the lesser shopkeepers who had forgotten their religion. Both establishments made money, more than his trading post in the Sudan, much more than his hard beginnings in the Plaka of Athens. "They are planning a discothèque, I hear."

"You have better ears than I. And guesses are wild. Rumors rise like dust storms in this part of the world."

Aristophanes shook his handsome head over his friend's amusement. "Dangerous things, these discothèques. Men and women, half-naked women, dancing together. Have your rich clients forgotten this is Muslim territory? Tell them, Pierre, what happened last year—just after your last visit. Or didn't you hear?"

Claudel shook his head.

"Tourists came off a cruise ship—they come for three hours and then they leave, and tell that to your rich clients, too—and there were some young women, stupid women. They wore short shorts and low-necked blouses and brought cameras to photograph the marketplace." Aristophanes dropped his voice. "They were stoned. They had to run for the taxis that brought them here from their ship. A crowd ran after them, jeering all the way. If the police had not arrived, there would have been a riot." Another rumor? Claudel wondered, but Aristophanes was deadly serious. "Tempers are short. Anger is quick. This place changes like the rest of the world. Ten years ago, when I came here, it was different. Now, politics—" He spat out a vivid oath. To hear a Greek curse politics was quite something, Claudel thought, but he kept silent. "All under the surface," Aristophanes went on when he had recovered. "So far, under the surface." He fell silent.

"What news do you hear from the outside world?" Claudel asked to shift Ari's dark mood away from Djibouti. Ari had, in his very private room on the top floor of his hotel, an excellent shortwave radio, high-powered, which could transmit as well as receive. Provided, no doubt, by Greek Intelligence in Athens; one of Claudel's educated guesses, bolstered by the fact that Interintell and Greek Intelligence had co-operated in defeating a terrorist plan to seize the airport near Athens. Friendly relations had been established, which possibly accounted for Ari's warm welcome on Claudel's visit last year.

It was, of course, a guess: Ari, who had a mania for gadgets, might very well have invested some money in a radio that would keep him in touch with Europe. He was an émigré who had become thoroughly attached to East Africa but dreamed back to the West. Neither Ari nor Claudel ever mentioned the word "intelligence." Their conversations were entirely focused on Djibouti or international troubles. But the fact that Ari had shown Claudel his radio was a definite hint: Claudel was welcome to make use of it should there be any urgent need.

Ari's dark mood refused to be shifted. He glared up at the large overhead fan, now motionless, and rose. "So I find a workman who will come, not at once but this evening. He will drive away my customers, fix the fan, and it will break down next week." Then he remembered his manners as host. "Do you need Alexandre and his taxi to drive you out to that godforsaken place?"

"Yes." Claudel glanced at his watch, saw it was ten minutes to nine. The day was half over for most people. By eleven, the streets were emptying; by noon, people were behind closed shutters or lying in the shade of a wall. In the early evening, after the long hot afternoon, life came back to the town. "Ask Alexandre to be here around ten o'clock." Claudel was on his feet. "I'll take my usual stroll to the market, stretch my legs, and buy a newspaper." It was his daily routine, like Alexandre's taxi, and it aroused no comment.

The Café-Restaurant de l'Univers stood at the corner of a broad street, once intended as a boulevard with two rows of trees down its middle. From here branched off some lesser streets, crossing other narrow streets at right angles, all part of neat French planning. After that, things went slightly haywire, but to reach the open marketplace was easy. One walked down a straight street, fairly straight at least, between two continuous rows of houses, mostly white, a few walls painted blue, all a little faded or discolored. Some had brief colonnades, little stretches of curved arches; most were plain-faced, unadorned, rising three stories above the street level, where a few shops had intruded; high-ceilinged stories, to judge by the tall windows, seemingly without glass, whose massive shutters were opened for the morning air.

The road was unpaved but many people walked there, for traffic was light—some neat cars, three small green taxis—and the sidewalks were uneven and raised by knee-high curbs. As if, thought Claudel, the planners of this street had feared torrential monsoon floods. Or, more likely, they had raised the sidewalks high to let people step out of their carriages without a jolt or a jump. What, he wondered, had this quarter been like fifty, thirty, even twenty years ago? Blue and white walls would have looked freshly painted, the shutters would have hung straight—not half off their hinges, comically tilted. Few chips and gashes on the arches, less peeling plaster, no large puddles at the side of the earth-packed road left from the morning's hosing of broken sidewalks. Bless the underground stream that gave the town its water, and pray that it flows forever and ever. Or did Nature's bounty change as men's did? Grow old and weary and tired of giving?

It was a sad thought out of keeping with the people he passed. Intent on their lives, on the immediate present such as the morning's marketing, the cost of buying, the price of selling, the earnest gossip with friends, they brought color and movement to the street. The variety of faces, of languages, of dress, always fascinated Claudel; and, above all, the women. They were young—and where were the older ones? So few to be seen—young and beautiful, very tall, very thin, their faces unveiled but their bodies enveloped by layers of floating muslin in bright flower patterns. Wide skirts fluttered to the ground and hid their ankles. Knee-length tunics, loose and thin, moved with each step. Vivid scarves covered their heads and then wound loosely around necks and shoulders in billowing folds. Their faces were extraordinary: smooth skin, deeply black, tightly drawn over fine-boned faces; profiles that were sculptured to perfection. But the eyes, briefly looking at him, then ignoring, were the hardest eyes he had ever seen, carved out of obsidian. Don't even glance at me, my proud beauties: you'd scare the hell out of me.

Strangely, the tall, thin, black-skinned men, with the same fine features as their women (but they never walked together; it was men with men, women either alone or with another woman), had eyes that seemed more human: clever-quick, deepset, not friendly, but not inimical, either. Some of the younger ones were dressed like Claudel, in trousers and short-sleeved shirts; the rest wore striped ankle-length gowns, drab in color.

He passed the floating dresses that billowed with the slightest touch of warm breeze, made way for a blind old man being led by a young boy, and came to the end of the shops and houses. Ahead of him, on open ground, with flowered muslin and striped nightshirts in mad confusion, was the encircling wall of the uncovered market. Outside the wall were two tethered camels and a few goats under the watchful eyes of eight-year-olds. The main entrance was a jostle of people moving in and out. Claudel took note of the time—five past nine—and removed his watch to the safekeeping of his hand. There was nothing of value in his pockets. The nimblest-fingered thieves were now around. Two pairs of black policemen in starched khaki uniforms were there to discourage the pickpockets if possible, arrest them if necessary. It was all part of the daily scene.

Claudel strolled into the market, rubbing shoulders, ignoring and being ignored. Casually, he looked around for the Old Arab's granddaughter. (But her skin was light brown and less smooth in texture, and her features were neither fine-hewn nor sculpted. Her eyes, however, could dance with delight, and her lips smiled.) If she were here at nine-fifteen, that would be the signal. His agents, one or other of them, had sailed into the bay west of Djibouti. The Old Arab ought to know; he owned both dhows, rented them to Husayn and Shaaban. A man of age, wisdom, and wealth, the Old Arab (his name had three hyphens and was a mouthful in any language) was respected by most, trusted by some, and feared by all. In his house tonight there would be a room set aside for Claudel's meeting.

Claudel's eyes kept searching. Bright dresses floated everywhere, their wearers bargaining shrewdly for the vegetables and fruit lying on the bare earth in the shade of the wall. Following its curve, pressed on all sides by black, brown, and vaguely white faces, he made his determined way. As usual, it was the strange smell that repelled him—a sweet sickly smell that he couldn't identify. A concentration of sesame oil or hashish? Or of aromatic resins from the gum trees in Djibouti, such as frankincense or myrrh? No one around him noticed it, except four seamen with red faces and Hawaiian shirts from some freighter docked over at the port. Their comments, in Dutch and German, were fortunately not understood.

The curving wall brought him to the meat market, a long covered platform with a table matching its length. Behind this counter, strong-armed men hacked away at hunks of goat, while a three-deep crush of women in three-tiered dresses argued and elbowed and pointed as they selected today's dinner. And no sign of the Old Arab's granddaughter. Emilie, she was called—an unlikely name but her own, given her by her half-French Somali father. (Her mother was of mixed origin, too: half-Arab, half-Sudanese. There were always complications in having four wives, as the Old Arab had found out, especially when he had spent earlier years in traveling southward from his native Lebanon, adding to his wives and his wealth.)

No Emilie today. No signal. No meeting at ten o'clock tonight. Tomorrow, he would have to visit the market again.

Behind him, an American said, "Jean! Just look at these black legs of lamb hung up behind the butchers. Coal black! Are they smoked or what? Look!"

Claudel turned his head and saw two women with faces showing horror and fascination. Quietly he said, "Not so loud, ladies. The butcher might throw a hatchet at us." And what the devil were two bewildered women doing here all by themselves? They had enough sense, at least, to clutch their handbags to their bosoms and not to wear short tight pants or low-cut blouses. Perhaps middle age had given them wisdom.

"Oh, thank goodness you speak English," said the older of the two. Her friend, Jean, was still astounded by the black legs of lamb. Suddenly her eyes stared in horror. "It moved—the black skin moved!" A butcher had slapped it with the side of his cleaver, leaving a wide streak of pale flesh.

"Flies," Claudel explained quickly, before any other exclamations would ring out. "Just large black flies." The two women stared in disbelief, but the butcher slapped again and again, ridding the meat of most of the flies before he heaved it off its hook and thumped it down on the table. Then he whacked away at the bone, cutting the leg into the right size for a muslin-draped customer. "And I don't think it's lamb. Goat, more likely." He looked around the market compound once more. No Emilie.

Jean said, "Irene, I think I'll leave. Which way?"

"Best follow the way you came in," Claudel said. "And watch out," he told Irene, who had nearly stepped on a piece of discarded offal, thrown to the dogs who roamed around like the half-naked children.

"At least," Irene said, looking at the children, "they don't suffer from malnutrition. They may be thin, but their stomachs aren't bloated." She took comfort from that, managed to regain some composure. "So very bewildering, so—so foreign!"

"Are you alone?" Incredible, thought Claudel: wandering into this market, two pleasant-faced women with faded blond hair under wide straw hats, the older one thin and fragile, the younger one (younger than he had first guessed) with a hesitant smile that softened her sharp features. Both of them were completely disoriented.

"We did have a sweet old Englishman along with us," Irene said, "but that awful smell—what *is* it?—discouraged him."

Claudel's eyes searched the compound once more. The rear exit ahead of him was closed, blocked by doleful-looking goats. Perhaps they sensed their fate if the butchers ran short of meat. Then, suddenly, he saw her—Emilie stepping carefully down from the chopping table, her white dress with its violent pink roses swirling around her. Briefly, she looked in his direction— she had probably been watching him ever since he arrived at the meat department—and then passed into a group of tall women, her own height now dwarfed.

"Oh, he's not here," Irene said, misinterpreting Claudel's glance. "He's waiting outside the market. We'll meet him at the camels."

If they hadn't moved off, Claudel thought. "I'll lead the way for you." He retraced his steps, the women following closely. Irene, the talkative one, was now mute, with her handkerchief covering nose and mouth. But delicately done, he was glad to see: no criticism made too obvious.

They passed the last of the vegetables, set out one by one. The women who had carried them here sat in the dust beside them in their shapeless dresses of drab gray or brown, their heads covered in coarse cotton. Tired faces, with nondescript features and resigned eyes, thinking of the few francs they had made or of the long journey back to their village. Claudel hurried his charges as much as possible, cutting short exclamations and questions. "The vegetables looked good," Irene was saying with some surprise, as they left the market. "But what *were* they?" Claudel, already regretting his offer to help, just shook his head, looked around for an elderly Englishman.

He wasn't near the camels. He was discovered after a five-minute search, and in some distress. He had lost his camera.

"Nipped off my arm by two small boys," he said indignantly. "And not one policeman around when you need him. Really!" He was a portly, florid-faced man with white hair showing under his rakish, if yellowed, Panama hat. "Anything you can do?" he demanded of Claudel.

"Not a thing," Claudel said cheerfully.

"Now where do we find that taxi?" Jean wanted to know. The heat was making her fretful.

"Wherever you left it."

"We left it somewhere along that broad street with trees," Irene said. "We asked him to wait—at least William did. He speaks French."

The Englishman cleared his throat. "I do my best," he admitted, "but the driver's French was worse than mine. However, he will be there. I paid him for the journey here, promised him more on our return."

"If he doesn't wait," Irene said in alarm, "how do we get back to the ship?" She burst into an explanation of their travels, partly around the world on a freighter; most comfortable, actually, a Dutch ship that could take twelve passengers. William had joined it at Singapore, they had boarded it at Sri Lanka, so much more interesting than traveling on a large cruise, didn't he think?

"Yes, yes," Claudel agreed hurriedly. "If you walk up that street just ahead, you will reach the boulevard with trees."

"There is an antique shop near here," Irene said. "I've got its address somewhere." She started searching in her outsize handbag.

William had other ideas. "After that, we could look in at that leather shop, the one we passed this morning. Attractive place."

This could go on forever, Claudel thought; am I supposed to find their antique and leather shops? "Pleasant journey!" he said with a parting nod, and left Irene searching for that address.

"A bit abrupt, wasn't he?" William said severely.

"Oh, dear!" said Irene. "We forgot to thank him."

It was eight minutes to ten when Claudel returned to the Café-Restaurant de l'Univers. There was no sign of Alexandre and his small green cab—the size and color of all the taxis in town; but no need to worry. "Around ten," Claudel had said, and for Alexandre that could mean eighteen minutes late rather than eight minutes early. He would park, as arranged, along the street, not immediately in front of the Universe, a name that Claudel enjoyed: it made him want to smile every time he heard it, and a good smile these days was hard to find. Apart from his sense of time, Alexandre (half-French, half-Issa) was someone to be trusted, almost as dependable as Aristophanes Vasilikis himself.

There was a message, a note discreetly folded, waiting for Claudel at Madame's desk. She was the Genoese wife of Aristophanes, a red-haired Italian whose ample figure dominated the scene whether it was the kitchen or the accounting office. Outside of them, her manner was genial and her expression amiable, contributing to Aristophanes' pleasure as well as his profits. Above all, she was uncurious about his guests or their business. "My little treasure," Aristophanes called her. Partly true: "little" was a peculiar adjective for five foot nine of solid flesh, all one hundred and sixty pounds of it. With a flash of yellowing teeth, a shake of henna-dyed curls, she sent Claudel on his way upstairs. Such a handsome young man, she thought, so pleasant in manner. Then she turned back to her desk and forgot about him as she corrected the office clerk's list of expenses. People came, people left, but bills went on forever.

It was a telephone message from Georges Duhamel, written down in Madame's fine italic script and uncertain French. *Will drop in for lunch one-thirty.* That was all. Meaning? Anything: it could be news, it could be a friendly visit. Yet, Duhamel wasn't the type to make contact openly unless it was urgent, and a meeting over a lunch table was less remarkable than two men talking on an empty stretch of beach. Claudel washed, changed his shirt, felt cooler—for the next half hour at least. Downstairs, Madame's head was bent over a ledger. Claudel gave a small wave to her briefly upraised face, passed through the deep verandah, ran lightly down its steps into the street.

Alexandre was there, standing beside his taxi, arguing with three people who didn't understand a word he was saying. And he certainly couldn't fathom what Irene's sweet old Englishman was telling him. "*Merde!*" Claudel said softly, and would have halted, turned, retreated, but Jean had seen him and was waving. So he kept on walking. Quick eyes she has, Claudel thought, and she isn't altogether surprised to see me.

"We want to hire this taxi," William announced, "to take us to the dock. Is that so difficult to understand?"

Claudel exchanged a glance with a much-ruffled-Alexandre, who prided himself on his French, and soothed his feelings with a kind word. "Thank you for waiting, Alexandre."

"You speak French?" Irene was amazed. "But aren't you English?"

"French is useful here, unless you know Arabic or Swahili. Didn't you go shopping?"

"Jean wanted to get back to the ship." Irene was the fretful one now. "And our cab didn't wait. So would you please tell this young man—"

"I engaged his taxi." It's always the way: he who helps, helps and helps. "Let me give you a lift. No bother. We'll be at the port in no time at all." At Alexandre's rate of driving, three miles could be covered in two minutes.

"Do you know it well?" William asked, and then covered his curiosity by adding. "Fantastic place. Ridiculous, though." He looked as if he were about to take the seat beside the driver—more space than being crammed into the back with two women, certainly much cooler—but Claudel forestalled him. Then his eyes bulged. "Look at that! Foreign Legion, aren't they?" He pointed to two athletic types crisply dressed in khaki, with flat white crowns on their visored caps. They were standing at ease beside a very clean jeep, also white-topped: quietly amused, seemingly impassive. "What nonsense!"

Claudel ignored the disparaging voice. "Where do we take you? What ship?"

"The *Spaarndam*," Jean said. She was relaxed and confident.

Irene was too busy pointing out the Café-Restaurant de l'Univers to pay attention to legionnaires. "Wasn't that the place where you said we'd have lunch—when we drove into town? Jean, you can't have forgotten. Stop the cab!" She spoke quickly to Claudel. "Please tell the driver to stop."

"No!" Jean was definite.

"We could eat and then do some shopping."

"I'm tired, and so are you."

"We've only been here two hours," Irene protested, looking behind her at a vanishing l'Univers.

"Quite enough," said William. "This place is a Turkish bath."

Claudel said, "All shops are closed until late afternoon." And that settled it.

Irene sighed and shook her head: no visit to a foreign country seemed complete without bargains to carry home as trophies.

William's well-worn Panama was off, his brow was mopped, as he shifted uncomfortably on the vinyl seat. "Ridiculous," he repeated as if to cue himself in to the observation he had been about to make when he was entering the taxi. He looked at the last of the town, abruptly ending, changing into a flat gray desert broken only by scrub. "I mean"—he leaned over to Claudel—"maintaining that port—all the money spent—all the enormous trouble. And for what? Why didn't the French let go of the whole place—town, port, everything—when Djibouti became independent?"

Is this, Claudel wondered, a sideways move to discover whether I am French or English? He didn't oblige William's curiosity. Instead of mustering a defense of the obvious—if Djibouti, left to itself, was taken over by a Communist regime as Aden and South Yemen had been, the entrance to the Red Sea would be locked, and what price free movement of shipping?—he merely said, "Haven't the faintest idea."

Irene said, "All these warships—it's madness, just asking for trouble."

Jean said, her voice soft and hesitant, "The Red Sea leads to Suez, doesn't it? I suppose if the Red Sea entrance was closed, the Suez Canal would be useless, wouldn't it?" She looked, ingenuous and appealing, at William.

"Ridiculous, though—all that money being spent," William maintained. "The French have better things to do than hang on to their empire. Say what you will," he told Claudel, "we English had the right idea with Aden. When you get out, stay out." Then, as he noted Claudel's boredom, "You aren't interested in politics, I see. Wise man. What business are you in?"

"I'm with a firm of advisers on construction abroad."

"Constructing what?"

"Hotels, mostly."

"Surely you don't plan a hotel *here*?"

"Our clients were considering the idea."

"Americans?" William was scornful.

"Not this time." Claudel was keeping his good humor without any show of effort. "I believe they are an English-German-Italian group." With relief he saw they were entering the port area.

There was an easy passage through the checkpoint: Alexandre was known and his passengers were accepted as tourists from the *Spaarndam*. But I slipped through there, Claudel thought worriedly; or did the duty officer recognize me from my visit three days ago? As Alexandre, at slackened speed, drove down the long dock past a Spanish freighter named *Juanita* to reach the *Spaarndam*. Claudel asked, "Is there a check as you board? Passports?"

Irene waved a card at him. "Just this. All signed by the captain and recognized by the authorities. We weren't allowed to take our passports on shore—there's a big trade, the captain said, in stolen passports." She glanced at William, couldn't help saying, "And he did warn us to take no photographs, either."

The allusion to his camera silenced William. He was the first to get out of the cab, his hat jammed down on his perspiring brow, the back of his shirt and trousers soaking wet, his bad temper increasing with the blinding heat that engulfed him.

"Where are the others?" Irene asked, pulling a damp skirt away from her hips as she looked up at a ship deserted of passengers.

"Where we should have stayed," William said. "In an air-conditioned cabin. Good-bye, sir. Thank you for the lift." Without waiting for Claudel's reply, he headed for the gangway.

Irene looked at some crew members who were disembarking, dressed for off-duty sightseeing. "I hope they remember we sail at midnight," she said. "Don't they mind the heat? Oh, Jean, hurry! The sooner we are indoors, the better."

"Not indoors. On board," Jean reminded her. "And the crew has worked hard—all night, all morning."

Irene ignored that, concentrated on her thanks to Claudel, exclaimed once more about the heat, and set out for the ship.

Jean's large handbag suddenly tilted as she stepped from the taxi. "Oh, dear," she said as its contents spilled over the hot asphalt. She knelt to pick them up. Claudel stooped, too, and was startled to see her brush a powder compact sideways, sending it under the cab.

At high speed, her voice low, she began speaking as he bent down to reach for a key ring. "Major Claudel—I received a warning last night by coded cable to pass on to you at the Café de l'Univers, where you are staying."

He had straightened up at her first words, then knelt to reach for a lipstick. "How did you learn that?" Who is she, and what?

"We intercepted a message sent from a business firm in Paris to The Hague." She was picking up a purse that had somehow burst open, gathering the coins as she spoke. "It concerned you. Paris requested full information about your presence here—was it Erik or was it shipments?"

He handed her the lipstick and the comb he had retrieved. Irene's voice called, "Jean! What on earth are you doing?"

"My bag upset. I can't find my powder."

Irene hesitated, looking back at the car in dismay. "Oh, Lord! You would! Forget it—you'll get sunstroke."

"It's the only compact I have." Jean's voice was cross, determined. She stood up along with Claudel, the two of them replacing the remaining items—wallet, mirror, landing and boarding card, traveler's checks, handkerchief—into her shoulder bag.

"It may have rolled under the taxi," Claudel called to Irene. "We'll find it." Irene continued on her way, as William paused almost at the top of the gangway to look and listen.

"He isn't English," Jean said, her head bent to search under the taxi. "Just imitates. A little too much, I think." She raised her voice to reach both Irene and William. "I see it! We'll have the taxi moved. Okay!"

She went on, lips scarcely moving, as Claudel caught Alexandre's attention. He had been leaning against his cab, arms folded, legs crossed, more interested in the unloading of crates from the *Juanita*. "He flew to Singapore from Bombay—hoped to contact Erik, probably." There was a brief smile as Claudel's eyes froze.

Alexandre, following Claudel's quiet instructions, had been having difficulty in starting the engine—enough delay to let her continue. "He made his millions out of greeting cards—was a Communist and one of Erik's early supporters in West Berlin. Lives in England now."

"His name?"

A small but determined shake of the head. "He's our business."

Our? "And who are you?"

The question was ignored. "When we were inside the market, he was meeting a man. Young. Dressed like an Arab. I saw them just after you led us out."

"Erik?"

"I wouldn't know. He's *your* business."

The engine had caught at last. The taxi edged forward.

"And Irene—are you two together?"

"Just another passenger—a schoolteacher—summer is the only time she has to travel. Been saving for this trip for years." She pointed to the small gilded box that was now exposed, and Claudel picked it up, dusted if off.

"And you?" he asked, dropping it into her bag.

"I write travel articles for magazines." Her voice was normal now. "Thank you, thank you so much."

"But who sent me the warning?"

"Friends. We sympathize. We may even join Interintell someday." She was moving away.

"That firm in Paris—whose?" he pleaded urgently.

"Klingfeld and Sons," she said over her shoulder and walked on.

Irene and William were out of sight. But William would be watching. So Claudel spoke a couple of words to Alexandre; they joked and shook their heads over the vagaries of women as they got into the taxi and drove back along the dock.

"Stop, at the entrance," Claudel said suddenly. "Just around the corner." And out of sight from the afterdeck of the good ship *Spaarndam*. "Wait there. About half an hour." His excuse for being at the port was nicely established. He might as well make use of it and see Georges Duhamel right away: there was urgent news to pass on about Erik.

Six

IF GEORGES DUHAMEL was surprised, he hid it well. Or perhaps his own excitement about the news he was about to give Claudel made other matters seem unimportant. He rose from his desk, which had several legal-size pages scattered over it. "Couldn't wait for lunch, could you? Just as well. I'd like you to see for yourself what is happening." He gathered the papers and clipped them onto a board. "Hope you had a good excuse for coming to the docks."

"Good enough. I gave three passengers from the *Spaarndam* a lift in Alexandre's cab back to the ship." And Alexandre was certainly describing them, right now, to his friends at the entrance to the pier. Alexandre's imitations were much enjoyed. Including one of me, Claudel thought wryly.

"Adequate," Duhamel conceded. "Now let's have a look at the *Juanita*'s cargo. Destinations: Ethiopia and Djibouti. Ethiopia's consignment consisted of twelve crates—they have already been moved to the railway depot. The freight superintendent, after some persuasion, authorized one of them to be opened. It was described in the manifest as containing typewriters. There were typewriters on top. That, my friend"—Duhamel's face, with its sorrowful dark eyes and long nose, looked sadly at Claudel—"was a bad moment for me. The second row, also typewriters. But the third row—well, it held some highly sensitive communication devices. American. We are checking now with Washington to find out if they are authorized for sale outside of its own military requirements. We"—and there was the Frenchman speaking—"haven't been allowed to buy them, even as America's friends."

"Any more rows in the crate?"

"A fourth one: typewriters."

"Neat. Any other crate examined?"

"The freight superintendent has authorized a full check. It is proceeding right now. Coming?" Duhamel's compact figure took three brisk steps toward the door. "We will have a firsthand view of the operation."

"One moment, Georges. Fill me in completely. Who sent these crates?"

"Didn't you guess? Why did I persuade—with some difficulty—the officer in charge to order a crate to be opened? Because, my dear Pierre, I recognized a name—a name you gave me." He held up the clipboard, riffled through the papers to the third one. "Twelve crates transshipped at Algiers on the *Juanita*, of Barcelona registry, from the initial shipment on a Liberian freighter out of New Orleans to Algiers. The shipping agent who handled this freight, from New Orleans to Algiers to Djibouti, is the representative of—yes, you guessed it!"

"Exports Consolidated," Claudel said, and took a deep breath. "But why the devil didn't you say so right away?"

Duhamel smiled. "Because it wasn't easy tracing all that in the last eighteen hours. I thought you ought to share some of the agony."

Now that Claudel looked closely at his friend, he could see a night without much sleep in the deep circles under Duhamel's eyes: always shaded, but today dark. "Pretty good work, Georges." We've got Brimmer, Claudel thought, we've got him.

"The *Juanita* is now unloading the four crates for Djibouti. Also shipped in the same way."

"Exports Consolidated again?"

"Again. It will be interesting to see what these crates contain. They are listed as office equipment: desk calculators, copying machines, typewriters. Of course"—Duhamel was thoughtful—"we do need these things in Djibouti: the Arab merchants are modernizing their business. And the consignment of crates is going to Asah, a regular dealer—so perhaps this shipment is quite legitimate."

"Asah?" The name tugged at a strand of memory. "Has he a son who trades in a small way—by dhow—called Husayn?"

"Yes. They are Afars, strong Muslims, sharp businessmen, but there is no question mark against Asah's name."

Until today, thought Claudel. And what about Husayn?

"You know him?" Duhamel's question was quick.

"Asah? No. I've met the son."

"He's more of a problem." Duhamel didn't expand that small statement. He went on. "About that other export house you mentioned—Klingfeld and

Sons—there is nothing from them on any current unloadings from the four cargo ships now docked here. But the freight superintendent tells me that Klingfeld does export office equipment; we've had several shipments from them in the past. It's a reliable firm, been in business for years. In fact, they supplied us with typewriters—and there's one of them!" He pointed to a machine on a small table near his desk. "So we can cancel out Klingfeld, I think.",

And I might be doing just that, Claudel reflected, if I hadn't heard that a message from Klingfeld's Paris office to The Hague had been intercepted. Now its meaning became not only clearer but threatening. Full information requested about Claudel's presence here: Erik or the shipment? "They may be involved. Office equipment is their specialty, you said. I've never heard of Exports Consolidated selling typewriters."

"Concealment of the Klingfeld name?" Duhamel shrugged. "Is that hard information, Pierre, or a guess?"

"A piece of information that might bolster a guess."

"A reliable informant?"

"I'm taking her on trust. But I think she's most reliable."

"She?"

"A professional, Georges," was all Claudel would say. And thinking of Jean, he led into the subject of Erik.

"Hasn't been seen." Duhamel was curt, slightly offended.

"He may be in Djibouti, though. Dressed as an Arab, talking outside the market with an Englishman, so-called, who is said to be a West German and one of Erik's early backers."

Duhamel recovered his usual sang-froid. "You *do* have your sources. Any that I can use?"

"Have you a list of the passengers on the *Spaarndam*? The Englishman is called William. William what?"

Duhamel found a sheet with the full complement of names on board the *Spaarndam*, ran his finger down the brief list of passengers. There was only one William. "William Haversfield." He looked up at Claudel, said with a shrug, "If you wanted him detained for using a false passport, sorry. He's a Dutch problem now. I think that I'll contact the captain of the ship."

"No. He isn't our business. So I was told. Most definitely. But I did need his name to add to details of his weight, height, eye color." That would help Interintell trace him back to his Berlin days, perhaps even lead to Erik if they made other contacts. Then another thought struck Claudel. "How many crew members are at liberty?"

"Day passes have been issued to eleven. Don't worry, Pierre. No one boards that ship without his pass being checked. If your Erik tries to slip in with a crowd of seamen, he won't get far"—the telephone rang and Duhamel picked up the receiver—"I can assure you," he told Claudel, and then began listening.

Claudel seized the chance to read the passenger list, upside down as it was on the desk. It was a trick he had long ago perfected. There were two Jeans. One was Barton from Boston; the other was Zinner from Brooklyn, New York. Which left him not much wiser, but you couldn't win all the time.

Duhamel's call was over. He repeated the report he had just received. A second crate for Ethiopia contained exactly what was stated on the manifest. But a third crate, on its bottom layer, had the latest equipment for long-range detonation of explosives. The entire consignment was being examined.

"Quite a scene at the railway depot," Claudel said. "What about the crates for Djibouti?"

"They are about to be opened. Let's go!"

Claudel hesitated.

"Don't you want to see what's inside them? Possibly nothing—as I said, the trader Asah is a reputable man. But the crates have to be opened; the name Exports Consolidated made sure of that. Come on, my friend."

"I don't think I should be seen—"

"There's no risk—for you. I didn't mention your name in connection with all this. Took the credit for myself in my usual modest way, said my information came from Algiers ten days ago. What more do you want, Pierre? You will simply be an old friend whom I brought along with me to see what's going on. The innocent bystander—you always were good at that." Duhamel clapped Claudel's shoulder, picked up his clipboard again, and Claudel's silent debate ended. Yes, he wanted to see the contents of these crates. Yes, it was necessary that he should see them if his report to Interintell wasn't to be based on something he had been told. But most of all, it was a very male reaction to a friend's remark: *no risk—for you.*

As they left, Claudel said, "Georges—take care for the next few days. There could be more danger in this than we think."

"Danger? You and I are used to that. Now let's talk about unimportant things, and relax."

They stepped into the bright burning sunshine, found refuge from it in the few minutes' drive to a mountain of cargo stacked on an empty dock. Duhamel was talking about cars—he was proud of his little white Renault that handled so neatly and behaved like something twice its price. "All in the maintenance," he was saying as they left it and found themselves faced by three Somali workmen and a gimlet-eyed Frenchman. One crate was already open. "It purrs along like a Mercedes," Duhamel concluded.

"Why not like a Citroën? Support French industries," Claudel said. "Of course, if we didn't, I'd choose a Jaguar."

"Uses too much petrol. Expensive, my friend."

The supervisor, eyes grimmer than ever at such a casual attitude on an occasion as serious as this, cleared his throat, said nothing, just pointed.

The top layer of the crate had been removed, a wooden shelf with typewriters in a neat row, each secure in its nest of Styrofoam. Typewriters definitely: their covers slit open showed carriages and keys. The crate's second layer was deep. It held large-sized boxes, each marked with authentic-looking labels, even with printed directions for the use and care of calculators. The boxes had also been slit. Inside, covered by a light packing of Styrofoam bubbles, were thin plastic envelopes showing the glint of metal. Not calculators. Weapons. Handguns, grenades, ammunition.

In the third and fourth layers of the crate, now ripped open, no longer carefully slit, there were M-16 rifles, automatic pistols, and enough ammunition to kill and maim hundreds.

Duhamel's face was white; the shadows under his eyes seemed to deepen. He spoke into his hand-size transceiver. To Claudel he said, "I'll wait here with the superintendent until the guards and other workmen arrive. Take my car to the entrance. I'll get a lift back." He looked at the crate, his lips tight, his jaw set.

Claudel said nothing. Duhamel wouldn't have heard him. He didn't even notice Claudel leaving in his little Renault, heading for the gate where Alexandre's taxi waited.

Trouble, thought Claudel, serious, deadly trouble . . . It was with an effort that he kept his talk with Alexandre away from politics in Djibouti, even produced several small jokes, and spent fifteen minutes looking at white herons grouped on a gray shore.

He left the cab near the Café-Restaurant de l'Univers. "Tonight," he told Alexandre, "I'll need you. Yes, double fare after dark. Around nine-thirty? And, Alexandre, be on time. *Please. No* later than nine-forty. I have an important engagement."

A meeting with a beautiful woman, Alexandre guessed. His smile was dazzling, a sudden burst of brilliant white.

"Wait for me until it's over. Perhaps an hour, or a little more."

So soon? wondered Alexandre. Europeans were strange. "There is no need to hurry. My brother will come to keep me company."

And will be handsomely rewarded, too, thought Claudel. Well, it's all on the expense account: insurance. Alexandre's brother was a policeman. "But not in uniform," he said quickly. No attracting of attention to a waiting taxi, thank you.

Alexandre looked disappointed. A police escort appealed to him, not only from the added status but also from safety. "Is it a quiet district where we wait?"

"Near the Old Arab's house. Tell no one, Alexandre."

"No one." The Old Arab arranged many things, even meetings with beautiful women. A wife of a high official? But one did not talk about the Old Arab's business. He did not like that. "I tell no one," Alexandre said, this time with complete truth.

Claudel left l'Univers one minute before nine-thirty. Its restaurant was beginning to function, its bar already crowded. Some able-bodied seamen, perhaps deciding that if they couldn't have a night on the town, they'd have the drinks they liked among people who talked in recognizable languages, were mixing with the Italians and French and their amiable women. Other hot and bone-weary seamen were about to enter, groups from various ships docked at the port. Outside, the taxis were already in line. What was a couple of hours spent in waiting when a bumper harvest was in sight?

Alexandre was on time, parked discreetly away from the crowd. His brother, in a loose white shirt, was his replica—neat-boned face, large eyes, a small mustache over a wide mouth, dark-skinned—but taller and even thinner. There was a flash of white teeth in greeting, and no word spoken.

The grave silence continued until Claudel gave directions. "Don't drive directly to the house. Let us take the road to the airport for ten minutes. Then come back through various streets." Alexandre's brother nodded his approval. The Frenchman was discreet. "And when we near the Old Arab's house, do not enter its lane. Park the car around the corner."

"The lane is ill-lighted," Alexandre's brother observed. He turned his head to look at Claudel's dark-blue shirt, long-sleeved; dark trousers, too. The Frenchman had come prepared for shadows, he decided, and said no more.

"But safe enough. If I need help, I'll yell," Claudel added lightly.

"Safe enough," Alexandre's brother agreed with some pride. "Only the cars are in danger." There was a plague of small-time thieves: an unattended car, even in daylight, could lose its radio and cassette player.

Was that why Alexandre wanted his brother along? wondered Claudel. No robbery possible when Alexandre was in that candy shop near the corner of street and lane, where a tantalizing variety of sweetmeats was for sale? We've all our own little plans, he thought, and laughed.

"It is," the off-duty policeman said in grave rebuttal to the laugh, "the most serious problem we have in Djibouti."

"Really?"

"Without a doubt." Alexandre's brother plunged into a series of statistics and examples, which brought them all the way to the Old Arab's lane.

It was a quiet street, narrow and short. The Old Arab's doorway was scarcely fifty meters away. All the houses seemed asleep, a delusion fostered by the blank plaster walls that were broken only occasionally by barred windows, one here, one on a floor above, built at random: the outside world, in Arab tradition, was to be ignored.

But once through an ornate wooden door, large enough for men on horseback to enter—another tradition remembered from another era—there was a paved courtyard with windows all around, and a stone staircase that led to the upper floor of the Old Arab's house. Instead of horses, there was now a car in the center of the yard. Claudel followed the venerable servant, black face looking even darker against his lengthy white shirt, who had opened the door before Claudel could even knock. Neither spoke. The man, quite impassive, led the way upstairs, gestured to him to wait at a low narrow door and disappeared inside. There were women's voices from other rooms; the smell of cooking and spices drifting up to the narrow balcony where Claudel stood, the sound of sad music from an Arab radio station. Apart from that evidence of life within the house, it was a cold, bleak place, dimly lighted by meager bulbs. But above the courtyard, in a square of ink-blue sky, there was a brilliance of stars to lift one's heart along with one's eyes.

The silent servant beckoned. He could enter. Claudel ducked his head to pass through the doorway into a small room; into another very small room; into a third where the Old Arab sat among rugs and cushions and soft lights. The formalities were brief, polite: your health, my health, a small cup of coffee served—and Claudel had to mask his astonishment—by a tall, thin beauty in a long, loose dress with chunks of gold forming necklace and bracelets. This couldn't be another wife, Claudel reflected as he praised the comfort and opulence around them—the Old Arab had outlived his allotted four. And a girl who wasn't even half Arab? Originally an Afar nomad, way back before city lights and city ways had brought her family to town. Poor little Emilie, he thought, once more an outcast, the quarterbreed granddaughter tolerated when the old man was completely widowed and needed a companion for his declining years. Declining? The eyes were shrewd and watchful, the hawk face ready to strike. Fortunately, he had taken a liking to Claudel last year. They were wary friends. Fortunately, too, he had liked Interintell's check discreetly deposited in his Cairo bank account.

The Old Arab waved a hand. The tall, thin beauty, as hard-eyed as ever, bowed and floated away. Once the door closed, he said, "Husayn is here. Shaaban, too."

"They came together?" Surprise mixed with doubt was in Claudel's voice.

There was a reassuring nod. "Husayn is now in the room from which you entered. Shaaban waits elsewhere. He will be brought to speak with you when Husayn leaves."

"With your permission," Claudel said, rising from the uncomfortable mass of cushions, and, with a small bow, left for Husayn. The Old Arab will hear everything we say, he reminded himself. There was a certain trick to the construction of some rich Arabs' houses: voices in an enclosed space could be heard, even a whisper, by anyone who stood in a certain corner of an adjacent room. The Old Arab was in that corner right now, Claudel was willing to bet; if not standing, then sitting.

Husayn's face was friendly even if its features were hard, thin, strongly pronounced. There was a welcome on his lips, but his eyes were uncertain. So were his replies to Claudel's questions. Yes, he had delivered coffee on his last voyage to Aden, and taken it right into one of the training camps. Yes, there were Europeans. Yes, one had escaped from India. Yes, there were some Cubans, too. No, he hadn't heard of any quarrel between two Cubans and the European from Bombay. (How did he know there were two of them? Claudel thought: I only asked about Cubans in general. And I never mentioned Bombay). Yes, the European had left camp. He was now dead. Yes, that was definite.

"Are you certain?" Claudel asked, his voice gentle and unchallenging. "Could the man not leave in a dhow? Sail to Africa? The distance is short."

Husayn agreed. The distance was short. But the man had not traveled it. The man was dead. So Husayn had heard. So everyone had said.

And so am I to believe. Claudel's face was expressionless. I've lost a good agent. Who doubled him? Or was it Asah, his father, who had influenced—commanded—him? Simple people had complex loyalties: complete obedience to the head of their family who was obedient to his sub-tribe, which in turn was obedient to the tribe; and the tribe itself was obedient to the main group which dominated all. The tight hierarchy of these Hamitic peoples was something hard to comprehend, and certainly difficult to deal with. Claudel pitied his friend Georges Duhamel. "One more thing, Husayn. When you visited the South Yemen camp, did you hear that some men there were of very different political beliefs? Men who were of two extremes: one to the right, the other to the left?"

There was visible relief on Husayn's tight face. What had he expected? A question about the weapons he had seen in the camp, or where did they come from? "To the right? To the left?"

He knows damn well what I meant. He's stalling. Afraid to give away his new political sympathies? "Do the men now in the camp all hold the same beliefs as the Cubans and the Yemenis?"

"Some keep apart when they eat and sleep. Very few. Three. No more."

"Thank you, Husayn." Claudel rose, signifying the end of the meeting, and gave a tactful handshake concealing a roll of Djibouti francs. It disappeared into Husayn's ankle-length shirt.

Husayn hesitated. "There was trouble at the port today."

"Oh?"

"None of the laborers have left the docks. That is strange."

So Husayn had heard no details about the actual opening of the crates, but he—and his family—had fears about the delayed delivery to Asah's warehouse. Did Asah's sub-tribe know of his dealings? Or was he acting alone, without their authority? Then who can be backing him? Someone he sees as powerful enough to protect him? Some nation with an eye on the port of Djibouti? Claudel's pulse heightened, but he kept his face disinterested. "Strange? They are working overtime perhaps. Is that unusual when many cargo ships arrive all at once?"

"Many cargo ships? You saw them?"

"I saw their seamen all over town today. Didn't you?"

"They make the Somalis work while they play."

"They unload, but they don't work on the docks. The Somalis wouldn't give up that job. Would they?" Claudel asked gently and added, "Good night, Husayn." Good night and good-bye, he thought as he watched Husayn bow and stalk out of the room. No mention of seeing me again, not even the polite formula for a safe journey home.

Three minutes passed. Then Shaaban arrived—strongly built, short in height, his dark flat-featured face beaming with pleasure. He could only report what he had seen and heard around Aden's harbor. There was talk of a big search for a man who had murdered and stolen. But the man had been too clever. He had slipped away from soldiers and police. Yes, he had escaped. In a dhow. But no one would even whisper the name of its owner, no one wanted to know where it was sailing.

"The man is alive?" Claudel asked.

"The man is alive."

Claudel studied the wide-set eyes that looked so innocent. Shaaban knew who had brought Erik out of Aden, but Claudel wouldn't embarrass him with a direct question. "Perhaps he sailed to Djibouti."

"Perhaps."

And that, Claudel thought, is as much as Shaaban tells. Yes, he knows; but he is afraid of the man who smuggled Erik into Djibouti. Or is this another case of tribal loyalty?

"To bring him here is a dangerous matter," Claudel said, and by the way Shaaban nodded, his dark eyes large and anxious, Claudel knew that it could also be dangerous for Shaaban if he had to answer any more questions. The man's relief was transparent as Claudel thanked him with the usual handshake; his good wishes for a safe journey were long-winded but sincere. Next time, he promised, there would be more news to report.

One long minute passed after Shaaban had left. Claudel glanced at his watch: almost eleven o'clock. Would he be summoned to the Old Arab's room for some polite questioning as usual, or had the old boy heard enough from his listening corner? Suddenly, remembering Shaaban's fear—and the man had courage enough—Claudel drew a sharp breath. Had the Old Arab helped Erik? He was most certainly no Communist; a devout Muslim, his hatred for the atheist Yemenis was now intense. Intense enough to let him hide anyone who was hunted by them? If your enemy is my enemy, then we are friends. . . .

Another long minute. The Old Arab won't see me again tonight, Claudel decided. Now he is caught in a predicament: I am hunting Erik, who escaped from the Yemenis, a man he has promised to help. How? With shelter and clothes, obviously. Money, possibly. False papers? To explain to the old man that Erik's hatred of religion was only equaled by his loathing for all capitalists, Arabs included, would be futile. Erik, true to form, would now be the most devout believer of all Muslims.

The door from the small outer room opened. It was a sad-faced Emilie who greeted him with stiff politeness. "My grandfather has sent me with his good wishes for a safe return home. He has retired for the night. Let me lead you downstairs."

Claudel nodded, followed her onto the balcony, said lightly, "No more jokes, Emilie? No tricks like this morning at the market? You let me search—"

She touched his arm, drew him quickly past the array of doors, women's voices, plaintive music. She began to whisper, her plain little face with its thick features looking up at him pleadingly. "Please—you must leave Djibouti. There is danger. A talk of kidnapping. My grandfather will have nothing to do with it. But he remains silent."

He stared at her.

She drew apart, led the way downstairs. Her voice was raised to normal once more. "I saw you at the market. But you were so fascinated by two old ladies—"

"Not so old. Just lost." A kidnapping? My God . . .

"Lost?" Laughter sparkled in her eyes.

"Very lost. They didn't understand a word of French."

"Of course you had to help them!"

"Who else was there?" Kidnapped how? he wondered.

"Where did they come from?"

"America—by their voices." Perhaps drugged and forced onto a dhow. . .

"You didn't ask?"

"We never got around to that." Taken to Yemen? Questioned? That would be no bloody joke.

"Will you see them again?"

"No. They aren't my type."

She laughed out loud, almost danced across the paved floor of the courtyard. The old servant emerged from behind a pillar, silently opened the heavy door just enough for Claudel to slip through.

He halted on the threshold. "Please give my thanks to your grandfather. I wish him happiness, a long life." And I hope the old bastard wishes as much for me—if it doesn't inconvenience him.

Emilie's face had lost its humor, her voice was almost inaudible. "Remember," she said. Careful, her eyes warned; be careful.

He nodded, kissed her wrist, stepped into the night.

Seven

In the lane, the houses seemed deeper into sleep. Their lights were out. The scattering of windows had become black patches behind iron bars. There was one lamp fixed to a plaster wall halfway to the street, aiming a bright circle on the unpaved ground. Outside of that solitary beam, deep shadows took over. But the distance before Claudel was short: only two doors to pass before he reached the corner.

He set a brisk pace, his eyes watching the first door on the right-hand side of the lane. Suddenly, he felt a warning, just a hint of the sickly sweet odor he remembered so vividly from the marketplace. His eyes switched to his left, to an indentation in the wall of a house, a shallow recess with a door half open, hidden by the shadows as he had approached it. A dark, thin figure leaped out, stick upraised, aiming at Claudel's head.

Claudel whirled around, caught the man's taut wrist, partly diverted the blow's strength and direction. It fell on his shoulder, a moment of intense pain, but he held on to the wrist, twisting it back, tried to loosen the man's grasp on the heavy stick. The door opposite had opened; a second man slipped into the street, a third . . . Claudel saw the glint of a knife and yelled.

For a moment, the three men stood motionless as the yell shattered the dead silence, reverberated between house wall and house wall. Claudel heard a wrist crack, seized the stick as it fell from the man's limp hand, aimed a blow that sent the thin figure reeling to the ground. The other two came on, two knives now shining. He backed against a wall, tightened his grip on the stick as he faced the two men, watched the glinting blades. One circled around him, avoiding the stick; the other lunged, gashing Claudel's left arm as he fended off the knife from his body.

Running feet. A voice shouting. The knives paused, as the two men turned to glance toward the street. A brief second, scarcely time to draw a breath, and they were gone, vanishing into the doorway opposite, with the third man following at a stumbling run. The door clanged shut as Alexandre reached it, a heavy lock turned.

"You are hurt?" he asked, coming over to Claudel.

"Blood—"

"Could have been worse. Where's your brother?"

"He had to leave." Alexandre looked around him nervously. "No use trying to follow these men. That is a spice warehouse they entered; it has other exits."

Strange, thought Claudel, now that the danger is over, Alexandre's fear of this lane is returning. Completely forgotten when he raced down here to help me. "Let's get out of here," he said, handing over the stick so that he could grasp the slit in his forearm, hold the wound together, staunch the flow of blood. His shoulder hurt like hell.

"They wanted your money?" Alexandre asked as they walked quickly toward the street. Some people had gathered at the corner. Three curious boys had followed Alexandre halfway down the lane.

My life, more like it, thought Claudel. "I guess so."

"Robbers . . . My brother would have arrested them. He will be sorry he missed all this."

"Too bad," Claudel said.

Alexandre looked at him sharply. "There was a call for all police officers to report for duty. An emergency." Then the defensive note left his voice. "It's something big. A special raid. Very important. The military will send units, too." A raid on Asah's warehouse—a search for previous deliveries of weapons that were being hoarded. For what?

"Come on," he urged Alexandre, who was besieged by questions from the curious. They pushed their way through the gathering crowd, the three small boys at their heels telling everyone how they had routed the robbers. Claudel looked at Alexandre's taxi, standing unguarded. "I tell you what— if your radio has been stolen, I'll buy you a new one."

Claudel entered l'Univers by its service door, reached his room by a rear staircase. He was bathing his arm when Aristophanes entered. "Alexandre told me," he said, his alarm growing. "Nasty, nasty," he pronounced as he looked at the wound. "It needs stitches."

"Haven't time." There's a report to be prepared for transmission to London, and I've to encode it first. Not that ciphers aren't easily broken by the new wonder machines, but a code keeps messages safe from the casual eavesdroppers—that new breed of radio buffs who listen to the world's private business with a twist on the dial and hope to make the headlines. Not with my report, thank you.

"The hospital—"

"No. I'll have Interintell's doctors look at it once I get home." No strange hospital for me; no quick injections, no truth serum.

"That may be too late."

"This wasn't any ordinary mugging, Ari. They meant to knock me over the head, kidnap me. When that failed, they tried to shut me up. Permanently."

"Kill you?"

"They weren't playing games." Claudel paused. "Ari, I need your help. Telephone Georges Duhamel. It's urgent. Ask if I can meet him at his office—within the hour."

Aristophanes nodded, his eyes on the blood-soaked towel around Claudel's arm. "I'll send Sophia—she knows about wounds," he said hurriedly as he left.

First, decided Claudel, I'll write out the message, keeping it short but clear. After that I encode it and take it to Duhamel. No one else handles it, and I'll stand beside him. Six items in all. He found his memo pad and pencil near the phone, began noting.

(1) Erik—alive, seen in town, has friends.

(2) Exports Consolidated—U.S. military supplies (illegal) for Ethiopia, and consignment of U.S. weapons (false declaration) to Djibouti; all crates shipped on S.S. *Juanita* (Barcelona origin) from Algiers.

(3) Klingfeld & Sons—sent message (intercepted) to their informant in The Hague, asking further details of my mission here.

(4) Klingfeld, again—may have engineered an attack on me tonight. (Arm sliced, but not to worry.)

(5) The agent Husayn—can no longer be trusted.

(6) Duhamel—Port Security, co-operating fully, help invaluable.

That about covered it, Claudel thought. The arm had to be mentioned (all wounds and severe illnesses had to be reported—Bob Renwick insisted on that), but no need to include the shoulder: not dislocated, not broken, thank God; just a heavy bruise, a tendon made painful for a week or two. No need, either, to name William, the sweet old Englishman, not until Claudel could report in detail when he was back in London and explain the little he had guessed about Jean. He owed her that delay.

The door opened. He tore off the page of notes and thrust it into his pocket. Madame entered, every henna-red curl in place, with a bottle of peroxide, antiseptic bandages, and a small first-aid box. "All we have," she said, and set to work. "This needs stitches."

"Later."

She shook her head. "There is so much infection—"

"I know, I know. I have visited the tropics before. Many times."

Madame raised a penciled eyebrow but asked no questions. "So much violence tonight! It comes all at once. A quiet week, and then nothing but trouble. You are lucky, monsieur. You are not dead like that poor sailor, all his clothes taken, left lying in a back street dressed like an Arab. Some Arab! Blue-eyed and face blistered by the sun."

"Navy or merchant seaman?"

"A sailor," she repeated. "From the *Spaarndam*. But that took an hour to find out. They say he was in the bar with the others. Then he left with someone. So many were here, no one could remember when he left. Or who was with him." She finished cleaning the wound, began bandaging the arm. "Hold still, Monsieur Claudel! Perhaps he went out to meet a woman. Men take such chances. But stabbed to death—so silently! No one heard even one small cry for help."

"The other seamen from the *Spaarndam*?"

"Never knew a thing. They left to join their ship before the poor boy was identified."

"Were they together?"

"Why, no—in small groups, some singly." She looked up at him in surprise. What made him interested in sailors who drank so much that they could hardly walk to a taxi?

"When was the body discovered?"

Her surprise increased. "About eleven o'clock."

"Near here?"

"A short distance away. Thank the Lord it wasn't found on our doorstep." She tucked the ends of the bandage neatly in place, said, "You ought to be a lawyer in court, Monsieur Claudel. So many questions."

"Sorry. And thank you. Perhaps you should be a nurse. You have gentle hands."

That won her completely. She even blushed under the circles of rouge on her plump cheeks.

"But you have," he insisted. "One last question, if I may. You said the man's clothes had been taken. Does that mean everything he owned?"

"Everything. Why else was it so hard to identify him?"

Stripped completely. Papers that he might have carried for safety in a belt under his shirt, his boarding pass—Claudel drew a deep breath. "A thorough job."

"A cruel one. So many evil people in the world!" She gathered up the last of her equipment. "I'll have brandy sent up to you, Monsieur Claudel. But the hospital would be the place—"

"Thank you, no. I have some things to do."

Both thin-penciled eyebrows lifted. "At this time of night?" The question had been forced out of her. She didn't wait for a reply, perhaps knew from her experience with Aristophanes that none would be given. With tact and a sympathetic look, she left.

Yes, Claudel verified from his watch, it was almost twelve-thirty. The *Spaarndam* would have sailed. With Erik? In the right clothes he could have slipped on board, mixing with a group of drunks who were hardly capable of noticing anything beyond their own footing. And the officer in charge? Like those at the entrance to the dock, he would be counting heads and passes. And the fake Englishman would be waiting to hide and help the stowaway. I may, thought Claudel, have to rephrase my report.

Angry and frustrated, he reached for the telephone and asked to be connected with the duty officer at the dock where the *Spaarndam* had been berthed. There was a tedious wait, of course, but at last he had his information. The *Spaarndam* had sailed, at midnight—no delay.

"Any of the crew left on shore?" He turned quickly as the door opened, but it was Aristophanes with a bottle of brandy and two glasses.

None. Those at liberty had all returned. Earliest arrivals at twenty-three fifteen; the last man at twenty-three fifty.

"Cutting it fine," joked Claudel and thanked the unknown voice. So the correct numbers were accounted for: between quarter past eleven and ten minutes to twelve, all crew members had gone on board. Including a dead man.

Erik . . . "God damn him to everlasting hell," Claudel said, and faced Aristophanes.

A moment for diplomacy, thought Aristophanes, and offered a glass of brandy to Claudel. "You sound more like yourself, my friend. Drink up!"

Hardly the right advice for brandy, thought Claudel, but he did. Aristophanes poured again, along with a glass for himself. Now what deserves two free brandies? Certainly not one small wound on my arm. "So you couldn't reach Duhamel. Or you did, and he couldn't see me tonight. Right?" He cursed softly, steadily.

Aristophanes waited. "He is dead. Duhamel is dead."

There was a long silence. "How?"

"His car went out of control. It crashed, exploded."

"Where? When?"

"Tonight. As he was leaving the port. He had been working late, so his assistant told me, and he was on his way to town—a special meeting."

An official meeting, guessed Claudel. If the raid on Asah's warehouse had uncovered a cache of weapons, then there would be one hell of a discussion. His thoughts broke off, and for a moment his brain seemed to have stopped functioning. He gathered his wits. "His car went out of control?" Georges was an excellent driver, and he babied that little Renault. "There was nothing wrong with it this morning. I drove it."

"I think," Aristophanes said slowly, "you should return to France. Tomorrow."

"Were there witnesses?"

"Yes."

"Which came first—the explosion or the crash?"

Aristophanes studied his glass, dropped his role as innkeeper. "They could have come together. The wheel could have controlled an explosive device. At the first sharp turn—and one is necessary when leaving the docks—there would be an explosion." He finished his drink. "Yes, my friend, you take the first plane to Paris. There is a flight leaving tomorrow."

"First, I must send an urgent message to London. May I use your transmitter, Ari?"

"Very urgent?"

"More urgent than ever."

"Perhaps send it to Athens? London may be too far."

"I'll try for London."

"I'll show you how to—"

"I have to encode it."

"Of course."

"Not because of you, Ari," Claudel said quickly. "But there are unfriendly ears. You understand?"

"Only too well. When will you be ready to send your report?"

"Give me an hour." He'd need all of that. The arm was throbbing, that damned shoulder hurt more than he had expected, and his mind was stunned.

"An hour," Aristophanes said as he left the room.

Claudel drew the scrap of paper from his pocket, lifted the pencil, and began to make the changes.

The first entry now became: Erik—was in Djibouti, most possibly has stowed away on S.S. *Spaarndam* sailing toward Suez, aided by early sympathizer (Berlin origin; false British passport in name William Haversfield) traveling as passenger same ship. Means of escape from Djibouti: murder.

The sixth entry was expanded. Duhamel—Port Security, co-operated fully, help invaluable, killed tonight in suspicious circumstances.

Claudel began to encode the report for Gilman in London. (Bob Renwick would hear the details in New York.) At the sixth entry, he paused. His eyes blurred. He closed them, passed his hand over his brow. What about Duhamel's wife? She was coming out here in November. In time for Christmas, Georges had said.

Claudel picked up the pencil, finished his task. He added a postscript: Leaving tomorrow.

Eight

"IT'S ALWAYS FANTASTIC," Nina said as she unpacked their traveling clock and set it back five hours before placing it on a night table.

"What is?" Renwick was studying the phone numbers he had copied down from Brimmer's Minus List.

"We left London at one and we were in New York by three." Fantastic, too, that she had managed to pack and close the flat in two days. Not bad for a beginner, she told herself. Bob had managed all these meetings at Merriman's, all the phone calls, all the clearing of his desk in his office, as if he had no more to worry about than keeping a dinner engagement. "How long do we stay at the Stafford?" It was a pleasant hotel, and Ronald Gilman, who used it on his visits to Manhattan, had been able to get them a room. "I mean, do I unpack completely or just for tonight?"

"That depends. Let me put in some phone calls first." It was now four-thirty, he noted. He could catch the Senator and the two businessmen before they left their offices. If not there, then he'd try their home addresses. The Minus List, with deadly efficiency, held both sets of numbers.

"I'll go downstairs and have a cup of coffee."

"No. I'd rather you stay here, honey. Will you? I won't be too long." He kissed her. "Keep that smile in place. And the door locked." Then he left.

There was a public phone in the lobby. Renwick, weighed down with a load of change, began his calls. The Senator was in Alaska on an ecological study. One businessman was fishing in Nova Scotia but would be home on Tuesday. The other had taken his family for a week in Wyoming.

Duty done, thought Renwick as he ended the three calls. Now he put in a fourth call, but this time it was to a car rental agency. The weekend was his. Relax, he told himself as he returned to their room. There never was any use worrying about something over which he had no control, and three characters wandering through the wilds of Alaska, Nova Scotia, Wyoming were certainly out of reach. Not just his but Brimmer's, thank God.

Nina was in the shower, her dress unpacked and ready for this evening—

optimist that she was. "Best of news," he called to her. "We can enjoy the Fourth like everyone else. Keep the water running—I'll have a shower, too."

Nina looked around the bathroom door, her hair bound in a towel. "Couldn't hear you, darling."

He stripped off the last of his clothes. "I said I'll have a shower, too."

"Your telephone calls—"

"All over."

"And everything is all right?"

"Very much all right," he told her, catching her around the waist. "Tonight, the town. Tomorrow, ocean breezes."

All worry banished, she thought, and she hugged him.

He pulled away the towel from her head, let the loose flow of golden hair drop over her shoulders.

"I'm in the middle of my shower," she protested as she kissed him.

"Are you?" he teased. "We'll turn off the water. There's a lot of time to put in before dinner."

Next morning, they drove to the far end of Long Island. The rented car performed well, and an early start from New York helped them avoid much of the holiday traffic on the expressways. "Miles of white beaches," he promised Nina, "and four days of sun. You'll be a beautiful bronze before Monday arrives."

"Or a peeling pink. But how on earth did you get a room at an inn for July Fourth weekend?"

"Friends," Renwick said with a broad smile. He hadn't felt as good as this in months. Four days with Nina and all problems pushed aside until they were back in New York. Communication with Interintell would be easy—again through a friend, Chet Danford, partner in the law firm to which Frank Cooper had belonged. Cooper was gone, killed two years ago, and could never be replaced, but Danford had stepped into that gap and was now a staunch ally of Interintell. He had bought Cooper's place on Sixty-first Street in New York, made use of it when he needed a town house, and—above all—kept Cooper's top-floor room secure. It contained a neat set of communication devices that had always astonished Renwick. (Old Frank had been a radio enthusiast since his days with the OSS when his life in Nazi-occupied territory had depended on it.)

"Friends?" Nina was asking. Bob seemed to know an amazing number of people in America—more than she did.

"One friend in particular. He has also offered us his house in New York. On Sixty-first Street. It's convenient." And safe, Renwick thought as he looked at Nina.

She was wide-eyed with delight. "But how marvelous."

"Just for a week or so. Until we take off for Washington. That all depends, really, on how my arrangements go." Such as the return of three marked men from their July vacations. Such as a visit to the New York office of Exports Consolidated.

"I ought to phone Father and warn him we'll—"

"And have your stepmother start arranging parties for us? No, thank you,

darling. Call him when we reach Washington. Time enough." And let's hope
Francis O'Connell and his Beryl will be miles away on the Maryland shore.
Then, feeling he had been too rough, he added, "I have guilt about not
seeing my own people. But that will come later—before we go back to
London." And by that time the danger may be over—it will damn well have
to be. He glanced at Nina. Horrify her by telling her the truth? Nina, my
love, my name is on a death list. All Renwicks are best avoided; all
O'Connells, too, until we get a certain matter straightened out. "That's an
attractive spot." He pointed to a windmill with a shingled house attached,
a garden with roses on a white picket fence, large maples and chestnut trees,
and a bright-green lawn.

"It's the third house today I've wanted to buy." This part of the world
was new to her. Even New York would be mostly strange: a pass-through
visit was all she had so far paid it. "Could we ever, do you think?"

"On second thoughts, too much grass cutting, too much leaf raking in
the fall."

"My wandering husband. Travel, travel—"

"Listen to that! From the girl I had to chase from Istanbul to Bombay
before she'd even kiss me." He slowed down for the mess of traffic in East
Hampton's Main Street, cars parked every inch of the way, trucks of all sizes
mixing with the slow stream of automobiles as thick as clotted cream.

Nina looked around her in dismay. "Don't tell me they've let the highway run right through their village."

"Good-bye New England, welcome New York's clutter." Including modern construction, new buildings for old. He shook his head as some real
inhabitants—you could tell them by their normal dress and stunned expressions—tried to cross the street, far outnumbered by all the brief pants and
yards of bare skin that pressed around them. "We've another village to
pass"—and another Main Street gone the way of all flesh—"and then let's
hope there are still some farms and woodland around. Can't be shopping
centers everywhere."

Twenty minutes later, once they cut away from the highway and took
the old road that edged the ocean, they could leave the procession of cars
speeding toward the happy hunting ground for shark and swordfish at
Montauk, the last tip of the Island's long finger that pointed at Europe. At
Portugal, actually. "I always forget how far south New York lies from London. If it weren't for the Gulf Stream, the English Channel could have
Labrador's climate."

"What, no playing fields at Eton? No swimming, no tennis, no strawber-
ries and cream?" Then Nina became serious. "Nature's mercies—we don't
think of them much, just take them for granted. Which means we're
ungrateful. Then Nature blows her top, just to remind us. A mountain
explodes or the earth cracks open or—Bob, is this hurricane territory?" She
looked out at the Atlantic with its perpetual breakers, high-crested even on
this hot summer day of blue sky and little breeze, that sent white surf crashing
onto the beach below the dunes.

"Later in the year. Don't worry, my pet. We won't waken tomorrow with
tons of salt water dumped on us and winds of a hundred and twenty-five
miles an hour behind them." He pointed to the small house that stood just

ahead of them, built on top of the dunes. Well beyond it, above some thin but determined trees, he could see the spreading roofs of a hotel. "Yes, this must be it." He drew the car up at the side of the cottage. "Chet Danford said the bed is made up, food is in the refrigerator, and the world is ours. No, to be quite honest, I added that last bit."

Nina stared at the cottage, stared at him, said, "But I thought—"

"Did I ever say we were going to an inn?" he reminded her and kissed her astonished mouth. "And no more thinking for the next four days, honey."

"No work at all? No worries, no—"

"Not even a phone call." He kissed her again, long and hard. "Surprised?"

"By everything," she said happily, her arms around him. "You're always surprising me." From the very beginning—when he had rushed her away from Washington to be married. To London, she had thought, until they were in a plane that was heading for Zurich. And from Zurich to Geneva, where they had first met. "Just an old romantic under this hard-boiled exterior," he had joked. But there was truth in that jest. Her arms tightened, holding him close.

"Why are we kissing in this damned machine as if we hadn't a place of our own? Come on, Nina." He was out of the car, his arm around her waist as she joined him.

"The luggage?"

"Later. No hurry for that."

She looked at the long stretch of white sand below the dunes, at the breaking waves so clean and cool. She glanced at Bob, wondering if he had read her thoughts. Of course he had. "Later," she agreed, "we'll swim later." And after that, lunch; then sleep and—"Oh, it's wonderful!" Four days together, no office, no meetings . . . "I love it."

"Be it ever so humble," he said as the front door stuck, its wood swollen with hot weather and sea air, and he had to shoulder it before they could enter. Inside, it was neat and sparkling clean, a simple place for plain living and high thinking: basic wicker furniture and packed bookshelves. But this is one weekend, he thought, when there will be high living and no thinking. For a moment there came flickering into his mind the memory of a list—nine names marked for death. He caught Nina into a tight embrace, holding her close. The memory vanished.

The weekend went as they had planned, except for the weather. Torrents of rain on the Fourth of July. "No fireworks," Nina said when they woke up to the sound of heavy drops sweeping over the roof. No picnic on the shore, watching the distant display of Catherine wheels and rockets bursting into the night sky from a village beach. Renwick took one look at the surge of dark sea and lowered gray clouds. "Back to bed—it's the warmest place."

"It's four o'clock—we've slept for hours. Aren't you hungry?"

"Aren't you?" he asked, and held out his arms.

She laughed and came away from the window.

On Monday, they drove back to New York. Not even the snaggled traffic and the waiting for mile-long jams to end could dampen Nina's high spirits. She would have plenty to do, she told him: museums and shops and so many things to see, even two of her old college friends who had come to live in New York.

"No, not yet, Nina."

Her euphoria vanished. Back to the real-world, she thought, and Bob is already deep into it.

"Wait a little, will you? Plenty of time to see them later," he promised.

"Are we here incognito?"

"That's one way of describing it."

"When will I see you? In the evenings?"

"As much as possible," he said vaguely and truthfully.

"We'll be sleeping together, won't we?" she asked in alarm.

"That I can promise you," he said. "And this business in New York may be over quite soon." How to approach the two businessmen, the government contractors who had become suspicious of Mitchell Brimmer and his Exports Consolidated? Phone them, arrange an appointment—yes, that was the first step. But after their experience with Brimmer claiming CIA backing, how would they react to a stranger saying he represented Interintell? Probably wouldn't believe him, wouldn't even listen to a warning about a death list with their names on it. Not until they had checked and double-checked Renwick, and that could take time. As for the Senator—he might believe, just might; but not quickly enough, perhaps.

Nina was saying, "Is this the Queensborough Bridge?"

"This is it. Takes us right where we are going. But first, I think we'd better drop the car at its garage. You stay there with the luggage while I find a cab and leave it around the corner from the garage. Then we'll walk to it. Okay, honey?"

"Really necessary?" She was startled, not so much by the maneuver itself but by what it proved to her: there was danger for Bob in this visit to New York. "Is there trouble ahead?"

"Might be," was all he said. "And I don't want it to reach out and touch you."

"Me?" She laughed that off. "Bob"—she was thoughtful now, blue eyes direct and serious, watching every small expression on his face—"why don't you recruit me? Let me join you."

He shook his head.

"I could help. I know it. Bob—I'm not joking."

"Nor am I, honey. No. And no, again."

"Don't you have women in Interintell?"

He looked at her, almost passed a red traffic light. "Where did you hear that name?"

From Pierre, she thought. Pierre Claudel would tell her almost anything that wasn't a deep and dark secret—if she pleaded with him long enough. And she had. "Partly because," she said, trying to keep to some truth at least, "I saw that report from Holland—it was in the London *Times*—"

"Oh, that!" Yes, there had been a mention of Interintell cooperating with West German authorities and the prevention of a terror-bombing in Greece. How international can one get? he thought. The report had come from

Holland, unauthorized but true. That was typically Vroom, now the head of a section of Dutch Intelligence at The Hague and one of Interintell's members. Johan Vroom, a good man in many ways but one who liked to talk about successes once a case was closed. But then, Renwick reflected, I've talked to Nina, too, about cases closed and filed away, only she doesn't go dropping hints to reporters. "Here we are," he said with some relief, swinging the car into the Fifty-sixth Street garage.

"You know, darling, you may keep too many secrets—"

"Not enough, I'm thinking." He reached across the seat and kissed her nose. She never had any answer ready for that.

He went searching for a taxi, his subconscious mind at work. And, as usual, if he just waited trustingly, it came up with the answer. Or at least one that might work. Certainly the surest and quickest way to contact a senator and two government contractors would be through the FBI. His friends there, Bill Wilson and Joe Neill, wouldn't have forgotten him; twenty months ago they had worked with Interintell and saved a president from being blown sky-high. They had been promoted for that: Joe to New York, Bill to Los Angeles. Not a case of passing the buck: he'd go with Joe to talk with the three men wherever that took him. Yes, they might begin to listen then. And keep their mouths shut. If they needed Brimmer nailed and Exports Consolidated out of all business, including assassination, they had better keep their mouths shut. But tight. Myself included, he thought as he caught sight of Nina waiting for him. My dear and beautiful Nina, don't you know how much I want to share everything?

The housekeeping couple at Cooper's one-time residence on Sixty-first Street were quiet and discreet. Breakfast could be brought up on a tray, a sandwich at lunchtime could be provided, but—

"We'll have dinner out," Renwick said quickly and sent them back obviously relieved to their ground-floor apartment. The house was in good order, and Nina explored it from the second floor up. "The top room used to be a study," he told her. "It's possibly shut tight." But the key was in the lock. For cleaning purposes? He only hoped the electronic equipment was safely stored away. Chet Danford had seen to that: a metal cabinet held all the components, with a door securely padlocked. Now Renwick could understand the small key that had come by special messenger in a thick sealed envelope to the Stafford Hotel on Wednesday night.

"Guns," Nina said in surprise, as she stared at their rack. "Mr. Danford's?"

"No. I think they belonged to the previous owner, a friend of his."

"Old, aren't they?"

Most were antiques, but Renwick's eye noted two usable models. He examined the bookcases and then the outsize desk. Paper and pens provided in the drawers.

"Well," said Nina, looking around her with pleasure, "you'll have a study at last, darling, even if it's only for a few days. Don't you like it?" she asked quickly. He was standing so still, a look of sadness on his face.

"Just a memory . . . My last visit here was when Frank Cooper was alive." He took her hand and led her out of the room. "Now what about washing up and unpacking? I'll make some phone calls, and then we'll go out to dinner. How's that?"

"Wonderful. I'll unpack for you and let you start phoning." She gave him a sideways glance, a small mischievous look. "You didn't bring *your* gun with you, did you?"

He stopped, looked at her. "I left it in Gilman's safekeeping. But how the devil did you—"

"I saw it. Hanging on our bedroom chair with your shirt draped over it. Last Monday, when you worked late and came in tired and worried and the Gilmans and Pierre were there."

Tired and careless and too eager to slip into bed. "Damn," he said softly. "Quick eyes, you have."

"I wish you didn't need to carry it around. It worries me, Bob."

"I don't carry it around. Only when there might be trouble."

"Have you had to use it?"

"I've never killed anyone, Nina. Just discouraged some."

"That worries me, too. You wouldn't be discouraging them if you weren't in danger. Oh, Bob—"

He put his arms around her, comforted her. "One hell of a life when you chose to marry me," he said, trying to bring a smile back to her lips.

"It's one hell of a beautiful life." And the smile had returned.

He went up to the study again and made his call to Joe Neill at the FBI office. A meeting in the Drake Room on Fifty-sixth Street was arranged for tomorrow at noon. A suitable place, cool and dark.

Then he unlocked the cabinet. Yes, all the needed equipment was there, and in good order. He examined it thoroughly, cut in the power to make certain the gear was operative. He was tempted to transmit. But there was a five-hour difference between New York and London. He would contact Gilman early tomorrow morning and set up their schedule for receiving and sending. He padlocked the cabinet and turned to have a look at the covered Telex machine standing near one of the new computer typewriters. These were Danford's additions. Lawyers certainly knew how to make themselves comfortable. He examined the gun rack, too: one of the pistols was his favorite type of Biretta, the other a neat twenty-two; both were clean. Chet Danford, in spite of sixty years and white hair, was as much a perfectionist as the weekend hostess who not only provided the usual soap and towels in your bathroom but toothpaste and new brushes, too.

All set at this end, he thought as he went downstairs. And there was nothing illegal about the communication system; Danford, lawyer that he was, would have registered anything that needed permission for his own private use. And if Renwick used them? His reports, sent and received, would not cause the United States any harm. On the contrary. Very much on the contrary. So let bureaucratic quibbles take care of themselves, he decided. He entered the living room that ran the length of the second floor, with windows at the front looking out at the trees along Sixty-first Street; at the back, two more trees in a small paved garden.

Nina was standing at the rear windows, looking wistfully down at the tubs of bright petunias and pink geraniums. "Out of bounds, I'm afraid." The garden belonged to the ground floor, no doubt. She sighed as she turned away. "Wouldn't it be wonderful—" She interrupted that sentence. Yes, it would be wonderful to have a house like this. But impossible on Bob's salary: it was strictly on the military level. "Wonderful to have so much space," she finished lamely. "How do I look?" She had bathed and perfumed, brushed her hair until it gleamed, applied just enough make-up to accentuate her eyes and lips, and was ready to step out for dinner in her ridiculous high-heeled sandals and soft silk dress.

"Ravishable. Come on, my would-be Mata Hari, let me show you off to the town."

"Darling, I was being serious about Interintell. And you don't have Mata Hari types. I know that. But surely—"

"Nina"—his voice was strained—"four years ago, in Vienna, there was a girl working with me. I recruited her. And she was killed. On a simple assignment."

"Killed?"

"Shot. She was trying to protect someone. She took the bullet meant for him."

"Were you there?"

"No," he said abruptly. "But since then I never recruit any women. Certainly never you, my love. Come on, darling, let's find some place to eat."

Her hand touched his cheek. "I'll never worry you again by bringing up—"

"Subject closed." He pulled her hand to his lips, kissed its palm. "Now, where do we go? French food, Italian, Greek, or a steakhouse? They're all around."

Discussing restaurants, they reached the front door. A key was hooked onto the wall. Renwick lifted it, tried it in the front-door lock, and pocketed it.

"I never thought of that," Nina said in wonder. But then, *it seems I never think of a lot of things. Shot . . . trying to protect someone. And Bob still feels responsible for her death.* She reached up and kissed his cheek. He looked at her in surprise. "I love you," she told him.

Arm in arm, they set off toward Lexington Avenue, just another handsome couple completing their holiday weekend.

Nine

GILMAN BEAT RENWICK to the punch. At six o'clock next morning, New York time, his call came by regular telephone from London. "Sorry to wake you so bright and early. All well? Settled in nicely?"

"Couldn't be better." Renwick kept his voice low.

"I'll be hearing from you?"

"As soon as possible. Good-bye for now."

"'Bye."

Renwick pulled on his dressing gown, left Nina sleeping undisturbed, found the padlock key, and ran upstairs, two steps at a time. Inside the top-floor study, he locked its door and then opened the cabinet. Now, he thought, as he got the dial set and made contact with Gilman's office at Merriman's, now for some real conversation. They would disguise names in a voice code that he had suggested before he left London. After all, the KGB listening post in New York was as alert as their interception unit in Washington.

Gilman's voice came through clearly. "We've just had a letter from Pete."

Letter meant a report. *Pete* was Pierre Claudel. "How is he? Enjoying himself?"

"Fantastic holiday—lots to see and do. I'll mail his letter on to you, let you read it for yourself."

Mail meant a coded message sent by transmitter. *Holiday* was Claudel's assignment in Djibouti. "I look forward to that. Any talk of Bright Eyes?" Renwick asked.

Bright Eyes was, of course, Erik. "Bright Eyes was passing through. They didn't manage to meet, not this time. Pete fell ill."

"Serious?"

"A nasty cut on his arm. Needs attention, I think. I've told him he'd be better at home with his own doctors."

Home was Interintell's offices in London. "So the holiday is over?"

"Just cut short. He intends to continue it elsewhere. I'll drop round to see him. By the way, some specimens of the Artful Dodger's work were on exhibition—Pete attended the grand opening."

The *Artful Dodger* was Renwick's choice of name for Mitchell Brimmer. "Glad Pete managed to see it." Illegal arms shipped to Djibouti . . . Ironic, he thought. We sent Claudel hunting Erik, and he found Exports Consolidated instead. "Impressive?"

"Significant. Confirms what your friend Warrior told you."

Warrior, Alvin Moore, that soldier of doubtful fortune. "Don't forget to send me Pete's letter. I'd like to keep in touch."

"I'm just about to mail it, right now."

What about Gilman's efforts with the Europeans on Brimmer's Minus List? "By the way, how are your five clients taking your advice? Or haven't you persuaded them yet about their future difficulties?"

"Not an easy job. I did make tentative suggestions to two of them, but I eased off when I felt they weren't receptive."

"Perhaps we had better talk with their respective insurance companies— get some reassurances about coverage for their requirements. In fact, that's what I plan to do here."

"Which company is that?"

The FBI, chum. Renwick said, "Federal Insurance."

"That's an idea. Keep me posted. Phone me at the office. I'll be here any day around three o'clock—just after I get back from lunch."

Subtract an hour, as pre-arranged, and Renwick would be at his transceiver at nine each morning, New York time, to talk with Gilman, courtesy of Telstar. "Okay with me."

"Over and out," Gilman said with a laugh. The phrase always amused him.

It was a cheerful note on which to end. Claudel's report must have held some pleasant surprises as well as the bad news. His arm—what had happened there? An accident? And Erik—elusive as ever, but at least he had been pinpointed in Djibouti. Come on, come on, Renwick urged his radio: the report is all coded and ready to send; give me the signal, dammit.

Two minutes later, it came.

It was in a code he had used before, but he was taking no risk of error. He went downstairs to the bedroom, found the page of ciphers which he had inserted into the copy of Frost's poems lying in his suitcase.

Nina was still asleep, head turned on the pillow, her hair—silken gold, he thought—falling loosely over slender neck and bare shoulders. Gently, he pulled the sheet to partly cover the lithe, tanned body. She stretched and sighed, fell more deeply into sleep with a last flicker of long, dark eyelashes. He left as quietly as he had entered.

Up in the top-floor room, he set to work. The report was startling. Claudel had really produced. But he shouldn't have been there alone. Yet, of the four other Arabic-speaking Interintell agents who could have passed as Frenchmen, two were in Chad, two in Mauretania.

Renwick pushed back his chair from the desk and concentrated on the changes that would now have to be made in his own plans. With the opening of those crates on a Djibouti dock, the whole perspective had been altered. Klingfeld was the important one, the one in command; Brimmer and his Exports Consolidated were secondary—used and manipulated by Klingfeld. But secondary or not, Brimmer had to be dealt with, and soon.

The Djibouti report had been sent early on Tuesday morning—just after the action there on Monday night. With time changes helping London, the report had arrived at Merriman's on Monday evening. Today, Tuesday morning in New York, it was in Renwick's hands. Even Brimmer, alerted to danger by Klingfeld, who in turn had been alerted by an informant in Djibouti, could not have received the warning any earlier than this. Renwick could only hope that Klingfeld didn't trust any informer to have direct contact with its headquarters: not likely, thanks to Klingfeld's obsession with anonymity. That could slow up the news from Djibouti reaching Exports Consolidated, a delay of a few hours possibly—or perhaps a day, with luck? Not more, certainly.

The French were now on the trail of Brimmer. No doubt about that. But by the time they had enlisted the help of the FBI to visit and search the offices of Exports Consolidated, what would they find? Just a set of legitimate business records. Brimmer would have destroyed his secret accounting of illegal dealings, and—with his precious Plus List, false passport, supply of ready cash—be on his way to Brazil.

You'd better make sure of those three pages of illegal transactions, Renwick told himself as he cleared the desk. Claudel's report and his own decoded version were torn up and burned in the metal wastebasket, their ashes flushed down the toilet bowl of the room's adjoining bathroom. All equipment, along with his page of ciphers, was locked behind the cabinet's strong doors. He gave one last check: everything secure, shipshape and Bristol fashion. The caretaking couple would find nothing to fault when they came up to sweep and dust.

Half past eight. He shaved and showered, was dressed before the breakfast tray arrived at the prescribed nine o'clock.

Nina, still dazed with so much sleep, barely roused herself to ask, "Are you going out? So early?"

"Some people to see. I'll be home before dinner."

He drank orange juice and black coffee, anchored them with a slice of toast. With a kiss and a hug and another kiss, he left Nina at her first mouthful of croissant.

At this hour, Sixty-first Street was only half astir, shaded from the sun coming over the East River by the small trees spaced at even distances along its sidewalks. Nearer Lexington Avenue, the shops that had invaded the row of red sandstone town houses were beginning to open. The offices downtown? Not until ten o'clock for the upper echelons. He would have time to walk to the building near Fifty-third Street where the firm Exports Consolidated was headquartered.

Lorna . . . Al Moore's girl, Brimmer's most trusted and very private secretary. It had been no problem for Interintell to discover her full name and particulars before Renwick had left London. He had insisted on it. Margaret Lorna Upwood of Beekman Terrace, a comfortable and expensive address, and merely a few blocks from her place of employment. Originally he had planned to visit her in her apartment tomorrow. But now speed was necessary. He only hoped she would be promptly at her desk, the place fairly quiet, routine just beginning for the day.

He reached the large block of offices, at least eighty firms doing business within this hunk of concrete and glass. The air-conditioned lobby was impressive, a good imitation of marble on its walls and floors, with giant green plants dotted around. He paused at the directory exhibited near a desk where a brown-uniformed guard sat, engrossed in a newspaper. A second guard stopped him as he started toward the elevators, pointed back to the desk. "The tenth floor—offices of Exports Consolidated," Renwick said, and hoped that would be sufficient. But no such luck.

The man at the desk laid aside the newspaper. "Have you an appointment?"

"With Mrs. Upwood."

"One moment." Middle-aged and overweight, he went slowly through the usual motions: telephone picked up; is Mrs. Upwood expecting anyone? A wait, then a reply. The guard looked at Renwick. "Your name?"

Renwick left his study of an inflamed mural, abstract patches of red and violent orange. "Al Moore."

"Mr. Al Moore," the guard reported to the office upstairs, nodded, said to Renwick, "Second bank of elevators to your left." He picked up his newspaper, went on reading about the baseball strike.

On the tenth floor, there were more potted plants, another frenzied mural (wouldn't like to delve into that guy's subconscious, thought Renwick), and a young receptionist. "Mrs. Upwood," he told her, and followed a pointing finger into one of the corridors. There were several open rooms with a drift of voices discussing the holiday weekend; and at last, in pride of place, dominating the end of the corridor were three doors, one narrow, two imposing, and all closed. There was a brass plate on one of them: MR. MITCHELL BRIMMER. The other had a neat name painted in gold: M. L. UPWOOD. The narrow door, beyond Upwood's, proclaimed its inferior status with no name at all.

He knocked, braced himself for any unexpected appearance of Brimmer in his most private secretary's office (I'm here to sell the newest in desk computers, Renwick reminded himself), and entered.

It was a scene of order, meticulous in arrangement, neutral in color: gray carpet, gray tweed curtains, a pale-gray wallpaper with darker roses climbing ceilingward in exact columns. A typewriter and a copying machine were on gray metal stands; a gray filing cabinet. No ornaments, no photographs, no plants. The one light-hearted note was in the gold frame of a painting—a misted river scene—hanging in the center of one wall. (Concealing a safe? There was none in view. Rather obvious, thought Renwick.) Two small neat chairs, chrome and leather, completed the room along with a small neat desk—a closed blotter, a pencil holder, a telephone on its dark-gray surface. Behind it, commanding the doorway, sat a slender woman in a black-and-white silk suit who had tried, quite successfully, to lop ten years from her thirty-five. Smooth white skin, fluffy auburn hair, a tip-tilted nose above vivid red lips, a general feeling of vagueness in a smile that never quite appeared, never vanished either. Just the helpless-looking type to bring out Al Moore's protective instincts. But he had never noticed her eyes in a moment such as this: as gray and hard as any filing cabinet.

Renwick selected a chair in front of the desk, drew it even nearer, and sat down. "May I?" At least they could talk without raising their voices.

"Mr. Moore?" She sat motionless, face expressionless, her hands folded over the leather blotter.

"Sorry about that, but it's a legitimate use of the name. I wouldn't be here if it were not for Alvin Moore."

Her eyes appraised him. "He sent you?"

"Indirectly. My name is Renwick."

There was a brief moment of astonishment but enough to reassure Renwick that no recognizable photograph of him was in circulation. In that case, he could face Brimmer if necessary.

He said, "I've some news—for your ears only." He pointed to the wall that separated them from Brimmer. "In? Or out?"

She hesitated, perhaps wondering which answer would be to her advantage.

"We've no time to waste. Is he in?"

"Out."

"For how long?"

"Until later today—he has been in Maine with his children for a week's vacation."

Renwick relaxed. "Has any message yet arrived from Klingfeld?"

Her face was unreadable. She shook her head. Her hands tightened.

"You would have seen it?"

"Of course." She paused. "What kind of message? Or don't you know?"

"I know."

"Well—what is it?"

"First, I'd like copies of three pages of Brimmer's illegal transactions." Then, as she remained silent, her eyes blankly innocent, he added, "Al called you from London, told you we needed these three pages as hard evidence. Didn't he?"

"Yes."

"You've photocopied them, haven't you? If not, I'll wait here until you do. Come on, Lorna, you're wasting time, and you haven't much of it left."

That startled her. "Why haven't I—"

"You haven't," he said grimly.

She rose, went over to the filing cabinet, selected a thick folder marked *Receipts for Office Expenditures*. From the middle of its numerous pages she extracted three. "I was going to mail these to you in London," she said diffidently as she handed them to Renwick.

"I also suggested a sample of Brimmer's profits—the ones he doesn't declare to Internal Revenue."

"I haven't had time to make a copy of that."

She doesn't intend to, he thought. Because she also hasn't paid taxes on excess earnings? No IRS investigators descending on this office until she has left and is beyond their reach?

"I'll mail it next week," she said as she turned away to replace the folder in the cabinet. Unlocked, Renwick noted. Clever girl: Brimmer would never look in a moribund file of simple expenses. The safe behind the painting was of more likely interest to anyone searching this office. And that safe, he was willing to bet, would contain nothing dangerous like the pages he held in his hand. They were authentic, all right. A quick scan down their entries shocked even him. She came back to the desk, studied him as he read.

"Next week," he said as he folded the three pages and slipped them into an inside pocket, "you will be with Al."

"No! I don't leave until—" She tightened her lips as if to keep any other revelation from slipping out. She eyed him warily. "Why should I be with Al next week?"

"Because Brimmer's luck has run out. The message from Klingfeld will give him the bad news."

Her hands, folded once more on the leather blotter, suddenly spread rigid. "How bad?"

"The crates shipped by Exports Consolidated to Djibouti were opened on the dock. By the French."

She must have known the contents of the crates, for she asked for no details, no reason why a search by the French spelled complete disaster. Now she was too preoccupied—with her own plans for escape, Renwick guessed—even to answer him.

"So," he went on, "Brimmer's day is over. All he can do, when he gets

Klingfeld's message, is to skip the country. But unless you leave ahead of him, you'll be in trouble. Deep trouble."

"How?" she challenged.

"If he finds that his little black book with that Plus List is missing . . ." Renwick shrugged, didn't need to finish his prediction.

The prospect didn't seem to alarm her.

"You think you can just walk off with it tucked into your handbag? But you're the first suspect—the only one: Brimmer and you shared its secrets. You and Al will be marked. Hunted down."

"By whom? By you? Brimmer can't—not now."

"By Klingfeld. The man in control there must know about Brimmer's Plus List. He may even have contributed some names of his own. He has been using Brimmer as cover, hasn't he? Why not in illicit payments, too?"

The idea disturbed her. Renwick pressed on. "That man in charge of Klingfeld and Sons has a long reach. In Djibouti, he had one man murdered—a French security officer—and another man attacked; two men who could possibly link him with the arms that Exports Consolidated sold."

"He arranged the sales," she said indignantly.

"He finds buyers abroad for Brimmer's exports—is that it?" A market made to order. . . "A name, Lorna. Give me his name."

She hesitated. "Would Interintell search for him? Find him?"

"Find him? That's the business we're in. He's arranging sales of arms to terrorists. He's providing instructors for these weapons—with Brimmer recruiting them as well as supplying the military and technological equipment. Brimmer must be making a couple of million dollars a year. Or more, Lorna?" *And you,* he thought, *have had your nice little share of it.*

She dropped her eyes. "It wasn't always like this," she said defensively, as if to excuse her own complicity. "Once, we—"

"Do you want to be rid of this man or don't you?"

Her voice lowered almost to a whisper. "Klaus. He ends his Telex messages with the name Klaus. That's all I know."

"Telex? Then the messages are in code."

"Only Mitch—Mr. Brimmer—knows how to read it. Even the name is coded. I wouldn't have heard it except that Mitch let it drop one day when he was angry. Klaus had sent a message, some suggestions that Mitch didn't like."

"But he followed them."

"There was no choice left." She sighed. "How much time have I got? A few days?"

"A few hours. There will be a Telex for Brimmer by the time he gets back here."

She opened the leather blotter and lifted a sheet of thin paper. "Then we had better destroy that message. I found it waiting on the Telex in Mitch's office this morning. No one else has seen it. I was here before anyone."

"Anyone? Are you sure?" The message was in no code he could recognize, but the key to it—part of the key at least—could be found in the name Klaus if that *was* the signature used. *At least, we do have a name.* Renwick drew a deep breath, folded the sheet carefully.

"Except for the supply-room clerk and an office boy," she replied. "What are you doing with that?" She pointed to the Telex, now disappearing into Renwick's pocket. "Destroy it!"

"Why not you?"

She looked most innocent. "How can I? I know nothing about it."

He could imagine the indignant protests if she were questioned: never saw it, you can search my room, I didn't destroy it, it must have been someone else on this floor. Just a girl who liked to have one truth in her story to bolster her confidence and make others believe in her sincerity. Renwick shook his head in amusement, rose to his feet.

"I said destroy it."

"Don't worry. I'll destroy it." When it had served its purpose: Interintell's deciphering machines would soon rip its secrets apart. "But I would worry, if I were you, about getting the hell out."

"I'm safe enough, for a few days at least. No Telex!" Then she added, "The FBI won't appear until they've gone through all the procedures to get a search warrant. And the French—well, they can't invade the office to arrest Mitch Brimmer."

"What about Klaus? One of his agents could have been inserted here—just keeping an eye on Brimmer's staff."

That was a possibility that had escaped her smart little mind. She stared at him.

"Has anyone come to work here since Klingfeld and Sons joined forces with Exports Consolidated?"

Her face whitened. "The clerk for the supply room."

"Where is that?"

She looked at the wall where the painting was displayed. "Next office—a small room," she said faintly.

"Keep talking," Renwick said and moved to the door. "Talk!" he told her as he opened it and left.

A man, young, with a windblown hair style and heavy glasses, a clipboard under one arm, a pencil stuck behind his ear, had just come out of the supply room. He was a friendly type who gave a nod and a "Hi, there!" as he paused to light a cigarette. Renwick had his handkerchief out and stopped a sudden sneeze, his face hidden as the man's lighter flicked. And failed to catch. And flicked again. By that time, Renwick had passed him. The young man walked on. "Hi, there, yourself," said Renwick as he entered the supply room.

It was cramped in floor space, its walls lined with deep shelving on which were stacked masses of envelopes, paper, every kind of replacement for office work from boxes of rubber bands and clips to a couple of spare typewriters. His eyes searched the dividing wall between this room and Lorna's. Here, the shelves had rows of filing boxes drawn up like soldiers on parade. And then he noticed the step-ladder, abandoned quickly, left in a precarious tilt against a column of boxes. Quickly, he scanned that column; the neighboring one, too. And *there* was something—a box well above his reach that broke the rigid pattern, retreated half an inch from the line-up. Replaced too hurriedly?

He pulled the ladder into position, climbed two-thirds of its height to stand on eye level with the filing box. It was of cardboard, not so light as it looked but easily pulled out by the leather tongue on its spine. Placing it on the top step of the ladder, he leaned forward to look through a hole drilled neatly into the wall. Judging from where he stood, the peephole must lie just above the painting next door.

He had a limited view of Lorna, sitting at her desk, sufficiently recovered from her paralysis to speak into a Dictaphone. He could hear nothing. He pulled out the next box; there was no mark of any listening device on the wall behind it. But this one was lighter in weight, much lighter. He replaced it exactly, opened the first box. Inside, fixed in position by a leather band—no slipping, no rattling when the box was lifted—was a cup-shaped item with a small earphone attached by a tube. An imitation stethoscope. It worked on the same principle, too. With the rim of its cup pressed against the wall, the earphone gave Renwick the clear sound of Lorna's dictation. He listened to only three words before everything was being replaced in its proper place and he could leave.

He opened Lorna's door, locked it behind him. She looked up at him, switched off the Dictaphone.

"Get out," he told her. "Leave now. As soon as you can, get out of New York. He could partly see us, and he certainly could hear us once he got his listening device working."

Her eyes showed fear. "Leave now? But there's no plane until this evening."

"Then get lost in New York until your flight leaves."

"He really saw us through that wall?" She could scarcely believe it.

Renwick walked over to the painting. It had been centered, logically enough, in a column of gray roses. They were shaded, lifelike except in color. Leaves sprayed out from their stalks, all carefully shaded, too, but darker than the flowers. One leaf seemed almost black, a deep shadow nestling so innocently among the intertwining foliage. That could be it, he thought, and pulled the picture to swing open on its hinges. The gilded frame with its antique curves no longer distracted the eye. The blackened leaf was definitely a hole. He pointed to it, then closed the picture over the safe. He heard Lorna's gasp. He chose that vulnerable moment to say, casually, "If you're heading for Europe, you'd better start packing."

"Yes, yes." She rose, distracted. "I never looked up when I opened that safe."

"No one does." One looked at a safe, not above it.

She reached for the telephone, told the receptionist, "No calls, no visitors. I'm going to see my doctor—a bad migraine. I'll be back here tomorrow." She replaced the receiver, opened a drawer, began pulling out its contents, jamming them into her shoulder bag. "You don't have to wait. I'll be out of here in ten minutes." Like her words, her movements were rapid. She brushed past Renwick, pulled the painting wide, and opened the safe. She reached for a neat stack of dollar bills. "What's delaying you?" Her tone was brusque. She had recovered.

"Curiosity. I'd have thought you would have made a beeline for Brimmer's safe. Or," he added, "have you already taken that little book with its Plus List?"

"It's secure. Beyond anyone's reach."

"Risky. What if he had opened his safe and found it missing?"

"A small black diary is easy to substitute. Two ninety-five in any stationery store." She closed the safe, then the picture.

"But inside"—Renwick persisted if only to hear her confirm his guess—"blank pages? A complete giveaway."

"Not so blank." She was much amused.

"I see. Brilliant. Names and dates and amounts of money—no relation to the real thing, of course." How long had she been preparing for this escape? The diary—and that was another detail for an estimate of its size—must have taken several weeks of careful imitation.

"Of course," she said mockingly, as she added the dollar bills to a zipped pocket in her handbag. "But good enough for any glance inside." She began filling a briefcase with a few folders from the filing cabinet, selecting them with care.

Beyond anyone's reach . . . So Brimmer's Plus List was not anywhere in her apartment but some place far from New York where she could collect it without fear of discovery. Some place, also, where she'd find more money: the dollars from the safe would pay her fare to Europe, would keep her for a week or two. On the run, no one risked leaving a trail with traveler's checks or a charge card: it was cash, nicely anonymous cash, all the way.

She closed the briefcase. "For God's sake, why don't you leave? You've scared me enough for one morning. What's keeping you?"

"A last piece of advice. I would avoid Switzerland. Klingfeld and Sons have offices in Geneva."

"Thank you for your concern, but Geneva wouldn't attract me." She was condescending, quite certain she had defeated him.

"Zurich could be safer. I hear it is a good banking town, too." That ended her assurance. "When you see Al Moore, give him a kind word from me." He will need it, poor guy.

"I'll do that. If I see him." She opened the door. Her voice sharpened. "Do I go first? Or you?"

"Ladies always first." He stood aside.

"Don't follow me!"

Renwick shook his head. But others might, he thought.

Should he warn her: another word of advice? The windblown-hair boy must have had time to contact a backup—if he had one. "Lorna—"

But she had left. Handbag strapped over her shoulder, briefcase in hand, pleated skirt swinging above excellent legs, three-inch heels clacking briskly on the tiled floor, she marched along the corridor, didn't look back.

Renwick followed slowly, gave her time to take the elevator before he passed the reception desk. He was still troubled by her last phrase about Al Moore. *If I see him.* Not when; if. Moore had served his purpose, so now . . . ? The money she intended to screw out of the men on Brimmer's Plus List would go twice as far if she were alone. Money . . . she had grown accustomed to its taste. There were two curses in life: money and politics. But no one—except the hermit in his cave—could live without them.

He stepped into a crowded elevator. No one edged near him; no one paid him any attention. He relaxed. But the sooner he emptied the inside pocket of his jacket, the better. For him as well as for those four pieces of paper.

Ten

B<small>Y THE TIME</small> Renwick reached the lobby, stepped into a whirl of people eddying around the elevators, Lorna Upwood had vanished. Almost half past eleven, he noted; he would be on time for his noon appointment with Joe Neill—Park Avenue and the Drake Hotel were only three blocks away. It would be a relief to talk with someone who was honest, straightforward, and with no avarice, either. How much did he make—twenty-five thousand a year? Everything was out of whack: Joe was worth more than any rock-and-roll singer or movie star in terms of the future of this country. But who thought much about the future? Me me me only thought about now now now. Renwick shook off the effects of his talk with Lorna Upwood and concentrated on reaching the entrance to this enormous building. The desk and its uniformed guard were just ahead. And there, too, was the supply-room clerk.

The man was alone, standing apart from the stream of people, watching. He had seen Renwick. He was either a fool or ill-trained: he wasn't even trying to melt into the background. At this hour the lobby was far from empty, yet this gas-head couldn't be missed, with his windblown hair and heavy glasses, posted as he was near the desk. Posted? A warning bell sent off its small alarm inside Renwick's head.

Quickly, he side-stepped behind two businessmen, ignored a friendly wave and a cheerful "Hi, there!" And where was the fellow's backup, ready to tail Renwick once identification was made? Renwick didn't wait to see. He turned on his heel, joined three lawyers arguing about torts on their way to the elevators, and broke into a short sprint to reach a closing door before it shut tight. He got out at the second floor, used the fire-exit staircase to lead him all the way down to a vast underground garage.

He had just managed it, but barely; no one could have had time to follow. This interest in him was to be expected. Inside his securely buttoned jacket there were four documents for which Mr. Klaus of Klingfeld & Sons would willingly murder. The clerk—and not such an idiot, Renwick admitted wryly—had seen him receive them from Lorna Upwood, had heard talk about illegal transactions and Telex messages in code. But the man hadn't stayed to hear a discussion about Brimmer's Plus List or Lorna's admission that she had taken it. Or, thank God, to hear Renwick leading her into the subject of Switzerland.

Plenty of problems, he thought as he made his way through row after row of cars—must have been hundreds of them parked here: the building was almost a small city in itself—but the immediate problem was a clean exit from this garage. Far ahead he could see a sloping ramp that led up to a wide mouth gaping into a busy street. He headed toward it. Waste no time, he told himself.

At the foot of the ramp's slope, a private ambulance was drawn close to a side wall. Door left open, waiting. But no one guarding it. Renwick halted, stepped instinctively behind a blue Chevrolet. A garage attendant had noted him, came forward at a leisurely pace.

"I was to meet my wife here," Renwick told him and forestalled any question. "But I don't see any sign of her—or her car."

"What make?"

"A Chevy. Blue. Like this one."

"Plenty of them around." The attendant was young, his voice not unfriendly. The glum look on his face was probably normal.

"An accident?" Renwick nodded toward the ambulance.

"Just an emergency in the lobby upstairs. Some guy had a heart attack. They'll be bringing him out any minute. They'd better. Can't have them parked here for long."

"Why not in the street?" Renwick was sympathetic.

"Couldn't find space." The attendant shrugged. "So what can you do? Turn away an ambulance?" He stared at the ramp where two men came hurrying down from the street. "What—no heart attack? Perhaps the guy's dead." He didn't seem to find it remarkable that the men wore no white coats, carried no stretcher. Or perhaps it had been explained to him and the other attendants, still engrossed in a heated discussion near the ramp: no stretcher required, the driver would take the ambulance to the building's entrance, the sick man could be helped to walk that short distance from the lobby.

Now the driver climbed into his seat, the other man about to enter. He paused—heavily built, round-faced, with a genial look and thick dark hair—and gave a friendly wave to the three garage attendants. "False alarm," he called as they approached him.

"Wouldn't you know?" the young man beside Renwick said in disgust, and left to get his share of the tip now being handed out.

Yet another figure had appeared, waiting at the head of the ramp until the ambulance would stop and pick him up. He no longer wore glasses, but he hadn't changed his hair style or seersucker jacket. Renwick bent to tie his shoelace, straightened up when the ambulance's motor merged with the traffic outside.

So the supply-room clerk had a mini-transceiver among his other little gadgets. When had he called for support? As soon as he saw me enter Lorna Upwood's office at ten o'clock? Or perhaps five minutes later, when he had started listening in? The ambulance was stolen temporarily, no doubt. It wasn't intended for Lorna Upwood—they must know her apartment in Beekman Terrace, could pick her up any time. So you're the candidate, he told himself as he walked toward the street level, leaving behind an argument resumed: who was to blame—owners or baseball players?

He hailed a taxi, directed it to First Avenue and Sixty-third Street. There, he walked three blocks back to Sixtieth Street, making sure Klaus's long arm was no longer reaching after him. Another cab took him west to Park Avenue. He left it one street away from the Drake. A small evasion, but he had little time for anything more elaborate. He was already ten minutes late for Joe Neill.

Neill was making his glass of beer last and beginning to worry. Renwick was always punctual. Then he saw him enter and quietly raised a hand to attract Renwick's attention to his table against the wall. One signal was all it took. Renwick sat down to face him. The room was dark and cool, the tables half empty at this hour. By one o'clock the place would be packed.

"Traffic heavy?" Neill asked, noticing Renwick's tight face.

"Complicated." Renwick ordered an ice-cold beer, suggested a couple of quick chef's salads, and let Neill make light conversation until they were served.

Neill had been waiting for that moment, too. He switched to a lower and more serious tone, asked, "What's the problem, Bob?"

"How do you get a healthy man into an ambulance—take him from a crowded lobby with few people noticing one goddamn thing?"

Neill said, "You know the answer to that." But his interest had been aroused.

"Yes," said Renwick, his voice intense even if it was held low. "A needle in his wrist, or a sting at the back of his neck. Sudden collapse, unable to talk, but possibly still able to walk enough—propped up by a friendly medic and a couple of ambulance attendants who just happened to be there."

Neill studied Renwick's face. "You? They tried it on you?" For once, his usual calm deserted him.

"They planned it. But I managed to keep a couple of steps ahead of them."

"Where did this happen? When?"

"In a highly respectable building in the smart business center of Manhattan. One hour ago."

Neill recovered. "You should stay in London. You always find trouble when you come over here. I've never known whether you go looking for it or whether it meets you."

"A little of both, perhaps."

"How bad is it this time?"

"Bad enough, and getting worse."

"Need some help?" Neill frowned, wondering how much involvement was necessary. He liked Renwick personally, admired him professionally, but there were limits to what could be done. Rules and regulations were rules and regulations.

"I think," said Renwick almost inaudibly, "that we both need each other's help. If you could prevent three Americans from being assassinated and—"

"What?"

"No exaggeration. Actually, there's a fourth on that death list—me, to be exact. But if you help me reach the other three, I'd be grateful. I've a copy of the list for you."

"My God," said Neill. A forkful of ham and cheese was poised in midair. "Do they live here?"

Renwick almost smiled. Regulations, regulations . . . "Houston, Palo Alto, Washington."

Neill nodded, went on eating. After a few minutes he said, "There was an 'if' in your last sentence. If we can help you, then what?"

"I can help you. About another matter. Highly sensitive. But immediate." For the last half hour Renwick had been trying to decide how much he could tell Neill—he couldn't hand over Brimmer's illegal accounts until he had made copies of them for Interintell's files in London. Tell Neill about them today, promise them for tomorrow? Not altogether satisfactory: evidence was best handed over with the facts. Yet, it was a pretty fair deal. He—and Claudel in Djibouti—had done all the groundwork on Exports Consolidated. "It would give you a head start on the others who'll be crowding into this case. A scoop, Joe, as our newspaper friends say." He pushed aside his half-eaten salad, looked around for the waiter. "The check is mine. Let's get the hell out. Some place where we can talk."

"My office?" Neill asked tentatively and wondered if Renwick would accept.

But Renwick did. "Not every day I get an escort from the Bureau," he said as they came out into the blinding light of the street and signaled for a cab.

He was back to his old form, thought Neill: finding a small joke in everything. In the Drake Room he had been as serious and intent as Neill had ever seen him. The information that Renwick could give must be a blockbuster. Neill's interest doubled. He noticed Renwick's glance at his watch as a taxi drew up. "We haven't far to go."

"Good." It had been a quick lunch. Now, it was only five past one. Renwick could catch Gilman in London at the end of his working day, alert him to expect a full report coming later tonight. "I have one phone call to make. I'll keep it brief," he said as they got into the cab.

A tactful hint. Neill grinned. "You can do that from my office. I won't listen. And I wouldn't understand a word of it anyway."

"I hope not." Renwick gave an answering smile. It broadened as another idea struck him. "By the way, how's your copying machine working?"

"It was fine this morning." Neill's amusement grew. "Taking over my office?"

"Just want to leave you with three interesting pages. Saves time—yours and mine."

As urgent as that? Neill settled back with his own thoughts.

Renwick fell silent, too, calculating the tight schedule ahead. His visit to Joe Neill's office wouldn't take long. The bare facts about Brimmer, complete with hard evidence, were ready to hand over. Also a full description of the supply-room clerk at Exports Consolidated and of his two accomplices. Also a mention of Klingfeld & Sons, whose agents they were. That was definitely FBI business. But details of Klingfeld and Klaus were unnecessary: they were based in Europe. That was Interintell's affair. So was Lorna Upwood's possession of Brimmer's Plus List, now in a safe-deposit box somewhere in Switzerland. And after his discussion with Neill about the best approach to the other three American names on that death list—what then? Some concentrated work on his report for London, every scrap of today's information made crisp and clear and then encoded for transmission this evening. He would send it out by six o'clock, six-thirty at latest, the Klaus Telex included.

And after that? Nina . . . Her safety, now with Klingfeld's agents in New York, was the biggest problem of all. If they couldn't get him, they would make a try to kidnap Nina; a hostage to hold and use as blackmail, force him to— He cut off those thoughts. Keep her safe, he told himself, keep her safe.

"Let's skip that movie tonight," Renwick said as they ended dinner at the little Italian restaurant not far from the house on Sixty-first Street. "Do you mind, Nina? I'm not much in a mood for it."

"I didn't think you'd be." She looked at him worriedly. He had been working in the top-floor study when she came back from shopping this afternoon, stayed there until after seven o'clock, and since then she had been making most of the conversation. He had listened, yes. Even joked with her over her first day's adventures in New York. But he had brought some problem to dinner with him—unusual. And instead of lessening, it had increased. Something I've done? she wondered, and her own anxiety grew.

Suddenly, watching her, he seemed to make up his mind. "Back to the house, darling. We'll put our feet up and talk. And tomorrow we pack."

That really startled her. She said nothing, only nodded. But, she thought in dismay, I was just beginning to settle down in New York. There's so much to see, and I'll never see it now. And as they left the restaurant, she glanced around the busy avenue—noisy, bustling, filled with a mixture of faces and clothes, everyone out for another evening of fun and pleasure—and repressed a sigh.

On the hall table there was a note, written in a large scrawl, waiting for Renwick. "Chet Danford," he told Nina, who was already halfway up the staircase on its climb to the living room. "He phoned us at eight-fifteen. Will call back later." Renwick frowned, wondering. At eight-fifteen, Danford must be phoning from somewhere outside his office. Then Renwick told himself, You're too much on edge: yesterday you wouldn't have sensed anything wrong about the placing of that call, felt any emergency. There probably wasn't.

Nina had noticed his frown, his slow step as he mounted the stairs. She glanced over the white banister at the kitchen door, which was ajar. "These shoes are a hideous mistake. They're far too narrow." She slid her feet out from them. "Now *that* feels good. This carpet is divine." Have I given a good excuse for our early return? It sounds vapid enough: the kind of remark Mrs. Whosis on the ground floor would expect from me. Why is it that strangers believe, if you're blond and twenty-three and wear a black chiffon nightgown, that you are a nitwit? "Do you think we should get a red carpet like this one? I rather like it. Of course, we'd then have to have a white staircase, too."

Renwick, having followed her glance, made no comment as he climbed after his barefoot wife. In the living room—two rooms, actually, knocked into one giant—Nina had chosen a central couch. He closed the door, said, "Has she been inquisitive?"

"No. Just a little critical—a slight sniff when she came to collect the breakfast tray and found I was still in bed. But I suppose she must wonder who we are and where we come from. Only natural, isn't it?"

Yes, it was only natural. He came over to sit beside her, slipped his arm around her, then disengaged it. "Can't think straight," he told her as he kissed her and rose. He pulled forward a small chair, faced her. "Hard to know where to begin. Look, honey—tomorrow morning, early, we'll leave for Washington. No, I don't know how long we'll be there. But my business in New York is finished. And there could be trouble if we stay."

She was about to speak. He leaned forward, kissed her lips lightly. "Hear me out, darling. Yes, I could be in some danger—and there was an attempt to waylay me today. No, no, nothing much. Just a warning—which I'm taking seriously. Because if I'm threatened at all, then the danger could spread to you. An unpleasant type, I'm up against. He has a long reach. Tried to have Claudel killed in Djibouti."

"Pierre?" She was aghast. "Was he hurt?"

"Not badly. A knife wound."

Nina drew a deep breath. "Will you be safe in Washington?"

The question was, would she be safe? "We'll have no contact with anyone linked to the O'Connell name, no one linked to the Renwick name, either. We'll call ourselves something original—like Smith."

"Where will we stay—in another friend's house? Or a hotel?"

"A motel to start with. Some place anonymous, where you won't run into any of your father's friends."

She said slowly, "Would it be better for you if I just cleared out? Went back to London?"

"No. Not that!" He quietened his voice. "The unpleasant type I mentioned—well, he knows about Interintell. You see, there's an informer connected with our outfit—no, honey, not in the London office, somewhere else. Don't worry, we'll find him." He took her hands in his. "Don't worry," he repeated, "or else I'll regret telling you all this."

"Don't, please don't. I wanted to be told—yesterday I pestered you with questions until you shut me up completely."

"I what?" He tried to laugh. "I must be worse than I thought."

"No, no. It wasn't you; it was what you said. About Austria four years ago, about the . . ." Her voice trailed off. About the girl who was killed there. And Bob, she saw, knew perfectly well what she had almost said aloud. She gathered her wits. "Well—if I can't go back to London, what about Connecticut? Aunt Eunice is there—mother's sister—so there's no O'Connell in her name. Besides, she's Mrs. Williams now."

"And there are three sons and a host of friends. How are you going to keep Renwick unmentioned? They'll never introduce you around as Mrs. John Smith, will they?"

She remembered her cousins. "Not without a wink or a nudge or a mysterious look," she admitted. "I'd be lucky if they didn't go off into a fit of wild jokes. The trouble is—they've never had to face anything like the dangers you face. Or Pierre. Or Ron Gilman. They just can't imagine—"

"Got it! I know someone who'd help us in Washington," he said, and then added more slowly, "if he's there at this time of year. He goes off to Europe in summer, looking at paintings—possible acquisitions. He's a museum director." Yes, Colin Grant had known threats and hidden danger and the grief they could bring.

"Museum?" That caught Nina's interest.

"Quite near Washington. Look, darling, let me telephone him—find out if he's around." Renwick had risen, was halfway to the door. "I'll use an outside line."

Nina made no comment about that. "Perhaps he won't want us."

"If he's there, he will." Renwick hesitated, then decided. "He was in Vienna four years ago—buying a painting. He wasn't Intelligence. Purely amateur standing. But with his help, we uncovered a secret funding for terrorists. He met the girl who was working on that case with me. They fell in love, were going to be married. She was killed."

The girl Bob had recruited . . . "So he won't joke when we use the name Smith," Nina said softly.

Renwick shook his head. "He will keep you safe," he said, and left.

Nina rose, walked around the room, and tried to divert her mind from Bob's last words. She concentrated on the outside call. Why use a public telephone near the corner of the avenue? There was nothing doubtful about Mrs. Whosis downstairs, except her natural curiosity. Or did Bob think the house phones could be tapped? Wanted his request for Washington Directory to be unheard by anyone? And a call to Washington tonight, followed by a hurried departure tomorrow, might—just might—give away their destination. Was that Bob's reason? Nina wondered. And with that, his last sentence came sliding back into her mind. *He will keep you safe.*

That could mean only one thing. Bob must be faced with the possibility of leaving her with someone he trusted while he traveled. A job that had to be done, and too dangerous for her to share. Or was she—as Gemma Gilman would say in her precise English voice—just a bloody nuisance?

Yes, Nina decided, I could be just that. There are times when I'm a total handicap. And having reduced herself to tears, she went upstairs to begin packing.

Eleven

HALF AN HOUR later, Renwick returned. "I had to find enough change, first," he told Nina. He was relaxed and natural once more. "So I went back to that Italian restaurant and got it."

"And your museum friend was at home. Not traveling?" Nina seemed equally relaxed. She snapped the locks on her suitcase. All ready to go, she thought, but where?

"Not until August."

"And he had no objections to having a lone female landed on him for three weeks?"

"Darling . . ." Renwick drew her away from the suitcase and with his arm around her waist led her to the chaise longue. "There, Madame Récamier," he said and settled her comfortably. He sat down facing her, his hands on her knees. "He had no objections at all. In fact, when I told him we were coming to Washington, he insisted we should stay with him. Plenty of room, he said. So we'll have lunch with him tomorrow, and I'll look the place over."

"Married?"

"No. He's alone except for a housekeeper."

"How old is he?"

"About a couple of years older than I am—forty-three, I'd guess." Renwick smiled. "Better looking, too. He's quite a guy. I'll tell you more about him on our way to the Basset Hill Museum. It stands in acres of gardens just outside Washington. And"—this pleased him—"it is well guarded. Valuable collection of paintings: seventeenth century, with French Impressionists in a new gallery he opened. You'll have plenty of beauty around you—inside the museum, outside in the woodlands. And—" he paused to emphasize his next words—"I shan't be away for three weeks, Nina. Three days perhaps, or ten at the outside. I may not have to leave you at all, and I won't unless—well, let's see how everything breaks. I'll be with you for the first day, at least. Some meetings in Washington."

She tried to keep her voice light. "How many problems left, darling? Only that man? The unpleasant type, you called him."

Klaus of Klingfeld & Sons. "He's the main one." There was Klingfeld's informant, too; the mole who had burrowed deep into Interintell. We'll have to unearth him first, Renwick thought, end his threat to us all: that should help to defang Klaus as far as information about Interintell is concerned. And there was also a third problem. Lorna Upwood and the black diary she had stolen from Brimmer. That little notebook, Brimmer's Plus List, could be the biggest challenge of all.

"Let's give the unpleasant type a name," Nina suggested. "One word. Something easy for me to memorize."

"Snake."

"That was quick. A snake in the grass, is that what he is?"

"A snake in long grass who needs defanging. But we'll just call him 'the opposition,' I think; keep the drama out of it."

Suddenly, she was upset. "And you—"

"I'm not alone in the search," he told her. "There's Interintell. And there are the intelligence agencies of at least twelve countries backing us up. We're in constant contact. Keep that in mind, will you?"

"And you direct the traffic."

He looked at her in surprise. "You overestimate your husband, my love."

No, she thought, I don't. Pierre's words—she had quoted him directly.

"Business over for the day," Renwick was saying, his arms around her. "Remember what George Bernard Shaw's girl friend said?"

"How much of a girl friend?"

"Never could tell with old G. B. S. Mrs. Patrick Campbell—yes, that was her name. Now, where does this come undone?" He opened her blouse.

"Bob—you'll tear it. My best—"

"All in a good cause." He unfastened her skirt, pulled it off.

"What did Mrs. Campbell say?"

"Can't recall the direct quote." Who could, he thought, at a moment like this? "Something about the marriage bed being so peaceful after the hurly-burly of the chaise longue." He threw aside the rest of her clothes, stood looking down at her. God, he thought, she's the most beautiful woman. He was about to tell her that as he bent down to take her in his arms. The telephone rang.

Renwick straightened up, swore softly. It rang again.

It was Chet Danford, speaking against a vague background of voices and laughter. "Sorry about this. One moment—I'll get the door closed." There was a short struggle; the noise diminished. "That better? A man came to my office late today—just as I was leaving. Knew Frank Cooper had been one of my partners and thought I must know you as another of Cooper's close friends. He had heard you were in town, wanted to meet you again, and where were you staying? He sounded quite sincere. Most plausible. Except that he hadn't seen you since your last visit to New York three years back. You weren't in New York then, were you?"

"No."

"Then thank God I had some doubts. Told him I hadn't seen you for the last two years, and if you were in New York—well, you hadn't called me. Sent him away convinced I was telling the truth. As I was."

"What was his name? His appearance?"

"Josh Grable. Medium height, thin, brown hair—a lot of hair. Heavy glasses. Seersucker suit. Late twenties, I'd guess, or early thirties. Ever met him?"

"This morning. He didn't know me, thought I was someone else." Until Al Moore's name had been questioned and Klaus had decided the description he had been given fitted me. "Just a try-on for size. Glad you didn't make it fit."

"Anything I can do?"

"No. We're about to take off, tomorrow. Sorry our stay has been so short. It was most comfortable."

"If you're anywhere near Washington, remember that Rosen is now heading our office there."

Wallace Rosen, another of Frank Cooper's partners and friends. Might be too much of a connection there, too. "Have you told him I'm here?"

"Not yet. I'll call him to—"

"Don't. I'll get in touch with him myself."

"Fine. Have to go—the intermission is just about over. Wish the play were, too: another clunker. Take care."

"You, too. What about that little key—where do I leave it? In an envelope in the desk?"

"Oh, yes, I forgot about that. Or you could mail it to—" Danford had turned to speak to someone who had opened the booth's door. "Just coming, my dear." Then to Renwick again, "My wife. 'Bye."

Mail it where? Renwick wondered, and shook his head over wives who yanked husbands away from telephones. "That was Chet. He's as sharp as a carving knife, the kind of lawyer I wouldn't like against me in court, but why the hell did he mention Washington and Rosen on a phone in a theater lobby?"

"He must have thought it safe enough. We can't be suspicious of everything."

"No," he agreed. "Not suspicious of everything. Just careful. There's a big difference."

"Bad news?" she asked, watching his face.

"A confirmation, actually. The opposition is trying to find out where I am in New York." Messages from Klaus to his informant in The Hague must have been frantic this afternoon. "At least I don't feel my hunch was so damned stupid about getting us the hell out."

"When do we leave?"

"About eight o'clock. We'll breakfast somewhere, then take a shuttle flight to Washington."

She looked down at the chiffon negligee she had bought this morning. Bob hadn't even noticed it. "When I was in Bloomingdale's today, I saw. . ."

He was thinking about The Hague. Yes, he decided, that has to be our first objective.

"Bob . . ." She had caught his attention. "Let's leave at eight, take a cab to a place where we can have breakfast at leisure, take another cab back in this direction—to Bloomingdale's. I'll only be a few minutes inside. The store can't be busy when it's opening. I won't delay us, really I won't. It's just something I didn't remember to buy today. And there are lots of flights to Washington, aren't there?"

He was amazed but he only said, "Okay—if it's important to you. As long as we leave this house early enough."

"Leave at seven? Just drive around the park? That would be fun."

That would be safe, too. "Okay," he said again. "Couldn't refuse you anything in that getup. New, isn't it?"

The telephone rang. "Shall I?" asked Nina. "You weren't expecting any more calls, were you?"

He shook his head. It couldn't be Danford: the theater wasn't over yet.

Nina lifted the receiver. "Yes?" Then she broke into a relieved sigh, handed the phone to Bob. "It's from London—Ron Gilman's voice."

Thank God, thought Renwick and took the phone. "Glad to hear from you. I was wondering if I could haul you out of bed."

"I've just finished reading your letter."

Pretty quick work. Renwick's report had been sent out just before seven this evening; Gilman receiving it around midnight in London, decoding, reading, and now able to make some comment. "Interesting, wasn't it?"

"I'd like to hear more as soon as possible."

"Working late? You sound tired."

"An all-night job, I fear."

So Gilman was in his office, and communication would be easy. "I'll write you at once. Good-bye for now." Renwick cut off the call.

He turned to Nina. "Sorry, darling. I've got to go up to the study, discuss some business. Ron is still in the office."

At half past three in the morning, London time? Nina's eyes opened wide. But she nodded, said, "We'll be here when you get back."

"We?" he asked as he kissed her.

"My new negligee and me." That sent him off with a broad smile on his face. Well, thought Nina, wives may be a bloody nuisance some of the time, but not always. With that comforting thought, she lay back on the bed and wondered about tomorrow.

Gilman was waiting for Renwick's call. They used voice code where necessary, but their fifteen-minute talk decided several things. It began with the serious problem of Klingfeld's informant.

Like it or not, Renwick insisted, they had to start with Johan Vroom at The Hague. First of all, Gilman had to find out if there was any close assistant to Vroom—one who might know about Vroom's association with Interintell; better still, one who had even been sent on a special mission to London. "Let's hope that is what we're looking for," Renwick said. "But if not . . ."

Then, like it or not, they had to make inquiries about Vroom himself. Was he in debt—had he received any large sums of money recently? Or was it a woman? An affair that could wreck his home life with wife and children if Klaus made it public? Or some photographs taken in a Rotterdam brothel, an unwitting connection with a Soviet agent that would ruin his career? "Either he's being blackmailed or—and I hope this is true—he has an aide who is milking him of information," Renwick concluded.

Gilman said unhappily, "I hope so. He is really a very decent man. Devoted to his family."

"Where else do we start?" Renwick asked bluntly. "Believe me, I've been thinking about it ever since we received that information on The Hague. There's no other solution."

"I'll begin a check right away."

"We haven't much time."

"Yes, I felt that when I read your latest report. In fact, that is what I wanted to discuss with you now. I'm concerned—"

"Don't be. We'll be leaving tomorrow." And Gilman knew his next stop after New York. "I've made safe arrangements for Beautiful." Nina, of course.

"Thank God for that. The present climate isn't exactly healthy, is it? Don't forget to pay a visit to my aunt. She's expecting you."

"Always a pleasure." Gilman's aunt in Washington was an elderly gentleman with an upstairs room as nicely arranged as this study.

"Also," Gilman went on, "about those accounts you found today—you gave three copies to Federal Insurance?"

"It saved time."

"What about your own copies?"

"I'll leave them with your aunt." And Gilman could have them picked up and sent over to London in a diplomatic bag.

"Good. But frankly I wish you'd return with them and stay here—you could direct things from the office. We could assign someone else to—"

"Forget it." Waste valuable time putting a new man in the picture? "I've been in on this from the first. I know the full story—all the particulars."

"I know, I know. Still—"

"No delays. We're at the stage when every hour counts. How's our friend's arm, by the way? Fit enough to join me?"

"He's been talking about that."

"Okay. Set it up. We'll meet in his old stamping ground." That was Paris, Claudel's home town. "I'll call you again—before I take off—arrange time and location."

"You're in a hurry, aren't you?"

"Our competition is setting the pace. He moves damn fast. And that reminds me—I'm looking for a good watchdog to guard the household while I'm away. I was thinking of an Airedale, like the one you liked in Ottawa." That was Tim MacEwan, one of the early recruits to Interintell, a Canadian who commuted between Ottawa and Washington. Nina knew him but hadn't met him in the last twenty months—a safe-enough time lapse for any contact between them in Washington.

Gilman was surprised into a laugh. Mac's bristling reddish hair was indeed reminiscent of an Airedale. "Easily arranged. You'll find him at my aunt's. Anything more?"

"Bright Eyes." Yes, what about Erik, little by little?

He was still on board the freighter, its rate of travel slowed by a faulty boiler, and wouldn't reach the canal for a few more days. The captain had been instructed to search the ship. One seaman was missing. No sign of Bright Eyes. The crew knew nothing. Could be a payoff, made by his very old and very rich friend.

"We could damn well question the friend as soon as we can board the ship." That would be at Suez, just as the *Spaarndam* was being cleared for passage through the canal.

"But we were told he isn't our business," Gilman said. "A quid pro quo. Remember?"

"Yes," Renwick said curtly, repressing his anger. Worry was causing it; deep worry. If Erik slipped away from the *Spaarndam* at the port of Suez, he could head easily for Cairo. And Cairo's sprawling airport, a vast stretch of complete confusion, was just made for Erik's talents. Once through there, he could be in Europe and practically home free. Renwick said, "I'll be in touch day after tomorrow. The usual time," he added and signed off.

His anger surged back. It had been Vroom, dealing with a Dutch ship, who had instructed that goddamn captain to make a quiet search of his *Spaarndam*. Why the hell hadn't he put the fear of demotion into the captain, made sure he really stirred his fat stumps? No doubt the man had assumed this was just another stowaway, what was all the fuss about? Stowaways were plentiful—a headache that could be expected. "Vroom," Renwick said aloud, "your mind just wasn't fully on your job. Was it? And why?"

His anger subsided as he concentrated on routine, restoring the room to complete neatness, remembering to remove his cipher list from safekeeping in the metal cabinet before he locked its doors securely. He hesitated in front of the gun rack, then lifted down the Biretta, slipping it into his belt. In the drawer below the rack, he found an extra clip of ammunition. He still hesitated. Danford would notice the small gap left by the borrowed pistol. So he went over to the desk and wrote a brief note to keep the house-keeper clear of any suspicion: *Something borrowed, something new. To be returned unused, I hope.* He placed the key to the cabinet inside the folded note, sealed them in a Manila envelope with wax and Scotch tape, addressed it in block letters, and left it with its edge tucked securely into the desk blotter. As satisfied as he could be, he went downstairs with the cold touch of the Biretta against his waist.

Nina had fallen into a light sleep. She stirred, said, "You, darling?"

"Soon be with you." Quickly, he packed his small suitcase. The Biretta and its refill went into a sock; the cipher list in between two pages of Frost's lyrics. As he stripped, he looked down at Nina. Then he stared. "Oh, no!" he said. She had cut her hair. It no longer fell to her shoulders, just to her ear level. "Oh, Nina!"

She half awakened. He slid in beside her. "Why, Nina? Why?"

"Too hot. It will grow," she said drowsily and fell completely asleep inside the curve of his arm.

Next morning, Nina kept her promise: she was less than ten minutes inside Bloomingdale's, hurrying out to the waiting taxi with a small shop-ping bag under her arm. She didn't explain a thing. Otherwise, Renwick had to admit, she seemed perfectly normal. He concentrated on making the short flight to Washington as easy and pleasant as possible. He didn't men-tion her hair.

Once they had arrived, there was a short delay. "Just five minutes," Nina pleaded, and left him at a newspaper stand while she hurried to the ladies' room. When she returned, she was wearing a silk scarf in turban style around her head and not a blond curl showing. Her lips were altered, too: pink had given way to coral.

"Look, Nina—" he began.

"I know. Silly, isn't it?"

In the taxi, she waited until they had left the airport well behind them. Then she drew the scarf carefully away, shook her head and let a smooth sweep of dark-brown hair fall to her shoulders. "Do you like it?" she asked, showing her first touch of uncertainty.

"You're incredible. But you're taking this too seriously. No need to—"

"Isn't there? Father has a lot of friends in this town."

True. It was also true that Nina's blond hair and blue eyes were memo-rable. But so was Nina transformed into a brunette. Unrecognizable, how-ever, unless you looked into her eyes and noticed their intense blue. "What about contact lenses?" he teased her. "And a cane to hobble with?" Then he kissed her gently. "As ravishable as ever, Mrs. Smith."

"Thank you, John."

"Not at all, Samantha."

She took out her sunglasses and put them on. "Better?"

He nodded. The transformation was complete. Best of all was her confidence: no sign of misgivings, of nervousness, of dejection. That could have been the case, he realized, and a wave of relief swept over him. "Incredible in every way," he said as he directed the cab to draw up at a pleasant-looking motel halfway to Basset Hill, and Nina didn't even ask one question. Not even one when he paid for two nights in advance, signed the register with "Jimson, Philadelphia," and they found themselves in a small sterile bungalow with a rented car waiting at its side.

"How?" Renwick asked the question for her. "Colin Grant booked the room and car this morning. We'll stay ten minutes. Next stop, Basset Hill."

"Are you sure his standing *is* purely amateur?"

"Quite sure. But he catches on damned quick—like you, my pet."

I've just had a medal pinned on me, thought Nina. She looked in the mirror and adjusted her new dark-brown wig. "Tell me about the museum," she said.

It had once been the late Victor Basset's eastern residence, a vast mansion standing on top of a gentle slope with nothing but parkland and trees surrounding its gardens. Four years ago its interior had been gutted and transformed into modern picture galleries, no expense spared in proper lighting and ventilation, a suitable place for the display of the valuable collection of paintings that Basset had gathered during his lifetime. He had lived to see his museum opened, to feel its future—handsomely endowed—was assured, and to know that his millions had been well spent. Fortunately for Basset now, he couldn't see the sprawl of a city forever creeping outward, turning countryside into bedroom annex. Basset Hill still stood apart in its twenty acres on the Virginia border—but it was only fifteen miles from Washington. Another few years and the tide of new housing would be lapping at its massive gates.

"Gates! But where are their walls?" Nina could only see thick high bushes leading out in a wide curve on either side.

"High iron fence disguised. Basset combined the practical with the aesthetic. It has an alarm system, too. There's valuable art inside that big house."

Nina studied it. An imposing entrance in the center of two outspread wings, built of silver-gray stone, decorative yet simple—if huge size could ever qualify for simplicity. "Big? It's enormous. And where does Colin Grant live? On the premises?"

"At the back." Renwick followed Grant's instructions, took the driveway as far as the museum and then branched off to his right. Up here, there were flower beds and two gardeners at work. Nina glanced over her shoulder, down the long slope of grass with its small islands of trees ending in the wall of high bushes. Even the trees, she thought, had been carefully chosen for shape and size, perfection in color and balance. "Basset had taste."

"And expert advisers," Renwick said. Not to speak of a billion or so in cash. "Here we are." Within its own wall and gate stood a neat house, built of stone, good architecture, with two small wings, nothing to detract from the overall scheme. Renwick studied it as he angled the car over a short driveway to reach the attached garage. There were some trees, but not close to the house. And the wall kept any visitors to the museum—there were many, judging by the parking area on its other side—from wandering into private territory. There had been an attendant on duty at the cars, a guard at the museum's front steps, and a guard down at the front gates. Yes, he thought, I could leave Nina safely here. "What do you think? Like it?"

"Yes. I just hope he likes me." She was looking at Colin Grant, who had come out to meet them. Tall, with dark hair turning gray, a friendly face, and—after a slight look of surprise as he saw her—a warm greeting. There was little doubt that he was a friend, a very good friend, of Bob's. But why be surprised about me? she wondered. She took off her glasses and shook hands.

Grant laughed. "Bob wrote me he had married a blonde," he said. "But the eyes have it. Come in. What do I call you? You're my cousin, you know—can't go around saying Mrs. Smith."

"Samantha," said Renwick, hauling the suitcases out of the car.

"No," said Nina. "Sue. Susan Smith is a very nice name."

Grant raised an eyebrow as Renwick accepted that, then took hold of a suitcase and led the way indoors. "We've twenty minutes before lunch," he said after he introduced the housekeeper—Mrs. Trout, white-haired and bustling—to his cousin, Mrs. Smith, and her husband. "Mrs. Trout can show you the house, Sue. I'll borrow your husband and let him see my own point eight nine four of an acre."

Outside, Grant said, "Now, Bob—put me in the picture. As you used to say, there's a need to know. God, how I used to bristle at that phrase."

They paced around the grass and trees while Renwick talked and Grant listened. "Sure," Grant said when Renwick brought up the subject of Tim MacEwan, "we can fit him in. He can be one of those foreign art experts who stay over in the guest cottage just beyond those trees—" he pointed to a roof near them—"whenever they come visiting the museum."

"Except that Mac knows little about art."

Grant thought over that. "Twice in the last eighteen months we had a scare about burglary. Each time we had an expert in security staying with us for about a week—he went over the alarm system, got to know the guards, the general layout. Is that more in Mac's line?"

"Much more."

"He can stay at the cottage. Or would he rather have a couple of rooms over the garage?"

"Whatever raises no eyebrows. Mac's probably the best judge of that," Renwick suggested. "I'll see him in the morning."

"When do you leave?"

"Tomorrow night, possibly. And I don't know how long I'll be away."

"Don't worry. We'll take care of Nina—Sue. Better keep calling her 'Sue.' She has a mind of her own," Grant added with a smile. "Did you have a hard time persuading her to wear a wig?"

"Her idea. She's like you, Colin: the inspired amateur. But don't let her get too inspired, will you?" Yes, he thought, everything will be all right.

After lunch I'll take a walk over this whole stretch of land while Nina explores the museum. Best not to be seen with me in public. Tonight we can stroll around the park—our last night together. "What about lunch?" he asked. "And you can tell us about the museum. It looks pretty impressive to me."

"A fine place to work. Strange—" Grant paused—"I wouldn't have accepted this job if you hadn't pushed me into it. You know—I really meant what I said back in Austria—about joining you, fighting those bastards from undercover—but you wouldn't recruit me, and so here I am."

"In your own right setting," Renwick said. "But you tempted me, Colin. You'd have been one hell of a smart intelligence officer."

"We made a pretty good team," Grant said slowly. However indirect, it was a reference charged with sudden emotion, a tribute to the girl who had fought along with them and had died. Avril . . .

They both fell silent, walked back to the house.

Twelve

By SEVEN O'CLOCK on a warm mist-heavy morning, Renwick was ready to leave Basset Hill. He stood at the side of their bed looking down at Nina as she lay asleep. A last memory to carry him through . . . Then he roused himself and kissed her awake.

"So soon?" she asked.

"The sooner I leave, the earlier I'll return."

"I'm coming down—"

"No, darling. I never like long good-byes. And I'll be back before you know it. I'll send you messages through Mac. Tim MacEwan, remember him? He'll be around to keep an eye on everything. And tell Colin I'll leave the car at Statler Garage—it's near the hotel. He can have it picked up there."

And after that? she wondered, but asked no questions. She slipped out of bed, threw her arms around him.

"You make it damn hard," he said, holding the soft lithe body tightly against him. A long kiss and he released her. He picked up the dark wig from the bedpost where he had tossed it the night before and clamped it on her short blond hair at an angle.

"Oh, Bob!" She was trying to straighten it.

That's how parting should be, he thought: a laugh shared. Without delay, he reached the door. "I love you," he told her as he closed it behind him.

Renwick timed his visit to Gilman's Aunt Chris for half past eight. Christopher Menlo, an Anglo-American who had spent early years in his native England and the remainder in Washington where he had served his new country well, was in his dressing gown finishing breakfast, tut-tutting as usual over the morning paper. White-haired, pink-cheeked, tall, and thin but now rounding substantially at his waistline since his retirement from the CIA ten years ago, he showed little surprise when Renwick arrived.

"I expected you," he said as he shook hands and returned to his bacon and eggs. He picked up his newspaper again. "Hardly as early as this, I must say. Breakfast? You'll find all the makings in the kitchen." He gestured across the small living room, a disorder of books and papers, to an open door showing a kitchen in equal disarray. Chris lived alone and—in between working on his book about the wars and politics of the seventeenth century—pottered. His word. He pottered around his small rose garden, he pottered with his large stamp collection, and he pottered with his electronic equipment in the spare room upstairs.

"Later perhaps," Renwick said. "But Gilman should be in his office by two o'clock. His time. I'd like to chat with him. Is that all right with you, Chris?"

"Of course. You know the way." Chris was relieved now he could finish breakfast in peace—a sacred hour. He eased his dressing gown more comfortably around him, went back to shaking his head over the news from Lebanon.

It was a small house with a strip of garden at the back: living room and den below, two rooms above. Halfway up the narrow stairs, Renwick halted as Chris called to him, "Your friend Mac got into Washington last night. He phoned me to say he'd be here around ten."

"I'll be downstairs by then."

"Oh—and another thing. Farley wanted to see you. He'll be here at noon. That's all right, is it?"

Maurice Farley was attached to operations at the CIA. "I'd like to see him, too." So Farley decided to accept my invitation, thought Renwick. Why? Yesterday afternoon, when I phoned him, he expected to have committee meetings all of today. "He's a friend of yours, isn't he?"

"Yes, yes. Drops in here whenever he wants to pick my old brains." Silence followed, broken only by the rustle of a newspaper.

End of conversation, Renwick decided, and mounted the remaining steps. He had twenty minutes to get his suggestions in good order before he made contact with Interintell at nine o'clock.

First, there was the problem of Erik. He might be able to disappear at Suez or in Cairo, but his movements could be traced. Through the fake Englishman, William Haversfield. And Haversfield's identity, past and present, was also traceable: an early supporter of Erik's Direct Action (and that meant in 1973 or 1974), a wealthy greeting-card manufacturer in West Berlin, where Erik had organized his anarchist group. Yes, Richard Diehl, of West German Intelligence, could start digging in the security files and discover Haversfield's real name and political connections. Gilman in London could start some digging, too: if Haversfield could afford to travel around the world, Haversfield had an income and must file a tax return. (People such as he, living under false pretenses, would most certainly obey the law and run no risk of arrest or inquiry.) The income-tax boys had his address, his business or profession, and his source of income. Enough, thought Renwick, to track down Haversfield, who could lead us to Erik.

Secondly, there was the problem of Klingfeld & Sons. Several problems, in fact, but these lesser ones could be better gauged once he and Pierre Claudel had a face-to-face talk about the events in Djibouti. However adequate a coded report was, it lacked the small details that could round out the picture, bring it into complete focus. The major question about Klingfeld & Sons was simply this: how had they known about Frank Cooper's connection with Interintell, his friendship with Renwick? That was the excuse offered by the supply-room clerk, Klingfeld's undercover agent in the offices of Exports Consolidated, when he asked Chet Danford about Renwick's visit to New York.

Renwick thought he knew the answer to that question. Apart from the Interintell group—Gilman, MacEwan, himself—who had been working with Cooper at the time of his death, there were only three others—and they had belonged to East German Intelligence—who had known about Cooper's connections. Two of them had engineered his death on orders from the third man; and he had been more than an East German Intelligence officer: he was KGB. And that, Renwick guessed, could be the source of Klingfeld's information.

An unpleasant deduction, but it could damn well be true. In the last few years the Soviets had become past masters in the art of remote control: never visibly present, working most effectively from the far background. Renwick could hear Gilman's groan when he heard about this new possibility in the Klingfeld puzzle. What? Gilman would say. Not them again? Which reminded Renwick to set Chris's transceiver on Gilman's wavelength and get ready for a dialogue in code. A blasted nuisance, he thought; but here in Washington he was in KGB intercept-territory. Their elaborate listening aids, set up quite blatantly on their embassy's roof, were part of the landscape.

At nine o'clock exactly he heard Gilman's voice, and the strange, seemingly nonsensical interchange began.

It went more or less as he had expected, even to Gilman's groan. There were initial objections, of course, to his interest in tracking down William Haversfield. ("Not our business, we've been told," Gilman reminded him.) But Renwick had his justification ready. "We won't touch him. Just use him to reach Bright Eyes. We'll leave him entirely to Pete's girl friend."

Gilman had agreed to that, even suggested that he could have some results of his inquiries by tomorrow. "See you then?" he had asked.

"No, better not. I'll go straight to Pete's home, meet him there. Same old place, same old time." And the same old place was one of the book-stalls along the left bank of the Seine. The time would be that of his last meeting there with Claudel.

Satisfactory, Renwick thought as he went downstairs and joined Chris, now with his last cup of tea and his first pipe of the day. The old boy was rustling his way through a second newspaper: he was an avid reader of small paragraphs, searching them out even among the shipping news, convinced—from years of experience—that many an important little item got lost in the back pages.

"Nothing remarkable today," he reported, "except that a man was found murdered in the Seychelles. He was an ex-Green Beret, which sounds strange. You'd have thought he would have known how to take care of himself."

Renwick, returning from the kitchen with a hastily brewed cup of instant coffee, looked at Chris sharply. "What was he doing in the Seychelles anyway? Snorkeling, skin-diving, or just lazing on the beach?"

"Doesn't sound much like the Green Berets I've met," Chris observed. "He was going to retire there, had just bought a house."

Renwick laid the coffee cup on the nearest piece of free space. "Let me see that, Chris, would you?"

Chris folded the paper to the proper column of print, pointed out the exact spot. "Really odd," he remarked. "Found dead in his bed. Throat slit. Was he drunk at the time?"

"Must have been." Renwick read the details, the more lurid of them already given by Chris. The man's name was Al Jones. Mystery around him was hinted at, but tactfully. He had bought the house on a secluded beach with a check drawn on a Swiss bank account immediately after his arrival on the island of Mahé only ten days ago. He was expecting his wife to join him in a few weeks. The authorities so far had not been able to find Mrs. Jones at the address on her husband's passport, which showed he had traveled by air to London and Zurich before he reached the Seychelles. Further inquiries were being made.

And they'll find the passport was false. Alvin Moore—is that where you ended, soldier of fortune, in bed with your throat slashed? You backed out from your contract with Brimmer, but you didn't handle it as neatly as you thought. You knew too much. Mr. Klaus of Klingfeld & Sons doesn't tolerate that. Where did they pick up your trail? At the airport in London when you were leaving, or in Zurich as you arrived? Or at the Zurich bank itself? Brimmer could have opened an account for you there—the usual procedure when payoffs were high.

Chris said, "You look thoughtful, Robert. Why? Did I miss something?" He took back the paper, scanned it again.

"Just a damned awful way to die," Renwick said. He drank his coffee and began talking about George Washington's victory at Yorktown, where the British were allowed to march in good order to their ships, their arms reversed, their band playing "The World Turned Upside Down." Gallows humor, wry and cocky. "Typically English, I'd say."

"And not lost on old George, either. He was born an Englishman." Chris beamed. "I've always taken consolation from that when some Idaho character called me 'an ersatz American.' The fact is, Robert, if the Americans and British don't hold together, the West will become unglued. Churchill believed that and so do—" The front doorbell sounded. "Ten o'clock. That will be our Scots-Canadian. D'you know what I like about your Interintell?" Chris was talking over his shoulder as he went to open the door for Tim MacEwan. "Your care for the West. Much too good a civilization to be thrown away. Come in, Mac, come in." He watched approvingly as MacEwan and Renwick met with real, if properly restrained, affection. "And now I must potter around my roses," Chris said. "Quite useless to work with them when the sun gets hot. Robert, tell one of your bright boys to invent an exterior air-conditioning unit: he'd make a fortune in Washington." He closed the livingroom door and went upstairs to change into his work clothes.

Mac hadn't altered much in the twenty months since Renwick had met him face to face, still the same cheerful pessimist, the romantic realist; but aren't we all? thought Renwick. He wasted no time on general chitchat but plunged into a complete rundown on Exports Consolidated's tie-up with Klingfeld & Sons and all it had entailed.

At the end of the briefing, Mac's square-set jaw was grimly serious. He hadn't even cracked one small pawky remark. He said, "What about Nina? Klaus is just the type to go after her if he can't get you."

So Renwick explained about Basset Hill and Colin Grant and Mac's role around the museum. "Okay?" Renwick asked.

"Sounds good," Mac said thoughtfully. "How long will you be away?"

"As short a time as possible."

"I'm on a two-week vacation. Got to be back in Ottawa by the twenty-second. Do you think you can finish your job by that time? It's complicated, Bob, damned complicated." And hellish dangerous. But there was no need to mention that. Bob knew.

"Oh, I'll just tie up some loose ends and then fade out."

"Like the way we tied them up in Sawyer Springs?" Mac asked with evident enjoyment. "Crawling on our bellies over a rough hillside, scouting around a terrorist camp in sunny California?" He spent a few moments remembering that foray, every minute a threat from danger. "Wish I were going with you," he admitted frankly. "Too much desk work nowadays."

"The price of promotion."

Mac smoothed his red hair, patted a waistline that was still firm. "Got to jog a couple of miles each morning. You look fine, Bob. How do you keep in shape? Karate? Running? Bend and stretch?"

"A little of everything. By the way, you didn't smuggle a revolver over the border, did you?"

Mac shook his head. "Hasn't Grant got a spare?"

"I don't believe he has any. So take this—it's Chet Danford's. You can return it to his office on your way home." Renwick drew the Biretta out from his belt and the extra clip from his pocket. "The guards at Basset Hill wouldn't think much of a security expert who didn't pack a pistol."

"But this leaves you short."

"Don't like smuggling any more than you do. If necessary, Pierre Claudel will provide."

Mac stowed away pistol and ammunition. They were a sign for him to leave, he decided. "I'll phone Chris each day, find out if he has any message from you for Nina."

"And you send Gilman a daily report about Nina. She's calling herself 'Sue—Susan Smith—Mrs. John Smith.' And don't be surprised when you meet her. She's a brunette."

"What?"

"Just temporarily."

"Your idea?"

"Hers."

"How much does she know?" That's the trouble with marriage, thought the dedicated bachelor; you never can judge where to draw the line.

"Only the reason why I want her out of the picture."

"Enough," agreed Mac. "I'll drive out to the museum after I've spent an hour dodging around town. I won't see you there this afternoon?"

Renwick shook his head. "I'll leave here by the first flight available."

And the farther away he travels, the less attention will be paid by Klaus to Basset Hill—was that it? Yes, Mac thought, that's his hope. He shook hands warmly, clapped Renwick's shoulder. "Don't worry about Nina."

"I'll see you when I get back."

"No fancy footwork, Bob. Stay safe." And with an encouraging grin once more in place, MacEwan headed for the small plot of roses and a last brief word with Chris.

There was half an hour to wait for Maurice Farley's noon visit. Renwick decided to give Chris a hand, cleared the window table of its breakfast dishes and picked up the scattered pages of newspapers. Chris didn't even notice the improvement when he popped his head around the door to announce he was going upstairs to listen to news bulletins from the Middle East. "Got Lebanon yesterday. Keeps my Arabic freshened."

Small wonder that Chris with all his side interests never managed to finish his book. Or perhaps he didn't want to bring it to a conclusion. Renwick glanced at the pile of loose manuscript on the writing desk, at the scattering of notes lying beside it. Is this what we come to when we retire? he wondered. Pottering? Then he shook his head: not with Nina around.

Maurice Farley was punctual and as crumpled as ever in a gabardine suit that hadn't stood up to this morning's humidity. He was Renwick's age, thin and balding, pleasant expression in place, a tall man who tried to disguise his height with a slight stoop. Black socks and brown shoes—a preppy touch like his narrow-shouldered jacket. But his voice still had traces of the bright boy from Kansas who had made it all the way into the sacred groves of Langley. The new breed, Chris Menlo called him, as sharp and quick as the brown eyes that were now covertly studying Renwick. New breed or old breed, thought Renwick, they both shared the same deceptive air of complete disinterest.

"Glad you could make it," Renwick said.

"My lunchtime, actually. Meetings all morning and again this afternoon."

"Another flap?"

"Aren't there always?"

"You've had your share recently."

"Inherited mostly." The polite sparring ended. They had been friends, after all, for almost ten years: military intelligence dealing with Soviet capabilities, before Farley had left for the CIA and Renwick had joined NATO. Farley relaxed into a genuine smile. "You wanted to see me," he prompted.

"Interintell needs a little information. Oh, quite harmless. No state secrets implicated."

"That's reassuring. You know, Bob, we're really sympathetic with Interintell's work. Just takes some convincing of the old boys before they agree to let you into our files. Come to think of it, you are rather aggressive, could try to take over a lot of our business."

"A case of a very small tail wagging a very large dog?"

"Files *are* sacrosanct, Bob. Hard won, hard kept."

"No interest in your files, Morry. Just in a little co-operation when it can do each of us most good and the opposition most harm. Reasonable?"

Farley nodded. "As I said, we're not unfriendly. What information are you hunting?"

"Was it one of your operatives who passed a warning message to an Interintell agent in Djibouti?"

Farley froze. "Isn't that asking too much?"

"No. For one thing, we don't want to complicate any of your investigations in progress. For another thing, if that operative—a woman—was yours, we'd like to thank you. She alerted Claudel and perhaps saved his life."

"Now what makes you think that she belongs to us?" Farley was amused.

"If not to you, then to either Swedish or Swiss Intelligence. I can make some inquiries there, but I thought you'd prefer not to have talk about Djibouti or the freighter *Spaarndam* become general gossip, if—" Renwick paused—"if you were interested in one of the *Spaarndam*'s passengers."

"Either Swedish or Swiss or us? How the hell did you pick on these three? Why not the French? Djibouti is their problem. And a big one, judging from the flack they've been sending."

"That's to be expected after what was discovered at the port last Monday—crates of arms and ammunition, some for Ethiopia, some for a secret cache in Djibouti itself. You know the map of that area. Djibouti is Ethiopia's one outlet to the sea. What could be more tempting than to possess that port? Especially if you have a political ally—Communist Yemen—just a few miles across the entrance to the Red Sea. That could really lock and bar the door to Suez, couldn't it?" As for his reasoning about the woman who had passed the warning to Claudel—that was best left unexplained. For her sake. She had said too much, just a small friendly remark: her people were sympathetic, might even join Interintell someday. The Swiss and Swedish were neutrals, didn't talk of possible affiliation with Interintell. As for other nations outside the West, those who were sympathetic were already co-operating. It had to be the CIA.

"What exactly in arms and ammunition? The French haven't been altogether forthcoming."

"Understandable. Illegal exports from America. Yes, illegal in every way. The French could be wondering how much that involves you."

That aroused Farley. "We're involved with nothing at Djibouti! Believe me, Bob."

"I believe you."

"What export firm?"

"You probably know it—if that *was* your agent contacting Claudel. She made an excellent job of it, I hear. Was she yours, Morry? Just don't want to foul up her mission."

Farley's eyes showed surprise. "I believe you mean it," he said slowly.

"I do. We have parallel interests in the problem of Mr. William Haversfield. Let's not have them tangle."

There was a slight stiffening in Farley's shoulders. "She's one of ours."

"Then Interintell thanks you. And in return I'll give you the name of the American firm that was smuggling illegal weapons through the port of Djibouti. Exports Consolidated."

Farley said softly. "So that explains it."

"Explains what?"

"You'll hear it on the evening news. Their offices in New York and Washington were raided yesterday by the FBI."

"Oh? Was Brimmer still there or had he taken off?"

"He was found dead. Heart attack."

"Where?"

"In the New York office."

"And his files?"

"Not mentioned on any news reports."

"Come on, Morry," Renwick said urgently, "did the FBI get his files?"

"As far as we've heard, the files were—innocuous."

"Then whoever killed him removed anything incriminating." And, in particular, anything that could involve Klingfeld & Sons.

"Killed him?" Farley pretended disbelief.

"When was he found? In the morning? Had his body been there all night?" That would give the supply-room clerk and his two friends enough time to search Brimmer's files.

"Now," asked Farley gently, "what makes you imagine he was eliminated?"

"He was no longer useful. In fact, he was a danger."

"To whom?"

"Now," said Renwick, equally gentle in tone, "what makes you imagine he wasn't a danger to someone?"

"To whom?"

So Farley didn't know as yet about the close connection between Brimmer and Klaus. "Is there anyone missing from Brimmer's office?"

"A private secretary, I heard. And some junior clerk. Both on vacation, possibly. The FBI isn't explaining. Your friend Joe Neill led the raid and—" Farley broke off. "Seen him recently?" he asked suddenly. "You're a wily character, Bob. Why didn't you come to me?"

"Brimmer's office is in the United States," Renwick reminded him. "And don't underestimate Neill—he moved as quickly as he could." In spite of red tape and regulations. "But didn't you have any information about Brimmer's illegal activities?"

"Rumors only." Farley was tight-lipped.

"No investigation of him when he went around claiming he was CIA?"

"Half the crooks are doing that nowadays," Farley said in a surge of anger. "Yes, there was an investigation started. We're now trying to find out where it got sidetracked. Well"—he rose—"time to move off."

He hadn't mentioned Klingfeld & Sons. Yet it was the CIA that had intercepted Klingfeld's message to its informer in The Hague requesting details about Claudel in Djibouti. A lucky accident, a chance interception? Not likely. More possible that all messages from Klingfeld's Paris office were being monitored. And the reason for CIA interest in Klingfeld & Sons? Something beyond any connection with Exports Consolidated. "Thank you, again," Renwick said. "Whose idea was it to warn Claudel in Djibouti? Yours?"

"Nothing at all. Glad it paid off. We're on the same side, aren't we? Can't go losing good men."

Renwick agreed with a warm handshake. "You know, Brimmer had partners abroad."

Farley's face became expressionless. "No doubt. Good-bye, Bob. And good luck with your terrorists."

The keep-off-the-grass sign was out: Farley had definitely a very special interest in Klingfeld. Renwick said, "One of them—Erik—but you know about him, of course."

That stopped Farley at the door. "I've heard several things. What should I know in particular?"

"He's on the *Spaarndam*. Courtesy of William Haversfield. Well hidden, too. Your girl on board could be in trouble."

There was a brief silence. "Now it's my turn to thank you," Farley said quietly, and left.

Chris Menlo heard the front door close behind Farley and took the cue to come downstairs and say good-bye to Renwick.

"Farley had to leave for a meeting," Renwick apologized.

Chris waved that aside. "He'll be around here any day. We don't stand on ceremony. Very decent fellow, actually, even if his friends edged me out. It was time, perhaps. Everything changes, as Bergson said. And when do I see you again, Robert? Or shouldn't I ask?"

"I really don't know," Renwick said frankly. "But I'll drop in whenever I can. And thank you, Chris, for—"

"Not at all, not at all. Always a pleasure. When you meet Gilman, give him my best. We *are* related, you know." The blue eyes had an amused twinkle. "Rather distantly. Not closely enough to be traced. Security, security. It's always with us—like the opposition, alas. Do you know a cure for blackspot, Robert?"

Accustomed as he was to Chris's conversational jumps, Renwick was nonplused. Chris was delighted. "Roses, Robert, roses. I've tried everything, but the damned spots won't out."

You and Lady Macbeth, thought Renwick, and left the old boy pottering happily through a garden encyclopedia.

Thirteen

THE FIRST AVAILABLE flight to Paris was at six-twenty-five. Renwick put in the waiting time as inconspicuously as possible: a fast-food eating place where no one he knew in Washington would choose to lunch, a visit to an out-of-the-way bank to cash traveler's checks, and enough time left to pick up his suitcase from a locker in a bus station.

By nine o'clock next morning he was in a quiet back room at a little hotel on the Rue Racine, unpacked and everything paid in advance, apparently settled for the next week. Must bring Nina here someday, he thought as he shaved and tried a telephone shower in the bathtub. The room was worth a visit—giant pink and purple peonies, reminding him of Bombay, climbing all over the wall behind a bright brass bedstead with green pillows. But even if the interior decoration raised an eyebrow, the place was neat and clean. There was sunlight, too, easing in through French windows from a small and peaceful courtyard, and the *café au lait* was excellent.

He stepped into the street just before eleven o'clock, glad to be back in tweed-jacket weather. Sunny but cool. He had always liked this section of the Left Bank, with its tight rows of ancient houses lining the narrow streets. At a steady pace, keeping his route complicated enough to discourage any-one trying to follow him, glancing at the small shops that edged the strips of sidewalk—ceramics, primitive masks, hand-fashioned silver ornaments, Greek sculpture, surrealist imaginings—he reached the Seine five minutes ahead of time. Claudel wasn't in sight.

Renwick slowed down, strolled a short distance along the *quai,* his atten-tion seemingly held by one of the excursion boats now passing under the Pont Neuf. There, the river branched around the Ile de la Cité—an island well worth a long look: the delicate spires of La Sainte Chapelle opposing the massive towers of Notre Dame. Nina, he began thinking—and cut off the thought. The sooner you finish this goddamned job, he told himself, the quicker you'll be back to a normal life. The job? It had to be done. Period.

He retraced his steps and paused naturally enough at a bookstall, with its overload of volumes, old and second-hand, that would attract any biblio-phile in search of treasure trove. Claudel was there, exactly on time, bur-rowing through a stack of dusty tomes, looking for a collector's item. Renwick chose to examine a pile of early maps, each of them to be slipped out and held up for a closer view. Claudel, still checking the bruised and battered books, drifted nearer.

Renwick studied a map of Paris in 1860. Voice low, he said, "Call Vroom at The Hague. Tell him I'm flying into Amsterdam today. I'll meet him at Schlee's Rare Books. Four o'clock."

"In the Bruna Building?"

Renwick nodded, apparently over a detail of the Louvre.

That, thought Claudel, will revive a lot of sad memories. It was in the Bruna Building that Jake Crefeld, Vroom's onetime boss, had been assassi-nated two years ago. Vroom had taken over Crefeld's job in intelligence at The Hague, and—as a matter of course—Crefeld's unobtrusive office in Amsterdam. Claudel picked out a likely book, began turning its pages. "Like me to fly you in?"

"If you can pilot with one arm." Renwick rejected the map, riffled through a few others, selected one that showed the River Loire.

"I could do it using one foot. The arm's mending, anyway." Dammit, Bob noticed the bandage bulging my sleeve. But at least he wants me along. Two could be needed. "And when Vroom asks where you are now—you aren't in Paris?"

"Right."

"See you at Orly, one-thirty." Claudel moved away, bought the book—a history of Montmartre when it was a village, apple orchards and all, before girlie shows and tourists had taken over. Then he set off along the *quai* to cross over the bridge onto the Ile de la Cité. Not only were there churches on the island but café-bars and small restaurants. Plenty of phones from which to choose.

Renwick put aside the maps, examined a collection of old magazines, bought a decrepit copy of *transition,* 1932. Those were the days when e. e. cummings declared all capital letters unnecessary, Renwick remembered—and then was astonished by the bits and pieces of nonsensical information that his mind had stored away. Like black spots on rose leaves. Still, they afforded some light relief on this somber day: the visit to Amsterdam would be grim. But if there was any setting that could make Vroom recall the decency and honesty of Jake Crefeld, it was the Schlee office in the Bruna Building. If he was Interintell's traitor, surely his load of guilt must double, make him more vulnerable to questioning when he faced Renwick across Jake's old desk. God, thought Renwick in sudden dejection, let it not be Johan Vroom.

He made his way to the nearest Métro, took a train that would drop him in the direction of Orly, and passed the journey by reading *transition.* So this was the magazine my father enthused over years before I was born, he thought in amazement. Strange sides to the old boy, always something new to discover about him. But he was glad his father couldn't see this sad copy: half its pages torn, a coffee stain blotting out a poem's lack of capital letters, a crude *"Me; de!"* scrawled over some impassioned prose on the purity of art. He propped it on a seat as he left the subway and took a taxi for the remainder of his journey.

Claudel was infatuated by airplanes. He had flown since he was eighteen. Renwick could relax, with the aid of a new hardcrusted roll filled with pink Normandy ham and his share of the bottle of Châteauneuf-du-Pape that Claudel had provided. His light plane, a twin-piston-engined craft, was kept well below ten thousand feet. "Flat as a pancake," he said of the country below them. "No need to climb."

Renwick had no objections. The neat squares of green and golden fields, the darker green of trees and forests, were stitched together by the wandering streams and rivers into a patchwork quilt. Even the man-made blobs of villages and towns looked pleasing from this height. "When do we arrive? Three o'clock?" We live with watches inside our heads, he thought, watches and maps, times and distances. Their cruising speed was being held to two hundred miles an hour; the distance between Paris and Amsterdam was two hundred and fifty-seven miles. "Want me to take over? I've done some flying, you know."

"My arm's okay." Not all that much okay; but no one, not even Bob, handles this little darling. "About forty minutes to go before we put down at Amsterdam's old airport."

"Then we talk. You can stop looking for your Djibouti friend, Pierre."

"How the devil did you know I was doing that?"

"You would. I found out who she is. She isn't working for the Swiss."

"No? She's Swiss-American. Mother lives in Brooklyn. Father in Basel."

"She's with the CIA."

"Jean Zinner? You're sure?"

"Maurice Farley admitted it. Reluctantly. In return, I tipped him off about Erik on board the *Spaarndam*."

"Thank God you did. She isn't there to keep an eye on Erik. We know that. But Erik doesn't." One small slip by Jean Zinner, and Erik would think he was her target. "She's in double danger."

"Farley is warning her, will probably get her to stay on board at Suez when Erik and Haversfield leave."

"Will they?"

"Wouldn't you if you were Erik? When does the *Spaarndam* reach Suez?"

"Should be there tonight."

"A cloak of darkness—that's all Erik needs." That was all Erik ever needed, not just for tonight's escape but for concealment in his world of conspiracy. Men like Erik, fit for treasons, stratagems, and spoils, cloaked their lives in darkness.

"Why is the CIA so interested in Haversfield? He's a small fish."

"Perhaps bigger than we think. What has Gilman found out?"

"Haversfield lives in Chelsea, London. Semi-retired. That lets him travel— he's fond of Paris, it seems. And he pays his taxes."

"Semi-retired from what?"

"A large stationery business."

"Office supplies? Such as typewriters? An agent for Klingfeld and Sons, typewriter exporters? Visits their Paris office?"

Claudel looked at him. "Now you're stretching a point, Bob."

"Except that the CIA is interested in Klingfeld and Sons."

"Did Farley tell you that?" Claudel was amazed.

"He wouldn't even let their name cross his tightly buttoned lips. I bet the CIA guys were onto Haversfield as a dedicated Communist in Berlin. So they wondered about his frequent visits to Paris, set up surveillance, and were led to Klingfeld's office. That's why they monitored the messages being sent from there."

"You could win that bet. What if the CIA had discovered Haversfield was more than a dedicated Communist—a KGB agent? That would interest it, all right." Claudel shook his head. "But does Erik know that he's being KGB-controlled? He had a fight with the Communists in Aden—so Moore said."

"He had a fight with two Cuban Communists. The KGB may have decided they handled him badly. So—its old rule: change of tactics. He's a valuable piece of property to those who plan trouble for the West."

"But will he go along with them?"

"If and when it suits him. It's suiting him right now."

"Alvin Moore said he'd never make it."

"Alvin Moore's political judgment was never very good. He didn't make it himself."

"What?"

"Throat slashed. In his Seychelles hideout."

Claudel was silent. Then he said, "Nearly forgot—Gilman sent you this." He reached into the pocket of his flying jacket, handed over Renwick's Biretta. "You brought your papers with you?"

Renwick nodded. There would be no difficulties at customs.

"What about Moore's girl?"

"Lorna got away. She's probably in Switzerland right now."

"Has she heard, do you think?" Throat slashed, my God. Klingfeld plays rough.

"She isn't worrying about Al Moore, just about her money and Brimmer's little black book."

"Fasten up! We're going in," said Claudel, ditching his thoughts about Klingfeld & Sons.

It was almost four o'clock before they approached the Prinsengracht, a street of gabled houses as ancient as the canal that ran down its middle. The building where Bruna Imports conducted its trade in pepper and coffee had been restored like its neighbors and now looked prosperous but restrained. Its fourth floor, a glorified attic, was unused by Bruna except for storage of outdated records, and Crefeld, Vroom's predecessor, had secured the front room for his more private and confidential business with Intelligence friends and contacts.

Renwick entered first. Claudel followed two minutes later to join Renwick waiting for him inside the very small elevator that took them directly and slowly to the fourth floor. They stepped out into a short corridor and reached the heavy wooden door where a small sign read: J. SCHLEE / RARE BOOKS / BY APPOINTMENT ONLY.

Renwick knocked, and as they waited he pointed to the cutout centered in a wooden rosette that was part of the door's carved decoration. So that's the peephole, Claudel thought, and we're now being checked. Johan Vroom was taking no chances.

The door swung open and Vroom, dark-haired and tall, impeccably dressed, was welcoming them into a paneled room. It was new to Claudel. He studied it covertly: a large desk, comfortable chairs, good lighting, three telephones, a filing cabinet, two long and narrow windows whose panels of diamond-shaped panes had been opened wide. Much the same as ever, thought Renwick, and took a chair to face Vroom, now seated at the desk. Claudel remained standing, keeping near the windows as if he were more interested in watching the canal traffic below than in any conversation.

Vroom was as voluble as ever, his American accent adopted at Georgetown University, where he had once been a student. He was slightly nervous, breaking into complete details about the search for Erik on the *Spaarndam* and its negative results. "We'll board the ship at Suez, of course."

Renwick nodded, said nothing.

Vroom hurried on. "I've sent two good men to make a thorough search of the *Spaarndam* there. I assure you, Bob, everything is being done."

"I'm sure it is."

"How was Djibouti?" Vroom asked Claudel, veering away from the *Spaarndam*.

"Hot. In every way." Claudel turned from the windows to look at Vroom. "When did you hear about Erik?"

"When we got Interintell's request to get in touch with the ship. Tuesday, I believe. It had already sailed." Vroom noticed the exchange of glances between Renwick and Claudel. "Something wrong?"

"Yes," said Renwick. "Are you sure you heard nothing about Claudel's visit before then?"

"Claudel's visit? Oh, is that what you were talking about? Yes, Gilman told me he was on his way to Djibouti—a highly sensitive matter, he said. So I didn't mention it to the rest of my department although my guess was Erik."

"Not even to your chief assistant?"

"To Van Dam? Of course not. There was no need for him to know."

Claudel asked grimly, "Did Gilman mention where I was staying?"

Vroom said impatiently, "He didn't have to tell me. I assumed it was at that Greek's hotel—l'Univers—the one where you stayed last year. You told me about it. We joked about the name when we had dinner together in Athens."

Did I talk about it? Claudel wondered. He couldn't remember much of that evening—he and Vroom had been celebrating a small triumph they had just shared. He fell silent, thoroughly embarrassed.

Vroom felt he had won a point. "What's this all about?" he demanded.

Renwick decided on brutal frankness. "There have been serious leaks of information in Interintell. We have an informant among us."

"And you come asking *me* questions?" Vroom was furious.

"Yes," said Renwick, "we are asking you questions, and we want some answers. Because last week a secret message was sent to The Hague from a firm in Paris. It requested details about Claudel's mission there, mentioned Erik by name. So, Johan, who else at The Hague knew about Claudel in Djibouti? Knew he was trying to discover Erik's trail? Who knew about Erik himself?"

Vroom's face became taut, his features sharpening. He said nothing.

"Who is in your confidence? Van Dam?"

Vroom's voice had thickened. "He would never betray us. Never! I trust him implicitly."

"Someone else in your department?"

"No." The word exploded like a bullet. Vroom's anger increased. "And I am not having an affair with a woman. Nor am I homosexual. I am not being blackmailed into betraying—" He stopped short, compressed his lips, suddenly avoided Renwick's eyes. "Nor," he continued bitterly, "do I have any surplus money. You can examine my bank accounts. No doubt you already have."

Claudel said, "Your wife seems to have some extra cash—"

"That was a legacy from an aunt in Virginia. Not much—just enough to pay Annabel's expenses—she likes to ski so she visits Chamonix for a long weekend just every now and again." Vroom was talking too much, his usual sign of nervousness. "I tried a visit there last winter, but I don't ski. Mountains upset me; I'm not accustomed to them. Annabel, of course, finds

Holland too flat." There was a forced smile on Vroom's lips. "The girl from Virginia, you know—grew up with hills all around her."

Renwick's gray eyes were thoughtful. "You skate, don't you? Surely you could have done that when Annabel was out on the slopes."

"Skate in a rink? Nothing more boring. I'm a long-distance man."

On the frozen canals, of course. Renwick nodded. "But you let her go alone to Chamonix?" That didn't make so much sense: Vroom was devoted to his wife.

"Perfectly safe. She has friends there."

"What about the children—don't they go with her?"

"They're away at school." Vroom's voice was abrupt.

So Annabel was restless, too little to do, and went off to Mont Blanc when the mood seized her. "Well," Renwick said, "your wife won't be leaving you for weekends at Chamonix now."

Vroom looked at him.

"No skiing," Renwick said quietly. Unless, of course, she was so proficient that she could tackle Mont Blanc's peak.

"She likes the mountains. The air does her good."

"She's still going there, in summer?"

"Not *every* weekend," Vroom reminded him.

Now what have we here? Renwick wondered. "No doubt she likes to go shopping in Geneva—it isn't far from Chamonix." Forty miles, perhaps even less.

Vroom stared at Renwick. "You are speaking too much about my wife. Why? You didn't come here to discuss—"

"No," agreed Renwick. "But now I do think we had better discuss Annabel. You talk with her a lot, don't you? Don't get angry! We all talk with our wives. And they ask questions."

"I resent this, Renwick, and I'll ask you to—"

"Do you tell Annabel much? Or leave your special notebook of very private addresses on the night table beside your bed? Along with your keys, or anything valuable?"

"Look"—Vroom was on his feet—"leave Annabel out of this! If I'm under suspicion—"

"We are all under suspicion," Claudel broke in. "All of us. Except Bob here."

"Why except him? Does he think that he's above—"

"His name is on a death list." Claudel controlled his rising temper. "He is marked for assassination along with eight other men—a list that the Paris firm has drawn up. The same firm, Vroom, that gets its information from The Hague."

"There are a thousand people it could contact in Den Haag. All the embassies. Or gossipmongers—professional spies—plenty of them."

"But," said Renwick, "how many among that thousand have their own private two-way transmitters that can reach Paris? Or Geneva, for that matter? You have one in your house, don't you? For emergencies? For your own convenience? Right?" Vroom was a man who liked his comforts.

Vroom nodded. He was no longer angry, just deeply troubled.

"What's more," said Claudel, pressing the sudden advantage, "who in The

Hague could possibly know about Bob's telephone number at Merriman's? Or his old address in London? Or the names of certain restaurants where he gave you dinner? Or the pub where you've met—the Red Lion? Yes, Vroom, they are all noted down on that death list."

"Oh, God—" Vroom groped for his chair, sat down. With an effort, he said, "What's the name of this Paris firm?"

Renwick said, "Klingfeld and Sons. Offices in Paris, Rome, and Geneva." Vroom shook his head. "Don't know it."

"Once it dealt in office supplies: typewriters, desk computers, copying machines. Now it's an arms broker. Illegal arms. It keeps in the background. Tries to pretend it is still the same old reputable dealer in office equipment."

Vroom asked quickly, "KGB control?"

Claudel said under his breath, "Careful, Bob, careful," and turned back to the window.

"Possibly," said Renwick, watching Vroom. "Its headman has several names, no doubt. But he uses one for very convenient cover." He paused, still watching. "Klaus."

"Klaus?" Vroom brushed that aside. "A common name. I must have met three or four of them—"

"Recently? Within the last six months?"

Vroom stared down at the desk. "One," he said, "one was seven months ago. In Chamonix. The weekend when I was there. Just one of Annabel's friends."

Renwick said gently, "Johan, why did you go to Chamonix when you didn't intend to ski or skate? Something was troubling you. Annabel?"

"Yes." With difficulty, Vroom added, "There was a ski instructor. I went there to—" He couldn't finish.

"Throw him down one of Mont Blanc's glaciers?" Renwick suggested. "I'd have done that with pleasure."

Vroom recovered himself. "But he wasn't there. Had gone. I thought the—the affair was over. Annabel swore to me that it was. Bob, she loves me. She loves the children. Believe me."

But there were photographs, thought Renwick sadly, of Annabel and her ski instructor teaching her new tricks in bed. Photographs, threats of exposure and scandal; then her acquiescence in supplying small pieces of information that seemed harmless enough. After that, bribery—just to make doubly sure of Annabel. Tactfully done, of course: expenses paid, pleasure weekends, and some extra spending money on the side. It was the old pattern, and Vroom hadn't even guessed what was happening. Or had he some vague suspicion, tried to ignore it? Silence it?

"Believe me," Vroom repeated. He took out his handkerchief and wiped his brow.

"I believe one thing. You've got to deal with her. At once!"

Vroom stared at Renwick. Then he panicked. "How?"

"Use your brains for a change. Feed her false information, try to trace her control—the man who pulls the strings and makes her jump." Brutal, Renwick knew, but his words acted like a bucket of ice water dumped over Vroom's perspiring forehead.

He blurted out, "Klaus. It could be Klaus."

"Second name?"

"Sounded like Sanuk or Sunek—I only heard it once. Annabel just calls him 'Klaus.' They are all first-name people—Klaus and Willi and Celeste and Pieter and Barney and Magda. Never met any of them separately. Klaus picks up the dinner checks, the bar bills. He drives a gray Ferrari; has a black one, too, for his friends. He's older than they are—almost fifty. But I didn't think he was important. I paid him little attention."

"What? Your wife stayed for weekends at his house and you didn't check?"

"I had other worries on my mind," said Vroom, and his lips tightened.

The ski instructor. "Where did all those first-name people stay?"

"With Klaus. But the weekend I went there"—the words were being dragged out—"Annabel and I stayed down in the town. There was no room at the chalet, and I thanked God for that."

"What chalet?"

"The Chalet Ruskin. It stands above—"

"Bob! Quick! Over here!" Claudel called out. "There are a couple of men in that building directly opposite. Fourth-floor attic. See?" He stepped to the side of the windows. Renwick kept out of view, too, and looked across the canal. Vroom joined them hurriedly. "They've been watching me for the last five minutes," Claudel said.

"Did you install a couple of men over there?" Renwick asked Vroom.

"No one."

Claudel's voice was tight with anger. "Who knew we were meeting you here? Your wife? Was she with you when I called at noon?"

"No. I—" Vroom turned on his heel, walked back to his desk. "I don't believe this. It can't be. It can't!" He crashed his fist down on the heavy mahogany top, sending a large glass ashtray splintering on the wooden floor. "All right, all right. I took Claudel's call at my office. I went home to see Annabel for lunch, explained I couldn't drive her to the airport this afternoon. A meeting, I said. Important. In Amsterdam. Four o'clock. Just couldn't drive her to the plane, she'd have to take a taxi or stay at home. She—she had her driving license suspended a month ago—a silly accident—not her fault really." He was picking up the fragments of ashtray, dropping them one by one into a wastebasket.

"You named us?" Renwick's eyes were watching the window across the canal. The two men—or was it just one man?—weren't visible now. But the window was still open wide.

"Not that way. No. Indirectly. Annabel asked if I couldn't postpone the meeting until later this evening. I said, 'Impossible—Renwick is already on his way, flying in from London.' And then, as I was about to leave after lunch, there was a phone call for Annabel. She took it in the library. I heard her say, 'Klaus?' Then she started explaining she might be late in arriving." Vroom straightened his back, threw the cigar stubs and some burned-out matches on top of the broken pieces of glass, looked with distaste at the white ashes left on the floor. "I didn't listen. It was talk about the weekend at Chamonix, I supposed. Well"—he looked at Renwick, who had turned to face him—"I was wrong. I'll resign from Interintell of course."

"What makes you think Klaus asks questions only about Interintell? Your own department in The Hague is of vital importance."

Vroom slumped, half seated on the edge of the desk.

Claudel was asking, "What's that? At the window. A telescope? Or some kind of rifle? You're the armaments expert, Bob."

Renwick swung around to look. Too heavy for a rifle. "Even heavier than a shotgun." And aimed right at these windows. He yelled to Vroom, "Get away from that desk! Move!" The three of them made a dive for the safest corner of the room, reached its shelter as a bullet exploded on the desk. A second followed. That was all.

"A shotgun never did that," said Claudel, looking toward the debris of a desk. The two chairs that once had faced each other were now tilted drunkenly on broken frames, the remains of their backs torn by shrapnel.

"Keep out of sight from the window," Renwick warned Vroom. "And do your telephoning downstairs. None of these on your desk could possibly work anyway. Come on, Pierre, we'll try to flush them out." They left at a run, using the staircase for speed, and descended through two floors of startled clerks and bookkeepers to reach the hall.

"Whatever that weapon was," Renwick said as they took shelter for a moment in the small crowd at the Bruna Building's front door, "it's too valuable to leave. They'll be dismantling it."

"We're dead anyway," Pierre said. "You and Vroom at the desk, me at the window. They won't expect us."

A voice said from the crowd, "What happened up there? Just look at that smoke. A fire?"

"Not smoke. Dust," Pierre said. "An explosion."

"Gas?"

Pierre's Dutch failed him. So he looked ignorant, and eased himself through the knot of people to join Renwick.

"We'll approach separately," Renwick said. "You take the bridge on our right, I'll use the one on our left. We'll meet inside the hall." Then, as he eyed the house across the canal—it looked abandoned, a candidate either for demolition or for complete restoration—he shook his head, restrained Pierre from leaving with a hand on his arm. A thin straggle of people had been walking along the opposite side of the canal, some carrying children, some carrying rolled-up bedding. Squatters. They were standing now at the door of the deserted house, a tall, long-haired young man urging them inside as if he were leading a charge over the barricades. "The police will soon be here," Renwick said with a sudden smile, "and our friends with the popgun won't like it one bit. Not one bit. Let's join the fun."

There was no need to separate. In the continual flux of movement and sound, they wouldn't be noticed. The squatters, about twenty of them, had already taken possession, the last of them entering the doorway. Except for the young man, who was addressing a group of worried citizens with flights of high rhetoric. Renwick and Claudel reached the center of the small crowd, kept watching the entrance to the house.

"Still inside?" Claudel murmured.

"Unless they left their weapon behind them—made a run for it as soon as they thought their mission was completed." But I doubt that: the gun is something they'll take to pieces, pack away, carry out. "Look for someone carrying a heavy suitcase."

"They'll never get it out through that little mob," Claudel predicted. "The staircase will be jammed."

"They can't wait in the attic, either. The police will search every floor." Interesting, thought Renwick. He shook the remaining dust from his jacket, smoothed back his hair. "We could both use a wash and a brushup," he said. "At least we don't look like a couple of cops," he added as two men, neatly dressed, were hustled out of the building in the grip of four squatters. A large suitcase was hurled after them.

The orator halted his impassioned plea, yelled, "*Agents provocateurs!*" He seized the suitcase, darted with it around the crowd just as a squad of police arrived, reached the canal railing, and heaved it over. It fell into the gray, still waters and sank.

"Too bad," said Renwick. "Okay, Pierre. The show's over."

They left, a fight and loud arguments starting up behind them. "You marked their faces?" Claudel asked.

"Got a firsthand view." But the two men might be out of circulation for some time. Policemen had seized them along with their four escorts, and they were trying to struggle free. A mistake. Resisting arrest. A bad mistake, Renwick thought as one of the men landed a punch. The orator, of course, had vanished completely.

Once out of the narrow street and away from Old Amsterdam's encircling canals, they could find a taxi to take them back to the airport. "We'll clean up there," Renwick suggested, "while you get the tank filled."

"We've enough fuel left to reach Paris."

"What about Geneva?"

"Tonight?"

"We'll get there for dinner. Four hundred miles away, isn't it?"

"Roughly. I'd better get the plane tanked up. Enough cash?"

"Yes. Passport and papers legitimate, too. You?"

"All in order. Transmitter and the travel kit that Bernie prepared. You know, Bob, our mad scientist at Merriman's might have heard of that gun. What the devil was it? Any guess?"

"I've none—needed a closer look." Exploding bullets? Some kind of high-caliber rifle? "It was damned accurate anyway. And the clinching argument as far as Vroom is concerned."

"Do you know Annabel?" The girl whose small pieces of harmless information led to murder and mayhem.

"By sight. She was at one of Jake Crefeld's parties three years ago." Black hair, roving brown eyes, long legs, and a noticeable figure. "She won't remember me—too many men around her." Men who were serious in face and in talk, men who didn't have much time for skiing and dancing. Poor old Vroom, thought Renwick.

Conversation became innocuous until they had left the taxi at the old airport in Amsterdam. Claudel was still thinking about Annabel. "She must use a private plane, too. Or else she'd have to take a flight from Schiphol Airport to Zurich—a long way round for a weekend at Chamonix. Does Klaus send his plane for her, I wonder?"

"No doubt. Part of her expense account."

"She's valuable property. Meanwhile. Until Vroom resigns from all intelligence work. Then she's useless. If he resigns, of course," added Claudel. "Will he?"

"End his career? But what kind of intelligence job would he get with Annabel still on his back?" Renwick shook his head. "He never deserved all this."

"It's the undeserving who often get clobbered. Yet I just can't imagine him teaching her how to use his transmitter. In fact, she wouldn't have risked asking him."

"Klaus probably gave her a lesson or two. It's not too difficult to master."

"And there was easy access to Vroom's study. He's only there for occasional meals and bed." Claudel fell silent for almost a minute. "How will he handle her?"

Renwick just shook his head.

"His problem," Claudel agreed.

And what did a man do when faced with that? "God help him," Renwick said under his breath.

Fourteen

They left Claudel's plane drawn up in its allotted space at the airport outside Geneva. Claudel, before locking up, had activated its alarm system: anyone attempting to enter it would set off a blast of sound that would bring out the fire truck itself. He had left behind his flying jacket, after removing a lighter that could photograph, a pair of eyeglasses that could amplify conversation from fifty feet away, a cigarette pack that could communicate within a three-mile radius. He was now wearing his tweed jacket that could take his neat automatic without bulging a pocket. His good arm carried Bernie's lightweight bag. (Duplicates of lighter, glasses, cigarette pack; a hairbrush whose back slid open to hold useful cipher lists; a talcum-powder tin that held spare film; and ordinary toilet articles such as toothpaste and brushes and shaving kit, useful for emergency stopovers. Also, infrared binoculars that could be used by night, a similar mini-telescope, and—of course—a book on bird-watching.)

Renwick was carrying the radio in its leather case, cut out in front to show an honest face, a portable that would keep a traveler abreast of the news and relax him with music. But remove the leather case and open the back of the radio, and there was a transmitter that could reach approximately a thousand miles—double the distance needed for communication with London. Its antenna, a thin wire minutely coiled and packed under the vinyl lining of the case, was easily strung around a room or dangled down the outside of a window.

If, thought Renwick as they reached the checkpoints for customs and passport control, by any son-of-a-bitching chance we are questioned here, I'll call Duval in Geneva or even Keppler in Bern. Keppler was one of Swiss Security's top men, a big wheel. Duval was an inspector of police. They knew him, had co-operated fully when he was tracking down a numbered bank account in Geneva four years ago—money reeking of conspiracy, theft, and murder—destined for international terrorists. He had been with NATO Intelligence, then, but Keppler and Duval knew about Interintell. Renwick believed in keeping allies informed, even those who were usually neutral except, of course, when Swiss serenity was threatened. And Klingfeld & Sons, with a flourishing office in Geneva, was definitely a real threat. Chamonix was across the frontier in French territory, but it was possible that Inspector Duval could provide some useful advice, if not unobtrusive assistance. After all, he must have contacts there: Geneva and Chamonix were neighbors, both French-speaking, both sharing the same problem—Klaus.

"Nothing to declare," Renwick said. Except a ton weight of worry. They passed through customs. Then passports were examined: two representatives of Merriman & Co., advisers on construction engineering. Business or pleasure? "Pleasure," said Claudel—no one ever asked what kind of pleasure. With a polite nod, they were waved on.

Renwick relaxed. Suddenly he decided: I'll phone them both, Keppler and Duval, tomorrow morning before we leave for Chamonix. But now, a room near the airport, and while Claudel rents a car, I'll make contact with London. A quick report on Vroom and Annabel, information on our destination, and what news from Basset Hill.

The Swiss are larks, up with the break of day. There was no difficulty in reaching Johann Keppler in his office in Bern by eight o'clock, Duval in Geneva at eight-thirty. Renwick gave only a strong hint of serious trouble connecting Geneva and Chamonix, together with an assurance that Keppler and Duval would be kept informed and a promise that the final action in Geneva would be theirs. This was, Renwick emphasized, a matter both for police and for Intelligence. Interintell could need help and would be much obliged.

Both men listened. Renwick was not someone to sound an alert based on flimsy suspicion. Duval even offered the name of a young police inspector in Chamonix whom he knew well—he would contact him right away. Renwick, he suggested, might use the code name Victor for use in any identification there.

"Victor," Claudel said as they left Geneva, and glanced with amusement at Renwick who was driving the Audi he had rented. He was in good fettle this morning: his arm now rested in a sling after being freshly dressed by a Swiss doctor. He had, of course, objected to all that, but Renwick had insisted, and Claudel must admit the result was bliss. So far, at least. "Victor. . ." Claudel joked. "Flattering."

"I doubt that. Duval's a sardonic type."

"Where's your own sense of humor this morning? Come on, Bob. Just look at these buses rolling toward Chamonix. Two of them loaded to the gunwales with Japanese. What draws them to Mont Blanc? The fellow at the garage said none of them miss visiting it—almost a kind of pilgrimage. The highest mountain in Europe, is that it?" But Renwick only nodded. He's worried about that report he got from London last night, Claudel thought. "Look, Bob, it doesn't mean a thing that the supply-room clerk—what's his name? Grable?—turned up at Cooper's old law firm in Washington and tried the same dodge on Rosen that he pulled on Danford in New York. He got nowhere once again."

"Unless someone in the Washington office heard Rosen telephoning Danford about that visit, or Danford's subsequent call to Gilman—" Renwick broke off, passed another busload of tourists, a truck, and two cars.

"A telephone tapped? Even so, you've got Nina well hidden."

But Renwick, eyes on the busy highway—the scenery so far was unremarkable—was worried. "Could there have been some link between Colin Grant and me that I forgot?"

"Not likely. Your memory is too damned tenacious. I know what's bothering you. It's having Grable snoop around Washington. But Nina wouldn't telephone her father, would she? Or visit him?"

"No. Not at present."

"Then let's start worrying about some real trouble. Erik, for instance."

Yes, he's still with us, thought Renwick. The *Spaarndam* had reached Suez ten hours ahead of expectations. Before Vroom's two men had arrived to search the ship, Erik had slipped away. Three hours later the bogus Englishman, Haversfield, had stepped with his luggage onto a launch and headed for shore. But he, at least, had been seen at the airport in Cairo. The Egyptians had reported yesterday he had taken a night flight to Rome. "They won't be far apart," Renwick predicted. "Haversfield needs to keep an eye on Erik, and Erik needs cash to get back to Berlin." Cash and false papers and changes of clothing; and a safe house, too, where he can hide while his identity is changed. "Terrorists don't travel far without a lot of help."

"I bet he learned that lesson in Djibouti when he found he had only enough money left to hire him a dhow as far as the nearest fishing village. Anyway, Bob, we've got the details on Haversfield, and that's something."

It was a considerable something, Renwick had to admit. West German Intelligence had come up with Haversfield's identity along with a photograph taken eight years ago, before he had vanished from Berlin. Its likeness compared nicely with the one on his British passport. And as a bonus to all this, Gilman had discovered the firms with which Haversfield's stationery business dealt. At the head of the list for office equipment was the name Klingfeld & Sons.

Suddenly, the highway shook off the octopus clutch of gas stations, cafés, small factories, same-looking neat houses, and began to climb. Hills heightened into savage peaks. Fir trees mounted the lower slopes, edging the fields and pasture lands in the valley, where a rush of water poured through its broad flat stretch. Above the tree line were precipices and giant ravines and the long gray rivers of ice that crept down from frozen mountaintops.

Claudel pointed to the glaciers. "They are white in winter. Snow covers all the debris they carry along with them—rocks, stones, trees—everything that gets in their way."

"Like Klaus." And what was his second name? Vroom, you left your brains behind when you came into these mountains and met Annabel's friends.

Claudel nodded. First, the killing of Georges Duhamel in Djibouti. Then Alvin Moore. Then Brimmer. Everyone who got in his way. "Who's next?" Claudel asked, trying to keep his voice light. "And where the devil do we find this Chalet Ruskin? Ruskin, Ruskin—that's a strange name for a French alpine village. Who was Ruskin? Anyone at all? Or is it a place far away?"

"He was an Englishman—a pundit on art, architecture, and moral values. Totally nineteenth century." Then Renwick smiled, his first real touch of amusement today. "Ever visited Oxford? There's a college built after his favorite style. My irreverent friends call it 'Ruskin Gothic': red brick, imitation of early Italian, the kind you see in medieval churches around Milan. But what red-brick Ruskin Gothic has got to do with a wooden chalet in Chamonix. . ." Renwick gave up.

And this is the man who worried all morning about a lapse of memory, Claudel thought. "Could Ruskin have ever been here?"

"It's possible. He traveled. A lot of well-heeled English writers did in those days—looking at monuments, looking at mountains." Renwick slowed the car, glanced at Mont Blanc hidden by mists. "Byron was here. Shelley, too. He wrote about that beautiful monster. Called all these mountains around it 'a desert, peopled by the storms alone.' Oh, Shelley—if you could see what we see now." Renwick looked at the row of huge buses, drawn up in neat arrangement before a sprawling inn. Its front garden, complete with long tables and benches, was ready to welcome the avalanche of tourists now pouring in for an eleven-thirty lunch. There was a car park, too, at the side of the inn. "A good idea?" he asked Claudel as he edged the Audi into a free space.

"As long as we don't pretend we're Japanese." But there was plenty of cover available in the Italian, British, German, Dutch, Swedish visitors, even in the few French looking lost in their own homeland.

"Wonder if we could find a room here?" Renwick said. The inn was on the outskirts of Chamonix, but it was a place where they would never be noticed. "Scout around, Pierre. Just see if anything is available—one with good walls where no ears can overhear." And if we're in luck, he thought as he watched Claudel thread his way through the mixture of foreign faces and voices, I can make contact with London before we walk into Chamonix for lunch and a general look-around. Ruskin. Why name a chalet after him? If he had been here, where did he stay? That could be a good angle to follow, however wild it seemed.

His mind branched off into Shelley's poem about Mont Blanc. It was twenty years since Renwick had read it, memorized parts of it. Now, odd lines came back to him, and trying to recapture them was one way to ease the worries that kept nagging at him. *The wilderness*—he remembered, and paused. Yes, the lines began with wilderness. And then?

> The wilderness has a mysterious tongue
> which teaches awful doubt, or faith so mild
> —that man may be
> in such a faith with nature reconciled.
> Thou hast a voice, great Mountain—not understood
> by all, but which the wise, and great, and good
> interpret, or made felt, or deeply feel.

He had lost some phrases there, a rhyme, too. But that was the gist of it. And it had worked. He was less tense, less troubled. He watched the garden, with its colored light bulbs strung among the trees, listened to a babble of languages mixed with the clanking of plates and cutlery. No one was hearing the great Mountain's voice. But, from this sheltered spot, no one could even see Mont Blanc.

"Where do we get a view of Mont Blanc?" he asked as Claudel returned. "From the hills opposite. Right?"

Claudel looked at him in astonishment. "Right. And what brought that on?"

"Shelley. He didn't sit under trees in a garden when he felt that poem. And if Ruskin was here—he wasn't the type to miss a view, either."

Claudel broke into a fit of laughter.

"What's so damned funny?"

Claudel recovered, produced three postcards. "Bought these while I was waiting at the concierge's desk. We have a room, too. Not much to look at, but it's on the back corner, top floor, and the walls seem adequate. I booked us for a long weekend—three nights—until Tuesday. Not many people stay here. Day tourists mostly. We're just ten minutes, walking, from the center of town. Okay?"

"Very much okay." Renwick glanced briefly at the first two postcards. One was of the Mer de Glace, the sea of ice on Mont Blanc, where the glaciers began; the other showed a statue of the local doctor who had been the first to climb the mountain in 1786. At the third postcard, he stopped. Surprise, followed by delight, spread over his face. It was a view from a high hillside, from a small, flat stretch of grass overlooking the crests of descending fir trees. Below them, the valley. Beyond it, Mont Blanc's white peak soaring into a very blue heaven. But it was on the stretch of grass that Renwick's eyes were fixed. At one side was a giant boulder, beneath which the caption read: *Ruskin's Chair.*

He turned over the card, found an elucidation printed in four languages: *The famous English nineteenth-century critic, John Ruskin, spent many happy hours here each day admiring the beauties of Mont Blanc. Come to lovely Chamonix! All winter and summer sports!*

"Well," said Renwick, "what about that?"

Claudel enjoyed a small moment of triumph. Then, "Come on, Bob. Let's have a look at the room. Its door has a strong lock. Also the wardrobe. We French like security, even on holiday. We can leave our baggage safely there when we step into town. Don't worry about our transmitter. Anyone who doesn't know how to open it is in for a nasty shock. Literally."

The room was as described: nothing much to look at inside; outside, a vegetable garden with trees behind it. "Couldn't be better," Renwick said, and began setting up communications with London.

There was a favorable report from the Washington scene. Nothing more on Rome, as yet. "Love to my girl. Tell her all is well," Renwick ended, and signed off.

"Lunch in the busy metropolis?" Claudel suggested.

"We'll aim for a central café, and then we'll wander as tourists do."

"Wonder if Ruskin's Chair will be any help. If he was a local celebrity a hundred years ago, his name could be popping up all over the place."

"Hope not." Renwick's depression of this morning had been routed. Even if Haversfield—and Erik—were arriving in Rome right now, Renwick's spirits were rising. No worrying news from Washington: Nina was safe.

Right in the heart of the little town, neat streets, neat shops and houses—no Tyrolean decorations here—they found a café with a rushing stream outside its door and a large statue of Dr. Paccard, the first to scale Mont Blanc, pointing triumphantly to its distant peak. He also blotted out any possible view of the mountain from the café's picture window.

No one seemed to mind. The people crowding the well-spaced tables were not day tourists; or local inhabitants. Weekend visitors and summer residents, young for the most part, some in jeans, some in tennis clothes, others in well-cut blazers or smart cardigans. "Strange," Renwick said, "how there's always one café in any tourist town where the well heeled and carefree gather. A kind of homing instinct. How's it done? By word of mouth or telepathy?"

"By the prices." Claudel was studying a scant menu. "They're enough to chase any busload away. I'll have an omelette, cheese, salad, and a carafe of white wine."

"The same." They were speaking in French, and with their tweed jackets, ties already removed, and collars unbuttoned, they were casual enough to fit into the scene. Renwick looked for a waitress, took the opportunity to glance around the room. He laid the menu aside, lit a cigarette, looked out the window at Dr. Paccard's coattails, and let Claudel do the ordering.

He has spotted someone, Claudel thought, and resisted looking around at the far corner of the room. From a table there, somewhere near the small bar, he could hear voices speaking in English. The words came in snatches. A mixed group: men with German or Slavonic accents, a woman's voice with a definite French intonation, another woman's voice. American? Slightly Southern in its soft drawl? "She's here," he said very softly.

Renwick nodded. Annabel Vroom, dressed for tennis, was holding court.

"Her protector?"

"Not here." Klaus—so Vroom had said—was around fifty. The men at Annabel's table were her age mostly, late twenties, early thirties. "Let's eat and clear out." And start our search. There must be several hundred chalets tucked into the hillsides around the town. At least we know the view from Ruskin's Chair, and that's a start. But we can't sit here in dead silence. "I'd have thought Chamonix would have been built closer to Mont Blanc," he tried.

Claudel caught on and started a long explanation. The town had once been farther along the valley, near the approach to the mountain. Then the glaciers disintegrated.

"How?"

"Never could understand that myself. But the valley below them—all the houses, all the farms—was completely destroyed."

"So the people took the hint. Rebuilt at a safe distance."

"Exactly. Now over near Zermatt, the danger is from avalanches." The talk went on about the hazards of mountains, about the men who climbed them, and lasted nicely through omelette and Roquefort cheese.

As they rose to leave, Claudel could risk a casual glance around the room. Four men and two women at the corner table. Dark hair, he noted, on the girl in tennis clothes—she was listening intently to a blond man similarly dressed, a possessive type, and athletic. Partners for the day or for the night? Had the ski instructor returned for the summer season? Claudel followed Renwick toward the door. And then Renwick surprised him, turning his head to speak as a man paused just inside the entrance.

"Who's the smaller figure on the Paccard monument—looking up admiringly at the doctor?"

"Ballat—" Claudel began and was interrupted by a surprised shout from the corner table: "Hey, Barney! When did you get in?"

Barney gave a wave of his hand and a cheerful greeting. "Hey there, yourself!" he called back and passed Renwick and Claudel, who was now explaining that Ballat was Paccard's porter, had trundled the heavy ropes all the way to the top of the peak, and some said he had climbed it ahead of the good doctor.

And then they were out, leaving a lot of handshaking and backslapping and general welcoming behind them, stepping into the heady mixture of warm sunshine and crisp air. They paused, as good mountaineering enthusiasts would, to read the inscription at the statue's base.

There was a delighted look on Renwick's face. "That was the guy I saw in New York handing out a tip to garage attendants before he drove away in a borrowed ambulance."

"That was on Tuesday—just after your visit to Exports Consolidated. Time enough for Barney to be called back to Chamonix. As a reinforcement?"

"Or to deliver any documents he filched from Brimmer's office. When the FBI visited it, nothing incriminating was found."

"Nothing to connect Klingfeld and Sons with Brimmer," Claudel said. "Clever boys. They move fast."

"Why d'you think we've been breaking our necks?" Renwick asked. "Yes, they move fast. We just have to be faster."

"Barney gave us a sharp look—not that he could see much of your face. Would he recognize you?"

"Don't think so. I kept well behind a blue Chevy." But it had been Barney, all right: same round cheeks and broad smile, same wave of the hand, same voice. A threatened abduction was one moment you didn't forget: smallest details were stamped into your mind. "Okay, Pierre, let's start our search."

They strolled through the crowded street, veering—once they were out of sight from the café—toward the hillside that rose on their right hand. Judging from the postcard, its viewpoint was somewhere up there. "Could be several roads up that hill," Claudel said. And chalets dotted around each of them. Couldn't ask directions, either: Klaus was bound to have a couple of informers planted here as a safeguard. No easy way to trace his chalet, yet it had to be found. It was the surest chance of seeing him. Without that, no surveillance would be possible. "It will be a long hot afternoon," he predicted gloomily.

"Can't imagine any of those chalet dwellers walking all the way down to a café and then climbing back uphill. We'll have a look at the parked cars. A black Ferrari is what we need."

"You don't expect Klaus's gray one?"

"Later. If Klaus were in Chamonix now, I don't think Barney would have time to relax with the gang." He must have a report to make—details of his successes in New York, plausible excuses for his failures. It was nice to be one of these, Renwick thought.

"It looked as if he had just arrived, found no one at home, dropped down to the old hangout for lunch. Quite a welcome he got."

From dupes and dopes, thought Renwick. "He's one of the three who murdered Brimmer. Possibly by a cyanide pistol. Heart failure as usual."

"A team of three? Is that a fact or a guess?"

"A little of both. I saw three of them working together: Barney, the man who drove the ambulance, and of course Grable. As the clerk in charge of supplies, he knew the floor plan of the office and could smuggle the others inside. He also could talk his way into Brimmer's office, get its door unlocked. It took more than one man to kill Brimmer and go through all of the files, yet leave them in good order as if nothing had been touched. Otherwise, Brimmer's death might have raised questions."

"Will the other two turn up in Chamonix?" Pierre speculated.

"I wish they would," Renwick said. Then Grable would be out of Washington, with no lead to Nina discovered. "I wish they would," Renwick repeated, and began searching for a black Ferrari.

Fifteen

THEY FOUND THE Ferrari parked among a group of seven cars at the foot of a quiet road leading off the busy main street. The road was unpaved, broad at its start, narrowing as it climbed. There had been a row of simple houses at its beginning, with a woman hanging out some family wash and another beating a rug even if this was the start of a Saturday afternoon. Farther uphill, only trees and bushes edged the road. There were no chalets in sight.

There had to be some, thought Claudel: too many cars at the bottom of this road; or had the Ferrari been left there simply because of good parking space? A discouraging notion. He stopped, eased his arm in its sling, and waited for Renwick, who was picking up a small wooden sign that had toppled on its face along with its support. Renwick held it out, and Claudel looked. The lettering was faded but it was still legible: RUSKIN'S CHAIR. And the arrow that followed the two words had once pointed uphill.

Renwick replaced the sign among grass and wild flowers, exactly as he had found it. Someone hadn't wanted this hillside too easily identified. Either that or poor old Ruskin was now a defunct celebrity. Certainly this route was little traveled nowadays by anyone on foot, but on the flatter stretches of the road, where the earth soaked by recent rains had turned into half-dried mud, there were traces of several cars.

"Must be a dozen houses up this way," Claudel said, examining the criss-cross of tread marks. "I bet you one thing: Klaus won't have any nameplate displayed at his gate." He looked around at the bushes and trees. "Houses, where are you?"

"Playing hide-and-seek behind clumps of firs. We've only walked about half a mile. Can't expect Klaus to choose a chalet so near the town." Or could we? With a man like Klaus, you could never guess.

But as they turned the very next curve, they saw a chalet lying quite openly on the right-hand side of the road with only a few bushes clustered around it. "Too small," Renwick said, and became more interested in a knee-high sign-post on the left side of the road.

"Too small and too exposed." Claudel studied it. "And no signs of life. All windows shuttered. But it's in good repair. Possibly used for winters only. Skiers?"

"Look at this," Renwick said and waved a hand toward the sign. It contained no name, nothing except a definite arrow pointing uphill. In size, age, and weathering, it matched the previous signpost they had seen, but this one stood straight and firm. Six feet beyond it, a definite footpath branched off to the left, climbing through thick bushes into a heavy fringe of fir trees. Surely that was the original direction of the arrow. Renwick was thoughtful as he looked at the sign. Yes, the arrow now pointed directly uphill. But that view on the postcard wasn't seen from any roadside.

"I spot two more chalets—over there, to the right—a short distance above the first one. Lots of trees around them. But," Claudel decided with regret as he pulled out his mini-telescope and focused on their rooftops, "not big enough to sleep Klaus's guests."

"Let's try this path," Renwick said.

In a few minutes they emerged onto a small stretch of grass that lay at the edge of a wooded cliff dropping down to the valley. And there, occupying most of this space, was a giant boulder. The view from it was identical with the one on the postcard. Renwick leaned against Ruskin's Chair, looked across the valley at a mass of soaring precipices and ice-filled ravines. But swirls of soft gray mist had started to circle around Mont Blanc's peak, blotting out its thrust into a sky of white clouds. "Will we ever see that mountain?" Renwick asked softly. Then he turned his head to glance behind him, noted the continuing hill that was thick with giant trees. "Could it be . . ." he began. Improbable yet possible. Yes, possible . . .

Claudel said impatiently, "Come on, Bob. We didn't climb up here to look at a view. Let's get back to the road, start searching—"

"There's an easier way to find Klaus's chalet. Safer, too."

"How?"

"Just answer me two questions, Pierre. Why was that arrow pointed uphill? It was meant to mark the path. But it pointed straight up that road."

"Someone angled it, fixed it firmly in place."

"To alert any visitor—anyone who is a stranger to that road—who is driving up to Klaus's chalet."

"A direction post? Warning him to be ready for the next opening he sees?" Claudel's voice had quickened.

"Next opening on his left," Renwick said.

"Why on his left? The next driveway could be on his right."

"Could be—except for the second question. How was Vroom going to end the sentence you interrupted, when you called us over to the window in his office?"

Claudel concentrated. Two men at a fourth-floor window opposite the Bruna Building, myself watching, Renwick and Vroom talking. "I heard Vroom name Klaus and then the Chalet Ruskin. As I called to you, he was saying, 'It stands above—' Right?"

"That's what I heard." Nice to be confirmed, Renwick thought. "Stands above—what?"

"The town."

"I thought so, too, until we came up here." Renwick patted the boulder against which his shoulder still leaned.

"Stands above Ruskin's Chair?" Claudel's voice quickened. "Could be, could be. The first driveway on the left would lead to a house just up there— above where we are standing now." He looked at the rise of land behind Ruskin's favorite perch. "Nicely wooded. Good protection for a chalet."

"And good cover for us. Let's have a look."

The climb might be steep, but it would have been easy enough if they hadn't been wearing leather-soled shoes. Underfoot, a heavy layer of dried-out pine needles coated the soft earth. It will be hell coming down, Renwick thought as they stepped into the wood; we'll be glissading all the way. Trees could be avoided; they were spaced enough, but there were scattered outcrops of rock. Pierre's wounded arm? We'll damn well have to take care, Renwick told himself: no headlong rush to lower and perhaps safer ground.

Suddenly, the dead silence was broken by a car at full throttle. They halted, concentrated on tracking its progress. It was traveling uphill, drawing nearer. And then it must have swung into a driveway just above these trees. It stopped abruptly. Claudel pointed straight up the slope in front of them. Renwick nodded: there was definitely some chalet ahead of them. In spite of the pine needles, their pace increased. Five minutes more and they were reaching the last of the trees, and beyond them a fence. Not a wall, thought

Renwick in surprise: just an eight-foot fence of thin iron railings, blocking nothing from sight.

They took cover behind the drooping branches of a larch and studied the house. Everything lay open, totally innocent. Three chalets joined together and modernized with wide picture windows, rising above a terrace fronted by a narrow garden; below that, a broad sweep of alpine grass and wild flowers reaching down to the fence. At the side of this converted group of chalets was a garage where the driveway ended. The four-doored garage was open and empty except for a small yellow car—could be a jeep, Renwick judged—while a black Ferrari stood outside, carelessly parked. At the other end of the house there was a tennis court; behind it, a screen of well-trimmed bushes. It must shelter a pool: sounds of splashing, of diving, of applause and merriment, and the excited barking of small dogs joining in the fun. Yes, thought Renwick again, everything open and totally innocent. Look at me, the house said, I've nothing to hide. He signed to Claudel. Carefully they backed away, made a safe retreat down through the wood.

Renwick went first, insisting that Claudel grasp his shoulder in case of a slip. "Sure, you're indestructible," Renwick told him once they were out of earshot from the house, "but just hang on to me, will you?" Claudel's annoyance was showing, partly due to his arm in that confounded sling—he'd get rid of the damned thing before tonight—but mostly because of his disappointment over the chalet. How do we get near enough to the place with all those picture windows? Bright lights in every room, no doubt, and a collection of yapping poodles who might not prowl around like Dobermans or German shepherds but who'd start barking at the slightest shadow. Renwick felt the same way: no more words were exchanged until they came out into the clearing. There they paused for some estimation of the scene.

"It's so goddamn innocent," said Renwick. "Something is strange about that whole setup. We'll get a closer look tonight."

"Not too close, I hope."

"Just enough to let us see Klaus. He wouldn't have invited these guests if he didn't mean to be there."

"What about an alarm system? I could see nothing."

"None around the fence as far as I could make out."

"Just barbed wire laced neatly along the top. How do we get over that?" We're traveling light, thought Claudel, we haven't got the equipment for any assault.

"A small mattress." Renwick had walked over to the edge of the clearing. Its drop was steep but not impossible. But by night? And with Pierre's arm out of real commission? "The local kids probably climb it every Sunday afternoon."

"We're not local. We're not young mountain goats, either. And Sunday afternoon is not full of black shadows. Tonight, we'll have to use the road again." And damn this arm.

"Let's get back to it now. We'll have to do some shopping in town." Rubber-soled sneakers, for one thing; dark sweaters and jeans, for another. Night work would leave tweed jackets and flannels looking fit only for scarecrows.

They had almost reached the road. They stopped abruptly as they heard the sound of cars coming uphill. "Two?" Renwick asked.

"Two," Claudel agreed. "Both high-powered."

Quickly, they chose the largest bush with a view of the road, stretched out under its cover.

"Look at that, will you?" Renwick said softly, his eyes on the small chalet opposite. Its shutters were still firmly closed but its door had opened. A woman stood waiting just inside the threshold and half emerged as the first car reached the path that led to the house. It drew up expertly—a silver-gray Ferrari. Its driver stepped out, looking around him, checking the road, and then signaled to the Mercedes that had stopped behind him. Tall, fair hair neatly cut, tanned face, strong features, decided movements. Klaus? Could be, thought Renwick. But we are not close enough to make sure of his age. From here he looks younger than fifty.

Renwick's attention swung away to the second car. Its door was open, but there was a delay. Why? Then he understood. Someone was being lifted out of the Mercedes by the driver and another man, someone wrapped in a concealing blanket. No movement at all. The still shape was being carried quickly up the path and into the chalet. One minute passed; almost another. Too distant a shot for his lighter's little camera, Renwick judged, and concentrated on photographing the face and build of the Ferrari's driver in his memory. Beside him, Claudel was doing the same thing, his brown eyes gleaming with excitement. He had his heavy-rimmed eyeglasses out, ready to slip in place as soon as the men reappeared and possibly started to talk.

But only one man came out, hurrying down the path to stop at the Ferrari. He reported briefly, was given in turn several instructions. Then the man—definitely young, strong-shouldered, quick in his movements—hastened to the Mercedes while the other slipped back behind the wheel of the Ferrari. The Mercedes made a precarious but competent reverse on the narrow road, drove downhill, almost grazing the bank on which Renwick and Claudel lay. The Ferrari's engine had started as the other car completed its bold turn and was about to continue its ascent. And at that moment a woman came racing wildly down the road. "Klaus! Klaus!"

The Ferrari braked. The driver stepped out, caught her wrist. "What's wrong?"

"I had to see you alone. Oh, Klaus, he knows! He telephoned! He said—" But whatever had been said on the telephone was silenced as Klaus shoved her into the car, took his seat, began driving. The Ferrari roared uphill, turned left within seconds, and soon came to a stop.

Claudel rolled onto his back, pushed aside some leaves from his face as he removed his glasses. "I got both car numbers. But couldn't hear one mumbling word of those instructions. Too far away." He pocketed the glasses carefully. "Didn't need anything to hear Annabel, did we? My God, she was terrified—hysterical. Wonder what Vroom did say on the phone." He sat up, drew a long breath. "What's next?"

"For us or for Annabel?"

To avoid being noticed by someone in the chalet opposite them, Renwick and Claudel had two choices. They could wait until darkness fell—possibly three or more hours—before they stepped onto the road. Or they could cut over the rough ground on the bank where they lay, reach the road a short distance downhill. "We've seen enough now," Renwick said softly, watching the chalet, which looked completely deserted once more. "Tonight we can risk a closer look." For that was where the real action was. The big house was a front, a cover, where Klaus played the country gentleman to a pack of informers and sycophants. But that woman at the chalet's door had looked more than a caretaker: as tall and strong as the man who had stayed with her.

With some difficulty, they made the scramble through the bushes, taking extreme care not to start any branches shaking. Soon they reached the curve that hid the chalet and could step down from the bank onto the road. They set out briskly.

Renwick was thinking about plain board shutters, no louvers, everything inside lit by electricity. Ventilation? Possibly at night when the back windows could be safely opened. "No dogs at least." No car visible, no bicycle, either; nothing to give the show away.

"Thank God," said Claudel. "Either they attack or they yap. Bloody nuisance. What shall we find in there? Two people on their feet, someone bundled in a blanket. But perhaps that third person is on his feet, too, now that he has been smuggled safely inside. What d'you think?"

"It's worth finding out." Renwick looked at his watch, slackened their quick stride to a more normal stroll. It was just after four o'clock. Ahead of them the road began to broaden. A little distance farther downhill, there was a cluster of parked cars, and then the busy main street.

"Well," Claudel said, "we can at last put a face to the name Klaus."

"We still need his second name. And not garbled this time."

"What about a visit to the local cop—get his help with that?"

"Later. We've plenty of suspicions, but Inspector Marchand will need more than them." So would Duval, his friend and mine, back in Geneva. So would Keppler in Bern. "Might be an idea to call Duval at once, get him to run a check on the gray Ferrari. You got its number—Geneva, wasn't it?"

"Yes. But the Mercedes had a Zurich plate."

Renwick raised an eyebrow.

"That doesn't mean it drove from Zurich today," Claudel reminded him.

"No. But it had collected more dust than the Ferrari." There had been mud spatters, too, above the wheels.

"Hate to spoil a good assumption. A black car does show more dust than a gray one."

Renwick's attention switched to the group of parked cars which they were now approaching. Against a white Renault, a man was leaning, watching them. He was of medium height, well proportioned, a neat figure in a tweed jacket, corduroy trousers, and turtleneck sweater. A cigarette was held in one hand while the other smoothed back a thick crop of black hair as he stepped away from his car and intercepted them. Dark eyes, quick and observant, studied them. Then he nodded.

"I'm Marchand," he said. "I've been expecting you since our friend Inspector Duval called from Geneva this morning. His description of you," he told Renwick, "was accurate. I don't think we need to use the word 'Victor,' Colonel Renwick." He bowed slightly. "Major Claudel."

"We don't use rank, either," Renwick said, keeping his voice friendly, repressing both surprise and annoyance.

"Nor I," agreed Marchand. "I hope I'm not interrupting your plans." He paused, his eyes watchful.

You know damn well you are, Renwick thought.

"But," Marchand went on, "I am curious why you're here. We have no terrorists in Chamonix."

Claudel said, "Let's walk while we talk. I feel naked just standing around. Perhaps a drink somewhere? After all, you're out of uniform." But always on duty, he thought.

"Saturday," Marchand said as if that explanation was enough, and opened the Renault's doors. "It is quite comfortable," he told them, noticing a slight hesitation. "No abduction, I assure you," he added. "I'll drive you to the inn where you are staying and save you a little walk. You've had enough exercise for one afternoon."

Smooth, thought Renwick, smooth; and he probably is a cop. With a telescope trying to follow us ever since we started up this damned road? "Thank you, but we've some shopping to do in town. Didn't bring a change of clothes with us."

"I think you'll find what you need at a place I know."

Claudel climbed into the back seat; Renwick sat beside Marchand. That way—if Marchand weren't Duval's friend, if he did try to drive them to some remote house—they'd be able to control him more easily. Marchand just nodded at this small maneuver, as if he himself would have done the same thing. The shop he had chosen for them was excellent: a small establishment that sold ski clothes in winter, climbing and hiking outfits in summer; and the sign over its door was ETIENNE MARCHAND. "My uncle," Marchand said as he noted Renwick's eyes on the name.

He waited in the car tactfully while they selected two warm outfits, both dark blue in color, and made sure that there were deep pockets. Navy-blue sneakers came next. "Glad we don't have to carry out a rolled-up mattress, even cot-size," Claudel murmured, remembering the project of climbing over an eight-foot fence laced with barbed wire. No need for that now. They had seen Klaus, could identify him. The chalet with the shuttered windows took priority. Always the way, he thought: you plan one thing, and then something else pops up. Like Inspector Marchand.

Renwick added a couple of lightweight turtleneck sweaters to their purchases, one navy and one black.

"Will the expense account stretch enough?" Claudel asked slyly.

"Barely—after your extravagance today. Three postcards when we needed only one."

"Couldn't draw attention to—" Claudel began, and then realized Renwick was joshing. That's a good sign, he thought. "Decided to trust our friend in the car?"

Renwick nodded. "What else?" As a friend Marchand would be helpful. As an opponent, difficult. The man was no fool; no small-town lackadaisical cop taking everything with a genial shrug, well that's the way life is today, what can you do about it?

Marchand had the doors open for them, ready to drive away. He didn't ask any questions about the packages, but he didn't need to. He can easily find out what we bought, Renwick thought in amusement, when he picks up a phone and talks with his uncle.

The distance to the inn was short. Marchand had only time enough to say that he had heard about Interintell, in fact had discussed it with Inspector Duval. They had worked with Interpol, of course—a matter of dealing with criminals smuggling stolen diamonds out of Geneva into Chamonix.

"Why Chamonix?" Renwick asked. But at that moment they arrived at the inn. The garden was empty—too early yet for dinner to be served—just three thin waiters wandering around like stray ghosts as they laid out the place settings. Renwick saw one table near the trees, a sheltered spot, still bare of forks and knives and paper napkins tucked into thick tumblers. "Have you time for a drink?"

"Why not?" Marchand stepped quickly out of the car.

"What brings diamond thieves to Chamonix?" Renwick asked when three beers had been placed before them.

"A choice of exits." Marchand hesitated, said, "Perhaps we should speak in English, no? I was a student in London—and later in America." He broke into English. "Our talk would go quicker. Right?"

Renwick, who had thought he was coping pretty well with Marchand's French, only nodded. But he wondered if the use of English was to encourage him to talk more. "A choice of exits from Chamonix?" he prompted.

"To the west you can reach Lyons, and south from there Marseilles. Or, if you go north from Lyons, quick access to Paris. If you prefer Italy, then the Mont Blanc Tunnel takes you east and you arrive in Milan. From there, Genoa or Rome. The roads are excellent and more difficult to watch than airports or railway stations. So many car changes are possible—wayside garages that can't be observed all the time." Marchand's English was precise. Claudel was impressed. A good student, he thought, and glanced at Renwick. But Renwick's mind wasn't on accents or vocabulary at this moment.

A choice of exits meant a choice of entries, too. Take Rome, for instance, as the starting point for a journey to this part of France. By air, Rome to Milan was a three-hundred-mile flight. Then by car from Milan to the Mont Blanc Tunnel? Not as difficult as it sounded—trucks used that route all the time. The tunnel itself, right through the giant massif of Mont Blanc, was about seven miles long. A total, perhaps, from Milan to Chamonix of just over two hundred miles—not much more. And almost a third of that distance was on the plains of Lombardy where the giant highway from Milan would let a car stay within the speed limit at eighty miles an hour. In fact, thought Renwick, I've traveled that *autostrada* at ninety miles an hour. "Interesting," he said.

Claudel was watching Renwick. Now what is he calculating this time? he wondered.

More waiters were arriving. Marchand waved away two who hovered near the table. "Later," he told them, "later." He turned again to Renwick. "Tell me one thing—why are you interested in Ruskin's Chair? Or, rather, why did you explore the woods behind it?"

"Your telescope couldn't follow us in there?" Renwick asked blandly.

"Unfortunately, no. Is there something I should learn about the Chalet Ruskin?"

"There is. But, first, tell us about its owner. What do you know of him? Klaus—what's his name?" Renwick looked vaguely at Claudel, whose memory also seemed to have lapsed.

"Sudak," said Marchand.

"Sudak?" Claudel repeated. "Where does he come from?" It sounded Czech, Polish, even Hungarian.

"Originally from Paris." Marchand hesitated. Then he said, "A professor I know at Grenoble University—a specialist in Russian history—tells me there is a small village called Sudak on the Black Sea. Not far from Yalta."

"Was he born there?" Renwick asked.

"I've never heard even a whisper of Russia. He is a French citizen, resident in Switzerland and completely neutral. Also, a most successful businessman. Now tell me why you are interested in his chalet. Or are you interested in Monsieur Sudak?"

"Yes," Renwick said frankly. "Interested in him and in the firm he now controls—Klingfeld and Sons. Head office in Geneva, I think."

"That's well known."

"Branch offices in Paris and Rome."

"Oh? Klingfeld and Sons are an old established business, of course. No doubt their market is widespread."

"Very widespread. Recently, Klaus Sudak has merged Klingfeld with an American firm, but secretly. He controls it, too."

"Oh?" Marchand asked again but added no comment this time.

"That firm, Exports Consolidated, is now under investigation by the FBI. Also, I suspect, by several other federal agencies. Its business has been the illegal export of armaments. Recently, since its amalgamation with Klingfeld and Sons, it has been supplying weapons—and instructors—for international terrorists in certain Communist training camps."

Marchand's dark eyes stared at Renwick, then at Claudel.

"Yes," Claudel said, "we have every reason to be interested in Klaus Sudak. And in his Chalet Ruskin. And in—" He hesitated, glanced at Renwick. Are we spilling too much? he seemed to be asking.

"And," Renwick finished the sentence for Claudel, "in the little chalet opposite the path to Ruskin's Chair. It's apparently closed."

"It is. It was bought recently by an Englishman, but he isn't taking up residence until the winter season starts."

"Klaus Sudak is occupying it."

"Sudak?"

"We saw his Ferrari arrive there, along with a black Mercedes. There was a woman, a caretaker perhaps, who opened the chalet door for two men from the Mercedes. They carried a bundle of some kind. Klaus Sudak waited until one of the men returned. They spoke. The Mercedes headed downhill. Sudak then drove to his house. The small chalet is still shuttered, looks completely closed and empty."

"But what—how—"

"We don't know as yet. But we'll keep you informed. If arrests are necessary, we'll need your men."

"You may need them before any arrests are made."

Meaning what? Renwick wondered. Marchand offering to help in our search, or Marchand giving a polite warning that we don't break the law? Suddenly the little colored bulbs above their heads were turned on although daylight was as yet strong. "We can take a hint," Renwick said, playing on words, and rose.

They walked back to the Renault to pick up their packages. Renwick said, "I needn't add that all this is definitely in strictest confidence. We aren't the only intelligence agency that has become interested in Klingfeld and Sons."

"Strictest confidence," Marchand agreed. "But I should inform Duval."

"Agreed. But inform him quietly. Very quietly."

"We do exchange top-secret information." Marchand's serious face relaxed into a small smile. "About jewel thieves. Not about terrorists." The smile faded. He stared again at Renwick, then at Claudel. "Can all this be possible? A reputable businessman like Sudak?"

"Not only possible but true. Tell me one thing. Why did he use the name Ruskin for his chalet?"

The question was so unexpected that Marchand actually showed astonishment. "It's always been used—ever since the first chalet was built there, one hundred and thirty years ago. It burned down, was replaced. That one also burned. Then three adjoining chalets were grouped on that site. The name has always remained the same. In fact, when Sudak bought the chalets three years ago and had them converted for his use, the people here would have been scandalized if he had not kept the Chalet Ruskin name. It's part of the history of that hillside. Sudak understood that."

"He was told? Politely, of course."

"Yes. And he listened. He wishes to please, shall we say?"

Which made it all the more difficult for a young police inspector to deal with this situation, Renwick thought as he shook hands and thanked Marchand for his patience. Claudel put it more bluntly but in his admirable French accent it sounded almost diplomatic. "We'll be glad of any assistance you can render us, direct or indirect."

Marchand nodded, looked at the packages they carried, and reached into the glove compartment of his car. He produced a hand-size transmitter. "This will find me wherever I am. Within five miles, of course. It's set on the wavelength I use."

"We'll keep it there," Renwick assured him.

"Remember, any difficulty at all, any problem . . ." Marchand shrugged, got into his car.

"We'll remember."

Claudel had taken out his notebook and pencil, was scribbling rapidly. He tore the page loose, gave it to Marchand. "Number of black Mercedes. Zurich registration." Marchand raised an eyebrow, but he slipped the page into his pocket. The car left.

Early diners, footsore and cold, were trickling into the garden. On the road outside, a line of excursion buses moved into place, reminding those on a package deal they would be leaving within the hour. There was a blare of rock-and-roll from hidden loudspeakers, a dazzle of little lights strung among the trees.

"Wild night life," Claudel said as they approached the inn. "We'll bribe a waiter to bring us hot food in the dining room. Chilly out there." And it would be colder on the hillside. "Wonder if we'll be alone tonight," he speculated once they had reached the privacy of their room. Everything, he noted, was in place; nothing disturbed.

"Marchand won't be far off." Renwick was busy setting up communication with London.

"We surprised him. He didn't expect to be told so much. Too much?" That worried Claudel.

"We need his help, and he needed to know. Don't believe in treating an ally as if he were the enemy."

"You're trusting him a lot, Bob."

"He's trusting us." Renwick pointed to Marchand's neat little transmitter, all set and ready to go, now lying on top of the bureau.

"He must have known we had a couple of our own," Claudel speculated, then added, "But not on his wavelength." He left to take a shower in the bathroom at the end of the hall. Renwick was already in contact with London.

"Good report?" Claudel asked when he at last came back into the room. "No shower. I soaked in the tub instead, with one arm held high." He had removed its sling.

Renwick finished packing the transceiver into its leather case. "Mixed." Something's wrong, Claudel worried. "You had plenty to tell them."

"That, yes."

"Any news of Erik?"

"Reported seen in Rome, in Naples, in Milan. Take your pick."

"And William Haversfield?"

"In Rome. Under surveillance for two hours. He dodged it."

Expert, thought Claudel: we're dealing with a real professional here. "Then Erik was in Rome, too. Disguised as a priest. Or perhaps a nun?"

Even that didn't raise any response from Renwick.

"How's Washington?" Claudel's voice was as casual as possible.

"Grable is hanging around."

The supply-room clerk . . . "Where?"

"The FBI spotted him. Lost him. In Georgetown—near O'Connell's house."

"Nina's father isn't there, is he?"

"No. In Maryland. Grable probably tried that, too."

"When was he seen in Georgetown?"

"This morning." Then Renwick roused himself. "I'll have that tub. Won't take long."

So the search for Nina was on. Claudel swore softly as he opened the parcels and began examining the clothes for tonight's job of work.

Sixteen

AT HALF PAST eight they were ready to leave. They made a rear exit through the inn's vegetable garden to reach the car park. It was deep in shadow. The buses had left, but over at the tables there were still a few determined romantics, local people with the sense to be well bundled up against the night air, drinking red wine by the light of colored bulbs, listening to a selection from Gounod. Overhead, the crescent moon was swimming through a sea of white clouds. Lucky for us, thought Renwick as he took the driver's seat: five days later and we'd have run into a full moon.

He eased the Audi into the road, took the direct route to town. Beside him, Claudel was in high spirits, his sling abandoned, his left arm free and less noticeable. Like old times, he was thinking, the two of us setting out, not knowing what we'll meet. Initial plans had been discussed, of course, over dinner in a dark and empty dining room with one small lamp to let them see what they were eating. As Renwick had said, "All we can do is to plan our first moves, but once we're up at the chalet, we'll play it by ear. There's always something you don't expect." The Audi would be left at the foot of Ruskin's road—what else did you call it when it wasn't even named on the town map that Claudel had picked up at the concierge's desk? From there they would use the road itself—probably unlighted—and be ready to dive for rough ground if they heard any car approaching. The silence of the hills would give them ample warning.

"Almost there," said Renwick as they came through the town, two figures in dark clothes that weren't noticeable. (On foot, Renwick had said, they'd make a weird sight: two joggers in the main street at this hour? Pockets filled with equipment, too?) A left turn and they were into the small parking space at the foot of the road. "What the hell's going on?" He had expected to find a couple of cars at this time in the evening. There were seven, and three of them almost blocked the Audi's way. Renwick edged through them, stopped just ahead of the leading car in the group. It was, of course, a small white Renault. He turned off the lights, switched off the engine. Marchand hadn't come out of his car to greet them, hadn't even looked at them as they had passed.

"Cool," said Renwick. "We'll play it cool, too." Without one backward glance, they started uphill past the row of houses with faint lights and sounds of television coming from their windows.

"Did you notice the two men standing at the car behind Marchand?" Claudel asked. "And the two inside the car behind them? No uniforms."

The men, who had let themselves be clearly seen, had worn checked shirts, sweaters, britches, heavy stockings, and boots.

"One of them sold us our tennis shoes today. Marchand has drafted his cousins." And he is hedging his bets: tonight may not be police business, but in case of action—then Marchand will be there. "They look as if they know their way around a rough hillside."

"He didn't give a damn if we noticed him or his troops."

"I like his style. He's reminding us to remember."

"But will you?"

"I'll try hard."

By the time they cut away from the road and traveled over a field of grass, small boulders, and bushes to reach the blacked-out chalet, their eyes were accustomed to the broken darkness. The moon in its first quarter was muted by passing clouds: now and again, a bright beam; then, just as suddenly, deep shadow. They moved carefully, taking cover behind a bush or beside a boulder whenever the half-moon's spotlight was turned on.

The structure of the chalet was simple. The first floor was raised slightly above ground level by squat supports; therefore, no cellar. No terrace; no garden, either. Just a pair of windows on either side of a front door reached by three steps. On the upper floor there was a balcony with three long windows under the overhanging roof. Two chimneys, but not even a trickle of smoke. The house was exactly as they had seen it that afternoon: shuttered tight. A desolate place.

They separated. Remembering the lie of the land, they would circle around the chalet and meet at the first line of trees some fifty feet on the slope behind it. Sparse trees, thin and small, but with enough cover to let them study the back of the house. Claudel, a few minutes late in reaching Renwick, was much entertained by something.

"Side windows?" Renwick asked softly.

"Two above, two below; all boarded up. No balcony."

"Same as my side." Nothing original about this place. Its rear view had three windows above, two below with a narrow door between them.

"Just over there"—Claudel repressed a laugh, pointed back to a group of bushes—"I nearly stumbled into their garbage dump."

Of course, thought Renwick, the people in the chalet might do without heat even on a cool night, but they needed food, and food meant garbage. "Small or large?"

"Only three bags, all neatly tied. They'll dig it in when they're good and ready. Not this evening, I hope."

Perhaps when the next delivery of food arrived—a night-time job, obviously. "I hope not," Renwick agreed fervently, his eyes studying the house once more. No balcony here, either, where it could have been useful, for this side of the chalet was in deep shade. "They must be suffocating in there," he added as he scanned the five shuttered windows, heavy black rectangles set into dimly white stucco walls. Then, "These bottom windows—something different . . ." And he unzipped a pocket to pull out his mini-telescope, and pressed its infrared release button. Claudel drew out his small binoculars and got them functioning for night work.

The two windows changed from dense black to the color of bleached blood. Every line on the board shutters was shown as a dark seam. And at the center there was a very broad seam—an opening, a definite opening. But it revealed nothing beyond, only a blank smooth surface, the same ghastly color in infrared as the shutters themselves.

Renwick and Claudel exchanged a glance, pocketed their pint-sized instruments. Quickly, they crossed over the rough ground—grass with some outcrops of rock—and reached the dark shadows of the chalet. Claudel took one window, Renwick the other.

And there his question about ventilation was answered. A black blind, opaque, covered the glass panes, but from the outside. Concealed behind it, the window could be opened wide. As it was now. There were voices.

He signaled to Claudel, who came hurrying to join him. Renwick held up two fingers, raised an eyebrow. Claudel nodded: two people were talking, a man and a woman. Not clearly heard, only an occasional word recognizable, as if the speakers were at the far side of the room. Renwick and Claudel drew out their heavily rimmed glasses, put them on, pressing the frames close above their ears. The words became as clear as if the man and woman had been standing beside them.

Words spoken in some small argument, complaining, bickering, using German—probably as a common language: the woman's accent showed traces of French, the man's was heavily Slavonic. She was saying, "Stop searching! And sit down. There's no more beer. You've drunk it all."

"What there was of it." Footsteps wandered over a wooden floor. "They send you plenty of food and nothing to drink."

"Nothing? You drank six—"

"Six bottles of nothing. Where d'you keep the cigarettes? They sent cigarettes, didn't they?"

"No. You had two packs."

"They're finished. Empty."

"Oh, sit down!"

"Can't even phone." The footsteps stopped. "Why shouldn't I try to—"

The woman's voice rose. "No phoning! Orders."

"Stupid orders."

"You're stupid. The calls go through the town exchange. Do you want someone down there asking who is up here?"

"The two-way radio doesn't go through the exchange. I'll call, tell them we need some real booze and cigarettes—it's a long night ahead."

"No! Only to be used in an emergency. Only then!"

A chair scraped on the floor. "Think I'll have a breath of fresh air."

"The car could arrive—"

"He won't arrive until midnight. Or later. It's a long haul."

"What about her? Don't leave me—"

"She'll give you no trouble. She's out cold."

"Do we keep her quiet until he leaves tomorrow?"

"He's in the big room; she's upstairs. And gagged. Who's to hear her? No one did today. If you ask me—it's a damn stupid mistake having them in this house at the same time."

"I'm not asking you. And it isn't a mistake. It wasn't planned. It just happened. She is—"

"She's a damned nuisance."

"An important nuisance. Remember that! Where are you going, Stefan?"

"Out." Heavy footsteps were crossing the room.

"Where?" she insisted.

"Up to the big house—get cigarettes and something to drink, find out what's new. You clean up here, have the place looking good for our visitor. Who is he? Did they say?"

"No. And tell them she isn't talking, won't speak. Yes, better tell them that."

"I'll tell them it would be easy to make her talk if they didn't want her kept alive. And how long will that be, anyway?" There was a grunt, short and contemptuous. "Switch off the light. Can't open the door until you've got that light turned off. Move it!"

Renwick and Claudel didn't wait for the light to go out. They raced to the nearest tree, glasses safely in their pockets, their rubber-soled shoes both sure and soundless on the grass, and slid behind its shelter. Propped on their elbows, they watched that back door. They were aware when it opened—in the stillness of the night, the turn of a heavy lock was audible. But it was only when Stefan stepped out from the house's shadow that they realized the door had closed. Not locked again, thought Renwick. Why?

They watched the tall, heavy figure in its dark clothes plodding slowly toward the road. Stefan stopped twice, looked around. Perhaps he really was enjoying the air. Perhaps he was checking to make sure everything was as peaceful as it should be.

And in the house he had left? The woman busy tidying the kitchen; someone in a room overhead, gagged and unconscious—a bad combination, thought Renwick. She could be smothered to death—orders or no orders from Klaus Sudak.

Stefan had reached the road, was lost from view as he turned to follow it uphill. "How much time?" Claudel asked. "Ten minutes to the big chalet. Fifteen minutes for supplies and some talk—and ten minutes back here. Give him half an hour?"

Renwick nodded. "The door wasn't locked. An invitation to enter, I'd say. Let's accept it."

"Marchand?"

"We'll scout around first. Time enough to call when—" Renwick, about to rise, broke off both words and movement. The door must have opened. The woman came out of the shadows, almost invisible in the dark cloak she had thrown around her. A shoulder tilted as she walked toward them. Carrying something? A large black plastic bag that glistened in a ray of moonlight as it bulged out from under her cape. They let her pass, scarcely fifteen feet away from where they lay under the tree. She veered to her left, up toward the bushes that disguised the garbage dump.

Renwick rose, gestured to Claudel, and they followed. She was out of sight behind the screen of bushes. "Deal with her now?" Claudel whispered and stood to the side of the path the woman had taken through the shrubbery. Renwick faced it. She came out, saw him, stopped. Her mouth opened, but she didn't cry out. Claudel's karate chop caught the back of her neck. She pitched forward, lay still

"Sorry about that," Claudel told her, "but how else do we keep you quiet for the next half hour? Come on, Bob. Lend a hand. She's the weight of two men."

Together they pulled her heavy bulk near some stones, dropped her head beside the largest of them. If any of her friends came prowling around, they might think it was a fall in the dark and a case of concussion. "All right, all right," Renwick said. "Let's go!"

They raced down the slope, stepped into a darkened kitchen with its door ajar. Renwick closed it, used his pen flashlight to find the switch and turn on a ceiling lamp. On the far wall was a narrow door. Quickly, they moved to open it: the woman's room—underclothes on a chair and a dress, smeared with blood, hooked onto a wall.

Back into the kitchen, out into the hall. A small place, stretching from back to front of the house, lit by a table lamp near the main entrance. Opposite them, a narrow staircase leading up the wall, beginning almost at the doorway to a back room. Stefan's room: city clothes dropped on the bed, a soiled towel on the floor near a washstand and a basin of red-tinged water. There was a front room, too, its door under the top rise of the stairs.

"Well," said Renwick as they entered it and switched on the lights, "all the comforts of home." It was larger, better furnished than the others, with even an adjoining bathroom. The wardrobe held a man's suit and overcoat—new, apparently unworn. New shirt, new underclothes, new shoes. A complete and natty outfit even to the dark-red tie. On the bureau, there was an innocent display of lace mat, brushes, and comb. Inside a drawer, at its back, lay a wallet packed with French francs and German marks. "Okay," said Renwick as he replaced it exactly and switched off the light.

They climbed the steep flight of wooden steps and reached the upper hall, lit by a lamp on a rickety table that stood almost at the head of the stairs. Hall? More like a corridor stretching the breadth of the house with a window at either end. Four doors here; and three of them half open, leading into unused rooms. The fourth was locked. With the key in place, Renwick saw in astonishment. But then, they hadn't expected any intruders and by habit had locked the door from the outside. Not that they had anything to fear from the inside: their prisoner couldn't have made even the feeblest attempt to escape. Renwick and Claudel paused at the threshold to the brightly lit room, stared at her in horror.

She was naked, bound with rope to a high-backed wooden chair, her body scored with vicious red slashes, one wrist broken, her legs covered with congealed blood. Her head fell sideways, as if she had tried in her last conscious moment to avoid the glare of light from a powerful lamp aimed at her face. Her mouth was savagely bandaged with a broad swathe of adhesive tape that stretched from ear to ear. Red hair, its loose tendrils lank and matted, had been hacked off at the neck and lay scattered with shreds of clothing thrown onto the bare floor.

Renwick thrust aside the lamp, began peeling the wide strip of plaster away from her cheeks and lips. Claudel had his knife out, was trying to judge where he could safely start cutting the rope that had bitten into her waist.

She moaned, tried to open her eyes, could only see two figures bending over her, didn't even hear Renwick's voice saying, "It's all right, it's all right." He grimaced in sympathy as he pulled the last shred of plaster away from her skin. The moan became a strangled sound of abject fear. Renwick looked at the white face now fully revealed. "God in heaven," he said. Quickly, he snapped his knife open, began freeing her arms. This must hurt like hell, he thought. The least touch is agony.

"No, no more—no more." She flinched away from the hands that were helping her. "No more—please. I'll tell you." Her eyes closed. "Zurich. Cathedral. Poste restante. Karen—Karen Cross." The hoarse voice became a whimper that ended in a strangled sob. Suddenly, it ended. Her head dropped, fell motionless.

"Dead?" asked Claudel.

Renwick felt her pulse. "Barely alive."

The ropes were cut. They carried her over to a cot, laid her on the gray blanket which had covered her on the journey here.

Claudel looked at Renwick's tight face. "You know her?"

"Lorna Upwood."

"Lorna?" Claudel stared at her. He drew a long breath. "And how do we get her out of here? I'm afraid to touch her."

Renwick nodded and took out Marchand's transmitter. "Five-mile radius," he said. I think I'd better find a way onto that balcony." This is one report that I want to go out loud and clear. "We can leave her here. You nip downstairs, Pierre, and find that two-way radio they talked about. Put the lights out of action, too." He locked the door behind them, pocketed the key, and hurried to the hall's French window as Claudel raced downstairs.

Renwick's exit onto the balcony was speed combined with destruction. He forced the window so angrily that a pane smashed, he slashed the opaque blind with his knife, he shouldered the shutters apart after a heavy kick at their lock. And now, his back close to the stucco wall, a wooden railing in front of him, he faced the view of the road as it wound its way down into town. He pressed the signal on the transmitter. Immediately, Marchand's voice said, "Identify!"

"Victor."

"About time. Where are you?"

"Inside."

"So that's where you went. Who welcomed you?"

"No one. The man left—"

"We saw him."

Saw? I ought to have guessed, Renwick thought: Marchand and his boys followed us up here. "Then you saw us, too."

"Until you vanished," Marchand admitted. "Anything interesting?"

"Police business now. We'll need a stretcher. Serious injuries."

"An ambulance?"

"Later. Can't alarm the neighborhood."

"Give us five minutes." Then Marchand's voice changed to a warning whisper. "Man coming down the road—another following, carrying a box."

Beer and cigarettes? "Better hurry."

"They'll be ahead of us." Marchand was worried.

"Bring flashlights," Renwick said and switched off communication. He stepped through the torn blind, found the hall now in darkness, and signaled Claudel with a whistle.

"Finished here," Claudel called as he left the ground floor.

"Fourteen steps," Renwick said softly as Claudel's flashlight pointed its beam on the stairs to bring him up at a run. "We've got company. Stefan and friend."

"You saw them?"

"Marchand did. He's out there somewhere—near enough."

"And the troops?"

"With him, I bet." Renwick raised a warning hand as the back door opened. Claudel switched off his flashlight. Footsteps entered the kitchen, stopped. Renwick glanced at the broad stream of moonbeams pouring through the hole he had slashed in the blind. He gestured to the head of the stairs and its wooden railing. Claudel nodded, took cover behind the balustrade. Renwick reached the window, leaned out through the torn blind to close the shutters. One of them balked. It would be easy enough to yank it forcefully if he could risk any noise. He altered his grip, pulled firmly. The shutter almost creaked. He stopped.

Downstairs, the voices sounded angry and baffled. One was American— Barney? The other was Stefan, his words more limited as he struggled with English. "Door unlocked! Magda, where are you? Magda!" He shouted upstairs, "Magda—you there?"

"Open the door, let's have some light in here," Barney said. Someone stumbled and dropped a heavy load. "Where's that goddamned switch? Got it!"

"She is not in her room. Outside, perhaps. I look."

"It doesn't work. A fuse? Where's your flashlight?"

"Two of them. Near radio. Beside stove."

Silence, while Barney searched and Stefan had his look outside. It was brief.

Too brief, thought Renwick, trying to persuade the shutter to swing inward. The blind hampered his movements, and he couldn't tear it fully apart without sending a warning down to the kitchen. Every sound seemed to travel in this tight little house. He tried another grip. Careful, he told himself, careful.

Barney swore steadily. "Won't work. Batteries are dead in both of them."

"We signal the house."

"That's what I'm trying to do, goddammit. I get nothing—nothing! The radio's useless. You telephone while I search this floor."

Renwick's silent battle with the shutter ended. He swung it steadily toward him. It tilted as he was about to close it—one hinge must have slipped when he had shouldered it open—and showed a gap, small but definite, a finger-wide streak of moonlight, bright against the hall's darkness. He tried to straighten it, force it even. And its good hinge, now bearing the shutter's weight, creaked loudly.

Instantly, footsteps hurried to the bottom of the stairs and stopped. From the kitchen, Stefan called, "Telephone out! Kaput."

Silence from Barney.

He's listening, thought Renwick and didn't even risk crossing the wooden floor to reach Claudel. Quickly, he drew himself to the side of the window. The table was near enough, a black shadow among shadows, flimsy protection but the only cover within reach. He stretched out his arm, ventured two careful steps, touched its corner. He felt the lamp tremble, steadied its base before it could topple. Then he crouched low at the side of the table, putting it between himself and the staircase.

Barney had started to climb the stairs, slowly, cautiously, trying to muffle the tread of his heavy shoes. Renwick counted the steps. One, two . . . He withdrew his hand from the lamp, tracing its cord to avoid tangling his heel and found that it ended at an outlet on the wall behind him. He eased the socket free. Then he took out his automatic. He was still counting. Eleven, twelve—and there Barney came to an abrupt halt.

There was no movement, no sound from Claudel or Renwick.

A minute passed. Barney relaxed. "Just the shutter. Lost its catch," he said over his shoulder, and took the last two steps in one stride. He flicked his lighter and held its flame high, his right hand grasping a revolver. He saw the slashed blind. "Someone *was* here!" he yelled, whirled around, stared at the man rising from the side of the table, and instinctively pointed his revolver.

Renwick hurled the lamp at his face, deflecting his aim. A bullet splintered the staircase wall behind Renwick as he fired, caught the man's right shoulder to send him spinning. His pistol dropped on the floor.

Barney regained his balance, threw his lighter at Renwick and missed, tried to pick up the revolver. One sharp blow from the side of Renwick's hand on the nape of his neck and Barney went down, lay motionless.

At the first shot, Stefan had bounded onto the landing with his pistol drawn and ready to aim at Renwick's spine. Claudel lunged at Stefan's legs with all his weight behind the tackle. It brought Stefan crashing down on his face. Claudel rose, stamped hard on the hand that still held the revolver, kept it pinned under his foot. He drew his automatic, pressed it into the back of Stefan's head. "One move," Claudel said softly, "just one move."

Suddenly, a blaze of lights. Powerful beams flooded into the dark hall from the staircase. Men's heavy footsteps clattered up the steps. And Marchand, reaching the landing, was looking at the splintered wall above his head, then at the two men on the floor, then at Renwick and Claudel. "Explanations!" Marchand said, his voice tight with anger.

Renwick walked over to the room where Lorna Upwood lay. He unlocked the door, threw it open. "In here," he said, and stood aside.

Marchand signed to two of his men to follow, and entered the room. He didn't stay long. He came out, visibly shaken. He even did some explaining himself. "We brought a stretcher. That was what delayed us." He looked at Stefan, at Barney. His voice hardened. "Are these the men responsible?"

"This one." Claudel released Stefan to the grip of two husky fellows. "And a woman. You'll find her on the hill behind the house."

"We found her. Are you positive she was part of this . . ." Marchand didn't finish, glanced back at the room. He couldn't believe it.

"Quite positive," Renwick said. "If it's evidence you need, you'll find a bloodstained dress in her room. Its blood will match the victim's."

Marchand nodded. "What about that one?" He looked at Barney.

"His revolver." Renwick offered it. "His bullet." He pointed to the wall.

Marchand signed to two men in police uniform. "Arrest all three. You know the arrangements."

One of the policemen was examining Barney. "This one can hardly walk."

"Make him!"

Renwick drew Marchand out of earshot. "The house must be cleared. Quickly. They are expecting a visitor to stay overnight."

"Who?"

"We don't know. But he's important. You'll find a complete change of clothes waiting for him in the front bedroom. Also a stack of money in the bureau's top drawer."

Marchand looked at Renwick. "You can leave police business to me," he said with a touch of acid in his voice. "We shall have the house cleared. Quickly. My men are quite capable, I assure you. But next time they'd prefer more action and less cleaning up."

Renwick accepted that rebuke with a nod.

"And what are your plans now, my friend? Sit out on a hillside and wait until this important but unknown visitor arrives?"

"Why don't you join us?" There was a smile in Renwick's eyes.

Marchand gave him another sharp look, began detailing his men.

Renwick followed Claudel downstairs, passed through a crowded kitchen where the woman sat handcuffed to a chair. "Quite capable," Claudel quoted. "And more of them, too."

Renwick nodded. "How's the arm?"

"Just beginning to remember it." Strange: he had forgotten the pain when he lunged at Stefan. There was nothing like real danger to distract the mind.

For a few moments they stood outside the closed door, breathed deeply of the cool clean air. Then, in silence, they started up the slope to the trees behind the chalet.

Renwick looked at his watch. Ten-fifteen. Almost two hours to wait . . . In Washington, another afternoon would be ending. And Nina? If only, he thought, I could get back to the inn, set up the transmitter, ask London what they've heard. But this is where I stay, wait out an arrival—it could come before midnight—nothing can be taken for granted—nothing. Not even Nina's safety.

Claudel halted at a group of firs where they would be protected from the sharp breeze and sporadic moonlight. "Okay?" he asked.

Renwick dropped onto the ground, his back against a tree trunk, his eyes on the path below them that led from the road to the chalet. "Okay," he said. But his face was taut. He tried to forget what had happened to Lorna Upwood, forced himself to concentrate on the Plus List she had hidden in a poste restante at Zurich. He should have felt excitement, even elation. All he could feel was exhaustion and worry. Worry about Basset Hill. About Nina. He had seen one hideous sample of what Klaus could do to someone he had abducted. I'll get him, he vowed. Before he wreaks any more harm, I'll get him.

Seventeen

I N WASHINGTON, IT had been another hot Saturday afternoon. Nina had spent most of it in the shaded porch of Colin Grant's house, working at her easel, trying to imitate the simple lines and delicate colors of the Dutch exteriors which had fascinated her in the Basset Museum.

At half past four she put aside brushes and palette—they had been supplied, like the easel, by Grant. Her interest in painting had delighted him, had created a sudden and warm friendship between them. The three days here would have been relaxed and pleasant if only she could stop worrying about Bob, if only she could telephone him, write to him. Tim MacEwan, looking the part of the security expert who was checking the museum's precautions against thieves, had brought her two reports from London. Bob was well. Bob sent his love. But, she wondered now as she went upstairs to change from her smock into something clean and cool for her daily visit to the museum, where *was* Bob? London never told her that. And if Tom MacEwan knew, he wasn't telling, either.

Quickly, she washed and dressed. She brushed her blond hair, left it loose for a few minutes. Then she replaced the dark-brown wig, added fresh coral lipstick, and put on her renovated sunglasses. Mac had brought them from Washington yesterday: dark lenses had been exchanged for a light color, enough to dim blue eyes but less faddish when worn indoors. Mac, she told herself, was—in some ways—much like Bob: he thought of everything. So did Pierre. A special breed—careful, watchful. Yet that didn't mean they could escape danger. Look at Pierre, for instance, with that knife wound in his arm. Of course, if he hadn't trained himself to be careful and watchful, he could have been killed.

"Don't even think of that!" she warned herself. "Don't!" She stared at herself in the mirror, forced her mind away from danger and death, concentrated on the girl who looked back at her. Not bad, she decided, just a little too serious at this moment. The eyeglasses emphasized it, of course. But they did change her appearance; so did the dark hair. Reassured, Mrs. John Smith—here on a brief vacation while her husband finished some business in Pittsburgh—ran downstairs.

She didn't use the front entrance. Mac had suggested that the back door, leading to the drying yard behind the garage and then through Mrs. Trout's vegetable patch, made a less noticeable exit. From there she reached the narrow gate on the boundary line of Grant's small property and entered the nursery, where a gardener worked on rows of seedlings and tender plants to replace, eventually, any wilting flowers in the museum's gardens and hall-way. Today it was Jim's turn to be there at five o'clock—by arrangement with Mac, of course. They exchanged cheerful good days and a sentence about the weather. Then she skirted the side of the museum to reach its impressive portico.

The guard, standing at the top of its steps, gave a friendly greeting. So did the two guards on duty inside the main hall. She was accepted, she thought, and was even more reassured. Mr. Grant's cousin, the art student, who paid her daily visit around five o'clock when the crowd of visitors had thinned. The sketchbook and pencils she carried weren't questioned. Neither was her habit of sitting before certain paintings, nor the notes and sketches she made.

She entered the gallery where the Dutch masters were displayed. Large, cool, perfectly lit, with elegant benches covered in green velvet, it attracted most visitors to the museum. Several were still here, slowly wandering, stopping, sitting. Voices were hushed, footsteps were soft. Watching this peaceful scene, a guard stood at ease by the gallery's wide entrance.

Nina chose her favorite bench. Nothing ridiculous about coming here to memorize the curve of a line, the balance of a composition. If Matisse, when young, could visit the Louvre every day for ten years to study its paintings—even copied them at an easel, right there and then—who was to say it was ridiculous? Training his eye, teaching himself, admitting he was an apprentice. Well, thought Nina, I'll never be a Matisse but this is something I love. She was so engrossed that she didn't notice Mac, who came to have a word with the guard—his usual practice around five o'clock these last three days. She didn't even see Colin Grant making a quiet tour of inspection along with one of the museum's trustees.

But her concentration was broken when two girls sat down beside her. "I'm dead," said one. "My feet—these floors. Oh, this bench feels wonderful!"

Her friend, a pretty face with blond hair falling to her shoulders, looked at Nina's sketchbook and then at the painting hanging before her against an ivory wall. "Is that Vermeer?"

"No. Van Ruysdael."

"I thought the Vermeers were here."

"On the opposite wall—the Dutch interiors are over there. Here, these are the paintings of exteriors."

The blonde looked puzzled, glanced over her shoulder. Her friend said, "Just sit here for a few minutes, Peg. We've seen enough for one afternoon anyway."

"I've got it!" Peg said. "Some painted what they saw *in* a room, some painted what they saw *from* a room. Is that it?"

"Well—" began Nina, but Peg's interest had ended as quickly as it had begun. She was talking to her friend about plans for this evening, and Nina went back to sketching. Difficult to concentrate with Peg's voice, light and subdued though it was, chattering away about Jeff and the discothèque they had visited last night. Nina bent her head, tried to concentrate on a long, low, sweeping view of the Rhine.

A young man entered the gallery. His seersucker suit, freshly donned that morning, was crumpled with the heat and as forlorn as he was. He paused, looked down the length of the room. He was of medium height, slight in build, his face undistinguished, his appearance ordinary except for his hair. It was thick and heavy. Uses a blower, thought the guard in disgust—his own hair was cropped close. Then the guard remembered: this guy had been here earlier today, gone through all the museum. Why back again? He was beginning to walk along one row of paintings—the Vermeers. Casing the gallery? The man looked harmless enough, and yet art thieves were clever, could send in a scout, someone to take notice and report. The guard frowned, watching carefully.

Josh Grable noticed the girl with long blond hair who was sitting across the hall between two others, a redhead and a brunette. He continued past the Vermeers, halted at the end of the gallery, gathered his thoughts.

For the last four days every lead he had been given had ended in failure. First, the lawyer Danford in New York; then the lawyer Rosen in Washington. Down to the Maryland shore: no Renwick staying at her father's usual summer home; no O'Connell, either—it was said he was lecturing in Boston. A check at his house in Georgetown, just to make sure. But no O'Connell or wife there, no Renwick, either. House closed for the summer. Then last night, a long message from Geneva, urgent enough to be delivered through the embassy. *Information from official files on Renwick show association, possibly close relationship, with Colin Grant in Austria. Grant now director of Basset Museum near Washington. CIA member known to have met Renwick in Washington, Thursday. Renwick reported in Amsterdam, Friday. Nina Renwick not in Amsterdam, not in London. Basset Hill? Investigate and report immediately.*

That message had troubled Grable. The amount of information given him by Geneva seemed to emphasize he had better succeed this time. Yet to him it appeared to be a wild, a ridiculous assignment, bound to lead to another failure. Only—he had to admit—the reference to "official files" was impressive. Geneva obviously put heavy weight on that information. Whose "official files" anyway? Straight from KGB? Better make this last effort to trace the Renwick woman he had decided, even if he thought it was another false lead. So that morning early he tracked down the museum and reached its gates as it opened.

He had explored the museum, then its grounds, checked every small building, told some inquisitive guards he was a reporter writing an article on Basset Hill, was told in turn (by a gardener) that Grant's house on the estate was occupied only by himself and his housekeeper. Grable had seen the housekeeper, an elderly white-haired woman, when he strolled around the wall that protected Grant's place from museum visitors. He had observed Grant himself in his office in the main building—door open to everyone. Grant's secretary was a woman, and so were two of his assistants. But none was near twenty-three years old or five feet four inches in height, or had long blond hair and blue eyes.

Now, on this final tour of the museum, Grable—tired, hungry, and thirsty—stood watching, wondering, waiting for the blonde sitting on the bench to turn her head, let him see her face. (The snapshot of Nina Renwick, given him in New York, was two years old, but it showed a vivacious girl with a bright smile.) Then he saw the museum director walking slowly down the gallery along with an elderly man, passing in front of the bench where the three girls sat, stopping just there to discuss one of the paintings on the wall. Colin Grant turned to look at the girls—definitely a friendly look. The blonde spoke to him,·laughed as Grant nodded and walked on with the elderly man, stopping to examine another picture. That's it, thought Grable: the blonde knew him. (If Grable actually had been born and brought up in America, he might have been less certain: the spontaneous exchange between strangers was something beyond his experience.) That's it, he thought again. He began walking to the bench.

Tim MacEwan had finished his appointed round to make sure the guards had nothing further to report. There had been talk this early afternoon when he had returned from business in Washington about a journalist who had been spending the day at Basset Hill. But reporters did visit this estate, did wander around trying to dig up some story on old man Basset, whose millions had created the museum. Wealthy eccentrics made good copy, and safe copy, too, when they were dead. Once more, MacEwan was standing at the entrance to the Dutch masters' gallery, making his last check on Nina. The guard said, "He's back again. Casing the museum. Don't like it."

"Where?"

"Just crossing the floor. Seersucker suit. See? He's more interested in the layout than in the paintings. Been looking around here all day."

"I heard reports about him. A journalist—" MacEwan broke off. The man's face was clearly in view at last. It was almost similar to the composite drawing that had been shown MacEwan at the FBI building this morning. By God, it was Grable! Grable—stopping just behind the bench where Nina sat. "Don't let him out of the museum! Pass the word!" The guard left. MacEwan spoke into his small transmitter, reached the nursery gardener. "Take action! Tell Neill to bring a couple of men. Fast! We've got someone he's looking for." MacEwan pocketed the transmitter, began walking slowly toward Nina.

She had closed the sketchbook as Colin Grant reached her, was ready to exchange a word with him. But Peg, the irrepressible blonde with a quick eye for a good-looking man, assumed his glance was for her. "Isn't this place divine? I just love these Dutch exteriors, don't you?" It was a charming gush, a sweet come-on. Grant gave a polite nod, walked on. Peg laughed to cover her disappointment. She was not the type, thought Nina, to feel embarrassment. Peg began talking once more with her friend. "Who is he, d'you think? I told you we'd meet the most interesting people here. No, don't go yet. He's looking this way." And Colin Grant was indeed looking back—at the man who had ended his slow step at Nina's bench.

Nina was deciding to leave: it was obvious that Peg and her foot-weary friend were going to stay. Suddenly a voice behind her said, "Mrs. Renwick!"

Nina almost jerked around, caught herself in time, sat still, her eyes on van Ruysdael's Rhine.

"Mrs. Renwick—how are you?"

Peg turned with a swing of loose blond hair. "Just fine, thank you. But would some other name do?"

Grable stared into her large brown eyes, stepped back in confusion. "Excuse me," he said, and retreated. Anger surged. A fool's errand. I knew it, I knew it, he told Geneva silently. I didn't fail. You did. You and your reliable information from official files. The Renwick girl is nowhere near Basset Hill, nowhere.

A redhaired man caught his arm above the elbow. "This way, if you please," MacEwan said softly. "No, don't struggle. You wouldn't win." There were now three guards at the gallery entrance.

"But why—what have I—"

"Just routine." MacEwan led him with a firm grip into the main hall. Two of the guards walked on Grable's other side. Ahead was the museum's front door. "No, no, I wouldn't try that," the quiet Canadian's voice said. "The men outside have been alerted, too. In here!" They had stopped at the secretary's office, empty at this hour.

"But what have I done? I'm a reporter. I'm writing a story on—"

"Tell us the story. We're interested." MacEwan tightened his grasp, urged him over the threshold. "You can sit there." MacEwan pointed to a chair beside the desk, released Grable. The guards entered, closed the door. "I'm the security inspector. We've reason to believe that an attempted robbery of valuable paintings is being planned. Today you've been seen wandering around. Why?"

Grable's relief broke into a stream of words. "I told you—I'm researching a story about Basset and his museum."

"What newspaper?"

"I'm free-lance." Grable had recovered. His voice was normal. No more indignation, no more anger. "I write for magazines; trade papers, too."

"Tell us all about it," MacEwan said, his light-blue eyes expectant. "We have plenty of time." Plenty, he thought. Joe Neill would need forty-five minutes at least to arrive here.

Grable looked at his watch. "But I haven't. I have an important dinner engagement tonight. At seven o'clock. In Washington. So you start your questions, and I'll answer them. I must leave in fifteen minutes."

"Perhaps. Perhaps not."

"But you can't keep me here. You've no reason to—"

"A threatened robbery gives us every reason."

"Do you think one man could plan such a theft?" asked Grable sarcastically. Such idiots—overzealous fools.

"No. But one man could check out our security arrangements."

Grable was all innocence again. "Is that what you think I was doing? I was only walking around, getting the atmosphere of this place. All part of the story's background."

MacEwan and the two guards just looked at him.

Grable glanced again at his watch. "At this rate, I'll never keep that engagement. May I use the phone—or is that denied me?"

"Not at all." MacEwan even pushed the telephone across the desk.

"Thank you." Quickly, Grable began to dial.

Now what will he tell his contact? MacEwan wondered. That he still has suspicions? That someone else must make a second visit to Basset Hill? Or that he was following a false lead? MacEwan waited tensely.

Grable let the phone ring twice, cut it off. "Think I dialed a wrong number. Guess I was hurried. Better try again. Do you mind?"

So that had been the signal to alert his contact that a vital message was about to be sent. "Go ahead," said MacEwan, and again noted the numbers that were being dialed with exaggerated care. They were exactly the same as the ones used previously.

"Sam? Josh here. Can't make dinner tonight—got a bad migraine. A rotten day altogether. Found no story, nothing worth writing about. Tell my publisher to come up with a better idea next time. I'm calling it quits on this one. See you in New York." Grable replaced the receiver, looked blandly at MacEwan. "Sam's my agent, usually a bright guy, but this time . . ." He shook his head.

MacEwan looked disinterested. Thank God, he thought. The search for Nina was over. Basset Hill had been declared a complete failure. He said to one of the guards, "Tell the Director that everything is under control here." As the man left, MacEwan lifted away the telephone from Grable's reach. "Now, let's start with your name and address. Then your agent's. Then your publisher's."

Grable stared at him. "Is this some kind of inquisition?" But his voice was less assured, his eyes less confident.

"Not yet," said MacEwan, "not yet."

Nina hadn't moved. She stared at the van Ruysdael, saw only a blur of blues and greens. Mrs. Renwick . . . And she had almost turned around. So near to disaster, just one small swerve of her head. Would he have noticed her eyes, noticed the startled look on her face? Could he have suddenly realized that the color of her hair might have changed, but that her expression was too alarmed, too concerned? She bowed her head, wasn't even aware that Mac had taken the man out of the gallery, didn't even know that Colin Grant had bid the trustee a hasty good-bye and was now coming quickly toward her. She heard the blonde speaking as the girls rose and moved away. What chased them off? she wondered. And then in panic, Is the man back here again? She raised her head. I'll brazen it out, she thought. But it was Colin who was standing before her. He took her hand, sat down beside her.

"The man has gone," he told her. "Mac took him in charge. We'll find out who he is. What did he say? Did he threaten you?" Her hands were cold with fear.

"He said—'Mrs. Renwick!' And I nearly looked around. Oh, Colin, I almost did!"

"But you didn't."

"He wasn't speaking to me, of course. But I *thought* he was. And I was so startled . . ." Nina shook her head. "But how could he have traced me here? There was no connection between you and Bob—not openly, at least."

"That's what I thought." Grant was frowning, trying to recall any time in Austria when he and Renwick had been seen obviously together. "Once—" he said—"no, it couldn't have been that."

"Once what?"

"We were trying to enter a small cottage—three men inside, armed. A girl upstairs. Kidnapped. So we made a little assault. I set the barn on fire—"

"You did what?"

"—with a grenade. Didn't expect the place to go up in flames." Grant was smiling at the memory. "Bob was at the house door, got the men as they came out with their Lugers waving. Quite a moment." He glanced around the gallery, and laughed softly.

"Killed them?" It was self-defense, she told herself.

"No, no. He's a damn fine shot. Picks his target. He got them on shoulders and knee, put them out of commission."

She stared at him in wonder—the man who was devoted to art, who wanted people to view the best paintings in the best of surroundings. "Then they saw you both."

"Only Bob. He was alone at the door. I shoved past them to reach the staircase and get Avril out—the whole place was burning fast. They didn't see my face, couldn't have identified me—a moment of complete chaos. Soon, some of our friends arrived and helped Bob with his prisoners. I wasn't there. I was with—" He stopped abruptly. The first time in four years I've ever talked of this, he thought. He drew a deep breath. "With Avril. After that we got safely away by car." He stopped again. This time there was no emotion on his face—just a blank look of astonishment. "That's it," Grant said softly. "Avril and Bob and I and two of his agents—all in that car, making good our escape. One of those agents—like Bob, he worked with NATO Intelligence—turned out to be in the pay of the KGB."

"One of Bob's people? A man he trusted?"

"Trusted and liked. He was a refugee, an anti-Communist. Escaped from East Germany. A good agent, reliable, honest. And then—well, he was blackmailed, threatened with the safety of his wife and child, who had been trapped in Dresden. So he passed information to the KGB in Vienna. When he was caught, he swore he had only supplied them with worthless facts, nothing they could use."

"Bob believed him?"

"Gave him the benefit of the doubt. His past record had been blameless. But one thing's certain: he never worked for Bob or NATO Intelligence again."

What could anyone do when his wife and child were held hostage? Suddenly she thought, was that man here today to identify me, have me taken as hostage—tomorrow, the next day, someday when I walked across the gardens?

"Are you all right?" Grant asked quickly.

She nodded. "Then it is the KGB who knew about the link between you and Bob," she said controlling her voice better than her fears. "They're the opposition, aren't they? Behind all this?"

"Must be." How else had that little bastard come in here today, all primed about my connection with Bob Renwick? There was no other source of information except through the East German and his KGB control. "I'll brief Mac. He'll send the word. Bob can handle this. Nina, please—don't worry. Please!" The name had slipped out. "You see," he said wryly, "how easy it is to make a mistake? But you were superb today. You didn't make one. Not one."

The gallery was almost empty at last. Thank God, there had been no alarms, no outcry, no scene, no violence. Mac had led the man away with utmost discretion. And the guards, too, had—Here was one now. Bringing bad news? I'm as nervous as Nina, Grant thought as he watched the somber face approaching him. But the news was good. Everything was under control.

"You heard that message?" Grant asked as the guard left. "Couldn't be better. We're in the clear. Come on, Cousin Sue, let's have a drink to celebrate."

In spite of herself, Nina was smiling. "Just how did you read all that into one little message."

"A formula Mac and I arranged. The man hasn't a clue that you are actually here. But don't ask me how Mac found that out. He'll tell us at dinner." He took her sketchbook and pencils, pulled her up from the bench. He steadied her.

"Just a cramp in the legs," Nina said lightly, "sitting there so long."

Yes, sitting there petrified, thought Grant. He began talking about her sketches as he led her out of the gallery into the hall, past his secretary's office with its door firmly closed.

Nina noticed the guard standing there. Guards, too, at the front portico. Usually they would be going off duty at this hour. "Where is Bob now?" she asked and startled Grant. "Did Mac tell you?"

"In Europe. That's all he said."

In Europe. "Well, that's nearer than Asia." Then she said, "You know, I used to think that all these precautions were just a little—" She hesitated.

"Excessive?"

She nodded. "Which only proves how ignorant I was."

"I know. I've been down that road myself."

"I don't think we should let Bob know about today, do you?"

"Mac has to send a full report to London," Grant reminded her.

"That, yes. But not about the incident—it was small, so very small." It would upset Bob, she knew. He would start blaming himself somehow. "Bob is the world's champion worrier. No need for him to know—until he's home—and it's all over."

She's Renwick's girl, all right, Grant thought. "No need," he agreed gently. He looked around the placid gardens, quiet, undisturbed, not one intruder and he drew a deep breath of thankfulness.

Eighteen

MARCHAND WAS AS good as his word. The chalet was soon cleared, and most efficiently. Renwick watched the cortège leave by the back door: two men carrying the lightweight stretcher (how often had they carried it down a mountainside with its wrapped bundle strapped in place, just as now?);

then four to guard a handcuffed trio—Marchand himself accompanying, with his hand close to his mouth. Using a transceiver, Renwick guessed, arranging his reception committee at the foot of the hill road. Which left two somewhere up here—he had counted six in the chalet in addition to a couple of police uniforms—to keep watch with us. Or to keep watch on us?

The slow procession took a shortcut downhill over the field. Darkness swallowed them. Claudel said, "Wouldn't be surprised if Marchand hasn't an ambulance halfway up the road as well as the van he mentioned. Hear that?" There was a distant sound of slow-moving engines. It ceased. "But even so," Claudel reasoned, "Marchand has a lot to do at headquarters. It's half past ten now. He'll never make it back here by midnight."

"He'll be back. He's curious."

"About us? That's nothing new."

"About Lorna. Why was she here? Did we know her?"

"And what do we say?"

"She was part of Exports Consolidated. Tried to quit."

Claudel listened intently. The low hum of engines had begun again, receded downhill. "Lorna," he said very softly. "Incredible, the way she hid that little black book with its Plus List. Not in a safe-deposit box in some big strong bank. Just in a private cubbyhole, guaranteed by a post office."

Karen Cross, Poste Restante, Cathedral, Zurich . . . The words couldn't even be spoken aloud; not here, not until I'm in Zurich, thought Renwick, and even then only to my old friend Keppler. He would be one man who could get at a poste restante box. Who would question a senior officer in Swiss Intelligence?

Claudel was saying, "You'd like to be opening that little box right now. Why don't you leave tomorrow? I'll hold the fort here if anything else develops."

"I'll stay. Wait. As if we had learned nothing tonight."

Claudel mulled over that. "Wise," he agreed. No one knew that Lorna had said anything, but some might begin to wonder if Renwick made a sudden dash to Zurich. After all, he thought, we were the ones who found her, had time alone with her. "Klaus Sudak—he's bound to have some ears and eyes down in Chamonix. How soon will they ferret out the story?"

"Marchand's men weren't a talkative bunch. Let's hope they keep their lips buttoned until midnight at least."

"Is Klaus just sitting up there in a comfortable room, ignorant of everything? Can't believe that. He's beginning to wonder now why Barney hasn't returned to the Chalet Ruskin."

"Unless Barney was expected to stay and make Lorna Upwood talk." And no more questions, Pierre: I'm depressed enough. Anything could go wrong at this stage; everything could slip away from us. "Take ten," he suggested. "Stretch your legs, keep the old muscles warm. But don't stumble over one of Marchand's men. Either they've slipped out by the front door and circled round to watch us, or they are still inside the chalet."

"Thought you said they were our allies." Claudel rose cautiously, straightened his back.

"Sure. The friendly adversary type. Competitive."

"Ten minutes and I'll be back here, let you wander around," Claudel said, his eyes now searching the trees behind him for adequate cover. "I can think of better ways to spend a Saturday night." He moved off, a silent shadow among shadows.

Ten minutes, thought Renwick, won't give him time to pay a visit to the Chalet Ruskin, try to see in his crazy way what is going on up there. I wouldn't mind having a look myself. Tempting. Klaus may be playing the genial host—bright lights, music, champagne, pretty girls and their handsome young men—but he is bound to be churning inside with worry. Too much at stake right here on this hillside: Lorna; the arrival of some overnight visitor; and don't forget Vroom's wife, Annabel—has he calmed her hysteria, solved the new problem she has given him? A very cool, capable customer is Klaus Sudak. Keeps apart. Gives his orders for Lorna's questioning, probably never even mentioned torture, just tells his thugs that her information is essential. He knows what they'll do—he chose his people, selected them carefully for just that type of work—and stays away. He won't even allow himself to be connected with this midnight visitor. Sure, he's giving him shelter, supplying him with new clothes, money. And that brings me to the question that has been nagging at me for the last half hour. Why doesn't he offer a room in his own house for an overnight stay? Either he doesn't want the man to be seen by any of his other guests, or he doesn't want the man to meet him. Whatever the answer is, one thing is certain: that man is not only important, he could be a danger to Klaus. In that case, why even hide him inside a shuttered chalet? On orders, perhaps: orders that even Klaus Sudak must take. This visitor is as valuable to them as that, is he?

Claudel returned. "Okay. All quiet up there," he said softly. "Just some lights from two small chalets above us." He grinned as he added, "And a lot of light from the Chalet Ruskin. Don't worry: I didn't risk that barbed wire. Hadn't time, anyway."

"Too bad," said Renwick and quietly left. When he returned, sat down beside Claudel, he said, "Pierre—try this on for size. We know that Erik has been traveling with William Haversfield. We know that Haversfield is linked with Klingfeld and Sons. We know that Klaus Sudak controls Klingfeld and Sons. We also know that Haversfield reached Rome from Cairo. He was seen, then slipped away after two hours from the men trailing him. Why did he lead them around for two hours? To draw them apart from Erik, let him get out of Rome safely?"

"I'd buy that," Claudel said. "But where would Erik go? He must have realized in Rome that they had been tracked down—the airport was under surveillance, that was obvious. So Erik wouldn't risk anything expected— such as taking a direct flight to Zurich or even Germany. All airports would be on the watch."

"Right. So what about a flight by private plane to Milan? With Haversfield meeting him there, also by private plane? From some small, out-of-the-way airfield?"

"Klingfeld has the money for that."

"Also an office in Rome—arrangements easily made."

Claudel nodded. "Milan? And from there? Not directly to Germany. Not by air. And a car—risky. He can expect the German and Swiss frontiers to be under tight surveillance."

"What about driving a hired car west? Leaving it at a gas station before the hill roads begin? Being met there? Brought into France?"

"By the Mont Blanc Tunnel?" Claudel stared at Renwick. "We are reaching, now," he said. "We've left our facts behind—they got us only as far as Rome." But he thought over Renwick's suppositions. Suddenly he said, "That wallet in the bureau drawer—francs and marks! Not Swiss currency for use in Zurich."

"Not Austrian schillings for a detour by Vienna. Not Italian lire for a freighter out of Genoa. That would take too long, anyway. He wants to get to West Germany fast. That's where the action is developing—anti-American feeling rising, protests against rockets and neutron bombs—Erik and his Direct Action terrorists would have their biggest chance in years. Might even be considered as fighting on the side of the angels."

"So that is why Klingfeld and Sons have gone along with him—not sent him into South America as they first planned." Then Claudel shook his head. "Bob—are you persuading me to believe that Erik will arrive *here*? Do you really expect him to step out of a car, all the way from Italy? What about the time factor—could he make it from Milan by midnight?"

"It could be done."

"You've calculated?"

"Roughly."

"You really are expecting him," Claudel said softly.

"Not expecting. Just thinking he's a good candidate for that big front room."

Erik was certainly that. The link with Klaus Sudak through Haversfield was a definite fact. And Erik never needed a safe house more than he did now. "All right. We don't expect. We just wait. And be ready." Erik—if it is Erik who steps into that chalet—will know there's something wrong the moment he opens the front door. He's too smart. He could take off like a shot. Where? By night, and darkness on this hillside for another four or five hours, Erik could disappear. He must have a pocket transceiver, could alert Klaus Sudak, be directed to safety. "We could lose him," Claudel said.

"Yes." Renwick smiled as he added, "If it is Erik."

"Almost thou persuadest me," Claudel said softly. He began trying to calculate, from memory, the distance from Milan to the Italian slopes of the Mont Blanc massif—then the tunnel right through into France, landing almost at the back door to Chamonix. "It would need a first-rate driver, one who knew that route."

"And one who knows the little chalet."

Claudel was thoughtful. "I'll move down closer to the road. There's a clump of bushes near the path. See it?"

"Not much cover," Renwick said. And where were Marchand's men?

"Enough. Pity there couldn't be a roadblock just halfway to Klaus's entrance. The car will make its delivery at the path to this chalet, then go on uphill. What do you think?"

"I think you've got something there." The car wouldn't be left standing outside an apparently deserted house. And if it tried to turn to go down to

Chamonix—that would be tricky. Even in daylight, a U-turn had almost ended stuck on the opposite bank. "A roadblock," Renwick said reflectively. He reached into his breast pocket, took out Marchand's transceiver. "Ten past eleven. He's just got time."

The connection was immediate. "Victor here," Renwick said as he identified Marchand's voice. "I have a suggestion. Could you borrow a couple of bicycles? Without delay? I saw several propped against a house wall near where I parked our car."

"Bicycles?"

"Yes. Two are needed. Three would be better. For a roadblock—just *above* where we are waiting. But not visible from the path. Got my meaning?"

"Yes. But you expect two men to pedal uphill?"

"No. Push. Mountaineers have pushed heavier loads than that up a steep slope. They could drop the bicycles across the road, make it look as if there had been an accident. That could let them stop the car's driver to ask for help to get back to town. But they'd have to work fast. Be here by eleven-thirty at latest."

There was silence from Marchand.

"Only a suggestion."

"Of course."

"By the way, where are the two men you left behind? We're moving our position—don't want to mess up things with them."

"Wait until I see you. Fifteen minutes. Details then."

"All is well?"

"So far." Marchand switched off.

"That is that," Renwick told Claudel and pocketed the transceiver.

Will he take your suggestion?" Claudel had his doubts.

"We don't move from here anyway."

"He's got us pinpointed."

"Yes. I saw one of his men watching us from the back door when we came up the hill."

"So we wait, dammit." Claudel, like Renwick, kept an eye on his watch.

Five minutes passed. Suddenly, through the night silence, came the distant hum of an engine.

"*Merde!*" Claudel said, sat up straight. Then, listening, he relaxed. The motor had stopped halfway up the hill road.

Renwick, too, relaxed.

"Did he actually bring bicycles in that van of his?" Claudel asked as the engine started once more and retreated downhill. "And now they're being pushed the rest of the way," he said, amusement growing. "God, for a moment there I thought our visitor was arriving early." He reached for his binoculars and trained them on the road.

"Give them ten minutes more," Renwick said. "It's a steep push!"

Actually, it was eight minutes when two dark figures shoving bicycles uphill came around the road's lower curve and passed the path.

"Beautiful!" said Renwick. "Just hope these two can get the driver out of his car before he sends any warning to Klaus."

"They will," said Marchand, and he sat down beside them.

"You're good," Renwick told him, recovering from his surprise. His hands, ready to reach out and strike, relaxed again. Claudel closed his knife, slipped it back into his pocket. And where, wondered Renwick, did a country-town cop learn that covert trick?

"Now," Marchand said, a touch of acid once more in his voice, "what else do you have to suggest?"

Claudel, still angry, said, "I'm moving nearer the road—to the patch of bushes beside the path."

Marchand remembered his glimpse of Claudel's knife. "Then I'll alert my man who is stationed there to expect some friendly company." He pulled out his transceiver, and as he made contact and spoke he watched Claudel already on his way, choosing every shred of cover he could find. "He moves well," Marchand conceded when his instructions were over. He didn't stow away his little miracle machine, kept it ready. "I have two men posted at the foot of the road. We'll have good warning if a car drives uphill."

"And you've still got one man in the chalet?"

"He was there. Now he is under cover, near the front door. Quite a search he had for the fuses you hid in the garbage pail. Not a bad idea. I doubt if much garbage will be collected from that house in the next week or so."

"Claudel's idea. So the lights are working again."

"Not upstairs. We must keep the house looking blacked out. That blind you slashed would show light and might alarm the midnight visitor." Marchand paused and added, "You were in a very unpleasant mood when you went out onto that balcony. Because of the woman?"

"We had just found her." And now the questions about Lorna, Renwick thought. Marchand's lead-in had been clever, but expected.

"Do you know her?"

"Met her once. Lorna Upwood. Worked with Exports Consolidated. She tried to quit."

"Ah, yes—the firm that Klingfeld and Sons took over. Did she say anything?"

"She thought we were her captors. A few words, a lot of pain and terror. Then she passed out. Has she been able to talk—tell you where she was kidnapped?"

Marchand shook his head. "Now under heavy sedation. Fortunately, we have good medical facilities here."

"You'd need them—skiing and climbing accidents, I suppose." Thank God that the conversation had turned amiable, friendly.

Perhaps the mention of Exports Consolidated had reassured Marchand, had given him the reason why a woman had been abducted and tortured. He dropped the subject of Lorna. "Of course those other three have said nothing at all. I have a feeling they will remain silent. They're afraid they could incriminate themselves still further."

"They've plenty to hide."

Marchand nodded his agreement. "But what is unbelievable is any connection between those people and Sudak. If you hadn't seen him arriving this afternoon along with the Mercedes that brought the woman here—Are you positive it was Klaus Sudak who drove the Ferrari?"

Briefly, Renwick described him. "We also heard his name called—by one of his house guests who came running down the road to meet him."

"Did they speak?"

"He pulled her into the Ferrari and drove uphill."

"He was angry that she had seen him there," Marchand judged. Then he brightened. "She might talk to us."

"Perhaps."

"That's the problem, isn't it? No matter what we discover about that little house below us, we have nothing to connect any of its happenings with Monsieur Klaus Sudak up there on his hill."

"So far."

"Yet, he must keep in contact with the house. Especially when the Mercedes leaves here, after depositing this mysterious visitor, and never reaches the Chalet Ruskin. That, my friend, is one weakness of your roadblock."

"It's worth the risk. You'll have a car whose route you can trace and a driver who was seen bringing a visitor to a chalet, ostensibly empty, shuttered tight. If you can identify the driver, link him with Sudak, then you've got something to go on."

"That depends on who the visitor is," Marchand said drily.

"He sure isn't Sudak's long-lost uncle."

"No. But unless he has some criminal connection, we haven't—" Marchand broke off as his transceiver gave its signal. He listened intently. "A car has just come through the town, started up the road," he told Renwick, and began checking with his outposts to make sure they had heard the warning, too.

"What kind of car?" Renwick asked.

"A black Mercedes. Zurich plate. Hear it now?"

There was a distant hum, strengthening, drawing nearer.

"There was another car with it," Marchand said. "It drove to a house on the outskirts of—"

"I'm going down," Renwick said, and was gone, running toward the back of the chalet, skirting its far side to reach its front.

Marchand had just time to warn the policeman stationed there to expect the American before he saw the Mercedes come around the curve, its lights dimmed to parking level.

The bush was lopsided and stunted, but it was the nearest cover that Renwick could reach. His run ended in a slide onto the ground, green leaves above his head. He rolled over to lie on his stomach and study the path. At this end it stopped at the front door—about twenty feet away, he calculated. At the other end was the road. And a car that was now drawing up.

A soft bird call came from a larger bush over to his left, farther away from the corner of the house where he lay. Marchand's man, he thought, but didn't risk an answering whistle, his eyes fastened on the black shapes and shadows that formed and unformed as the moon's shrouded light played over them. The car, a hard, dark mass, was definite. He heard its door close, saw a black figure separate from its bulk and start slowly toward him. Slowly, carefully, although the path was even; stopping once, to listen and look. The moonlight strengthened briefly, was clouded over again. Enough to let Renwick see that this was an elderly man in a long black coat, white-haired, stooping slightly, walking with difficulty. So you guessed wrong, Renwick told himself; all right, you win the booby prize. Too eager, too quick to play your hunches.

The Mercedes had waited, perhaps to make certain its passenger reached the house safely. He halted near its steps, faced the road, let one small beam flicker from his flashlight, and the car moved away. So he's satisfied everything is safe, Renwick thought, as the flashlight disappeared into the man's pocket and his hand came out empty. No key? Is he supposed to knock? If so, we've had it. He will get no answer, and he'll take off—he's been studying the lie of the land ever since he started up the path.

Then a change came over the man. With the car gone—and no one to see him as frail and old—he straightened his back, took the steps nimbly, tried the door handle.

Renwick's body tensed; he lifted himself into a crouch, his legs braced to move. God, he was thinking as the door was rattled again, was it supposed to be unlocked? Unlocked as soon as Stefan heard the Mercedes arrive, locked once more as the visitor slipped into the bedroom? Renwick drew a long breath.

The door opened.

Renwick's spine stiffened. Marchand—it could only be Marchand. Bloody fool, what does he think he's dealing with? An unarmed jewel thief? Now we'll have a goddamned shooting match, blast it to hell; and Klaus alerted—the last thing we wanted.

Marchand must have stepped aside to let the stranger enter. "Your room is over there," he was saying.

That does it. Stefan can't speak French. Just bad German and halting English as well as his native language. Renwick half rose, moved quietly to the side of the bush, freeing his legs from a grasping branch, and drew out his Biretta. Had the midnight visitor been briefed about Stefan? Surely, with all these exact preparations, he knew what to expect—must have been told. Well, thought Renwick as he straightened up, you just can't win them all. And to corroborate his words, at that very moment the moon chose to emerge from the clouds.

Yes, the man had been told. His hand went into his pocket, came out with his gun, and crashed it down like a bludgeon. He turned to run.

Renwick called out, "Don't try it. You're completely surrounded." Marchand's man—police uniform on this one—had risen from cover. From the other end of the path, two men loomed into view: Claudel with his automatic drawn, and a solid type with a rifle.

Renwick watched the man's right hand as it let the revolver droop—a powerful weapon made all the uglier by its silencer. Of course he'd use a silencer. This man was a planner, left nothing to chance. Tonight he had made no mistake; he had just stepped into the mistakes made by others.

For that long moment, he stood still. He seemed to have listened to Renwick's words. His eyes counted the odds against him, then his head bowed in acceptance. In a split second, his head raised and he fired, his body swerving around in a halfcircle as he aimed at each man. Four bullets in rapid succession: at Renwick, the policeman, the rifleman, Claudel.

Renwick had seen the man's right hand tighten and swing up, dodged sideways. The bullet aimed at his chest grazed the inside of his arm. The policeman, stepping forward to arrest the man, was not so lucky: he was knocked backward, lay motionless. The rifleman had dropped prone, taken a sight as the bullet intended for him whistled above his head. Claudel, too, had fallen flat on his face, raised his pistol. But before either he or Renwick could fire back, the rifle bullet had bored a hole through the man's heart.

In silence, Renwick and Claudel walked over to his body. It had been slammed backward against the steps, jolted so hard that the white wig had slipped. Renwick pulled it aside, shone his flashlight on the startled face that stared blankly at the sky above.

"Erik," said Claudel.

Renwick switched off the flashlight and entered the hall. Marchand was alive but unsteady on his feet. He had sensed the blow coming, tried to avoid it, and had almost succeeded. There was a savage weal across one cheek, a jaw beginning to swell, perhaps a collarbone smashed. Renwick helped him down the steps, past Erik's body, left him by the dead police-man to hear the rifleman's explanations.

Claudel closed the chalet's door and came over to join him. "I thought you had packed it in," he told Renwick. "You weren't hit, were you?"

Renwick raised his left arm, looked at the singed streak across its inner sleeve.

"Too close for comfort," Claudel said. "Where did he learn to shoot like that?"

"In a South Yemen training camp," Renwick said grimly.

"What now?" Claudel looked in the direction of the Chalet Ruskin. "He heard that shot."

"A rifle. It could be explained, perhaps." Renwick tried to think. "Acci-dental discharge by a—hunter or poacher—someone out on this hillside." Renwick made an effort. "Tell Marchand to phone Sudak and the neigh-boring chalets. Explain—reassure them all."

"Reassure Sudak?" Claudel was disbelieving.

"Try it, anyway. What else?" Renwick's voice was sharp. "If Marchand has a better idea, let him use it." Then he sat down, legs crossed, and stared out over the patchwork of faint light and dark shadow that covered the hillside. Behind him, Erik lay staring up at the stars.

Nineteen

MARCHAND WAS ANGRY, obdurate, and in pain. He had lost a man, and noth-ing compensated for that. Not the Mercedes driven back downhill with bicycles and prisoner intact, an easy capture. (Its chauffeur—perhaps ex-hausted by a day of hard traveling, perhaps surprised by a totally unexpected danger almost at the entrance to the Chalet Ruskin—had been slow to resist.) Not the death of a murderer, the leader of a vicious gang of West German terrorists. Not even the fact that he, himself, had escaped that savage blow and remained alive. He had lost a man.

"Enough," Marchand said. He had rejected the idea of explaining the rifle shot to any chalet on this hillside. Instead, he had ordered his van partway up the road, and, with it, two stretchers. "Enough," he repeated. "Tonight we rest. I have a report to make. Tomorrow, early, we shall visit Sudak."

"We will lose him," Renwick said quietly.

"How? The road ends above the Chalet Ruskin. If he tried to leave, he must drive downhill to the town. I have cars blocking the exit. He will be stopped. And what evidence do we have against him if the Mercedes' driver won't talk? A dead terrorist? He can't talk."

"He never would have."

"Sudak will claim total ignorance that the man was ever here. As for that guest—the hysterical female you saw today—what excuse could we offer to drag her out of bed at this time of night? No, tomorrow morning, early, we can prepare a reason, visit the chalet—"

"And why should we expect to find Sudak there?"

"I told you—"

"There's no way out by car except by this road." Renwick held down his impatience, kept his voice even. "But are there footpaths—through the trees—like the one we took today from Ruskin's Chair? A path that doesn't end in a cliff or a steep drop to the valley?"

Obviously, there was one. Marchand fell silent.

"What part of town does such a path reach?"

Marchand's eyes widened, then narrowed.

"You had a report about a second car—one that followed the Mercedes into Chamonix. It stopped at a house on the outskirts—isn't that what you said?"

"A wild guess, if you mean Sudak will try to reach that house."

So it did lie somewhere near the end of a path from the Chalet Ruskin. "Have you a map you could show us?"

"Haven't you one of your own?"

"Forgot to buy one today." The only map they had been able to find was one of the town with surrounding hills and mountains named, but with no details such as paths or trails. "We all make mistakes," Renwick added with considerable tact.

That admission was accepted with a nod. And a small confession followed, making a nice diversion from the subject of maps. "I thought we could trap that man—Erik?—inside the house. But"—Marchand shrugged—"there may have been an identification signal necessary. Yet, he gave no time for that, I invited him to enter, and he attacked."

Renwick refused to be diverted. "Have you a map you could show us?" he repeated. "One with ski trails and climbing paths clearly marked?"

"Not enough light to look at it here. You can study it in the van. Unless, of course—" Marchand's sardonic mood was back—"you insist on visiting the Chalet Ruskin now."

"No interest." The visit should have been made forty-five minutes ago, just after the rifle had been fired. "By this time, Sudak—"

"Sudak will have sent someone to investigate this small chalet. But I have already ordered two men to keep watch around it. And two more near the Chalet Ruskin. Sudak will wait for a report, and when none reaches him—my men will take care of that—he will then assess the situation, and perhaps move. Or stay, to face us and play the complete innocent." Marchand nursed his jaw, now so swollen that even talking was difficult. But he persisted. "And we still have our problem. What connection between all this—" he tried to gesture to the house, flinched as his collarbone's pain sharpened— "and Sudak? He will send no one here whom we can identify. His men never were known in the town. If they appeared there, it was as tourists, day visitors."

Renwick nodded his agreement on that point. But he exchanged glances with Claudel, and they shared the same thought. Klaus Sudak wasn't the type to wait and assess any situation. His assessment would be done when he reached safety. He moved on instinct.

"The van has arrived," Marchand said, listening. He began walking rapidly to the road. "We'll take it down, send it back for the stretchers."

Renwick gave one last look at the chalet, tightly shuttered, deserted, a sad and lonely place, with two men lying still and another standing guard. And amid that silence, among the dark trees lost in shadows? Someone moving around, trying to guess what could have happened? If Sudak had even stayed this long to receive a report, then let him. This was one defeat he'd never repair.

In the van, they studied a detailed map. "Now, where's that house on the outskirts of town?" Renwick asked.

"There!" Marchand pointed to one of the neat small squares that were dotted over the layout of the valley like a scattered flock of sheep. "It was rented two weeks ago for the rest of the summer."

"Occupied?"

"Not until tonight, except for an occasional caretaker."

"What kind of car arrived there?"

"A white Fiat. Italian registration."

"Milan?" Claudel asked quickly.

Marchand looked at him, then at Renwick. "Perhaps my biggest problem is that I've been told so little. How did you know about Milan? Why didn't you tell me?"

Renwick finished memorizing the position of the house reached by the Fiat. It was among a cluster of five, the last group on the road from town. Fields around their sides, a wooded slope behind them. And the path that could lead from the Chalet Ruskin ended not too far away—close to a run-off stream from the hillside: a good marker, he thought, in a valley that was as flat as a billiard table.

"Why?" Marchand repeated, his lips tight.

"We didn't know," Renwick said. "Just another wild guess."

Marchand's look sharpened, but the American was rolling up the map, handing it over with a polite thank you.

"What color is the house?" Renwick asked.

"White. Blue shutters."

"Not tightly closed, I hope," said Claudel. He was feeling a delayed elation. Even if we win nothing more, he was thinking, we found Erik. We found him. And no sharpshooter in Marchand's outfit would have been there to get him if we hadn't flushed him out.

"Keep away from that house," Marchand told them. "There's no need for you to go near it. I have posted two men already. If anything develops, I'll know at once."

'So we just go to bed and enjoy sweet dreams?" Claudel asked.

"Yes. You're lucky. I have work to do."

"First," Renwick said, "have that shoulder looked at."

"Then what? You'll write my report for me?" Marchand's temper was fraying rapidly.

"Tomorrow, when there's a quiet moment, we'll sit down with you in a closed and very private room. We'll answer your questions if we can." Renwick looked at his watch as the van came to a halt.

Marchand opened its door. "If you can," he mocked, but he was partly mollified. "Tomorrow morning we meet here at the foot of the road. Six o'clock sharp. That will give us time to make our plans before we pay a visit to—" He broke off, staring uphill.

A small vehicle, headlights blazing through the darkness, had swerved around the last turn on the steep slope. It was out of control, driving right at them with incredible speed, its horn blasting as its powerful beam swept over the group of men near the van and parked cars. Barely ten yards away, a violent twist of its steering wheel sent the yellow jeep careening over to the road's left side. It hit the low bank, leaped wildly, turned over, came to rest on its side in the field beyond.

Renwick and the van's driver reached it, Claudel and Marchand at their heels. "Light here!" Marchand yelled over his shoulder to the men at the roadblock, who had been standing as if paralyzed. It came on full strength.

The driver was dead, still held in position by a safety belt. His passenger had been thrown clear—a young woman, dark-haired, wrapped in a traveling coat. A suitcase was some distance away, its contents spilled onto the bank and field.

Claudel went over to her. "Alive," he called to Renwick, who was looking at the driver, partly unrecognizable. But he was the blond young man who had sat and joked with Annabel in the café that early afternoon. The ski instructor. Renwick had named him. Whoever he was, he had saved some people from injury, perhaps some lives, and lost his own.

"Annabel?" Renwick asked very quietly as Marchand and he reached Claudel. Claudel nodded. "She's hurt but alive."

Annabel's eyes had opened. She said, "Oh! My leg! I can't move it."

"Don't," Renwick said. Her voice had been natural. Nothing too seriously wrong. A broken leg, perhaps. She would live. "Why were you leaving, Annabel?" he asked gently.

"Wait until we get her to the hospital," Marchand said, and turned away to direct the removal of the body from the jeep.

"Annabel," Renwick repeated, dropping on one knee beside her, "why were you leaving? At this hour?"

"He told me—told me to pack and leave. Oh, my leg!"

"Don't move it. Lie still. You'll be all right. When did Klaus tell you to leave? What time?"

Her voice was angry, indignant. "Midnight—after midnight. Didn't stay around to say good-bye, can you believe it?" She was suddenly worried. "Where's Jerri? Hurt, too?"

"What went wrong? Isn't Jerri a good driver?"

"The best. It was the jeep—the brakes." She struggled to rise, cried out with pain. She began to weep. "Where is Jerri? Where is he?"

Renwick rose. "You handle this," he told Claudel and went over to the jeep, interrupting Marchand, who was ordering an ambulance. "Yes, again!" Marchand almost shouted into his transceiver. "Return here! At once!" He switched it off, looked at Renwick. "Brakes, did you say? Tampered with?"

"Get your best mechanic to find out how they were put out of commission, and you'll have a case of homicide against the Chalet Ruskin." Renwick was speaking rapidly, signaling Claudel to join him. "Who gave the order? Question them all. Jerri's death may loosen some tongues. The girl—name is Annabel Vroom—could be a good witness." And with that, Renwick moved quickly to his car.

He was already in the Audi, had its motor running, by the time Claudel reached it. "Slightly abrupt," was his comment on Renwick's speedy departure. "I suppose Marchand guessed why."

"He didn't try to stop us anyway." That was a relief: no more argument, no more wasted time.

"Now he will be warning his two men who are watching the house in the valley to expect a couple of lunatics in ten minutes."

"Five." The street was empty of traffic.

"Even at this hour there's still a speed limit." Claudel flinched at a sharp corner, added, "We'll enter for Le Mans next year." Then he turned serious. "Do you really think that Klaus Sudak is now climbing down a dark path over a rough hillside?"

"No. I think he is at the end of the path by this time. You saw the map."

Claudel nodded. The path would only take about an hour of walking, even by night. We may be too late, he thought as he looked at his watch. It was almost ten past one. If Klaus had set out as soon as Annabel had orders to leave, he could now be reaching the meadows at the foot of the hill. From there to the house with blue shutters was a short distance. "Let's hope he delayed."

"For what? For news that two people had been killed in a car crash? He believes they're dead. A jeep without brakes on that hill road at night? A disaster. But Jerri could drive." And with his hands gripping the wheel he hadn't a second to unbuckle his safety belt. "If there hadn't been a roadblock, he might have made it. He just might."

They took the road that lay on the right bank of a narrow river that ran through this broad, flat valley toward the town. Houses were now sparse, set down here and there, sometimes singly, sometimes in groups, square blobs of ghostly white, and all neat and solid and fast asleep.

"This might be it," Renwick said as he saw a cluster of houses ahead of him. He wasn't sure. They weren't the close group he had expected. Three seemed more or less together, fields at their sides and backs. Then two followed, slightly apart. Behind all the stretch of fields was definitely a dark hillside, heavily wooded. By daylight it would be easy to identify a path coming down from the hill; by night, impossible. "See any blue shutters?" he asked as they passed the first three houses at reduced speed.

"Can't tell color by this light." Claudel was depressed. No cover anywhere—just small gardens and rough hedges, shrubbery, no large sheltering trees. Then his voice quickened. "There's a white car—parked at the side of that last house."

"You're sure?" Renwick kept on driving for another fifty yards before he brought the Audi to a stop. Still no cover around them—flat fields reaching the hillside on his left, the River Arve flowing far to his right.

"The car was the same color as the house. Shutters looked gray. Could be blue by day. But I'm damned well not sure of anything at this moment. Do we risk it? Go in?" And if the car isn't pure white, if it isn't a Fiat, we could be in trouble.

"We risk it," Renwick said. He was looking at the flat road just ahead of them. It rose slightly as if it were bridging some small tributary to the river. A man-made stream, a runoff for the torrents of spring from the hillside. His eyes followed its straight line, as far as they could see by the half-moon light. Yes, it ran toward the woods. "The path is just over there," he said, pointing to the hill. He switched off the car's lights, reversed, and drove back to the houses at low speed. "No sign of Marchand's men."

"They are keeping well out of sight."

"They know this territory. We don't."

"Where do we park?"

"Just beyond the house—near its neighbor. It's the best we can do." And damn all this maneuvering: it was taking as much time as the drive through the town and its outskirts.

They passed the house where Claudel had glimpsed a possibly white car in the driveway. It was there, all right. The next house had no shutters, its upper windows open for air; no lights, everyone asleep; and the car at its side was black.

Renwick brought the Audi to a slow and soundless halt, drawing it close to a hedge. "The best we can do," he said again as he turned off the engine. "Now we check the car we saw. If it is a Fiat, you deal with it. I'll cover you."

"If Klaus did use the path to reach the house, why the hell did he delay? Why not take off in the Fiat?"

"Change of clothes, change in appearance."

Claudel nodded. "It would be too much to hope he had sprained an ankle coming down that hill."

"Or broken his neck," Renwick said grimly. "Let's move it. After the Fiat's dealt with, we'll have a close look at the house, see what's stirring. You take a look around the back. I'll watch the front. Then we meet. Okay?"

"Okay."

They left the Audi at a half-run, reached their target in a few seconds.

The shutters were closed, but a streak of light came from the ground-floor rooms. So people were awake. And moving around; one room darkened, another lit up. How many of them? Klaus—if he were there; the man who had driven here tonight—alone or with a chauffeur? And possibly the caretaker. Not too many, thought Renwick. Still, Marchand's men would be useful. Were they both at the back of the house, keeping watch from the field or a vegetable patch? The front garden, small, was absolutely still.

Renwick and Claudel exchanged a nod, separating as they started up the short driveway, one on each side of it, crouching low behind a rosebush or shrub as they advanced cautiously toward the white car that was pointed toward the road. It was a Fiat.

Claudel bent down to check its plate: Milan. He signaled an okay to Renwick and opened the Fiat's hood. Renwick waited until Claudel had dealt with the distributor—taken off its cap, removed the roto inside and thrown it over the hedge, replaced the cap—and closed the hood again. In spite of Claudel's extreme caution, there was a small click. Renwick's hand went to his automatic, rested there. But no one in the house had heard anything. No door opened. Claudel signaled once more as he disappeared around the side of the house to reach its back, and Renwick relaxed. Now he could move to a bush that seemed a likely spot: larger than most, not too high but thick and heavy, a good piece of cover with a first-rate view of the front door.

He reached it, head and shoulders well down, and dropped into its shadow. His hand fell on a sleeve, a rough sweater, an arm that was still and lifeless. My God, he thought, my God . . . He had found one of Marchand's men.

For a moment, Renwick froze. Then he drew his Biretta. He glanced at the body lying beside him. Face down, it had been pulled or shoved under the spread of branches. To be got rid of later, when time was less pressing? Gingerly, he reached out to the man's back and felt a heavy dampness between the shoulder blades. The man had bled a lot, but the blood was cold. A knife wound.

He eased Marchand's transceiver out of his pocket. Risk it? He'd better. This house was more than suspect now. He looked around him, listened. Nothing stirred, only the dappled light of a moon struggling to free itself from the clouds. They thickened, grew. As the garden was plunged into darkness, he made contact with Marchand. All he said was, "Victor. Send help." And Marchand, after a second of shock, said, "Understood."

Renwick put away the transceiver. Marchand knew he was here. Marchand knew he wouldn't call for help if it weren't urgent. Marchand knew it was police business if he made such a call. Marchand, thought Renwick, must be cursing the day when Claudel and I arrived in town.

He had to move away from here. He tried to recall the layout of this patch of ground as he had seen it in the last burst of moonlight. The heavy clouds would last another two or three minutes. He rose and began a cautious approach in the temporary blackout over the ill-kempt grass to reach a dwarf tree that stood, all seven feet of it, in the corner of the garden. Its branches were thin, its leaves sparse, but they would blur any clear view of him when the moon came out of its cloud cover. From here he would be able to see one side and the front of the house. He looked at his watch. All this—the approach to the driveway, the Fiat, the body, and now a sheltering tree—had taken only nine minutes. Yet up on the hill beside the chalet there had been almost two hours of waiting, and worrying and waiting. It was always the same: hurry up and wait. When the action did come, it could be counted in seconds—like a torrent bursting out from a breaking dam.

The cloud was passing, the moon reappearing. Renwick caught sight of a dark figure standing at the side wall of the house, right at its front corner, barley twenty yards away. Claudel? Yes, Claudel. He had taken his time; but there he was, every sense alert as he looked around. Renwick tried a hand signal, stretching his arm beyond a branch, holding it there briefly. It was enough. Claudel's quick eyes had seen it. He made a desperate dash before the moonlight strengthened, racing in his rubber-soled shoes to reach the thorn hedge that bounded the garden, and then the long grass beside Renwick. He fell prone, lay still, regained his breath.

Slowly, Renwick dropped to a kneeling position, keeping his body behind the trunk of the tree—however small, it gave some protection from the house. Something was wrong. Claudel wouldn't have come directly here if it weren't. Once he had noted Renwick's position, he should have chosen shelter farther away. And now they were breaking their second rule. Claudel was speaking. In a whisper. Renwick bent his head to catch the words. They were certainly less loud than any murmur into a transmitter—couldn't Claudel have risked even that?

"One of Marchand's men—looked dead. But he isn't. Still breathing."

"Where?"

"At the back of the house—near a truck. I dealt with it."

"How was he hurt?"

"A knife between the shoulder blades."

"The other one is dead. Knifed, too. I've called Marchand. Must have happened just after they got here, took their positions." Renwick paused. "A throwing knife, I'd guess."

Claudel thought over that. Then he said, "I think we'd better stay together."

"Back to back, if possible."

Claudel nodded. "I'll laugh at that tomorrow."

Renwick put a hand to his lips for silence. A light footstep had sounded. They turned their heads toward the house and watched the man who had emerged from its front door.

He looked young and trim, walked with a spring in his step. Like them, he wore dark clothes, and became barely visible as he reached the shadows of the bush where the dead man lay. He was checking, thought Renwick in a sudden rise of anger. Checking to make sure nothing was disturbed, everything just as he left it. Then Spring-heeled Jack walked on, starting a tour of inspection around the garden, pausing to look briefly at the road outside. It must have been empty—and where the hell is Marchand? Renwick asked himself—for he walked back, up the short driveway toward the Fiat. Once past it, he was lost to sight.

It was a quick tour of inspection. He reappeared from the back of the house, walking down its side, reaching the spot where Claudel had stood before his ten-yard dash to the hedge of thorn bushes. He stopped at the corner, looked around. Satisfied, he walked on. At the front door, he paused again and knocked twice. Then he stood aside, waiting.

The inspection tour was over—no more trouble had been expected, so no more trouble had been found. The signal had been given: it was safe to leave. Renwick reached for Claudel's shoulder, touched it. Claudel nodded, his eyes on the house, his automatic ready. Renwick released the safety catch of his Biretta. He glanced up at the sky—no clouds to cover the moon for another three or more minutes. We are in luck, he thought: enough light to see by. His attention switched back to the house. Its door had opened.

Two men stepped out, barely pausing to look around the garden before they hurried to the car. One was white-haired, stoutly built, wearing a suit that was silver gray in the moonlight. The other was tall, broad-shouldered, his hair hidden by a chauffeur's cap. He was appropriately dressed for the part he was playing: a white shirt under a dark-blue or black suit. At that moment, as they reached the Fiat, Renwick heard a distant hum—the sound of a car, two cars perhaps. Marchand? But the sound stopped.

Claudel was staring. "Haversfield," he whispered. That dear, sweet old Englishman in Djibouti. "He's mine."

Renwick nodded, still listening. Only silence from the road. Perhaps the cars had been bringing people home from a Saturday-night dance, he thought wryly.

Silence, too, from the Fiat. No response from its engine. The chauffeur must be cursing it, but his voice was held too low to be heard. Just Haversfield in the back seat, his driver at the wheel, and a car that was dead.

Now? wondered Renwick but hesitated to move. Spring-heeled Jack was still standing by the house door. (One warning from him and the other two would be heading for the back field.) He was looking toward the Fiat, wondering why it wasn't moving. Then he ran to help.

"Now," said Renwick. Jack had his back turned, his head bent, as he argued with the driver. Yes, the car had been in good running condition all the way from Milan; Jack had checked it after he had dealt with the interlopers; Jack was sure. A quick command sent him hastening to the hood. He started raising it.

He caught sight of Renwick and Claudel, halfway across the garden, fanning out as they approached the car. He yelled a warning, his hand reaching toward the back of his neck. The gesture was unmistakable—a throwing knife. Renwick took no chances. He fired as the man's hand brought the knife out of its holster and threw it in one quick sweep of the arm. The blade sliced past Renwick's head as the man fell to the ground and doubled in pain.

Everything burst loose. At the sound of the shot, two men raced up from the road. The chauffeur was out of the car, running, firing at Renwick, then at Claudel, but unable to aim properly as he bolted toward the back of the house. He never reached either the field or the truck. Renwick's bullet caught his hip, sent him sprawling into the grip of two more men who had just burst through

the hedge at the side of the driveway. Claudel, now at the Fiat, pulled
Haversfield out. "Unarmed, unarmed! No weapon!" Haversfield was saying,
his voice as high as the arms raised over his head. "Not worth the trouble,"
Claudel said in disgust, and handed over Haversfield to a newcomer.

Renwick slipped his automatic back into his pocket. Yes, he thought,
everything happens at once: the dam broke and the torrent swept over us;
danger counted in seconds. He turned to greet Marchand, who had appeared
at his elbow.

Marchand's anger was against himself. "We parked farther along the
road—wanted to give them no warning."

"You didn't. It was a good idea." And Renwick meant it. If the cars had
approached any nearer, all three men would have made a dash for the field.
And Claudel and Renwick, over by the dwarf tree, couldn't have hit them.
There would have been a chase after them, a scattering across the field into
the woods. The Englishman, so-called, could have been taken, but the other
two? Renwick looked at the chauffeur, lying on the ground a short distance
away. That's the one we want, he thought; but first things came first. "You
have a wounded man at the back of the house. He needs help—fast. Claudel
will show your men the place."

"How? When?"

"Before we arrived. He was knifed." Renwick waited until Marchand had
detailed two men to leave with Claudel and was, himself, about to follow.
Renwick caught his arm, said very quietly, "Another over here. Come!" He
led Marchand to the bush under which the body lay. "Knife in the back.
There's the man who threw it." He pointed at Spring-heeled Jack, now
moaning and clutching his groin.

Renwick left Marchand kneeling beside the body and went looking for
the knife that had just missed him. The sky darkened—more of those damned
clouds—he'd have to use his flashlight. A brief search, and he found the
knife buried hilt-high in the earth. He handed it to Marchand. "Evidence,"
he said, and went back to the driveway and reached the fake chauffeur, still
face down on the ground, two men pinning his arms and back. His leg was
out of commission. "Turn him over!"

Renwick flashed his light on the man's face and pulled off the cap. The
hair was blond, but it belonged to a young man. Up close, his resemblance
to Klaus Sudak was superficial. Oh God, thought Renwick, and he felt suddenly exhausted, exhausted and sick. All this for nothing, and my fault. I
was so damned sure. And I was wrong.

He turned away, walked toward the Fiat, leaned against it. The moonlight strengthened. He forced himself to watch as Marchand's man, barely
alive, was carried away; as a body wrapped in a bag was taken out; as two
wounded criminals were removed along with an elderly gentleman who had
nothing to say but was almost smiling in silent triumph. Renwick noticed
that smirk. His depression deepened.

Claudel, and then Marchand, joined him. "Let's go back to the inn,"
Claudel said.

Renwick nodded, straightened up, left the Fiat. All three walked slowly
down the driveway.

"We've searched the house," Marchand said. "Klaus Sudak is not there." Never has been, said his eyes. "So tomorrow at eight I shall visit the Chalet Ruskin—as I originally planned."

Renwick's voice was flat, expressionless. "He won't be there."

"You still believe that?" Marchand was incredulous. Tactfully, he didn't add, "After tonight?"

"If you were Sudak, would you wait?"

"I'll telephone now. Speak with him. About the accident to the jeep."

"Someone else will answer and tell you that he can't be disturbed at this hour."

Marchand's anger broke. "If he isn't there, and he isn't down here, where *is* he?"

Renwick roused himself. "I don't know. But if you've watched the roads, checked the cars—"

"We have!"

"—then the path from the hillside down to this valley is his only escape route. Logical."

"Logical?" Marchand looked at Claudel for support, but Claudel was keeping silent. Besides, his arm had started acting up again: he couldn't ignore any longer that it was far from healing, had gone on a rampage of its own.

Renwick said, "Yes. And when he got to this house and heard that two men had been watching it, he wouldn't stay. Sure, they had been dealt with. But the fact that they were here proved the house was under suspicion. He'd take off within a couple of minutes."

"Where?" demanded Marchand. He held out his hand. "My transceiver," he reminded Renwick, and took it from him. "No more need for that!"

"Let's get back to the inn," Claudel said again. "We are dead on our feet."

"And I have another report to make," Marchand said grimly. Then he relented, put a hand on Renwick's shoulder. "Mistakes can be made. Don't be so hard on yourself. Tonight, we gained something. And lost something." But the biggest loss was in my two men. And Renwick knows that, he realized, watching the American's face. "Good night."

"A quarter to three," Claudel said when they reached their room. "Bed— and a long sleep—that's for me."

"I have to contact London," Renwick said wearily. He was too exhausted, physically, emotionally, to make out a detailed report of today's results and put it into code. That would have to be done tomorrow. Now he'd give the basic news, and briefly: about Erik; about Haversfield; about Klaus Sudak. And ask for the latest word—if any—from Washington. Nina . . . If something had gone wrong at Basset Hill, then I'm to blame for that, too. His depression turned into an agony of despair.

He began to set up the transceiver. Gilman, he told himself, would be sleeping on a cot in the office: standard procedure for a crisis situation. And the delay in sending this report was possibly keeping Gilman awake with anxiety.

He made contact. Gilman was there. Renwick, with an effort, tried a voice code. And Gilman's reaction was one of frank astonishment. "Splendid, splendid," he said and didn't even let the news about Klaus dampen his optimism. But much of that came from a report he had recieved only two hours ago from Washington. "All is well," he said. "The supply-room clerk has been arrested by the FBI. Everything is normal. Under control." And with that, he signed off.

Renwick's heart lifted. Nina was safe. Josh Grable was no longer searching. Nina was safe.

Claudel, unable to sleep, watched him. Bad news? Renwick's head was bowed, a hand over his eyes. He rose, began putting the equipment safely away. He glanced over at Claudel, saw he was still awake. "Everything is under control at Basset Hill." That was Mac's phrase—when he said "under control" he meant it. Then Renwick laughed, the first real laugh he had given in two days. "Nina's okay, Pierre. The FBI have caught Grable. She's safe." And Renwick laughed again.

Twenty

RENWICK WAS ASLEEP as soon as his head hit the pillow. Claudel envied him. There was a throb in his arm that not only kept him awake, tired as he was, but worried him. For the first time he was admitting that he had better do as the doctors had told him. A six-inch cut in his arm—nothing to it, he had thought: in the past he had suffered more serious wounds than that and recovered quickly. But this time his body was being beaten. It troubled him and it angered him. He closed his eyes, tried to forget the London doctor who had said, "East Africa? You can pick up the worst infections there. You should have had stitches in that wound within hours of receiving it. Be careful!" And the Paris doctor had said much the same, adding with Gallic realism, "Be careful you don't lose that arm." As for the doctor in Geneva, he had prescribed two days in the hospital. Like hell I'll go there, Claudel thought. But the next three hours were misery.

Suddenly there was a shout from across the room. Renwick was sitting bolt upright in bed, totally awake within that split second. He looked over at Claudel, saw he wasn't asleep. "That house next door—the one without shutters—with the windows open for air. People sleeping inside. Why the hell didn't they wake up with those pistol shots? They didn't even stir." Renwick was out of bed, grabbing a towel on his way to the bathroom.

"Didn't want to become involved," Claudel tried.

"Not one light turned on, dammit."

"There was hardly a light turned on anywhere."

"In the nearby house there were some." A few. But in the place right next door? Nothing. "Where were our eyes, blast them?" Renwick left.

Claudel struggled to rise. Our eyes were working, Bob, but our brains were scrambled with frustration. And disappointment. Disappointment? Too mild a word. We don't enjoy losing, Bob. And underneath all that exhaustion—God, were we tired! A long, long night. We had our own troubles, repressed, held down, until the job was over. Then they surfaced. Mine about this blasted arm, a small thing compared to Bob's. Deep inside him there was anxiety and fear—for Nina.

Claudel sat on the edge of his bed, made an effort to reach his clothes, began pulling on socks and trousers. He was trying to ease his arm into a shirt sleeve when Renwick returned.

Renwick dressed quickly, looked at Claudel. "No go," he said quietly. "I'm taking you to a doctor."

"I'm all right."

Renwick picked up the phone, had to wait for a slow answer from the lobby before he got the number of the police station. There, he asked for information about Marchand's home address. It wasn't needed. Marchand was at his desk. Poor old Marchand and his reports, thought Renwick as he heard a tired and irritated voice. "Yes," he told Marchand, "it's me again. Where's your hospital—or a clinic? Claudel's arm needs attention."

Marchand's annoyance vanished. "Was he hurt?"

"A knife wound on his arm—a week ago. Yesterday didn't help it."

"I'll send someone—"

"Just give me the directions. I'll get him there." A few seconds more, and Renwick could put down the phone.

"Look," began Claudel, "you may need me."

"I'll leave you at the clinic. Marchand uses it for himself. Good doctors. I'm only going to have a look at the next-door house anyway. Klaus—if he was there—has left by this time. But I'd just like to check. Okay?"

Claudel nodded. That's a bad sign, thought Renwick as he helped Claudel with his jacket: not one argument.

It was ten minutes to seven by the time Renwick had dropped Claudel at the hospital and could follow the right bank of the Arve, glacier gray and ice cold, into the flat spread of fields. By day, everything had changed. The surrounding hills, their peaks lost in last night's darkness, had become mountains piling up one beside another, flying buttresses to Mont Blanc's cathedral. Blue sky, cloudless, and the silence of Sunday spread over the valley. Few people were stirring either in the houses or on the highway.

Renwick's furious speed slackened as he approached the last two houses on the road. He hadn't been quite accurate when he had told Claudel he was coming here merely to look at the place. Klaus might be still around, using a two-way radio—communication was a necessity—to receive the last possible reports. He had never been alone here, never isolated. He must have installed one or two of his people in the town to keep him informed of any interesting newcomers or developments when he was absent in Geneva. Or in Paris. Or in Rome. Renwick could hope that no details of yesterday were being bruited in Chamonix, but even the best of Marchand's men—not knowing what was at stake, only what had actually happened—could let a few words slip. So could a nurse or a medic, and they had plenty to talk about. Impossible to seal all lips: curiosity, excitement, speculation made sure of that. Our one advantage was in speed, he decided. In one day we arrived and the action was begun. By tonight, even this afternoon, whispers will be circulating.

He passed the house without shutters. Its windows were open. And the car was gone. Too late, he thought, and drew the Audi into the driveway where the white Fiat still stood. Then he walked back to the neighboring house and strolled around it.

No signs of any caretaker, no movement or sound from the kitchen windows. The back door was locked and, although he dealt with that easily enough, it was also bolted from the inside. He would have to try his skill on the main entrance and hope that no early hikers were on the road.

Breaking and entering, he thought as he loosened the lock on the front door; now what would Marchand say to that? He began looking into each room. All was in order, barely furnished, a light film of dust on the wooden surfaces, but nothing disturbed. No food in the kitchen, no signs of cooking, just the stale smell of disuse. And a two-way radio.

He mounted the narrow stairs, treading softly. The upper floor, thanks to the open windows, had fresh air circulation that held the cool touch of night. Three small rooms were neat, unused. The fourth had been occupied: the bed was rumpled. Heavy clothes—flannel shirt, thick sweater, loden britches, wool stockings, strong boots—were dropped in one corner. So Klaus had come down from the hillside dressed like one of the local guides—except that all these items were dark in color. No white stockings, no yellow plaid shirt here. On a chair was a rucksack, empty. Last night he had backpacked a change of clothes down the hill path. Something to transform him into a gentleman of leisure? Or into a businessman in his town Sunday best?

Possibly the businessman, Renwick thought as he entered the bathroom. There was the scent of lemon and traces of lather in the basin. Inside the cabinet above it, a barely used tube of shaving cream and a discarded razor lay on one shelf beside a small bottle, half empty, of verbena toilet water. Trying to get rid of the smell of blood on his hands? But not all the perfumes of Arabia . . . Renwick went downstairs.

He was shaping last night's scenario in his mind. Klaus had reached the house next door safely and planned to change clothes there and use the Fiat. Which meant he had given Erik up as a total loss—perhaps had tried to reach the shuttered chalet by its two-way radio after he had heard a rifle shot: no response. And if he had risked a telephone call, there would only have been a dead line. More than enough to warn Haversfield and Spring-heeled Jack to expect him within the hour instead of Erik this early morning. He arrived. And left as soon as he heard two men had been watching the house. So he slipped over here, played possum, congratulating himself on always taking extra care, extra precautions: a neighboring house readied for any emergency. Possibly, thought Renwick, the bastard even had four hours of solid sleep—one more than I got. So he is now in that car—it looked either black or dark blue—and traveling. Where?

At that point the scenario ended. He opened the front door and faced Marchand.

"Good morning," Marchand said. He had discarded the stained windbreaker he had worn last night and was now back into his dapper tweed jacket, but he wasn't a pretty sight. He had an arm in a sling to take the pressure off his collarbone. The weal on his cheek was covered by a broad strip of plaster, the swollen jaw was turning black with jaundice-yellow undertones. His eyes were ringed and heavy from lack of sleep.

"Good morning," said Renwick with equal politeness.

Marchand's attempted smile was lopsided but friendly. "Claudel told me you were here."

"Talkative this morning, isn't he?"

"He was afraid you would run into danger." Marchand looked at the patch of fresh oil stain on the driveway. "You might have."

"Are you still watching the roads?"

"All of them. When did he leave, I wonder—just after we did?"

"As soon as he had rested—perhaps slept. He's cool, very cool. But why don't you have a look upstairs? You'll find it interesting. Front bedroom on your left." Renwick stood aside and watched Marchand climb the stairs. Tenacious—my little French bulldog, he thought, and sat down on the front doorstep to wait. The sun felt good. His eyes traveled up the mountain mass in front of him. He could actually see Mont Blanc's white-topped peak. It does exist, he told himself and laughed.

Marchand was back again, staring at him in amazement. The change in this man was startling: what had he to laugh at?

Renwick said, nodding toward the mountain, "Thought I'd have to leave without ever seeing it."

"You're leaving—when?" Marchand took a seat beside him.

"After I pack and pay the bill and visit Claudel. How is he, actually?"

"In bed."

"Strapped down? Better keep him there until the doctors clear up that arm. Not good, is it?" Renwick was serious now.

"Not good."

"But they got the arm in time?"

"Just in time, they think. Didn't you warn—"

"Sure, I tried to tell him. He wouldn't listen. Said he was okay. He's stubborn, you know."

"So are you, my friend. And now you are going after Sudak?"

"If I knew where a black car was traveling early this morning. Have you had any reports?"

"I'll check as soon as I get back to my office." Marchand rose, and Renwick with him. "I'll leave word for you at the hospital if there is any information. Might drop around again myself. The woman Upwood is on the critical list but conscious now. This morning she even managed a few words."

"Oh?" Renwick kept his impatience in check. He closed the door. The lock wasn't too badly damaged, he saw with relief. "Anything important?" he asked as they walked slowly toward the road.

"No, no. Just like a woman, she wanted to have her clothes fetched from her hotel in Zurich." Marchand was preoccupied. "By the way—" he began.

"What hotel?" Not only clothes but all her possessions were there.

Marchand eyed him, hesitated, then said, "The Bürkli."

"Where was she kidnapped?"

"As she left her hotel. Yesterday morning. Drugged and brought here." Marchand's voice sharpened. "Why are you so interested in Upwood?"

"Just wanted to complete the picture. I saw her arrival at the chalet and wondered where her journey began. Did she say why she was kidnapped?"

"She hadn't the strength for any more answers." Just her name, nationality, where she had been abducted and how. But she had pretended to sleep again when she was asked *Why?* "She may have known too much about Exports Consolidated." That seemed to remind Marchand of something, or perhaps his introduction of Lorna Upwood into the conversation had been leading up to this point. "By the way," he repeated, "there have been inquiries from Paris." He lowered his voice, although the road which they had now entered was still empty. "From French Intelligence."

"Sent to you?"

"No, no. Inquiries sent to my friend Inspector Duval in Geneva. And to his friend Keppler in Bern. Do you know Keppler? He is with Swiss Intelligence."

"We've met. Four years ago."

"Keppler and Duval are now interested in Klingfeld and Sons. You see, French Intelligence has been investigating Exports Consolidated—a matter of weapons being smuggled into Djibouti."

And a matter of the murder in Djibouti of one of their own, Georges Duhamel. "So Paris has traced the connection between Exports Consolidated and Klingfeld and Sons?"

"Actually," said Marchand with appropriate modesty, "I mentioned that connection in my report to Duval yesterday evening."

Just after I had given him that information at the inn, thought Renwick. No objections. I expected it. "But why didn't French Intelligence ask Interintell's help directly? We've worked together before. Did they think this time there was no need to contact us? They could handle everything themselves? Or that we wouldn't move quickly enough?"

Marchand's face was expressionless. He changed the subject. "Keppler is with Duval right now."

"In Geneva?" That was surprising in a way. Keppler rarely traveled out of Bern nowadays. He must have decided that the case of Klingfeld & Sons needed special attention.

"Yes. They are meeting in Duval's office for a close consultation."

"Surely they don't expect to find Sudak in Geneva."

Marchand went further. "Switzerland is the last place he would visit."

Yesterday Renwick would have agreed. This morning he wasn't so sure. Not Geneva, certainly. But Zurich? Would Sudak risk that? If the stakes were high enough, the risk might be taken. And what greater prize than—Renwick shut off that thought. No more guesswork, he warned himself. At this moment he had nothing on which to base any sound deduction.

Marchand's car was parked near his. Renwick said, "I think I'll go to the hospital first."

"Anxious about your friend?"

"Wouldn't you be?"

"Yes. But he is in good hands."

"I'll have to persuade him to stay in them."

"I may see you there." Marchand looked back at the house they had just left. "But first I send two men out here. Fingerprints, of course, and a thorough search."

"And, of course," Renwick said blandly, "to detain the man or woman who comes to collect Sudak's clothes and remove all evidence."

"That, too," said Marchand, and climbed into his car with a smile that cost him considerable pain. What would have irritated him last night now seemed comic.

Not just a matter of sunshine and blue skies instead of night shadows under cold moonlight, thought Renwick as he backed out of the driveway. The reports Marchand had made yesterday would be enough to bring a smile to his lips even if his jaw had been broken. And the report he would send this morning? Marchand, you'll be the brown-eyed boy of French Intelligence.

Suddenly, Renwick was startled. French Intelligence? Well, well, well . . . He must try that idea on Claudel: nothing like a good joke to cheer up a hospital room.

Claudel was resisting sleep. "Hoped you would come," he told Renwick. "What did you find?"

"He was there overnight. He was gone this morning."

"And now?"

"I'm waiting for news of a black car. Marchand says he will tell us as soon as he hears anything." And if his superiors allow him, Renwick thought. "French Intelligence is now in on the game."

"I half expected that. Do they know about Lorna and her—"

"Kidnapping?" Renwick's glance around the room was marked. He raised a warning hand: no talk about a poste restante in Zurich, it said. "They must have heard. They're in Geneva. Probably here, too. They've connected Exports Consolidated with Klingfeld and Sons."

"They may resent us being here."

"They're just friendly adversaries. You know the type."

Claudel's eyes widened. That had been Renwick's phrase yesterday for Marchand. And if he was connected with French Intelligence, this room was surely bugged.

"And why any resentment? We filled in the facts for them about Klaus Sudak. And who gave them some brand-new leads and half a dozen arrests?"

"Marchand's damn smart," Claudel said. He was beginning to smile. "Knows his way around here."

"A natural for the job. Relatives, too, to help him out."

Claudel's grin was wide. "Visited his police station?"

"I haven't been invited. He was in his office there when I phoned this morning. One thing I admire: the co-operation here between police and Intelligence. Or vice versa," he added, suddenly seized by the imp of the perverse. "The name of Sudak, for instance. Traced by a professor at Grenoble. Doing research for French Intelligence?"

Claudel burst into a laugh.

"I thought that idea would cheer up the invalid."

"Shall we tell Marchand?" Claudel was enjoying himself.

We've already told him. Renwick said, "And destroy his faith in his professor? Perish the thought. How's the arm?"

"Forgot it in these last five minutes. You're better than any antibiotic." Claudel turned serious. "I'd like to leave right now with you. Don't like the idea of you taking off alone. Where are you going? Sudak—" He compressed his lips; he had almost said too much there, almost asked about Sudak. I'm half doped, Claudel thought; brain's not working.

Renwick said lightly, "First, some breakfast. Then I pack and pay the bill. Next, I'll drive to Geneva, see Inspector Duval. A matter of saying thanks. Marchand has sent full reports, of course, with more to follow." He paused, reflecting. He never had met any police officer who made so many reports within fifteen hours. "Of course, I'll only be repeating Marchand's information. We told him everything we knew. Interintell will think we've lost our marbles."

Claudel had stared in amazement as the unnecessary recital began. It wasn't Bob's usual style. Then Claudel understood and he relaxed. *We told him everything we knew.* Except about Zurich. "And now Klaus Sudak is on his way to East Germany." Claudel was all innocence.

Renwick was just as bland. "No doubt. But that's a problem for Geneva. And Paris. And Rome. Klingfeld's offices will need a thorough investigation. We've done our part, Pierre. So get some sleep. I'll push off, can't spend all day hanging around for Marchand. In fact, I think I'll drop in at the police station and pay him a call. I'd like to hear where that black car headed this morning. Always curious; you know me. Besides, it would complete my report on Chamonix."

"Wonder if Marchand will tell you."

"Why not? Unless, of course, he is working with French Intelligence. They might think we are trying to muscle in on their act."

"After Interintell completed their case against Sudak? They didn't even know his connection with Exports Consolidated until we—"

The telephone rang. It was Marchand speaking. He was still in his office, a mountain of paperwork. But he had checked on all cars leaving Chamonix this early morning. There were only three that were black. One, a Fiat, had taken the road to the Mont Blanc Tunnel into Italy. The second, a Porsche, had traveled southwest to Grenoble. The third was a Citroën using the Geneva route.

"Leaving when?"

"The Fiat at five-forty-five, the Porsche at six-twenty, the Citroën at six-fifty-four. What do you think?"

"Anyone's guess."

"I agree. And where are you going?"

"Geneva, actually. I'll see Duval and thank him. And, of course, I'll mention your invaluable help to Interintell's friends in Paris." Then Renwick's formal voice changed to something more natural. "Our thanks, Marchand. You're one helluva good cop. *Au revoir.*"

And he was. Whatever Marchand really was, he made one hell of a good cop. Claudel was half asleep.

"I'll phone you. So will Gilman. Just to make sure you're doing well."

Claudel nodded and closed his eyes. Renwick give up the chase for Klaus Sudak? The man who had placed his name on a death list, threatened Nina, too? "I should be with you. I'll be out—soon—I'll . . ." His voice drifted. The antibiotics took over. He fell asleep, didn't even hear Renwick leave.

Twenty-one

Renwick had hoped he could cover the short distance from Chamonix in sixty easy minutes. But Sunday drivers were already on the road by nine-thirty, and he didn't reach Geneva until almost eleven o'clock.

The delays didn't irk him. It was a more pleasant journey by far than the one he had made with Claudel yesterday morning. Then, the news he had received from Washington had him worried sick: Grable was on the prowl, circling round Nina's old home in Georgetown—too close to Basset Hill for any peace of mind. Now, Grable was safely under arrest; Basset Hill was not in danger; everything, according to watchdog Mac, was under control. Renwick's intense anxiety was lightened, and he could concentrate on Klaus Sudak. On Sudak and on a poste restante in Zurich.

Were they connected? Not quite. Not yet, at least. One thing was certain, though. When that little black book with Brimmer's Plus List had disappeared from his office just as his most private and confidential secretary had taken off for Zurich, Klaus Sudak was interested. Interested enough to have her traced, abducted, brought to a remote chalet in France, and put to torture. Her abject terror when Claudel and Renwick had been trying to cut her loose gave the answer to Sudak's questions: Where was the book, where, where? Yes, Sudak wanted that list of names.

Wanted it? Sudak needed it. It was his last chance.

His cover was blown; his network—with seven agents captured, seven and a half if you counted Annabel Vroom—was fractured. Total failure, even in the loss of Erik, the prize terrorist who was to have started raising hell for the West Germans. It was a bleak and icy future for Sudak, unless he could arrive in Moscow with that Plus List safely in hand. Its value was incalculable: men of importance, all named and ready for blackmail and manipulation. Brimmer's diary would give him a reprieve; not a full pardon, not until he could reorganize his network and have it functioning again. Klaus Sudak was just brilliant enough to be given a last chance—if he could deliver the Plus List.

He has to head for Zurich, Renwick decided: he has no other choice. But what does he know?

Not the name of Karen Cross. Lorna's handbag was searched. It didn't hold any false passport; otherwise Stefan and the Godzilla woman wouldn't have ripped Lorna's clothes to pieces in search of a note with a bank account number, a key to a locker, anything at all that would give them some clue. Sudak got nothing out of Lorna Upwood.

He does know her hotel. He will search her room there. Thoroughly. Tear it apart if necessary, go over it inch by inch. That takes time. And it's precarious—a forced entry could be discovered. So will he try to search now, or wait until the hotel is notified by Marchand that Lorna Upwood isn't returning? Then he could engage the room himself. A hefty tip to the reservations clerk could make sure of that.

And when do Marchand's friends in French Intelligence enter the scene? Are they on their way to the Bürkli Hotel to make their own search, trying to solve the question why Sudak had ordered abduction and torture?

It would be tempting to let Sudak and the French have a battle of wits all between themselves. What branch of French Intelligence? wondered Renwick. Anyone I know?

Well, whatever they find in Lorna's room—the name Karen Cross, the receipt for rental of a box in a poste restante—they have two disadvantages to overcome. Just as I have. We are all foreigners in Switzerland. And today is Sunday: a day of rest, and official business closed. Monday morning could be a fascinating time when the post offices in Zurich open their doors.

Renwick gave up his thoughts for some skillful maneuvering of the Audi as he approached the city. He knew Geneva well—what avenues to follow, which of them to avoid for a quick run into its center. Eight years ago he had spent weeks here along with a NATO delegation to a disarmament conference with the Soviets. At that time his intelligence work had been directed at the military developments in the Warsaw Pact countries. Four years later he was back in Geneva, now concentrating on the spread of well-organized terrorism, the latest weapon in the Soviet secret arsenal. That was when he had met Duval and Keppler, who became as concerned as he was with a numbered account in a Geneva bank, millions of dollars culled by theft and murder in Vienna, a nicely anonymous source of income for international terrorists. Then almost two years ago he had returned here. With Nina. That memory brought a smile to his lips.

He skirted the head of the lake, crossed over a bridge where its waters poured into the beginning of the Rhône, and drove to the railway station. Duval had a small office not far from there, useful for his own special conferences; and if he was indeed spending his Sunday morning at work instead of boating on Lac Leman, that's where Renwick would reach him.

With the Audi legally parked and Claudel's air-travel bag safely at his feet, Renwick began dialing with zero two two and added Duval's private number. Automatically, he was through. Duval's voice answered.

Delighted to hear from Renwick, but only too sorry he couldn't manage to see anyone today—not even for lunch.

"Next visit, then," Renwick said, much relieved. This call to thank Duval was a necessary gesture. But he, himself, had an eye on his watch—eleven-forty-five now—and another idea in mind.

Duval was talking of Chamonix: a busy night they all seemed to have had, and congratulations to Renwick.

"Not yet," said Renwick. "Later perhaps. With luck. By the way, Marchand mentioned that Johann Keppler was in town."

"He's here," Duval said, "and wants to speak with you. One moment, then. And, again, felicitations, my dear fellow." With that, a dead silence followed.

His hand is over the mouthpiece, thought Renwick with amusement. *He and Keppler are discussing whether my words*—*Not yet. Later, perhaps. With luck*—*mean I have more information to add to the reports they've been studying all morning.*

The telephone came alive again with Keppler's deep-throated voice. As usual, he was quick and direct. "I have a feeling we should meet."

"So have I."

"Then twelve-fifteen in the café of the hotel where you and your wife stayed. Suitable?"

"Perfect."

And the call ended.

The old boy actually remembered about Nina and me, Renwick thought with astonishment. But the fact that he had known about their visit to Geneva was not surprising. It only reinforced Renwick's belief that Keppler was the sharpest ear that Swiss Security possessed.

Renwick left his bag in a locker at the station, safer there than in the Audi's trunk. He could scarcely carry it into an elegant café on the Place des Bergues and pop it under a table. The well-drilled help would try to carry it off to the cloakroom, where it belonged. And Keppler himself would wonder what was so important in that bulging carryall. Just everything Claudel and Renwick had brought into Chamonix, with the addition now of a Biretta wrapped inside Claudel's jogging outfit. There had been no room for Renwick's clothes, not with the addition of the radio transmitter in its leather case. Anyway, he had been glad to get rid of his suit; that singe streak on its undersleeve kept reminding him he was damned lucky to be walking around today.

As for the spot chosen by Keppler for this meeting, Renwick wasn't enthusiastic. But Nina and he had never used the café, or the restaurant. And with the constant turnover of visitors in a hotel with two hundred bedrooms, it wasn't likely he would be remembered. The only excuse he could find for Keppler's choice was that his Swiss friend hadn't wanted to name either a café or an exact street for their rendezvous. Certainly he had kept it anonymous enough and guarded against anyone trailing him. As Renwick had done. No one had been following him. He had made sure of that.

Avoiding the hotel lobby, he entered the café directly from the street. Keppler was already settled in a corner where the neighboring tables were as yet unoccupied. *We'll have about half an hour to talk before the place fills up,* Renwick decided; *I'd better waste no time.* He gave a warm greeting, a firm handshake, and took a seat with his back to the room.

For almost a minute they studied each other. Keppler was of medium height and solid build, his close-cropped hair now white. His features were strong—a well-defined nose, a long chin, a firm mouth. Heavy eyebrows, usually knitted in a small frown above clear blue eyes, eased slightly as he nodded his welcome. His promotion three years ago—but not all the way to the top, as his friends had expected; perhaps he was too near retirement age for that—had brought him definite prosperity. In his well-cut, dark-blue suit, he looked like a most respectable burgher who had spent the morning in church and was only contemplating a large Sunday dinner surrounded by grandchildren.

A waitress arrived with two bottles of Spatenbräu, a beer Renwick had favored four years ago. The time was exactly twelve-fifteen. "You haven't lost your touch," Renwick said.

"And you haven't lost your knack of finding trouble. I thought you were safely upstairs in Merriman's head office." Keppler's English was good, its accent tinged with the German spoken in his canton.

"It was there, in my office, that the trouble began."

"When?"

"Thirteen days ago."

Keppler's eyebrows lost their frown, shot up. "Thirteen days? You move fast, Robert."

"The opposition set the pace. And it isn't over yet."

"No? I've read the Chamonix reports. They seem full, but there are gaps. Big gaps, I feel. Why don't you fill me in? Tell me how it all started."

"How much time do you have?"

"I am expected back in Bern by five o'clock."

Renwick said, "Unavoidable?" His disappointment showed.

"Where were you hoping I'd be?"

Renwick looked at the nearby tables: still empty, but he lowered his voice even more. "Zurich."

Keppler slowly drank some beer, lit a cigarette. "Tell me how it started," he said again.

"It will take half an hour at least," Renwick warned. "A brief rundown. But with all the essential facts."

Keppler noticed his second glance at the tables around them. "The weather is on our side. A warm Sunday in summer means picnics or open-air cafés. We won't be disturbed."

So Renwick began with the phone call to his office from Alvin Moore, the ex-Green Beret who had thought he could outwit and outrun both Exports Consolidated and Klingfeld & Sons. The essential facts, he had promised, and these he gave: Brimmer's lists, both Minus and Plus; the lead to Klingfeld & Sons, to Klaus Sudak, to Chamonix; the death of Erik. (Keppler knew who he was, had followed his career, and had put out an alert at Swiss frontiers in case Erik had tried to cross them.) Lorna Upwood, Renwick kept to the last—she was the natural lead into Zurich.

Keppler didn't speak, let him finish without interruption. Even then, Keppler remained silent for almost two minutes. At last he said, "Are there any Swiss names on Brimmer's Plus List?" His face was grim.

"There could be. It's international, I understand."

"And if you find that list? What will you do with it?"

"My first impulse was to burn it."

"You've changed your mind?" Keppler asked quickly.

"I'm not sure. If one of those names, American, belongs to a politician who hopes to run for president—" Renwick broke off, shrugged his shoulders.

"A problem," Keppler agreed. "You wouldn't want that kind of fellow in your White House." He lit another cigarette, his frown more intense than ever. "And we could have a similar problem if one of those names belonged to an ambitious Swiss politician. Particularly if . . ." He paused, then questioned, "Are you positive the KGB is involved?"

"Sudak had information that only their files could contain. And London confirmed it—at three this morning. I don't know how Interintell learned that fact, but they sent me a definite warning."

"You know that there are others who are trying to solve the mystery about Lorna Upwood?"

"The French. Naturally."

Keppler nodded. "Two of them were with Duval when you telephoned him."

Renwick raised an eyebrow. "They move fast, too." But let's get back to the question of Zurich. "What's the usual procedure for a foreigner collecting mail at a poste restante?"

"You produce your passport."

"No signature?"

"Not if the passport photo and physical description are identifiable."

"But if someone is ill, sends a friend?"

"The passport is still needed along with a written authorization."

"That could be faked."

"Penalties are heavy."

"If the fraud was discovered right then and there." And Klaus Sudak wouldn't delay one minute. He would be out of the post office at the first premonition of danger. "Couldn't it be possible," Renwick said, choosing his words carefully, "that the Zurich post offices be notified? Anyone trying to collect Upwood's mail must be refused unless he shows proof of authorization?"

"*All* the post offices?" Keppler prodded. "Did she not name one in particular?"

"Cathedral," Renwick admitted.

"Then," said Keppler, pleased with his small victory, "she was referring to Fraumünsterpost. It is the main post office, opposite the cathedral, which is called Fraumünster. Not far from her hotel. The Bürkli, I believe?"

Renwick nodded.

"So," Keppler went on smoothly, "you would like me to notify Fraumünsterpost. But how do you come into possession of her passport? Do you know where it is?"

"No."

"She was registered at the hotel under her own name, but I do not imagine she used it for the poste restante address. I suppose you must know her assumed name?"

So he's already been in touch with Zurich about Lorna Upwood, thought

Renwick. Encouraged, he dodged an answer to Keppler's question and said, "If I do happen to find her fake passport, would you back me up when I present it at the Fraumünsterpost?"

"Say that you are her brother? Her lawyer?" Keppler was curt. His eyes were hard.

"No. A matter of national security, as it may well be. You could vouch for me at the post office. When I get that Plus List, you'll read it along with me." That was a fair-enough deal, but Keppler was still brooding over his glass of beer. What had got into him? Had he become the complete bureaucrat after all—afraid to take chances? Surely not Keppler . . .

Keppler said, "One difficulty. A telephone call from Chamonix—a request from Marchand to Duval just before you phoned. He wants Duval to contact Zurich police and have them hold Upwood's possessions until he can have them collected tomorrow."

"Until his friends in French Intelligence collect them." Some people made it the easy way, Renwick thought bitterly. "They won't even know the importance of what they are taking. Dammit all, Marchand hadn't even heard the name Lorna Upwood until Claudel and I—" He stopped short. No use whining. Bellyaching was something you kept to yourself.

"Until you and Claudel . . . ?"

"Found her, cut her loose, dealt with three of Sudak's thugs." Renwick's voice was brusque.

Keppler said in surprise, "That wasn't in any of Marchand's reports. And you didn't mention it when you—"

"It wasn't part of the essential facts."

"Then you must tell me all about the unessentials when we meet again." Keppler was on his feet. "Order more beer. And some ham and cheese. We will keep our waitress happy—and have lunch, too. Don't worry if I'm delayed. I may be ten or fifteen minutes absent." He left their table, walking with his usual brisk light step through the half-empty café, and vanished into the hotel lobby.

Telephoning, thought Renwick; but he put all speculation aside. Enough to know that Keppler was interested. Keppler was still Keppler, and no bureaucrat. He had been right, too, about a warm Sunday in July: they had peace to talk in this most unlikely place for a serious meeting. Renwick glanced around at the green-and-gold room, pink-frilled lampshades on every elaborate panel, velvet-covered chairs, lace mats under glass on the spindle-legged tables. A change of scene. Sixteen, fifteen hours ago, he and Claudel had been entering a squalid room with one blinding light focused on a woman tied to a chair. In ten years of his work in intelligence he had seen many appalling sights. But that was the worst. The worst.

He pulled himself back into the present, signed to the pretty blond waitress, and had food and drink waiting on the table by the time Keppler returned.

They ate as they talked, and—conscious of the need for haste—had completed lunch and conversation by half past one. Keppler's news was encouraging. He had phoned Duval and suggested that—as a matter of national security—he, himself, would contact the Zurich police, and Duval had agreed. "I shall notify them at seven o'clock. I cannot delay beyond that. You understand?"

Renwick nodded. By seven-thirty, he could expect the police to seal off Lorna Upwood's room. "I'll take the first flight out."

"And are you staying overnight at the Bürkli Hotel?"

"If I can get a room at such short notice."

"You have one. I took the liberty of arranging for a room for you there. Talk with the manager when you arrive. Your name for your visit is Brown."

"That takes care of one big problem." Sudak had never seen him, but he knew the name of Renwick.

"You are on your own until tomorrow morning. I'll meet you at Fraumünsterpost when it opens. Seven-thirty."

Renwick nodded. "I'll be there. Can't thank you enough."

"Always a pleasure to work with Interintell."

Renwick pushed back his chair. "Do I leave first or do—"

Keppler stopped him with a gesture. "Some bad news. I kept it to the last. Duval has just received another call from Chamonix. About the hospital."

Renwick went tense. "Claudel?"

"No. Not Claudel. The woman Upwood—she's dead."

There was total silence.

Keppler said, "Marchand is blaming everyone. Fortunately, Claudel was asleep, and you were about to meet me here." Keppler enjoyed his little joke. "A priest visited the hospital at noon. He came, so he explained, in place of the regular parish priest, who was taken ill that morning."

"A priest? Or a man dressed as a priest?"

"Priests do visit the sick."

"And what about the nurse in Lorna's room?"

"He sent her away so that he could hear Upwood's confession. He left before the nurse returned fifteen minutes later."

"And found her patient dead."

"With her throat slit."

"Good God!"

Keppler said nothing.

If the nurse had believed confession was possible, then Lorna must have been conscious and able to speak. So Klaus Sudak's agent had found the information he needed, and made certain—quickly, surely—that no one else would have it. Renwick said very quietly, "Sudak now knows."

Keppler nodded. "He will be in Zurich."

Renwick rose, shook hands, said nothing.

"*Auf Wiedersehen!*" said Keppler as Renwick left. *Auf Wiedersehen?* Or was this a last good-bye? His frown deepened. Sudak was a dangerous man, too prone to violence. Ruthless and merciless. Power had corrupted him completely. Grim faced, Keppler watched Renwick enter the street, and called for the bill.

"The gentleman paid everything," the waitress told him.

Independent young cuss, Keppler thought, relaxing into a polite nod. Yes, he decided, definitely another phone call to Zurich: Renwick going in alone, his partner hospitalized, needs more help than he has requested. And he

must stay alive until he finds that Plus List: I can't be involved with that—
not directly. Besides, he never did mention Lorna Upwood's assumed
name—not only an independent young man, but careful too. I've always
liked him; that's the difficulty. I'm risking a lot in helping him. I'm risking
everything. That's my problem. How do I handle it?

Keppler rose and made his way into the hotel lobby toward a public telephone. His movements were slow and heavy.

Twenty-two

THERE HAD BEEN a mixture of good and bad luck today. Good, when
Renwick found a taxi leaving its fare at the door of the Geneva café, persuaded it to wait for him while he picked up his bag at Cornavin Station.
Good luck, too, as they drove past his parked Audi and saw a sharp-eyed
man who had nothing much to do except lean against a neighboring car,
his ankles crossed, his arms folded, complete picture of innocence. Bad luck
this morning, though. If Claudel's arm hadn't acted up, if Renwick hadn't
taken him to the clinic, then Renwick would have arrived at the house in
the valley before Klaus Sudak left. A matter of minutes—ten, perhaps fifteen at the most—and Sudak, caught by surprise, a bullet in his knee as
discouragement, would now be under lock and key. And there would be
no need for this race to Zurich. But at least Claudel was worried enough
about his arm to listen to the doctors. He'd be all right. And that was a
major consolation.

Strange, thought Renwick as the taxi drove through broad avenues with
glistening shop windows, passed small parks of trees and flowers, skirted wide
sidewalks, I've always liked this town, and yet today I barely noticed anything in it—had no time to stop and look at any of its pleasing prospects.
Next visit, he told Geneva, I'll see you properly. Next visit? Would there be
one? He blocked that question, kept it out of his mind.

At the airport he had a wait of twenty minutes. Five of these went in a
telephone call to Claudel.

"Better by the hour," Claudel told him with his usual Gallic optimism.
"I'm fine. What about you?"

"Fine."

"Where are you?"

"In honeymoon city and watching some fireflies. Not much of a show
until their tails light up at night."

Claudel caught the allusion to Geneva's airport and laughed. Then his
laugh ended abruptly. "Some bad news here."

"Yes. It travels fast. I heard."

"Marchand would like to know what you think. Could it have been Sudak himself? The priest was tall, fair-haired. Sudak might have stayed in town, got someone else to drive away by seven o'clock, and then left by another route in a different car."

"It wasn't Sudak—unless the priest used verbena toilet water," Renwick said. "Ask Marchand—he'll explain." And he slipped up on that one. "Where was he, anyway, when it happened?"

"Catching some sleep. He had been up all night."

"You lie down and do the same."

"I'll be out of this bed by tomorrow. Wait—will you?—until I can join you?"

"What—aren't the nurses pretty enough? I saw one that was a knockout." At least he had Claudel, now talking about the sparkling brunette who liked to ski, far away from the topic of joining him. "I'll call you tomorrow," he told Claudel and hung up the receiver.

The next five minutes were spent in a lavatory, typically Swiss in its neat cleanliness. There, he removed Claudel's outfit, rolled pants and shoes and tops into a tight bundle, jammed it into a trash bin. His Biretta was secured in his trouser belt. And space was now waiting for a few purchases: he'd buy a shirt and underclothes as soon as he had time and saw a likely shop. Not at this airport—in Zurich, if he had a few minutes to spare, where there were giant arcades and goods of all description for sale. He might not know Zurich, but he did know its airport. Which reminded him to stop briefly at the tourist information booth and pick up a couple of folders dealing with that town. One of them had a map of the streets, a complete layout with public buildings named. Just what the well-briefed intelligence officer needed. Renwick gave a wry smile over his present state of ignorance as he jammed the tourist folders into his pocket and made a dash for the plane.

Zurich and Geneva: two contrasts with much in common. They each lay at one end of a large lake from which waters poured to divide the town and begin giant rivers—the Rhine from Zurich, the Rhône from Geneva. Each had long histories of siege and war ever since their Roman days—plenty of courage and determination in those independent-minded cities. Even in religion, Geneva had its Calvin, Zurich its Zwingli. And both had bankers, boats on the lakes, boutiques and shops with enticing displays. But Geneva spoke French and Zurich German, and Geneva's broad avenues ran straight while Zurich's streets curved and twisted. Thank God for that tourist folder, thought Renwick.

First, he taxied to the railroad station as a simple precaution. A second taxi took him down the Bahnhofstrasse—the main thoroughfare—past fashionable shops and tramway junctions into a medieval city where the thirteenth-century cathedral, the Fraumünster, was faced by a giant twentieth-century post office. The Bürkli Platz lay just beyond, and there the street ended and Lake Zurich began.

The Bürkli Hotel was not, of course, on the plaza. That would have been too logical for this constantly surprising city. He left the taxi there—he hadn't wanted to drive up to the hotel door, in any case—and, turning away from the astonishing view of lake and hills, he started back into Bahnhofstrasse.

Again he blessed the tourist folder with its list of hotels and their locations. The Bürkli was on a small street branching off to his left, and should be only a two-minute walk. It was, he noted as he reached it, a close neighbor to the national bank as well as the Fraumünster post office. Lorna Upwood had enjoyed convenience. She also had chosen a quiet, self-effacing, and wholly respectable hotel. Staying here, she must have felt secure.

He entered the Bürkli. No doorman at its well-polished entrance, and only one elderly bellboy—a porter, or both? At the reception desk, there was a young, dark-haired man poring over a heavy ledger. Clerk, concierge, and accountant? Not exactly overstaffed. Renwick crossed the immaculate floor, barely glancing at the scattering of guests—three men, two women, all separate, each in a comfortable armchair—and reached the desk. Only one of the men had paid him much attention. Okay, he thought, I'll know you again, too, buster. To the clerk he said briskly, "I believe you have a reservation for me. The name is Brown."

The young man came to life. He pressed a bell, trying to disguise the movement of his foot, and wherever it sounded, it wasn't in this lounge. Renwick studied the wall behind the desk, with its pigeonhole slots for keys and mail. Four floors, judging by the room numbers, and only ten of them to each floor: forty rooms, no more, in this hotel. Then his attention switched to the manager's door (designation and name—Wilhelm Goss—clearly printed) that lay adjacent to the pigeonholes. It had opened. A gray-haired man in a dark suit came forward; his features bore a marked resemblance to the clerk's, and his manner to that young man was definitely family. "I'll attend to this, Hans! Better finish these accounts." He turned to Renwick, gave him a quick but thorough inspection. "Welcome, Herr Brown. Glad to see you again." His voice had carried across the lounge.

Not bad, thought Renwick, not bad. He relaxed slightly. "Glad to be back."

"Formalities, formalities," Goss said and pushed the register toward Renwick, but he laid aside the pen it held and kept it under his hand. "Passport?"

Renwick, his back to the room, hiding any movement of signing or not signing, hesitated but reached into his breast pocket. He didn't like this one bit: no need for the name Renwick to be left at a reception desk.

"Thank you," Goss said, and turned away without waiting for the passport. He reached for a third-floor key, said, "Now, if you'll just follow me? We are short-handed today. One of my clerks was called up last week for military service, and my accountant is doing his annual two weeks back in the army. Next year, fortunately for us, he will be forty-nine and won't need to do any more military duty. Just keep his rifle and uniform, like me, and have shooting practice once a week." Goss was talking too much, a sign of nervousness, but at least the flow of words got them out of the lounge and into the self-service elevator. At one side, Renwick noted, was a flight of stairs; at the other, an entrance to bar and restaurant. A compact place.

Silence broke out and lasted all the way upstairs and down a narrow corridor to its end—Room 305. "Thank you for your help," Renwick said as he took the key and unlocked the door.

But Goss followed him inside. Quickly he said, "You aren't staying here overnight—just passing through."

"Oh?" And where do I sleep tonight?

"Otherwise you would have to sign the register. And then—your passport?" Goss shrugged.

Yes, Renwick on the passport and Brown on the register would have been an embarrassment. "How did you know I was legitimate?"

"A good description of you and your clothes."

Keppler, thought Renwick, was thorough.

"I understand this is of national importance?" Goss queried.

"Of security."

Goss's face, usually placid, with its broad cheekbones and square-shaped jaw, was heavily creased with worry. "I haven't been told—except that this is an emergency measure. It won't last long?"

"Not long."

Goss lowered his voice. "There is a man from Bern—from Security—in the lounge."

"The man with reddish hair and a thin face?" Renwick asked quickly.

"No. That one is waiting for one of his friends. Your man is reading a newspaper."

"He hid well behind it. His description?"

"Dark hair but half bald. Eyeglasses. Medium height. . ." Goss floundered.

"That's enough," Renwick said reassuringly. "One other thing, Herr Goss. A friend of mine has been staying here—a Mrs. Upwood. What is her room number?"

"Frau Upwood? Room 201. She had stayed with us before—three weeks ago. And then returned last Wednesday. But she wasn't here last night, and that is strange. She was so quiet, regular in her habits, always back for dinner and the evening in her room. Oh, yes—that reminds me, Herr Brown. We aren't supplying room service on Sunday. Shortage of help. But what can one expect these days?" He was about to leave. He paused at the door. "If Frau Upwood isn't here tonight, I shall call the police tomorrow. Don't you think?"

"It wouldn't do any harm."

"Very difficult, very difficult. She may have spent the weekend with friends." Goss sighed, now concentrating on his own problems.

Renwick said nothing at all. The door closed quietly. He placed his bag inside the wardrobe and locked it, then looked around him. It was a small room, furnished simply, with one window overlooking a courtyard, all neat and clean, a place for an overflow of guests. But there was an adjoining bathroom fitted into cramped space, and a toilet that worked.

Almost five o'clock. Klaus Sudak must be installed in Zurich by now. Yet, even allowing for his seven o'clock start this morning—letting him cross the frontier before the alert went out—his journey here couldn't have been simple.

He would have to stop, once over the French-Swiss border, to get rid of the Citroën and rent another car. As he skirted Geneva, it must have angered him to know his own plane was parked at that airport. But he would avoid all airfields, all railway or bus stations: these were now under observation. Would he risk the main highways which would let him cross Switzerland at high speed? No, decided Renwick, he would calculate that they would be too easily watched. It would be safer to keep to the smaller roads where there was less chance of checkpoints. But on them he could only travel around sixty miles an hour with constant drops to thirty-five as he reached the villages. And there were plenty of villages. He would make sure he kept within the speed limits. Infringement brought instant arrest and fines: the Swiss took their traffic laws seriously. There were other delays, too, for Sudak. Sunday drivers and tourist buses.

So, thought Renwick, probably Sudak hadn't reached Zurich until midafternoon. There, at last in some apartment or house, he could safely make contact with his agent who had forced the name Karen Cross out of a terrified woman with a knife at her throat, then silenced her swiftly, permanently. Communications took time. His agent hadn't stayed around Chamonix to send an immediate report but would have made his escape far to the west, where he'd find a safe house, secure enough for his top-secret information to be transmitted in code. (Karen Cross and her Zurich poste restante were not names to be openly trusted to telephone or radio.) Sudak's planning would need time, too, before he made his move. Or perhaps he had already made it. Renwick locked his room door and set out for the staircase.

The second floor had a wider corridor and higher ceilings, a relic of the days before elevators were installed, when lower rooms were considered superior and upper floors were only engaged by those who had less money but stronger legs. In keeping with the age of the building, there was a slight creaking at each step, which even the crimson carpet couldn't quite muffle. The rooms themselves were silenced by their old thick walls: Renwick could hear no sound from any of them. There was no maid around, either; the service door was firmly shut. It was a somber corridor, wood-paneled like the entrance foyer downstairs, decorated with carved heraldic emblems, lighted by parchment-shaded bulbs fixed to the walls, a peaceful place in a quiet hotel on a Sunday afternoon.

He tried his room key in the simple lock and—as he half expected—it worked. No thieves were supposed to wander around this family-run hotel. If Lorna Upwood had only known, she'd have barricaded her door at night with table and chairs. But no danger had touched her here. It was on a little street just off a busy thoroughfare, with people all around her, that she was in jeopardy. Had she been thinking how well she had planned everything? The numbered account in a nearby bank, growing in its tax shelter year by year; Brimmer's little black book mailed to Karen Cross, Poste Restante, here in Zurich. And why the hell hadn't she been content with an ill-gotten million safely banked. Another possible million or two from blackmail— had that been too big a lure for her greed?

Quickly, Renwick opened the door of Room 201, stepped inside, locked it. A very pleasant place with two windows and bright chintz and a large couch behind a coffee table at one end of the room. Opposite, a double bed with nightstands. On one side wall, a wardrobe and dressing table. On the other, near the door, a small desk. Everything was in order. Yesterday's newspaper on the coffee table was neatly folded, and beside it lay tourist brochures in a small stack close to a guidebook. Nothing looked disturbed, even to the perfume bottles and powder box that were precisely arranged along with brush and comb on the lace mat of the dressing table.

It would be a long search: too many drawers, too many shelves. He had a full hour of safety, perhaps an hour and a half with luck. From the Zurich police, he reminded himself. Not from Klaus Sudak—he could appear any minute.

Renwick set to work. By ten minutes to six he had completed the unpleasant task. He had not only examined the drawers but felt their undersides for a taped passport or envelope. The wardrobe had only a row of suits and dresses, with nothing pinned to their folds or deep in any pockets. The bed's covers and mattress hid nothing, the pillows were soft and innocent. Nothing inside the bathroom's cistern; and its cabinet's shelves contained only a few items that couldn't have concealed even the new-style U.S. passport, barely five by three inches. Nothing was taped behind two pictures of rustic Switzerland or behind the dressing-table mirror; and the hairbrush had a solid back, unremovable. The desk drawer was locked—a moment of expectation—but when opened it was only protecting Lorna Upwood's regular passport, a bankbook, a list of traveler's checks, a note of purchases made and of expenditures for meals and tips. The window-length cretonne curtains concealed nothing in their pleats. Not one thing under the coffee table. The couch was firm, tightly upholstered; so were its three cushions, with no side openings, no zippers. Under the couch? Too heavy; she could never have turned it over by herself. He reached under it as far as his arm could stretch, and found not even a hairpin.

He sat down on the edge of the couch, looked around him. Nothing. What had he missed?

An idea flashed into his mind and was almost dismissed as fantastic, even stupid. Yet, yet . . . He had been searching in every place where he, a man, might have hidden something. But—with all deference to equality of the sexes—Lorna Upwood was a woman. He remembered Nina's ingenious ploys: her solutions to a problem were always simple, seemingly ridiculous, but they worked. Nina, he asked silently, where would you have hidden a passport?

Quickly, he reached for the stack of travel folders and guidebook. Nothing. The newspaper hadn't even been read. Then he went over to the desk, where at one side was the usual hotel literature: prices for laundry, dry cleaning, and breakfast menus—all too thin and light to conceal a passport. There was also a leather folder, well worn, containing a shopping guide and advertisements. He had a moment of hope when he picked it up but—like the desk blotter he had already examined along with the underside of the telephone—it hid no secret. A leather folder . . .

He glanced at the telephone on the other side of the writing table. It sat on top of a local directory encased in a mockleather cardboard binder, faded, unremarkable. He set aside the phone, opened the binder. The directory was secured by two long, thin wires, attached at the top of the binder's spine, that snapped down between the book's pages and divided them into three sections. The first division held nothing. But spread-eagled under the grip of the second wire was the passport.

He pulled it loose, shaking his head. Dammit all, you just searched in the stupidest, most ridiculous place and you find it in two seconds flat. No—

not so stupid. Not ridiculous, either. Just so simple that it couldn't even be suspected. The passport seemed slimmer than usual: its twelve pages had been reduced to eight by removal of its two center folds, carefully done so that the stitching had been left intact. Who would notice except a U.S. immigration inspector? Certainly not a Swiss post office attendant.

He slipped the passport for Karen Cross of Wilmington, Delaware, into the deep inside pocket of his jacket. The directory, with telephone on top, was replaced exactly. One glance around the room: everything was just as he had found it.

Seven minutes past six. He was about to unlock the door. Outside, he heard the creak of a floor, a tentative fumbling at the keyhole. Police? They were prompt. Too prompt, unless Keppler had called them earlier than he had promised.

Soundlessly, Renwick stepped well to the side of the door. No escape by the window: no balcony, no ledge out there. The bathroom? A trap.

The hall floor creaked again. A smothered curse. Then a man called in German, "Room service!" There was a knock.

Renwick slipped his Biretta loose from his belt, held it behind him.

"No one there," the voice said more quietly, and the lock was burst open. Two men entered. One was ferret-faced, with reddish hair, gaunt cheeks. The other—tall, hair now darkened, but with that unmistakable profile—was Klaus Sudak. He pushed the door shut, looked around the room, saw Renwick.

He stared, backed a few steps, kept his eyes fixed on Renwick. "What are you doing in my room?" he demanded, his hand slipping inside his jacket. Ferret-face, keeping parallel with Sudak, was quietly reaching for his gun, too. There was a fixed smile on his lips.

Renwick shot twice as two long-nosed pistols were whipped out and took aim. Their shots, muted by silencers, missed: Sudak fell even as he fired, the other man crumpling in pain as he pulled the trigger. But he would live.

Renwick kicked the red-haired man's pistol clear of his loosened grasp, sent it spinning across the room. There was no fight left in him anyway. And in Sudak? None at all. His hand still gripped the revolver, but he would never fire it again.

Renwick placed the Biretta in his pocket and closed the door behind him. Along the hall a man came running at full speed. Dark-haired, half bald, eyeglasses, medium height, well built. He couldn't have been waiting downstairs, must have posted himself on this floor. Renwick relaxed his grip on the Biretta, ignored the revolver in the other's hand. "You're Keppler's man?"

"Security," he answered abruptly, showing his identification as he replaced his gun in its holster. He turned his head to glare at two opening doors, answered a jumble of alarmed questions. "No need to worry," he called to them. "Just a car backfiring." And then to Renwick quietly, "One shot, it sounded like. One shot and an echo."

"Four shots. One in the chest, one through the heart, two in the wall behind where I stood."

"Who was killed?" The question was quick, angry.

A man who had listed nine men for assassination. "Klaus Sudak."

Keppler's agent stared. "Well, now—we've been searching for him."

"Better get your cleanup squad here—as fast as possible."

"Won't take long. We were expecting some trouble. And where do you think you're going?" He stopped Renwick, who was about to leave. "Give me the facts. You saw them enter the room?"

Renwick nodded. "They broke the lock."

"So you were suspicious?"

"They could hardly be the Zurich police."

"They had their guns out?"

"You'll find one in Sudak's hand, the other is under the wardrobe."

"Who fired first?"

"Well, let's say they were just a split second too late." Gently, Renwick disengaged his arm from the restraining grip. "I'm going up to my room. You'll find me there if you have any more questions." He added impatiently as Keppler's agent still blocked his path, "Look—last night I had three hours of sleep. Today I've traveled across Switzerland. And five minutes ago it was kill or be killed."

The man nodded, walked quickly along the corridor toward Room 201. His transmitter was already out in his hand.

Renwick reached his room, sat down on the edge of the narrow bed. Suddenly, he was exhausted, so drained of physical energy that he couldn't move, couldn't even draw off his clothes to lie down and sleep. He sat there staring at the thin carpet at his feet. The first time he had ever had to kill a man.

Not planned. And no choice offered. A split-second reaction that had saved his own life. He had nearly packed it in. He drew a deep, long breath. Yes, a moment's hesitation and he would have been dead—as dead as if Brimmer's Minus List had been given the chance to become a reality.

The first time, he thought again as he drew out his Biretta. He looked at it. Then he threw it onto a chair across the room. The hell with it, and the hell with a report I should now be encoding to send to London; or this waiting for questions now from Bern Security; or with this room which I'm supposed to leave—pack up, get out, walk into a cold street. The hell with all of it.

But he remembered to take the passport out of his pocket and slip it under his pillow. He pulled off his clothes, fell into bed, and slept for ten hours.

Twenty-three

THE EARLY LIGHT that flooded into the room awakened Renwick. For a few moments he lay on the narrow bed staring at the plaster walls, wondering where the devil he was. The Bürkli . . . This was Monday. He thrust his hand under the pillow, relaxed as he found the passport there. It was ten minutes past five by his watch. And a lot to be done.

Briskly, he rose; showered, shaved, and washed in record time; and even had a change of shirt to make him feel still better. Before he set up the transmitter he began making notes. His last message to Gilman in London had been sent at three in the morning, yesterday. My God, he thought, how do I pack all that has happened since then into one brief report?

He solved that question by just giving basic facts. Elaborations and elucidations, words as tiresome as the processes they begat, could wait until he reached Paris. The emergency was over; danger, too. His relief—and the deep, unbroken sleep of last night—sharpened his wits. The coding of the information for Interintell went easily: Sudak dead, Upwood dead; necessary passport discovered, diary to be retrieved today, Keppler co-operating; Claudel in hospital but recovering. He ended with, "What news Washington? Immediate reply requested. About to leave."

It came within two minutes. No comment about the report he had just sent—that was still being decoded. But the reply to his question couldn't have been better. "Washington all clear. Nina safe and well."

That was a thought to keep him happy as he packed everything—including the Biretta—into Claudel's bag. By six-fifteen he was ready to leave. Time enough for a quick call to Chamonix and reassure Claudel.

"Can't talk much now. But all is well."

"The show is over?" Claudel's disappointment was clear in his voice.

"Mostly. Should be simple from here on out. So relax. I'll drop in to see you as soon as I can."

"No need." Claudel's voice became decisive. "I'm signing out."

"Too soon."

"The doctors have fixed the arm. So where do we meet? I mean it, Bob. I mean it. Now, where?"

"Where we arrived. Early afternoon, possibly. Say two o'clock?"

"We'll have to buy a couple of tickets. But don't talk me out of leaving! Meet you at two—or whenever you can. I'll wait."

There was no arguing with that mood, even if it belonged to a man whose arm wasn't fit enough to let him pilot his own plane. "Okay," said Renwick,

ending his call. He understood what Claudel was feeling: if he had missed
the action, then he damned well wanted to be the first to hear the details.

The telephone rang as Renwick was halfway to the door.

It was Keppler. And angry. "You should have kept this line open."

What has got into him? I was only on the phone for a couple of minutes.
"Sorry."

"Did you find what you needed?"

"Yes."

"You will be met outside the Fraumünster at seven-twenty-five."

"The cathedral?" Renwick asked to make sure.

"Yes. Main door. It's only a few minutes to the Fraumünsterpost."

"Met—by whom?"

"You know him. He spoke to you yesterday evening. He will accompany
you and see everything safely through."

"Won't you be there?"

"Later."

"When?" Renwick's voice sharpened.

And Keppler's voice eased. "As soon as I can get away from my office.
There are several urgent problems."

So he was still in Bern. "I thought you wanted to see that list."

"I do. A little delay won't matter, provided the list is safe. It won't be in
any danger now."

"I hope not."

"But you took care of our major problem last night. Most efficiently, I
hear."

"There could be other interested people."

"As far as I can learn, you are way ahead of them." With that piece of
encouragement, Keppler ended their talk.

And am I supposed to hang around Zurich until he can leave Bern? Then
Renwick's annoyance subsided. He had asked for help, he had got it, and
now—it was always the way—he would have to go along. Gracefully, he
told himself. He picked up his bag and left the room.

As he started downstairs, he had other worrying thoughts. It could be
that Keppler might have co-operated too willingly with Interintell and was
now trying to pacify his chief in Bern or the Zurich police. But if Keppler
was meeting difficulties, had overstepped his authority—well, whatever he
learned from the names on the Plus List should get him out of that fix.
And if no Swiss names were on that list?

Renwick paused at the second floor, looked down the corridor. A workman was busy at the door of Room 201. On impulse, Renwick strolled along.
The man was installing a new lock, didn't even lift his head to glance at
Renwick. The bloodstained rug had been removed. Another workman had
filled two holes in the opposite wall with plaster and was now touching them
up with cream-colored paint. A woman was packing Lorna Upwood's possessions into two suitcases while a young policeman watched her carefully.
Renwick, at the threshold, didn't wait for any questioning. He left as quickly
as he had appeared.

He felt the better for that brief visit. Keppler had taken care of every-

thing. And if Keppler had any difficulties in Bern, he was capable of dealing with them, too. With that reassurance, Renwick could blame his attack
of bad temper on the fact he needed a good solid breakfast.

In the empty lobby Manager Goss, even at this early hour, was busy at
the reception desk. He was posting sealed envelopes—no stamps on them,
no addresses, just names in large handwriting—one by one in each correct
pigeonhole. Renwick said, "Good morning," and received a glare. Herr Goss
placed the last bill in its allotted space and faced him.

Renwick laid his passport on the counter. "I think you need this. Temporarily. I'll be leaving as soon as I've had something to eat. And"—he drew
the register toward him—"I should sign here." Not Unknown Brown,
either, but Robert Renwick, London.

Goss stared blankly. His glum expression changed, first into surprise, then
to relief. He took the passport, compared it with Renwick's signature, made
a note of its number and address, returned it most politely. "I am afraid the
dining room is closed, Herr Renwick—until seven o'clock."

"Then where is the nearest place where I can find something to eat?"

"Not near. It's early, you see."

And in less than an hour I've to meet Keppler's man—Losch or Lasch or
Lesch. He flashed his identification so damned quick, or I was so damned
tired, that I didn't read it properly. Karl was the first name. That I did see.

Goss was watching him. "Perhaps," he said slowly, "we could stretch our rules."

Considering the rules that had been already stretched, Renwick could only
smile. "Very kind of you."

"You did not come down to dinner last night," Goss observed.

True, true. "I fell asleep."

"Yes. So we saw. This way, Herr Renwick. May I suggest you eat at my
table? That would be the easiest place." He led the way through a small
bar into a small dining room, and reached a corner table near the kitchen
door. His son, finishing a last cup of coffee, rose to his feet, said, "Yes,
Father, I'll attend to the desk" even before he heard the command, and
hurried away.

And now, thought Renwick as he sat down and placed his bag close to
the leg of his chair, I'll be questioned. Goss is curious, wants to talk. But I
have a question of my own: who saw me asleep?

Goss fulfilled the prediction. He took an opposite chair, summoned his
daughter from the kitchen (the family likeness was strong), and ordered a
substantial breakfast for Herr Renwick. "So much happened last night," he
began.

"Sorry I missed it."

Goss dropped his voice. "Two men—burglars, we think—attempted to
rob one of our rooms. When they were intercepted, they fired their pistols.
Yes, they were armed!"

Renwick shook his head in wonder.

"Fortunately, Inspector Lasch was there. He was with the military for
several years—an expert marksman."

"Oh?" Renwick's interest was real.

But Herr Goss's information stopped short of one man dead, another wounded and arrested. Such things did not happen in his hotel. "You didn't hear anything last night? Nothing at all?"

"As you saw, I was asleep." Renwick tried to keep everything light and easy. "Were you actually in my room? I never heard a thing."

"Just for a moment. When Inspector Lasch saw you were so soundly sleeping, we left."

"Lasch was there?"

"This is the way it was. After the—disturbance, he was checking the rooms."

I bet he wasn't. Not rooms plural. Just mine. But why? "Of course," said Renwick.

Goss rushed on, feeling the need for an apology by way of an explanation. "He came to me for a key to your room. He hadn't been able to get any reply when he knocked at your door. Naturally, I insisted on going upstairs with him. No one enters a guest's room without his permission—or mine."

"So you stayed with Lasch when he entered my room?"

"Certainly. But you were deeply asleep. He couldn't ask you any questions. So we left."

An honest man, thought Renwick as he looked at Goss. Perhaps Lasch is honest, too: all he wanted to do was to ask me some questions for his report on the disturbance, as Goss had put it so eloquently. Perhaps. But I'll keep an eye on Inspector Lasch.

Yet why hadn't he broken the lock instead of trying to borrow a key? One answer could be that a broken lock would have had me tight with suspicions when I discovered it this morning. Or perhaps I'm in a doubting mood until I get something into my stomach.

Breakfast arrived. Herr Goss rose tactfully, prepared to go back to supervising his son. "I'll have your bill prepared for you when you leave."

"In half an hour. And, by the way, Herr Goss, could I trouble you for a strong envelope? I'll collect it when I pay the bill."

"An airmail envelope?"

"A Manila envelope, if possible. Heavy."

"Certainly, Herr Renwick." Goss didn't seem mystified. Guests make stranger requests than this one.

Renwick poured the coffee. Once he was in possession of that little black book, once Keppler had been shown its contents, as promised, he would mail it from the airport. He wasn't going to carry it around with him halfway across Europe, that was for damn sure.

He began eating. It was an excellent breakfast.

There was a fresh touch to early sunshine that invited a brisk walk along the lakeshore. But with regret Renwick turned north on Bahnhofstrasse. He passed Fraumünsterpost, an imposing edifice, lying just across a side street from the cathedral buildings. He reached the Fraumünster itself, ten minutes early.

So was Inspector Lasch. He looked friendly, even if his face was white and tired. He couldn't have had much rest last night. Yes, definitely friendly: and very correct. "Colonel Renwick—good morning!"

"Good morning, Inspector Lasch. Or should I say Colonel, too?"

Lasch's eyes wavered. "Perhaps it is better if we do not use rank."

He's a major, Renwick thought with amusement. "Much better. I prefer it. Shall we walk a little?" Or just stand here and look obvious.

They strolled around the cathedral's precincts. "Were you," asked Renwick, "with military intelligence before you joined Keppler's outfit?"

"Outfit?" Lasch's English, good, didn't stretch that far.

"Section—department—whatever he heads. He is chief of operations, isn't he?"

"Of his division, yes. But of the whole department—no. Last year when our new chief was appointed—" He broke off; he may have felt that his politeness had let him say too much. His voice changed. "These are matters we do not talk about."

"Sorry. You know my status. I'd like to know about yours. But if it's a state secret, then we'll drop the subject."

"Not a state secret. Just security."

"I don't think we are being overheard here. Do you?"

Lasch smiled too.

"So you are with Keppler's antiterrorist division, and not with the department. You couldn't have a better boss—probably the most capable man I've met in any intelligence service. Certainly, he carries a lot of clout."

"Clout?"

"Important, powerful."

"Yes, indeed."

"Why was he passed over last year?" The question seemed aimless.

"Never had any training in military intelligence," Lasch said abruptly.

"And that disqualifies him? Permanently?"

"No, no. With Inspector Keppler's record, that may be overlooked next time. Changes are happening. But he may reach retirement before that position is open again."

"That's a problem in all careers." The man who makes it to within touch of the top job, Renwick thought, and then is defeated by age. Retirement on what? Half pay? And a life of pottering around a small garden like Gilman's Aunt Chris in Washington. "He never married, did he? Lives with his sister, as far as I remember."

"She died last year. A long illness." Lasch shook his head in sympathy.

"Sorry to hear that. Well, I just hope Keppler gets that final promotion before he retires. But of course there will be other competitors for it, too. There's always a lot of infighting between various intelligence departments. That happens in every capital I've visited."

"Does Interintell suffer from that?"

"So far not, thank God. But we aren't large-scale; we are more concentrated. On terrorist activities. And we don't pull rank. We began as friends—people who knew each other—and we keep it that way."

"Interesting." Lasch liked the idea.

"I just hope that Interintell's request for help hasn't put Keppler in a difficult position. His competitors might—"

"Inspector Keppler can handle all difficulties." Lasch looked pointedly at his watch. "I think it is time."

Time to close a delicate conversation? "I believe it is," Renwick agreed. They retraced their steps and began to approach the Fraumünsterpost. "So you're my bodyguard, as it were," Renwick joked.

"There is nothing to guard. Just formalities."

"Do you know what I am collecting?" Renwick watched the man's face.

"An envelope. But it is of some importance, I understand."

He's telling the truth; he has no idea what the envelope contains. "It's damned important," Renwick said, and saw Lasch's eyes open in surprise. "Just keep a sharp lookout, will you?"

"There is nothing to worry about, I assure you."

But there he wasn't telling the truth. The sharp eyes were suddenly uneasy. The white face was strangely taut. "Good," said Renwick, "good." And as he seemed to forget any possible danger, Lasch relaxed also. One thing I did find out, thought Renwick: Keppler has enough power to handle any difficulties. If some quibbling is going on in Bern this morning, Keppler can take care of it. And thank God for that. If I had got him into some real trouble, I'd have had that on my conscience for a long, long time.

"Everything is arranged," Lasch was saying as he led the way into the post office. "You have also your own passport? Identification papers?"

"What about the authorization?"

"That has been given."

It sounded easy. Although there could have been complications from the current renovation of the Fraumünsterpost's interior, with scaffolding and work-in-progress around, Lasch knew exactly where to head for the poste restante section. The actual transaction was simple. Renwick and Lasch were expected, and at this early hour they had the place almost to themselves. Lasch flashed his identification, then turned everything over to Renwick, who showed Karen Cross's passport. Yes, he said, he was acting on behalf of Karen Cross, and signed a paper to that effect. Then there was his own passport to be examined briefly, and his signature compared with the one he wrote on the receipt. That over—a matter of minutes—he was in possession of an envelope, addressed to Miss Karen Cross at this poste restante in Zurich, and mailed in New York two weeks ago. "One moment!" he told Lasch and opened the envelope. It held a thin black notebook, four by three inches, no more, in size.

He riffled through some pages. This was it. The Plus List.

Suddenly, Lasch's arm shot out, his hand trying to grasp the book. Just as quickly, Renwick jammed it into his inside pocket. He stared at Lasch as he closed its zipper, made the pocket secure. "What the hell were you trying to do?"

"You are to give me the book."

"I what?"

Lasch gave a worried glance around the room. "No argument here, please. Keep your voice down. My instructions were that you give me the book."

Renwick walked on. He reached a long row of grilled windows now open for business and stopped abruptly. He dropped his bag at his feet, took his stand. He lowered his voice but spoke with a fury that startled Lasch. "Whose instructions? Whose?"

"We should leave. We talk outside."

"We talk in here. Whose instructions? The Chief of Intelligence? Or some-one who wants Keppler's job?"

"No, no. Please. I can't tell you. You understand?"

Renwick was recovering. The book was still in his pocket. Lasch was armed—that formidable Swiss army pistol he had drawn last night was in its holster under his jacket—but he hadn't tried any threats with it to force Renwick to walk outside into a waiting car. Renwick's voice lost its intensity, became low but clear; and he didn't move from where he stood.

"No," he said, tight-lipped. "I don't understand. And you don't under-stand, either. This book, which you tried to grab, was Interintell's discov-ery. We learned about it, we risked a lot for it—one helluva lot. Including yesterday evening. Do you think I enjoy having to fire to kill? Do you? If I hadn't, I would have been dead. Sudak would have searched my pockets, discovered the passport. And he would have found a way to get this book. Oh, yes, he would have. He must have had his plan all arranged: a woman who resembled Karen Cross, who'd pass muster. Easy enough."

Lasch only stared at him.

Renwick went on, "What is more, Major Lasch, I signed for this enve-lope. My name is on record. If there is an inquiry and I can't account for the contents, what then? I got it and I lost it, all within forty seconds. Is that what I say?"

"Inquiry?" That astonished Lasch, horrified him, too. "No need for any—"

"What do you expect if someone is trying to prevent Keppler's future promotion? Sure, there will be an investigation, an inquiry. So whose orders were you following? Your general in charge of operations who—"

"No." The sharp rebuttal was spontaneous, indignant.

"Then whose orders?" Renwick was curt, authoritative.

Lasch looked the unhappiest man in Zurich. "Inspector Keppler's. It was understood that you should get the book for him."

"It was not!"

"But—"

"Look," said Renwick, becoming the civilian again, "you must have misun-derstood Keppler's instructions. He was to see the names in this book and act on them—if any of those names do belong to Swiss citizens. That was all. There was no talk whatsoever that the book was going to Bern." Then Renwick paused, said, "You haven't been told why these names are so important, have you? They belong to men of several nations—several. Not just Swiss. They took money to aid and abet the illegal business of Exports Consolidated and of Klingfeld and Sons. You've heard of them, haven't you?"

"Of them, yes." The tight control over Lasch's face was slipping. There was anxiety now, mixed with doubt and uncertainty.

A man who is loyal, obeys orders, but he's not stupid: if he let me talk, it was to find out what I could tell him. And he's listening. Renwick said,

"When did you hear of Exports Consolidated? In the last few days? But not in the last two weeks when you should have heard."

Lasch looked at him sharply.

Renwick said, "Who could have smothered any report on Exports Consolidated? Who could have sidetracked its link with Klingfeld?"

There was a long silence. Lasch glanced at the hall's entrance. Two men had stationed themselves there, blocking its exit.

Renwick noticed the glance and the men.

Lasch said crisply, "You refuse to hand over that book to me?"

"Yes."

"And if you were to be threatened with arrest, with questions about the death of Klaus Sudak, you would still refuse?"

"Yes."

"For the reasons you have given me?"

"Yes." No other exit, thought Renwick. But the business day had begun: people moving around, lines forming in front of the grilled windows, stamps being bought, packages mailed. If he could mix with a group as they left, reach the street?

Quietly, with an abrupt hand sign, Lasch signaled to the two men. They moved away.

Dismissal. Renwick's breath came more easily.

Lasch said, "You wait here. I shall telephone Bern."

"And tell Keppler to stop playing hard-to-find. I promised to show him the names in the Plus List, and I'll keep that promise. Tell him also—"

"Plus List?"

"Exports Consolidated's list. The man who kept it had a peculiar sense of humor. Useful friends were a plus," Renwick explained patiently. "So when you call Keppler in Bern, tell him to get over to Zurich as fast as he can. I'll wait—until noon. That gives him four hours."

Lasch's eyes were hard. "Inspector Keppler is not in Bern."

"In Zurich? Has he an office here, too?" *As soon as I can get away from my office.* Keppler's words.

"No." Lasch turned and hurried toward the doorway.

Renwick's face tightened. He took out Brimmer's diary. Thirty-eight names were on the Plus List, one to each page. There were only two Swiss names. One was Johann Keppler.

For a moment, Renwick felt paralyzed. He hadn't wanted to believe it. It couldn't be, he had told himself in those last few minutes, it couldn't be. But it was.

He snapped the book shut, picked up his bag, and reached a counter. There, with the bag safe at his feet, he pulled out the Bürkli envelope. Into this he slipped the Plus List, sealed and addressed it to J. P. Merriman & Co., with *Attention Ronald Gilman* across one corner of the envelope. He marked it *Luftpost—Par Avion—Airmail.* Then he had the envelope weighed and stamped and registered. He asked for special delivery. Contents? A personal diary. And so noted. And so mailed.

It was with mixed emotions that he let the envelope fall out of sight through a slot for delivery abroad. I'll rely on the Swiss, he thought as he walked back to the spot where Lasch had left him: their mails, like their trains, run on time. No sign yet of Lasch; or of any self-effacing men standing against a wall, watching.

How could Keppler have done it? Thirty years or more of honest service, and then this. What made him? Why? Disappointment over promotion? Savings vanished with the expenses of his sister's illness? Retirement on little money? But other men had faced these questions and hadn't answered with betrayal.

It was a recent involvement. The first payment came last October: fifty thousand deposited in a Nassau bank. A second deposit of fifty thousand in March. The third was made two weeks ago: seventy thousand. Peanuts compared to what some of Brimmer's helpers had been paid. Keppler would never know how cheaply he had been bought.

And then, in one last desperate hope, Renwick wondered if Keppler could have mounted a secret investigation of his own into Exports Consolidated and Klingfeld. Had he thought he could infiltrate, get proof of their bribery and corruption? Yet, that wasn't Keppler's style: he never took wild chances. Everything he did was calculated. One of the most capable and reliable men I've ever met, thought Renwick. He was all of that, four years ago, when we first worked together. What happened? Or did it happen? Am I condemning a friend who took a fantastic risk to furnish real evidence?

Heartsick, he stood motionless, scarcely heard Lasch's voice at his elbow. "Inspector Keppler will meet you at noon."

Renwick nodded.

"At the Belvoir Park, north entrance."

No park, thank you. Renwick shook his head. "At the airport. Twelve o'clock. I'll wait one hour. Then I leave."

"Where do you wait?"

"Inside the terminal—the corridor with the long stretch of shops." And plenty of people around. "There's a café at its far end."

"Which end?"

"If you stand looking out toward the runways, then it's to your right-hand side." Not brilliant, but the best he could do at this moment.

"I know the café." Lasch paused. His face was impassive, but his eyes were worried. "Did you look at the Plus List?"

"Yes."

"Were there names of Swiss citizens?"

"Two."

"Will you show the list to Inspector Keppler?"

"I will tell him."

"You promised—" Lasch began. And then, "So you don't trust us."

"At this moment I trust no one." Renwick said bitterly.

Lasch wasn't too surprised. "The list does concern our national security?" he persisted.

"Very much so. Interintell will keep your government fully informed."

"Then," said Lasch softly as he gestured in the direction of the poste restante where Renwick had received the envelope addressed to Karen Cross, "all that was of importance?"

"Of vital importance to Switzerland. And to six other countries."

Lasch's relief was transparent. "There will be no inquiry about this morning."

"Not concerning you and me, at least." Renwick picked up his bag, and they walked out together.

"May I give you a lift?" Lasch asked as they left the Fraumünsterpost. Renwick looked at the olive-green car that waited by the curb. The two men inside it were those who had blocked the exit from the main hall. "Very kind of you, but I think I need some air. By the way, what changed your mind about giving me a lift earlier today?"

Lasch hesitated, seemed to take Renwick's measure, said very quietly, "Your questions: who smothered any reports on Exports Consolidated—who sidetracked its link with Klingfeld?" There was another hesitation. "That happened two weeks ago. But I thought it was a mistake in judgment, an error."

Seventy thousand dollars two weeks ago. Renwick's small hope grew fainter. "You have a phone call to make. I won't delay you any more. Goodbye, Major Lasch."

Lasch smiled, showed a small transmitter concealed in his hand. "No need to telephone. *Auf Wiedersehen,* Herr Renwick."

So Keppler isn't far away. He could have met me here and now. Grim-faced, Renwick made his way toward the crowded Hauptbahnstrasse.

Twenty-four

IT HAD BEEN a long morning of walking, of thinking, of trying not to think, but eventually Renwick took a taxi and reached the Zurich airport. He entered the café in the terminal building at twelve o'clock exactly.

It was almost filled. People waiting for planes, people spending time between connections, people concentrating on their own worries—schedules, safe transfer of luggage, delays. People everywhere, but no sign of Keppler. Renwick made sure of a table, vacated in near panic by an elderly couple as they heard their flight being called, by sitting down as the remains of their lunch were being cleared away. He ordered a pot of coffee.

By half past twelve he ordered more coffee and a sandwich as his pretext for occupying the table. Its position was too good to lose. He lit his fourth cigarette.

He had always liked this café, a pleasant place to relax in the middle of an airport's turmoil. It wasn't walled in; it needed no door, no windows. It was simply a large space roped off from the broad indoor avenue, lined with shops, that ran the length of this giant terminal. Its decorative plants didn't block the view of anyone walking outside its boundary; its tables were jammed together: Keppler would see him easily. And Renwick had taken a chair that let him have clear sight of anyone who stepped out of the crowd to enter this oasis.

So there he was, sitting in a place he usually liked and hating every minute of it. He stubbed out his ninth cigarette. It was one o'clock. He pushed aside the uneaten sandwich, looked no more at the entrance in front of him, began counting out Swiss francs to cover the bill and tip. Five past one. Keppler wasn't coming. No talk; no clarification. But, then, there was the old-time rule for intelligence officers: never apologize, never explain. If your friends couldn't take you on trust, they were no friends at all.

He reached for his bag—that goddamned bag filled with old Bernie's little goodies he had been lugging around Zurich as if it were Fort Knox in miniature. He sensed a movement toward his table, looked up sharply. It was Lasch who stood there, his face set and his arm stiff as he indicated the chair opposite Renwick. "May I?" he asked.

Renwick straightened his back. What now? A last-minute summons to a police station? Questions about the shooting of Klaus Sudak?

Lasch sat down. "I am glad I found you. I only heard half an hour ago. I came at once."

Renwick waited.

"He is dead."

"Dead?"

"Drove into a stone marker at the side of the road. He was traveling at high speed. It was a dangerous curve."

"On the highway to the airport?" Renwick could remember no sharp curves.

"No. On the road to Luzern. He must have left Zurich just after—just after I talked with him." There was a long pause. Then Lasch forced himself to say, "He knew that road well. He used to say he could drive it blindfolded."

Renwick's last shred of hope was gone. He felt stifled, couldn't speak.

"In Luzern—there was a woman. Very young. Forty years younger."

"Since when? In the last year?"

Lasch nodded. Again a pause. He said slowly, "Death was instant. He made very sure. It was one solution. The only one perhaps?"

Yes, Renwick answered silently. For Keppler it was the only solution.

Lasch went on talking, but his voice was now brisk. "You said there were two Swiss names on the list of men who had taken bribes from Exports Consolidated."

Renwick nodded.

"You said that Interintell would send these names to my government. Will they?"

"Yes. I think that's the way Interintell must handle that list: names to each government of its citizens who have taken those bribes. The government concerned can keep an eye on their future ambitions—it won't want men like that running for public office or occupying positions of power and trust. But," Renwick added, "there would be no need for Interintell to send a dead man's name. He would no longer be a—" and this was difficult to say—"a security risk."

"I agree," Lasch said, and relaxed. He looked at the American's tight face, then at the heap of cigarette stubs and the uneaten food. "One more thing. It is important. To me."

"Yes?" Renwick had pushed back his chair, was about to leave.

"Yesterday evening—at the Bürkli—I had no idea you were in Upwood's room. No idea. I wasn't told you could be there."

Renwick stared at him.

Lasch rushed on. "In the lobby I saw the red-haired man keep looking at his watch. At six o'clock he rose and went through the bar into the restaurant. A tall man, dark-haired, arrived within a few minutes. They took the service stairs from there—without a word, moved quickly. I followed. Discreetly. When I reached the second floor, they were already at the door of the room. I was calling for my backup as they broke the lock and entered. I thought—I swear before God—that I would let them start searching, and then I would surprise them, hold them until my two men arrived. I did not know you could be in there—facing them—alone." Lasch's eyes hardened at that thought. "Believe me," he said, his first sign of anger showing against Keppler, "I wasn't told. That is not how I work."

"I believe you."

"My report reads that there was an exchange of shots. You were standing to the left side of the door. Facing the men. They had their backs to the couch at the window. Yes?"

"Yes."

"I knew it! The two bullet holes were in the wall of the room, just behind you. The bullets we extracted were matched with their revolvers. There will be no doubt that the two men fired at you. But missed, *Gott sei Dank*. So, Herr Renwick"—Lasch actually smiled—"as you were acting for Interintell, there should be no difficulties, no unpleasantness for you. It was self-defense, in the line of duty."

Then I'm free to leave, Renwick thought.

Lasch said, "More important, your actual name will not be mentioned. There is no need to have it recorded for the benefit of any KGB file."

"No need," Renwick agreed. "And thank you for that."

"The least we can do. You have done us a service."

"Not one of my choosing."

Lasch said quickly, "You didn't destroy him, Herr Renwick. He destroyed himself."

Yes, last October, Keppler destroyed himself. "Good-bye, then. I'm glad we talked." Renwick was rising to his feet. He couldn't resist adding, "And thank you for letting me sleep last night."

Lasch's white face flushed. "I entered your room to ask if you had found the passport."

"And to persuade me to entrust it to you for safekeeping?" Renwick asked gently.

"I was instructed—" Lasch broke off. "You understand?"

"Fully."

"Of course, if you hadn't found the passport, then all our plans for this morning would have been changed. *Nicht wahr?*"

"True," Renwick agreed, and eased the look of embarrassment on Lasch's unhappy face. Plans would have been changed, and Keppler would have been still alive, still undiscovered. He would have searched for the passport, and when he had found it, he'd make sure this time that Brimmer's Plus List would be delivered into his hands. As it was meant to be, this morning. Renwick resisted one final question. Why didn't you grab harder at that little black book, Karl—or force me with a gun at my ribs into your car? Instead, he put out his hand. "It was good working with you, Karl. Fortunate for me, too." And that was the solid truth.

"A pleasure to work with Interintell." Lasch was on his feet, his hand crushingly strong in its firm grip.

"Good-bye."

"*Auf Wiedersehen.*"

Renwick was three paces away. "Herr Renwick!" he heard. What now? he wondered as he turned around.

"You forgot your bag, Herr Renwick." Lasch handed it to him with a bow.

Renwick took it, shook his hand, and walked on, back into his thoughts about Keppler. Strange: they had talked about him for the last fifteen minutes and never once had they mentioned his name. Yet not so strange: Keppler, as they had known him, had died nine months ago.

Now, where was a telephone? In Washington it would be half past eight. He would waken Nina with the best news in his life: he was coming home.

Twenty-five

In ZURICH, RENWICK hadn't been able to reach Nina. There was only the housekeeper's voice, cool and impersonal, telling him they had left Basset Hill. Yes, Mrs. Smith had left. And Mr. MacEwan. With Mr. Grant driving them in his car. No, she didn't know where they were going.

The short flight to Geneva became a long plunge back into frustration and anxiety. He had expected too much, he told himself, when he hoped to find Nina waiting by the phone for his call. Everything was all right, must be. But the last message from Basset Hill, relayed by London this morning, had been sent out from Washington last night. Anything could have happened in that time-lag. Anything.

At the Geneva airport, he found a cheerful Claudel with an arm heavily encased in bandages and a bright word of welcome. "I was delayed," Renwick said. "Sorry to be late."

"Nothing to it. Got here early." It didn't seem the right moment, judging from Renwick's face, to mention Claudel's own efficiency. He had put the hours of waiting to good use. His plane was tanked up, ready to soar. And for once he was going to allow someone else to take over the controls.

Leave his sweet darling alone and abandoned at Geneva until he could come back to fly her out? No, thank you.

"How's the arm?" Renwick asked as they walked through the terminal.

No explanation given for the delay, no mention of what had happened in Zurich. Claudel controlled his impatience. He'd hear the details once they had taken off—another good reason for flying private. On a commercial flight there would be no serious talk. He began describing the wire cradle in which his forearm was resting, a neat piece of medical engineering to hold the wound together and let it mend naturally. "There will be a scar, of course, but the girls never object to that—intrigues them. It will cramp my style for a week or two. Can't move it around."

"You'll think of ways," Renwick told him. He was abstracted, his eyes searching for a phone booth.

"Gilman reached me this morning and—"

"Have you any spare Swiss francs? I'm running short."

"Sure. But—"

"I'm calling Washington. Where's the nearest phone, dammit?"

"No need, Bob. She's en route. To Paris."

Renwick's voice sharpened. "Alone?"

"Bob—the danger is over. Anyway, Mac is traveling with her. That is, if they made the shuttle to La Guardia in time to reach Kennedy by nine-fifteen. She's taking the Concorde. It doesn't fly from Washington on a Monday." Claudel laughed. "Nina decided it all—must have been studying timetables for days. Gilman was slightly astonished—especially by her last question. Couldn't understand it quite, but he said yes anyway. She asked, 'Then the snake has been scotched?' What the devil did she mean? Klaus Sudak?"

Renwick nodded, a first smile playing around his lips. "Thoroughly scotched." He calculated quickly. "Arriving at DeGaulle just before six. When's the first flight out of here?"

"We can do better than that. I've got my plane all ready to go. You can take her up, can't you?"

"You bet I will." Renwick was already moving off.

"Easy, easy," Claudel told him as he caught up. "Gilman has booked Nina into the George Cinq—he knows the management. He will be there himself tomorrow—he's eager to get the full details. Who isn't?"

"He'd better be back in Grace Street by the day after tomorrow. There's a registered envelope on its way from Zurich."

"You mailed Brimmer's Plus List?"

"Seemed the safest bet."

"Rough going this morning?" Claudel was astounded.

"Well—let's say it could have been."

"Didn't Keppler deliver?"

"He sold out."

"What?"

"Later, Pierre, later. When did Gilman call Nina?"

"Just after he got your report and had it decoded."

"At half past one in the morning?"

"A telephone call means good news." Bad news would have been sent in a message to MacEwan and let him break it, face to face. "Bob," Claudel said most seriously, "don't you know how worried we've all been?"

And there were moments when I was damned worried, too. Renwick said, "What's the best flying time we can make?"

"We could—with this good weather—reach Orly by five o'clock."

And then traffic delays. "We'll try for De Gaulle."

"Problems, Bob. I usually fly into—"

"You work them out."

"Well, well. Delegating authority, are you?"

"From now on there will be plenty of delegating."

"I think I've heard that before."

"This time I mean it." Renwick's face went taut.

Claudel looked at him quickly. I believe he does, Claudel thought. I really believe it. I didn't even have to tell him how near Nina was to danger. That news can wait, like the other items Gilman gave me on our double-talk over the phone this morning. Vroom, for instance: Vroom resigning from Dutch Intelligence as well as from Interintell, Vroom taking a job with Bruna Imports, leaving next month for Indonesia and the problems of the spice and coffee trade. Or perhaps I won't mention the threat to Nina, let Gilman do his diplomatic best with that. What Bob needs now is an hour in a decompression chamber. This time he went too far down below the surface. And he knows it. Goddammit, why did he go in alone? With such speed? But Claudel knew the answer: the only way to deal with Klaus Sudak was to be one jump ahead of him. "Okay," he said as they reached the plane. "Sure you won't strip her gears?"

They arrived at De Gaulle Airport, as Claudel had predicted, with time to spare. They even managed a very late twenty-minute lunch of sandwiches and beer, and still had half an hour to wait. Midway through the flight, Renwick had begun to talk. Back to normal or almost, thought Claudel, and thank heaven for that. Now it was he who began worrying. It was more than possible that Nina hadn't managed the distance between La Guardia and Kennedy airports before the Concorde lifted off. In that case, Claudel could see his own plans for tonight evaporating. Tomorrow morning he would be waiting again with Bob at this bloody airport for the arrival of an overnight flight from New York.

As they paced along the exits from customs and immigration, Renwick said, "No need for you to hang around, Pierre."

"No need," Claudel agreed cheerfully, but he stayed. No need? After all that he had heard this afternoon? But the decompression chamber was working: Bob was out on deck, breath normal, and it only needed Nina to complete the cure. My God, what if she didn't arrive? Quickly, Claudel began talking about next January. If he could manage it, he might be back in Chamonix for some skiing.

"The brunette nurse?"

"Yes, the knockout—the one that caught your roving eye."

But at that moment, Renwick's eyes were riveted. The first arrivals were beginning to appear.

Claudel said, "Give me that bag, and I'll see you tomorrow. In Gilman's room at the George Cinq. Around eleven?"

"Two o'clock." Renwick's eyes were searching.

"Gilman will be there by ten."

"You can start with Amsterdam and hold him with Chamonix. You've got plenty to tell—" Renwick broke off as his eyes found a girl with fair hair cut short and curling. Nina. Nina, more beautiful than ever, with her large eyes and the tilt of her head and the smile on her lips. She hadn't seen him yet as she walked—high-heeled sandals tapping lightly, cream shirt open at the neck, cream skirt slightly swinging at each step—beside a red-haired man, and listened to him talk. Mac, thought Renwick, I like you; I like you a lot, but you don't have to be so damned fascinating.

Mac, quick as ever, had seen them both and caught Claudel's high sign to follow him out.

Renwick didn't even notice. Nina had halted, her blue eyes widening as she stared at him in wonder. Renwick scarcely heard Mac say, as he dropped Nina's suitcase beside him, "All yours, now. Glad you're back, Bob."

Renwick put out his hands to grasp hers. For a long moment they stood looking at each other. Then he drew her into his arms, tightening them around her as they kissed. Soft lips, soft cheeks, soft silken hair against his mouth. Suddenly, he was alive again. He laughed with the joy of it. He released her, held her back from him to look at her once more. "Magic, you are pure magic, darling." He picked up her suitcase and slipped an arm around her waist as they began walking toward the street.